ISBN: 0615653243

ISBN-13: 978-0615653242

This is a work of fiction. Names, characters, places, businesses and incidents are either the product of the author's imagination or are used fictitiously. Any resemblance to actual persons, living or dead, businesses, events or locales is purely coincidental. No actors were harmed in the making of this novel.

.

*This book is dedicated
to the cast and crew of Gilligan's Island.*

INTRODUCTION

Readers of this book will most likely come to notice that the format is a bit... different. The chapters are lengthy and at times seem to employ a different style of storytelling than the rest of the book. For this, there is good reason.

Starlette was originally released as a serial novel, one chapter every other week. Each chapter was meant to provide the reader with a fulfilling experience of its own, while adding to the overall novel—like episodes of a TV series.

This book is the complete Starlette novel. While you are now free to read the story from beginning to end, its serialized spirit lives on.

STARLETTE

Hollywood. The glitz and glamour of movie stars, shining down upon the world from giant two-dimensional thrones. Projections of majesty. Icons. Myths. For years, they told us how to dress; how to speak; how to feel; how to think... And in one night, they were gone...

CHAPTER ONE
THE FINAL SCENE

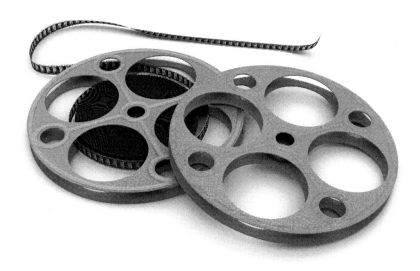

Hollywood, California. 1:43 p.m.

Dorian Harker cast his eyes downward, trying to find the right words. He should have been used to this by now. This was hardly the first time he'd been in this situation, yet here he was. Lost.

Chiseled features will only get you so far, he told himself. No amount of ab definition, sparkling blue eyes, or perfect hair would save him if he couldn't find the words... No, seriously, he could not *find* the words.

Finally, he found the lines and spoke, "Stop. Please. Just wait."

He skimmed ahead, finding his next line in the script so that he could avoid yet another drawn out pause.

Dorian was sitting at one of three tables, set up in a U-shape in the center of the room. There were no windows. There were only drably painted walls, a ceiling fan which hummed far too loudly, and people. Lots of people.

No matter how long he had worked with this cast and crew, or how comfortable he was performing scenes on the actual sets, in front of actual cameras, table-reads always made him nervous. They were unpolished and sloppy. They made him feel like he was back in high school, about to take a test without having studied.

Nobody expected perfection from the table-read. It was a simple verbal run-through of the script so that the writers and producers could hear the words spoken aloud and discuss any possible changes. Some actors didn't bother to consider how they might deliver their lines during the table-read. There was no reason to care... except that Dorian couldn't stop his mind from thinking about the delivery. He couldn't pretend that it didn't matter how the words sounded to him, because this was a fickle town, and you always needed to be at your best. Nobody's job was secure on television—by its very nature, television is temporary —and in Dorian's mind, every scene could be his last.

Luckily, Dorian's discomfort was not as obvious to others as it was to him. Sweaty palms and the sound of his own heart beating in his ear were not evident to everyone in the room, and he could control the tone of his voice during the read. He was a slightly-trained professional, after all.

Sitting around the table were other actors, as well as writers and producers. A few of the people sitting in the back of the room were unfamiliar to him, but they still had scripts. Everyone knew when he missed a line or fumbled over a word, and he would beat himself up over that. This was good. It forced him to learn fast and always be prepared when the cameras were rolling.

Dorian wasn't always an actor. In another life, he was a high school quarterback. Where he came from, a mistake meant extra laps after practice. There was a price to pay for dropping the ball.

"Why should I stop?" demanded the voice of his co-star, Casey Dale, which was as smooth and effortless as if she'd had a week to prepare her scenes.

Dorian had a special fondness for Casey. She was beautiful, with her natural dirty-blond hair, milky white skin. She wasn't the type of actress who had glided through life on her looks. In fact, most people wouldn't have called her beautiful just by looking at her, but when she spoke and her personality came through... she was flawless.

"I love you," Dorian told her, but only because those were the words written in the script.

"I know you love me, but that's not enough. Not anymore. We can't keep doing this to ourselves. I'm sorry. I just can't."

One of the producers, Shawna Price, sitting several chairs down read the non-dialogue portion of the script, "Dane walks toward the door. Astin grabs her arm and spins her around, kissing her passionately."

While table-reads made Dorian nervous, he enjoyed many aspects of his job. Amongst these perks were the romantic scenes that he was able to play with Casey. Holding her. Kissing her.

"I love you," Dorian read.

In real life, they were friends who hung out together after work and goofed around on the set. It was their real chemistry which inspired the writers to make their characters a couple on their popular television show, *Dream Town*.

"They continue to kiss as we fade to black. End of episode," Shawna read, before looking up from the script and moving her glasses to the top of her head.

Casey turned toward Dorian, and stared at him with exaggerated passion in her eyes, and in a Spanish accent, she said, "Kiss me, you wild, saucy animal man."

She then proceeded to lick the air, as though she were being passionately kissed by a wild, saucy animal man.

"Oh, you couldn't take this heat," Dorian assured her. "The type of passion that's all up in here would melt your face off."

On the other side of the U-shaped table setup, one of the show's other stars, Lotti Trusse, snapped her fingers in the air and told them, "Y'all could make a killin' if you released a sex tape. That's all I'm sayin'."

Lotti played the sassy best friend of Casey's character on the show. She'd originally started out as a professional African-American business woman, meant to inspire young black girls across the country, but somewhere between seasons three and five, the character had been turned into a stereotype, who regularly ended her boardroom meetings with the catchphrase,

Zuh-zam.

Lotti performed the part well either way, but Dorian could tell that she preferred the original concept for the character. Now, she hammed it up, because the popularity of the character meant more work in the long run, and deep down she knew that typecasting was better than no casting at all.

"We should totally make a sex tape," Casey agreed. "I call topsies!"

Dorian shook his head in disapproval, "Are you kidding me? Do you know what I look like in night-vision? There's no way I'm doing a sex tape."

Casey nodded in agreement, and thought for a moment before saying, "We don't need to do it in night vision. Full color, high-def, baby."

Shawna shook her head and turned to the rest of the room, saying, "Do I have the most professional cast in all of television, or what?"

"Pssh," Lotti smirked. "A *professional* would find a way to work around the night vision thing."

~

As everyone walked out of the table-read, Casey noticed that Dorian was standing by the door. He did this often, and never seemed to notice that he was waiting for *her*. She figured that this was part of his proper southern upbringing, which she thought was as adorable as the fact that he still got nervous over a simple read-through.

When they started to walk toward the door, Dorian asked, "So, how did that audition go? Did you hear back yet?"

Two days earlier, Casey had auditioned for the role of a drug addicted prostitute in a star-studded art film. It was a role that she really wanted to throw herself into, because it was the type of role that could turn a minor television star into a major Hollywood player. There was even nudity involved, and if she showed some boob, surely she would be taken more seriously as an actress.

Sadly, her rise to the A-list would have to wait a little while longer.

"They said I looked too sweet," Casey replied with a frown.

"Too sweet? Have they seen the tabloids lately? You're a total skank."

Casey's eyes widened, "I know, right?!"

"They don't know what they're missing. I've felt your boobs and they're awesome."

Somehow, Casey imagined that conversations between co-workers were probably different in Hollywood than they were in most places. It amused her to think of two accountants discussing boobs and sex tapes. Surely, there were rules and regulations that would apply to them. Fortunately, Hollywood was all about breaking the rules. The more drunk driving arrests a girl had, the more the press loved her.

If only Casey could bring herself to endanger the lives of countless innocent people on the streets of Los Angeles, she might have gotten to play that prostitute.

She liked Dorian. Normally, if she liked a guy, she would act on those feelings. But there was something about him that was different. She had dated every type of guy, ranging from Wall Street tycoons to crazed Australian rock stars, but Dorian was the first one to ever scare her. Being with him, she felt the same way she did the first time she performed before a live studio audience. He was her future.

Of course, she had to go through at least one practice husband before she would even consider marrying the man that she was meant to be with. That meant that she would need to meet a guy and invest a few weeks getting to know him before getting married. After that, it would be another two months of living together, and four of being legally separated before she would file for divorce. An annulment would be better, but that wouldn't have the same type of headline appeal.

In the meantime, she enjoyed spending time with the guy that she would eventually spend the rest of her life with.

"At least you have the show to come back to," Dorian told her.

Her thoughts having trailed off, Casey was now blanking on what they had been discussing. She had no idea what he was talking about. Apparently, he could read her like a trashy novel, because he quickly added, "Since you didn't get the movie, I mean."

"Oh," she replied, "Which sucks."

Dorian seemed a little hurt by her reaction, as he said, "You don't like it here?"

"I like it here just fine. I love working with my best friend in the entire world. And you too, I guess."

Dorian smiled. She really wished that he would stop doing that, so she could focus on her first husband.

"I like working here. I just had a really good way of getting out of my contract," Casey continued. "I was going to be a total diva."

"Ah," Dorian nodded, understanding how she might have enjoyed that, "Well, I'm sure you'll get to be a diva someday."

"You think?"

"I do. And if it makes you feel any better, I hear that most of the wardrobe department already hates you."

As they exited the building and walked toward Casey's car, she wrapped her arm around his and rested her head on his shoulder, asking, "You're not just saying that?"

"Nope. I swear."

There was a long silence as they continued to walk, but as they approached Casey's car, Dorian finally spoke once again, saying, "You know, if you want to sulk, maybe you could come over tonight. Watch the awards. Eat some carbs. Trash talk people we'd kill to work with."

Casey pulled her keys from her pocket as they reached her silver hybrid SUV, and though she may have wanted to take Dorian up on his offer, she looked to the ground and said, "I can't. I have a date."

"Oh," Dorian replied, with a tone that said much more than that one word. It asked her why she would waste her time on another guy. Why she felt a need to delay something that they both knew was right. Why she couldn't just give in and be happy.

Of course, most of these questions were in Casey's head, but Dorian had to be wondering the same things too.

The answer to these questions was simple. Casey was scared at the finality of dating Dorian. He was it. When she looked at him, she saw the house and the kids, and the bake sales and the family vacations and deathbed goodbyes when they were old and their faces had been pulled tight by some of the world's finest plastic surgeons. When she looked at him, she didn't need fame or fortune, and that scared the crap out of her.

With a nod of acceptance and pretending not to care, since they never allowed their feelings to interfere with their friendship, Dorian asked, "Is it the male model again?"

Casey nodded, "He sings too."

"Cool," Dorian replied. "Tell his cheekbones I said 'hey.'"

"Yeah," Casey answered, feeling more awkward than she'd like. "I will. But, um... I guess I should go. I have to do some stuff."

"Yeah. Totally," Dorian said, opening her car door for her and allowing her to get in. He added, "Call me later if you get bored."

"I will. See ya."

Dorian closed Casey's car door and stepped back as she started the engine and pulled away with a quick wave goodbye.

As she drove off the lot and down the street, Casey's mind was spinning with thoughts of Thanksgiving dinners in the suburbs, and trying to sneak dollar bills under the pillow of a small child with missing teeth.

She never noticed the black motorcycle following her, or the shady man riding it.

~

Los Angeles, California. 3:18 p.m.

Tessa Baker was beauty personified, in her day. She was the envy of actresses all over the world, due to her ability to command attention without uttering a word. Her mere presence added weight to a scene.

When she looked into the eyes of a costar, she could melt a thousand hearts. When she shot an angry glare their way, the audience would hold their breath without even realizing it. Pick an accent, and she could deliver a performance that made you believe that the director of her movie had flown to whichever foreign land the role required, and had plucked the rarest talent from amongst its grassy hills or city streets.

Nobody would have guessed that Tessa Baker had been born Irina von Haus (a name that was quickly changed because producers decided that it sounded like she was a communist Nazi), the daughter of an elementary school teacher from New Jersey. Nobody seemed to mind that her face was just a little bit more round than the typical Hollywood actress, or that her nose was perhaps a tad more pointed. When she was on the top of her game, Tessa became the image of beauty, and the rest of the world followed in her footsteps.

While Tessa was gracing the covers of all of the major magazines, the notion of the Hollywood actress who needed platinum blond hair and a pouty lower lip were dispelled. She had strength about her, which men found appealing and women aspired to recreate. She had brown hair, which was often plainly styled, to better suit her characters. Sometimes, she would perform with only a small amount of makeup and unimpressive clothes.

She did not drip glamour from her every pore, as some actresses did. At least, not on screen. In real life however, she enjoyed dressing lavishly. She happily wore designer outfits and applied a respectable amount of makeup when she appeared on talk shows to promote her movies. She enjoyed attending every award show and film premiere. She was not simply an actress, she was a *star*.

On this particular night, all of the important names in Hollywood were gathering for one of the most prestigious award shows of the month: the Golden Me Awards. These were the awards which set the tone for all other award shows. Those who took home a Gimme (as they were commonly known) could expect raises in salary and opportunities beyond their wildest dreams. Much more importantly, they would win adoration. *The spoils of awards*, as Tessa loved to proclaim.

The GMAs were watched by tens of millions of people around the world. The actors, actresses and miscellaneous crew members who received the awards would be the envy of every small child who dared to look into their bathroom mirror while clinging onto their mouthwash bottle and delivering an imaginary acceptance speech.

On this night, royalty graced the streets of California.

Meanwhile, Tessa Baker sat in a small waiting room, on an uncomfortable chair which had a questionable stain on it. She sat in a room full of women who all looked vaguely like her, and each of them was looking down at the same script pages that Tessa's agent had sent her, each silently mouthing the same words which Tessa had committed to memory the night before.

Somehow, over the years, the shine of her stardom had worn off. Now, she wasn't offered starring roles in major motion pictures, she was offered the opportunity to audition for supporting roles which only serve to propel some younger, more attractive actress to stardom.

She had aged gracefully. Even in her late fifties, Tessa could play younger. She hadn't officially had a stitch of plastic surgery. She had full use of her facial muscles, unlike many of her contemporaries. She still had talent and weight to her performances. The only thing that she lacked was an outlet for her art.

The office door opened, and one of those actresses who looked vaguely like her walked out. An assistant called Tessa's name and every woman in the room looked up to see if this truly was *the* Tessa Baker.

There was some part of Tessa that wanted to shrink down and pretend that she was not the woman that they just called. It was only a small part, however. Tessa was not one to shy away from uncomfortable situations. She was not easily humiliated. She was a celebrated actress and her work spoke for itself. It *demanded* respect.

She rose from her seat and straightened her skirt as she looked toward the assistant with all of the strength and determination that she was known for. As she walked forward, there was not a sound in the room. All eyes were on her, and she imagined all of those other women convincing themselves that they didn't stand a chance against a star of Tessa's magnitude.

She walked into the office and the door was closed behind her.

In the office, two men were sitting at a table that was set up on one side of the room. One of these men was a casting director and the other was the director of the film for which she was auditioning. To Tessa, they both looked like little children who were playing filmmaker with their daddy's camera.

There was another man in the room, sitting behind the video camera that would capture Tessa's performance.

None of these men seemed to be interested in conversation.

None of them had any hint of the respect for Tessa that the women in the waiting room had.

"Could you slate for us, and then go for it whenever you're ready," one of the men instructed.

Slating was when an actor or actress would look at the camera and give their name, and their agent's name. It was an introduction. It was a note, so the people reviewing these auditions later on would know who each actor was. It was a far cry from the days when Tessa would sign onto a movie over lunch with the director; when she would be offered countless roles without mention of the word *audition*, outside of a joking context.

It seemed to Tessa that once an actor's age range changed, and the parts that they could reasonably expect to get were different than what they had played before, they might as well be fresh off the bus from Kansas—their whole career suddenly became worthless.

"My name is Tessa Baker," she told the camera. "I'm with the Penzer, Dall and Hart Agency."

There was a slight nod from one of the men at the table, and she wondered if he was nodding to let her know that she had done an adequate job of slating. Did he presume to suggest that she didn't know how to do her job?

She ignored this and moved into her audition.

Taking a deep breath, Tessa looked to the ground. A moment later she turned her attention to the man beside the camera, with tears in her eyes.

"I have given you everything I have," she said with a perfect blend of pain and anger in her voice. "I have loved you. I have supported you in spite of everything you've done to this family. I have waited years for you to become the husband and the father that we deserve... ... ... and what do I have to show for it?"

The man beside the camera read from the script without any hint of emotion, saying "What do you want from me. I have tried."

"Tried? You call this trying? You call drinking yourself into a stupor every night *trying*? You call missing every one of your son's football games *trying*? You call going to your daughter's wedding drunk and taking a... a *piss* on one of the centerpieces *trying*?"

"Yes. I do. I do call it trying. I am sorry if I am not up to your standards."

"My standards have been pretty fucking low!"

"Oh. She can cuss now."

"I can do a lot of things. I can walk out of this door and never look back. I can take my children out of your life and I can promise you that you will never see them again. You have caused this family enough pain. Now you can rot alone. You can die alone!"

"You are nothing without me."

"I've believed that bullshit long enough. Now I know the truth. I know that I'm nothing *with* you, Roger. When I walk out of this house, I will stop being nothing. I will stop being the laughing stock of this neighborhood. I will be a person again, for the first time in twenty-five years. Goodbye, Roger. I hope you enjoy dying alone."

There was a long pause. The scene was over, and Tessa's heart was pounding. She wasn't nervous in the slightest, but she was angry. She was scared. She was the character that she was auditioning for, and she felt every word that was written in this rather sub-par script. For a true actress, it wouldn't matter if the script was horrible. Actors were like Midas, with the ability to turn shit into gold, if they were truly gifted.

Once Tessa pulled herself out of the scene, she looked to the men sitting in the room, who were lazily taking short notes. Then one of them—possibly the director, but it didn't really matter—looked at her and said, "Thank you. We'll be in touch."

For Tessa, discussing business without a meal in front of her was unusual enough. But to perform a scene and receive not even the slightest hint of a response, as though her performance were the same as every other actress who walked through the door...

She had been to many auditions in recent months. She had seen many fresh-faced directors who believed that they could change the course of the industry with their keen ability to make their movies look cool by adding computer-generated monsters instead of actual talent. She was sick and tired of actors being reduced to supporting roles, while silly blue cartoon creatures frenched each other.

Tessa was sick of watching her beloved craft wither and turn into trash. Film was to be respected and appreciated. Its stars were to be cherished. When Christmas rolled around, people looked forward to spending time with their families; but they also looked forward to spending time with James Stewart and Maureen O'Hara. When people were heartbroken after a bad breakup, they turned to Audry Hepburn. So few of the movies that Tessa had auditioned for were attempting to be anything but emotionless fluff.

Each audition she attended would end with the same promise: That they would *be in touch*. It was a joke.

She wanted to be angry. She wanted to throw a fit, the likes of which today's female celebrities were applauded for. Everyone loves a diva nowadays. It's a sign of an empowered woman, not simply the sign of a bitch.

More than merely throwing a fit, however, she wanted to teach these boys what it meant to be an artist; to inspire them to greatness.

However angry she might wish to be, her attitude was merely a mask for the ugly truth hiding beneath it. She was sad.

"No," she told the men at the table. "You won't be in touch."

One of the men looked up from his notes and said, "I beg your pardon?"

"I have been in this business for decades. Since before either of you were a glimmer in your mother's eye. I know how this works. You're going to decide to go in another direction. I'm not quite what you're looking for. Despite the fact that your leading man is three years younger than me, you want a sexy young thing for him to fondle on camera, not some *worn out* old woman."

Neither man said a word, and this frustrated Tessa. She wanted to scream, but she could only grin.

"I have acted in over seventy-five films. I have won countless awards. I have signed my name to more than one fucking sidewalk in my day. I have made this studio and others more money than either of you can dare to dream of. Yet there you sit, honestly believing that you are better than me," Tessa went on. "Well, gentlemen, I will leave you now. I will leave you to take your fucking movie and shove it up your fucking asses... which is undoubtedly where you found this script in the first place."

She raised her chin and walked tall as she exited the room. If her career were to go down, it would go down in a glorious ball of fire, not a pathetic drip.

As Tessa left the room, her performance demanded the attention of all those who were near enough to witness. She walked with the weight of every starring role she had ever performed, and she was proud of herself, whether she won this role or not. She was Tessa Baker, star of the silver screen.

"Thank you. We'll be in touch," repeated the voice from behind her.

~

Beverly Hills, California. 4:30 p.m.

Amanda Hoit-Martin stood in a guest bedroom which had been converted into a second closet in her mansion, and studied her reflection in the full length mirror that she managed to find for only fifty thousand dollars at an antique auction house. Her hair was up in curlers, but her makeup was finished and she could not deny the fact that she looked beautiful, even before she put on her dress.

Amanda was one of Hollywood's shiniest stars of the present day. She had three hit movies in the last year alone, two felony arrests, and several strategic nip-slips. Her hair was the color of spun gold, according to the label, and the swelling from her last nose job had gone down just in time for her to enjoy award season. Life was good.

Hanging on a mannequin in front of her was the gown that she would be wearing to the GMAs, and what she imagined herself wearing as she accepted her very first Gimme.

If she angled herself just right, she could put her own head on the reflection of the mannequin and it was as though she were already wearing it. Plus, she looked super thin.

She looked into her own eyes and widened them with shock, putting her hands to her mouth and pretending to cry. She never could do real tears on demand, but she was good at miming them.

She mouthed the words "*Oh my God*" but didn't bother to say them out loud, since nobody at home would be able to hear her initial reaction anyway. She practiced this surprised face several times, as well as the opening of the acceptance speech in which she would insist that her win was a complete shock and that she was honored to be considered in the same category as the other nominees. Whoever they were.

"You should practice your losing face too," advised a voice from behind her.

Amanda's happy face turned into an angry face when she heard this.

"You don't think I'm going to win?" she asked Danielle Cortez, her personal assistant of nearly three years.

"I think you will... but your losing face is very important if they pick another name. You remember *what's-her-name* a few years ago, when she got that really pissy look on her face?" Danielle asked.

"Who? I don't remember that."

"Exactly! If the public sees you as snobby, they won't support your movies. They want you to be gracious, like you'd be happy if *they* won the award instead of you."

"But I want the award. I've earned that award. Do you know how many takes it took to get that sex tape just right? Plus, I had to do a movie that I could be nominated for."

"I know you deserve this, but you should be prepared for anything."

"Fine," Amanda said, and she began to practice her gracious loser face in the mirror.

After about three seconds of playing the loser, a giant smile formed on her face, and she looked at Danielle in the reflection.

"Isn't my dress the most beautiful thing you've ever seen?" Amanda asked, feeling up the mannequin which had the sparkling pink dress on it.

"It is stunning. Just don't forget the name of the designer. They're going to want to know that," Danielle reminded her.

"Right. Who is that again?"

"Enrico Van-Solis."

"Uh-huh. And... who is he?"

"He's nobody. I made him up, but the name sounds damn fancy."

"Yes it does," Amanda smiled. "Y'know, I really think I have a chance at this."

Danielle smiled back at Amanda, "You do have a chance. You

were playing a lesbian, in a period piece, where you were committed to an asylum, where you led a revolt and found true love. How could you not win?"

"Yeah, but do you think I was ugly enough?"

Danielle nodded reassuringly, which made Amanda feel good about her chances, and her art in general. She loved doing work that *really* made a difference in the world... and she wanted to remember to say so if she got the chance during her acceptance speech.

Her preparation time was quickly disappearing. Amanda still had to finish her hair and get her jewelry. She had a million things to tape down, tape up and tape together if she wanted to look her best in the dress. There was no more time to simply stand around looking at her reflection.

"Okay," she said to Danielle, "where are my shoes?"

Though Danielle was normally quick to jump at any task that she had to tackle, she did not move. She did not say a word. The only reaction that Amanda got from her at all was a look of fear in her eyes.

"Danielle, where are my shoes?"

"I thought *you* picked out your shoes without me, when I went to get the dress."

"I didn't pick out the shoes. I thought you picked out the shoes!" Amanda yelled. "Oh, God! I don't have any shoes to wear!"

"Don't panic," Danielle told Amanda as she looked around the enormous closet for a pair of shoes that would be suitable.

The room was lined with shoes of all different styles and colors. There must have been a thousand that would have gone with Amanda's dress, but each of the shoes in the closet had been worn by Amanda before, and she could never be seen in public wearing the same shoes twice.

There was no time to go shopping for shoes. There was no time to have them delivered. No time to do anything.

Quickly, Danielle looked down at her own feet. She was wearing a pair of plain brown clogs. With no other option available to her, Danielle kicked off her clogs.

"Wear these," she told Amanda.

"Eew, but they're clogs."

"What other option do we have?"

Amanda looked at Danielle's clogs with disgust in her eyes. She wanted some other option—any other option—but there was nothing she could do and she knew it.

"It will be a funny story for you to tell on the red carpet," Danielle told her. "They'll be playing clips of it all over the place."

Still resisting, but slowly coming around, Amanda pouted as she asked, "Like Sharon Stone's t-shirt?"

Danielle smiled and put her hand on Amanda's shoulder, "Just like Sharon Stone's t-shirt."

~

Random English Countryside Location, 2:21 a.m.

Victoria Sanders was neither here nor there when it came to her career. She had been acting since she was three years old, mostly in commercials as a child, but then in more and more television roles. When she was nineteen, she was cast as the lead in a television series about a high school student whose father was killed by corrupt oil tycoons, leading her to become a masked crime fighter by night.

The series was a modest success and ran for eight seasons, during which time she appeared on magazine covers and even had her own action figure.

She was not the type of girl that you would normally expect to find fighting crime in the bad part of town. She had big green eyes and a slender build. At the moment, she had long blond hair, which was styled in the fashion of a nineteenth century woman of high social standing.

Victoria was standing next to one of the giant lights which made the surrounding area appear as though it were daytime, despite the fact that it was the middle of the night. In post production, it would be made to look like night once again through the magic of filmmaking.

This is stupid, she told herself. *Just ask somebody.*

She was starving. She would have sacrificed a limb for a bagel, but she had somehow lost track of where the food truck was. Looking back at the road, she could see trailers lining both sides, but it was dark, and the food truck was nowhere to be seen. If she wandered aimlessly, she would look lost and pathetic. If she got lost for too long, she would be missed when it came time to film her scene.

She was not famous enough to have a personal assistant who could be sent on such missions. She could ask one of the lower ranking crew members, but this was her first day of filming and she worried about the impression that she would make if she asked the wrong person to fetch her a snack.

Victoria needed this job to work. She needed to be known as something more than the girl from a campy TV series which was aimed toward the teenage girl/adult fanboy demographic. Somehow, her two decades of working in front of the camera were now meaningless. All that was left was an actress whose name had already been forgotten by the director twice on that very day.

Her male co-star was an A-list film star. His movies routinely pulled in less money than expected, but his name had pull and his films were respected amongst the Hollywood elite. If Victoria could manage to not look like an idiot when she attempted an English accent, she would have her work played before an audience of the most influential actors, directors and producers in the industry.

The film would be played for them even if she did suck, but she chose to ignore that fact. To consider this too often would only make her suck even more and she could not risk that.

She watched as her co-star discussed the scene with their director, Jan de Jan. The first *J* was pronounced, the second was more of a *Y* sound. If he hadn't been famous for years prior to Victoria meeting him, she was sure that she would have messed up this pronunciation more than once.

If she were on her television series, she would have walked to them and joined the conversation. She would have discussed lighting and camera placement. She would have joked with them and asked where the damn bagels were. She was not normally the type of girl who tried to shrink while on the job, but this was different. This was her first day on the most important project she had ever worked on. This was a day that would change her life forever.

A woman walked to Victoria and stood with her as she watched the director. This woman, Julie Patterson, was wearing the same nineteenth century dress as Victoria. She was wearing the same jewelry. She even had a wig which matched Victoria's hair perfectly... if you squinted enough.

Julie was Victoria's stunt double, and the two of them had worked together before. Though they weren't particularly close, Victoria welcomed the familiar face with a smile.

"So, that's him?" Julie asked, nodding in the direction of Victoria's co-star. "He seems shorter in person, doesn't he?"

"They all do," Victoria replied.

"So, why are you hiding by the lights? Trying to keep warm?"

"Sure. We'll go with that story if anyone asks."

Julie smiled more widely than before, "They're just people. They all flinch when the explosives go off."

Jan turned toward the women and motioned for Julie to join the conversation.

Julie started to walk, but turned around to face Victoria for one last comment. "Big stunt. Horses and fire. I guess they want to figure out how to do it without my incredibly flammable wig changing the genre of the movie by mistake."

"At least one of us gets to talk to them... Any idea where the bagels are?" Victoria asked her.

"Follow the road. Three trailers down, then cut between them and you'll see the truck."

"Thanks."

As Julie joined the men for their conversation, Victoria turned to walk toward the food truck. Having been close to the lights for too long, her eyes were not properly adjusted to the darkness of night behind them, and she accidentally bumped into a man who was wearing all black.

"Sorry," she told him, hoping that she was looking at his face, though all she saw were swirls of color.

He came back with a quick "Pardon me," before moving around her and moving on.

Whoever he was, he seemed to be in a hurry, but this was not unusual on the set of a big budget movie. Victoria thought little of it. Looking back, it would be one of the biggest regrets of her life.

~

Dorian was settling in for a night of junk food, relaxation, and mocking all of the celebrities whose careers were on a far more successful path than his own. He wasn't jealous. As long as he had a steady paycheck, he was happy. Even if his show were to be canceled—which seemed to be a major possibility every season that it was on the air, in spite of its popularity— he had enough money saved up to get by until another opportunity presented itself.

The GMAs were where the superstars went. It was where you'd find every celebrity whose face was on the cover of every tabloid on a bi-weekly basis. They were more famous than him, sure, but most of them were also attention craving maniacs who would do anything it took to get their picture taken with their hand up to the lens of the camera (though never actually covering it) as though they were annoyed by the attention. Because of this fact, he felt no remorse in laughing at their stupid outfits and mocking their lame acceptance speeches.

Jealous? Never.

As he paced across his kitchen floor, wearing his most comfortable sweat pants and old worn down t-shirt, waiting for the popcorn to finish popping in his microwave, Dorian tried to calculate how much time he would have to spend on the treadmill the next morning, paying for his night of off-diet eating.

On the counter, next to the empty box from the frozen pizza that was baking in the oven, sat the script for the next episode of his series. He still had to learn his lines and figure out his character's motivation, but he would put off his work for as long as possible. It was more fun to run lines with Casey in the makeup trailer anyway.

Watching award shows was better with Casey too, but she was on a date. Once again, he was at home alone, wishing that he was with her, while she was off dating some other guy. Dorian could respect that she only wanted to be friends with him, and he could take the constant hints without requiring her to actually say it out loud and humiliate them both. Still, he didn't have to like it.

When the popcorn was finished popping, Dorian stopped the microwave. He poured the popcorn into a large bowl and grabbed a cold root beer from the refrigerator. He then headed into his living room, where the red carpet show was already playing on the TV.

As he sat on the couch, Dorian caught only the last part of some comment that Amanda Hoit-Martin was making about taking clogs off of some poor woman's feet so that she wouldn't have to attend the awards barefoot. The story did not sound fascinating in the least, but Amanda Hoit-Martin sure did seem entertained by herself.

Of course, Dorian suspected that a ball of yarn would have kept this woman busy for at least a few hours.

"My sex tape would be so much better than hers," Dorian said to the TV, since there was nobody else in the room with him. "I mean, the lighting on that thing was horrible. The camera work was sloppy. And the acting was... Actually, it was better than most of her movies."

His humor would have been more fulfilling if he weren't alone. He considered calling Casey to make snarky comments over the phone, or maybe texting her so that she could read his comments without her supermodel boyfriend noticing... but if Casey wanted to spend the night making fun of the A-listers, she would have been there with Dorian in the first place.

There were others that he could call. His male co-stars enjoyed a good joke now and then, but they were married and had small children, so calling them during the evening hours was usually a mistake.

A few of the crew members were pretty funny. Of course, he didn't have any of their cell phone numbers.

For a moment or two, Dorian considered posting his jokes on one of the social networking sites, which was always a popular outlet for celebrities, but he didn't want his insults to end up on the entertainment news shows. His mother would never let him hear the end of it if she thought he was starting to sound like a Hollywood snob.

He reached for his cell phone and quickly typed up an e-mail to the one person that he could count on to appreciate his sense of humor. He wrote: *Amanda Hoit-Martin sucks as a porn star!*

A moment later, his cell phone alerted him to an incoming e-mail. After reading it, he quickly replied to himself: *God, you're lame.*

Dorian had owned a dog named Mr. Howell for many years, so when a *thud* came from the bedroom, Dorian didn't immediately react to the noise. It took his brain a few moments to even notice the noise, and another second to remember that Mr. Howell had died three months earlier.

~

Casey was sitting at her regular table in a small, unimpressive Chinese restaurant. She was alone, which was not how she had planned to spend this evening. She had expected to meet her date, Juan, at the restaurant and enjoy a pleasant meal with him. Afterward, they might take a walk or catch a movie. It was a simple plan, which even the dumbest of guys should have been able to understand, and yet she was alone.

She had spent the first hour waiting for Juan to show up. Fidgeting with her hair. Checking her watch. Texting him to see if he was caught in traffic, which wouldn't be surprising or beyond the scope of good excuses.

Every ten minutes, a peppy waitress would stop by the table, asking if she was ready to order. Casey would delay by ordering another root beer.

After an hour of waiting, Casey ordered her dinner, making sure that she would have food left over to replenish her refrigerator's supply at home.

As she waited for her food to arrive, Casey dialed Juan's cell phone number, but he did not answer. Instead, all she heard was his thick Irish accent, telling her to leave a message after the beep.

"Hey," she said, after the beep. "I'm here. Where are you? Call me when you get this."

She ended the call, but kept her cell phone in her hand. She wanted to call Dorian and see what he was doing, but she had already turned down his offer to hang out, and surely he would have had other plans by then. Even if he didn't, calling him would mean talking about being stood up. Discussing relationship problems with him could only serve to complicate their situation.

She took her time eating her food. It wasn't the fanciest restaurant in town, and there were no celebrities fighting to get through the door, but it was the best Chinese food in town, whether or not it came with free publicity.

After eating, she had the remaining food boxed, and she walked to the front counter to pay her bill. Behind the counter, there was a small TV which was tuned into the Golden Me Awards. On the screen, the show's host, comedian Barnie Spalding, was making a joke about staying home and eating Chinese food. There was something humorous about hearing the joke while standing in a Chinese restaurant, but only mildly so.

Just as Barnie was introducing the people who would be presenting the award for outstanding performance by a lead actress in a dramatic motion picture (formerly just *best actress*) Casey grabbed her bags of leftovers and walked toward the door. She didn't need to hear which actress would be earning even more money than her in the next year.

With her bags in hand, Casey left the restaurant and began walking down the street, toward her car, which was parked several blocks away. She kept her head down and avoided making eye contact with people. She was not regularly swarmed by masses of adoring fans, but because she occasionally got recognized by someone who was familiar with her work, and she made a habit of smiling and being polite to anyone who cared about who she was.

She was not in the mood to smile and be friendly on this particular night. She had been stood up, had eaten dinner alone, had turned down an offer to spend time with her best friend, and was beginning to think that the shrimp might not have been as fresh as she would have preferred. Meeting even one fan at this moment would have been a test of her acting abilities.

"Oh my God. You're her!" came a voice from behind, and Casey knew that her cover had been blown. "You're Casey Dale! I love your show. I never miss it."

Casey stopped walking and pasted a smile on her face before turning around to face her fan.

When Casey saw the woman, she was surprised to find that this was not her supposed target demographic. She was a woman in her 30's, wearing a Hawaiian shirt and flip-flops; obviously a tourist. Few people who lived in the area cared one way or the other when they saw a celebrity. At least, this had been her experience.

"Hi," Casey said, holding up her bags of food, one in each hand. "I'd shake your hand, if I could."

This was a lie. Casey hated shaking hands with strangers. She thought that it was a horribly, outdated ritual, probably responsible for most of the outbreaks of horrible diseases which spread around the world. She wasn't a hardcore germaphobe, but the thought of shaking the hands of random strangers on the street gave her the creeps.

"You're one of my favorite actresses. The chemistry you have with Dorian is amazing," the woman continued. "Can I have a picture?"

In the past, not every person on the street had a camera. If they met a celebrity, it could be a quick and painless encounter, and both could be on their way. Now, everyone had a cell phone and every cell phone had a camera. Now, everyone needed a picture.

Casey would have loved to turn the request down and walk away, but she did not want to be one of *those* people, so she agreed to stand with the woman while the woman's husband, who apparently had no idea who Casey was, took their picture.

"You should have chosen Toby though," the woman told Casey, "I mean, between Astin and Toby, Astin is way hotter and you have more chemistry. But I get that the timing wasn't right. But this whole *'I choose me'* thing was just aggravating... as a viewer."

"I will be sure to tell the writers," Casey replied.

"Oh, I have. I've emailed them and told them exactly what I think," the woman came back. "But I'd like to know if you agree. Do you?"

"I think that you'll be happy with the upcoming storylines, but don't tell anyone I said that."

"Was that a spoiler? I didn't want a spoiler!"

"It wasn't a spoiler," Casey assured her. "It was just... Watch the upcoming episodes."

As Casey dealt with this oddly rabid fan, she failed to notice the man standing behind her, dressed in black. It wasn't until she finally managed to pull herself out of that conversation and she started to walk down the street once again, looking into the store windows along the way, that she saw the man's reflection. He was matching her pace, and while she couldn't get a clear view of him, there was something about him that didn't sit right in her mind.

In the next window that she passed, there were several video cameras on display, and she could see the video that they were capturing in the monitors that sat beside them. She could see the man behind her, and she could see that he was wearing gloves.

Aside from some of the more eccentric personalities in town, few people wore gloves in Los Angeles. It was a generally warm climate, so there was little need for them. Coupled with the black outfit, the man looked like he belonged in a spy movie.

Hoping to let the man pass and leave her life forever, Casey ducked into the electronics store. As she walked, she hoped to hear the automatic doors close behind her, but judging by the sound, they only closed partway before opening again to let someone else in.

Casey closed her eyes, cursing the situation, but trying to talk herself into believing that everything was normal at the same time. The man hadn't done anything to her. He hadn't spoken to her. He hadn't tried to grab her. There was no reason to believe that there was anything unusual about him, except that she had a feeling. When she saw his reflection in the window, she felt as though he was more than a random stranger on the street.

Casey walked through the aisles, pretending to browse at movies and TV show box sets. As soon as she got an opportunity, she turned to look behind her. She expected to find the man standing there, waiting to grab her, but he wasn't there. He was nowhere to be seen.

Still pretending to browse, Casey picked up a box and looked across the store, now hoping to see security guards or off-duty policemen, as well as the man with the gloves.

There was a slight giggle beside her, which drew her attention. She saw a teenage girl standing nearby, looking at the box in her hand and then to Casey, as though there was something funny about her movie selection.

Looking down, Casey found herself looking at her own picture. She was holding the third season box set of her own series in her hand, and the girl beside her found this funny. Normally, Casey would feel the need to explain that she didn't routinely buy her own show and that she couldn't even stand to watch herself on screen, but she had more pressing concerns.

There was a feeling in her gut which told her that the man with the gloves was nearby, and the fact that she could not see him was only making matters worse. If only she could look across the store and find him looking at vacuum cleaners, she would be so relieved.

Putting the box set down, Casey wandered from that particular aisle, and moved through the store. She walked toward the wall of television screens as she pulled her cell phone from her pocket and dialed 9-1-1.

She put the phone to her ear, wondering what she was going to say when the operator answered and asked her what her emergency was. Somehow, she didn't imagine that the operator would find news of a man wearing gloves to be as alarming as Casey did.

A voice came over the phone, saying, "You have reached 9-1-1 emergency assistance. Your call is very important to us. If you are currently in an emergency situation, please stay on the line and an operator will be with you shortly."

This recording was followed by some horrible 1970's music, which only served to make the current situation seem even more creepy than it already was.

Casey hung up the phone and dialed another number. As she put the phone to her ear, she whispered to herself, "C'mon, Dorian. Pick up. Please pick up."

There was no answer.

~

On the other side of town, popcorn covered the floor of Dorian's living room, mixed with the broken glass from his root beer bottle, the contents of which now covered the television screen that displayed only a network logo over a black background.

The air was thick with black smoke and the smell of burning pizza, but the fire alarm did not sound. Its batteries had died long ago.

Beside the couch, the popcorn was soaked in blood. Beside that, Dorian lay dead.

The phone rang.

~

Casey was now ducking behind a display for the latest and greatest video game, hoping to remain hidden long enough to get someone to help her avoid the man with the gloves.

Dorian was not answering his phone, and the fact that it hadn't quickly gone to voicemail told Casey that his phone was still on, and he had not simply pressed the *ignore* button.

It was not like Dorian to ignore her calls, and just as she had felt that something was wrong when she saw the reflection of the man behind her in the window, Casey now felt that something was horribly wrong with Dorian.

The feeling that something was wrong with him was almost worse than the feeling that something was wrong with her own situation. She wanted to find him and to make sure that everything was okay. In order to do this, she would have to leave her hiding place and get to her car.

She slipped her cell phone back into her pocket and placed her bags of leftovers behind the cardboard cutout of a large alien robot nearby. After taking a deep breath, she prepared herself to stand up and walk toward the exit.

It required a second deep breath before she could actually get the nerve to make her move. When she did manage to pull herself up, it was not with the fierce determination that she had always imagined herself having in this situation. It was with fear and hesitation. As it turned out, this fear was justified.

As Casey stood and made her way around the video game display, she found herself standing face to face with the man with the gloves. Now, he wore a ski mask as well, in keeping with the standard *bad guy* dress code.

She gasped as she saw the man, and took a step back.

"Oh God," she said, as the random thoughts filled her mind, preventing her from any sort of logical reaction. "Please don't do this. I have a photo shoot in the morning."

The man took a step toward her, and Casey's survival instinct kicked in. She turned and ran in the opposite direction, yelling "Help me! Somebody please help me!"

Customers around the store turned to see who was screaming and why.

Somewhere in the store, Casey heard the voice of a young man ask, "Is that the chick from TV?"

And another young man replied, "Damn, she's hot."

"Someone, please call the police. He's trying to kill me!" Casey cried, as she reached the wall, which was covered in televisions.

On each of these TVs, Casey's show was being displayed. On each screen, she was smiling and holding onto Dorian.

There was no time to stop and admire the coincidence of this situation, or consider the odds of her finding her own show being played at a moment like this. There was no exit on this wall, and that meant that she had to keep moving.

With the man following closely behind her, Casey ran down an aisle on which the video cameras were being sold. Each of these cameras had a small TV screen hooked up to it, and each of these screens displayed the live image of Casey, running from the man with the gloves and the mask.

Unfortunately, none of these screens displayed the image of anyone coming to her aid. Instead, the other customers in the store, as well as the employees, stood back and watched as the man with the gloves reached out and grabbed Casey by the hair.

He pulled Casey backwards, causing her to fall to the floor.

She screamed, but didn't cry. She struggled, but his grip on her hair was strong and she could not escape. Though she tried to claw at his hands and his arms, they were covered, so her efforts yielded little result.

As Casey kicked and screamed, and tried to get away, she happened to see one young girl with her cell phone in hand. She was not calling the police. Instead, she was recording video of this incident, which would undoubtedly wind up online.

The more Casey fought, the more phone cameras she saw, and for some reason, she couldn't help but appreciate the fact that there would be multiple angles, giving the editors more options for the final cut.

She knew it was over. There was nobody to help her, and she could not win the fight on her own. She only hoped that Dorian was not suffering the same fate.

The man with the gloves grabbed one of the video cameras from nearby, and though it was attached to a strong tether, there was enough slack for him to swing the camera through the air.

The last thing that Casey ever saw was her own image, on one of the display screens, getting larger as the camera grew near.

He hit her in the face, and everything went dark. She could feel blood dripping down her head.

He hit her again, and she could feel her skull breaking.

He hit her again, and again, and again, until she was finally dead. And then he dropped the camera beside her body, so that she could film her final close-up.

~

Victoria had finally found the food truck, and the tent in front of it which had tables set up where a selection of food was made easy to grab for those who didn't have time to wait for French toast to be made fresh.

On the table, she found a variety of bagels with a large selection of jams and cream cheeses to spread on them. There were trays full of scrambled eggs and tater tots. There were bowls of fruit and vegetables, and even a juicer, for those who were inclined to drink their way through life.

Aside from one or two smaller projects that she had worked on in her day, the food that was made available on the set was always reliably good, though not always reliably healthy. What she saw before her now was what was available between meals. At lunchtime, there would be pie.

If only she didn't have to squeeze herself into an impossibly tight corset, she could have had a good time with the food that was made available to her. As it was, she would settle for a little bit of fruit and a plain bagel to pick at.

She found herself standing alone, as she looked over all of the food that had been put out. For some reason, there seemed to be very few crew members moving about, which was unusual. In the makeup trailer, which was several trailers away from where she stood at that moment, Victoria could hear the GMAs being broadcast over the radio, with cheers and whistles rising from the audience. Perhaps this was where all of the crew members had gotten off to.

She grabbed a paper plate from nearby and spooned several pieces of melon onto it. As she reached for a fork to aid in her eating, and hopefully prevent her from dropping any melon juice on her costume, Victoria dropped a piece of melon to the ground.

Reaching down to pick up this piece of melon, Victoria noticed a spot on her dress, just above the waste. At first, she thought it was dirt, or perhaps a wet spot from the falling melon, but the more closely she looked at this spot, the more it took on a reddish hue.

Blood, she thought to herself.

As the realization came over her, the sound of the award show playing in the background seemed to become louder, and she realized that what she had originally heard as cheers and whistles now sounded like screams of terror.

In her mind, Victoria walked backward through her day, trying to imagine where the spot of blood might have come from. She thought that it might have been a crew member who had cut their hand without realizing it. She thought that maybe she had a cut of her own, so she checked her hands, but saw no cuts.

She then remembered the crew member who had bumped into her, on her way to the food truck; the man who was dressed in black. She remembered feeling him touch her as he moved around her, but she hadn't thought anything of it at the time. Now, she was certain that the spot must have come from him.

The strange thing was, the spot seemed to grow bigger by the moment. It also seemed to grow more and more wet.

She thought that it must have been her eyes, adjusting to the darkness after being in front of the lights for so long, but this was not a case of her eyes playing tricks on her. When she touched the spot, she could feel the wetness of the blood. She could feel the warmth.

As the stress of finding this blood on her dress came over her, she began to feel a cramp in her side. It was dull at first, but soon grew sharper.

In what seemed like the most obvious realization of her life, combined with the most stupid she had ever felt, Victoria realized that the spot grew larger because the blood was not merely a stain on her dress. It was her own blood.

The bastard stabbed her.

She didn't feel cold or weak. The blood was not oozing from

her at an alarming rate. She was not going to collapse at any moment, never to wake again. So... why?

She could not, for the life of her, figure out why a man would stab her in passing, if he didn't intend to kill her. What possible purpose could there have been?

Victoria needed to find help. There was a medic somewhere on set, but she needed to find him. She needed to find security and warn someone that there was a lunatic going around stabbing people.

She walked between two of the trailers, hoping that someone would notice her and call for help. Nearly everyone had a walkie-talkie, so if she could manage to find a production assistant, she could just sit down and allow everyone else to come to her. Unfortunately, this was easier said than done. As she walked around the trailers, the only people she saw were too far away, still discussing how they wanted to frame the next shot.

Victoria turned and walked to the door of the nearest trailer. It was an office trailer, where schedules were being drawn up for the next day, and call sheets were being prepared for distribution. Surely there would be someone inside who could help Victoria.

She climbed the steps, wondering if she should announce herself before entering, as she was always taught to do when entering the hair and makeup trailer, but deciding that this was no time for rules and preferences. This was an emergency.

She grabbed the handle of the trailer door and pulled it open. There were two female production assistants inside. Both were sitting in chairs in front of a table, where papers were scattered all around. Neither of them turned to see her.

"Hello?" Victoria said to them, hoping to get their attention. "I'm bleeding. I need help."

As she climbed the remaining steps and walked into the trailer, Victoria realized that there was blood on the floor of the trailer, dripping from the hand of one of the production assistants.

It took her a moment to realize that both of the women in the trailer were dead.

She gasped, but it was not the type of gasp that she had been portraying on screen for most of her life. It was not the sharp, dramatic gasp that was familiar and expected. This gasp was quiet, and lacked dramatic flare. If she had delivered a gasp like this in front of the camera, she would be told to try it again, and to make it more realistic this time.

By now, Victoria's heart was pounding in her chest. She was no longer the sole victim of this brutal attack, she was also a witness. She was a survivor, when others had been savagely killed.

But why? Why would he stab her and not kill her, as he had with these other women?

There was a silent walkie-talkie on the table beside the dead women, which Victoria figured the killer had turned off. Normally, communications were bouncing to and from crew members, so when she picked up the walkie-talkie, she was surprised to find that it was already on.

She pressed the button and spoke into it, saying, "Hello? I need help. Two women have been murdered and I have been stabbed. Please, someone, help me."

Releasing the button, she waited for a reply, but the radio remained silent.

She let out a groan under her breath as she turned toward the door and began to make her way out of the trailer.

As she exited and looked out at the other trailers, which lined the road on both sides, Victoria could see a pair of legs sticking out from between two of the trailers on the opposite side of the road. Just as she saw them, they were dragged between the trailers and out of sight.

She had to think fast. People were being murdered, and there was no safe place to go. If she ran for another trailer, she would be running through the darkness, open to another attack. Who knew where the killer was, or even how many killers there were?

Turning in the other direction, she saw Julie and Jan talking in the well-lit area of the field where they would be filming. Her co-star was off to the side, reading his script.

As far as Victoria was concerned, they were the only living people in the area. They were the only ones who could possibly help her. So, as quietly as she possibly could, she closed the trailer door behind her and she began to walk toward them.

Behind her, the radio broadcast had changed. Now, there was nothing but the emergency broadcast signal, minus the informative message that was supposed to follow.

She walked, hoping that someone would turn and see her before she reached them, but nobody turned. Even if they did, the lights between them would have made it hard for them to see her approaching, holding onto her still-bleeding wound.

Each step she took felt as though it was a step through quicksand. Never fast enough for her liking. She felt like screaming to them, but to do so would only draw the attention of her attacker, who had left her alive for some unknown reason.

If they're killing people, why only wound me?

It was the same question that had run through her mind over and over again since finding the dead bodies in the trailer.

She assumed that the crew members they had killed so far might have just gotten in the way at the wrong time, and some might have been killed to prevent an alarm from sounding, but where were the others? There had to be more.

As she kicked the questions around in her head, walking toward those who she could see were alive, she was suddenly stopped by a loud *BANG!*

Victoria watched as Julie fell to the ground. She had fired enough guns in her days as a television action hero to know that Julie had been shot. Watching Julie fall from afar, dressed in the same clothes as Victoria, and with the same hair—meant to look like Victoria on camera—was like watching herself fall dead from outside of her own body.

Jan tried to catch her, but he was not fast enough. As he leaned down to check on her, another shot was fired. Jan fell next.

While Jan struggled to breathe, choking on his own blood, a third shot was fired, instantly killing Victoria's co-star.

Victoria felt numb. Not because of her wound, but because of the situation. She had now witnessed a mass murder, and had managed to escape, thus far, with a relatively minor wound.

Escape.

If her attacker had wanted to kill her, he easily could have, but he had something more important to attend to. He hadn't killed everyone right away. There was something else.

It occurred to Victoria, as she stood in the darkness, that the killer did not stab her repeatedly because he did not feel a need to kill her in that moment. A wound would distract her and slow her down, but he was not worried about her escaping.

Why?

This time, as she asked the question inside of her own head, the answer came to her. This was the same answer which she had spent six seasons pretending to figure out for the first time, just before the second commercial break. The killer was not worried that she would escape because he had a bigger plan, and this bigger plan would ensure no survivors.

Victoria turned and hurried to get out of view by walking between two of the nearby trailers.

"A bomb," she whispered to herself. "It's always a bomb."

But where? Where would the killer, or killers, hide a bomb? Where could they be sure of an explosion that would leave no survivors?

Suddenly, Victoria felt as though she were standing between two large sticks of dynamite. The trailers. All of them. That is where *she* would hide the bombs.

As she came to this realization, Victoria hurried to get away from the trailers. On the far side, there were hills and open land. She would be exposed, but to go the other way would mean entering a minefield, so she quite literally ran for the hills.

Once the trailers were behind her, Victoria felt as though she had a target on her back. She expected to be shot dead at any moment, but no gunshot came. Instead, the world around her turned into a shaking, violent mess of shrapnel and fire.

And then there was black.

~

The Golden Me Awards were even more boring in person than they were on television. At home, you could change channels to avoid particularly lame jokes or repetitive acceptance speeches; you could pig out on junk food while wearing your pajamas; and you could heckle those on stage until you were blue in the face.

Heckling was frowned upon when you were in the actual auditorium. Junk food was strictly prohibited. You could sneak out to the bathroom in order to avoid listening to whoever was on stage, but if you were nominated for an award that night, you ran the risk of becoming one of those actors who was in the bathroom when they won the award; that actor whose friend or co-star would have to accept in their place, turning you into a laughing stock.

Amanda had not devoted her entire life to becoming famous, and the last several months to developing acting skills, just to have it all thrown away at the last minute. So, she sat in the audience, patiently waiting for her award to be announced, and politely pretending that she cared who wrote what song, or who designed which dress. Nobody at home cared, which was why most award shows had started granting some awards in a separate ceremony, for those really boring aspects of filmmaking. Amanda just wished that the Gimmes would have learned that lesson so that she wouldn't have to sit through some boring foreign director talking about how great his movie was, in an accent that made it nearly impossible to understand a word that he was saying.

Foreign films were so lame, in Amanda's opinion. Hardly any of them were ever filmed in America, so she didn't know why she should have to watch them win awards in America.

To occupy herself during these less interesting presentations, Amanda took to her cell phone, where she wrote updates to her fans, via the popular social networking sites. In response, her biggest fans told her how much they loved her. Little girls told her how much they wanted to be just like her. And some guys asked her to take off her clothes.

She loved her fans, because they loved her. And to Amanda Hoit-Martin, anyone who loved her could not possibly be all that bad. Even if she didn't win the award—which she figured was a small possibility—she would have the praise of her followers, numbering about six hundred thousand when last she checked.

On the stage, comedian Barnie Spalding was going on and on with endless jokes that Amanda was too distracted to hear. Every so often, she caught the name of a politician or foreign leader with whom she'd had dinner and she would clap or laugh, depending on the reaction of the rest of the crowd. She didn't have to worry too much about accidentally clapping at something that she should find offensive, since a lot of the people in the room used the same political consultant that she did. Their opinions would be the same as hers.

So much easier than thinking of opinions on her own.

At long last, Amanda heard Barnie announce the presenter for the award in her category, and Eva Pipp walked onto the stage. She was a heavier woman, but they called her beautiful anyway. She'd won the award the year before. She was wearing a long, flowing gown, with beautiful duck-shaped shoes which Amanda thought would have gone perfectly with her own dress.

When Eva reached the microphone, she read the teleprompter, which said, "For decades, we have gathered to celebrate the brightest stars in Hollywood, and to honor their most memorable performances. Last year, I was honored to receive my own Gimme for my portrayal of Dominic Lillipad, a woman who fought the hardships of the Dust Bowl, while coming to terms with her homosexuality and leading a revolt. This year, we honor a new crop of actresses who have managed to shed an even newer light on some completely different social issues. And so, it is my pleasure to introduce the nominees for outstanding performance by a leading actress, portraying a female character, in a film or motion picture—"

Before Eva could complete her speech, the power to the auditorium was cut, and the place went pitch black.

From the darkness, a shriek arose, the likes of which could shatter glass. It was a chilling, pain-filled scream.

When the emergency power kicked in and the room was once again visible, everyone turned their attention to Amanda, who had let out the scream. She looked around at them, at first hoping that nobody would be able to tell that it was her, but then admitting, "I just really wanted to hear her say my name."

There was no time for anyone to respond to her before the gigantic television screen behind Eva came to life. On it was the silhouette of a man, sitting in a large leather chair. Behind him was a room that was filled with books.

A chill ran up and down Amanda's spine. That chair was not pleather, and that meant that this man was a murderer. She couldn't figure out what was happening, but she knew that it was not good.

"Good evening," rose the deep, menacing voice of the baby cow killer. "Right now, you are all thinking to yourselves, 'Oh, my God. I wonder if my hair looks okay.' However, at any moment, you will look up at this screen and you will realize that something is not going according to plan. You will see that there is a rather ominous looking man speaking to you from an undisclosed location, and this is rarely a good thing. You will wonder who I am, but it does not matter. You will wonder why I am doing what I am about to do, but in truth, that will matter even less, so I won't bore you with my reasoning. I will simply tell you that ours is a world corrupted. Corrupted by greed. Corrupted by envy. Corrupted by celebrity. Our children grow fat and waste away, while watching endless hours of television. Our lives have become meaningless and hollow. We offer sacrifice to you, our false gods, and that sacrifice is all of us."

Around the auditorium, gasps could be heard. People tried to refute what the man was saying, but apparently he could not hear them through the television screen.

Whispers were heard. All around Amanda, people ranted about the craziness of Christian extremists, while wondering what he was going to do to them.

Amanda turned to her cell phone once again, writing to her fans: *OMG. Smthing ttlly wrd hppng.*

The man continued, "And right about now, you're all regretting the fact that you had neglected to see how your *'frightened'* face would look with your fancy outfit. Let me assure you that it could not possibly look bad on any of you. I know what you are all asking yourselves. You're all wondering *who* I am wearing. Well, I am going to ignore that question and instead give you the answer to the question that you *should* be asking: What am I going to do next? This answer is simple. I am going to kill all of you and bring an end to the reign of Hollywood buffoonery."

Amanda was horrified by the blasé manner in which he wrote off the hard work and creativity of fashion designers. It seemed so typical of the cow-murdering Christian who wanted to kill her, and it made her sick inside.

Well, it was either that, or the fact that he wanted to kill her. Amanda was having a really hard time deciding what she was reacting to. All she knew is that she wanted to get away from the man on the giant screen. She wanted to run, but there seemed to be a rule against running, because nobody had gotten out of their seats yet. So, she stayed put.

"Do not try to open the doors, for I assure you that they are all quite locked. There is no escaping your fate," the man told them. "They say that the stars we admire in the night sky might have been dead for centuries before we ever notice. The same could be said for all of you. You see, I was once a follower of your cult of the moving picture. I was enamored with the beauty; enchanted by the idea of mindless entertainment which required little or no effort on my part. I believed that there could be intelligence to your work, and I sat through countless hours of *Lost* because of this belief. I watched movie after movie, directed by M. Night Shyamalan, because I truly believed that there must have been something that I was missing. Some deeper meaning. Some hidden key which would make those movies worthwhile."

"Did you see *The Happening*?" someone mumbled behind Amanda, "What the fuck was that?"

"So lame," someone else replied.

The man on the screen continued, speaking over the people behind Amanda, but she could only listen to one conversation at a time. When she returned her attention to the man on the screen, he was saying, "—something clicked for me. I had an epiphany, and I began to see the world in a new light. Our culture has become a culture of cultureless buffoons. Now, I realize that I just used the word *culture* three times in that one sentence, but I assure you that I am the right man to bring..." he seemed to choke on his own thought before continuing with, "...*culture*... back to the world. This is why I have spent years passing my philosophies on to my students, and why I have worked tirelessly to place my pupils all over the world, in jobs relating to your beloved entertainment industry. Through these pupils, I have gained all of the knowledge necessary to bring your industry to its knees. Tonight, I put that knowledge to use."

The stage erupted with pyrotechnics, which reminded Amanda of the *Wizard of Oz*, only way more scary. She wrote to her fans: *Bg blls f fr. Vry scry.*

The fire began to spread across the stage, eventually setting fire to the curtains which surrounded the oversized screen on which the mysterious man was delivering his message.

People began to stand from their seats and panic. Amanda stood, wishing that she could go back in time and prevent the people from installing that giant TV, so that none of this would have happened.

As the room began to erupt in both fire and panic, people began to push Amanda in an attempt to slip by her, out of the row of seats, and to the open aisle.

She wrote: *Jst gt shvd by Ptr Jcksn. Wy cl.*

She followed that with: *Mt hv bn Kvn Smth.*

Either way, she was stoked to be in the presence of some really good movie makers.

"This is your final act, Hollywood," the man on the screen said, now surrounded by smoke and flames, making him seem even scarier than before. "Prepare yourselves. For, the curtain is indeed about to fall. Your lives have reached their climax and you must now prepare to fade to black. Roll credits. Cue the wretched music which never actually played during the movie and nobody will stay to listen to, but which will undoubtedly be the foundation of every soundtrack and television commercial you produce. Special thanks to the city of Hollywood. Several animals *were* harmed in the making of this video."

I knew it! Amanda thought to herself as she struggled to get past the swarms of people who were shoving, poking and grabbing her.

The screen went black, but the auditorium remained lit by the flames. When Amanda finally reached the main aisle, and all of the other celebrities hurried to push their way toward the exits, Amanda wandered toward the stage instead.

"I want to thank my wonderful cast and crew," she said in a quiet voice, which nobody would hear.

Around the room, the fire spread quickly. Several more explosions rocked the building, this time taking casualties. Cries and screams could be heard. Somewhere in the distance, someone yelled, "Did you see that guy? He wasn't even reading from a teleprompter. He had those lines down!"

"I want to thank my mother and father, for always supporting me," Amanda continued.

On the other side of the auditorium, a woman's hair caught fire. The woman screamed and hurried to pull the wig from her head and throw it to the ground.

"But most of all, I want to thank my fans," Amanda said, watching the chaos unfold.

Amongst the hundreds or thousands of screaming people, only a handful of specific voices could be made out. They said:

"My breasts are melting!"

"Somebody call my agent!"

"I want to direct!"

"Oh my God, look! Real tears!"

The smoke began to burn Amanda's lungs, and the fire was beginning to claim lives. The smell of burning flesh filled her nose and turned her stomach. She was, after all, a strict vegan.

"My fans have always been there for me. Supported me, through good times and bad. So, thank you. Thank you for believing in me. Thank you for loving me."

In the following minutes, some burned to death. Some were trampled. Some killed by others who believed that they could kill their way to freedom. Some passed out from inhaling too much smoke. Most, however, died when the auditorium collapsed in on itself.

In the end, Amanda Hoit-Martin found herself trapped beneath the rubble of the auditorium, with a Gimme somehow piercing her chest. As she slowly bled to death, she looked at what remained of the world that she loved so dearly, and a single tear fell down her cheek.

"Remember me," were her final words, as she slipped from this world forever.

~

From her apartment, high above the city, Tessa could see the chaos unfolding. She could see the explosions and the smoke rising into the night sky. She could smell the burning city below her.

She had lived in that town for decades. She had spent the best years of her life there, and the worst as well. It was her home. It was everything that made her who she was.

All she could do was watch. The television screen which had been tuned into the GMAs was now showing nothing but a network logo. Tessa held her cell phone, which received updates from many of the celebrity social networking accounts. She had set it up that way so that she could be in touch with the world that she was once a part of. So that she could hear about opportunities. So that she could dream of the days when she was one of those actresses that she now followed online.

On this night, most of the updates were the same. They spoke of the pain that came from multiple stab wounds; the feel of blood dripping down various body parts; the smell of one's own flesh burning off of the bone.

Each account. Every celebrity. Every director, writer, producer... Every person from every level of the entertainment industry was reporting live from the scene of their own death.

The sky was lit by the fires burning below, and darkened once again by the smoke that came with those fires.

Embers were blowing through her window and littering her balcony.

What was there for Tessa to do, except wait? She sat in her chair, wearing her finest silk night gown, with her hair and makeup done just right, and a glass of red wine in her hand.

The will to live was strong. She wanted more than anything to reclaim the life that she had once had. She wanted to go back to the world that she loved. But the life that she dreamed of had been gone for years already, and the world that she loved was now in flames. What more was there for her?

After pondering what the future might hold for a faded actress in a world without film, Tessa pulled herself to her feet, and put on her high-heeled slippers.

She could not be a suburban housewife. She had no husband.

She could not be a farmer, nor a teacher, nor a doctor. She could not be a soldier. She could not be anything of any use to anyone, except an actress. But there were no more actresses, and might never be again.

If her world were to end, she wanted to go with it. If this was to be her fate, she would not run from it. She would not hide. She would embrace the final scene and play it for all that it was worth.

She walked to the door which led to the hallway outside of her apartment, and she turned the deadbolt to unlock it. She unlocked the second deadbolt, and the third, and finally, she unchained the door and opened it.

If death were to pay her a visit, he would be welcome in her home, with a glass of wine waiting for him.

She returned to her chair and sat down, with her back to the door. Waiting. Wanting.

Unfortunately, this was still Hollywood. In this town, an actress of Tessa's age couldn't even get herself murdered.

Death would not be coming for her.

~

The morning sun rose over what remained of the trailers and film equipment, now scattered over the English countryside. The fires had burned out long ago, and now a cool breeze scattered script pages across the hills.

Under the charred remains of the food table that had knocked her to the ground, Victoria remained unconscious, but breathing. The bleeding from her wound had stopped. Though she would be in pain for days or weeks to come, Victoria would find herself a survivor of the Hollywood apocalypse.

Chapter Two
A STARLETTE IS BORN

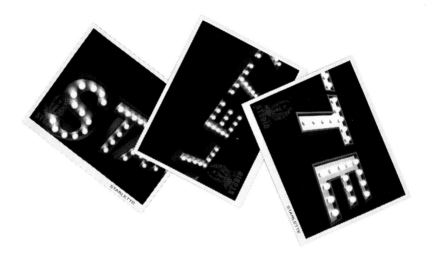

Dawn had already passed by the time Victoria Sanders began to come around. The sun was hanging high in the sky, which was deceptively beautiful that morning. As her eyes began to open, she didn't have a memory of what had happened the night before. All that she was aware of was the sky.

For the most part, the sky was clean and clear. The few clouds that hung overhead seemed to glow whiter than normal, nearly hurting her eyes just to look at them. Several birds were taking advantage of the cool morning air. For a moment, it was a wonderful awakening.

Victoria wasn't unfamiliar with the feeling of waking up in a strange place. Her career as an actress required her to travel often, both for filming and for promotion of her films, so she seemed to wake up in strange hotel rooms more often than not. She had even slept outside during the filming of one low-budget film, shot in the middle of the woods of some fly-over state. So, as unusual as it was to wake up outdoors, that fact alone did not immediately stir her memory and throw her into a panic.

There was a feeling in her side, as though she were laying on a rock or some other hard and uncomfortable object. Without thought—but with far more effort than it normally should have taken—she put her hand to the ground and tried to move this object, but all she felt was grass. When she put her hand to the spot on her body where she still felt this phantom object, she was shocked by the sting of her own touch and the sudden awareness of the weight that was pressing down on her.

Within a split second, the night came back to her. She remembered her stabbing, and the discovery of the dead bodies in the trailer. She remembered witnessing even more murders, and the explosion that followed. These memories hit her harder than the warming tray that had been thrown from the food table during the explosion, and struck her in the head, leaving her unconscious. They weighed heavier on her than the debris under which she was now buried... Though, the debris was a far more literal weight and a more pressing concern in that moment.

Covering her stomach, there was a piece of wood, blackened by the explosion. To Victoria, it looked like a piece of a folding table which had been blown apart, but she couldn't be entirely sure of this. Not that it really mattered. All that mattered to her was that it was heavy, and on top of her.

There was something else which prevented her left leg from moving, but she could not see this second object, due to the piece of table which obstructed her view of her leg.

She needed to get free. She needed to get to a hospital. She needed to get home, to her own country, to her own house, and her own bed. She wanted to hug her dog. She wanted to call her family.

Her first instinct was to call out for help. If anyone else had survived the killer's attack and the explosions, maybe they were still in the area and could help her get free. Perhaps they could also help her figure out what the hell was going on.

She remembered hearing the award show the night before, and the screams that came over the broadcast. She remembered hearing the emergency signal. She wanted to tell herself that none of these things were related to what happened to her and her coworkers, but there was a nagging feeling in her gut, right beneath the chunk of table, and a few inches to the left of the stab wound, which told her that something big had happened. The world looked different to her. The air smelled different.

Actually, the air smelled like smoke and burning flesh, but metaphorically speaking, these smells smelled differently to her than they would have smelled, had she not experienced what she had experienced.

Victoria didn't call out. She knew that this would be a mistake, because everything from every script for every horror movie that she had been offered a role in (but turned down) since the cancellation of her series told her that if someone did hear her and came looking, it would be the wrong person, and she would end up dead, with a single bullet between her eyes.

Instead, she maneuvered her hands beneath the piece of table, and she pushed with every ounce of strength that she could muster. Had she been at the top of her game, unwounded and fully nourished, she would have had an easier time of this. Regardless of her weakened state, Victoria managed to push the piece of table off of her and lay it on the ground beside her.

Her stab wound was now throbbing, and she could feel fresh blood trickling from it. She knew that if she did not get medical care soon, the wound would become infected and that would make this situation infinitely worse.

Left leg still pinned, Victoria tried her best to pull herself up, so that she might assess the situation. She ached. It seemed as though every muscle and joint in her body was rebelling against her, but she ignored the pain. She had no choice.

When she saw what was pinning her leg down, she nearly threw up.

Thrown across her leg, staring back at her with the hollow gaze of the dead, was a man—or possibly a woman—whose face had been torn, bloodied and burned beyond any recognition. The body's clothes were blackened by fire, and the shirt appeared to be melted onto their skin. Had they lived through this, the pain would have been beyond anything that Victoria could have imagined. Part of her was glad that the dead person would not have to endure that pain.

She hesitated before moving the body. She did not wish to be disrespectful, and in the back of her mind, she was worried about hurting this person whom her conscious mind knew could not possibly feel pain. Also, she didn't want to *touch* the dead body. She was not squeamish to the point of fainting at the sight of blood, but this was something else entirely.

If anyone asked, she would tell them that her nausea was caused by head trauma or loss of blood, but seeing that body made her stomach turn even more than it already had been.

Gently, she reached down, and tried to push on the shoulder of this dead person, hoping that they would simply roll off, as bodies often seemed to do in her line of work. This body did not roll. It did not move at all, with the exception of a portion of flesh and t-shirt which slid off the bone beneath her fingers.

Victoria pulled back, and out of instinct she jerked her leg as hard as she could, freeing it from under the corpse, which slumped to the ground and now stared up into the beautiful morning sky.

She was free now, but did not immediately rise. Instead, Victoria pulled her knees to her chest and breathed deeply, trying not to cry or scream or vomit.

One of her strongest assets as an actress was her ability to compartmentalize her feelings. She had gone to work the day after her beloved father had died, for example, and she played a fun comedic scene as though she were the happiest person in the world. She had played raging hatred toward men that she had fallen in love with off camera. She had cried in agony on some of her happiest days.

In that moment, amongst the rubble and the corpses, she could have fallen apart, but she had trained for years for situations like this. She knew that she could pull herself together if she could just take a moment to get into character.

Deep breaths. Careful concentration. Blocking out the world around her, and pretending that she was back on the set of her low-rated action series, Victoria was becoming the type of person who could handle this situation.

Slowly, she rose to her feet, ignoring the pain in her side and the pounding in her head. She was dehydrated and hungry but none of that mattered, because more than anything in that moment, she was a professional.

She took her time when looking around the damaged area, which was still smoking in several places, though she saw only one small fire that still burned. She looked for movement of any kind which might lead her to another survivor, or warn her of an attacker, waiting to stab her once again.

There was no movement though. There were no cries or screams. No coughing up blood while delivering a heartfelt monologue during a drawn out death. What she heard was the gentle breeze blowing through the wreckage, blowing lighter pieces of debris around, and the sound of birds circling overhead; *like* vultures, but *not* vultures.

Victoria took a step forward, trying her best to avoid stepping on debris, but failing. At the very least, she hoped to avoid stepping on human remains. She hoped that whatever bodies she found would be whole, like extras who had been dirtied up and scattered around to add atmosphere to the background of a scene, but as she moved around, she found bits here and pieces there. Most of them were charred, but still recognizable as human.

As she passed through what had once been the line of trailers, she saw an arm sticking out from beneath a pile of debris. There was a watch on this arm, which reflected the sunlight, drawing her attention to it. She didn't move toward it, because she knew that whether or not she found it attached to a person, that person was dead.

She recognized the watch. It belonged to the woman who ran the wardrobe trailer, and made sure that all of Victoria's dresses and accessories were correct for the period which they were trying to portray.

Victoria pushed her initial reaction to the back of her mind, preventing herself from lingering on the memory of that woman's voice warning her not to wrinkle her outfit, and she moved on.

As she examined the site of this attack, she could not believe the level of destruction that had been done to this location. Every camera, or light that she found seemed to be damaged beyond repair. Even the walkie-talkies all seemed to be broken. It was as though someone had come back while she was unconscious and had made a final pass through the rubble to make sure that nothing of this operation remained intact.

What she also could not believe was that there were no helicopters in the sky. No fire trucks, spraying water across the smoking mess. No police officers calling out for survivors. No news vans. No gawkers. No studio representatives coming to assess the loss of profits that might arise from such an event, or the negative publicity that might be associated with it.

Victoria was alone. The only company that she had now were the dead bodies on the ground, and the birds up above. She felt like a ghost, haunting the site of her own death, but she had yet to come across her own body.

She walked up the hill, losing track of where the trailers had ended and where the filming was meant to be done. In the explosions and the resulting fires, everything seemed to merge into one pile of wreckage.

For a moment, as she looked down, she almost believed that she did find her own body. She saw a dress that matched her own, and hair that looked like what hers had once looked like, before the attacks.

It might have been a relief to find herself dead, and to be able to move on to whatever came after, but she was not as stupid as some former costars would have led the public to believe. She knew that the woman on the ground was her stunt woman, Julie. She knew that the hair was a wig. It had slipped since Victoria last saw Julie alive, the night before. Now, Julie's naturally dark hair was showing through.

Victoria had known Julie for years, since working together on television. They weren't close. Half the time that Julie was filming Victoria's stunts, Victoria was somewhere else entirely, filming a different scene. But they were friendly toward one another, and to see Julie dead made this tragedy seem more real than it had before.

After being stabbed, Victoria had wondered why she had been allowed to go on without being finished off by the attackers. In their hurry to shoot every major cast or crew member in the area, they had simply slowed her down, so that she would be killed in the explosion.

By the time Victoria was stabbed, it was only a matter of minutes until the bombs would go off. Whoever had planted them would have wanted to get their primary objectives accomplished and move away quickly.

Victoria was the female lead of this movie, so at first, she wondered why she hadn't been a priority. The answer soon came to her: The killer did not know that she was the star. Julie was talking with the director and male lead. Julie was wearing the same outfit as Victoria. Julie was killed in Victoria's place. The fact that Victoria was alive was a mistake on several levels.

Victoria stared at the body of her stunt double as she ran these realizations, which were really just theories and speculations, through her head. She felt guilty for living. It might have been Julie who could have gone on, but as usual, and for the last time, Julie took the hits for Victoria.

"I'm sorry," Victoria said, knowing that this was the point where she was supposed to bend down and close Julie's still-open eyes... but Julie's eyes were closed already, so Victoria simply took a moment to say her goodbye and then moved on.

From where she now found herself, Victoria could look back and see the full scope of the attack area far more clearly than she could while standing in the middle of it.

She asked herself how this could have happened. She asked why they had chosen to attack this specific set, especially considering that they had taken every possible measure to ensure that their production was animal friendly and that their carbon footprint would be offset by the purchasing of several trees and small shrubs.

As she tried to figure out the specifics of the situation in which she now found herself, without any means of collecting data or putting clues together, she waded through the wreckage once again, just in case there was someone still breathing.

"Hello?" she called out, now relatively certain that there were no shady murderers lurking about. "Can anyone hear me?"

The silence that she received in response seemed somehow more quiet than it had been before she called out.

"If you are alive and you can hear me, make some sort of

noise!" she called out again. Again, there was no response.

Victoria turned and looked into the distance, where the day seemed to be going on as usual. Beyond the burnt grass and fragments of trailer that was scattered across the field, everything appeared to be normal and peaceful. There was no smoke in the distance, which might suggest more attacks and mass casualties.

Deep in the distance, she could see a small grouping of houses, too small to be a town, but large enough to be of use to her, in her present situation. Surely, they had seen the explosions the night before. Surely they could see the damage in the clearness of day.

If Victoria wanted to know why those people had not come to help, or why the authorities had not been called, she would need to make her way to those houses. All she would need to do was walk a great distance in hot, heavy period clothing which impeded her ability to breathe, while making sure that her stab wound did not start bleeding too badly.

She could have fussed about this, or screamed at the fact that people should have come to help her, but she chose not to do those things. As an actress, she was forced to swim in freezing waters. She was forced to be uncomfortable and tired and hungry on a regular basis. If she wanted to survive this day, she would have to rely on those instincts. She needed to put aside her concerns and her pain until this was over.

She needed to take control. She needed to be in the lead. Whoever had tried to kill her had failed. She would not be as clumsy. After all, she was a star.

As she walked toward the cluster of houses, a low rumble began to rise in the area. Victoria recognized this sound as the engine of a car, and quickly turned to see who might be coming. With luck, it would be help, but given her situation, she was not inclined to trust in luck. She hurried to get behind a nearby scrap of trailer.

Once behind this cover, Victoria peered out, toward the road. The trailers had been lining both sides of the road, and when they exploded, they blocked the path of any vehicle attempting to pass through. As it turned out, this was a good thing.

Despite the fact that the vehicle she saw coming up the road was a black SUV, which was built for rough terrain, it would need to stop at the edge of the debris. This would give her time to hide.

Victoria didn't think that the fire department would be driving big black SUVs, nor the police, and certainly not an ambulance. Whoever was inside that SUV was someone else, and that meant that there was a good chance that they would want her dead.

She only had a few moments to figure out a plan. She needed to get herself out of sight, fast.

Nearby, there were bodies thrown, and covered with pieces of debris from trailers and equipment. Their faces were not visible. This gave Victoria the idea of pulling fragments of the trailers on top of her and playing dead. Surely, if this SUV contained people who wanted to see her dead, they would not bother to sift through every single body. They would be looking for survivors in the debris, and possibly down at those nearby houses.

She got onto the ground and began to pull whichever scraps of burned wreckage she could find on top of her. She covered her torso and one leg. The last piece of debris that she pulled over herself was pulled over her head, but she left an opening big enough to see out of.

Victoria wanted to see who had attacked this place. She wanted to look into the eyes of the man who had tried to kill her, and she wanted to repay the favor. Ordinarily, she was a peaceful woman. She ran marathons to raise money for charitable organizations. She even appeared as part of a montage of lesser-known celebrities during a telethon, raising money for disaster relief in a foreign country.

After everything she had seen and been through, she could no longer choose to be that woman. Instead, she needed to survive, and to survive, she would have to be angry. She would need to hate the people who had done this to her, not ask them which childhood trauma had driven them to lash out in such a manner. In order to survive, she needed to want to see the blood of her enemy.

Lucky for her, the part came naturally.

She heard the SUV come to a stop at the edge of the debris, and the engine was left running. She heard one of the doors open and close. She might have imagined hearing the footsteps of the man, since she was not very close to him, but she could have sworn that she heard them.

"Hello?" came a man's voice. "Is anyone here? Can you hear my voice?"

He was not speaking with a British accent. Victoria did not respond to him, and wouldn't have even if he did have the British accent, because she did not wish to die in a blaze of stupidity. She merely thought that if this man wished to sound like an authentic passerby, or member of local law enforcement, he should have at least tried to sound the part.

Amateur, she thought to herself. She had worked long and hard prior to taking on the role that brought her to the English countryside, perfecting the accent that would be required for the role. At the very least, the man could try to sound local.

"If there are any survivors of this horrific and tragic event, I am here to help you! Make a sound!" the voice came again.

Deep within the rubble, there came a sound. It was the sound of knocking. Victoria couldn't tell if this sound came from another survivor or if the man himself was doing the knocking, in an attempt to draw attention to himself.

"I hear you!" the man called to the sound, and Victoria could hear him moving through the debris. "I'm coming!"

There was more knocking, and more scurrying through it. Victoria could not see anybody from her position, but if there truly was another survivor, they hadn't made a sound when she called to them.

"I'm here!" the man called to the sound. "I'm coming to get you!"

For a moment, all of the sounds stopped. Victoria could imagine that the man had come across another survivor and was digging them out, but she heard no evidence of this.

As long as the voice had been calling out, Victoria knew where he was. Now that he was silent, she had no way of knowing what was going on around her. He could have been standing right on top of her and she wouldn't have known it. He could have been aiming a gun at her, and she could do nothing to stop him from pulling the trigger.

What Victoria could hear was the sound of her own breathing. Against the debris, her breath sounded louder than any banging or stomping. She worried that if she could hear it, the man could hear it as well. She imagined him walking closer and closer, being careful not to make a sound. She imagined that he knew exactly where she was and how to avoid being seen in her limited view of the area.

Trying her best to stop breathing didn't work. The more she tried to hold her breath or slow it down, the more out of breath she felt and the heavier she breathed.

BAM!

The shot rang out, and seemed to echo through the debris on top of Victoria. She had been so uncertain of where this strange man was that she had allowed herself to believe that he was standing on top of her. He wasn't.

Somewhere, far enough away from Victoria to let her know that he wasn't aware of her presence, but still close enough to be too close, the man had fired a gun. Presumably, he had killed another survivor.

Someone had survived, and she had failed to find them before the attacker came back. Though she called out and tried to look around, she had failed. Now, someone was dead.

As much as this might weigh on Victoria's conscience, she didn't have time to linger on feelings of guilt or remorse.

When the shot was fired, and Victoria was nervous enough to believe that it might have been meant for her, she flinched. This small flinch caused the debris on top of her to shift and slide. It made noise.

She had to assume that the man heard this noise. She had to assume that at that very moment, he was looking toward her from wherever he happened to be, and he was waiting for some further indication of life amongst the rubble.

She held her breath and remained as still as she could possibly remain. She wanted to close her eyes and squeeze them tight, as though this could make the man go away, but she knew it was an irrational desire. She needed to keep her eyes open. She needed to know if he was coming for her, because if he was, she needed to take action of some sort.

For several moments, there were no other sounds. There did not appear to be anyone rushing toward her, waving a gun and preparing to shoot her. If she could remain perfectly still, she thought that she might be able to recover from her mistake.

After holding her breath for as long as she could, she tried to let it out as slowly and quietly as possible. The exhale was shaky at best, but she thought that she did a fine enough job of being quiet.

The man with the gun was doing an equally good job of remaining quiet. She would have preferred that he stomp around and cause a lot of commotion, but there was nothing.

"Hello?" came the voice of the man again, this time much closer to where Victoria was hiding.

How he had gotten so close without making a sound was beyond her, but he was there. Not directly on top of her, but close enough to hear if she were to flinch again. If this happened, she would surely be killed.

"Is there someone here?" he asked, not even calling out, but speaking plainly. "That wasn't a gun shot that you heard. It was just a piece of garbage falling."

Did he expect anyone to believe him, or was he just having fun at this point? His cover had been blown by the firing of his gun, so he couldn't possibly expect to have people willingly calling attention to themselves.

Victoria prepared herself for what seemed like an inevitable confrontation. She expected the man to suddenly throw the debris off of her, and aim his gun at her face. After some sort of pun or sarcastic comment, he would shoot her dead.

"You can trust me," the man said. "I drive a tiny electric car."

After this, there was silence. No footsteps or further calls into the rubble; only the sound of the breeze blowing past the scrap of trailer, which she had pulled over her head.

For what seemed like an eternity, she waited for the next sound, and half expected it to be the final sound that she would ever hear. Her muscles were aching to do something beyond playing dead. Her legs wanted to run. Her arms wanted to fight. Her voice wanted to scream, but she resisted. Patience was a virtue, and if there was one lesson that she had taken away from her years as an actress, it was how to lie down and remain still, come what may.

The silence was broken by what sounded at first like chirping to Victoria's ear, but which she soon realized was a cell phone ringing. When it stopped ringing and the man spoke, it sounded as though he was standing right on top of her. The slightest mistake on her part, and she would be doomed.

"Yeah?" the man said to whomever it was that was calling him, "I'm just double checking the place now, tying up any loose ends. I'll be on the plane tonight, don't worry. I think he'll be happy with my work."

There was another moment of silence before the man said, "Oh, I did. I had a *blast*."

Yup. There it was. The required sarcasm and punning that comes from the over inflated ego of a mass murderer.

The man apparently ended his call and began to walk away with much less care and stealth than he'd used when approaching Victoria. She was relieved to have distance put between herself and the man with the gun, and listened for the sound of his car driving away. Soon, she would be able to get up and run.

The SUV door slammed shut a moment later, and Victoria heard the sound of its tires rolling through the debris. It sounded like a dirt road, with rocks being kicked up by the tires. Soon, the sound faded into the distance, but Victoria did not jump right up and take a deep breath of fresh air. Instead, she played dead until she could be damn sure that she could not be spotted through the rearview mirror, should the killer decide to look back.

Minutes passed, and the longing for escape did not once dull. Her heart was pounding as she waited for the moment when her brain would convince her that it was the right time to leave, but no signal came.

Each time that she thought of standing up, she also thought of the SUV stopped by the side of the road, waiting to see if anyone would get up. She pictured the man with the gun, now replaced by a high powered sniper rifle, waiting to take her down the second that she felt safe.

As those minutes passed, she came to realize that there was no *safe*. She would never feel safe again. All there was now was *fight*.

Though her brain told her to stay down, Victoria threw the scraps of trailer off of her and got to her feet. She was careful to stay low, to minimize the target area, should someone be watching her through the sight of a rifle.

Angles were a talent of a good actor. Always know where your camera is, and know how to play your angles. Usually, you want to be as prominent as you can possibly be when a camera is pointing your way. To hell with natural behavior, you angle your face toward the camera. Major corporations pay millions of dollars for ad space during the airing of a popular television series. They get thirty seconds to flash their product. An actor, in a primary role, gets much more than thirty seconds, but the idea is the same: show your product.

In this situation, the best course of action seemed to be the opposite. Remain small. Minimize visibility. For once in her life, Victoria's goal was to ruin the shot.

Once behind a larger chunk of metal, Victoria carefully took a look at the road. She saw no SUV. She saw no sniper. Then again, that was usually the point of a sniper.

She had no options left to her. She could not remain hidden in the rubble for the rest of her life. If she wanted to leave, she had to do it fast.

Pushing aside all of the instincts in her head that told her that she would fail, or trip or get herself killed, Victoria lifted her rather bulky dress and ran toward the cluster of houses in the distance.

With each step, she expected to be shot through the back. She imagined herself tripping over her own feet and rolling down the hills, causing her wound to bleed yet again.

Her hair, which had been well pinned and sprayed by one of the top professionals in the film industry, was flopping down across her face. She brushed it aside and tried to tuck it behind her ear, but time and time again, it got in her way.

Considering the night that she'd had, and the morning that followed, Victoria was not going to complain about her hair, but the annoyance was still there.

Her shoes hurt too. They were insane. Constructed for *look* rather than *function*, with heels that were not made for running up and down hills, and sides which felt like they were growing tighter by the second.

The worst piece of her wardrobe had to have been her corset. It constricted her movement. It made it hard for her to breathe. It pinched and dug itself into her skin around its edges.

Victoria longed for the day when she could wear a pair of jeans and a sweatshirt once again.

The houses seemed to grow farther away at first, rather than nearer. When she began her run, she had all of the energy that came from lying still and wanting to break free. Once she was in motion, this energy was replaced by the hunger of not having eaten, and the thirst that came from denying herself water the night before, for fear of having to climb out of her costume in order to use the restroom. In spite of the difficulties, she pushed herself. She would not allow her body to slow her down, and she would not allow her clothes to get her killed.

It took her longer than she would have liked, but Victoria reached the cluster of houses at long last, and rounded the nearest of these houses, so that she could bang on the front door.

Once again, she brushed the hair out of her face. It was now soaking with sweat, as were her clothes. She could only imagine what her face looked like, with dirt and ash mixed sweat and whatever blood had been drawn during the explosion.

At least she didn't have to worry about her makeup, which was a revolutionary new product, made to survive a day in the life of the most active woman. From tears to sweat, the new ultra resistant formula would keep a woman looking fresh and alive, from morning to night... According to the magazine ad that she was reading while the makeup woman was applying her face for the day.

There was no answer at the door. Victoria pounded a second time, but still, nobody came running to answer.

She moved to a window and looked inside. Within the house, she could see a cup of coffee sitting on a table, next to a half-eaten plate of food.

The television was on, but displayed only static. Beneath the television, a lamp was on the ground. While the bulb of this lamp was still shining brightly, the glass lampshade was in pieces on the ground.

Victoria came to the conclusion that someone had come to this home, most likely during the night, before the attacks, and there had been a struggle. The fate of those who lived there was a mystery, but there did not seem to be anyone inside at the moment.

Victoria returned to the door and tried the knob. It turned and the door opened with ease.

Inside, the house was quiet. It was decorated simply, with a somewhat rustic influence. The floors were wooden, and looked as though they had been there for centuries. The fireplace was surrounded by stone, with a wooden mantle. It was beautiful.

The house could have easily seemed like home to Victoria, on any other day. She could imagine herself sitting at the kitchen table, with a cup of tea, listening to the sound of *nothing*.

On this day, however, she wanted *something*. She wanted a telephone and a computer with internet access. She needed information, but more than that, she needed help.

On the floor beside the sofa, she found the phone. It was broken into several pieces, and stood no chance of working. She could tell that it was useless from a distance, but tried to use it nonetheless.

As expected, the phone didn't work.

Victoria wandered through the house, hoping to find another phone, or a person who could tell her what was happening, but she found none of these things. What she did find, in the master bedroom, was a laundry basket, full of a woman's clothing.

The pants were ten sizes too big in the waist, and short in the legs, but there was a large dress with a string that tied in the back. Though baggy, it would work for Victoria much more than the dress that she'd been wearing all morning, so she began to strip.

Getting out of the corset was more work than she would have liked. She felt exposed in the house. Knowing that there had been an attack there already, she still expected to be shot at with every second that passed.

It took far too long for her to get out of her costume, and into normal, much more comfortable clothing. Luckily, the shoes that belonged to the woman in this house were within range of her own, so she found a pair of sneakers and put them on.

On her way out of the bedroom, she found a radio sitting on a shelf by the door. She went to it and turned it on, hoping for news at last. What she got was more static. Channel after channel was filled with nothing but deadness. The world was beginning to feel like a very lonely place to her.

Just as she was beginning to lose hope, a voice came over the radio. It was the low, ominous voice of a man, midsentence, which said, "—will wonder why I am doing what I am about to do, but in truth, that will matter even less, so I won't bore you with my reasoning. I will simply tell you that ours is a world corrupted. Corrupted by greed. Corrupted by envy. Corrupted by celebrity. Our children grow fat and waste away while watching endless hours of television. Our lives become meaningless and hollow. We offer sacrifice to you, our false gods, and that sacrifice is all of us..."

As Victoria listened, the man went on to say how cultureless our world had become, and how he would restore our society. With each word, Victoria's stomach turned.

The man on the radio spoke of the pointlessness of *Lost*, and Shyamalan movies, and by this point, Victoria's hands were balling into fists.

He was insane. He presumed to judge everything that she had based her life around. He had apparently targeted every corner of the entertainment industry, wiping out everything that Victoria had ever loved, and for what? Because he never thought to watch *The Happening* in black and white, thus bringing the whole theme of the movie into focus? Because he could never connect the dots of Libby's backstory on *Lost*? Because he just didn't *get* it?

Victoria had witnessed a great deal of suffering in her day. She had seen reports of terrorism that were beyond imagination, but she had remained politically neutral in an effort to avoid alienating foreign markets. But this was different. Whoever this man was, he had attacked Hollywood, and that made it personal.

When the message on the radio began to replay, Victoria turned it off. As she did this, she became aware of a sound coming from outside. It was the sound of an engine.

Victoria carefully walked to the nearest window, trying her best to avoid being seen by anyone who was outside. She hoped to find a normal person, coming home from the market with a bag full of groceries, but nothing on this day would turn out to be ideal.

What looked like the same SUV that she had seen coming up the road earlier, carrying the murderer with the gun, was now sitting on the road that connected the small cluster of houses.

The driver's side door was open, and he was nowhere to be seen, but the engine was running. Whatever he was doing, he was not planning on sticking around for very long.

Victoria angled herself for a better look at the surrounding area, and saw a house across the street, with the door swinging open in the wind. For a moment, she kept an eye on this door, waiting for the man to come through it and return to his car. As she waited, the anger within her built. She could choose to remain hidden, and hide for the rest of her life, or she could take action... She could make this son of a bitch pay.

She left the bedroom and hurried through the house, keeping an eye out for anything that might be used as a weapon. Though she was staunchly in favor of strict gun control, Victoria would have preferred to find a rifle hanging over the fireplace. This was an emergency situation, after all, and she was a trained professional.

There were no rifles that she could find. There was not even a poker near the fireplace, which she could use to spear the murderer with. The best she could find was a large, somewhat dull knife, which she came across in the kitchen.

For people who lived in the middle of nowhere, the residents of this house did not seem very well equipped; certainly not for self-defense.

After grabbing the knife, Victoria made her way through the back door of the house, hoping to sneak around and between houses, making her way to the house with the open door without being noticed.

The important lesson that Victoria learned on this day was that a door that was swinging in the wind did not necessarily mean that the bad guy was in that house. As she exited the back door and made her way to the side of the house, Victoria stumbled upon a group of people, bound together and gagged, with a darkly dressed man standing over them, holding a gun.

Before the man could see Victoria she hurried to get out of

sight, hiding around the corner of the house once again. She knew that the other people had seen her, and that one of them had probably recognized the dress that she was wearing, but if they were smart, they would not let the man with the gun know that she was there.

"I am not intent on killing you," the man told his captives. "In fact, to do so would violate the orders that were handed down by my superior. We only needed to keep you here and keep you quiet until our attack on the Hollywood machine could be carried out."

There was a slight pause, which made Victoria uncomfortable. When she took a quick look around the corner once again, she saw the man looking to the ground, deep in thought.

The man was extremely well dressed for a terrorist. His black cargo pants appeared to be tailored to his specific measurements, and his black sweater had a black dress shirt underneath it, accented by a black tie. His hair, which was perhaps a little too blond to be natural, was neatly combed.

The only thing that made her pause and question his look were the army boots that he was wearing. They did not seem to fit the look that he was going for.

As Victoria looked around the corner, she also looked more closely at the people who were bound together. Four men and three women were tied to each other, preventing them from coordinating any sort of escape. Next to them, two little girls and a little boy were tied to each other.

While the children could not take their eyes off of the man with the gun, Victoria could see two of the men looking directly at her. With a nod, she told them that she was there to help, and they quickly looked away again.

Victoria ducked around the corner and took a moment to think through her situation. Normally, she would have a consultant of some sort, telling her how to properly hold her weapon or free the hostages in a stealthy fashion. This time, however, she was on her own. She needed to draw from her past experiences and devise a plan of her own, trying her best not to get anyone killed in the process.

When she looked down to the ground, Victoria saw an assortment of children's toys scattered around the lawn. Toy soldiers were mixed with baby dolls. Sand box shovels were mixed with twirling batons. Most importantly, she saw a cheap plastic slingshot, half buried, having been neglected for too long.

She pulled the slingshot out of the ground and looked it over. Despite being covered in dirt, the slingshot appeared to be in working condition. Though Victoria was better versed in the use of a baton, the slingshot would provide her best chance of success.

As a plan began to form in her head, Victoria questioned her ability to take down an armed gunman with a child's slingshot, but there was another way for her to use the slingshot to take the man down.

She tucked the knife that she'd taken from the kitchen into the string of her dress. She grabbed a rock from the ground and placed it in the little plastic basket that was meant to make the toy easier for children to use with water balloons or some such object.

She took a deep breath as she pulled back on the little basket, stretching the rubber straps to their limits and hoping that they wouldn't snap.

Victoria looked around the corner one last time, to make sure that the gunman wasn't looking in her direction. When she did this, one of the bound man began to attempt to talk to the gunman, drawing his attention.

The man's words were muffled by his gag.

"You can't talk," the gunman told him. "That's the whole point of the gag. I specifically did not want you to talk."

While the gunman's back was to her, Victoria aimed the slingshot high, and shot the rock over the corner of the house next door. A moment later, the sound of the rock hitting some hard object drew the attention of the gunman.

"What was that?" he asked the people, who only shrugged in return. "Do you have a dog or something like that? Someone who might come poking around?"

The people shook their heads.

The gunman put his hands on his head, trying to decide what the best course of action to take would be. He seemed nervous, which Victoria hadn't expected, based on what she'd seen and heard of him earlier in the day.

"You know, if they had just sent someone with me like I asked, I wouldn't have to worry about going to see what that noise is. I wouldn't have to worry about leaving you here, or wonder if someone's waiting around that corner with a shovel, ready to smash my face in," the man told his hostages. "But, no. They send me alone."

Victoria liked the shovel idea. She looked around for a shovel, but there didn't seem to be one nearby.

After a deep, annoyed sigh, the gunman started to walk toward the corner of the house next door, holding his gun firmly. As he walked, he turned to his hostages and warned them, "I don't want to kill you, but if you try to do something stupid, I won't have a choice."

With that said, he walked around the corner and out of sight.

Victoria knew that she only had a matter of seconds before the man came back. Without taking the time to think, she hurried toward the hostages, pulling the knife from her dress. Keeping an eye on the corner, waiting for the gunman to come back, she hurried to get the knife to the ropes which bound the hostages.

"Stay quiet," she told them. "Don't let him know anyone is here."

She sliced back and forth on the ropes, but the knife was horribly dull, and her progress was slow. She was beginning to think that she would not have enough time to free the hostages before the man came back, and if they could not be freed, she would have to think of some other plan. This other plan would require her to take down the gunman on her own. It would not be easy.

"C'mon," she said under her breath, but the knife would not cut fast enough. "You people really need sharper knives."

Seconds were ticking away. She knew that the sound of the rock would not distract the gunman for long. There was no option but to hand the knife to one of the bound women. As she did this, Victoria looked the woman in the eyes.

"Keep working on this," she told the woman.

The woman nodded as she took the knife from Victoria and began to attempt slicing at the ropes herself.

Victoria tried to think of another plan as she walked toward the corner of the house, where the gunman would soon be coming back. The only option she had was to take him by surprise, and hope that he didn't fire any stray bullets into any random victims.

Looking around the area, Victoria could find nothing that would make an ideal weapon. No shovels or gardening sheers. All she could find nearby that had any bulk to it at all was a wooden bucket, three-quarters full of rainwater. She picked it up by the sides, not the handle, and put her back to the wall, hoping to remain unseen until the man was in front of her.

Her fingers were slipping on the bucket, so she moved one hand to the bottom, hoping that it would allow her to get some more thrust when she needed it.

She really hated this plan.

Each second that passed seemed like an eternity. Victoria wanted to look back and check the progress of the hostages, hoping that they would free themselves in time for some of them to help her jump the gunman, but to look back would mean letting her guard down. Letting her guard down would result in her death.

From around the corner, she heard the sound of feet on grass. He was coming.

She steadied her stance and prepared to take action as the man rounded the corner.

Within moments, he was there. The first thing she saw of him as he rounded the corner was his gun. He held it in front of him as he came around the corner, ready to shoot at anyone who tried to surprise him.

As Victoria had learned in her early days as an actress playing an action hero, this form was entirely incorrect. While it may look pretty in the movies, it will get you killed when someone attacks your gun before your eyes are around the corner.

Case in point: Victoria swung her bucket of water once she knew where the man's face would be. His arms had given him away, and there was no way for him to be prepared for her attack.

The gun went off, blowing a chunk out of the house next door, but there would be no casualties from that bullet.

The bucket connected with the gunman's face, and he fell backward as the water sloshed out of the bucket and onto the ground.

Victoria rounded the corner as quickly as she could, and swung the bucket again. This time, the gunman blocked her attack with his hands. This told Victoria that he had no means of blocking another blow, so she stepped toward him and kneed him in the stomach, though she was aiming for the groin. He doubled over, and she swung the bucket one last time.

As the bucket connected with the gunman's head, it shattered. It would be of no more use to her, though it had performed much better than the piece of shit knife.

The gunman fell backward as pieces of wood and drops of water flew in every direction.

Victoria was surprised that she was able to hold her own against a man who had killed so many people, but she wasn't going to let that pride slow her momentum. She stepped forward, grabbed the gunman's arm, and twisted it until the gun dropped to the ground.

She meant to push the gunman away, pick up his gun, and spread his brains across the English countryside with it, but the gunman swung back this time. She was caught off guard as she was struck in the side, just above her stab wound. She couldn't help but wince and suck air through her teeth, which gave the gunman an opportunity to hit her again, this time in the face. Hard.

Victoria fell to the ground, trying to gather her senses and resume the fight. She was not fast enough. Soon, the gunman was on top of her, grabbing her by the throat and pinning her to the ground as he choked her.

She tried to kick him, but her legs only made contact with air. She tried to punch, but her arms were pinned to the ground. She tried to breathe, but she could not.

Soon, every muscle in her body relaxed, and her body went limp. Her eyes lost focus, and there was no more struggling.

The gunman grinned as he released her neck. He remained on top of her as he leaned in close and said, "Nice try."

As he began to sit up and climb off of her, Victoria could hold her breath no more. She took a deep gulp of breath and looked the gunman directly in the eyes, and said, "Thanks."

She grabbed him by the sweater and flipped the gunman over her head. It was one of the first moves that she'd learned when taking the self defense classes that were required for the role of a street-smart girl, raising her siblings on the harsh streets of Chicago, in the made for TV movie, *Woman Of The Hood.*

Once the gunman was away from her, Victoria turned herself over and grabbed his gun as she hurried to pull herself off of the ground.

The gun wasn't good enough. She wanted to hurt this man. She wanted to feel what it was like to beat the crap out of him.

She walked to him and kicked him across the face, saying, "You like killing people?"

He did not respond. He seemed to be dazed.

She stomped her foot down as hard as she could on his gut. "You enjoy causing pain?"

She kicked him again in the side, so hard that he nearly rolled over. He coughed and spat blood onto the ground.

"You wanted to wipe out my people? Well guess what," she said to him. "You failed."

As the gunman flopped to his back once again, Victoria stepped back and aimed the gun at his head.

"What does it feel like to be on the other end of this thing?" she asked him. "And how the hell did you get a gun into England anyway? Aren't they, like, *really* strict about that?"

He didn't answer her. She didn't want him to. She just wanted him to suffer. She wanted to pull the trigger and be done with him. She wanted to go home and have all of this behind her forever, but he had taken her home away. He deserved to die.

She looked at him, down the barrel of the gun, and with the sight aimed directly between his eyes. She tightened her grip on the gun and held her breath, ready to pull the trigger.

But she couldn't. She was not a killer.

The pain that rose in her gut was not from any of her wounds, it was the emotional pain that she felt, finally catching up to her. Her eyes filled with tears, and a scream rose from her throat.

She swung the gun and hit the murderer over the head. He was knocked unconscious, but unlike all of those that he killed, he would live to see another day.

~

As the day wore on, Victoria found herself sitting in the first house that she had visited. The woman that lived there with her two children had offered her a meal and a place to sit for a little while.

Victoria's wound still required medical attention, but she couldn't bring herself to travel at the moment. She needed time to stop and to think about what she was going to do.

To the world, she was just sitting, staring out a window with a blank expression on her face and cup of room temperature tea in her hand. In her mind, she was racing, running, fighting, planning... Her thoughts were chaotic and jumbled. One moment, she would be wondering how to get home and the next, she would see an image in her mind of the body that had been draped over her leg when she woke up that morning.

"We were attacked yesterday afternoon," said a soft voice from behind her.

It was the voice of one of the men that she had freed earlier. She hadn't heard him come into the house and didn't turn to see him now. She just looked out the window and listened to what he had to say.

"When they came, we didn't know what the bloody hell was going on. We thought they wanted money or something like that... but it never made sense. We're not rich," he told her, and his accent reminded her of how far from home she really was.

"We were all so excited to have you lot filming out there. I guess maybe we thought they were with you, or wanted to watch you work. But then they had the guns, and it was around that time we sorta thought they might not be your normal spectators."

The man pulled up a chair and sat next to Victoria, taking the tea out of her hand and putting it on the table. He was in his late forties, with hints of gray starting to show in his otherwise black hair. As he spoke, Victoria felt no need to keep her guard up. She simply listened.

"Then we saw the explosions and the men were *excited* about it. They'd been planning it for a long time. Living it. Breathing it every day; probably for years. They knew exactly who was out there and exactly how to go about killing all of you. 'Cept, I think something happened and it went slower than they planned. Jet lag or something like that. If they weren't in a hurry, I'm willing to bet that they would have taken the time to make sure that you were good and dead."

Victoria looked at the man as he began to get around to the point of why he was saying all of this. She had a feeling that she knew what he was about to tell her. It was what she'd been thinking about ever since she had been able to put together what was going on around the world. She could have cut the man off, but she didn't want to. She wanted to hear someone else say it, just to make sure that she hadn't gone crazy.

"Now, the point I'm trying to make is that you are *meant* to be dead. All over the world, those like you were murdered and these people have nothing better to do now than clean up the scraps that they left behind. They know who you are. If you just go back to your normal life, they'll find you and they will kill you. As we stand now, only one of them knows that you survived... and let's just say that he's not going to be talking to anyone when he's done here," the man said, in a tone that could have easily been scary but which Victoria found oddly comforting. "To the rest of them you are dead."

"And I'll stay that way," she finally cut in. "The person I was is gone. I have nothing to go back to. And you're right; they will kill me if I try. They'll kill my family. They'll kill my friends."

Victoria stood from her seat and walked to the kitchen counter, where she picked up the knife that she had taken earlier. She looked down at this knife, and saw her own reflection in it.

Victoria held the knife tightly in one hand as she gathered her long, golden hair in the other, "Victoria Sanders is dead," she said to the man, and slashed at her hair with the knife.

What should have been a smooth cut and a dramatic moment soon deflated as the knife failed to cut more than a small chunk of her hair, and only pulled on the rest, making her wince.

"Seriously, what the fuck is with this knife?" she asked, continuing to slash and chop at her hair.

When all was said and done, she put down the knife, believing that she had done an efficient job of cutting her hair off. In spite of this effort, one patch of longer hair still managed to flop down over her eye.

~

Eleven months had passed since the attacks on the Hollywood empire. Eleven months since the death of Victoria Sanders, and the birth of something new; something which was not named until much later.

It took weeks for her to find her way home, traveling from town to town on the kindness of strangers, and then from boat to boat without asking permission at all. She could not flash her passport and could not risk someone asking for it.

Along her travels, nobody had recognized her. She'd never been very famous to begin with and now her hair was shorter and her eyes were surrounded by dark, smoky eye shadow which made it even harder for anyone to see what she had once been.

Upon her arrival in Los Angeles, she discovered a wasteland. The attacks had wiped out many of the beloved landmarks in the area, and masked killers had tracked most of the stray celebrities down to stores or restaurants, killing them in full public view.

At first, some thought that this was an elaborate flash mob, or promotion for a movie that would be released at some later date. As time went by, intrigue turned to fear. The economy collapsed as people fled the entire region. Hollywood was a ghost town.

Around the world, actors went into hiding; doing whatever it took to survive. For some, this meant staying in a dark room, waiting for it all to end. For others, it meant trying to fight back. Some actors had guns, which they waved around in public, whenever they were in need of a headline. Their attempts to use these guns for self-defense failed because they neglected to *load* them... Waving a gun in the middle of a crowd may have gotten publicity, but waving a *loaded* weapon around could have led to serious charges being filed.

Most who survived the initial attacks wound up dead just the same.

Those that remained were faced with new threats and challenges. At first, the federal government sent troops to aid in the recovery of this once great region. Soldiers marched the streets, attempting to keep peace when violence was just waiting to erupt.

The aid did not last long. Soon, the streets were lined by protestors, marching against the use of military force on American soil. A sympathetic government soon recalled their forces, and once again the streets were empty.

Before long, small but snotty theatres began to pop up, where refugee actors and directors would produce plays that they had written themselves. Small movie theaters opened, playing old films which had been salvaged from the rubble of studio vaults. Musicians played their songs on street corners. Dancers danced. Comedians made jokes.

These attempts to revive the now-dead land failed.

Within days of each theatre opening, and theater opening, shots were fired and buildings were bombed. The performing arts would not be tolerated, and so marches were held, promoting tolerance for the performing artists. Those that marched were easy prey.

When shots were fired, some saw opportunity. They saw the chance to look their attackers in the face and to open a dialogue that might help the two sides better understand each other. Peace through communication did not work either.

Eventually, the streets became home to the dark and menacing forces that always seem to pop up in the wake of tragedy. When people no longer have anything to live for—no hope, no dreams—they turn into animals. They hunt for survival and for the mere pleasure of it. They kill to feel alive.

Thuggery was rampant amongst the displaced commoners who had nowhere else to turn when the city died, but the most horrific of all the creatures born of the attacks were those who once dared to dream. Former waiters and valet parking attendants took to the streets, killing, looting, blowing things up and doing unimaginable things to those who were unfortunate enough to cross their path.

Across the country—and the world—citizens were rocked by the events of the Hollywood apocalypse. Their televisions went blank. The few radios that remained in the modern world now broadcast only static. Videos no longer streamed over the internet. The only entertainment that the world had was what they already owned, and some were murdered for attempting to hold public displays of these relics.

Even teenagers with camera phones hesitated to post videos of themselves singing horrible pop songs, or jumping off of tall buildings and smacking into the sides of swimming pools on streaming video sites. Parents were forced to monitor their children, in order to prevent them from posting potentially dangerous videos.

Families across the world began to lose touch with reality.

Fathers threw balls at small children who then threw the balls back.

Younger children went insane, insisting that they were pirates, army men, or grown family units, pouring invisible tea from small plastic tea pots.

Mothers packed food into baskets and forced their families to abandon their homes on dangerously sunny days, and made their kids eat this food off of paper dishes, spread out over blankets on the ground.

Books became the only form of entertainment to be spared by the attacks, and bookstores were swarmed by people of all ages, undoubtedly damaging their eyes by reading far too often and sometimes with insufficient light.

Nothing was as it should have been. Nothing about the world was right or good anymore. Something needed to be done. Someone needed to fight to win back what they once had...

From the ashes of Victoria Sanders rose a new woman. She dressed in tight black pants, with a useless belt hanging loosely around her waist. She had knives strapped to her calves, and guns holstered at her thighs. Her pink tank top was two sizes too small, and the black leather jacket that she wore over it made it difficult for her to move her arms.

She was no longer a victim. She was a fighter.

She was *Starlette*.

~

The night was unusually cold, and made even chillier by the lack of life. What had once been a bustling city street—with bumper to bumper traffic and scantily clad women walking the sidewalk with bags full of new designer clothes—was now littered with the remnants of buildings that had been blown up and cars that had been crashed.

In the distance, Starlette could see a garbage can, glowing with a fire that burned inside. There were no homeless people warming themselves around this fire. There was no purpose for its being there, except one: it was a sign. Someone was paying respect to the many set designers who had worked on apocalyptic wastelands in the past; most of whom were now dead.

She liked to walk the streets, though many had advised against it. For Starlette, it was a chance to think. It was a chance to remember what it was that she was fighting for. It was a chance to picture things as they were, and as she hoped they could be again.

In the months that followed the attacks, she had become something that she never could have imagined in her previous existence. She did not fear the streets, as many did, because she did not need to. The streets feared her.

When a moment of calm came over her, and she began to feel anything but anger, she walked these streets. When the rest of the world seemed to be dragging their heels in the fight to win back what had been lost, she looked at the theaters that had been destroyed, and the designer clothing stores that no longer required a person to be buzzed in. Their doors swayed in the wind. Their hangers were bare. Their designers now clothed the politicians, philosophers and scientists who were becoming the new celebrities of the world.

She walked the streets to keep her fire burning, because to wander through the haunted city was a promise of violence.

In the distance came a cry for help.

The promise had been kept.

~

Candy Applewood had lived in southern California her entire life. Now seventy-six years old, she was not about to be run out of town by a couple of kids with a penchant for firecrackers.

In her youth, Candy moved amongst the golden era celebrities that modern filmmakers could only dream of becoming before their demise. She ate at the same restaurants as them. She passed them on the street as they walked their dogs or cheated on their spouses. She knew they were gay before any of the newspapers ran with the story, and though she had never befriended them and she had never even tried to join their ranks, she considered them a part of the extended family. This was her home, and she was not going anywhere.

She was sixteen blocks from her apartment building, shopping at the only grocery store that still operated within her ability to reach. They specialized in canned foods these days, because nobody was going to be importing fresh fruits, vegetables or meats. The best they could hope for was a bi-monthly delivery of whatever the hell they could get, and they rationed off those supplies to the few fools who wished to remain in the city, and even then, they would not accept customers who were unknown to them. It was too dangerous.

As she walked to her car, Candy tried her best to hold onto her groceries while fishing through her purse for her car keys. It was unwise to wait until reaching the car before finding the key. In general, it was a bad idea to stop moving for any reason at all.

She was relieved to find the key with plenty of time to spare, and she prepared to open the door, get inside, and lock the car once again, all in one fluid movement which she had practiced many times over the months.

Her plan was scrapped when one of the straps on her reusable shopping bag—made of 100% recycled materials—snapped, sending cans to ground, rolling in every direction.

"Oh no," she said to herself, looking around the area carefully before stopping to pick up her food.

As she scrambled to pack all of her cans back into the bag from which they had fallen, another voice cut through the silence of the dark. It was the voice of a man.

"Having some trouble?" he asked her.

Candy turned and looked at the man from her low position, and immediately rose to her full height upon seeing him.

Before her stood three men. Each of them was wearing torn jeans and t-shirts, with their leader wearing a leather vest. One of the men had a purple Mohawk, which Candy thought was entirely ridiculous and the third man was bald, either by choice or by nature.

Somehow, these did not seem like good natured citizens who were going to help her gather her groceries and get to her car safely.

"I'm fine," she told them men. "You don't have to bother hanging around here. I can take care of myself."

The man with the leather vest smiled and said, "I bet you can. I bet you can take care of yourself *real* well."

"I don't know what that means," she replied.

Behind the man in the vest, the man with the Mohawk laughed and said, "Yeah, she don't know what that means."

The bald man didn't smile. He pounded his fist into his hand and said, "Maybe we should show her what it means."

"That made no sense. Show her what it means to take care of herself real good?" the vest man asked his friend.

"Well, it didn't make sense that you said that she could take care of herself real good in the first place," the bald man replied.

"Look, are we gonna rob this bitch or are we gonna talk about it all night?" the vest man asked, turning his attention back to Candy. "'Cause I say we rob her."

"Yeah," giggled the Mohawk, "I say we rob her *real* good."

Candy dropped her groceries and stepped back, keeping her purse close and preparing to reach in and grab the pepper spray that she kept inside.

"Stay back," she warned them. "Stay back or else."

"Or else, what? You'll *old* us to death?" the bald man asked.

The man with the vest looked at Candy, shaking his head as he said, "See? This is what I deal with all day long."

Candy's only response was, "*HELP!* Somebody please! Help me!"

The vest man stepped forward and grabbed Candy by the blouse, pulling her closer to him. He looked her in the eyes and said, "Scream all you want, bitch. Ain't nobody here can help you."

Candy reached into her purse and pulled out the pepper spray, but by the time she could take aim and think of pulling the trigger on it, the man with the vest had already grabbed her arm and twisted it. The pepper spray fell to the ground.

Candy was beginning to get scared, and asked him, "What are you going to do to me?"

"I'm gonna make sure you know better than to walk down these streets alone from now on."

"Or..." a voice from behind him interrupted, "You could leave her alone and you just might get out of here without ever knowing what your own intestines look like."

When the man turned to see who was talking to him Candy could see the woman who had come to her aid. She was a young woman, with choppy blond hair, and enough weaponry to tell Candy that this was not a woman out on a casual stroll through town. This was a woman with a mission.

All three of the men smiled, seeming to be much more interested in the pretty young girl than the homely old woman. The man with the vest released Candy, and she backed away from him.

"Well, look at this," the man with the vest said to the girl. "Sweet young thing like you shouldn't be out here all by yourself at this time of night. Could be dangerous. Might find yourself interacting with the wrong sort of crowd. What's your name, sweetheart."

"They call me Starlette," she replied. "And I don't see anyone here that strikes me as a threat."

The leader of the men nodded his head slightly and said, "*Starlette*. I think I've heard of you. Aren't you famous or somethin'?"

"I've been a lot of things in my day. Famous isn't exactly one of them," she shot back, and from the Candy's angle, she could see a shimmer in Starlette's hand that the men could not have seen.

The man with the vest smiled, "No, you are. People 'round these parts have been talking about you. They see you out here at night. They've seen what you do to people."

Her voice was calm and steady when she replied. The look in her eyes unwavering. Candy could tell that this was a girl who either thought she stood a chance against these men, or didn't care either way when she said, "And yet, here you are, acting all intimidating. Either you think the rumors are false, or you're just a very special kind of stupid."

"Hey," the bald man chimed in, squinting and cocking his head just slightly. "Anyone ever tell you that you kinda look like that chick from that show that was on a long while back?"

Starlette turned and looked this man in the eyes. She did not seem pleased to be meeting one of her fans.

"Not for a long time," she told him, right before throwing a knife, which planted itself in the bald man's leg.

The bald man grabbed his leg as he fell to the ground, screaming in pain. His friend with the Mohawk couldn't help but laugh at the bald man's pain. His giggle was high pitched, and grating on Candy's nerves like nails on a chalkboard.

The man with the vest did not seem as amused with Starlette's attack. He said, "You stupid bitch," as he rushed toward her, pulling a knife of his own from his belt.

As the man with the vest neared Starlette, Candy took a deep breath, wondering if there was anything she could do to help the poor girl who was obviously going to get slaughtered by these men who were much larger than her. However, to Candy's surprise, Starlette easily deflected the first attack and threw the man with the vest to the ground with what appeared to be great ease.

Candy knew that any interference in this fight would only result in more bloodshed, and more likely than not, that blood would be her own. She took the opportunity to hurry behind her car, where she could be protected from the violence that was erupting in front of her.

In times like these, Candy wished that she believed in a god, so that she would have someone to pray to. She found herself praying out of instinct alone, though she wasn't quite sure where these prayers were being directed. In the 1960's, she was deeply interested in the religions of the east. The 70's were her pagan phase. In the 1980's, she had joined a Christianity-based cult for a short time. By the time the 90's rolled around, she figured that if she could be so fast and loose with her religious beliefs, she probably didn't believe in much of anything at all, so she gave up entirely.

The regrets people have in the heat of the moment never ceased to amaze her.

When Candy was finally behind the car and had the opportunity to look back to the fight, the man with the Mohawk was swinging a billy club at Starlette, which she managed to avoid with a series of ducks and by just plain smacking the club away from her.

With a spin, Starlette attempted to sweep the feet out from under the man, but he jumped over her leg as though it were nothing more than a jump rope. He even laughed playfully after he was once again on the ground.

"You're a spry little thing," the man with the Mohawk told Starlette. "Almost kinda wish I didn't have to, like, kill you and stuff."

While Starlette was focusing her attention on the man with the Mohawk, the man with the vest pulled himself off of the ground. He pulled a gun from behind his back and took aim at Starlette.

Starlette kicked the man with the Mohawk in the groin with enough force to make him double over in pain.

"Watch out!" Candy called to her, from behind the car.

Without missing a beat, Starlette grabbed the man with the Mohawk and trapped him in a headlock, spinning him around just in time to catch the bullet that was fired by the man with the vest.

As the gunshot rang out, Candy jumped and grabbed her ears. She'd heard gunshots before on television and in the movies, but she had managed to live her entire life without hearing one in person. The sound echoed through her head like a banshee's scream, warning of an impending death.

Candy's eyes were closed, and she was afraid to open them. For as long as she remained unaware of what had happened, she could imagine that there was no blood and that everyone who had been alive a moment ago was still breathing.

Guns had always scared Candy, ever since her mother was killed by a stray bullet when Candy was just a little girl. She hadn't witnessed the actual event, but she saw it thousands of times in her dreams over the years.

When Candy finally managed to force her eyes open, she did not see the splashes of red that she had pictured in the seconds since she heard the gun fire. Instead she saw Starlette forcing the man with the Mohawk forward, using him as a human shield as she charged the man with the vest.

As this was happening, the bald man was getting off of the ground, having pulled the knife from his leg. He seemed very upset.

Starlette rammed the man with the Mohawk into the man with the vest, who fired two more bullets into the night, but his aim was not true and his bullets did not strike flesh.

As both of these men fell to the ground, the man with the Mohawk grabbed his arm, and Candy realized that he had indeed been struck by the first bullet.

Starlette spun and threw another knife, striking the bald man in his other leg. He did not fall to the ground in pain, as he had before, but he was slowed in his charge toward her and howled as he pulled the second knife from his leg.

The man with the vest threw his wounded friend off of him and began to pull himself off of the ground, still clinging to his gun, which he attempted to aim at Starlette.

She moved too quickly for him and kicked the gun, causing it to once again fire into the darkness and strike nothing that bled.

Starlette kicked the man with the vest in the face and grabbed his arm, twisting it until he released the gun, and then twisting just a little bit more until the sound of bone snapping could be heard even from where Candy was standing.

The sound made her jump nearly as much as the first gunshot had.

As the man with the vest winced in pain, he slumped back, onto the man with the Mohawk, making it impossible for the man with the Mohawk to get back up.

The bald man was now holding two knives as he rushed toward Starlette, screaming both in pain and in anger as he neared her.

When he reached her, he went at her swinging the knives through the air in an attempt to slash her throat. She ducked, avoiding these swings, and punched the man in the stomach. But he did not relent. With his knee, the bald man hit Starlette in the chin and she stumbled back, losing her balance and nearly falling over as she did.

He went at her again, jamming his elbow into the side of her head and throwing her against the car.

Candy gasped as she tried to think of something—anything— she could do to help Starlette out of this mess. She could think of no realistic way for her to help, and she cursed the weakness of her age.

"Leave! Please, just leave her be!" Candy cried out, but nobody seemed to care.

The bald man raised both knives high in the air as he closed in on Starlette. Her back was to the man and Candy feared that there was nothing that she could do to stop him.

As the man began to bring the knives down, two more gunshots rang through the air, shaking Candy to her core. She hated those sounds and would die happy if she never heard them again.

Candy expected Starlette to slump over dead, and to see the man with the vest aiming his gun. She expected to see its barrel smoking, just as it would in any of the movies that she had grown up with. However, when she looked to the man with the vest, he was still stumbling to get off of the ground.

The bald man stumbled backwards, screaming again as he tried to take the weight off of his left foot first, and then his right. He fell to the ground, accidentally stabbing himself in the right leg as he did.

Starlette straightened up and Candy saw a gun in each of her hands. She looked at Candy with a smile, and said, "These days, a girl's gotta make sure she brings enough protection. Know what I mean?"

Candy smiled at the joke. She liked the moxie that this girl had.

Starlette turned to face the two men who were still trying to get off of the ground.

The man with the vest tried to raise his gun, but Starlette shot it out of his hand with little effort at all. The gun hit the ground, and Candy half expected it to go off again, but it did not.

Starlette walked to it and kicked it out of the way. She holstered one of her guns and used this free hand to produce two zip ties from one of her pockets. She tossed one of them to the man with the vest.

"Put it on your friend," she told him.

At first, the man with the vest hesitated, but Starlette aimed her gun at his head, and his mind was at once changed. He tied the hands of the man with the Mohawk behind his back.

"On your knees," Starlette then said to the man with the vest.

"Yeah, on your knees," the man with the Mohawk said to the man who just tied him up. He laughed at the humor of it all.

The man with the vest got to his knees and Starlette walked around him, saying, "Hands behind your back."

The man put his hands behind his back, and Starlette moved to tie them there. As she did this, he swung his elbow toward her head. She blocked this move with ease and smacked him over the head with her gun.

After he fell over, Starlette finished tying him up. She then turned to Candy and said, "Get your things and leave. Now."

Candy walked around the car and looked at the men on the ground with a smile.

"You sure did kick their asses, didn't you, dear?" Candy said to Starlette, bending down to pick up her groceries.

Starlette stood back and kept her gun aimed at the men as Candy picked up her things. "Yes, I did," she replied.

Once Candy had her groceries in hand, she opened her car and put them inside. She then turned to Starlette and said, "What do we do with them?"

"I'll make sure they get where they need to go," Starlette told her. "Just go home, ma'am. Lock your doors and eat your soup."

Candy nodded in understanding and prepared to walk around the car and get in. She couldn't resist the urge to give the man with the multiple knife and gun wounds one last kick before she left. Starlette seemed amused by this.

Candy hurried to get to the driver's side of her car and opened the door. She said "Thank you," to Starlette as she got into the car and closed the door.

As quickly as she could, Candy started the engine of her car and began to back away from the scene. She looked over her shoulder to make sure that the coast was clear. Finally, it was all over.

BAM! BAM! BAM!

Candy turned around once again, putting the car into *park* on instinct alone. When she looked forward, she saw Starlette standing in her headlights, with a gun in each hand and three dead bodies at her feet.

Candy's eyes widened at the horror of this sight. She wanted to scream. She wanted to cry. She wanted to go back in time and undo what had just happened.

Instead, she did all that she could do. She got out of her car and she looked at Starlette with tears in her eyes.

"What did you do?" she asked.

"I did what I said I would do. I got them where they needed to go," was Starlette's reply.

Candy could not believe this. She could not believe that this girl had just killed these men, who were helpless at her feet. They were tied. The fight was over.

Her look of shock turned to anger as she said to Starlette, "Do you think this was *just*? Do you think you're *better* than they are now? Do you think this makes you a *hero*?"

"No ma'am. I'm not a hero," Starlette said, as she turned and started to walk away, "I'm an actress."

~

The night had been full of violence and bloodshed, but she wouldn't have called that unusual at this point. In a world where each day was a battle to survive, she had to do what needed to be done. Sometimes, that meant killing... Okay, *usually* that meant killing.

Starlette walked home that night, and let her mind wander. She allowed herself to think of green fields and starry nights, with little to worry about. This is what she was fighting for. This was the future.

As she arrived home, she opened the heavy metal door which led into the poorly lit cement staircase, and down.

Deep beneath the city, far from all that anyone had ever known, there was another metal door. This door opened with a loud squeal, and a bright light filled the stairway behind her. As she stepped onto the metal stairs which would lead even further downward, she looked out at the expansive hidden world that had become her life now.

Within this underground world lived hundreds of other people, each of whom had been a member of the film or television industries.

Each a survivor.

Each a soldier in the war that raged on.

CHAPTER THREE
STUDIO TOUR

Most didn't dare to venture out into the night by themselves. They didn't even dare to venture out into the daylight. They didn't want to risk their lives unnecessarily, and who could blame them? A good number of them risked their lives often enough as it was.

For Starlette, walking the streets alone at night wasn't about getting fresh air, though the air in The Studio could get rather stuffy. It was about the danger. It was about reminding herself what they were fighting for. It was about never letting go of that initial need for justice.

The Studio was where she lived now; at least that's what they called it. It was not a large lot of stages and offices with a beautiful front gate, as some might imagine. It was an underground hangar, which only a few people had known about before the attacks.

The size of The Studio was beyond anything that she could

have imagined being underground. Not exactly an entire city, but perhaps large enough for a small gated community. Originally, it was designed by an eccentric billionaire, for the purpose of building highly experimental film equipment. After this billionaire died, he left the hangar to one of his many Hollywood mistresses. Since she had no idea what to do with a giant underground hangar, she used it as leverage to escape a rather oppressive studio contract. For decades it became extra storage space for used sets, large props and crates full of unproduced screenplays.

After the attacks, the hangar became the one place where nobody would ever find the survivors of the Hollywood apocalypse, because only a select few of the Hollywood elite knew that it existed. It became The Studio.

As survivors began to surface in the days following the attacks, they were picked off by the terrorists who had failed to kill them in the first place. Studio executives allowed word of The Studio to trickle down through the network of Hollywood insiders. Soon the place was populated by actors, writers, directors... anyone who had worked in the industry prior to the attacks and could no longer go home for fear of being killed was brought to The Studio (assuming they were in a union).

Once these people were gathered, a new project was greenlit. Each of them knew that they could not sit idly by and allow those who had destroyed their way of life to go unpunished. Vengeance must be had, and if anyone could bring those bastards down, it would be the Hollywood elite.

Actors were auditioned and casts were soon assembled. Each member of these casts was uniquely qualified to be sent out on location and fight the evil forces of the man that the writers had named *Bookworm*.

Eleven months had passed since the attacks, and while some of the actors in Starlette's cast had been replaced for various reasons, she was now comfortable with the team that she had in place. As their female lead and the most qualified of their team—due to her years of working as an action star on a low-rated superhero series—Starlette would take top billing on their missions. While she reported to superiors of her own, Starlette was responsible for keeping her cast in sync while on location. It was a job that she took very seriously these days, as she had witnessed more than her share of actors being either killed or dropped from the cast.

"Where were you?" came a voice from her right, just as Starlette had stepped into The Studio after a long night of prowling the streets and kicking the asses of the thugs who now lived there.

She didn't need to look in order to know who it was. She was familiar with the sound of The Director yelling at her. She would know his voice anywhere.

She stopped walking, but didn't turn. Eventually, he would catch up to her and he could yell as they walked.

"I asked you a question, Starlette. We've been looking all over the place for you," he said as he reached her side.

She began to walk. He kept pace.

"I went out for some fresh air," she told him.

"Fresh air? Your knives have blood on them."

"Would you believe that I was helping an old lady get her groceries home?"

"This isn't a joke. Lives are on the line here, and if we can't count on you to be here when we need you, maybe we need to think about recasting."

Starlette stopped walking and turned to face The Director. She looked him in the eyes, wanting to make some smart-ass remark, but she chose not to.

"I was helping an old lady get her groceries home," she told him again, with a serious tone, "She was jumped. I stepped in. One of the punks recognized me from my show."

The Director's look seemed to change from that of anger to concern.

In the past, The Director had been an actor. When he was in his early twenties, he starred on a popular TV series which earned him high praise and popularity. He could have ridden that fame all the way to the top of the acting A-list, but he wasn't content to simply act. He wanted to craft movies and episodic television with his own hands. He wanted to *direct*.

As time passed, he began acting less and directing more. Before the attacks, he was still known to take the occasional acting role, but his directing resume was growing larger and larger each week. He had a talent for it. He could see how each scene would play out before the actors ever arrived and he knew how to get the best out of them.

Though he had put on a few pounds, his hair was a little shaggy and he wasn't known to shave on a regular basis, The Director still had the same good looks and charm that had won over audiences two decades earlier. When he saw a potential threat to one of his actors, he did not just feel the concern of a normal director, he felt the concern of a fellow actor. He knew that someone recognizing Starlette could be dangerous for her.

"What did you do?" he asked.

"What do you think I did?" she replied, "If *he* knows I'm alive, *they* might find out. I wouldn't put The Studio at risk like that, so I killed him."

The Director looked off, thinking the situation through carefully for a moment. He then turned back to Starlette and said, "I'm glad you're safe and you handled the situation without anyone important getting hurt. The fact remains, this wouldn't have happened if you weren't out there, walking the streets. Are you trying to get photographed, Starlette? Are you trying to tip off the tabloids?"

"I'm careful."

"Doesn't sound like it."

"I am," she assured him. "I need to be out there. I need to be a part of the world and see what it's like to be normal. I can't just be an actress. I need to know what we're fighting for. I need to know that there's something to go back to after we wrap this project."

"Does walking around make you normal?"

"It makes me *feel* normal, even for just a little while."

The Director accepted this. He obviously didn't like it, but he accepted it. Starlette knew that she wasn't off the hook entirely, but for now he appeared to be cutting her some slack.

"We'll talk about this later," he told her, "Right now, I need you to get everyone together in the conference room."

With nothing more to add, The Director walked away from Starlette. As he walked, he pulled a baseball cap from his pocket and put it on. Now she knew he was in a deep state of concentration.

Before Starlette could assemble her supporting cast, she needed to check her weapons back into the prop department. It was always the first place she went after returning to The Studio, partly because she needed to assure Prop Master that she hadn't lost any of his beloved weapons, but also because she needed to assure him that she hadn't been killed.

When Starlette was first starting out in the business, she worked on a low budget horror film called *They Eat Your Entrails*. Prop Master also worked on the film.

The two of them later worked together on her television series, which lasted for several years. He was the one person that she knew from her previous life. In some twisted way, Prop Master was like a father to her. He kept her from losing sight of who she was beneath the costumes and makeup.

Prop Master has been working in the film industry since before Starlette was born. He got his start in the mid 1970's and built a name for himself over the years. He had worked on projects, both high budget and incredibly low. He did it for the thrill.

"Do you have all of your knives this time?" Prop Master asked, as Starlette walked into the walled off area that made up his department. In the front, there was a standard room with a few weapons hanging on the walls, next to mirrors, making for a nice presentation. Behind a door on the back wall, there was a large storage room where various weapons and other useful props and pieces of evidence were kept in carefully labeled boxes.

"I have all of my knives," Starlette assured him, as she started to place her weapons on his desk.

When she got around to taking off her knife holsters and placed them in front of him, Prop Master shook his head.

"I give you weapons for these walks because you need protection out there. I give them to you so that you'll have something, just in case," he told her.

"And I appreciate it."

"So, why is it that every single time you come back here, you're either missing some knives—which aren't easy to make down here, by the way—or they're covered in blood? And don't give me any stories about sweet old ladies being in mortal danger this time."

"It's actually true this time. I swear."

"Sure it is."

"I have a meeting to get to. I'll probably be back for more weapons later on."

"I'll try to have the blood cleaned off by then."

"I'd appreciate it. And please make sure they're sharp. I hate a dull knife," she said with a tone that suggested snobbery without sounding snobby.

She smiled and joked, but there was something not right inside of her. She liked Prop Master and their conversations, but even when she laughed with him, or anyone else, she felt like it was all an act. Inside, she knew the truth. She knew that the only time anything felt real to her anymore was when she was fighting. Everything else was just a pleasant distraction.

Starlette started to walk out of the prop department when Prop Master spoke again, saying, "So tell me... How many did you kill tonight?"

Stopping by the door, she didn't look back. She hated when he tried to get all deep and analytical with her.

"Three," she told him.

"Did you feel it? Do you feel any of them anymore?"

"They were going to kill that woman."

"I'm asking about *you*, not *them*."

She turned and took a moment to think about what she wanted to say to him. She thought about whether she wanted to lie or to tell the truth.

"I feel it," she said at last, before walking out the door.

When she left the prop department, one of her supporting cast members was waiting for her. He was wearing jeans and a t-shirt, covered by a gray hoodie. His hair was messy. He was unshaven. They called him Wacky Best Friend, and it more or less summed up his relationship with her while managing to overlook all of the important parts.

He handed Starlette a paper plate which had a warm quesadilla on it.

"Thought you might be hungry. Long nights of walking and manslaughter always make *me* hungry," he said. "Not that I judge. I just hope you're careful. 'Cause it'd suck if you died out there and then we had to go on without you and then we all got axed. Dying is selfish when you're part of a team, Starlette."

She took the plate from him and started to eat as they walked.

"I'm not going to die out there, Ethan."

She called him Ethan. Stage names like his were a mouthful during casual conversation, and most preferred to hold onto their former selves, if only when they were wrapped for the day. Out in the world, one slip could reveal their true identities. Families could be slaughtered. Weaknesses could be abused. Out in the world, like it or not, he had to be *Wacky Best Friend*.

It wasn't a name that he was fond of, but names were chosen by type, not by choice. Casting directors worked long and hard to assemble casts with the proper balance of character and skill. When they needed a Wacky Best Friend to fight by Starlette's side, he just happened to land the role. He had been fighting to break free of the typecasting ever since.

Ethan Wehrli was in his early twenties at the time of the attack. He had been working as a professional actor since graduating from high school and coming out to Hollywood to live the dream. Somehow, the possibility of being slaughtered by a group of terrorists who were bent on taking down the industry never did factor into that dream.

He was a natural, with charisma and charm that won him roles almost immediately. Nothing big, of course. Guest spots on the numerous procedurals mostly, but he managed to land a sitcom pilot just before the attacks, so he figured that he was on his way.

Ethan wasn't an unattractive guy, he just didn't fit into the mold of the *leading man* types. He was of average height. Muscular, but with a build that always seemed to make him look lankier than he was. He had a kind face, which made him seem... safe.

Throughout his childhood, Ethan had been enrolled in different types of martial arts classes. He was a native Texan and grew up around firearms. He had the skills to bring him to the top on this project, but the casting directors were less interested in who he *was* than what he *appeared* to be. This is how the *Star System* worked at The Studio.

Starlette enjoyed spending time with Ethan. He was easy to talk to; didn't ask too many questions; didn't give too many answers. He was the type of guy who reminded her of who she had once been.

He was also the person who came up with the idea of changing the spelling of her name from *Starlet*, as it had originally been, to *Starlette*. He thought it would give her the sense of individuality that most of their screen names lacked.

Before long, this spelling had become the title of their entire cast, and it was being splashed across crew jackets and script covers.

Starlette found all of this fuss humorous at first, but as it began to take hold she realized that this persona that Ethan had created for her allowed her to be the person that she was already on a path to becoming. It gave her role in this fight a point of focus, and the rest of the cast and crew members responded to that.

Of course, ask anyone at The Studio and they'd tell you that one of the writers had come up with the name. To give Wacky Best Friend credit would mean altering the terms of his contract and any sort of contract negotiation would give him more power than The Studio wished him to have. After all, he was only meant to play a supporting role in any of this.

One of the things that Starlette liked best about Ethan was that he didn't *seem* to mind. He would try to work his way up the ladder and lash out in his own passive-aggressive ways. Until he could make his move, he was willing to play the part that he'd been given and he never resented those who got the better deal. Perhaps he would have gotten a better stage name if he'd had a bigger ego, but if that were the case, Starlette would have been without one of her most trusted allies. Truly, he was her wacky best friend.

"You would not believe what I found in a box, in a corner, in a shadowy neighborhood of The Studio," he told her, seeming to be very excited by his news.

Starlette waited for Ethan to continue with his story, but he did not continue. He was waiting for her to ask him what he'd found and for some reason he was very unwilling to let her slip by without playing his game. If she hadn't been chewing her food, she might have caught herself smiling at this.

"What?" she asked, at long last.

"Good lord, it took you long enough to ask me," he replied, and then answered, "I found scripts. Lots of scripts. For what seems like every oft-forgotten scifi series of the 1995 season on *Fox*. I'm talking *Sliders*. I'm talking *Strange Luck*. I'm talking *VR.5*. I'm talking... Well, pretty much just those three. But still, how awesome is that? I'm pretty sure that some of them were never even produced."

"You're far too excited about this."

"You're far too *not* excited about this! Two of them weren't even available on DVD *before* everyone we know and love was murdered horribly. Now? Well, I think the chances of ever seeing them again have taken a pretty deep plunge. I'm thinking of putting together a table read. Wanna play?"

"Play what?" came the voice of Starlette's other beloved sidekick, Girl Next Door. "Board games? 'Cause, probably not."

Girl Next Door was an interesting person to observe. Her real name was Ember Leigh, changed from her original surname, *Li*, in an attempt to sound less ethnic prior to the attacks.

She was twenty-two years old, with ten years of professional acting experience under her belt. She was well versed in the art of sitcom line delivery, sympathetic looks, and technobabble. Though she often played the typical Asian character who came from a strict family with deep roots in their country-neutral Asian culture, Ember was a modern American woman. She enjoyed loud music, stiff drinks, and texting her besties while driving down the freeway.

She had a sweet look to her, which kept her out of roles which required a sexy, strong female. No matter what type of makeup she painted on, or which outfit she poured herself into, Ember always seemed to remind people of the girl they knew back home, or their kid sister. During one audition for an alien-themed B-movie, she even had one casting director ask her to put on a warm sweater, because it made him uncomfortable to see her in a form-fitting crop top. Needless to say, she didn't get the part of the slutty cheerleader who died midway through the first act.

In The Studio, she was Girl Next Door, despite herself. She tried her best to be the character and to live up to the expectations that came along with it, but she could never quite fit the role. Somehow, The Studio Executives didn't seem to notice or to mind.

As she caught up with Starlette and Ethan, Ember was wearing a plaid skirt, which was perhaps just a little too short, and a nice sweater, which was a bit too tight. Her hair was in pigtails.

"Ethan found scripts for some old *Fox* scifi shows," Starlette told her. "He was thinking about having a table read."

"Pass," Ember replied. "Why bother? The table read would probably be canceled after the first script anyway."

Ember turned around and started to walk backward, so that she could face Starlette while they continued on their way to the meeting. She asked, "Are the pigtails too much? I'm trying to do this straight-up wholesome, but I'm not always sure about the point where it wraps around and becomes slutty again."

"Does she look like Hair to you?" Ethan quipped.

Ember glared at Ethan and replied, "Do I look like I wanted to hear your thoughts on the subject?"

"You're breaking character."

"You're breaking... wind."

"Ouch."

Starlette remained quiet, content to listen to the bickering that shot back and forth like a ping-pong ball. They were like siblings when they argued, and they reminded Starlette of better days, with loved ones that she would probably never see again. Even if they passed her on the street, she wondered if her family would recognize her. Would she want them to?

"Seriously, I'd say ditch the pigtails and go with a ponytail. It'll come off as less desperate and more tomboy. Everyone loves a tomboy," Ethan eventually got around to telling Girl Next Door.

"I *bet* you like boys named Tom," Ember replied.

"And insults are not your shtick. Be nice and smile. It's disarming, which will make it easier for you to kill people because your aim is shit," Ethan told her in a tone that made it difficult for Starlette to tell whether he was being honest or just insulting.

Ember pulled the bands off of her pigtails and began to pull her hair into a ponytail as she faced forward once again and walked with her friends. She came back with, "My aim is totally better than your aim. You shoot like a girl."

"Which is only insulting if by *girl*, you mean *you*."

"Keep talking, Wacky Best Friend. Keep talking and we'll see how good my aim is."

"Like that extra that you shot last week?"

"Oh, please! It was an extra! It's not like I shot someone who actually mattered. They don't even get names."

"Yeah, well because of you, he was bumped up to a speaking role."

"'Cause it's my fault the guy couldn't get shot in the stomach without whining about it."

As they neared the conference room, Wacky Best Friend and Girl Next Door slowed their pace, to allow Starlette to enter the meeting first. Their exchange of insults came to an end as they entered the room and Starlette tossed what remained of her food in a nearby trashcan.

The conference room was dark. Its main sources of light were the three large LED TVs that hung on the wall to the back of the room, and four blue-tinted lights which sat in the corners of the room, for added atmosphere.

The lighting department had been trying to perfect their approach to the conference room for several months, but The Director never seemed pleased. He always found the room to be either so bright that it killed the atmosphere that he was going for, or so dark that nobody could read their scripts.

In the room, there were three tables set up in a U-shape. The Director sat at the center of this setup. Starlette and her supporting cast sat to the right side of the room, and directly across from them were writers, and producers. Various department heads stood along the walls, listening to what was being said so that they could plan their work for the day.

Prop Master entered just after Starlette sat down. He stood by the door, in a spot that was normally reserved for him. It was an unspoken rule of The Studio; one of many.

At first, there were rumblings in the room, amongst the writers and various members of the crew. The three actors remained silent. The lighthearted conversation that they had on their way to the meeting was left outside. Within this room, they were not friends. They were not normal people who joked and laughed and ate greasy food. While on the job, they were in character, and they rose above the nameless, faceless crew members. They were the *stars*, shining brightly, guiding the wandering industry professionals back to the home that had been lost to them.

"Three hours ago, I received a message," The Director told the room, though his eyes were on his actors. "A rogue agent contacted me with information regarding an actor who wants to come home."

"Rogue? So we're talking unsolicited?" Wacky Best Friend asked.

The Director nodded, "Yes."

Unsolicited inquiries from rogue agents were not typically reliable. Starlette's instinct was to disregard it entirely, but she knew that The Director must have some reason for assembling the cast and crew. So, she asked, "How do we know we can trust the information?"

"We can't," The Director told her.

Her faith in his good reason was beginning to fade.

"Well, I think that if there's the slightest chance that we could save a life, we should do it," Girl Next Door offered, now fully owning the roll that was given to her.

"Yeah. Sure. We can go in with guns a-blazing. Not *our* guns, but y'know... guns that are aimed at us. With bullets that blow holes in us and make us dead," Wacky Best Friend replied, using *his* role to its full advantage.

"We're not committing to anything. Right now, we're just researching the project. We're going to have lunch with this agent and see what he has to say. If we think we can trust the information, we act on it. If not, we pull the plug before it has a chance to catch on."

"It's like *Lone Star* all over again," Girl Next Door sighed.

On the other side of the room, Head Writer reached into his messenger bag and pulled out a stack of papers. He began to pass them around the room.

Head Writer was not someone that Starlette had a particular fondness for. He was a man in his mid-thirties, with shaggy hair and thick-rimmed glasses. He never looked well rested and there was something about him that seemed off to Starlette. Whenever she looked at him, she could see him plotting. He dictated the lives of all of the actors, and while they occasionally went off script, they were forced to adhere to his outline.

There had been a Head Writer before this Head Writer. She had been far more open to ideas from the actors. She appreciated the fact that they were the ones under the spotlight, and they were the ones whose lives were on the line when the shooting began. She tried her best to tailor her writing to their strengths.

The original Head Writer's work had been well received by the actors and had generally been successful, but she had been torn apart by the critics one too many times, and The Studio had pressured her into returning to formula.

She tried to fight them at first. She tried to remain true to her craft and her storylines, but the Studio Executives, whose faces remained hidden even from the Producers, kept the pressure on.

The original Head Writer had given in to the pressure *one time* and returned to formula. *One* script for *one* random bottle episode, which seemed safe enough, as it took place entirely within an elevator. Apparently, it had been a mistake and Bookworm's minions had seen each twist coming from a mile away.

This was why Starlette's spinoff team had only lasted six shoots before being killed. Her original co-star, Headliner, managed to survive the bloodfest... but not for long.

The original Head Writer's failure consumed her. She ended her own contract before giving The Studio the chance to give her the ax.

The new Head Writer was unpredictable. He lived to please the Studio Executives. He often resorted to formulaic outlines, with the opinion that actors could always be recast.

As the pages were passed across the room, Starlette was already thinking about how she wanted to play this scenario. Head Writer never went out on location, so until she returned to The Studio she could do whatever she wanted, as long as she hit her mark. Usually, if she got good reviews, the writers would take credit for a job well done. Starlette rarely got bad reviews.

As predicted, the script called for Starlette to take the lead in the meeting with the rogue agent. Wacky Best Friend would remain by her side during the discussion, while Girl Next Door would remain out of sight, able to provide backup if needed.

Despite the jokes that were made about her recent flub with the extra, Starlette always had faith in Girl Next Door and her ability to do whatever was needed.

The plan was standard. Formulaic. Cliché. Starlette only had to glance at the script and knew her lines within a minute or two. Though she knew it would only cause more annoyance for everyone to continue to ask questions, she looked up to The Director and asked him, "What's my motivation?"

The Director hesitated for a moment, as though he thought she might be joking, but Starlette rarely joked with him. She took her job very seriously.

"What do you mean?" The Director asked. "Your motivation is saving a fellow actor."

"A fellow actor who apparently doesn't even know how to find his light, or else he would have known how to stick to the shadows. Why should we put three of our lives on the line for one of his?" Starlette pressed.

"I believe I can answer this," Head Writer chimed in.

Starlette didn't really care to hear what Head Writer had to say. She did not trust him. She did not care why he did the things that he did. She wanted to know why The Director would invest in this plot, but she remained silent. If she wanted to speak to The Director later, she could. Until then, she had to pretend to respect Head Writer's role in all of this.

Head Writer pressed a button on the table and the three LED TVs came to life with images of a man that looked only vaguely familiar to Starlette. He had a chiseled jaw and sculpted abs. Dark hair. Clear blue eyes. Just the right amount of stubble.

His headshot was displayed on the center screen, and on either side, his reel was displaying his skills in action. For some reason, he was shirtless on all three screens.

"Ooooooh," Girl Next Door said, under her breath and seemingly without realizing it.

"His name is Ben Hurley," Head Writer told them.

"As in *the* Ben Hurley? Star of the popular television drama,

Sacred, and dabbler in the craft of underwear print ads?" Girl Next Door asked, before hesitating and finally adding, "Yeah, I think I might kinda recognize him... From somewhere."

"That's because he's the wallpaper pattern in your trailer," Wacky Best Friend whispered to her.

"Ben Hurley was the star of that television series, but it ended two seasons prior to the attacks. During his first pilot season after his series ended, Ben was offered roles in three series. He chose a police procedural and underwent several hours of intensive training in weapons handling. He also sat in on three real police interrogations, making his experience invaluable to us. Sadly, the pilot never made it to air, and Hurley left television behind in order to pursue a film career. After three romantic comedies, he landed the lead role in a superhero film, which required him to add nearly twenty pounds of muscle to his already impressive frame."

Girl Next Door nodded as Head Writer spoke, seeming to be very interested in the information that was being dispensed. Starlette and Wacky Best Friend were less impressed.

"The role also forced him to spend two months training in three forms of martial arts, as well as wire stunts," Head Writer continued. "His profile—as well as his training—could make him one of the most exciting prospects that we've seen in The Studio in... A very long time."

"If the information is real at all. If not, we're sending three proven talents out into the field to be killed," Starlette countered.

"Sometimes, we have to take risks in our line of work," Head Writer shot back.

"Is that really the path you want to take with this conversation?" Starlette asked. "Because we can talk about the *risks* you've taken in the past."

The Director cut in, saying, "If the last minute details check out, the decision's made. The pages are locked. The van will take you to the location in three hours. Be ready."

Starlette didn't like this. She had a feeling in her gut that told her that something was very wrong with this information. Still, she was a professional and would take risks when told. She hadn't gotten this far by playing it safe.

She tuned out the rest of the meeting, where the many department heads would ask questions and get answers from The Director. Surprisingly few of them ever seemed to care what Starlette had to say on any given subject.

On the way out of the meeting, she walked with Ethan and Ember, but said nothing. She stared at the pages that had been given to her, trying to figure out the best way to go about playing a scenario that she had no faith in whatsoever.

"I don't normally get star struck, but this is pretty cool," Ember said. "Ben Hurley is super talented."

"I don't like it," Ethan replied, seeming to be thinking along the same lines as Starlette. "I mean, *wow*. The guy has abs and a good enough spray-on tan. Woo-hoo. That doesn't make him better than me. But there they go, bending over backwards, throwing us to the wolves, just so they can give him all of the good storylines."

Okay, so he wasn't thinking along the *exact* same lines as Starlette after all.

Ember looked over to Starlette and saw the sick expression on her face. She repressed her excitement and took on a more sympathetic tone.

"Are you okay?" Ember asked. "You look... pale."

"My stomach is turning," Starlette replied.

Ember nodded her understanding and said, "I get stage fright too sometimes. Not a lot. Throwing up helps."

"This isn't stage fright, Ember. It's disgust. We have no clue whether or not we can rely on this information. Some random guy, claiming to be an agent—but obviously not a *legit* agent—tells us that this pretty-boy ab model wants to sign with The Studio and we just rush to believe him?"

The three actors stopped walking and huddled together, keeping their voices low, so that nobody else would hear them. It was routine for them to discuss how they wanted to play a scene together, so nobody would think twice about seeing them talking in hushed tones. Nobody would know that Starlette was badmouthing the writers. If they did, the writers would surely begin petitioning The Studio to kill her off.

"If it's true, he could be a huge asset," Ember argued.

"If it's not true, we all die," Ethan countered.

"There's that," Ember said with a slight nod.

Starlette added, "No matter how we look at it, this isn't being played wisely. It's desperate."

"Are you saying that you want to back out for creative differences?" Ember asked. "Because I always thought that was code for something else."

"Right now, I'm just saying that we can't count on some hack writer to tell us what we need to do and how to watch our backs. When we get out there, we have to play things in the moment. Be smart," Starlette told her.

"And don't shoot any of us in the gut," Ethan said, looking to Ember.

Ember rolled her eyes, but tried to keep her voice down as she shot back, "Oh my God! *One* guy! One *stupid* little guy! And it was totally because of those crazy little sparkly gloves they gave me to wear, with the blinking lights. Who wants blinking gloves in that situation?"

"I can name at least one ICU patient who'd be opposed to the idea," Ethan smiled.

Starlette turned and started to walk away from the others. As she left, she told them, "I'll be in my trailer, prepping. I suggest you do the same."

Ethan and Ember barely acknowledged Starlette's exit as they continued their conversation.

Starlette listened to their back and forth banter as she walked toward her trailer. The ease with which they amused each other was something that Starlette sometimes envied. They had the ability to leave their work behind at the end of the day; to turn off their characters and walk away, maintaining their own lives and personalities in spite of all that had happened.

For Starlette, it was harder to let go of each day. She felt as though letting go of the character that she had spent so much time building would make it difficult to find again when she needed it. To laugh and play would be a betrayal to who she was meant to be and the job that she was supposed to do.

Only when the final shot had been taken could she be released.

~

As he sat in the chair, the light which shone in his eyes was blinding.

Scissors and blades littered the counter in front of him, as well as bottles of mysterious, multicolored liquids, pastes and gels.

Wacky Best Friend had already shaved the stubble from his face, and now he watched as his messy hair was slicked back into a suave and cool style by a man known only as Hair.

Hair was in his mid forties, with hints of gray starting to show in his short, once-black (once-blue; once-green) hair. He was a little on the pudgy side, but not so much as one could call *fat*. He, like so many non-actors, simply did not take care of himself with strictly monitored diets and training routines. Instead, he wore loose-fitting Hawaiian shirts and brown cargo shorts.

Hair wore horn-rimmed glasses, which sometimes hung by a string around his neck.

He looked like a tourist, but somehow, it worked for him.

"I don't know why you refuse to comb your hair in between shoots," Hair said to Wacky Best Friend. "Look at this. Look at how it frames your face now. You look so much better. You look clean and sexy, considering the limitations of your character."

Hair flicked at Wacky Best Friend's hair—just a little bit—to add a hint of messiness that was becoming of a man with his second-rate name.

"People don't want to see me looking clean and sexy. They want to see me with a bag of potato chips, playing video games," Wacky Best Friend replied. "Not that I can ever actually eat potato chips. I just have to *look* like I'm eating them."

~

Girl Next Door looked cute as a button, and she was getting cuter by the moment. A ponytail would not do, so Hair had given her a cute little bun on the top of her head, with stray strands to frame her face.

Makeup was standing in front of her now, with a brush in one hand that danced across Girl Next Door's face, tickling the skin and giving her a pinkish glow at the same time.

Her eyes were lined, but softly, and accented by pink and blue eye shadow. Her lips were her own natural color, but now shimmering with a high gloss.

Makeup was an artist. She was in her late thirties, with bottle blond hair that hung midway down her back when it was allowed to hang free, and streaks of various colors let the world know that this was a woman who didn't care what the world thought of her ugly hair.

How Makeup could be married to Hair without his going insane over her chosen style, Girl Next Door could never understand. Then again, it was hardly the most puzzling aspect of their relationship.

Makeup wore surprisingly little makeup for a woman in her profession. She seemed to spend more time thinking about the face in front of her than she did about the face that was attached to her. Yet, somehow, she never looked horrible. Smooth and clear complexion. No horrible lines or wrinkles.

Girl Next Door chalked Makeup's overall youthful and fine appearance to the fact that she didn't wear makeup or follow the strict tanning procedures that she had set in place for all of the Studio talent. They had to look good on camera, while she could simply look good in person.

"Have you had any trouble with running lately?" Makeup asked.

"Not since you switched brands," Girl Next Door replied.

Makeup nodded, "Any clumping or smearing?"

"Not that I've noticed."

"How does it feel? Can your skin breathe?"

"I think so."

"Good."

Makeup was in the zone, and until her job was done, she would focus on nothing else. Smalltalk could be saved for touchups.

Makeup and Hair shared a trailer, so Girl Next Door was only a few feet away from where Wacky Best Friend was getting his hair prepped for their next mission. Though she was looking straight ahead so that Makeup could ready her face, Girl Next Door could see his reflection in one of the many mirrors that were hung in the trailer.

He caught her looking his way and gave her a nod. The look in his eye wasn't the typical, sarcastic look that he normally had about him. He was focused. He was preparing.

~

Wardrobe was a skinny, short, older woman who wore half-eye glasses which sat at the end of her nose, forcing her to look down her nose at everyone as she evaluated them. Somehow, she intimidated Starlette as much as anyone she'd ever met.

Starlette had walked into Wardrobe's department, hoping to get in and out quickly, without the need for a long discussion.

As Starlette walked into the department, she was still wearing the outfit that she'd worn for her nightly walk on the town. When Wardrobe spotted her, she walked her way and stopped in front of her, arms crossed, and looking over Starlette's entire outfit.

"Any rips to report? Tears?" Wardrobe asked.

Starlette shook her head, "No."

"Good. Because the last time you took an outfit without my permission, you neglected to tell me about a tear. I didn't notice until it was needed for a scene."

"Sorry."

Wardrobe reached over to a nearby rack and grabbed a hanger which had another outfit on it, wrapped in plastic. She handed it to Starlette.

"Go put this on and come back here so that I can have a look," Wardrobe told her.

Starlette nodded and slung the outfit over her shoulder. Wardrobe immediately tensed up.

"No! Hold it by the hanger. You're going to wrinkle it!" Wardrobe scolded.

Starlette corrected herself at once. She felt stupid for even thinking of slinging the outfit over her shoulder. She should have known better by now.

Starlette looked Wardrobe in the eye and like a newcomer, fresh off the bus she said, "Sorry."

She took the outfit and left Wardrobe's department, headed for her own. As she walked, she thought about all of the bullet holes that could destroy the outfit. The blood stains. The flames. The knives. The explosions.

Whatever happened, she would not allow this outfit to get wrinkled.

~

The scene would be interior; an old rundown fast food restaurant; night.

As they approached the restaurant, Starlette, Wacky Best Friend and Girl Next Door were checking the area out. It was dark and quiet. Sirens sounded, but nowhere nearby. The smell of smoke hung heavy in the air, but it always seemed to anymore.

The restaurant had once been a hot-spot of activity for Hollywood. Celebrities would roll up to its drive-thru window on their way home from award shows or live performances. Everyone loved to be photographed at this restaurant, because it made them look and feel like one of the normal people and that was good for publicity.

Now, it was as dead as the city in which it was built. It had been closed for business since the attacks and a fire had taken a good sized chunk out of its structure. The sign in front, which once read GIANT MOUTH BURGER, now simply read *N OUT BURGER*.

The three actors stopped walking, with enough space between themselves and the restaurant to scope it out and discuss their staging before heading in. With Wardrobe's color scheme for this shoot favoring the color *black*, they were secure in the knowledge that they could not be seen hidden within the shadows.

Starlette now wore black jeans with a black tank-top and black boots.

Wacky Best Friend, with his perfectly styled, messy hair was wearing a black t-shirt with a black hoodie, black cargo pants, and black sneakers. He had a black messenger bag slung across his chest.

Girl Next Door had black capris and a black cardigan, with cute little black tennis shoes.

Each of them had guns in holsters, and were ready for action.

"Not exactly the type of place we normally do lunch meetings," Wacky Best Friend noted.

"The more expensive places are too obvious. Bookworm would be expecting actors to show up in those restaurants," Starlette told him.

Girl Next Door shrugged, "I just thought The Studio was cheap."

"I don't see any of Bookworm's minions anywhere, do you?"

Starlette asked, scanning the restaurant, surrounding streets and whatever she could see of the nearby buildings.

Wacky Best Friend nodded, "Looks clear."

"Girl Next Door, you should get yourself around back, to the kitchen exit. Wacky Best Friend and I will meet with the rogue agent, but you stay in the background, out of sight. Wait for your cue before entering."

"What's my cue?"

Wacky Best Friend jumped in, saying, "If we start shooting the guy, you come help us."

Girl Next Door nodded, "Gotcha."

Starlette looked over at her fellow actors and said, "Let's roll."

"Rolling-rolling," Wacky Best Friend replied.

As she broke away from the group, put on her sunglasses, and started to make her way around the restaurant, Girl Next Door confirmed, "Background."

Preparing his own sunglasses, Wacky Best Friend looked to Starlette and said, "Action."

~

Starlette and Wacky Best Friend walked into the restaurant, unsure of what to expect. They were ready for anything, with hands on their guns, and sunglasses obscuring their vision but making them look super cool.

Starlette had been talking to Wardrobe for months about getting night vision in their sunglasses, but the budget and technology just wasn't there. Unlike Prop Master, Wardrobe didn't enjoy sitting around, thinking up cool new gadgets. She had a more important job to do, and that job was making the team look awesome as they went about their jobs.

As they made their way through the restaurant, both actors removed their sunglasses, making sure to look incredibly spy-like in the process. Neither of them wished to die for the sake of looking cool for the duration of the meeting.

The restaurant was darker than the street outside, thanks to the lack of moonlight. There was no electricity, so no working lights. There were no cooks frying up burgers in the back. All that remained was the ghost of what the place had once been. Brightly covered stools, covered with dust and ash. Chrome-lined counters, no longer sparkling.

Toward the front of the restaurant, sitting in a booth with one of the few tables that remained standing, was the rogue agent.

In the darkness, he was little more than a shadow, but it was unmistakably the shadow of a man and not an empowered woman.

Starlette took the lead as she and Wacky Best Friend approached the table.

"Are you the agent?" Starlette asked, standing over him.

"I am," he replied in a low, almost whispered voice. "Please. Sit."

Without hesitation, Starlette sat on the bench across from where the rogue agent was sitting. Wacky Best Friend remained standing by her side.

The rogue agent reached to his side, and the actors reacted by preparing to draw their weapons.

"Calm," the agent told them. "I'm simply reaching for my food. This is lunch, after all, is it not?"

The agent pulled a small brown paper bag from a briefcase that sat on the bench next to him. He placed it on the table.

"Forgive me," he said, removing a wax paper-wrapped sandwich from the bag and placing it on the table. "I didn't bring enough for everyone."

"We don't eat carbs on Tuesdays anyway," Starlette replied. "We're here for what you promised us. The actor."

The agent smiled and said, "Of course you are."

His smile lingered for longer than seemed natural. He looked Starlette in the eyes, and in the darkness of night, his eyes reflected what little came through the window and seemed to glow.

"Of course, there is the matter of my compensation," the agent told her.

"You'll get your cut once we have the actor."

"No deal. I want my money up front."

"That's not how this works."

"It seems to be now."

"Then no deal."

"No deal."

"Fine."

Starlette remained at the table, staring down the rogue agent that sat across from her. He calmly went about eating his sandwich. Silence fell between them, which lasted several seconds.

Once the agent swallowed a bite of sandwich, he said to her, "You see, I know how these negotiations work. You're desperate. You need something, and as long as there's a chance that I can help you, you will pay me whatever I ask."

Starlette sat back on the bench and replied, "You seem to think that I'm hanging around here because I have no choice but to deal."

"Why else would you still be here?" the agent replied, cocking his head just slightly, as though feigning curiosity.

"I'm letting you finish your sandwich..." Starlette replied, "... and then I'm going to blow your fucking head off."

The agent smiled, and his teeth now caught some of the light that his eyes had been reflecting. He said, "See, now we're negotiating."

"The actor who contacted you—" Starlette started.

The agent cut in, clarifying, "—Ben Hurley."

"Ben Hurley. He should have known better than to go to someone like you. You're not even a real agent."

"I seem to be having lunch with a Studio rep as we speak," the rogue agent quipped.

"You are. But you're out of your league. Because for every Ben Hurley that's out there, I could show you a dozen other actors who could do the same job just fine."

"Then, why would you come here?"

"Because..." Starlette hesitated and looked to the table for a moment, before looking back to the rogue agent. When she did, she had tears in her eyes as she said, "Do you know what it's like to watch everything you know and love vanish from the face of the earth? To have every person you saw on a daily basis gunned down in front of you? We are tired of losing people. We are tired of blood and violence. We need hope. And you allowed people to feel that hope for just a little while. You let us believe that there was more out there than death and explosions. We needed hope, and you were there. You're our hope."

"Oh my God. Who wrote that? Do we have a writer from *Grey's Anatomy* on staff?" Wacky Best Friend blurted from beside Starlette, causing her to smirk.

"Son of a bitch," she said. "I had that one! I was delivering it with a straight face and everything."

"Sorry, but I think I know who we have to kill next," Wacky Best Friend told her, before taking out his gun and aiming it at the rogue agent's head. "I mean... After this guy."

Starlette's look hardened as she turned back to the agent, who had no idea what was going on anymore.

"See, we're supposed to read these lines that they gave us. We're supposed to play you, because the people back there think that maybe someone like you has a soul. But the two of us—my wacky best friend and I—we know better. Don't we?"

"Sure do," Wacky Best Friend agreed.

"We know that you will sell us out in a heartbeat, because that's what people like you do. You'd be just fine seeing us all die, as long as you got paid for it."

"That is true," the agent replied, now taking a juice box from his bag and poking its tiny straw into it.

He squeezed the box just a little too hard as he put the straw in, and juice squirted out onto his shirt and pants. As he took a napkin out of the bag and used it to clean himself off, he spoke softly to the actors.

"The fact remains," the agent told them, "your fellow actor will die. I have feelers out with other interested parties, and I could just as easily tell them where he is. But I came to you first, because The Studio has money and you have a good reason for wanting this man alive."

Starlette glared at the rogue agent for a moment before leaning in and asking, "Yeah? What's that?"

The agent leaned closer and whispered to her, "He's a card-carrying union member."

Starlette sat back once again, thinking about the situation and what was being said. After some deep consideration, she scooted out of the booth and stood next to Wacky Best Friend.

"The way I read the situation, you're stuck in this booth with a window on one side and a gun on the other. You can try to make a break for it, but only if you think you can break the glass and get away from us faster than we can shoot you. You will die. I promise you that. So, the question is... Crap, I forgot the question."

Wacky Best Friend leaned in and whispered in Starlette's ear, "How much is your life worth to you?"

"Right," Starlette nodded, and then turned back to the rogue agent. "How much is your life worth to you?"

The rogue agent took a sip from his juice box and considered the question for a moment. After careful thought, he turned to Starlette and said, "Right now, there are packs of C-4 strapped to this table, to the front door, and to several of the chairs in this restaurant. Additionally, my personal assistant, Jennifer, is sneaking up behind whatever backup you had enter through the back. You could kill me, but neither you, nor your wacky sidekick here are going to make it out of this building alive unless I do."

Starlette and Wacky Best Friend looked around the restaurant, but it was too dark to see any C-4. There was no way of knowing whether or not the rogue agent was telling the truth.

~

Girl Next Door was trying her best to listen to the conversation that was taking place in the restaurant, but she could barely hear a word that was being said. All she could make out was that Wacky Best Friend had apparently caused Starlette to break character for a moment.

He would undoubtedly pay for that when they returned to The Studio.

In addition to not being able to *hear* anything, Girl Next Door could not *see* anything, because she had missed her opportunity to remove her sunglasses during her entrance to the scene, and to remove them in the middle of the take would come across as awkward.

She assumed that if violence broke out she would be able to hear it and take action. Until then, she would remain in the kitchen, trying not to be seen, and hoping that her sense of hearing would be improved due to her inability to see. She hated not knowing what was going on with her co-stars, but she was a team player, so she would remain content to watch the dailies when they returned to The Studio.

As she listened, she heard slight mumbling from the restaurant, which was useless to her. She heard the sound of her own breathing, which seemed to grow louder and more annoying with every breath. She heard what sounded like a mouse, scurrying through one of the metal cabinets nearby. And then she heard... something else.

This last noise was hard to place at first. It was a shuffling of some sort. It was behind her. It was...

At long last, the sound registered in her brain and she recognized it was that of a person, creeping up behind her.

Girl Next Door spun around, just in time to see a dark figure take a swing at her.

Girl Next Door fell to the ground and her sunglasses were knocked off. They broke as they hit the tile floor and the room was suddenly much more visible, though still dark.

She could see now that a woman was standing in the kitchen with her. The woman was wearing blue jeans and a long sleeve t-shirt. On her belt, she had two cell phones in holsters. In her hand, she had a metal bar, which looked as though it had once been a towel bar in the kitchen.

She lunged toward Girl Next Door, screaming as she took another swing.

Girl Next Door rolled out of the way, just in time to avoid being hit in the head by the bar. With a sweep of her leg, she knocked the woman's feet out from under her, sending the woman to the ground.

Adding a spin to the kip-up that she had perfected over the year, Girl Next Door managed to get to her feet, facing the woman who had attacked her. She jumped in the air, raising her fist and bringing it down hard, aiming for the woman's head.

The woman shifted out of the way, hoping that Girl Next Door would hit the tile with her fist and possibly break her hand, but Girl Next Door caught herself in time.

With a flip, Girl Next Door brought her foot down on the woman's chest, knocking the air out of the woman, but this did not buy her much time.

The woman grabbed Girl Next Door's foot and twisted it, causing Girl Next Door to fall to the ground.

Both women used a kip-up to get to their feet, where they stood, eyeing each other in the darkness.

"Who are you?" Girl Next Door asked.

The woman smiled the type of maniacal smile that was usually reserved for comic book villains and said, "I'm Jennifer. The agent's personal assistant."

Girl Next Door's eyes widened. Agents could be difficult to deal with. They were sneaky and underhanded. They could twist words and get people to agree to things that they would never agree to normally. Agents were bad.

What was *worse* than an agent was a personal assistant. It didn't matter who they worked for, or which side of the battle they were on, a personal assistant was fierce. They did the dirty work that nobody else wanted to handle. They cleaned up messes. They took a beating, but kept coming back for more. They didn't make enough money to explain their willingness to do anything for their bosses. The sort of abuse they sustained on a daily basis could only be explained through insanity.

Personal assistants felt no pain, or at least they didn't let on if they did.

Jennifer grabbed a metal tray from one of the counters and swung it at Girl Next Door, screaming as she attacked.

Girl Next Door blocked the first swing with ease, but Jennifer kept coming at her, again and again. Jennifer would not relent.

~

Something was happening in the kitchen. Starlette and Wacky Best Friend both knew that Girl Next Door was in trouble, but neither of them could leave the rogue agent. For the moment, Girl Next Door was on her own.

The rogue agent wiped his mouth with a napkin and placed all of his garbage back into his brown paper bag. Lunch was over.

"It's not too late to make this work," the rogue agent told Starlette and Wacky Best Friend. "Give me my money and I will tell you where you can find your actor. Otherwise, his location goes to Bookworm."

"You know how to contact Bookworm?" Starlette asked, not entirely believing him.

Nobody knew who Bookworm was, much less how to contact

him. If they could get a lead on communicating with him, they might be able to drive him out of hiding and finally take him down.

"I have many methods for contacting many people," the agent told her in response. "But that is one person whose information you will not be getting from me. Now... Do you want your actor, or not?"

Starlette carefully considered her options. She wanted to turn him down. She didn't think that Ben Hurley was worth the price that was being asked of them; not just in terms of money, but in terms of violating everything they believed in.

Never pay an agent up front. It was the first rule that any actor learned when trying to go pro. Some were lucky enough to learn this lesson the easy way, through acting classes or the advice of other actors. Some young actors learned this lesson the hard way and wound up with nothing, but their good looks and a career as a mid-level prostitute.

Nobody ever said that acting was for lightweights. If you got burned, you got burned bad.

She had to repress everything that she had learned in her life, but she did this because she had directions to follow. She could play loose with her lines, but the scene still had to move in the same direction, regardless. She needed to make this deal and walk away with the location of Ben Hurley.

She placed her hand on Wacky Best Friend's gun and pushed it down. He lowered it to his side and while she did not look at Wacky Best Friend, Starlette could tell that he was no more happy with this decision than she was.

The rogue agent smiled and stood from his booth. He put the brown paper bag into his briefcase and pulled a manila folder from it. He opened the folder and took a glance inside. Starlette could see Ben Hurley's headshot as he did this, but nothing else.

"My money," the rogue agent reminded them.

Starlette held out her hand, in Wacky Best Friend's direction. He hesitated. He didn't want to do this, but knew that he had no say in the matter. He hadn't yet earned the right of final script approval.

He took off his messenger bag and handed it to Starlette. She proceeded to open it and show the rogue agent what was inside. It was money—a lot of money. Something which The Studio often seemed very willing to toss away in favor of half-assed plots.

"Very good," the rogue agent said to Starlette. "Now, give it to me."

She clenched her jaw and every muscle in her body tightened, but she handed over the bag. The rogue agent happily accepted it. He placed the folder on the table as he stepped past Starlette and Wacky Best Friend.

"As soon as I'm safe, I'll disarm the explosives," he told them. "Good luck."

Starlette picked up the folder and opened it, looking at the information inside. The headshot featured Ben Hurley with a warm expression in his eyes and a slight smile. Behind it, there were papers with all of his credits and special skills, and written on these papers, in black marker, was an address.

"I can't believe we just did that," Wacky Best Friend told her.

"At least we have what we came for," she replied.

Standing in the doorway, with his bag of money and a smile on his face, the rogue agent turned and said to them, "That's what Bookworm said too."

He left the building and Starlette's expression turned to hardened steel. She gave Wacky Best Friend the folder.

"Help Girl Next Door. I'm going to kill that son of a bitch," she told Wacky Best Friend, and she ran for the door.

~

Jennifer was screaming in Girl Next Door's face, throwing punches so fast that she looked as though she were swimming a marathon. They were sloppy punches, and without much force, but they proved to be distracting enough to keep Girl Next Door occupied for several seconds.

She had been forced backwards, and now had her back against one of the stainless steel countertops. She waved her hands in front of her, blocking the punches as they came, and waiting for her moment to strike.

When that moment came, Girl Next Door grabbed both of Jennifer's arms, stopping them mid-punch. Jennifer immediately attempted to head-butt Girl Next Door, but Girl Next Door acted quickly, and used her foot to shove Jennifer to the other side of the room.

While Jennifer was attempting to regain what little senses she had, Girl Next Door grabbed a baking sheet and swung it at Jennifer, hitting her in the face with enough force to make Jennifer stumble to her side.

Jennifer came back quickly, and though Girl Next Door took another swing with the baking sheet, Jennifer ducked to avoid it, and rammed Girl Next Door into the racks behind her.

Girl Next Door dropped the baking sheet as she hit the racks, but wasted no time in feeling around for another weapon that she might use. What she came up with were two pairs of tongs; one in each hand.

Jennifer took a swing at Girl Next Door's face, but Girl Next Door avoided the punch and grabbed Jennifer's wrist with the tongs.

Jennifer tried to take a swing with her other hand, but Girl Next Door repeated the maneuver and grabbed her other wrist.

Girl Next Door then used Jennifer's own hands to smack her in the face. She then kneed her in the gut, causing the personal assistant to double over.

Girl Next Door dropped the tongs and grabbed Jennifer by the neck. She spun around and slammed her face into the stainless steel countertop behind her. She then noticed the deep fryer a few inches to the side.

Though the fryers hadn't been used in quite a while, the oil remained. It was dirty and smelly now. Debris from the building had fallen into the oil, as well as a rat which had been attracted by the smell of food, but which had not survived its plunge into the oil. It had been there for several weeks, at least.

Girl Next Door pulled Jennifer's head up by the hair, and plunged it down again, this time into the deep fryer.

Jennifer kicked and fought to get free, but Girl Next Door had her pinned.

As Jennifer struggled, oil sloshed out of the fryer onto the ground.

Wacky Best Friend hurried into the kitchen, and saw the fight in progress.

"I'm here to help!" he yelled, as he hurried across the room.

As he neared Girl Next Door, Wacky Best Friend slipped on the oil that was on the ground, and fell. Hard.

Girl Next Door turned, and asked, "Are you okay?"

"I'm fine," he replied, trying to get back up, but falling once again. "I'm good."

Hearing that Girl Next Door was distracted, Jennifer managed to pull her face out of the oil and spit the dead rat out, hoping to hit Girl Next Door, but failing.

Unfortunately, the rat wound up near Wacky Best Friend's hand, just as he was once again trying to get up. Seeing it, he flinched and fell for a third time.

Girl Next Door tried to push Jennifer's face back into the oil, but Jennifer was able to get her arms under herself and stop Girl Next Door's attempts.

Finally, Wacky Best Friend pulled himself off of the ground and got to his feet.

"Okay," he said, taking a deep breath. "That was gross."

He pulled a gun from one of his holsters and aimed it at Jennifer's head, "You'd have the right to remain silent, but I'm not a cop. So, you best talk now and save yourself the burden of a bullet in the brain."

~

Starlette ran out of the restaurant with gun in hand and ready to take down the rogue agent.

As the night breeze surrounded her and made her realize for the first time just how stale and dank the restaurant had been, she expected to see the agent getting into a car or running down the street. Instead, what she saw was nothing.

The rogue agent had somehow managed to walk out of the restaurant and vanish into thin air.

Starlette was unwilling to accept this. She would not believe that a man such as that could so easily escape her. She had faith in her ability to figure out where the rogue agent had gone, she just needed to *think*.

The night was cold and the streets were empty. The only sound that Starlette heard was the sound of her own breathing.

She closed her eyes and allowed the world around her to slip away. In her mind, she brought up an image of the surrounding streets and the exterior of the restaurant. She recalled her approach to the building and her meeting with the rogue agent.

She remembered his suit and his briefcase. She remembered the sound that his shoes made on the tile floor of the restaurant.

Within The Studio—and especially with actors—it was customary to wear shoes with softer soles, in order to reduce the noise that was made on the floor and increase the quality of any audio that was being recorded at the time.

The rogue agent was not an actor. He fancied himself a businessman. He wore shoes that presented a look of authority and which produced a *click-clack* sound with each step.

Starlette listened for the sound of the rogue agent's shoes on the sidewalks and streets. At first she didn't hear anything. Wherever he was, he was walking softly, so as not to be heard. But as any actor knows, you can only reduce the sound of a leather sole so much.

From off to her right came the *click-clack* of his shoes and before she even opened her eyes, she was moving.

Turning the nearby corner, Starlette made her way to the side of the restaurant, scanning the night for any sign of the rogue agent.

On the side of the restaurant, there was a parking lot. Though there were no cars parked in the lot on this night, there was a dumpster, six overgrown bushes, two sleeping dogs and a homeless man, reading an ancient copy of *People* magazine. Their sexiest man alive had been a corpse for nearly a year and Starlette highly doubted that he had managed to maintain his boyish good looks.

She saw the rogue agent moving down the street, partially obscured by the dumpster. He was headed for a dark alley.

Starlette ran after the rogue agent, keeping her gun at the ready. Her shoes did not make a sound on the pavement as she moved, and she hid herself under the cover of darkness and behind whatever object would allow her to remain unseen, should the rogue agent decide to look over his shoulder.

By the time he entered the dark alley, Starlette was not far behind.

He had a car waiting for him. It was black and sporty, which meant that even if he did manage to slip into the alley without being seen, his location would be revealed by the roar of the engine as soon as he turned the key.

As he pressed the button which unlocked his car door and reached for its handle, the rogue agent found the barrel of a gun placed against his ear.

"Freeze," Starlette said to him, with more sass than a law enforcement officer might have used.

The rogue agent smiled, "You know, I'd hoped we might meet again, but I never could have imagined that it would be so soon."

"You sold the information about our actor to Bookworm. I want to know how you got in touch with him," Starlette demanded.

"Networking, my dear. It's all about networking. I know a guy who knows a guy, who put me in touch with an old roommate of his younger sister's best friend... or something like that. Nobody's hard to track down if you can just find that one small piece of the puzzle that sets you on the right path."

"Well, congratulations. You've just been selected to be my first piece."

The rogue agent shook his head, "It doesn't quite work like that. You see, if I help you, I burn a bridge. I sully the name that I've built for myself."

"You're a scam artist. You use desperate actors for profit and leave them to die. I think your reputation will remain intact."

"I do what I have to do in order to survive. Unless you find murder and violence to be an honorable life choice, I wouldn't be casting any first stones if I were you."

"I didn't start this war."

"But you plan to finish it. No matter what the cost."

"Tell me how to contact Bookworm or you won't need to worry about your reputation. As you've pointed out, I'm a killer these days."

"Yes, well... Aren't we all?"

"What's that supposed to mean?"

"It means..." the rogue agent didn't bother to finish his sentence. He simply raised his hand, which had his car's remote control in it and he pressed another button on the remote.

A violent *BOOM* shook the entire neighborhood. The glow of an explosion turned night into day. Debris began to rain from the sky, along with fire and ash. The restaurant had been blown up.

Starlette's first instinct was to duck and cover, but she repressed this urge. She couldn't repress her second instinct however; which was to turn and look down the alley, toward the explosion.

She had left Girl Next Door and Wacky Best Friend behind when she went to find the rogue agent. She left them in a restaurant, which she knew to be rigged with explosives. She left them... and for what? The off chance of finding a clue that might lead her to Bookworm and allow her to get her revenge once and for all?

Everything she had ever been or known had been destroyed nearly a year prior. Since that time, she had experienced more pain and more loss, but she had also discovered a new family for herself. She had met people who had been in the same situation as her. People who were just as desperate. Just as capable.

They weren't dead.

Starlette turned back to the rogue agent with every intention of pulling the trigger, but as she turned he smashed his briefcase into the side of her head. She stumbled just enough to allow him to jam a stun gun into her side.

As the jolt of electricity surged through her, Starlette dropped her gun.

The rogue agent threw a punch, which landed squarely on Starlette's jaw. It was a girlie punch, which she normally would have blocked with ease and amusement, but her reflexes were thrown off by the stun gun. Instead of laughing, Starlette went down.

From behind her, shots fired. Bullets bounced off of the rogue agent's high-end sports car, but the agent himself remained unharmed as he hurried to get into the car.

Wacky Best Friend and Girl Next Door rushed through the alley, firing shots as they went along. The bouncing that went along with their running prevented them from hitting their target, but they managed to provide cover for Starlette.

Within seconds, the rogue agent started his engine, which

roared through the alley and made Starlette's teeth feel as though they were vibrating.

She struggled to pull herself together and to get up off of the ground, but by the time she brought herself to her knees, the rogue agent was speeding down the alley and away from the actors.

Wacky Best Friend was the first to reach Starlette. He smelled like dead fish.

She took his hand and he helped her to get back to her feet, but none of them were particularly happy with how this had gone down.

"He got away," Girl Next Door said. "Great."

"We got what we need," Wacky Best Friend came back. "We have Ben Hurley's location. Mission accomplished."

"Are you guys okay?" Starlette asked, more concerned with her co-stars than she was with herself.

"We're good. Kicked Jennifer's ass and got out of the restaurant right before it exploded," Girl Next Door told her.

Wacky Best Friend looked back down the alley, toward the restaurant. The glow of fire was still lighting up the entire area as he said, "I guess the pipe that we cuffed her too probably didn't provide adequate cover."

"The personal assistants always end up suffering the most," Starlette told him, bending down to pick up her gun.

Starlette holstered her weapon and began to walk toward the street, where the van would be coming by to pick them up at any moment. Wacky Best Friend and Girl Next Door followed her.

"I don't know. They're scrappy little things," Girl Next Door said. "I wouldn't be surprised if she did manage to get out of there before it exploded."

They walked for another moment or two before Starlette stopped and got her first good look at the fiery restaurant. She put her sunglasses back on as she watched it burn.

"So tell me then…" Starlette mused, "…why would you cuff her to a pipe and leave her alone if you thought she'd escape?"

"Because I hadn't thought of it until just now," Girl Next Door replied, "There were all kinds of lock picky things in there too. I bet she escaped."

Starlette nodded, "Great."

"Well, Wacky Best Friend was there too! He could have said something."

"I wanted to shoot her!"

"You wanted to shoot her in the knees."

"Yes. And she would have been blown up then, wouldn't she?"

"That is a good point. I don't shoot people in the knees often enough."

"You shoot them in the gut a lot though."

"*One* frickin' extra!"

~

"The Critics are reviewing your work now," The Director told Starlette as they walked across The Studio.

She was tired and dirty, having just turned in her weapons to the prop department. She still needed to turn in her wardrobe and take a shower before climbing into bed for what little sleep she could manage to get.

"But I'm going to say that you did well tonight," he finished.

"We let a rogue agent get away. He was our best chance at contacting Bookworm," Starlette disagreed. "Whatever The Critics say, I know we could have done better."

"You're too harsh on yourself. When the rogue agent thinks he can turn a profit off of it, he'll tell us what we want to know," The Director assured her.

"Since when do you give pep talks?"

"I don't. I'm just telling you that you have to let this one go. Clear your mind so you can focus on your next job."

Starlette stopped walking and turned to face The Director. She asked, "Ben Hurley?"

The Director nodded. He had a script in his hand that she knew was meant for her, but she didn't want to see it. All she wanted to do was shower and sleep.

"We're working on the final revisions now, but your cast heads out in six hours," The Director told her.

Starlette was a little surprised by this order, "Daylight?"

It was unusual for their shoots to take place during the day. The tone of their work and the style of their wardrobe usually lent themselves more to night.

"This is a very special shoot," The Director told her.

"Bookworm knows we're coming. They'll be waiting for us."

"And we know that, which is why we're sending in the A-listers."

"As much as we appreciate being killed because we're the best, it's still a fool's errand. We're talking about *one* actor."

"We're talking about the opportunity to breathe new life into a project that could very well be in danger, Starlette. Our Nielson surveillance units are telling us that our ratings are down. People around the country are looking toward other options. Inside The Studio, people are beginning to feel that our work is futile."

"And you think that introducing a new character is the way to change this?"

"Some do."

"Do you?"

"I think that every actor we save is another kick in the nuts to Bookworm. He wants us dead. All of us. Since the attacks, they've been hunting us down like animals and the more rare we become, the more brutal their killings become. The last actor's body that we found showed signs of being tortured for days before finally being allowed to die. His pec implants were on the other side of the room. You may not care about Ben Hurley, and that's fine. You may not think that he's worth it. But this is the war. This is what we're fighting against and if you aren't interested in saving one actor's life, you're just giving up on all of it."

Starlette didn't come back with a quick and sarcastic response. She didn't turn and walk off. She stopped and seriously thought about what she was doing and how hard she was willing to fight.

War had been declared and it wasn't her decision. She hadn't signed up for this war, she had been drafted. Not by The Studio, but by Bookworm. He made it impossible for her to turn her back on this fight when he decided to kill everything and everyone that she had cared about; when he made it impossible for her even to go home and see her family.

She was tired. She wanted to curl up and go to sleep, but more than anything else in this world, Starlette wanted to put a bullet between the eyes of the man who had stolen her life from her. She would stop at nothing to make sure that she got what she wanted.

Ben Hurley was out there, somewhere. He was exactly like Starlette had been when all of this started, only he hadn't yet found a way to fight back. He wanted to come in from the cold, and to join The Studio as they waged their war. He wanted Bookworm dead as much as she did.

Who was Starlette to turn down the wishes of such a pretty face?

Chapter Four
BLEEDING HEARTTHROB

Ben Hurley was not the type of guy who normally waited around for someone else to jump in and save him. He was a go-getter. He set goals for himself and he achieved. The night of the attacks was a turning point in his life. In that one night, every ounce of confidence was lost to him. Every achievement was made irrelevant.

One part of the actor's life that Ben Hurley hated was the publicity tours. He hated giving interviews to magazines and blogs, but what he hated more was appearing on talk shows to promote his new films. The interviews usually consisted of two minutes worth of plugging his project—including the short clip that was shown—and then eight minutes of discussing some aspect of his personal life.

Usually, the story that was selected was some humorous

anecdote about shooting the project, or something that he'd done recently. The anecdotes were meant to draw the audience in and allow them to relate to the actor on a personal level.

These anecdotes haunted Ben. Every day that he went about his normal life, he wondered if that day would be the topic of conversation. Would he wind up talking about his trip to the grocery store? Would someone bring up a photograph of him walking out of the movies?

He hated talking about himself on a personal level. He felt stupid when he told a story about his life and people laughed. He felt uneasy every time he took a bite of a muffin, because surely there would be a comment made about his abs. People would take pictures of him at the beach and if they weren't perfect, he would wind up on the side of the page which read: *Worst Beach Bodies.*

Ben Hurley loved his job. He loved becoming other people and living other lives. He loved the energy of the set. He loved the rush of stepping in front of a camera and losing himself as the entire crew melted away and all that there was was *that* moment and *those* characters.

He loved his fans. He didn't feel comfortable being recognized on the street by any means, but he appreciated the fact that people enjoyed his work.

At least, he hoped they enjoyed his work. At least fifty percent of the people who recognized him on the street found some way of referencing the fact that they had seen him in nothing but his underwear. In those moments, he wanted to shrink into nothingness. Not because he was ashamed of his body, or embarrassed by it, but because those people didn't recognize him as a person. They recognized him as a fantasy. He could never live up to that.

He was not the most famous person in the world. He wasn't even one of the top fifty. He wasn't recognized by everyone or swarmed, as an A-list celebrity would be. He was only recognized enough to make him feel different. He wasn't always being watched, but he felt as though any moment could be that moment when he would be recognized. He judged and criticized every move he made, even if nobody else did.

On that cold night as he walked down the streets of New York, on his way to one of those horrible interviews on a late night talk show, Ben felt like any normal person.

He was bundled up in a heavy coat, with a scarf and a hat. He kept his head down—not to hide, but to capture some of the warmth of his breath in the scarf.

Nobody looked twice at him. Nobody recognized him. For that one brief moment, he allowed his guard to be let down and he enjoyed the night. He savored it.

He arrived at the studio where the talk show was going to be filmed and he was shown to the green room, where he would get ready for his appearance and sit through the entire show until it was time for his introduction. He was famous enough to be on the show, but only for the last ten minutes or so.

He went out on stage and the audience cheered, mostly because they were told to. He told his funny story—which revolved around the pet hamster that he had as a child—and he said goodnight.

This was considered a day off for him, since he was on a strict schedule of dieting, weight training and martial arts lessons for his upcoming movie, which was a high-budget superhero film, and there was no rest for those who played heroes.

As he left the studio and walked back into the cold night air, a voice came from behind him. Someone called his name.

Ben was all too happy to turn and greet a fan. He would pose for photographs (though not shirtless or pantless photos, as some fans requested) and sign autographs. He would show interest in those fans, because they cared enough to show interest in him.

When he turned, he had a smile on his face.

When he saw the knife that was cutting through the air toward his chest, his smile quickly turned to one of those awkward expressions that one hopes to never see captured on film.

Out of reflex, Ben raised an arm and blocked the attack. He grabbed his attacker's arm and pushed him against the wall of the building.

He had no idea where this instinct to fight came from. He'd never been involved in so much as a bar fight or a schoolyard brawl in his life. He hadn't been beaten up. He had certainly never had to fight for his life. So, to find himself fighting for his life was a surprise that should have resulted in his death. Yet... it didn't.

Somehow, those hours of training found a way to bubble to the surface. He wasn't dealing with the threat of a foam-covered stick, but his constant push to do better and to look more realistic when performing those fight scenes was now turning into something more real.

"You're going to die tonight," his attacker told him.

"Why?" was all that Ben could bring himself to say in response.

The rush of adrenaline and the shock of the moment were making it hard for him to think. If he *had* been thinking clearly, he probably could have thought of several more intelligent questions to ask his attacker, but that one word was all that he could force out.

"You are the vermin who walks this earth. The filth that dirties us all. You and your kind are the plague and we are the cure," his attacker said.

Perhaps it was that adrenaline making him foggy, but for the life of him, Ben could not make heads or tails of what the attacker had just said.

Confused, Ben asked, "Is this, like, a religious thing?"

"No, you fool. This is about your kind devouring the intelligence of our race. This is about the wasted hours and the loss of potential. Do you realize how stupid people have become since the rise of Hollywood?"

"Well, we have better computers now. More fuel efficient cars. Satellites that can capture pretty impressive pictures of distant—"

"I am talking about true intelligence! True brains! I am talking about the fact that our children don't read anymore..."

"Are you kidding? All they do is read the internet all day long. Read, read, read. It's hard to get them to *stop* reading."

"Books! I'm talking about books!"

"Oh. Yeah. That's probably true."

His attacker tried to fight Ben and get himself free of Ben's grip. In response, Ben shoved him against the wall one more time. He was about to continue the conversation and demand more answers from his attacker, but something stopped him.

In the distance, a rumbling began to rise. It was an unnatural rumble, which shook something deep in Ben's core.

Overhead, explosions began to destroy the building which Ben had just walked out of. Glass and debris began to rain down upon him.

"As we speak, your world is falling, actor," the attacker went on. "Your *kind* will not exist by morning."

"Is this a racial thing? Or a gay thing? Because those rumors aren't—"

"No!" his attacker cut in. "*ACTORS!* Hollywood. The whole entertainment machine will fall by our hands."

"Oh," Ben said, with a nod of understanding.

Before he could think of anything else to say, Ben saw the eyes of his attacker look to something behind Ben and the slightest of smiles formed on his attacker's face.

Once again, instinct kicked in and Ben spun his attacker around, using him as a shield against the blade of a second attacker who had been aiming for Ben. The first attacker fell to the ground, mortally wounded by the knife of his ally.

The second attacker pulled his knife from the body of his comrade and wiped the blood on his pant leg. He looked to Ben, and Ben could see the murder in his eyes.

Ben stared down the second attacker and he tried to use all of the bad-ass training that he'd endured, hoping to intimidate the second attacker, but it didn't work. The second attacker did not want to make conversation or run on about their evil plans. He did not even show remorse for killing his own friend.

The first attacker groaned on the ground. He was dying, but his friend did not seem to care. There was a part of Ben—the part which had not yet processed the events of that night—which wanted to call an ambulance for the dying man. Even if such a thing had made sense and he did place that call, no help would come.

The city shook with the chaos of death and explosions. People screamed in terror and ran for cover. The reality of the situation set in at last and Ben Hurley knew that death was coming for him on that night.

So, he ran. He ran like hell.

Of course he knew that the second attacker would not just let him run off into the night. They wanted him dead and they would not stop until they had accomplished this mission.

As he ran down the street, people watched. They could clearly see that there was a man with a knife chasing after him, but their world was in chaos as well. Nobody knew who the good guys were and who the bad guys were. People wanted to save themselves and their families.

He wasn't the only person running as fast as he could. In fact, as he ran down the street, Ben witnessed a red-headed woman in the middle of the road, being stabbed to death by an attacker. He knew this woman—not by name, but by face. He had just seen her performing on Broadway the night before.

If the woman hadn't already been dead by the time he saw her, Ben would have rushed to help her; no matter what the cost to himself. She *was* dead however and this meant that there were more than two attackers. He didn't know how many there were, but according to the first man who attacked him, the plan was to wipe out the entire entertainment industry. That meant that there could be an entire army. The streets could be swarming with men and women who wanted him dead.

He ducked into an alley. This wouldn't get his primary attacker off of his trail, but he hoped that he could avoid drawing the attention of others who might come to help the man with the knife. If they brought a gun into the mix, he would be in trouble.

He had seen—and acted in—countless movies and television shows where someone attempted to escape down a dark alley, only to run into a fence along the way. He expected to run into a such a fence as he ran down that alley, and to turn around just in time to see the attacker's blade come down on him, but there was no fence. In front of Ben, there was open street and the chance for freedom. Yet, he stopped running and turned around just the same.

The man with the knife was not far behind and as he got closer, Ben grabbed the lid of a metal garbage can. He prepared himself for battle.

His attacker reached him and attacked with full force and fury. He swung the knife wildly, attempting to do as much bodily harm to Ben as he could.

Ben blocked the knife with the lid of the garbage can time and time again. With each swing, he expected the attacker to try something new and clever, which would catch him off guard, but the man with the knife just kept swinging.

After Ben had blocked several of these swings, the attacker raised the knife into the air one more time. Before he could bring it down, Ben saw his chance. The attacker's balance was thrown off by the raising of the knife and Ben used this opportunity to shove the lid of the garbage can into his chest, causing the attacker to stumble back.

Ben followed, swinging the lid again, hitting the attacker across the face.

He dropped the lid and moved toward the attacker with nothing to come between them. When he reached the attacker, Ben threw a punch as hard as he could and landed it squarely on the attacker's face. He could feel the attacker's nose breaking beneath his fist and he could hear the *crunch* of that break.

The attacker dropped his knife and stumbled, blinded by the pain of his broken nose, but Ben did not relent.

Ben spun around and kicked his attacker, just as he had been taught for scene thirty-two in his upcoming superhero movie; only this was not a stage fight and there were no camera cheats. When he kicked, he kicked hard and he made contact.

His attacker fell to the ground, holding one hand to his face and the other in the air, hoping to block whatever blow was coming next.

Ben squatted next to the attacker and grabbed him by the neck, squeezing.

The attacker waved both arms through the air, trying to breathe, but unable to. He dug his fingernails into Ben's arms and Ben began to bleed.

He swung at Ben's face and grabbed Ben around the neck, but his grip was too weak to make any difference. Ben would not relent. He squeezed tighter and the attacker's arms fell to the ground. He squeezed tighter and the life drained from the attacker's eyes. He squeezed tighter and tighter, until his muscles hurt and he could not squeeze any more and he held this grip for several minutes, as the events of the night caught up to him and fear mixed with rage. Dead was not enough for the man who attacked Ben, but it was all that could be dealt.

As Ben held the body of the man who had attacked him and he looked into the dead eyes of this man with fire running through his blood, a snowflake fell from the sky and landed on Ben's hand.

Another snowflake fell nearby and soon he was surrounded by them.

In the morning, the world would be glowing with freshly fallen snow. The death and destruction of this night would be a distant memory for most, but there was an army out to destroy Ben and everyone like him. There was no going back to the way things were.

As the snow cooled his senses and rational thought returned to him, Ben looked toward the street from which he had run. Sirens could be heard in the distance. Screams. The smell of smoke hung heavy in the air.

Both of the men who had witnessed Ben coming out of the building were dead now. As far as their army was concerned, he could have been inside the building when it exploded.

Ben Hurley died that night, as far as they knew. He would remain dead to them for as long as he possibly could.

It was a night that would be blurred in his memory, but which forever changed him. Up until that point, it was the worst night of his life, and it would remain the worst night of his life for seven months.

~

Eleven months later.

Starlette tossed and turned in her bed, unable to sleep. It had been a long time since she'd slept in and five hours of uninterrupted sleep was more than she knew what to do with.

In her mind, she was walking through the steps of her upcoming outing. She was still no fan of Ben Hurley and the idea of sacrificing her entire cast for him did not sit well.

An addition to the cast would mean spreading their resources even thinner than they already were. They would have less resources for location shoots, and shooting in The Studio had proven to be pointless in the past, no matter how Head Writer had attempted to spin it.

Starlette might not have liked the script that she had been

given, but she was a professional and as long as she had a contract to fulfill, she would never deliver a half-assed line. She hated when actors did that. Poor acting was what got people killed these days and she would have nothing to do with that sort of underhanded contract renegotiation tactic.

The location scouts had returned from the address that had been supplied by the rogue agent. What they found was a rundown apartment building in the middle of the city. It was abandoned, as far as anyone could see. No lights were on inside.

The location scouts were not trained to go into these buildings, because they might run into dangerous situations. They were merely trained to be stealthy observers, reporting back whatever information they could, so that the actors would have some idea of what they were getting into.

Location scouts were chameleons. They were ghosts.

An updated call sheet had been slipped under Starlette's trailer door and there was now an extra hour of prep time worked into the schedule. The Executive Producers were taking no risks and cutting no corners. They wanted to sign this actor.

She sat up in bed, anxious to get the show on the road. Her mind was racing. Her palms were sweating. She hated to admit it to anyone around her, but Starlette craved the fight. She longed for action. It wasn't a love of killing or bloodshed that drew her in. It was the fact that each bullet fired brought her that much closer to the end of this war.

There were days when her only job was to sit around and wait. On those days, Starlette found herself pacing endlessly, while Ethan and Ember watched from the lawn chairs that they liked to keep in front of their trailers.

She could work out and train for battle, but even this did not feed her thirst because it did not move the story forward. She deeply hated those days off. She hated fluff and filler.

She pulled herself out of bed, brushed her teeth and slipped on some loose-fitting sweats and slippers before heading out the door. Outside, Ember was sitting in one of the lawn chairs. She had curlers in her hair and was sipping a steaming cup of coffee. Starlette took the chair next to her.

"You've been to Hair already?" Starlette asked, grabbing

Ember's cup of coffee and taking a sip.

"Early bird catches the worm," Ember smiled. "Plus, today is so important. Check it out..."

Ember reached into a bag that she had sitting next to her chair and pulled out a magazine that featured a cover story about Ben Hurley. She told Starlette, "He had a hamster when he was a kid, named Stoner. Isn't that adorable?"

Starlette raised an eyebrow and asked, "Are you, like, a stalker?"

"I'm not crazy or anything. I just think it's cool when you get to work with an actor that you've really admired for a long time. His technique was totally underrated. The subtle expressions in his eyes."

"The subtle flexing of his pecs."

"Oh, that was super sweet too, don't get me wrong, but Ben Hurley was an artist. He just happened to be stuck on a crappy TV show. You of all people should be able to relate."

"My show was a cult classic."

"A depressingly small cult."

"We had a panel at Comic-Con."

"That's awesome."

Starlette shrugged it off, "I hated doing big events. Signings. Interviews."

"Yeah," Ember smiled. "And now you'd give anything in the world just to get back to that life. That person you used to be."

Starlette looked toward the ceiling of The Studio, stretching her neck and handed Ember's coffee back to her, "The show's over. She died in the last episode."

She got out of the chair and started to walk toward Hair and Makeup's trailer. As she walked, she waved back to Ember and said, "See ya in the van, Girl Next Door."

~

As she sat in the chair on Hair's side of the trailer, Starlette looked at herself in the mirror. Her hair was a mess. She had not even a hint of makeup on her face. No guns. No fancy clothes. Yet, everything that made her Starlette was still there, in the eyes.

As Hair came in and made small talk about his *chi-poo* puppy and how it ran around in its fluffy angora puppy sweater, pooping on everything in sight, Starlette's hair changed from a bedhead mess to a stylish, hard-ass style, with a streak of black that added extra cool factor.

Throughout this process, Starlette remained silent. She didn't know what a chi-poo was and she didn't seem to care. She kept her focus on the reflection of her eyes, which failed to become more glamorous.

Once she was done with Hair, Starlette moved over to where Makeup was setting up her assortment of *Starlette* colors. Again, Starlette kept her eyes on the mirror.

Her lips became a dark shade of red, glossed over. Her eyes took on their normal, slightly seductive, smoky edge, with a slight shimmer added to the mix, which was out of the ordinary. This was a sweeps-level outing and The Studio expected nothing less than the best from everyone.

Even Ethan—who was sitting in Hair's chair by the time Starlette was midway through her makeup application—was getting an extra wacky hairstyle. With an added edge, naturally. He didn't seem to love it.

"Can't we just do the comb-and-mess, like we always do?" he asked, as Hair was whipping out the straightening iron.

Hair simply huffed and told Ethan to hold still if he didn't want to get burned.

"I'm pretty sure my hair's not long enough for this," Ethan told Hair.

"Do you want me to tell you how to read lines, find marks and shoot people?" Hair replied. "Because if not, I suggest that you shut your mouth and let me do my work."

Ethan huffed and muttered a musical line from *The Wizard of Oz*, "Stuff-stuff here, stuff-stuff there."

When Starlette was done with Makeup, she looked like a 1970's disco assassin, in her opinion. But she was not one to question the work of the other departments. She had her own concerns to consider.

With a quick glance to Ethan and a smile that she couldn't seem to repress at the sight of him squirming in the chair, Starlette left the trailer and headed for Wardrobe.

~

There was nothing but black. Ben had a bag over his head, preventing him from seeing anything or anyone in the room. He could hear footsteps and whispers. Every so often, someone would walk into the room, ask him questions and find some way to inflict pain when he refused to give them the answers that they wanted.

His arms and feet were bound to the chair where he was forced to sit. There was no escape. No way to warn those who might come looking for him, assuming anyone knew he was there.

When Ben contacted the rogue agent, he knew the risks. He knew that he was opening himself up to lies and betrayal, but he had no choice. There was nowhere to run anymore. The only hope he had was finding others like himself.

For months after the attacks, Ben heard nothing about other survivors. He didn't know whether or not he was the last actor on the planet and he certainly had no idea of how to go about finding any other survivors.

He ran and hid as well as he possibly could. From time to time, someone caught wind of where he was through some method that he could not figure out and they came looking for him. Somehow, he always managed to avoid death, if only narrowly.

A time came when things calmed down and he had been left alone for long enough to lull him into a sense of security. That was a mistake that he would carry with him forever.

Following that incident, he ran once again, to the only place he had left to run. He ran to the place where all of this had first taken root. Hollywood.

He'd hoped that his comeback would be easy and that the struggles would be behind him, but he was wrong.

The streets were cold and cruel and the town was crawling with people who wanted nothing more than to kill him. Laying low was his only option. So, he observed the new order of the town and listened to what was going on around him.

After some time, there were rumors of survivors. Nobody knew who they were or where they were, but the criminals, thugs and murderers whispered the stories which had been whispered to them; stories of incredibly attractive people, fighting back.

Hope swelled in the heart of Ben Hurley and he felt as though there might be a chance for him to find a world where he could belong and exist without the constant need to look over his shoulder. Where he could join forces with others like himself.

If they were fighting back, he wanted a role in that fight and he was willing to do whatever it took to land that role.

Desperation led him to make a stupid decision. He trusted an agent who claimed to know how to contact the elusive Studio, but this agent required payment for his services up front. Ben gave it to him and he waited.

Eventually, people showed up at the agreed upon location, but they were not his fellow actors. These were minions of the man now known as Bookworm on the streets; the man whose real name was never revealed and whose location was a mystery.

In his attempt to contact The Studio, Ben had opened himself up to attack. He had been aware of the risks going into this deal, but he had not considered that he could also be used as bait to lure The Studio into the open. His mistake could now cost the lives of others.

After Ben was captured by the minions of Bookworm and the bag had been placed over his head, the minions began to interrogate him. They wanted to know who he was, how he survived, if he'd seen other survivors, where they were, where The Studio was located and many other answers that he either could not or would not give them.

His lack of knowledge and cooperation led them to more drastic methods of interrogation. At first, he was simply beaten. Then, his shirt was ripped off and he was electrocuted. Then, he was cut into.

Even if he'd had the answers that they wanted, he would not have given them to the minions of Bookworm. They could torture him all they wanted, but there was nothing left for them to take. He had already had everything taken from him and in the places within him which had been hollowed by those losses, the seeds of rage and vengeance had been planted. If left untended to, these seeds would continue to grow until they consumed everything else within him and rage was all that was left.

He was tired and weak by the time the questions came to an

end, but he was not relieved that they did. When the minions stopped asking him about The Studio and the acting community, Ben began to worry.

He heard a whisper in the distance, which sounded like the whispered voice of the rogue agent that had given him up to Bookworm. What the agent was saying, he couldn't make out entirely. He did hear enough to tell him that the agent had contacted The Studio and planned to double his profits by luring them to this building.

When he heard that conversation, Ben's stomach began to churn. If someone came to get him and they died in the process, he would feel even worse than he already did. There was no remorse felt when he killed the minions of Bookworm, but when the blood on his hands was innocent or good, Ben could feel it forever. No amount of atoning could remove that feeling.

He pulled at his bindings and tried to get free, but he could not. As he did this, the voice of a man whispered in his ear, "You fight. You struggle. You pull and tug and scream all you want. In the end, we kill you just the same."

~

They walked through The Studio, now in the clothes that Wardrobe had given them and with a wind machine in front, so that their hair and clothes would look as breezy as they possibly could.

Starlette was wearing tight leather pants, a leather jacket and high-heeled boots. As she walked, she could see all of the vegans in The Studio glaring at her with their disapproval. Leather was frowned upon in their community, but Studio Head had demanded it for this occasion and nobody questioned his requests. Especially because nobody had ever seen him face to face. He was merely a voice on the phone.

Girl Next Door and Wacky Best Friend were dressed in equally uncomfortable, yet incredibly nice smelling clothes which Girl Next Door struggled with, because leather was murder.

Their natural impulse was to walk in slow motion, allowing the rest of The Studio crew to watch in awe of their sexy inefficiency, but they fought this urge and walked at normal speed.

Each of the actors had been wired with a microphone, which

was taped to their chests and ran underneath their clothing, to a battery pack which was strapped to the back of their belts. It would be hard to sit down and there was no two-way communication available with this method, but when it came to audio recording in The Studio, bluetooth was simply not an option. Starlette just assumed that there was a good reason for this.

Before Starlette and her fellow actors ever reached their location, The Director sent out a team of camera men. He selected several positions for them to set up their rigs, on rooftops and in abandoned buildings along the street, where they would remain hidden from view. Their orders were to keep an eye on the building and if they ever had a clear shot of the enemy, they were to take it.

The final product from the various camera angles would be edited together with the audio recordings and used to review the work that was done. Eventually, it would also be released in a DVD collection of all of the *Starlette* cast's work, with addition footage, bloopers and commentary from The Director.

Near the van which would drive them to their location, Prop Master waited with a cart full of weaponry that they would use for this shoot. As they approached, he handed Starlette a six foot long black bo, with chrome accents.

"What the fuck?" Starlette asked as she took the bo. "Please tell me this shoots people in really creative ways."

"Sorry. This is a sweeps-level shoot, which calls for full glam and maximum dramatic effect," Prop Master told her.

Starlette looked at Prop Master with disbelief, "Did Head Writer put you up to this?"

"Orders came straight from the top," Prop Master assured her, before leaning in closely and saying, "I put six handguns, your throwing knives and two grenades in the back of the van."

Starlette allowed only a small grin in response, so that she wouldn't raise any suspicions, "Oh my God, that's exactly what I told Santa I wanted this year."

Prop Master turned to Wacky Best Friend and handed him a pair of nunchucks. Wacky Best Friend was put off by this, "Nunchucks?"

"Nunchaku," Prop Master replied.

Wacky Best Friend nodded and said, "I am going to die today."

For Girl Next Door, Prop Master pulled out two beautiful swords in sheaths and handed them to her.

"Oooh..." Girl Next Door said as she took the swords. "Pretty."

"I'm really going to die today," Wacky Best Friend told Starlette as Girl Next Door took the blades.

"You're just jealous because my weapons might actually do something," Girl Next Door snipped.

"Yes. I kinda am," Wacky Best Friend agreed.

The Director approached them and put a hand on Starlette's shoulder as he said, "The three of you are about to embark on one of the good scripts. Today, we're not putting our focus on death and despair, but on the possibility of life. I'd say that's a nice change of pace. So, go. Find us an actor and bring him home safely."

None of the actors chose to respond. Each of them looked as though they were about to laugh at his attempted sincerity.

The Director took a deep breath and said, "On *action*, you enter that building and you shoot the living shit out of whoever gets between you and Ben Hurley. I want him back here alive. We only have one take with this, so no messing around and no stepping on each other's lines."

"Yes, sir," Starlette nodded and she headed for the van.

As Starlette attempted to climb into the van her bo knocked against the side of the door. She turned it so that the top of the bo could go in first, but this resulted in the bottom of the bo hitting the side of the van. She turned it again, attempting to put it in once again, nearly taking out Wacky Best Friend's eye in the process.

With one last try, Starlette managed to get the bo into the van and climbed in after it. Sitting was not easy in her tight leather outfit and she could barely breathe when she did sit, but she was a professional and she would not let something as silly as breathing get in the way of her job.

Wacky Best Friend followed her into the van, tossing his nunchucks in before him. When he saw the back seat of the van, his eyes lit up and he said, "Guns! Awesome!"

When Girl Next Door climbed into the van, she was thankful that her swords were sheathed, because they seemed determined to knock into everything and everyone that they could possibly come into contact with.

Once she was settled in, the van doors were closed and the driver pulled away from The Studio, into the bright streets and off toward their location.

~

It was afternoon when they left The Studio and the sun shone down hard upon them. Unfortunately, sunglasses did not fit the style of their wardrobe on this shoot.

The street on which the van dropped them off was—like most of the streets around Hollywood—rundown. It was a dead neighborhood, with buildings that had been abandoned, looted and sometimes burned.

Once the van pulled away, all three actors knew that they were on their own. There was no way out until they finished their work.

Starlette led the way down the street, feeling very exposed in the daylight. The chrome accents on her bo were reflecting the sun and she worried that this might tip off whoever was in the building to the fact that they were about to make their dramatic entrance.

While in the van, each actor had taken two guns and strapped them on. Wacky Best Friend kept the grenades for himself, while Starlette had her trusty throwing knives. Girl Next Door was content with her guns and swords, which gave her a misplaced sense of power.

Starlette could not see the camera men and dared not look up to the rooftops in order to find them, for fear of tipping off the enemy or possibly ruining a shot by looking into the camera, but she knew that they were there and that they had her covered. She adjusted her angles accordingly.

The building that they were about to head into was seven levels, with a closed-down bakery on the first floor and five levels of apartments above it. Below, there was a basement.

Starlette stopped her team just as they reached the building and looked back to her co-stars, saying "I'll head in through the front and work my way through the bakery before heading upstairs. Girl Next Door will take the back and work her way through, eventually meeting up with me. The location scouts say that there's a set of stairs around the side, leading up to the other levels. Wacky Best Friend, you take those stairs, start at the top floor and work your way down. We'll eventually meet up with you."

"What about the basement?" Wacky Best Friend asked.

Starlette replied, "Once we've cleared the upper levels, we'll head down there. There are no windows or rear exits down there, so it'll be a harder escape if we do run into trouble."

Wacky Best Friend nodded.

~

Starlette entered through the front door of the bakery and scanned the area for potential bad guys. She had her bo at the ready, just in case she found herself under attack, but the bakery was empty and quiet.

Slowly—and as quietly as possible—she worked her way toward the kitchen. In the dust on the ground, she could see footprints, but not enough to give her a full trail to follow. Only enough to tell her that there were people in the building.

~

Girl Next Door walked with Wacky Best Friend as they moved down an alley on the side of the building. Both of them held their very stylish weapons firmly, expecting to be jumped by minions of Bookworm at any moment.

They did not say a word as they walked along the side of the building. They scanned the area and covered each other's back without a need to communicate. They had been working together for long enough to know how to work off of one another.

On this side of the building, there was a door which had a broken window, through which they could see the stairs that led up to the other levels of the building.

While Girl Next Door kept moving around the building, Wacky Best Friend went to the door and quietly attempted to turn its knob. The door was locked.

Still scanning the area for enemy attackers, Wacky Best Friend reached through the broken window and felt for the lock on the inside. Once he found it, he unlocked the door and opened it.

He moved into the building and closed the door behind him. Inside, there was another door which would lead into the bakery, but he ignored this door and moved up the stairs.

At the first landing, there was a door which had a smaller window on it. Through this window, Wacky Best Friend could see part of the hallway beyond. It gave him an idea of what the layout would be when he did eventually exit the stairwell, but he did not go through this door. He continued to move upward, holding one end of his nunchucks with his right hand and allowing the other end to wrap over his right shoulder and under his arm, where he held it with his left hand. He had never used nunchucks before, but this always seemed to be the way they held them in the movies and he trusted Hollywood with his life.

He moved up to the next level, where the door had been busted off of its hinges and now leaned on the wall beside the doorway. He could see nobody through the doorway, so he continued up the stairs.

His movements were fast, but quiet. He had taken one miming class in his life—which lasted for about three hours—and he had given up on the class because he did not believe that it would further his career. Oh, how he laughed at that thought now. Each step was feather-light and he made not a sound. He was a three-hour miming prodigy and all who would cross him had better beware.

When he reached the final level of the building, he took a deep breath and opened the door, moving quickly out of the way, just in case someone was waiting on the other side and attempted to blast a hole through him with a machine gun.

There were no shots fired.

Wacky Best Friend moved out of the stairwell and into the hallway. The building was not incredibly large and there were only two apartments on each level, as well as doors which led to a utility closet and the other stairwell.

He moved to the first apartment. The door was already open, so he walked through it without breaking the stealthy but brisk pace of his search.

Despite the daylight outside, the apartment was dark. Several of the windows had been broken and boarded over. There was no carpet on the floor; only the subfloor which squeaked beneath him, despite his mad miming skills.

Someone had lived in this apartment. Furniture remained behind, as well as knickknacks. There was a television cabinet on one wall which was big enough to house an old-fashioned, bulky, heavy TV set. Judging by the dust patterns in the cabinet, a TV had been there recently. It was now missing. The same was true for either a VHS player or a DVD player, because one of the shelves in the cabinet was missing another piece of equipment.

These missing pieces—coupled with the fact that other potentially valuable items in the apartment remained behind—told Wacky Best Friend that Bookworm's minions were indeed inside the building. Now, it was just a question of where they would be found.

~

Girl Next Door entered the building and found herself in a storage room behind the bakery. She held her swords in front of her, ready to take action against any person who might cross her path, keeping in mind that there were two allies and a potential new boyfriend in the building that she should probably try not to slice in half.

The room was dark and quiet. Nobody was in there, but Girl Next Door was not going to take this fact for granted. She kept her guard up and reminded herself that angry ninjas could drop from the ceiling at any moment.

None of Bookworm's minions had ever seemed to be ninjas in the past, but she was not going to let that stop her from expecting ninjas. She had swords after all and that demanded some ninja action.

As she made her way toward the front of the building, she could see Starlette walking in her direction. All seemed calm, which was usually not a good sign.

She walked toward the staircase which led upward, making note of a door directly across from that staircase, which would take them down to the basement when the time came.

Starlette said nothing as she met up with Girl Next Door. She simply joined her and began to walk up the stairs.

The stairs creaked as Starlette stepped onto them. Though

Starlette was light and walked with stealth, the building was old and there was no way to prevent these noises. If someone were in the basement, there was a good chance that they already knew that the actors were in the building.

Girl Next Door stepped onto the first stair. Keeping to the right side of the stair, she hoped to avoid making the same squeaking sound that Starlette had made. She failed. Now, the Bookworm minions would know that at least two actors were there.

On the wall beside her, Girl Next Door noticed a bloody fingerprint, still wet. The smear pattern suggested that someone had reached for the wall while moving past the stairs, not up them.

She doubted that they would find anyone on any of the upper levels of the building, but the scene had been blocked in a very specific way and Girl Next Door would follow her directions.

Her own image reflected back at her from the shining blades of her swords and she snuck a glimpse of herself from time to time, to see if she looked as badass as she felt. When she saw the wholesome image staring back at her, she was reminded of what her role was in all of this. She was not meant to be the badass. She was the sweet and cute girl next door. She adjusted her performance accordingly.

The swords also provided a sort of rear-view mirror as she climbed the stairs. If anyone tried to sneak up and attack her from behind, she would be ready and they would pay the price of underestimating her.

Starlette's bo smacked against the wall as she climbed. The sound broke the silence of their stealthy search and seemed about ten times louder than it would have under any other circumstance.

"Son of a bitch," Starlette murmured under her breath and then resumed her walk as though the mistake had never happened.

The next time Girl Next Door saw Starlette turn a corner, she watched Starlette spin the bo around her back and grab it with the hand farthest from the wall. It was becoming more and more a part of her with each step and each mistake.

When they reached the door which led to the first hallway, Starlette stopped walking and signaled for Girl Next Door to proceed up to the next floor while she searched this one alone.

Girl Next Door shook her head in silent protest. This was not the way they were supposed to do it.

In response, Starlette held up her wrist and used her other hand to tap it where a watch would be. Time was of the essence and the sooner they searched the levels that they all considered low-priority, the sooner they could head into the basement and finish the job.

Girl Next Door pursed her lips and cocked her head. The down-home sensibilities that she was meant to bring to the group continued to protest. Safety in numbers, after all. Yet the badass within wanted to cut to the action just as badly as Starlette did.

She remained in character and shook her head again. Starlette came back with an icy stare. At the end of the day, Starlette was the star of this show and Girl Next Door was just a supporting player.

With a huff of reluctance, Girl Next Door gave in and followed her orders. She watched as Starlette walked into the hallway and began her solo search.

Girl Next Door continued up the stairs. Walking with Starlette always made her feel more confident somehow. Without the support of her female lead, she felt exposed in front as well as behind. She glanced into the reflection of her swords more often as she made her way to the next floor. She saw nothing behind her.

When she reached the next doorway which led to the hall that she would be searching, Girl Next Door felt no sense of urgency. She felt no immediate threat. These searches were strictly meant to build tension and provide material for the montage that would be compiled at some later time.

She walked into the first apartment that she came across and scanned the room as she entered. It had apparently been the apartment of a college-aged tenant, because the posters on the wall were all Che Guevara and marijuana leaves. There was not much by way of furniture in the room; just beanbag chairs and a bookcase made out of cinderblocks and scraps of wood. On them, Girl Next Door saw text books and a worn copy of *War and Peace*.

On one of the walls, there was a TV mount, which was empty. Beneath it, there was a relatively new gaming console, which had been smashed into uselessness.

Someone had been here and had taken the TV, but simply destroyed the console. A common thief would have taken both. A Bookworm minion would destroy the console out of rage and disgust toward the violence that such video games taught to today's youth.

The books and posters were untouched, signifying an appreciation for the intellectual side of the apartment's former tenant.

As she moved toward the tiny kitchen area of the apartment, Girl Next Door spotted magnets on the refrigerator, in the shapes of letters. Some of these magnets had been rearranged to form the word *nevermore.*

The poetic word on the refrigerator, coupled with the text books and the lack of television began to give Girl Next Door the creeps. She glanced at her swords once more and this time the eyes that she saw staring back at her were not her own.

The woman standing behind her had shortly cut hair and a piercing on her brow. She looked at Girl Next Door with a maniacal smile across her face.

"We weren't expecting you until tonight," the woman said.

Girl Next Door spun around and jumped back out of instinct. She swung her swords wildly through the air, but the woman stepped back, avoiding the blades.

Girl Next Door shook off the initial shock of seeing the woman, composed herself and stared down the woman with a steely gaze as she moved into a more traditional sword-wielding pose and said, "Well then, I guess I have the element of surprise."

"Do you even know how to use those swords?" the woman asked.

"I'm Chinese. Of course I know how to wield the mighty katana."

"Katana are Japanese."

"I know that," Girl Next Door lied. "I am a master of all of the Asian-American martial arts and you stand no chance against my ethnically inappropriate, somewhat racist weaponry."

"I'm impressed that you could say all of that without tripping up."

Girl Next Door glared, "I am an actress, after all."

With that, Girl Next Door attacked, spinning around and slashing through the air with the mighty blades of her swords.

Her swords slammed into the doorway that led from the kitchen to the living room, hurting her hands just slightly. She gave no sign of this pain as she let out a warrior's cry—inspired by the swords in hand—and proceeded to kick the woman in the gut.

The woman stumbled backward and pulled a knife from her belt.

Girl Next Door quipped, "Mine are bigger."

To which the Bookworm minion replied, "I know how to use mine."

The woman lunged at Girl Next Door with every intention of jamming the knife into Girl Next Door's chest.

Girl Next Door responded out of instinct alone and flailed the swords mindlessly. This method proved to be effective, as the woman screamed in pain and her knife-holding hand fell to the floor.

Blood squirted across the room and across Girl Next Door's face as her mouth fell open in shock.

The woman grabbed her badly bleeding, handless arm and fell to her knees, crying.

"Oh, God!" Girl Next Door said. "I didn't mean to do that. I just wanted to kill you. I am so, so sorry. That's... gross."

Girl Next Door no longer felt the coolness that she had once associated with her swords. They now seemed like sloppy, dangerous weights, tied to her hands. She dropped them to the ground and freed herself of that weight.

The woman looked up at Girl Next Door and screamed, "My hand! You cut off my hand! You stupid bitch."

The woman continued to bleed onto the floor as she took a moment to gather herself and she eventually looked back to Girl Next Door, saying, "I'm sorry. I didn't mean to call you a bitch. That is a sexist, vile term and I am above that."

"I appreciate your apology," Girl Next Door told her.

"This has nothing to do with disgusting labels, but when Bookworm kills every last one of you, the world will truly be a better place. You are the vermin that spread the disease of stupidity across the world. You and actors like you will be remembered as the tyrants of the current generation."

"Aww..." Girl Next Door said in an adorable tone, pulling out her gun and shooting the woman in the head. "That's sweet of you to say. Bitch."

The minion of Bookworm slumped to the ground and blood poured from her head wound, puddling on the floor; along with the blood from her severed hand. Girl Next Door walked closer and stood over the dead body.

"Gosh," Girl Next Door said. "That is a lot of blood."

~

In his mind, the nunchucks were like the invisible balls that he had been taught to juggle in his mime class. They spun and moved through the air with grace and ease. Wacky Best Friend held them as he searched for enemies within the building and allowed them to pick up speed, as though he were adding more balls to his impressive act. Each increase built upon the energy of his weapon and this energy could only be dispersed through combat... Or by being locked inside of an impenetrable invisible box.

As his search progressed, the frequency of his smacking himself in the face with the nunchucks was lessening. He was starting to think that he was getting the hang of them.

Wacky Best Friend had already cleared the floor that he was on and was moving toward the stairs when he heard a shot ring out, somewhere below his current position. He immediately dropped the stupid nunchucks and pulled a gun as he listened for more shots, or any sign of what might be happening. He would have loved to run out of that room, but he knew that rushing into the unknown was a bad idea. He had to play this situation wisely, or risk becoming one more actor that Starlette would need to save on this shoot. He had to be smart.

Still listening and trying to make as little noise as possible, Wacky Best Friend took a step forward. In doing so, he tripped over the nunchucks that he had dropped on the ground and found himself in one of those cartoonish falls, with feet over his head and back landing squarely on the ground.

It was not his finest moment, but at least this shoot was not being filmed before a live Studio audience. He quickly grabbed his weapons and pulled himself up.

He picked up his pace as he entered the stairwell, holding his gun at the ready and keeping his nunchucks tucked safely in his belt.

He moved down the stairs with stealth and speed and entered the hallway of the next level, knowing that this was not the floor on which the shot had been fired. One of his fellow cast members was in trouble, but he could not neglect the directions which had been given to him.

Had he been the one blocking this scene, Wacky Best Friend might have kept the team together, because there was safety in numbers. He might have added more background actors, to add support to the main cast and to add credibility to the idea that this was a high priority shoot.

But he was not The Director. He was merely a cast member and his job was to take direction, not give it. All he could do now was work with the material which had been written and that meant that he had to clear the upper levels of the building before rejoining his team. To simply run down the stairs in search of the source of the gunshot would have left them exposed to anyone who might have remained on the upper levels.

He breezed through the hallway with the focus of a wolf, the grace of a dancer and the speed of an actor from the 1980's, coked out of his ever loving mind.

He checked the first apartment and cleared it without incident, while noting that the television was missing and a radio was smashed on the ground, next to an MP3 player. There was an empty brandy glass on the kitchen counter, with just a hint of brandy remaining in the bottom. Next to it was a receipt, which came from a bookstore.

The enemy had been in that apartment and the stench of their loafers still hung heavy in the air.

The second apartment showed no signs of missing televisions. The place was decorated with antiques and there were bookcases lining each wall. Potpourri sat in bowls on tables, next to candy dishes which were full of hard candies that had melted together. There were doilies on the arms of the chairs and a corded telephone with a rotary dial.

The apartment made Wacky Best Friend sick to his stomach.

He hurried through that apartment and got the hell out of there as quickly as possible. The entire floor was clear of Bookworm minions. He hurried for the stairs.

~

Somewhere high above him, a shot was fired. All he could see was blackness, from the bag that covered his face. His hands and feet were bound. He could not react to the sound of the gun being fired in any proper way, so Ben tugged at his bindings and let out the closest thing to a yell that he could manage with a gag in his mouth.

Immediately, he was hit on the side of the head with what felt like the butt of a rifle. He wasn't knocked out by this blow—as he had seen happen in so many movies—but it did hurt like hell.

He continued to struggle, but there was nowhere for him to go. There was nothing for him to do.

At that moment, someone could have been dead because of him and that thought struck him harder than any weapon could. He was tired of being the cause of so much suffering. He wanted to put an end to this. He wanted to fight.

He pulled harder at the ropes that kept him immobile, but he could not free himself. In the blackness before his eyes, Ben's mind projected images of pain and suffering. He saw the blood of innocents pooling at his feet and his heart pounded in his chest so hard that he thought it must be visible to anyone who was looking his way.

He tried to scream again, this time in an attempt to shake the images in his own mind and once again, he was struck. The pain helped to bring him back to the real world and away from those horrors within himself. He preferred the pain to the darkness and so he screamed again.

If only his captors knew that they were helping to ease his true torment.

~

Starlette had searched one apartment, where she found nothing but the mess that someone had left behind as they gathered their most treasured belongings and rushed out the door. Rotting food remained on the kitchen counters and half used tubes of toothpaste had been left in the bathroom.

There were no bad guys, so she moved on.

The second apartment that she entered was similar in some respects. It was not incredibly well decorated and it seemed as though the people living there had left in a hurry. Starlette could only imagine what it must have been like for these families on the night of the attacks, sitting at home, going about their normal routines, only to have the night shattered by explosions and gunfire that was never meant for them.

One of the bedrooms in this apartment was painted bright pink and it was filled with all of the most valuable possessions of a little girl, which her parents would not think twice about leaving behind. Dollhouses and princess lamps. Art supplies and plastic tiaras.

As she entered this room, Starlette was flooded with mental images of this little girl, screaming and crying as her parents pulled her from the only life that she had ever known.

There was a doll on the floor, near the bedroom door. It was an off-brand doll whose face and name would not be featured on theme park attractions or DVD collections, but it seemed well worn from use.

The doll was of the typical thin, blond variety. It was dressed in a sparkling blue gown, with painted on jewelry. Her shoes were missing. Her hair was messy and streaks of it seemed to be colored red by marker ink.

A thick layer of dust had collected on top of this doll, but the image of what she had once been could still be seen, shining through the mess. She could be cleaned off and loved again, but Starlette left the doll on the ground. The girl who once loved her was not coming back anytime soon.

Besides, Starlette figured that the little girl had probably outgrown such silly things. It was a cruel, dark world out there these days.

A shot rang out on the level above Starlette and she could hear the sound of a muffled thump as a body fell, lifeless.

She pulled herself away from thoughts of little girls and their dolls as she ran from the apartment, keeping her bo at the ready.

Starlette was ready for action. Her heart was racing almost as fast as her mind. Her muscles yearned to be pressed to their fullest abilities.

As she entered the stairwell, Starlette could hear Wacky Best Friend hurrying through the doorway of another level and she heard Girl Next Door on the stairs above her, calling out, "I'm fine. Just killed a woman, that's all. Keep doing what you're doing."

There was a flaw in the logic of her friends. Starlette was not rushing to the stairs in order to rush to the side of Girl Next Door. She had enough faith in Girl Next Door's abilities to know that she could handle the situation.

Starlette's primary concern was that the gunshot had carried through the entire building. From top to bottom, everyone would know that the fight had begun. The element of surprise was gone. There was no longer time for stealth.

She was rushing for the basement. She knew that if Ben Hurley was still alive, he would be held down there and the longer she took to reach him, the more time the Bookworm minions would have to coordinate their defenses.

Sooner or later, Wacky Best Friend and Girl Next Door would figure out what she was doing and they would rush to her side. Until then, she was content to go about this on her own. With fewer lives to worry about, she would be willing to take more chances. She was officially dead, after all. That meant that there was nothing left to lose.

The door to the basement was just as she had left it. There were no enemies rushing to investigate the sound of the gun being fired. If they had been pouring through the doorway, Starlette would have the opportunity to take them out, one at a time. There would be no chance for all of them to gang up on her at once.

One of the biggest lessons that an actor had to learn upon entering The Studio was that bad guys did not play by any set of rules. They did not come at you one at a time. They jumped you all at once. If you took even a moment to gather your thoughts, you were dead.

The key to survival was an instinct for improv. Never second guess your decisions. Never undermine the logic of what you have created in the moment. Just clear your mind and go. There would be time for reflection once the job was done.

Without skipping a beat, Starlette pulled open the basement door and rushed down the stairs.

The basement was dark and cluttered with shelves and boxes. In another life, it had been used to store supplies for the bakery above it. Now, it was a makeshift dungeon.

The light in the basement was dim, coming from only two overhead bulbs. The first of these bulbs was in the center of the room. The second bulb hung inside the walk-in refrigerator which was now nothing more than a large closet with a heavy door. From what Starlette could tell, the only electricity working in the building was that which powered the bulbs. It probably came from a generator somewhere, but this detail was of no concern to her.

She could see Ben Hurley inside the refrigerator, tied at the wrists and ankles, with a bag over his head. He was shirtless and bloody, but he seemed to be alive. Starlette couldn't help but think that the situation would have been made easier if she found him dead. At least then she could fight her way to freedom and never have to wonder where his loyalties lay. His being alive could only serve to complicate her life.

She had only enough time to catch a quick glimpse of Ben Hurley before she was attacked by the minions of Bookworm. There must have been ten of them and they all charged at her at once.

Starlette stood her ground and prepared for the fight. She gripped her bo tightly and waited until the Bookworm minions were close enough before putting her weapon to good use.

When Starlette was a little girl, she wanted to be a fairy princess. She had a magic wand, which she would wave through the air and she would pretend that she could turn her sister into a toad.

As she grew older, she traded her wand for a baton and taught herself to twirl it and throw it and catch it with ease.

Her bo was not a baton. It was bigger and heavier, and far more prone to hitting things that she did not mean to hit. However, as she had progressed through the building, some of the same principles that had been instilled through her baton had worked their way into her relationship with her bo.

When thought of as a large stick, the baton was clumsy. However, once she could turn that stick into an extension of her own body, its form began to take on a new logic. Her hands were merely joints, which she could flex in order to bring movement to the bo. Though her blood did not flow through the bo, her energy did.

As she spun the bo through the air, the dim light of the room reflected off of its chrome highlights and it looked as though she controlled lightning itself.

She made contact with the first of the minions to come within reach of her bo and the skin on his left cheek tore. He twisted in pain and slammed into one of the other minions.

Another twist of her wrists and another minion doubled over, unable to breathe.

She spun the bo through the air and tried for one more minion, but this time the bo was caught. Her intended victim grabbed the bo and pulled on it, but Starlette refused to let it go. She was drawn closer to the minion, who raised his foot off of the ground and planted it in Starlette's stomach as she came near.

Starlette had solid abs, so the kick to the stomach was not as bad as it could have been for some, but she was off balance and unable to swing her weapon freely. In that moment she was at a loss for what to do next. Her brain offered no suggestions. All she could do was rely on her body to pull her through this.

She leaned on the bo and used it to support herself as she kicked one of the attacking minions in the face. She then flipped over the bo, shifting the angle from which she was pulling on it and throwing the minion who held it off balance, but not for long. He soon recovered and his grip became strong once again.

Starlette raised her knee and used it for leverage as she snapped the bo in half, using the piece that she now held to club the minion who was holding the other half. As he went down, she bent over and grabbed his piece of the bo, now holding one half in each hand.

She swung and kicked and flipped her way through several more blows to the Bookworm minions, but for each minion that fell, another one pulled himself—or herself—up off of the ground and resumed their attack. Starlette soon found herself not only outnumbered, but surrounded.

She fought hard and drew blood from many of those minions, but she could not last forever. Eventually, she was grabbed and held and though she kicked and struggled, she could not break free. She was caught.

"Hey!" came a voice from the direction of the basement stairs —and not a moment too soon.

Nunchucks flew through the air—clumsily and without great force—and bounced off the head of one of the Bookworm minions who was holding onto Starlette.

Wacky Best Friend and Girl Next Door stood by the basement stairs, guns in hand and ready to fire.

"Who's got two thumbs and loves her some violence and apple pie?" Girl Next Door asked. "I'll give you a hint… The chick upstairs doesn't have two thumbs anymore."

Wacky Best Friend and Girl Next Door opened fire and most of the Bookworm minions scurried for cover while one remained, using Starlette as a human shield.

"Put your guns down, or your friend dies!" he yelled as he gripped her tightly, keeping his full attention on her friends.

Starlette twisted around and jammed the jagged end of one half of her bo into the side of his head. The minion went down and she pulled the bloody weapon out once again.

Rather than grab her gun, as her friends probably would have liked, Starlette threw herself into the battle with the other minions, charging toward them with half a bo in each hand.

She found herself fighting three minions, who each had weapons of their own. Tasers, knives, chains… no guns. Starlette took this to mean that their mission was to bring actors back to Bookworm alive.

She was tempted to give them what they wanted. If she could be taken prisoner, they would take her to him. She could stand face to face with the man and eventually, she could snap his neck. Unfortunately, she figured that she would also be drugged, bound, or both. They wanted answers, not confrontation. If she were taken, it would be difficult to break free and end this war once and for all. So, she fought. Hard.

A smack to the head for one minion sent her into a spin, which allowed her to sweep the feet from beneath another. She came face to face with the third minion, just as his chain made contact with the side of her head and she was thrown off balance, stumbling to the side. The pain was great and her ear began to ring, but Starlette would not be taken down by a stupid chain. Who the fuck used a chain as a weapon anyway? Was this a 1980's video game?

Then again, she had come armed with a stick.

She reached for the knives on her belt and threw one at the third minion with her left hand, where it planted itself in his arm. This seemed to make him angry and he charged at her, growling like a wolf. She could see the veins bulging in his neck. His face was red with fury. He didn't seem to notice that she had thrown two more knives at him, using her right hand. One was sticking out of his chest and the other had planted itself in the minion's inner thigh.

When he saw the knives in his chest and thigh, the minion chose to pull free the knife in his thigh. Soon, his entire leg was dripping in blood. She had severed his femoral artery. He gripped his leg in a desperate attempt to stop the bleeding, but he could not.

Behind this minion, his friends were pulling themselves back up. Soon, Starlette would have to face the two of them once again.

Starlette jumped into the air, grabbed an overhead pipe and used it to add force as she swung her feet forward, landing both of them in this angry minion's chest and driving the knife into his heart. He fell dead.

With the brief time that she had before being attacked again, Starlette looked around the room to check the status of her supporting cast. While they had charged into the room with guns drawn, Starlette had made it difficult for them to open fire in the basement. She had run right into the swarm of Bookworm minions. In doing so, she turned a fight that was easily resolved through bullets into a hand to hand battle, which would quite possibly last into the night. Surely, she would be accused of over acting when she returned to The Studio.

Girl Next Door had her back to a wall and three minions of her own walking toward her. She had only taken her swords and her guns into the building and her swords were nowhere to be seen now. She smiled nervously at her approaching attackers.

"Can we talk about this?" Girl Next Door asked them. "I'm sure that if we just sit down with some ice-cold milk and a plate of fresh chocolate chip cookies, we can work through our differences. And hey, we *are* in a bakery."

The minions didn't seem to be impressed with her cutesy banter. Perhaps it would have been better received if Girl Next Door had gone into this fight with her usual down-home wardrobe and not the sexed up version of her character that Studio Head had ordered for this shoot. Undermining the character never worked well, but the lesson always seemed lost on the bosses in the suits.

Girl Next Door was a constant professional and a talented actress, however. When the minions couldn't be swayed by her cuteness, she kicked one in the balls, punched one in the face and leaped on top of the third, wrapping her legs around his neck and throwing her weight backwards, pulling him to the ground.

Wacky Best Friend, meanwhile, was facing down minions of his own. He kept his guns in hand, always looking for a clear shot that didn't risk hitting one of his co-stars, but finding little such opportunity.

As minions charged toward him, Wacky Best Friend spun and twisted his way out of danger, while using his guns to block knives and smash faces. Where the nunchucks had failed him, his handguns now succeeded.

Minions were dropping steadily. An end to the battle was within sight. Starlette could see Ben Hurley, still struggling to break free of his bindings. He did not seem to be in any immediate danger. All they needed to do now was finish off the Bookworm minions, free Ben and waltz out of the building. It was easy. Too easy.

As she continued to fight, Starlette glanced back to the stairs one more time. She could see a stream of light break through the darkness as the door upstairs was opened. She saw shadows against the wall as more minions began to make their way down the stairs. This didn't surprise her in the least.

Still fighting, she called out, "Heads up! We have more incoming!"

Both of her co-stars caught sight of the incoming minions. Wacky Best Friend was squatting over the limp body of his third attacker at this point, having turned a Taser on the minion who had been wielding it. He seemed to be going through this minion's pockets as Starlette called to him. When Wacky Best Friend saw the minions on the stairs, he stuck the wallet of the limp minion in his own pocket and opened fire on the stairs, taking out more than one of the bad guys as they came down. Despite his true and steady aim, there were too many minions coming down the stairs and the attacks from within the basement had not yet been settled.

Girl Next Door pulled out her own gun and began shooting. One of her bullets struck a Bookworm minion, but before she could take down any more, she was hit from behind by a metal bar which one of the minions had found on the basement floor. She went down. The minions who were attacking her began to move closer.

Starlette hurried to get to Girl Next Door, pulling a knife from her belt as she ran. When she reached the minions who were attacking Girl Next Door, she wasted no time in grabbing one of them by the hair, pulling his head back and slitting his throat.

Blood sprayed across the basement and over Girl Next Door.

"Oh, gross!" Girl Next Door yelled as she wiped the blood from her face. "Why do people keep bleeding on me?!"

Girl Next Door then turned and saw the minions pouring down the stairs. Her eyes filled will panic.

"There are a lot of them," Girl Next Door said to Starlette, looking for some idea of how they might get out of this.

"The refrigerator!" Wacky Best Friend called. "Get in there. Now!"

They were not clear to simply run into the refrigerator. There were minions attacking them and they had to fight to break free, but eventually each one of them managed to fight their way to the refrigerator.

Wacky Best Friend was the last one inside. As he entered the refrigerator, Starlette closed the heavy door behind him. They were safe from flying bullets for the time being, but they were still trapped.

Girl Next Door went to Ben Hurley as soon as the door was closed. She pulled the bag off of his head and removed the gag from his mouth.

"Are you okay?" she asked him.

Ben didn't make eye contact with any of the other actors as he said, "I'll live."

Starlette didn't particularly care if Ben was hurt or not. If not for him, none of them would be trapped in a basement full of Bookworm minions, wearing ridiculously uncomfortable clothes.

She looked around the refrigerator, assessing their situation and what tools they might have to aid in their escape. The shelves were empty. There were no meat hooks that could be used in creative and bloody ways. All that she saw was the chair that Ben was tied to and a stack of televisions that had been collected from the apartments above and thrown into the corner of the refrigerator. They were broken now, rendered useless to anyone who tried to entertain the world through the magic of rerun syndication.

No weapons. Nothing that Starlette could use to fight her way to freedom, no matter how much duct tape she threw at it. All they had was what they brought with them.

"Give me a knife," Girl Next Door said to Starlette, holding out a hand.

Starlette gave her one of her throwing knives and Girl Next Door went to work, freeing Ben.

"How long have you been down here?" Girl Next Door asked him.

"A couple of days, I think," he replied. "It was stupid. I'm sorry I got you into this."

"This is what we do. Don't worry about it," Girl Next Door replied, with a warm smile.

Wacky Best Friend looked in Starlette's direction and they exchanged thoughts without a word spoken. Neither one of them was a fan of this situation and both of them had their doubts about Ben Hurley.

Ben stood with Girl Next Door's help. He was weak and bleeding, but he was trying to push through it.

Girl Next Door touched his chest softly and asked, "Does this hurt?"

He shook his head, "No. I'm fine."

She pressed on his abs, "How about this?"

"I'm good. Thanks."

"There are too many of them out there. They'll take us out as soon as this door opens," Wacky Best Friend said to Starlette.

"Give me a gun. I can handle some of them," Ben told him.

Wacky Best Friend looked at Ben with a good amount of doubt in his eyes. He didn't trust the new actor any more than Starlette did and wouldn't until a more detailed interview could take place. There was too much missing time between the attacks and Ben's attempts to contact The Studio. Too much unaccounted for.

"I'm fresh out of bullets," Wacky Best Friend told him.

Ben looked at the ground, very aware of the situation that he was in and the first impression that he had made.

A gun was held out in front of him. Girl Next Door was handing him a weapon, though her eyes were on Wacky Best Friend.

"Oh, look," she said. "I just happen to have a spare on me."

Ben looked at Girl Next Door, who reaffirmed her warm smile. He took the gun, but still seemed uneasy about it.

Starlette walked to the center of the room and looked at the dim lightbulb. She then swatted it, breaking the bulb and casting the room into darkness.

"Why did you do that?" Girl Next Door asked. "Now we're totally blind!"

Starlette turned on a flashlight, which Prop Master had gotten from the lighting department and routinely included in her supplies. It was fitted with a filter which filled the room with red light.

"When we get out of here, we're going to take out the bulb. Their eyes will need to adjust. Ours won't," Starlette told the others.

Girl Next Door nodded, "Oh. That's pretty cool."

"I can fight. I'm trained for it and I'm up to it," Ben told Starlette, catching on to the fact that she was the lead in this cast.

"That's sweet, but we need something more than fists and bullets," Starlette replied.

"Like what? We don't exactly have an abundance of supplies in here," Wacky Best Friend came back.

Starlette walked to him and looked him in the eye as she pointed to the grenades that he had strapped to his chest.

Wacky Best Friend smiled and said, "Oh. I totally forgot that I had those."

"We'll open the door and stand back to avoid any gunfire that comes our way. Wacky Best Friend will throw the grenades; take out the bulb and as many of the enemies as possible. We run in the chaos. With luck, we can make it out of the building while their ears are still ringing," Starlette ordered.

Everyone seemed to understand the plan, though Starlette had to doubt Ben's ability to follow through. Even if he could be trusted not to sell them out to Bookworm, he was weak and vulnerable. Girl Next Door may have sympathized, but Starlette did not.

Wacky Best Friend moved to the wall beside the door and pulled the grenades from where they were strapped, yanking the pins in the process. He held the safety levers, ensuring that the grenades would not explode inside of the refrigerator and kill them all.

The first time that Wacky Best Friend ever held a live grenade in his hands, Starlette remembered seeing a look of fear in his eyes. He didn't seem to trust himself to hold them. He worried that he would do something stupid and blow himself up in the process.

These days, he was an old pro with explosives. He handled them with ease and used them with talent. Just one of the many changes that she had taken note of since the attacks.

She put her hand on the door's handle and looked to Wacky Best Friend. He gave her a slight nod.

Starlette then looked back to Girl Next Door and Ben Hurley. She told Ben, "Get through the front doors. A van will pick us up and take us back to The Studio."

Ben nodded and gripped his gun tightly. Girl Next Door put a hand on the small of his back and said, "Don't worry. I've got you covered. Just run and don't look back."

Starlette readied her guns and took a deep breath to ready herself. She then looked to Wacky Best Friend once more before pulling the door open.

Before the metal door was fully opened, bullets were bouncing off the outside. The Bookworm minions preferred to have one prisoner, but they probably didn't need all four.

Wacky Best Friend ducked low as he turned into the doorway and threw the grenades. A bullet struck him in the arm as he pulled back into the refrigerator and waited for the explosions to pass.

Starlette assessed his wounds in the second before the grenades exploded. It was not an in-depth assessment for sure, but it told her that he was not bleeding horribly. There was probably not any serious damage done.

The grenades exploded and the whole building shook. The light in the basement went out. Smoke and dust poured through the doorway.

Starlette led the way through the refrigerator door and through the basement. Ben Hurley was behind her, followed by Girl Next Door and Wacky Best Friend.

As they rushed through the basement, Starlette kept her eyes peeled for any enemies who might attack. Most of them were either blinded by dust and darkness, or wounded from the explosions. The few who raised a gun did not live long enough to pull the trigger.

She led the way up the stairs, where they were met by several Bookworm minions who were guarding the exits. More gunfire ensued. Windows shattered. Blood spilled onto the floor.

Wacky Best Friend punched an older minion in the face and seemed to take great pride in this minion's defeat as the minion fell to the ground, unconscious. He quickly made his way to each of the fallen minions, taking their weapons off of them, in order to ensure that none would be able to use their dying breath to fire off one last shot.

Starlette tried to make her way toward the sunlight and fresh air, but more gunfire came from the buildings nearby. She was stopped in the doorway of the bakery and forced to take cover.

"How do we get out of here?" Ben asked, ducking behind an overturned table.

"Just wait for it," Starlette replied, turning to him and never doubting for a moment that they would make it out of the building alive.

The van drivers who worked for The Studio were trained to handle all types of situations. Their vans were armored. Their windows were bulletproof. In a pinch, one could always count on a van driver to get them where they needed to go.

Before long, a van screeched to a stop in front of the bakery. Bullets were cutting through the air and striking the vehicle, but the actors were close to safety. They hurried to the van and climbed inside.

As soon as the doors were closed, the van peeled away from the bakery and sped down the street. Evasive actions were taken just in case they were being followed, but there were no signs of Bookworm minions.

The action was over. Shooting had wrapped for the day.

Now safe in the van, sitting next to Starlette, Wacky Best Friend examined the objects that he had taken off of the dead men in the bakery. The knife was old, with an ivory handle, which would be highly illegal if the ivory was not pre-embargo. However, given the fact that the knife had come from the pocket of a genocidal maniac, illegal ivory would be a relatively minor offense.

There was an inscription on the gun which he had pulled from the scene. On the side of the barrel was a line that read: *What strange developments of humanity, what wonderful advances upon our rudimentary civilization, I thought, might not appear when I came to look nearly into the dim elusive world that raced and fluctuated before my eyes!*

The line might as well have been written in Klingon for all the meaning it held for Starlette as she looked at it. After studying the line in silence for a moment, Wacky Best Friend tucked the gun away and rifled through his pockets for more spoils of war.

Starlette looked to Ben, who was sitting in the seat directly in front of her. He was bleeding onto the upholstery and breathing heavily as he watched the world speed by through the windows.

He seemed worn and tired.

Girl Next Door offered him a bottled water, which she pulled from a cooler in the front passenger seat. He drank, but did not drink deeply. He took his time.

~

The days following the attacks were a blur to Ben. He had taken cover wherever he could manage to stay hidden. He cowered in the shadows, feeling as though someone was watching him at all times. He did not know where to go or what to do. He had survived the attacks, but he knew that those people were still out there and if he was found they would try their best to kill him once again.

When hunger overcame him, Ben ventured out of his hiding spot and into the city. He pulled his collar up high, wrapped a scarf around his face and kept a hat on his head so that he would be impossible to recognize.

Times Square was alien to him now. Still bustling with people, the place seemed empty to him somehow. The giant television screen that once displayed images overhead was now showing nothing but static... Apparently, nobody could remember how to turn the thing off.

As Ben walked along the sidewalk, he found himself standing outside a store window, looking in at more televisions which displayed nothing but snow. He couldn't look away.

Next to him, a little boy approached. This boy could not have been more than four years old and he placed his hands on the glass of that store window, looking at the same televisions that Ben was staring at.

"Let's go. Your father and brother are waiting," the boy's mother called from behind.

"No!" the boy cried. "I want to watch TV!"

"Get over here, now!" his mother called, getting more frustrated with her son.

"No!" the boy yelled back.

The boy's mother walked to her son and grabbed his arm, pulling him away from the window.

"I want to watch TV!" the boy screamed.

"There is no TV!" the mother replied, angrily. "You can't watch

TV! It's gone!"

"No, Mommy!" the boy screamed. "You're a bad eyeball!"

"Fine. I'm a bad eyeball. That won't bring back the TV," the woman replied, dragging her son away from the store and down the street.

Ben turned and watched the boy kick and scream as his mother pulled him away. This would be the first clear memory of life after the attacks that Ben would hold onto. He would be able to picture it clearly, hear the voices and smell the street for months after. It was the moment when he fully came to understand the scope of what had happened; not just to himself, but to the world.

~

Starlette wasn't sure whether or not she could trust Ben Hurley, but when she caught a glimpse of the look in his eyes as they drove back to The Studio, she could tell that whatever he had been through had taken its toll on him. Only time could tell how big a toll it had truly been.

Chapter Five
THE GOLDEN AGE

Starlette walked the streets of Hollywood, as she often did in those days, nearly a year after the attacks which had brought her industry to ruin. The night air was cool and there was a breeze which washed over her and soothed her. If she closed her eyes, she could imagine that she had traveled back through time.

She had walked those streets many times before the attacks. She would grab a quick cup of coffee or browse the clothing stores while chatting on her cell phone or trying not to trip over her incredibly awkward shoes when a photographer noticed her. It was rare, but it happened... Once. Maybe twice. She was the star of a television show, after all.

Looking back on the person that she once had been was like thinking back on a movie. It was vivid, but without great depth; as though her mind was filled with the memories of a person who was completely unrelated to her. In truth, they barely had anything in common. The way they thought and felt was completely different. Their hopes for the future. Their opinions on world politics and micro-minis.

The girl she had been was a vague notion to her now, like Audrey Hepburn's character in *Breakfast At Tiffany's*. She was a person that Starlette might like to be if she could dare to dream, but it was a goal which seemed unattainable. Stars burned bright, but died out fast in the real world; and it could take years for anyone to notice that they were gone.

It was a quiet night, which did nothing for Starlette's mood. She wanted to run. She wanted to fight. She wanted to feel as though she were moving forward, even if she would eventually return to The Studio and realize that nothing had changed at all. She was an actress after all, and actresses enjoyed a good fantasy every so often.

In her logical and reasonable mind, she doubted that anything would ever change. The world that she knew was gone, and what remained now was a desperate group of people, clinging to the past. They were few, compared to the great culture they had once been. They were weak, compared to the power and influence they had once wielded. They now lived in a state that was entirely counter their nature... They were hiding.

The idea of the fight kept them alive. The goal of reclaiming the world of immortal screen legends, and their standing in the world of the mere mortals was what saved many of them from putting a pistol in their mouths and pulling the trigger. How realistic a goal this was, nobody ever really discussed. Nobody wanted to know the answer.

In their defense, their entire lives had been spent ignoring the odds. Getting on a bus in the middle of some fly-over state that nobody of importance had ever even heard of, and stepping off of it in Hollywood was like buying a lottery ticket. Many will enter, few will win. The chances went down even more if you happened to be ugly, no matter how talented you might be. Yet they persisted. Some of them beat the odds and became steadily working industry professionals.

Others merely earned union cards through bit parts here and

there, and happened to survive the attacks, which led to more substantial work in The Studio due to the low number of living actors in general... but they had beaten the odds as well.

Each night that she walked the streets of the city, Starlette asked herself the same questions, over and over again. Could they pull this off? Was there a point to any of it?

She longed for a fight, because the fight presented the clear and simple answer: In the end, it didn't matter if there was a point to any of it. People fight because they have to. They fight to live, or they fight to die for something they believe in. They fight because without it they have nothing left at all.

The best that Starlette had found on that night was a can, which she thoroughly kicked the ass of as she walked along the street.

She looked up at the buildings, remembering what it was like to hear the sound of horrible music being blasted at the highest possible volume, as an overpriced car passed her on the street. Nobody ever seemed to blast good music.

She remembered seeing through the windows of stores and apartments, as people went about their lives. She remembered avoiding dog poop on the sidewalk. She remembered weather forecasts on television.

The windows were dark now. There was no music to be blasted. There were few televisions at all, and nothing being broadcast to them. The shop windows had been broken and the stores had been looted long ago. The families—if they were smart —had moved away from the city and the violence that had overtaken it. Few remained, and most of those who did were not the types of people that you would smile a polite *hello* to as you passed them on the street.

In the sky, the moon was shining brightly and the few clouds that hovered over the city glowed with its silvery light. The stars could be seen in the spaces between those clouds, which seemed unnatural to Starlette. This was a city that should be hazy with smog and the sky should be dulled by light pollution. The stars should not be shining brightly in Hollywood.

As Starlette turned a corner and continued her walk, her eyes were still cast upward. She caught sight of a tall building several blocks away. Like most of the others, this building was a shadow of its former self. She could see windows broken on several floors. It was dark and ominous, looming over the city like an ancient relic. There was something else which caught her eye, however.

High on one of the upper levels of this building, Starlette saw a light shining brightly and a figure standing in the window, looking down over the city; perhaps looking down at Starlette herself.

She stared at this window and the person who was standing in it for several seconds, wondering why this person would advertise to the world that they remained in this building.

She'd seen people in the city before, of course. Some people had chosen to remain behind, rather than abandon their homes and the lives that they had built over years or decades. Those lives were usually lost anyway, but she had to respect the level of stupidity that would cause someone to make that decision and stick to it.

The figure in the window seemed different than those other people somehow. The way this person was lit and the manner in which they looked out across the city seemed dramatic and intriguing.

Starlette began to move toward the building. If she could not have a fight on that night, she would have to settle for exploring the mystery of this figure in the window. At the very least, she had to tell this person how stupid it was to draw attention to yourself in the times in which they lived.

She made her way to the building with speed that would just barely fall short of being called a *run*, counting the windows of the building as she went so that she could know which floor they were coming from.

It would be a long walk up the stairs of this building, but Starlette was in the mood for a challenge.

~

Thirty hours earlier...

The van pulled up to the entrance of The Studio and all four actors poured out in a hurry. There were no blindfolds or bags placed over Ben Hurley's head. If he was discovered to be untrustworthy, he would not live to reveal the location of The Studio.

As they walked through the door which led into The Studio, and down the stairs to the main floor, they were greeted by dozens of people from all departments, coming to see the latest addition to their cast.

Ben walked behind the others, trying to avoid the attention but failing. He kept his eyes on the ground and his mouth shut. Starlette had to wonder if, through all of this hustle and frenzy, Ben's awareness of the fact that he was not wearing a shirt was at all heightened. The way he was carrying himself, it seemed as though he felt completely naked out there, in front of all those people.

"We need help here!" Girl Next Door called into the crowd. "He's been hurt! Someone help us!"

"Let us through! Move aside!" came the voice of a woman in the middle of all those others who were buzzing over the new actor.

Hair and Makeup made their way through the crowd, each carrying a small black bag full of supplies, and followed by assistants. Makeup approached Ben first, taking his arm and leading him to a stretcher that had been prepared for his arrival, just in case he couldn't walk. He sat on it, and the other actors watched as he was tended to.

Makeup looked over Ben's wounds, studying them closely. She asked him, "When was the last time you used bronzer?"

"I don't know. A year, I guess," he replied, with a blank expression.

Makeup shook her head. She pulled a tissue from her bag and dabbed his wounds.

"I need mousse foundation, now. Satin ivory!" she called, holding a hand behind her and waiting as her assistant looked through the bag of supplies for the foundation.

"Is he going to be okay?" Girl Next Door asked, standing behind Makeup.

"I don't think there will be any permanent scarring," Makeup replied, looking Ben in the eyes. "You got lucky this time."

Ben stared at Makeup with a look that could only be described as incomprehension. Somehow, the idea that he had gotten lucky after everything that he had been through seemed puzzling to him.

The Director pushed his way through the crowd and to Ben's side. When Ben saw him, he squinted slightly, as though he recognized The Director.

"I'm The Director here, Ben. I run things down here on the floor while the Producers are busy with other business," The Director told him.

"Ben Hurley," Ben said, extending a hand, which The Director shook.

"You've been through a lot, and we're eager to have you sit down and tell us all about it. As soon as you're all fixed up, you'll be taken down to the waiting room where you can wait for your meeting with the casting department. We'll also want you to give an interview with Queen of Talk. It won't be fun, but we need to know more about what's happened to you and where you've been."

Ben nodded his understanding.

Starlette turned and walked away from the crowd. Wacky Best Friend was close behind her.

"What, you don't want to stick around for the publicity tour?" he asked her.

"I'm sure I'll get the gist of it later."

They made their way toward the prop department, so they could turn in what remained of their weapons, talking as they went along.

Wacky Best Friend asked her, "Do you trust him?"

She considered her answer for a moment before saying, "Do I think he is working for Bookworm? No. Probably not. Do I think he'll be a good fit for us?"

She took another moment to think about what her answer would be to that question. During the time she had spent with Ben Hurley, in the bakery and in the van as they drove back to The Studio, she had watched him. She had looked into his eyes, trying to get a feel for the person that she was bringing into the one safe haven that the film and television industry had left. She ran through all of the mental notes that she had taken in that time, and finally, she turned to Ethan and said, "I think he's damaged. I think he has a lot of questions to answer about where he's been and what's happened to him over the past eleven months. I don't trust him not to break down in the middle of a fight. I don't trust his ability to hold his own, even if he is strong enough in body. A lot's happened between the time he spent training and today, and I'm not about to bet my life on his ability to watch my back."

She walked into the prop department, and Ethan was still with her as she put her guns on Prop Master's desk. Prop Master was nowhere to be seen at the moment, so Starlette and Wacky Best Friend were alone.

"The big question I have," she told him, "is whether or not he was worth the risk, even if he is a good fighter. What he did was stupid. It was amateurish. It was dangerous. He put this entire organization at risk for the sake of saving his own ass, and I'm not about to forget that."

Ethan nodded in agreement with everything that she said as he put his own guns down on Prop Master's desk. Starlette continued by placing her throwing knives on it as well and she observed as Ethan checked his pockets for any further items to add, but eventually chose not to.

During the fight, he had taken a few items off of the bodies of the men that they had killed or wounded. A knife. A gun. Perhaps more that she hadn't seen. He chose not to turn these items over to The Studio.

Ethan noticed her watching him. He hadn't hidden the knife or the gun from her in the van, so he had nothing to hide from her now.

"Are you a fan of film noir?" he asked her. "Or, I mean... Were you a fan, back when there were noir movies to watch?"

"Some, I guess. Not a lot," she replied.

"People think of them as these straight up detective stories, because a lot of them were. But it wasn't just about walking around, asking questions. It was about putting pieces together. It wasn't just about solving the mystery, it was about understanding the story."

"So, you're collecting evidence?"

Ethan pulled the knife that he had taken from one of the minions out of his pocket and held it in his hand, running his thumb over its ivory handle as he said, "I'm trying to figure out who these people are and why they're so bent on taking us down.

It's not just about solving the mystery. It's about understanding the story."

He slipped the knife back into his pocket and smiled at Starlette. He said, "Plus, it's super pretty."

They walked out of the prop department and toward Wardrobe's department. As they went along, Starlette said to him, "You know what I've learned from my years of working in this business?"

"What?"

"Sometimes, there's no sense or logic. Sometimes we just do what we're told because we're being paid enough money to not think about *why.*"

"Touché."

"Yup. I'm deep like that."

"Wait... You're getting paid?"

~

Starlette approached the building, studying its design as though it were some ancient structure that she had found in the middle of an uncharted jungle. There was a classic look to the building, with marble along the walls of its entranceway and revolving doors, which were broken and nonfunctional. Gold and silver gave the place a deco flare, and red carpeting gave the building a touch of old Hollywood, even if it was dirty, torn, and worn from age.

This was the type of building that Starlette could imagine seeing in an old Ginger Rogers movie. She could imagine plucky women walking through the lobby, exchanging banter with their romantic lead, ending it all with a smack to his face.

She could imagine well-dressed businessmen, wearing fedoras and fine suits, walking off to eat their lunch in the drug store down the street. She could picture them going off to have drinks at some fancy nightclub, where a beautiful woman would sing an enchanting song while wearing a slinky dress. Of course, it would all end with a shocking murder and the frenzy to cover it up.

As she walked into the lobby of the building with her flashlight in hand, Starlette was disappointed to see how badly the building had been damaged. The front desk was broken to splinters and a safe rested on the floor bedside it, blown open by some sort of explosives. It was empty.

There were files and envelopes scattered around the desk, and a telephone which was on the floor. Somehow, the receiver of that telephone was neatly placed. The fact that it was not broken, or that the receiver was not off of its cradle made Starlette feel as though the phone would start ringing at any moment.

The rest of the lobby oozed with style and the spirit of the Hollywood glory days, though it was all rundown and falling apart now. There were sofas, which were ripped to shreds. There were giant pots, where dead plants were rotting. There were fish tanks that Starlette felt no rush to get a better look at.

It was an old building, and was quite possibly falling apart long before Bookworm and his evil minions had ever even thought of killing off the entertainment industry, but in Starlette's eyes it was just another casualty. One more shot of fuel for the fiery rage that was building inside of her.

She looked forward to seeing what would become of the rage. When the attacks first happened, Starlette had been scared. Then, she got mad. And the more time that passed—the more she saw of the world that had been created by the attacks—and the more she wanted to kill the man responsible. She wanted to make him suffer the way that he had made her and everyone else around her suffer. She wanted him to die slowly and painfully for what he had done. Not only to those who had died in the initial attacks, but for all those who had died in the months that followed; for the co-stars that she had fought alongside and cared about, only to lose.

She walked to the phone which was resting on the floor and bent down to pick it up, being sure not to leave herself vulnerable to attacks from behind.

Once she was holding the phone, she picked up the receiver and put it to her ear. Most phones in the city had been dead for months. She didn't know what she expected to hear when she put the phone to her ear, but she had to do it, if only to put to rest the small part of her mind that expected it to ring.

It was silly. She was acting as though the image of the person that she had seen in the window high above the streets had been a ghost, rather than a living human being. She was acting as though she were expecting to hear some disembodied voice on the other end of the line, reenacting the bloody death of some unfortunate soul who had perished in the attacks.

She walked the streets every night, whether on a shoot or on her own time, and she sometimes felt the presence of those people who had died. She had occasionally seen shadows in the corners of her eyes, which she tried to brush off. But, the city was haunted. Whether by ghosts, or just the memories of the people who had lived and died there, the place had an energy to it that was not right. It wasn't natural. The city was dead, and yet Starlette never quite felt alone when she walked those streets.

She listened to the other end of the line, trying to convince herself that she didn't believe in ghosts. She was not religious, though she did consider herself spiritually curious. She studied meditation and yoga, on and off. She bought a crystal once, to hang from the rearview mirror in her car. She almost bought a rabbit-foot keychain, but then she remembered that killing animals was wrong and she did not want any animal rights groups trying to blow her up.

Looking back, she now thought that she'd be willing to risk it. The threat of heavy explosives was not as frightening to her anymore.

On the other end of the line, she heard nothing. There was no dial tone, no recorded message. No ghostly voice crying for help. There was silence... and yet, there was something to the silence that wasn't quite right. It was the silence of a live connection, which nobody was speaking on.

"Hello?" Starlette said, though only in a half-assed way, because she felt stupid for talking to nothing.

There was no response. The silence continued, and while this should have eased that sense of creepiness in regards to the phone, the silence only seemed to make things worse.

She hung up the phone and placed it on the ground, being sure to leave things more or less as she had first found them. The less she disturbed, the less of a trail there would be behind her.

As she turned to move away from the phone, a flash of light in the distance caught her eye. At first, she thought that it must have been a light bulb on the fritz, but as she walked deeper into the lobby of the building she saw no flashing bulbs. The light had been a reflection of her own flashlight on the glass of a framed picture, which was hung on a door on the far end of the lobby.

The discovery of the unbroken picture frame was as suspicious to her as a blinking light would have been, so Starlette moved toward it.

At first, her own flashlight prevented her from seeing the picture that was framed, but as she moved closer and closer she could see that it was an old black and white photo of a man.

The closer she got, the more details she could make out. Eyes which conveyed life and humor, hidden behind round-framed glasses. Wild black hair, sticking out from beneath a far-too-small hat atop his head. He had raised eyebrows and a smile on his face, and looked like any normal person off the street. It could have been the picture of a former owner or someone who had meant something to the history of this building, back in its glory days. Starlette should have quickly moved on, but there was something about the picture that captured her attention.

It took her a moment to realize exactly what it was about this picture that caught her eye, but second by second the image became more clear to her.

Studio lighting. The personality in the eyes. The combination of wardrobe elements. The picture was too perfect. Too *in-character*. There weren't many pictures taken in the moment, *by* amateurs or *of* amateurs that would look like this.

The man began to look familiar to Starlette. She couldn't place the name, but she knew that she had seen this man many times before. He was not a famous superstar by any means, but he was an actor. A *character* actor, from the golden age of Hollywood.

It was a sign. The picture told Starlette that Hollywood lived in this building. Not many people would catch on to the subtle details of that picture, and Starlette thought that the picture must have been meant as a message. *Come through the door.*

She turned the doorknob and walked through the door and somehow the darkness became darker than it had been before. Her flashlight cut through it like a knife, showing her the stairs in front of her. They led upward, toward the light that Starlette had seen from the street.

She looked up the stairwell, hoping to see some sign of that light now, so that she could keep her eye on it as she grew closer, but there was not so much as a hint of it above her and the light from her flashlight faded into nothingness as she shined it upward.

She moved toward the stairs, not looking forward to the climb, but determined to explore whatever it was that called to her. She wondered if this was an elaborate trap, set up to lure actors and actresses to their demise, but the hint was not strong enough for that in her opinion. Bookworm was usually more obvious in his actions. He lacked the subtlety of the artists that he had sworn to kill, and even the more obvious artists usually had more style and flare in their delivery.

Starlette was not a big book reader before the attacks and she sure as hell would not be giving Bookworm the satisfaction anytime soon, but writers were artists—in their own way—and she imagined that they would have a more subtle approach than Bookworm had ever shown.

As she pondered these thoughts and stepped onto the first stair of many, Starlette heard a *click.* Her heart skipped a beat as a *beep* came from beside her. A number of blinking lights came to life on the wall next to Starlette, and she found herself face to face with a large block of what she could only assume was not merely clay.

A display of numbers appeared on the device, and it began to count down.

Ten. Nine. Eight. Seven. Six. Five...

~

Twenty-five hours earlier...

After he had turned in all of his props and wardrobe, Ethan ate some food, worked out in the gym and found himself sitting in the lawn furniture that he and Ember had set up outside of their trailers, twirling the ivory-handled knife that he had taken from one of Bookworm's minions and waiting for the final word on their new recruit.

As he did this, Ben Hurley was undergoing a rigorous casting process, with auditions and interviews. Everyone, from Head Writer to the Executive Producers were in on the audition. They were even conducting conference calls with various affiliates that

The Studio was networked with around the country. For some reason, which escaped Ethan entirely, Ben Hurley was a high level recruit.

Ethan didn't like the feeling that he was getting from this process. An audition and interview process was normal for any new cast member, but from what he could tell, Ben Hurley wasn't just a recurring member of the team. This was the casting process for a full time cast member; possibly a lead.

Ethan had spent far too long building his role on the team. He had put up with being called *Wacky Best Friend* through it all. He had put in the hard work, and built a relationship with his co-stars. They could rely on each other. They knew how to work off of each other without a second thought. They had chemistry and a rhythm, which had survived the loss of several of their original co-stars.

Bringing in a new lead was not only dangerous, it was just not fair. Ethan deserved to be given a more prominent role on the team. He had put in the hard work. He had earned the trust and respect of his co-workers, both on cast and on crew. But none of that counted when it came to the writers and the suits. All they cared about were higher ratings, and in their opinion, that would come from shaking things up.

Ben Hurley was well known around the industry. He had a proven record of success before the attacks ever happened, and those in charge of casting would take that history into account while overlooking the hard work of someone who had been on their team since the start. To them, Wacky Best Friend was just a supporting player, and that was all he would ever be. If they ever needed to shake things up and inspire everyone else to push themselves harder, Ethan suspected that they might even decide to kill him off in some shocking and gory manner. He suspected that it had happened before.

Whatever the decision of those in charge, Ethan would try his best to simply ignore Ben Hurley. If he was given a new leading role on the team, Ethan would take his cues from Starlette. He trusted her. He liked her. As far as he was concerned, Ben Hurley would just be an extra, brought along for the ride. He would try his best to avoid speaking to Ben.

"Wacky Best Friend," came the voice of The Director, from off to the side. "I need you to do something very important for me. It's not going to be a fun job, I know, but it needs to be done."

Wacky Best Friend stood up, ready for whatever dangerous mission The Director had decided to send him out on.

"What do you need me to do?" he asked.

"Ben Hurley's been through casting and he's just finishing up his interview now. A decision has been made, and he will be coming on board."

Wacky Best Friend was disappointed to hear the news, but didn't show it. He was a better actor than that.

"In what capacity?" he asked The Director.

"Final details are still being worked out. We should know more once he's through with the interview. But what I'm going to need from you is to show him around The Studio. Take him to Wardrobe so we can get him some clothes. Get him acquainted with his co-stars..."

"So, he's on *my* cast then," Wacky Best Friend replied, more for his own sake than anything else.

"There was some thought of putting him in with one of the lower rated teams. Lord knows, Stoner Comedian isn't exactly pulling in a lot of wins these days, but we think that he's more suited to Starlette's style."

"He seemed a little... distant."

"As with any new cast member, there will be a period of adjustment. You're all going to have to get used to working with each other, and I'm sure that there will be some revelations and twists in that process. I think your cast is where we need him to be. If he isn't capable of mounting a comeback in this industry, you're the team to figure that out."

Wacky Best Friend nodded in understanding, though he silently wished that he could raise hell over this casting decision. He did not wish to be the source of any behind the scenes drama. He was not secure enough in his own role at The Studio to make such a bold move.

"I'll do what I can," Wacky Best Friend told The Director.

For a moment, it seemed like The Director had something else to say to Wacky Best Friend, but whatever it was, he chose not to say it. Instead he said, "Head down to the green room. Ben will be taken back there after his interview and we should have a full description of the role that he'll be playing by then."

With that said, The Director walked off. Ethan was not in any hurry to get to the green room. If Ben had to wait a few minutes for Wacky Best Friend to arrive, perhaps it would send a message of some sort. Maybe it would get the point across that Wacky Best Friend was Starlette's sidekick, not Ben Hurley's.

He took his time getting there. He passed the craft service table along the way, and picked up some cookies. He stopped to chat with a production assistant. He took five minutes to try to come up with his best guess for exactly how high the ceiling in The Studio was. And then, finally, he made his way to the green room.

When he got there, Ethan found Ember sitting on the floor just outside the door, waiting for Ben Hurley to return. She had changed her clothes and returned her props, and now she was just waiting.

"Did The Director send you to escort our new cast member around too?" he asked her, taking a seat on the floor beside her.

She looked at him with a little bit of surprise and said, "New cast member? So he's definitely in? And with us?"

"Yeah. I thought you'd have heard by now," Ethan replied.

"I've been sitting here, waiting, but I haven't heard anything. Wait... The Director told *you* to show him around? Why *you*?"

"I've been asking myself that same question. Only when I asked, it had a slightly different inflection to it."

"Oh, come on. How can you not think it's awesome? We get a new co-star to cover our asses out there, and he also just happens to be super hot."

"Well, hotness aside—since I'm thinking he's not my type, barring a major reworking of my character—I just don't trust him."

"You mean, you're totally jealous of him coming in here and getting all of the good scenes while you play backup?"

"No!" Ethan insisted. "I'm only concerned with what's best for the team."

In a world full of actors, you would think that you'd find better liars. Ethan was particularly bad at it. His delivery of that line definitely could have been better.

"You're such a diva sometimes," Ember told him, while rolling her eyes. She then flagged down a production assistant and asked, "Hey there. Could you maybe get me a double-shot half-fat iced soy mocha, with just a sprinkle of cinnamon on top? Thanks a bunch."

"Right. *I'm* the diva," Ethan commented, while holding up two fingers at the P.A.

As the production assistant left them, Ben Hurley approached. He was still shirtless, but his bruises had all been properly tended to with makeup, and he seemed to be less malnourished now.

Ember stood when she saw him coming. She put on a sympathetic expression, and she asked, "How did it go in there?"

"Fine," Ben replied. "I've been through worse."

Wacky Best Friend stood up and nodded as he said, "Yeah, I'll bet that line's gonna come up a lot for you... until the next time you're tortured."

Wacky Best Friend then cocked his head slightly and asked, "They couldn't find a shirt for you to wear? Really?"

"I think they wanted to see me shirtless for the audition. It happens a lot with me," Ben told him.

"Yeah," Wacky Best Friend agreed. "Totally. Me too."

Ember smiled at Ben. She said, "So, I guess we should show you around. Let you get a feel for the place."

"Sure," Ben nodded.

Just as Ember was about to take his arm and lead him through The Studio, the P.A. came back with the iced mochas. As he handed one to Wacky Best Friend and the other to Girl Next Door, he told her, "Head Writer wanted to see you for a minute."

"What?" Girl Next Door replied, seeming to be very upset by this news. "Can it wait?"

The P.A. shook his head and replied, "He said it was pretty urgent."

He then held up a finger, telling Girl Next Door to hold on for a moment as he listened to someone talking to him through an earpiece that was plugged into a walkie-talkie on his belt. After he was done listening, he replied by talking into a microphone that was attached to the earpiece, saying, "Girl Next Door's on her way to the office now."

He then looked at Girl Next Door and asked, "Would you like me to walk with you?"

It was a subtle way of telling Girl Next Door that she was going to meet with Head Writer, whether she wanted to or not.

"What does Head Writer want with her?" Wacky Best Friend asked the P.A. "He never wants our input. He doesn't care about what we think of his scripts."

"I just know that he needs to speak with her," the P.A. replied.

Girl Next Door smiled at Ben and said, "We'll talk later. It'll be nice for us to get to know each other. Y'know, since we're going to be working with each other and all."

"Yeah," Ben replied. "Sure."

Girl Next Door walked off with the P.A. close behind her. This left Ben Hurley alone with Wacky Best Friend.

The two of them looked at each other for a moment. Wacky Best Friend was sizing up the new guy, trying to get a read on him. Ben, it seemed, was... tired. Possibly bored.

"We have a lot to go over about The Studio and how things work around here," Wacky Best Friend told Ben, as they began to walk. "I'll be your co-star and tour guide for this evening. They call me Wacky Best Friend."

Ben seemed puzzled. He asked, "That's your name? I mean, I heard people being called Director and Head Writer, but I thought it was just a title."

"It is and it isn't. We use stage names here. Each of us are given a name based on the role that we play at The Studio. For them, it's based on their job titles. For us, it's more about typecasting. I'm Wacky Best Friend. You've met Girl Next Door. And Starlette... She's our lead."

They entered a more open area of The Studio, where hundreds of people were going about the business of their daily lives, and Wacky Best Friend stopped walking. Ben stopped beside him. As they looked across the floor of The Studio, Ben caught sight of a little girl, walking up ahead. She was only seven or eight years old, with golden braids; cute as a button.

"Kids?" Ben asked.

"That's Up-And-Comer..." Wacky Best Friend answered. "Or... Well, the latest of them anyway. Don't underestimate her. Also, don't schedule her for really long missions. She's only allowed to work for four hours at a time."

"What happened to the other Up-And-Comers?" Ben asked.

Wacky Best Friend chose not to answer that question. He simply said, "There's always another Up-And-Comer," and moved on, continuing on his walk.

He said, "There have been a lot of people working at The Studio. Some go on to lead wildly successful careers, like Starlette. But for every Starlette, there's a Bombshell. They burn bright, but burn out fast."

"You've lost a lot of talent?"

Wacky Best Friend looked to the ground and grew somber as he said, "Yeah."

Ben saw Starlette walking in the distance, and said "I guess that's why she's so pissed off. She's tired. Tired of the fighting and the death."

"Like I said, we've lost a lot of people. Good people. Sometimes, the people we loved the most just went out and never came back."

"What was his name?"

"Who's?"

"The guy she lost."

"His name was none of your damn business," Ethan told Ben, looking at him with a steely glare. "The only thing you need to know is that you're here to do a job. You don't need to understand the inner workings of anyone here, because none of it matters. Studio Head doesn't care what we think or what we feel. The Executives don't care who you are, they only care who they *say* you are."

"What happens if I'm not who they think I am?" Ben asked, looking into the distance, with that tired look about him once again.

Wacky Best Friend shrugged, having no real answer for him except, "They found out that Token Black Guy was a Republican, and I haven't seen him since. So I'd just keep it to myself if I were you."

Ben looked around the place. He took in the people and the

trailers and the equipment that filled The Studio. He then looked upward, as though noting the fact that the place was a giant hole in the ground, and asked, "What makes this place any better than out there?"

Wacky Best Friend didn't answer that question. While there were many things that he could have chosen to say in response to the question, he decided to remain silent on the subject.

Instead, he directed Ben to Wardrobe's department, and followed him inside.

"First things first, we need to get you set up with a shirt," Ethan told him.

When they entered, Ethan looked around for Wardrobe. She was nowhere to be seen, which might be inconvenient, but was also a bit of a relief. Wardrobe could be a tricky person to get along with at times.

Like Prop Master's department, this department had a room out front, which served as a general office where Wardrobe could fit clothing on people, and conduct her business. Behind this was a larger storage room, filled with countless numbers of shirts, pants, skirts, shoes and anything else that might be needed to go along with them. Wacky Best Friend did not want to even think about trying to navigate the storage room, and would probably be murdered in his sleep if he dared to.

Fortunately, there was a rack of clothing in the front room, which had apparently been pulled specifically for Ben. A style had not been chosen for him yet, so the rack was full of many different looks. Wacky Best Friend walked to the rack and started to fish through it.

"Should we wait for someone to come back?" Ben asked, hesitant to jump in and start pulling things for himself.

"We could do that. It would also come with a lecture about proper care for each shirt, and directions for how to sit, stand and move without wrinkling or ripping anything. Wardrobe is hardcore, man. Seriously," Wacky Best Friend replied, still looking, but finding nothing that he liked.

He went on to tell Ben, "Besides, this gives us the chance to choose clothes for you. We can set the tone for who you'll be around here. Clothes make the man, right? And we need to find something that tells the rest of The Studio how you want to be seen. Ooh! How 'bout this one?"

Wacky Best Friend pulled a shirt off of the rack and held it up. It was a bright red turtleneck, made of heavy wool. Ben cringed.

"No? Really? I see you as a red shirt kind of guy," Wacky Best Friend commented, putting the turtleneck back and pulling a red long-sleeve tee from the rack. He held it up, but Ben didn't seem to like that one either.

Ben walked to the rack and began looking for himself. After only a few seconds of looking, Ben grabbed a blue plaid button-up and put it on. Wacky Best Friend had been hoping for something less suited to the *macho leading man* type, but he said nothing as Ben put the shirt on.

"We can come back later and get a full load of supplies," he told Ben, as he headed for the door. "We still have to set you up in your trailer and all that fun stuff."

Once they were out of Wardrobe's department, The Director caught up to Wacky Best Friend and Ben. Wacky Best Friend noticed a folder in his hand as they walked.

The Director wasted no time before getting to business, saying, "We have the full breakdown of the role you'll be playing here at The Studio, Ben. Based on your skills and previous experience, we think you'll be a nice asset to Starlette's team."

The men stopped walking and The Director handed Ben the folder. Ben didn't open it right away. He looked at The Director, and seemed to know what role he'd been given without even looking. Wacky Best Friend knew as well, but held out hope for some miracle of casting that would place Ben as the eccentric neighbor or the wise homeless guy who people look to for sage advice, but who rarely joins the team in their zany adventures.

Ben smiled halfheartedly and said, "Thank you, sir. I'll do my best."

"If you have any questions or want to talk about the direction of your character, or motivation, or anything like that, let me know. I'm around if you need me," The Director told him.

Ben smiled his *thanks*, and The Director walked off. Ben took a deep breath, and then continued to walk, without ever looking at the folder.

"You're not even curious?" Wacky Best Friend asked.

"It's always the same role for me, Wacky..." Ben started, before stopping once again and turning to face Wacky Best Friend. "What's your real name, by the way?"

Ethan hesitated. He wasn't used to introducing himself to strangers. Out on location, if someone slipped and used his real name, there could be a price to pay.

Ben picked up on the hesitation. He looked downward, just slightly, revealing his insecurity with being new and unfamiliar.

"You know what? Never mind. You can tell me once you trust me," Ben said. He handed Wacky Best Friend the folder and said, "And as for me...Well, I guess this is who I am now. Who I've more or less always been."

Wacky Best Friend opened the folder and looked inside. On top of the file that was in the folder, there was a headshot of Ben, but the name on the picture was changed. It now read: *Heartthrob*.

Wacky Best Friend was disappointed. No matter how hard he worked or how long he had been with the team, he would never be thought of as anything but Wacky Best Friend. A new guy, brought in off the streets, somehow gains a more prominent role on the team.

"I'm never going to get to be a wacky best friend or an eccentric," Heartthrob said as he smiled half-heartedly. "You're lucky. You play the part that they'll always need around. But, the second the shine wears off that eight by ten glossy in my folder, they'll just turn around and bring in a new guy who can fill the same exact role. I'll be phased out or killed off."

~

Five...

Four...

Three...

The device on the wall, with its fancy blinking lights and its countdown to destruction, was quite intimidating. Starlette watched it count down, and the first instinct that she had was to run and take cover. Her second instinct was to look closer.

Wires coiled around wires, and plugged into the brick of what looked like C-4. Battery housings were protected by switches and triggers. The beeping that accompanied the counting down of each number was from an independent sound source, having nothing to do with the countdown itself. The lights that were blinking were tied directly to the battery supply, and seemed to serve no purpose.

If one were to see the device and run for the hills, they would miss all of the fine details, which made the device look intimidating, but which assured Starlette that it was utterly harmless.

If the bomb were to go off, the stairwell would be destroyed. Seeing as how the elevator was probably not functioning at the moment, Starlette was willing to wager that the person who was living in this building would not willingly destroy their only way out.

She waited for the countdown to reach *zero*, and she watched it closely as it did. If she was wrong and it did explode, it would explode right in her face. There was little chance that she would survive such a blast, and an even lesser chance that she would maintain her stunning good looks if she did.

Once the device reached the end of its countdown, the beeping became more urgent and the lights blinked a little bit more quickly. Yet, after all of that, the device simply went dead, waiting for the next time someone came along to activate it.

Starlette smirked, but paid the device no more attention as she walked up the stairs.

The stairwell was dark and cold. Every step she took—no matter how stealthy she attempted to be—seemed to echo through the stairwell, killing any chance she had of sneaking up on anyone.

Spider webs littered the corners, and dead cockroaches, crickets and other miscellaneous insects crunched beneath Starlette's feet. The air smelled of dust and mold. There were no obvious signs of life in the building, aside from the bomb. The lobby had been a mess. From what she could see of each floor that she passed, based on a quick glimpse through the door and down the hallway, the building appeared to have been looted and torn apart already. There would be no motivation for a normal person to look much farther, if they were simply out for goods to sell on the black market.

The more she pressed on, the more Starlette began to feel as though she had been summoned into the building. The question now became whether she had been summoned by friend or foe.

If she were a good and proper Studio actress, Starlette would have reported this strange finding to The Director, who would then pass it by the Producers. If they decided to explore the strange figure in the window, they would send a logline to Head Writer and he would lead his team through the outlining and scripting process. Location scouts would check out the area and report back to The Director, who would incorporate their findings into a storyboard, which he would use to walk the actors through the scene and block their movements, so that when they were finally ready to act on the information, they would have a clear idea of what they were doing there and how they were to handle their findings.

To Starlette, this seemed like a lot of work to go through for a job that was potentially pointless, and to seek out a person who may very well die of old age before the scripting process was completed. She decided to improvise her way through the scene.

She had to wonder what kind of person would lock themselves away in a tower such as this, and hide away, far above the world. She half expected to find a fairy tale villain or a crazy person who kept a collection of human skulls in their bedroom. But she couldn't help but think that this was the desired reaction to everything she had seen so far. There was no welcome mat on the front porch, and no smell of freshly baked cookies, because this person wanted to keep away the riff-raff. If the fake bomb didn't deter them, the fruitless ascent through the crumbling carcass of a building would.

As she reached the nineteenth floor, Starlette's mind was spinning with all of the possible outcomes of this exploration. She ran through various scenarios and how she could react to each of them. She pictured gunplay and drawn blood. She pictured the discovery of a band of orphaned child actors that would require a proper upbringing in The Studio. She even imagined—for a brief moment—a teary-eyed reunion with her own sister, whom she hadn't seen since before the attacks.

She quickly squashed that thought. *Starlette* could have no family. No hope of going home. No dreams of settling down in her hometown and raising a family with her high school sweetheart. That girl was dead, and needed to remain that way. Forever.

A light went on ten floors above her, like a spotlight being shined into the stairwell, cutting through the darkness like a blade. As she looked up at this light, music began to play. It was an old tune, which sounded as though it was from the 1930's or 40's. It was heavy on the big band in the background and the sweet, somewhat ghostly voice of a woman singing, long before the age of digital recordings and computerized pitch corrections.

The music echoed through the stairwell, seeming to surround Starlette as its vibrations bounced off of the walls around her and came back toward her from multiple directions.

If the intention of the person above was to scare her off, they failed. If their intention was to draw her closer through mystery and intrigue, they had succeeded masterfully.

Starlette picked up her pace and seemed to cover the distance between herself and that light in no time at all. As she neared it, she wrapped her hand around the grip of her gun and prepared to open fire on anyone who might seek to cause her harm.

As she stepped onto the landing near the lighted doorway, the bright light shut off, and the stairwell fell into darkness once again. Her eyes needed time to adjust to the renewed darkness, but when they did, Starlette saw the source of the bright light that had shined through the stairwell. It was an old stage light, plugged into a series of extension cords, which led down the hallway.

Starlette followed the extension cords with her eyes, and saw that they led to another doorway, which was lit by a much dimmer light. The music was still playing, as loudly as ever, and seeming to come from that same doorway.

She walked toward the door, pulling her gun from its holster, but keeping it by her side as she went along.

When she reached the doorway, she stopped just short of stepping in front of it. She put her back to the wall beside the door and prepared herself for whatever she might find inside.

She took a deep breath and held it as she turned and raised her gun, crossing through the door, into the great unknown.

What she found upon entering the apartment was not what she had seen in the rest of the building. There were no spider webs, and no debris scattered around. What she found was a rather nicely furnished apartment. Sure, it looked like its style hadn't been updated in a while, but the glass sparkled and the leather sofas looked fresh and new.

The wood floors seemed to be recently polished, and the bar was fully stocked.

Giant windows lined one wall of the room, though they were covered by heavy curtains, which prevented Starlette from seeing the view outside.

She walked deeper into the apartment, and found an absurdly old record player, sitting on an antique table, blasting the music that she had heard from many floors below.

She walked to the record player, and lifted the needle from the record that was playing. The room fell silent, aside from the light *hiss* and *pop* of the record player's speaker.

Starlette scanned the apartment, looking for any sign of the person that she had seen from down below, and at first she saw nothing. She thought that the person who had lured her to that apartment might have been hiding, but she did not know why. It was a lot of trouble to go to, only to remain hidden.

She didn't feel as though they were hiding. She felt the eyes of a person watching her every move. She knew that she was being observed, but could not see the person who was watching her.

Smiling, Starlette turned to face the one dark corner of the apartment. Her eyes had initially skipped over the dark corner, just because it seemed insignificant to the passing eye, but upon closer inspection, the shadow began to take form. A chair. Legs. The form of a woman.

"You climbed those stairs faster than I expected," said the woman sitting in the corner, whose face Starlette still could not see.

"I'd have been here sooner, but I got distracted by the fake bomb," Starlette replied, holstering her gun.

"You don't think I'm a threat?"

"The bomb. The lighting and music... Dramatics like this usually mean one thing."

"That I'm a flaming homosexual?"

"Or an actress."

"What's the difference, am I right?"

"That's homophobic."

"How so?"

"You... mentioned gay people."

"That's retarded, dear."

The woman shifted in her chair, and Starlette tried to get a better look at her face, but the shadows still hid the details. The woman was doing this on purpose. She was waiting for the moment when she could finally reveal herself to full dramatic effect. She navigated the shadows masterfully. She had full control of her vocal inflections, lending just the right amount of charm to her shadiness.

Starlette took several steps closer and looked around the room. With the woman revealed and no more threat of an attack from behind, she could now take in the finer details. The photographs. The awards. On the shelves of that apartment, there was an entire life on display. It was a life of success and achievement—It was the life of a star.

Her eyes found their way to a shadow box on the wall, which contained the poster for a movie called *The Sacrifice Of Ingrid*, and beneath it was the film's script.

Starlette's jaw wanted to drop, but to allow it to do so would betray her steely character. She knew this movie. *Everyone* knew this movie. It set the 1978 award season on fire as it singlehandedly consumed just about every trophy in sight.

On a nearby shelf was a collection of awards shaped like various planets, and creatures, and naked people holding all manner of objects. There was only one person who would have this collection of awards, coupled with that movie's poster and script.

Starlette turned and looked at the woman in the shadows. She said, "It's you."

The woman leaned forward, allowing a beam of light to wash over her face. With a grin that captured the essence of every Hollywood legend to ever grace the silver screen, Starlette's suspicions were confirmed. Before her now sat a master of her craft; a woman whose beauty shined through, despite the ravages of time and lack of proper plastic surgery.

Before her now sat Tessa Baker.

~

Seven hours earlier.

"Who?" Ember asked as she sat on the lawn furniture outside of her trailer, with Ethan in the chair beside her.

"Heartthrob," Ethan replied. "Ben Hurley. Only he's not Ben Hurley anymore."

"That name is awesome. Have you noticed that our names are really long, and there's no way to shorten them without sounding stupid?" Ember noted. "One time, Starlette and me were being shot at and we were hiding behind this car, and she wanted me to run behind this other car. So, she'd like 'go, Girl,' trying to shorten my name. But to me, it just sounded like 'you go, Girl' and I was like 'yeah, that's right' and she looked at me like I was on crack."

"Fascinating story."

Ember fell silent for a moment, with nothing more to say on the subject of their long and stupid sounding names. After the topic had thoroughly died off, she asked, "How long has he been asleep?"

To which Ethan replied, "Long enough for me to sleep, wake up, and sit around waiting for his ass to get up. I thought he woke up a while ago. I heard someone yell something and I thought it came from his trailer, but I guess not."

"What are you going to do when he gets up?"

"Finish showing him around, I guess. The Director made me the welcome wagon."

"No fair."

"Life's not fair."

Ethan checked his watch, eager to get on with his day. Waiting around was something that one had to get used to when it came to life in The Studio. When there was no location to rush off too, or some scene to shoot up, the life of an actor could be boring as hell. One could only waste so much time working out and running lines with their co-stars. It was no wonder to Ethan that Starlette usually chose to break free of The Studio and wander around the city, but she could get away with things that he couldn't even think about doing. She was the star, after all. He was just a sidekick.

A production assistant approached Wacky Best Friend, carrying something in his hand that he couldn't make out right away. As he neared, the P.A. said, "Wardrobe wanted me to drop this off for you. She said that you left it in your pocket after your last shoot. She also said that you tore a sleeve."

"Umm... Sorry?" Wacky Best Friend said, not quite sure how to respond to the news of a sleeve that was torn in the middle of a gunfight, which featured heavy stunt work, the use of explosives, and the shedding of his own blood.

The P.A. handed Wacky Best Friend a wallet, and turned to walk away.

It was the wallet that he had taken off of a Bookworm minion during the mission to rescue Heartthrob. Wacky Best Friend took it and stuck it in his pocket, hoping that nobody would make a big deal out of it.

"What's that?" Girl Next Door asked.

"Just a wallet," Wacky Best Friend replied.

"It's not your wallet. Your wallet has Velcro on it, and little cartoon birdies."

Wacky Best Friend ignored Girl Next Door, hoping to catch the P.A. before he got too far. He said, "Hey, P.A. guy..."

The P.A. turned around.

Wacky Best Friend continued by asking, "Could you knock on Heartthrob's trailer. Tell him he's needed on set or something?"

The P.A. shook his head, and replied, "Heartthrob's not in his trailer. I saw him walking around about an hour ago."

"Oh," Wacky Best Friend said, as he started to stand up. "Crap."

~

Heartthrob had been wandering The Studio for a while by the time he finally made his way to an area where not many people were scurrying around, looking his way and whispering. Somehow, he doubted that they were talking about his keen acting abilities and his rock hard physique.

He was the new guy. People had a lot of questions about him, and he wasn't sure that he wanted to answer all of them right away.

The place where he found himself looked like a scene out of a movie about the gods of ancient Greece. There were pillars and arches, which looked as though they were made of marble. In truth, they were probably made of some sort of foam or painted wood. Despite this truth, the fact remained that it was a stunning set... If perhaps a smidge over the top.

"We call it the *stage*," came a voice from behind Heartthrob.

When he turned, he found Starlette, standing with her arms crossed, as though she was evaluating him from a distance.

"It's where we come to train," she continued. "Sometimes that means a nice, relaxing yoga class. Usually—for me anyway—it means sparring."

She started to walk closer to Heartthrob. He kept his eyes on her, not sure whether she was speaking as a nice, friendly co-star, or an untrusting skeptic.

She went on, "Long before we made this place our basecamp, The Studio was used as storage for all sorts of things. Old scripts that people wanted to forget. Props that they just didn't know what to do with..."

Heartthrob cocked his head just slightly as he looked at the stage and said, "Wait—is this the set they used at the '08 convention?"

"Legend has it," Starlette replied.

Heartthrob smiled just slightly, "Neat."

"I guess... if you're the religious type."

"Listen," he replied, switching topics as she got closer, "I just wanted to say that I'm looking forward to working with you. I know you didn't ask for a new addition to your cast."

Starlette placed her hand on one of the fake pillars and replied, "It's not about what I want. It's about whether or not you can get the job done. Are you all fluff and filler, or is there a real actor in there?"

"I think my past speaks for itself."

"What past? I've heard all this talk about your training, but I can't remember seeing any of that on screen."

"The attacks—"

"I know. They cut my career out from under me too. I was going to be a real actress—I had a dialect coach and everything.

Now, none of that seems to matter very much. I'm back to doing the same thing I was doing years ago. Kicking. Fighting. Chewing up the scenery, while wearing skin-tight leather. It's what I'm good at, I guess."

She walked away from the pillar and circled Heartthrob, evaluating him. He knew what was coming, but he allowed her to continue.

"What are you good at, Ben?" she asked him.

It was funny, but the name no longer seemed to fit him. When she spoke it, there was no connection for him. Ben Hurley was gone.

"Where have you been? What have you been doing? Because, for the life of me, I can't seem to figure out why the hell I should trust you to have my back out there."

"I trained with—"

"I don't care who you trained with, or what project it was for. Eleven months is a long time."

"I'm still alive."

"How?" she asked. "Show me."

~

"You're Tessa Baker," Starlette said, stating the obvious, but in keeping with her training as a professional television actress.

"I am. Or, I was," Tessa replied, taking a sip of brandy. "I haven't quite figured that part out yet."

Tessa's glass was empty. She stood and walked to the bar, where she poured herself another drink. She asked Starlette, "Would you like a brandy?"

"No. Thank you. I don't drink."

Tessa seemed amused by this statement. She took another sip of brandy and turned to face Starlette once again.

"You don't drink? And you call yourself an actress?" Tessa asked. "Please tell me, at the very least, that you smoke."

"Not really," Starlette replied.

"Dear God. What is this town coming to?" Tessa quipped, before peeking out the window and saying, "Oh. I'd nearly forgotten."

"Have you been hiding here all this time?"

"I've been hiding here for longer than that."

"Why?"

"Where the hell else am I supposed to go?"

"Come with me. There's a place."

"The Studio?"

"You'll be safe there."

"Safe there? Are you out of your fucking mind? Look at me, and tell me how many of my kind you've seen wandering around that Studio of yours."

"You're a legend."

"And do you think that matters? Do you think that there is any loyalty or honor to The Studio?"

"We can talk to them…"

"They left me to die! Before the bombs or shootings, they left me out in the cold. They left me to rot. And if you don't think that they'd do the same thing to you, my dear, you have quite a rude awakening to look forward to."

~

Six hours, forty-five minutes earlier…

Starlette circled Heartthrob, studying the way he stood, the way he breathed, the way he kept track of her position. He didn't turn his head to watch her. He simply allowed her to position herself behind him, seemingly unaware of the fact that she was about to attack.

Only, he was not unaware. The way his muscles reacted to her position, Starlette could tell that Heartthrob was preparing himself.

"Where have you been all of these months?" she asked him.

"Running," he replied.

She leaped into the air, and brought her fist down as hard as she could, aiming for his head.

Heartthrob ducked out of the way, grabbed Starlette's arm and twisted it until it was behind her back. He then pushed her away, allowing her to regroup and come at him again.

As she prepared to attack him for a second time, Starlette asked, "Running where?"

"It's a big country. Lots of space to run."

"Lots of space to hide too. So, why aren't you?"

"Why aren't *you*?"

Starlette rushed toward Heartthrob and threw a punch, which he easily avoided. She was expecting this, and quickly followed the punch by attempting to sweep his legs out from under him.

Heartthrob flipped backward, avoiding the sweep. He took on a more offensive stance and looked Starlette squarely in the eyes, daring her to come at him again.

"Do you have family?" she asked.

Heartthrob rushed toward Starlette, and attempted to tackle her. In response to this, she grabbed him, kneed him in the gut, punched him in the face, and threw him to the ground.

"Do you have family?" she asked once again.

Heartthrob gathered himself and got off of the ground. He sucked on his bleeding lip and prepared for the next attack.

Starlette heard footsteps on the catwalk above them. She looked toward the sound and saw Ethan and Ember watching her spar with Heartthrob.

Ember took a seat on the catwalk, allowing her feet to dangle over the side. She pulled a box of Gummi bears from her pocket and offered some to Ethan, who took a seat beside her and shared the snack.

"I hear you've lost some people," Heartthrob said to her.

Starlette's eyes shot back to Heartthrob, and then briefly back to Wacky Best Friend. He winced, regretting the fact that he'd spilled some information on Starlette.

She turned her attention back to Heartthrob and said, "We've lost a lot of people."

"Yeah," he replied. "We have."

Starlette went after Heartthrob again. First, she threw a punch, which he easily blocked. She followed this with a roundhouse kick, which he ducked to avoid.

He threw a punch of his own, which Starlette easily blocked before grabbing his arm and attempting to twist it. He twisted harder, and pulled his arm free.

He grabbed her arm.

She kneed him in the gut.

He punched her in the face.

One of her co-stars accidentally dropped a Gummi bear on Starlette. She ignored it.

Starlette tried to side kick Heartthrob in the chest, but he grabbed her leg and attempted to throw her to the ground instead.

She turned his attempt into a backflip, followed by a forward flip that landed her right in front of him.

He managed to punch her in the gut, but she quickly recovered and punched him in the face with enough force to send him stumbling sideways.

"You can handle a punch," she told him. "How 'bout a knife?"

She pulled a throwing knife from her boot and threw it at Heartthrob's head.

~

"For years, I played their games," Tessa told Starlette, running her hand along the curtains that blocked her view. She wanted to open them and gaze out at the city, but she didn't dare reveal herself to anyone who might be passing.

Starlette took note of this.

"I was their perfect little puppet. I could perform any scene that they gave me, no matter how absurd it might be. And after all that hard work and dedication, do you know what happened to me?"

Starlette watched as Tessa turned around and glared at her awards with hatred brewing deep inside of her. She took another sip of brandy and swallowed it hard.

"Here I am," Tessa continued. "All these fucking years later, and what do I have to show for it? A bunch of worthless, gaudy gold statues and not a soul alive who cares whether or not I'm still here."

Starlette asked, "How did you survive?"

"Nobody ever came for me," Tessa replied, with a tear in her eye. She then smiled and waved her arms in the air, in the fashion of the great dramatic actresses of Hollywood's golden age, saying, "Here I am, living in my secluded tower. I haven't moved an inch in fifteen years. I might as well put a fucking neon sign outside my door, welcoming guests and murderers alike, for all the good it would do."

"Nobody came for you?"

"Nobody cared. Look at all of these posters and scripts. Look at the awards, and tell me what they all have in common, sweetheart."

Starlette wasn't sure whether or not Tessa was being rhetorical when she gave this order. She turned toward the walls and shelves, and looked at a lifetime full of accomplishment. She saw the person that she had always dreamt of being.

She didn't answer Tessa, for fear of saying the wrong thing and sounding stupid. Instead, she waited until Tessa walked up beside her and looked at the collection of her own trophies.

Tessa said, "Point to one of these items that came to me within the last ten years."

It was as though the room shifted, and suddenly Starlette could see what Tessa was saying. Where she had seen a dream life only moments earlier, she now saw relics.

Tessa Baker had always been a hero to Starlette. She was a master of the art, capable of crossing, and sometimes blurring, the lines between drama and comedy. She could be strong and vulnerable in the same second. She was the type of beauty that screamed of Hollywood royalty. Starlette had never known a time before Tessa Baker, and Tessa's work would always be a part of her own character. Literally. Starlette actually studied Tessa's work for inspiration while developing her own skills.

When looking at Tessa's life from the outside, everything sparkled. Yet, when Tessa invited Starlette in for a look around, the shine began to wear. Starlette became very aware of the fact that she hadn't seen Tessa Baker act in any movie or television series for years.

Tessa read the look in Starlette's eyes and turned to walk into the kitchen. Starlette followed.

"I was a starlet once too. Young and full of life. Now look at me. I'm living in a rundown penthouse, living off of expensive booze and cans of caviar," Tessa said to Starlette. She looked off to the side for a moment, and then shrugged, saying, "Though I guess when you put it that way..."

"Why did you bring me here?" Starlette asked.

Tessa leaned against the kitchen counter, looked Starlette in the eyes, and said, "I brought you here to warn you."

~

Six hours, forty minutes, and seventeen seconds earlier...

Heartthrob barely managed to avoid the knife that was thrown at his head. As it stuck into the pillar behind him, he had to look and make sure that it was the real thing. Once he confirmed that it was, he looked to Starlette, wondering just how crazy she was.

By the time he looked back to her, Starlette was holding a throwing knife in each hand.

On the catwalk above, Wacky Best Friend and Girl Next Door were watching the show. Girl Next Door's eyes widened.

"Oh my God," she said, "Starlette's totally trying to kill him."

"I think she's trying to make sure he doesn't kill us," Wacky Best Friend replied.

Starlette stared down Heartthrob. She watched as he assessed her, and the situation that he was in. She watched as his eyes scanned the room around him and his mind went to work, formulating a plan.

"In the real world, we don't have the luxury of playing nice," Starlette told him. "Out there, we don't always have time to run our lines and block our scenes. Sometimes we just have to act."

Starlette threw one of the knives at him, aiming for center mass. Before she could see whether or not this knife found its target, she threw the second knife.

Heartthrob twisted out of the way of the first knife. Starlette couldn't track the second knife, as Heartthrob jumped and rolled through the air, which she imagined would have looked really cool in slow motion.

When he landed, Heartthrob revealed that he had caught the second knife mid-air and he threw it back at her before she had time to process the fact that he had it at all.

Starlette fell into a split, and could feel the knife zip over the top of her head. She quickly got back up and smiled at Heartthrob. He was staring her down now.

"You want to do this?" he asked her. "You want to see what I'm made of?"

"I do," she replied.

"This is going to get ugly," Girl Next Door whispered to Wacky Best Friend.

"This is going to get awesome," he replied.

Heartthrob nodded at Starlette, and said, "Okay then. Let's do this."

He pulled off his shirt and threw it to the ground, as he prepared to fight for real.

"Oh, come on!" Wacky Best Friend groaned. "Who does that?"

Girl Next Door smacked his shoulder and said, "Shh!"

Heartthrob walked to the pillar where one of the knives was stuck and pulled it free. He held it in his hand, feeling the coldness of the metal against his fingers.

Starlette pulled another knife of her own. Her grip was not that of a person preparing to throw a knife. It was the grip of a person who was about to charge. She wanted a real fight.

She charged at Heartthrob like an animal, raising the knife as she neared him. He greeted her attack by standing his ground, and blocking her knife with his own.

Metal slid across metal as their knives met and quickly parted once again. Starlette sliced through the air as she aimed to make a mark on Heartthrob's face. He avoided the blade and lunged his own toward her gut.

She pulled back, and used her free hand to deflect the attack.

He took a swing at her with his own free hand and followed this up by bringing his knife down at her from above.

Starlette allowed the punch to make contact with her shoulder, choosing to block the knife attack instead. As her knife met his, she grabbed his arm and held onto it, preventing him from taking another stab at her.

He grabbed onto her arm with his free hand as well, and for just a moment, they remained locked in this position, each waiting for the other to take action.

Finally, Starlette leaped into the air and kicked off of Heartthrob's chest with both feet. She flipped backwards, landing steadily on the ground as Heartthrob fell backwards, into one of windows that had been built into the set. He nearly went through it, but managed to catch himself just in time.

Starlette threw her knife at his face once again. He avoided the blade, but was thrown off balance in the process, and wound up falling through the window after all.

~

"You've become something of a legend in this city, Starlette," Tessa told her, still leaning against the kitchen counter.

Starlette was surprised by this news. She knew that she was known within The Studio, but had been unaware that the rest of the world even knew about the war that was being fought. She asked, "People have heard of me?"

"Oh, yes. And not just because of your work in The Studio. You walk these streets at night, patrolling. Some people believe you're the ghost of one of the slain actresses, come back to seek vengeance against those who destroyed your beloved city. It's a clever story. Just the right amount of truth, wouldn't you say?"

Tessa walked to the refrigerator and pulled some lettuce, tomato and ham from it. She placed the items on the counter, and pulled a loaf of bread from a nearby cabinet.

As she went to work, making two sandwiches, Tessa continued, "You've become an icon. Someone the world can look to."

"That's a good thing, right?"

"In a way, I suppose it is. But, you see, you're dying in the process."

"What do you mean?"

"I know this industry. I know the people you work for, and I see a lot of myself in you. I see you making the same decisions I made years ago. Oh, it was a little different back then. The names they gave us weren't quite as colorful, but the game was the same. New name. New hair. New identity. And what happens to the person we were?"

"The person I was died before The Studio ever gave me a new name. Bookworm took away the life I had, not them."

"He did. And that fucking bastard deserves every ounce of pain that I imagine you'll someday deal him. But I am warning you. Keep your eyes open and don't walk blindly into the jaws of the scavengers who come to pick at the carcass that he left behind. They're just as vile as he is."

Tessa finished putting together the sandwiches that she was making and put one on a plate, which she slid over to Starlette.

Starlette looked down at the sandwich, but didn't pick it up right away. Tessa smiled at this and said, "Let me guess. They have you on a specific diet so that you'll look your best when they pour you into one of those outfits of theirs."

Starlette didn't respond. Tessa was right. Starlette's nutritionist would have a fit if she exceeded her daily carb allotment.

"The Studio preys upon those that they perceive as weak. They see your desperation. Your drive to become the actress that you know you can be. They promise you the opportunity to become that actress, but they have plans of their own. First, it will be little suggestions here and there. The name's all wrong. The hair isn't quite right. Before you know it, nothing about you is *you* anymore. And those dreams that you had? Oh, you'll be a successful actress if they want you to be. But will you be playing the sort of role *you* want to play, or will you be playing the role that *they tell* you to play?"

Tessa picked up her own sandwich and took a bite. As she chewed and swallowed, Starlette thought about what Tessa was telling her. She thought about the life that she was living at The Studio.

She *was* Starlette. She *was* the person who fought the war. She *was* the woman who wanted to track down Bookworm and drive a knife through his chest... Wasn't she?

~

Starlette walked to where Heartthrob had fallen, and she stood over him. She watched as he rolled over and began to pull himself off of the ground.

She could see in his eyes that he hated himself for falling, and the funny thing was, she didn't fault him for it. She didn't think any less of him for losing the fight.

She extended a hand, which he looked at, but didn't take right away. He seemed to be asking himself whether this was some sort of trick, or if he could trust her to help him up. Finally, he took her hand.

Once Heartthrob was standing, Starlette looked him in the eyes and told him, "We've all fallen. Since the attacks, it seems like that's all we do sometimes."

They walked away from the window and onto the open floor, where Girl Next Door and Wacky Best Friend were already coming to meet them.

As they walked, Starlette told Heartthrob, "The thing you have to learn—now that you're a part of this cast—is that when you do fall, there's always going to be someone to help you back up. When you miss your mark. When you flub a line. When you mess up a shot..."

She turned and looked Heartthrob in the eyes once again, and told him, "Stop running. Accept your role here. The Studio is a lot of things, and you'll draw your own conclusions about that soon enough. But you're a part of my cast now, and you have to accept your role on it. Because it's not always you that's going to fall, and if you're not there to help one of them back up... I will shoot you myself."

~

Starlette looked down at the sandwich that was on the plate in front of her. She could feel Tessa's eyes on her, waiting to see what she would do next.

Tessa spoke softly, saying, "You have to ask yourself, dear... Are you a follower, or are you the star of this show?"

Starlette looked at the sandwich, knowing what it would mean for her to take a bite. She thought about her options. She thought about who she was and who she wanted to be.

Finally, she looked at Tessa and replied, "I'm a ghost."

With that, Starlette turned and walked out of the apartment, leaving Tessa to eat her sandwich alone.

In the meantime, Starlette would be hunting down the man who had destroyed their world. To do this, she would be using every resource that The Studio had to offer.

Chapter Six
ON LOCATION

It had been a week since Heartthrob joined Starlette's cast. He had gone through the audition process and several rounds of interviews. He had been tested more than once by his co-stars, which was understandable. He didn't expect them to trust him without any question of his abilities. This latest test though—assuming that it was a test at all—was one that he did not know how to handle.

"Tell the truth," Girl Next Door told him, handing him a plate of... something. "I need to know if it tastes okay."

"Hasn't he been tortured enough?" Wacky Best Friend cut in.

They were sitting in front of their trailers. Since arriving at The Studio, Heartthrob had spent a lot of time sitting in the lawn chairs that were spread out on the actors' cement lawn. Each day, he waited to hear about a shoot that he might go on. He wanted to prove himself. He wanted to show his castmates that he was capable of pulling off the role that he'd been assigned. More than that, he wanted to show the Bookworm and his minions that there was a new actor to fear in this town. He wanted to *fight*.

Girl Next Door—*Ember*, during her off hours—had been cooking for what seemed like forever. She started by baking a batch of oatmeal cookies, which turned out thin and runny.

She followed this by trying to make some homemade lemonade. While she did remember to sweeten the lemonade, she had forgotten to strain the seeds from her freshly squeezed lemon juice.

Now, she was supposed to be making lasagna. Heartthrob assumed that this was what he was looking at on the plate, but he couldn't be quite sure. Usually—in his experience—lasagna had some sort of red sauce. This sauce was greenish.

"I don't normally cook," Ember told him. "I know it's ugly and horrible, but I just have to learn how to do this stuff."

Wacky Best Friend looked down at his own plate, sniffed the food, and asked, "Why?"

Girl Next Door took a seat next to the men and let out a sigh. She told them, "Head Writer has been driving me crazy. For the past week, he's kept calling me into his office to discuss my character."

"Does he even have the authority to discuss that with you? Shouldn't he be taking it up with The Director and maybe one of the Producers?" Wacky Best Friend replied.

All of this was still new to Heartthrob. He had spent the previous week doing whatever he was told to do and asking few questions, because he was never quite sure how each crew member fit into the structure of The Studio.

Wardrobe wanted to meet with Heartthrob on his second day at The Studio, and he spent a good amount of time being measured for specially designed outfits that he could wear while shooting. She also gave him a bag of more casual clothes; all of which seemed to be super trendy and awkwardly fitting. He was stuck wearing scarves with plain white v-neck t-shirts, and pants that fit far too tightly around his calves and didn't seem long enough in his opinion. But who was he to tell Wardrobe how he should be dressing? So, he wore the clothes that he was given.

On his third day in The Studio, Heartthrob went to Makeup to have his bruises and cuts looked at. She checked him out—taking an especially long time to examine his chest wounds—touched up his concealer, and told him that they were healing well. She was done with him in a matter of minutes.

On his way out of Makeup's side of the trailer, her husband, Hair, called Heartthrob over and told him to sit down. He spent three hours with Hair, having his hairstyle changed and photographed several times. Once they had found just the right style, Hair gave Heartthrob a quick trim, neglecting to cover him with a hair cutting cape. Despite Hair's best efforts to clean him off, Heartthrob was forced to walk through The Studio and back to his trailer without a shirt, due to the itchiness.

By the time his first week had passed, Heartthrob was beginning to feel more comfortable in his new surroundings. He was starting to understand how things worked. He was also beginning to feel like he was a part of the team with most of his castmates.

Though Wacky Best Friend hadn't offered his real name yet, Heartthrob respected him and his role on the team. He always seemed to be thinking and planning, which Heartthrob appreciated. The last thing he wanted was a co-star that had no interest in doing the job to the best of his abilities.

Girl Next Door was as forthcoming as one could reasonably be while not coming off as a crazy person. She told Heartthrob her real name. She told him stories about her time at The Studio and before. She joked with him as though he had always been there. She—more than anyone else—had made Heartthrob feel welcome. Sure, she was an excessive hugger, but he could live with that.

The only member of his cast that Heartthrob could not quite get a handle on was their lead actress, Starlette.

She was reserved and quiet. She often wandered off on her own, and Heartthrob had seen her leave The Studio by herself. He said nothing about this to anyone, but he knew that solo gigs were frowned upon within The Studio. In filmmaking, there's no such thing as a one woman show.

Starlette was a mystery. She was troubled and full of pain, but who wasn't in those days after the attacks? The world of each person in The Studio had been chewed up and spat out. Nobody had made it out of that experience entirely whole. The closest that Heartthrob had come to seeing an almost normal person was Ember, and he was pretty sure that she could crack at any moment.

"Oh my God," Wacky Best Friend said, interrupting Heartthrob's train of thought. "This might be the worst thing I've ever tasted. Did you make it out of plastic?"

Girl Next Door pouted as Wacky Best Friend put his plate down. She turned to Heartthrob and said, "You don't have to eat it. I can't even get the right herbs that I need for the recipe, so I don't know why I bothered trying."

Heartthrob looked at the defeat in Ember's face and he felt bad for her. She was trying to be something that she was never meant to be. It wasn't her fault that she didn't know how to cook.

He took a bite of the lasagna and swallowed. It was not good. It was chewy. It was grainy. It was oddly minty. He took another bite.

Wacky Best Friend watched Heartthrob eat the lasagna, cringing with each swallow that Heartthrob completed. He said, "Damn. What kind of mind games did those monsters play on you?"

"It's fine," Heartthrob replied. "A lot better than some of the stuff I've eaten lately."

That part was true. On the run from Bookworm's minions, Heartthrob had been forced to slum it. He had resorted to eating whatever he could manage to dig up, and sometimes *dig up* was not just a figure of speech.

"You don't have to be nice. I know it sucks," Ember told him, with a look that expressed concern for his health. Her eyes drifted to the plate of food in front of him, as though she was worried that he might take another bite, just to make her feel better.

Heartthrob took another bite, and Ember smiled just a little bit at the sweetness of the gesture. She then grabbed the plate from him and tossed the food into a nearby garbage can.

"If he dies," Wacky Best Friend told Ember, "it's on you. Just like that extra you shot."

"He did *not* die!" she screamed back at Wacky Best Friend, before turning to Heartthrob and explaining, "He did not die. I shot *one* stupid little extra by mistake, and he did *not* die."

She turned and smacked Wacky Best Friend over the head. Wacky Best Friend laughed at this, which only seemed to annoy Ember more.

"Shut up!" she yelled.

As Wacky Best Friend continued to laugh, Heartthrob couldn't help but smile too. The two of them reminded him of his life back home.

Quickly, the smile faded as his happy memories were replaced by those of more recent events. His eyes drifted down to the ground.

~

Inside her trailer, Starlette sat with her back to the window. She could hear everything that was being said by the others. She could hear them discussing the horrible food, which she had no desire to try. She could hear Ember yelling at Ethan. It put a smile on her face, if only just slightly.

She kept herself inside her trailer, listening to the others because she still hadn't made up her mind about Heartthrob. She was supposed to trust him as though he had been there all along, but the simple fact was that he was new. He was unproven. She had tested his fighting skills, and he seemed like a nice enough guy, but she didn't know where he had been since the attacks and he often seemed to grow distant when the subject was brought up.

Starlette wanted to trust him. She couldn't claim to be an open book herself. She couldn't dislike him just because he pulled back at times, or seemed troubled. If these were traits that would lead an actor to be written off, she would have been in serious danger.

While she waited for a shoot to go on, Starlette collected as much information about Heartthrob as she could. She'd looked over his resume and bio, but it didn't tell her much that she didn't already know from her first briefing regarding his recruitment. So, she listened and watched him closely. She could form impressions based on the subtle movement of his face and eyes. She could see when he got uncomfortable and shifted. She could hear when his voice became shaky and when he redirected conversations. He seemed good at that.

Though all of this was helpful, it was only once she was able to see him work in an actual location, on an actual shoot, that she would be able to see how well he handled himself. She wasn't worried that he was a spy from Bookworm's camp. She was worried that he was broken to a point that made him more of a risk than an asset.

She heard laughter. The unmistakable tone of Ember's laugh was recognizable to everyone in The Studio. Her laugh was real. Though some of the actors in The Studio tried to laugh in order to help sell their characters, Ember wasn't faking it. One had to wonder if she was just a really good actress, or breaking character each time she smiled. Either way, it usually put a grin on the faces of everyone around her.

Starlette could hear Ethan laughing outside her trailer as well. His was the laugh of a man with a lot on his mind. True, but with reserve.

Heartthrob didn't laugh at all, it would seem. She listened to see if he might have a softer laugh, but she heard nothing.

Starlette moved closer to the window so that she could get a look through the blinds and see whether or not Heartthrob was laughing. She needed to know if he was taking part in the good humor of the moment or if he was so distracted by something else that he couldn't even enjoy the company of his co-stars.

When she saw Heartthrob, he had a smile on his face. He watched Ember and Ethan interact as though they were putting on a show, and he shook his head slightly as he grinned from ear to ear.

Watching her co-stars enjoying their afternoon, Starlette couldn't help but admire them for their ability to leave their work at the office. In their off hours, Ethan and Ember seemed more in touch with the people they had once been than Starlette could imagine feeling herself. When Girl Next Door and Wacky Best Friend turned in their props, Ethan and Ember were the ones who went home for the night.

She didn't even realize it at first, but when she started to move away from the window, she found that she had a slight smile on her face. She appreciated it. Of all the people in her world, her co-stars were the only ones who could keep her grounded. Without them she would be lost.

Though she had moved away from the window, Starlette could still see through her blinds enough to notice that The Director was approaching. He walked toward their trailers with a script in hand and when Starlette saw that script, her heart began to beat just a little bit faster.

She was just preparing to walk to her trailer door and meet The Director outside when she saw that he was not there to talk to her. He was there for Wacky Best Friend. He motioned for Wacky Best Friend to come with him, and the two of them left Heartthrob and Girl Next Door sitting by themselves as they walked around the trailer and away from the ears of Wacky Best Friend's co-stars... Or so they thought.

The walls were thin on Starlette's trailer, and the acoustics between trailers allowed voices to carry even more. As The Director met with Wacky Best Friend, Starlette could hear every word.

~

"You've read it?" Wacky Best Friend asked The Director as they reached a quiet place between the trailers.

The Director looked down at the script in his hand. He didn't seem to know quite what to say at first. He looked back to Wacky Best Friend and struggled to find the right words. At long last, he said, "Head Writer would call for your contract to be terminated if he found out that you were handing me scripts on spec. You know that, right?"

Wacky Best Friend nodded, but in a manner that seemed to shrug off the warning as he said, "It's a solid piece though. You'd know that if you read it."

"I did read it. And while I don't normally approve of my actors stealing the boots off of the enemy, the wallet you found was... interesting."

"And the address on the license?"

"That part was interesting too. But we're talking about a Bookworm minion that you killed in that building."

"Actually, I just stunned the crap out of that one. He's still alive.

Which means, he will go home. When he does that, we can find him. We can make him answer questions."

The Director took a long pause in order to think about what he wanted to do next, and to make sure that his initial reaction was the best possible reaction. Wacky Best Friend waited with bated breath to see what The Director would say.

After thinking for a good long while, and allowing the tension to build to a level which was appropriate to the situation without becoming overly dramatic, The Director said, "I sent two location scouts out there about an hour ago. I haven't heard anything back yet, but if we do, I'll make sure that your script gets the green light."

Wacky Best Friend smiled like he hadn't smiled in nearly a year. He said, "So you think this is legit? We might actually have a lead on Bookworm?"

"I think that we need to take this opportunity, but let's not get ahead of ourselves," The Director insisted. "We still have a lot of work to do between now and then. So prepare your team. Fill them in, but let them know that this is just me *optioning* your script for now. We don't need spoilers spreading around The Studio before we've even finalized all of the details."

Wacky Best Friend smiled and nodded in understanding. The Director turned to walk away, but stopped himself at the last moment. He knocked on the wall of Starlette's trailer and said, "I expect you to back Wacky Best Friend. Pull your cast together for him."

"Sure thing, boss," came Starlette's muffled voice, from within her trailer.

~

Starlette left her trailer and met Ethan just as he was returning to their makeshift patio. He still had a smile on his face after his meeting with The Director, and Starlette patted him on the shoulder as she met him.

"Looks like you're building a writing resume," she told him.

"What?" Ember asked from her lawn chair, before rushing to stand next to Starlette. She asked, "Are you serious? You're a Writer now?"

"I'm not a Writer. I just pitched one script to The Director.

That's all," Ethan explained.

Ember pouted and shifted slightly, saying "God, I can't even bake cookies and you're off writing... I suck."

"You do suck," Ethan told her, in that brotherly way in which he always spoke to her. "But I got lucky. An opportunity presented itself and I took advantage. Simple as that."

Heartthrob joined them and started listening. He seemed curious, but didn't ask any questions. Starlette figured that he didn't feel comfortable jumping into their business talk just yet. She saw him look to her, expecting her to ask the questions. So, she did.

"What opportunity?" she asked Ethan.

Ethan walked back to the lawn furniture, looking around The Studio to make sure that his co-stars were the only ones within listening distance. They followed him and each took a seat.

Once he was sure that they were alone, Wacky Best Friend explained, "When we went to get Heartthrob out of the building full of Bookworm minions, we came under fire. Bullets flying. Teeth breaking. Knives being thrown every which way. And since we weren't in any hurry, I decided to investigate the minions and see if I could find anything of use on them."

Girl Next Door nodded in understanding and concluded, "You mugged them."

"No," Ethan insisted, "I was just *investigating* their pockets for anything that might be of some value... To our cause."

"You totally mugged them," Girl Next Door pushed.

Wacky Best Friend seemed annoyed by her and snapped, "Well, they killed everyone we knew, so I figure we're square."

Girl Next Door crossed her arms and shook her head in playful disapproval.

"One of the things I took was a wallet," Wacky Best Friend continued.

Girl Next Door made a quiet *mm-hmm* sound as she continued to listen for more information.

"Wallets have personal information inside. Credit cards. Identification. That was good thinking," Starlette told him, ignoring Girl Next Door completely. "Kinda makes you wonder why nobody has thought of checking their pockets for nearly a year now."

"I'm gonna chalk that up to crappy writing," Ethan replied. He looked at Heartthrob and explained, "I mean, every time we go into one of these shoots, we have to pretend that we forget half the lines they want us to say, just so we don't wind up standing in front of the armed bad guys, making puns for five minutes instead of shooting them."

Girl Next Door looked over her shoulder, checking to see if anyone was listening to their conversation. Starlette said nothing in response to the points that Wacky Best Friend was making. Heartthrob looked to each of his co-stars, taking in their reactions and seeming to make mental notes of them.

Ember leaned in closer to Ethan and in a very low voice said, "Please tell me that you didn't say any of this to The Director or any of the writing staff."

"No, I didn't," Ethan replied. "But I also couldn't wait around for them to come up with some contrivance that would get us Bookworm's location. So, I did it myself. I found an address inside the wallet. It's outside of our normal shooting area, but I think it's worth the travel expenses if we can get more information on Bookworm."

"So, why aren't we hopping in the van?" Ember asked.

"Location scouts are checking out the area now. Once they report back, we can start formally putting the script into production. Until then, we should start prepping on our own," Wacky Best Friend told them.

For a few seconds, nobody said anything. Starlette's mind began racing with the hundred different ways that she might be able to play the scene, once she knew for certain what that scene would be. She began running down the list of interrogation techniques that she might be able to use on the Bookworm minion, once they had him secured.

Girl Next Door stood up and began to pace nervously. She put one hand over her mouth, as though doing so would help to keep her thoughts internalized and not tip off anyone else in The Studio as to what was going on.

Heartthrob did nothing. He said nothing. He didn't react at all. The coldness with which he absorbed the information did not sit

well with Starlette. She wanted to see him respond. She wanted to
see a healthy desire for action. She wanted to see some reluctance
to get back onto the streets. She wanted any reaction that meant
that he felt *something*, because an actor *needed* to feel. To close
himself off to the emotional side of their work would mean
placing the entire shoot in jeopardy.

~

Hours passed before the actors were called into the conference
room. When they walked in, they found The Director sitting next
to Head Writer. None of the other crew members or department
heads had arrived yet.

The room was full of smoke, which was against state
regulations. In her younger days, Starlette had done a public
service announcement about the dangers of second-hand smoke.
She didn't like it. She didn't like it at all. But there it was, and she
could do nothing about the horrible deeds which had already
been committed.

She and her co-stars took their seats at the table. The Director
and Head Writer said nothing at first. Head Writer glared at them
with disdain, which told Starlette that he was not happy. An
unhappy writer was dangerous to an actor out on location. They
could get an actor killed with the stroke of a pen.

The entire situation was a mess, but it was one that Starlette
was willing to navigate. The pitch that Wacky Best Friend had
made was a valid one. It was a chance to move their plot along for
the first time in what seemed like forever. If that meant that Head
Writer wanted them all to die, then she would have to keep her
eye on him. One more enemy would hardly add to the stress of her
life.

"Glad you could make it," The Director finally said to the actors.
"We'll be joined by the other department heads in a little while,
and we'll go over the finer points of this sequence with them.
However, I think the situation warrants some added discussion
between all of you, Head Writer and myself."

The Director walked to a messenger bag that was sitting on the
floor and he pulled four scripts from the bag. He handed each
actor one script.

Starlette looked down at the title page of the script and read what it said. She was eager to see Wacky Best Friend's name. She was proud of his effort.

What she saw under the title was something else entirely. The title page read: *SUBURBAN ADVENTURE, written by HEAD WRITER, story by HEAD WRITER.*

"What the fuck?" Girl Next Door blurted, without even thinking about what she was saying. "I mean, what the *heck*?"

Catching herself and her break from character, Girl Next Door looked up to The Director and said, "The suburbs? We're going to the suburbs?"

Wacky Best Friend looked at Head Writer, who was sitting on the far end of the room. Head Writer met his glare and didn't flinch at the obvious displeasure on Wacky Best Friend's part.

The Director said, "Obviously, we have a lot of issues to discuss."

"Why isn't Wacky Best Friend getting the credit he deserves?" Starlette asked. She was the lead actress on their cast. If nobody else would say anything about what was happening, she would.

"I don't know what you're talking about," Head Writer replied. "Wacky Best Friend did do some evidence gathering on that last shoot which *I* scripted. I suppose he might get a special mention in the *thank yous*, after the credits. But really, he was just doing his job."

"You know damn well—" Starlette began, before being cut off by Wacky Best Friend.

"It's cool," Wacky Best Friend said, still looking Head Writer directly in the eyes. "We have a job to do, and whatever gets that done is best for the team."

Starlette was not happy at all. "But—" she started again, before being cut off by Wacky Best Friend once more.

"I said, it's fine," he told her, now looking her in the eyes and shaking his head slightly so that she would not press the issue.

The decision was his to make, but Starlette didn't have to be happy about it. She didn't have to enjoy watching her friend get his hard work trampled.

She balled her fists, but remained silent.

"Our location scouts have confirmed that the address is good. They've sent pictures back to us, and we've started blocking the scene. They'll set up basecamp at an abandoned grocery store, about a mile away from the location itself. From there, we will monitor your work and make sure that we get all of the coverage we need to make this a successful shoot."

As The Director went on, he gave them all of the information that they would need. He broke down the location details and the layout of the home that they would be invading. He told them how he wanted them to play the scene, which was not exactly their normal style.

Other department heads came in and listened to what would be happening. A few asked questions, but most simply listened.

Through this all, Starlette kept her eyes on Head Writer. She may not be allowed to kill him, but she could sure as hell let him know that she wanted to.

~

When the meeting was over, everyone began to leave the conference room and head off to their various departments to prepare for the day's shoot.

Wacky Best Friend was on his way out of the room with his co-stars when Head Writer caught up to him and grabbed his shoulder.

Wacky Best Friend turned and smiled politely, saying, "You might want to move that hand, friend. My character breakdown does call for bloodshed on occasion. I just have to make sure to crack a joke while doing it."

"You think *you've* been offended in all of this?" Head Writer grinned. "I have a job here. I do that job well."

"I get that you're all worried about job security in these harsh economic times, but there's work to be done here and I don't see us making a lot of progress."

"You make it sound so simple. Like we should just march out there and finish this thing off once and for all," Head Writer replied.

The tone with which Head Writer said this amused Wacky Best Friend. The tone suggested that this was *not* what they should be doing, and that all of the poor plotting that had been done so far was all just part of some master plan. He couldn't help but chuckle.

"I'm all for going after Bookworm," Head Writer told him. "I want to kill that son of a bitch, the same as everyone else in this Studio does; the same way that every person who works with The Network wants to. Now, I think it's great that you want to plow through this half-cocked and guns a-blazing, but there's a reason why we do things the way we do."

"There is? Really?" Wacky Best Friend replied. "There's a reason why friends of mine have gotten killed or just disappeared? There's a reason why we get shot at day after day, and still have nothing to show for it? We've been at this for almost a year, and how much closer to taking down Bookworm are we?"

Head Writer just shook his head and looked to the ground. He seemed to be looking for some way to make Wacky Best Friend understand the situation. He started to speak, but stopped himself. He couldn't seem to find the words right away.

When he did finally find those words, Head Writer looked to Wacky Best Friend and said, "Do you remember when you shot the pilot? Do you remember the way your hand shook when you held a gun? How you hesitated? It took that pilot nearly three hours to die."

Wacky Best Friend listened to what Head Writer was saying. For the first time since Head Writer arrived at The Studio, there seemed to be a point to what he was saying. There seemed to be some sense to what he was thinking.

"There's a reason why we couldn't get that information. It's because you weren't ready. You didn't know *how* to get the information. Do you think you would have known what to do with it if you did get it?" Head Writer asked.

Wacky Best Friend didn't answer. He simply listened and thought about what Head Writer was saying.

"Characters need arcs. You need to progress from point *A* to point *B*, because you learn something with each step along the way. You become better at what you do. You become more certain of what you need to do. Now, tell me… If Bookworm were sitting in this room with you right now and you had a gun to his head, do you think that your hand would still be shaking?"

Wacky Best Friend intended to answer this question, but he wanted to answer it in the right way. He wanted to fully convey the meaning of what he was saying, so that Head Writer would be very clear on his point.

"No," Wacky Best Friend replied. "But my hand hasn't done that in a very long time. My hand stopped shaking before Bombshell died. My hand stopped shaking before Headliner disappeared. We could have ended this a long time ago, but we've been spinning our wheels instead."

Head Writer nodded, letting Wacky Best Friend know that he understood what he was saying. He told Wacky Best Friend, "I wasn't here for all of that. But let me assure you, I have an endgame. We know where this is going, and what we need to do along the way in order to make sure that this ends the way we want it to end."

Wacky Best Friend nodded, letting Head Writer know that he understood as well. He replied, "There is a difference between pacing the arcs, letting the characters develop naturally along the way... and just drawing things out. We need details, not framework. We cannot win this war if all we have on our side is good intention."

"It seems like some people around here agree with you," Head Writer told him.

Wacky Best Friend looked Head Writer in the eyes. There were a number of things that he wanted to say to Head Writer, about the level of writing that they'd been dealing with lately, the lives that were put in jeopardy due to bad plotting, and the downright stupid lines that they were asked to deliver when dealing with their enemies.

He wanted to let it all out, but there was a line that had to be drawn. Wacky Best Friend was not the star of his cast, and he could easily be replaced with someone who would be more compliant. He needed to watch himself now more than ever, because he'd already made some pretty bold moves just by submitting a script of his own. So he chose not to say any of those things that immediately came to mind. Instead, he walked away and let the situation settle wherever it would settle.

~

On her way out of the meeting, Starlette had the urge to raise hell. When she saw that Head Writer had taken credit for Ethan's work, she wanted to punch someone. Badly.

When it came to the production aspects of The Studio, Starlette routinely kept her eyes on her own homework and let everyone go about their business. It wasn't her job to judge their work, and frankly she didn't care much about what they did. When she was on a shoot, she might be surrounded by cameramen and sound techs, but her job wasn't to worry about whether or not their equipment was functioning properly. Her job was to hit her marks and to hit them hard. She had to worry about enemy fire, and protecting the lives of her co-stars.

If she had time after all of that was finished, she might try to think about her lighting and double check to make sure that she didn't forget any of her lines.

When she first arrived at The Studio, she wondered why they needed lines at all. While they were few and far between, often scattered between pages of stage directions, she thought it absurd to have those lines in there at all.

Even all those months later, Starlette still placed her lines low on her list of priorities and usually improvised whatever dialog she had with the enemy. After all of the explanations about controlling the situations and attempting to manipulate her foes, Starlette couldn't bring herself to care.

In spite of all this, it pissed her off when she read through that script that Ethan had written, and she saw someone else's name attached to the words that had come from his mind. Her palms were aching; the result of driving her nails into them and sitting that way through the entire meeting.

She somehow managed to remain composed throughout the meeting and to conduct herself in a professional manner, but the fact remained; she wanted to do someone a great deal of bodily harm.

"I don't get it," Heartthrob said to her, in a hushed tone, as they walked out of the meeting and through The Studio. "How can they just take his work like that? Does that happen a lot around here?"

"I wouldn't know," Starlette replied, wanting to say little else for fear of saying too much.

"Shouldn't we do something?" Heartthrob shot back.

Starlette gritted her teeth, "Yes, we should. But we won't."

Because we're not paid to think, we're paid to read lines and fight bad guys."

Heartthrob looked puzzled as he asked, "Are we paid?"

Catching up to them, Girl Next Door kept pace, while turning and walking backwards in order to keep an eye out for Ethan. She said, "I can't believe the nerve of these people."

She turned and faced forward as she continued to walk beside Starlette and Heartthrob. She said nothing else on the subject. She put a pleasant smile on her face and she assumed the image of the happy-go-lucky girl next door.

As they walked, The Director hurried to catch up with them. He placed a hand on Starlette's shoulder, stopping her in her path. Girl Next Door and Hartthrob stopped beside her. Neither Starlette nor Heartthrob looked happy at that moment. Girl Next Door looked pleasant as ever.

"There's something you should understand," The Director told them. "The name on the script…"

"You mean the name that wasn't *Wacky Best Friend*?" Starlette asked, with enough attitude to let The Director know that she was not happy. Of the three actors standing there, she was perhaps the only one who thought they could get away with such boldness.

"Head Writer wasn't the one who changed the name. I was," The Director explained. "It was a decision that was reached between myself and the Producers. So, if you're going to be angry, just know who you're directing that anger toward."

"Why would you do that?" Starlette demanded. "I want to know why you would take the hard work of one person and slap someone else's name on it."

The Director struggled to find the right words to explain his actions. When he finally spoke, he said, "Everyone in this Studio has a role to play. Wacky Best Friend has his name for a reason. He's not here to think. He's not here to write. His job is to back you up when you're out there."

"That's it? Just like that, he's not allowed to do anything else with his life?"

"Just like that, none of us are. It's not ideal, but it's the way things have to be right now. We have a system, Starlette. I want you to think about that and really understand what I mean when I tell you this... We have a system. Each person here has a role to play and a job to do. We have structure. The *second* people start crossing the lines and doing someone else's work, that structure will crumble. Every single person here wants the chance to kill Bookworm and his cronies..."

"*Minions*," Girl Next Door corrected. "We call them *minions*. It's more fitting."

The Director gave Girl Next Door a *does it really matter* look and continued to speak to Starlette. "You and your cast are trained for this fight. You're professionals. Your job is to be out there, front and center. You might not understand what it's like for everyone else, working behind the scenes to help you succeed in this, but knowing that they will never get the glory. They will never get the chance to draw blood and avenge their loved ones. If they see one of you doing their job, they will see a chance for them to do yours. When that happens, we will have hundreds of people on the streets, unprepared for what they're going to find. And they will die."

Starlette allowed The Director's words to sink in. She listened to them very carefully and did not resist them, just for the sake of being argumentative. But once she was done considering his words, Starlette looked back to The Director and said, "You don't know that. We've all become something that we could never have dreamed of before this happened. I don't believe that those people would die. I think they would fight."

"I respect that opinion," The Director replied, nodding his head just slightly as he listened. "But you are not running this show. So, while we value your thoughts and opinions on the direction of your character... ultimately, the decision will be ours. And we've decided that this is the best course of action."

"Then we'll have to agree to disagree," Starlette concluded.

With that said, Starlette turned and walked away from The Director. Heartthrob was close behind her. Girl Next Door hesitated for a moment, missing her chance to make a proper exit. As she lingered, she smiled awkwardly at The Director and said, "That was a really good speech."

The Director turned and walked away.

~

The sun was shining brightly through the windows of the Carter home. The smell of freshly baked apple pie filled the air. The floors had been freshly polished. The laundry had just been folded. It was a beautiful day in their home.

Betsy Carter sat on the living room sofa, having kicked off her shoes so that she could cuddle up with her seven year old daughter, Emma, and read a story.

"The witch climbed through the window of the little girl's room, and crept across the floor. *Creeeeek*, rose the sound of the old wooden floor as she walked across it. *Squeeeeeeeak* came the sound of the heavy old door as she pulled it open. The witch moved as softly as possible, but it seemed as though the house was refusing to allow her presence to remain unknown to the little girl whose parents had been put to sleep by the witch's spell..."

"Mommy, is the witch going to kill the little girl? Because if so, I'd like to stop reading this now," Emma cut in.

"Of course not, sweetie. This is an age-appropriate book. That means that the witch will lose in the end and the parents will wake up, and everyone will be happy," Betsy assured her daughter, petting her daughter's precious gold curls as she did so.

"Mom! You just ruined the end!" Emma yelled, getting off of the sofa.

"I didn't mean to. I just answered your question," Betsy tried to explain. "I'm sorry, dear. Do you want to read another story?"

"We might as well," Emma sighed, walking to the bookcase, for another book.

As Emma shuffled through the many titles on the shelf, completely oblivious to the fact that they had pretty much all been spoiled for her already due to a lack of originality on the part of each author, there came a knock at the front door.

Betsy placed the book she had been reading on the sofa and slipped her shoes back on. As she stood, she straightened her dress and walked toward the door.

There was another knock.

When Betsy opened the front door, she found four young people standing on her front stoop; two girls and two boys. They were all rather darkly dressed, but she wasn't one to jump to conclusions about people based solely on their clothing.

The girl up front had a hairstyle that was lopsided, and she had dark makeup around her eyes. This girl was the one who spoke first, saying, "Mrs. Carter?"

Betsy smiled and said, "Yes. Are you kids from the local high school?"

"No ma'am," said the second girl, who was Asian and seemed far more pleasant than the first. "We often pass for teenagers, but we're actually quite older than we look... But not too much older."

"I see," Betsy replied, still smiling. "Who are you then?"

The first girl spoke again, saying, "We're looking for Michael Carter. Does he live here?"

Betsy wasn't sure what to make of this request. She was told to always be skeptical of strangers who came to the door, but there was something about that second girl. She seemed familiar somehow, and Betsy assumed that she must have seen the girl around the neighborhood without ever even realizing it.

"My husband is upstairs. He's been a little under the weather lately. If you'd tell me who is asking after him, I'd be happy to pass along a message."

"Oh, that's okay, ma'am. We'll just come in and talk to him ourselves," that first girl told Betsy as she pulled a gun and stuck it in Betsy's face.

~

The house was the type of place that made Starlette sick. The hedges were perfectly trimmed. The lawn was green. There was a freshly delivered newspaper on the front porch and a yappy little dog next door that annoyed the hell out of her.

She didn't hate it for what it was. She hated it for what it represented. It was a world that had moved on. It was a life being lived in the sunlight, while she and her people were forced to hide underground.

As she held the gun to the woman's face, Starlette's mind flashed with images of her childhood. She came from a neighborhood similar to where she now stood. Her home looked different on the outside, as she came from a completely different part of the country, but it had a similar feel to it. It was... safe.

She remembered sitting in the sun, as the smell of her father's grill filled the air and children played in the swimming pool next door to her childhood home. She remembered going to sleep with the windows open, and allowing the cool night air to wash over her.

The Starlette who stood in the doorway of this home was not that girl. She was something else entirely, created by men like the one who was resting comfortably upstairs.

She gripped her gun firmly and told the woman, "Get inside. Now."

"Please. Don't hurt us. I have a daughter," Mrs. Carter said, moving aside so that Starlette and her co-stars could move into the house.

Once inside, Heartthrob closed the door and locked it. He and Wacky Best Friend moved to each window and closed the curtains so that they would not be spotted by prying eyes.

From the living room, there came a small voice. It was the voice of a little girl, frightened and hiding. She said, "Mommy, who are these people?"

Mrs. Carter looked into the living room, to the corner where her daughter was hiding behind a potted plant, and she said, "It's okay, baby. They're just people who want to talk to Daddy. Don't worry."

Girl Next Door walked into the living room, scanning the area. She had a gun in hand, but it was at her side. She said, "This place is really nice. I love the wallpaper. And... is that apple pie that I smell?"

"Y—Yes," Mrs. Carter replied. "I baked it this afternoon."

Girl Next Door nodded and continued to scan the room. She then walked to the dining room and had a look around in there.

"I'm going upstairs to talk to the husband. You keep them down here, and don't let them out of your sight," Starlette told Girl Next Door, just as Wacky Best Friend and Heartthrob returned from covering the windows.

"I'm going with you," Heartthrob told her.

Starlette's initial reaction was to tell Heartthrob to stay put and let her do her job. She didn't need the annoyance of babysitting the new guy while she was trying to interrogate a minion of Bookworm. She didn't turn him down though. Instead, she decided to take this opportunity to test Heartthrob in the field.

She nodded, and then turned to Girl Next Door. She told her, "Keep your gun on her."

Girl Next Door nodded and raised her gun to Mrs. Carter's head.

"Mommy!" screamed the little girl in the living room.

"It's okay, Emma. You don't worry about Mommy. I'll be fine," Mrs. Carter told her daughter.

"That's right, Emma. Mommy will be fine," Girl Next Door told the girl, and then lowered her voice and told Mrs. Carter, "As long as Mommy doesn't upset me."

Starlette and Heartthrob moved toward the stairs, keeping their guns ready. There was no way of telling whether or not Michael Carter knew that his house had been invaded. He could be waiting for them, ready to open fire.

They moved up the stairs swiftly, but quietly. Once reaching the second floor, Starlette took a look down the hallway, making sure that the coast was clear.

There were four rooms on the second floor of that house. Three of the doors to those rooms were open. The first door on the right had bright pink paint on the walls. It was so bright that its color seemed to glow, staining the hallway directly outside with its pinkness. Starlette highly doubted that this was the master bedroom.

On the left, there was a bathroom. She could see the tile on the floor and the mirror on the wall—Also not the master bedroom.

Next to the bathroom was a door, which opened into a room that was painted a sage-like color. It could easily be the color of a master bedroom, but Starlette was willing to bet that this room was a spare. A parent seeking rest while a young child ran free in the house would not leave their door open. They would want quiet. They would want to leave their spouse to watch the kid.

This led Starlette to the door at the end of the hall, which was closed. She turned to Heartthrob and motioned with her head, toward that bedroom. He nodded in agreement.

Together they moved down the hall, hoping to rush into the

bedroom and catch Carter by surprise while he rested in his big suburban bed.

When they reached the door, Starlette and Heartthrob each put their back to a wall and tried to leave the doorway clear, just in case they were shot at upon entering.

Heartthrob put his hand on the shiny brass doorknob and turned it slowly. She could hear the mechanisms inside the door moving, but hoped that Carter wouldn't be paying enough attention to notice.

Heartthrob took a deep breath and looked to Starlette, in order to make sure that she was ready to charge. She gave him a nod.

He threw the door open and Starlette burst into the room, gun leveled on the bed. Heartthrob was right behind her, scanning the room and making sure that nobody else was in there with them.

Michael Carter was in bed, with a cast on one arm, and some week-old bruises on his face. He had blankets pulled over him, but Starlette could see both hands, and there was not a weapon in either.

"If you move so much as an inch, I will blow your face open," Starlette warned.

"Who are you?" Carter asked, coming to the realization that he was being held at gunpoint.

Heartthrob walked to the side of the bed and aimed his gun at Carter's head. He asked, "You don't remember me?"

When Carter looked at Heartthrob, he knew at once what was happening. He took a deep breath and said, "I'm sorry. I'm sorry. Please, I'm sorry."

"Sorry for holding me hostage and torturing me? Or sorry for killing everyone I knew, hunting me for a year and destroying my life?" Heartthrob asked.

Starlette was impressed by his delivery of those lines.

"I'm sorry for... I'm sorry for all of it. Please, don't kill me," Carter cried.

"We won't kill you. All you have to do is answer some very simple questions for us," Starlette told him.

Carter started to cry harder, "If I tell you anything, they'll kill me."

She shrugged and said, "Well, I guess you should have thought of that before you allied yourself with an international terrorist organization, shouldn't you?"

~

Girl Next Door kept her gun aimed at Mrs. Carter's head, ready to pull the trigger at any moment, should the woman make any threatening move at all.

Though she kept her guard up, Girl Next Door looked around the house, studying its details and absorbing as much of the essence of that place as she could. This was exactly the type of place that a girl next door type would grow up in, and far from where Girl Next Door had actually grown up. She was a city girl. She knew apartments, not two story suburban dream homes.

Wacky Best Friend sat on the stairs; gun in hand, but hardly on guard. Every so often, he would turn and glance up the stairs as though he expected Starlette and Heartthrob to come down at any moment. Girl Next Door knew better. She knew that whatever they had to do up there, it would probably take a while.

"Tell me," Girl Next Door said to Mrs. Carter. "Did you know what your husband does for a living?"

"What he... does?" Mrs. Carter replied, as though she were about to break into tears.

"You know, terrorizing people. Locking them up in basements, and torturing them. Did you know?" Girl Next Door asked.

Mrs. Carter's eyes went to the living room, where her daughter was still hiding behind the plant. She then looked to Girl Next Door and said, "My husband is a good man. He's an honorable man."

Girl Next Door nodded, playing along with her response. She said, "I bet he's the life of every cocktail party."

Girl Next Door fell silent for another moment, but there were hundreds of questions that were bouncing around inside her mind, and she wanted answers. She needed to do something besides wait, and she knew that the woman standing in front of her could provide her with information. She just needed to force that information out of her.

She gripped her gun a little bit more tightly, and said to Mrs. Carter, "I'm going to give you one chance. You will do everything I tell you. You will answer every question I ask you. If you don't..."

she then lowered her voice to a whisper, so that the little girl wouldn't hear, and said, "I will shoot you between the eyes and completely ruin the wallpaper behind you."

Mrs. Carter looked at Girl Next Door, growing nervous. She obviously wasn't sure what to expect next, but she believed that Girl Next Door would follow through on her threats, and that was a good thing as far as Girl Next Door was concerned.

"What are you doing?" Wacky Best Friend asked, standing and walking closer to Girl Next Door. "This isn't part of the script."

"I know," she replied. "I'm going off-book. I have to. This woman knows things."

Wacky Best Friend seemed uncomfortable with the situation. He looked toward the living room, and then back to Girl Next Door, trying to decide whether to back her play or not. Once he decided, he gave her a nod.

Girl Next Door had the support of her co-star, so she pressed on with her plan. She put the barrel of her gun directly against Mrs. Carter's temple and said, "Now... You're going to tell me everything you know about making an apple pie, and you're going to tell me right now. Understand?"

Mrs. Carter had tensed up a great deal when Girl Next Door put the gun to her head. Her hands were at her side, gripping her legs as though this would provide her with added support. Her eyes were wide with fear. She couldn't speak. Instead, Mrs. Carter sucked air through her teeth, trying to keep herself from crying, and she nodded.

"Good," Girl Next Door said. "Now, we're just going to go into the kitchen, and you're going to show me how to make a pie crust. Mine always turn out mushy and I'm not sure if it's because the place I live is kinda hot, or if I'm not mixing the dough right... It's just a mess."

Wacky Best Friend walked to Girl Next Door's side, and leaned close enough to whisper to her. He said, "Apple pie?"

"You have your job and I have mine," Girl Next Door replied.

"My daughter," Mrs. Carter said. "Please, let me take her with us."

"No deal," Girl Next Door told her. "Your focus will be on answering my questions and telling me what I need to know. If you do that, you and your family will be just fine."

"I'll watch the kid," Wacky Best Friend offered. "I used to babysit all the time, back when I was in high school."

"How do I know you won't hurt her?" Mrs. Carter asked.

"Your husband is a terrorist with links to an organization that murdered literally thousands of people around the world. Men, women and children. You suddenly have standards now? I'm not the kid killer in this house," he replied.

Girl Next Door looked to Mrs. Carter and nodded in agreement with Wacky Best Friend, "He does make a valid point."

"Fine," Mrs. Carter said. "But if you hurt so much as a hair on her head, so help me..."

"I don't shoot kids that don't shoot me first. It's kind of a rule I have," Wacky Best Friend smirked, seeming to grow more and more annoyed with the woman with each word exchanged between them.

Girl Next Door grabbed Mrs. Carter's arm and shoved her in the direction of the kitchen. She said, "One wrong move and you die. Got it? I want this crust flaky."

~

While Heartthrob kept his gun aimed at Michael Carter, Starlette went to the window and closed the blinds. The sun was bright, and still seemed determined to creep into the room, but at least there would be no prying eyes from the neighbors.

Starlette turned and kept her back to the window, hoping to appear as more of a dark figure than a person, for the added air of mystery and intimidation.

In a quiet, calm voice, Starlette said to him, "It's a funny thing, to have someone force their way into your world, isn't it? To have this life, this home, this comfort zone that seems as though it's so impenetrable. Then, in one moment, every ounce of comfort that you took from that place is gone. What's left?"

"Look, I get that you're upset—" Carter began. Starlette cut him off with a laugh.

"I'm *upset*?" Starlette asked. She turned to Heartthrob and asked him, "Do I look upset to you?"

"Cool as a cucumber," Heartthrob replied.

"See? I'm cool like produce. If I were upset, you'd be bleeding by now," she told Carter. She sat on the windowsill with her gun in hand, but pointed toward the floor, as though she had all the time and patience in the world. She went on, saying, "Now, my friend here... I think he's a little upset. Is that fair to assume, Heartthrob? Are you upset?"

"I'm fucking pissed," Heartthrob replied, tightening his grip on his gun even more than it was already.

Starlette shrugged and said, "It's understandable. Don't you think it's understandable, Mike? You and your kind went to town on this boy. Made him just about as ugly in the face as this one can get."

"Please. Don't hurt me. I don't know anything. I'm just a lackey."

"We prefer to think of you as a *minion*. Sounds more evil and less sad that way."

"But I'm not evil. I just... I wanted a better life for my little girl."

"So you killed someone else's little girl?"

"I didn't!"

"You did. Oh, if you could see the pain and the suffering you caused. Not to mention the people who didn't quite die, but wish they had because they hurt so much. That's what you and your kind brought to this world, Mike. Now, I'm pretty good at keeping my emotions in check, but this guy here is new. He's untested. Probably a little unstable, and who could blame him for that? I don't blame you, Heartthrob."

"I appreciate it," Heartthrob replied.

Starlette moved from the window and took a seat at the foot of Carter's bed. She looked at him and then down to her gun. She said, "I could make you talk. It wouldn't even be hard. But what I want to do is give you the opportunity to talk to us without the need to resort to violence and bloodshed."

She paused and waited for Carter to reply, but he said nothing. He looked at her gun, and to Heartthrob's gun, and his eyes filled with tears.

Starlette could tell by the way Carter was breathing that he was scared, and she liked it. She enjoyed knowing that she could make a person fear her without so much as raising her voice.

"Will you talk to me?" she asked once again, rather politely in her opinion.

"I can't..." Carter replied, with a tear falling down his cheek.

"Okay then," Starlette said, standing up from the bed.

She walked to a nearby chair, where a pair of pants had been tossed after being removed. She pulled the black leather belt from these pants and looked it over, moving toward Carter once again.

Starlette folded the belt in half and pulled it tight, which resulted in a loud *snap*. She looked to Carter, whose eyes were on the belt, wondering what Starlette was going to do with it.

She ran the belt over his legs, which were still covered by his blanket. She tapped the belt on his legs, but only lightly. She wanted to draw out the suspense. She wanted to make him fear what she was going to do next, because fear was just as powerful as pain.

"Do you have a high pain threshold?" she asked him.

Carter didn't respond. His eyes went from the belt, up to Starlette's eyes and back to the belt once again, as his mind filled with possibilities. She could see his mind racing, and she imagined all of the different ways that he could think of being hurt. She allowed him to ponder the many options for a while as she held the belt.

Just before her dramatic pause turned into an awkward delay, Starlette moved past Heartthrob, getting between his gun and Carter. He said nothing, but lowered his gun so that he wouldn't be aiming it at her.

Starlette folded the belt once again and told Carter, "Bite on this."

Carter apparently hadn't thought of that as a possibility, which amused Starlette just a little as she shoved the belt in his mouth.

"Try to be quiet, so you don't scare your kid," she told him.

Carter tried to say something, which was muffled by the belt. It sounded like "Whm arm thm ghm dm?"

She figured that he was asking what she was going to do to him. She didn't answer.

Instead, Starlette pulled a knife from her belt. She turned to Heartthrob and told him, "Start with the tip of a finger. No need to do the whole thing if he becomes more agreeable. If he doesn't... Well, I'm sure you can improvise something."

Heartthrob holstered his gun, took the knife and replied in a cool tone, saying, "I'm a bad eyeball."

~

Wacky Best Friend paced back and forth in the living room, staring at a Carter family portrait with each *back* and the loaded bookcase with each *forth*.

He had holstered his weapon, with little fear that young Emma would be able to overpower him. Now, he was relegated to babysitting the kid while waiting for everyone else to obtain the information that they'd come for. Somehow, this had never been worked into the script that he had pitched. In that script, his role sounded much more exciting.

If all had gone as he had planned, Wacky Best Friend would be covering the front of the house, keeping out potential bad guys while Starlette rushed to get the intel. Since no alarm had been sounded and apparently the neighborhood was not overrun by Bookworm minions as he had theorized, there was nothing for him to do but wait. And pace. And babysit.

The shelves of the bookcase were filled with books, both for children and for adults. There were leather bound copies of all of the fairy tale classics, which Wacky Best Friend could just picture the Carters sitting down with and reading to their impressionable child. Within those books there was imagery that no child should be exposed to. Grandmothers being eaten by wolves who could hold conversations with little girls. Poisoned apples. Children baking in ovens. Evil step mothers... Wacky Best Friend had a step mother growing up, and she was a rather nice lady. She didn't deserve to be stereotyped as some evil witch who wanted to kill kids.

He had seen the recordings of Bookworm's award show speech so many times, the voice was etched into his mind. The smugness of it all, with its super judgmental demonization of the entertainment industry. The claims that they were poisoning society with their work. Yet, look at the greatest works of literature and you will find some of the most horrible violence, immorality and corruption around... At least, that's what Political Advisor had said in their last awareness seminar. It seemed to make enough sense to Wacky Best Friend, which was perhaps the first time he'd been able to follow anything that Political Advisor had ever said.

He had resisted the general consensus that had swept The Studio in the time since the attacks. He tried to keep a clear mind and think things through logically and rationally. So, he was not entirely on board with the notion that books were for bookworms and Bookworm had killed his people, so books were inherently evil. The logic in his industry could be muddy and difficult to follow at times, and he usually tried to think on his own.

Yet there he was, pacing back and forth, and keeping his eyes on that bookcase as though Hemingway might open fire on him at any moment.

Each time he turned around, Wacky Best Friend caught a glimpse of Emma, sitting behind the potted plant. He thought about the sort of lessons that she must have been exposed to in that home. He thought about what an upbringing must be like in the world of terrorism, and he shook his head in disapproval.

"What's your name?" the girl asked.

"I don't have a name," he replied, continuing to pace.

"Everybody has a name," she shot back.

"Not me."

"Then how do people get you when they want you?"

"Usually by snapping their fingers."

Emma giggled at his response.

He stopped pacing and looked at her with a straight face and said, "It's not funny. They actually do that."

There was a *thud* from upstairs, followed by the muffled scream of a man in great pain. Emma gasped when she heard this and asked, "What was that?"

Wacky Best Friend looked toward the ceiling and replied, "Sounds like Daddy got a boo-boo."

~

"They're hurting him!" Mrs. Carter gasped as she pulled her dough-covered fingers out of the mixing bowl.

"Oh, he'll live," Girl Next Door assured her. "I mean, I don't *know* that, but he'll probably live. I mean... it could happen. Do you ever put ginger in your lasagna?"

Mrs. Carter looked at Girl Next Door with terror in her eyes, and Girl Next Door honestly couldn't figure out whether this look was based on what she'd said about Mrs. Carter's husband, or the lasagna. Wishing to clarify, she said, "My mother used to put ginger in everything. I don't think it was an Asian thing… it might have been. I don't know. She didn't really make lasagna, since it's Italian and my mother was a raging racist, so I'm never sure where the ginger will work and where it's just kinda gross."

Mrs. Carter continued to look at Girl Next Door with fear in her eyes. Tears began to form and her hands began to shake.

"Oh, you're still worried about your husband? Forget that for now. My people have it covered," Girl Next Door said with a smile. "Now, keep smooshing the dough. I want to see how this works out."

Despite Girl Next Door's orders, Mrs. Carter did not move. She was frozen in place. Girl Next Door sighed and rolled her eyes. She then raised her gun and pointed it at the woman's head. She said, "See, now you made me threaten to kill you again, and I *really* don't like repeating myself."

"How can you be so cold?" the woman asked.

"Cold is killing thousands of people, just because you're not a fan of their work. Cold is making us live in fear of being hunted and slain, even though we can't possibly continue with that work at this point. Cold is what the butter should be when you add it to the dough, so it melts in the oven and makes the crust super flaky," Girl Next Door replied. "I learn my lessons quickly and I adjust my life accordingly."

Girl Next Door wished that this woman would just get back to work and show her how to roll the dough without it breaking. Instead, Mrs. Carter continued to look into Girl Next Door's eyes, and her expression changed from one of fear to one of questioning.

"I can't place you," Mrs. Carter said. "I know I've seen you, but I just can't place you."

"Yeah, I have one of those faces," Girl Next Door sighed. "Which sucks when you're an actress, by the way."

"You used to act as a child, right?"

"Yeah."

"On a cable show?"

"*The Happy Fun Time Club House Cable Hour!*" Girl Next Door smiled. "We didn't last very long though. And then I did *Camp Uh-Oh* for three seasons, but I doubt you saw that."

"How do you go from being a bright young girl, so happy and care-free, to... this?" Mrs. Carter asked.

"I just told you, stupid. I don't like repeating myself. Blah-blah terrorism. Blah-blah murder," Girl Next Door shot back. "Crap, now you made me miss my chance for a teary-eyed monologue. Thanks a lot, whore."

Both women paused for a moment, after the considerable change in character for Girl Next Door.

Girl Next Door winced at the mistake and then looked back to Mrs. Carter and said, "Can we do this again? Let's start from the whole cable show thing."

~

The sheets began to soak up the blood that poured from Michael Carter's hand. Heartthrob had just cut off the tip of his left pinky, and Carter was screaming like a little girl.

Starlette held a pillow over his face, muffling the scream.

"You really need to shut up now," she told him. "Otherwise, I'm probably gonna kill you by mistake."

Heartthrob wiped the bloody knife on the sheets. He asked her, "Do you normally cut off body parts?"

"I think I've done it twice before. Something like that," she replied, in a ho-hum tone. "I usually try to avoid it, just because it's loud and messy. I prefer straight-out killing."

Carter began to kick and flail his arms, still screaming in pain. Starlette turned to him and said, "I could let you breathe if you stopped screaming. Do you think you can do that?"

Carter stopped struggling and screaming.

"Well, he's either over it or he's dead," Heartthrob said.

Starlette shrugged, "Either way."

She took the pillow off of Carter's face. He gulped down air as quickly as he could, and grabbed his injured hand with the uninjured.

"Now," Starlette started in again, "if you tell us what we need to know, we can be out of here. You can go to the hospital and they can put that pinky tip back on. Before you know it, it's like we were never here."

"I can't tell you," Carter said once again. "I can't."

"How much do you love your wife, Mike?" Starlette asked, as she grabbed a pillow, stripped off its case and used that case to wrap up Carter's hand. "How much do you value the life that you have here? The kid... the car..."

"Don't hurt my family, please." Carter begged. "Leave them out of this."

"The way you left our families out of this?" Heartthrob replied.

Starlette looked back at Heartthrob and she could see the hate in his eyes. She noticed him tighten his grip on the knife, as though he wanted to stab Carter to death right then.

The way he'd responded to the mention of families raised a flag in Starlette's head. She sure as hell hadn't lost family in this war. Most people knew to steer clear of their real lives once the attacks started. They took on new names, just to be sure that nobody would connect them to the people they had once been. If she had the time, she would have considered Heartthrob's reaction more, but she had more pressing business now. She moved on.

Starlette turned back to Carter and continued, saying, "Your family will be fine. As long as you tell me what I need to know."

"What do you want from me?" he asked her. "What can I possibly tell you? I'm nobody."

She stood and went to the window once again. She asked, "Do you have a boss?"

"Yes," Carter replied.

"Do you have an office?"

"Yes."

"Will you tell me where this office is, and what your boss' name is?"

Carter began to cry, "I... Please, I can't. Please."

After taking a moment to look at the sunlight that was coming through the blinds, Starlette turned and asked, "Do you enjoy killing people, Mr. Carter?"

Carter hesitated. He didn't know what to say.

"Do you enjoy causing pain, Mr. Carter?"

"I... No."

Starlette walked to Heartthrob's side and put her hand on his shoulder. She asked Carter, "Where were you when my friend here was being tortured?"

Carter did not respond. He looked to the bedroom door, as though he was considering rushing toward it.

"Did you hear my friend screaming in pain, Mr. Carter? Did you hear him cry?"

Carter remained in his bed, holding his wounded hand. Starlette could tell that he was in fear of what came next. She enjoyed that he had no way of knowing, and that his imagination was scaring him in ways that she couldn't possibly do herself.

"In the end, you're going to have to ask yourself... *Was it worth it?* Joining the ranks of Bookworm's minions and setting out to kill all of those people seemed noble, I'm sure. You probably had some twisted logic to live by at the time, but what do you think of that logic now? How do you feel knowing that you didn't kill us all? That those of us who remain are not only pissed off and want you dead, but also have nothing left to lose? Does it scare you, Mr. Carter?"

Carter's lower lip was beginning to tremble. His breathing was shallow. He looked away from Starlette, and she expected him to sob.

"When I was a child," he told her, "my mother used to sit me down in front of the television while she did her housework for the day. As she cooked dinner, I watched television. While she vacuumed, I watched television. Instead of living life, I wasted away. I was lost in a world of senseless cartoon violence, which my young mind could not understand. How could an anvil drop on a rabbit's head and not kill him? How? I watched those television programs, and as I grew older, the cartoons became real people. They shed what appeared to be real blood. They cried what appeared to be real tears. They died... and then they came back. Just like that. You love and you lose, and in the end you get a happy ending. You lie to us. You make us feel and give us hope where there is none. You are fundamentally evil. So, you can threaten me. You can torture me. I don't care. Torture my family. My kid. It will just prove my point."

Starlette watched him speak, and she listened to every word. She imagined whatever pain he must have been put through and how that must have left him vulnerable to the influence of classical literature. She didn't care.

She couldn't believe that Carter just invited her to torture his family. Any normal person should have been begging them to let their family go. At the very least, he should have begged them not to hurt his little girl. She wondered what kind of person would put that thought out there and it made her realize just how disgusting this man really was.

And then she realized that she had made a vital mistake. Michael Carter's expression changed. He no longer looked at her as a monster. He saw her limitations. The image that she had projected up to that point was gone. Her disgust at his comment must have been revealed in some look that passed through her eyes. She had broken character. She had failed.

"You murdered thousands of people," she told Carter. "They never came back."

She turned away from Carter, beginning a search of the room in an attempt to salvage whatever she could from this shoot. As she walked, she told Heartthrob, "Go to town."

~

Wacky Best Friend was sitting on the sofa, waiting impatiently for Starlette and Heartthob to come down the stairs with the vital information that would lead them back to Bookworm.

Emma was still sitting behind the potted plant, but she had moved slightly to one side, so that she could see Wacky Best Friend more easily.

"Why are you here?" she asked.

"Selling candy for school," he replied.

"Mommy and Daddy don't like me to eat candy. They say that it rots teeth the same way that Hollywood power couples rot society."

"That's nice."

"But I eat candy when I go over to Alicia's house. And we play with dolls and pretend that they're people and that they like to eat candy too."

Wacky Best Friend turned and looked at Emma. He asked, "You like playing make believe?"

"Yeah," Emma replied, in a tone that sounded as though she

was incredibly disinterested in the conversation, but she continued to speak anyway. "I like pretending that I'm all grown up and I have a family and I can bake cookies and I like to kill actors."

"Well, aren't you just... horrifying." Wacky Best Friend smiled.

"Daddy says that when I grow up I can go to work with him," Emma went on, completely ignoring what Wacky Best Friend had said.

When she said this, a light bulb went off in his head. He imagined himself as a little boy, with his father sitting on the floor with him, telling him all about deli meat. His father loved to go on about the family business and how it would all one day be passed down to the next generation.

Thinking back, Wacky Best Friend decided that he probably should have considered this option more carefully. Now, he wondered... What would it be like to grow up in a house that was led by an evil Bookworm minion? What ideals would be passed down? What information?

"Do you want to work with your Daddy?" he asked her.

Emma nodded, "Yeah. Daddy gets to drive a really cool car when he's at work. And he gets to tie people up. And he gets to cut into them. I like pretending that I work with Daddy and I use squirrels like they're actors."

"Aww. That's adorable," Wacky Best Friend cringed, moving just slightly farther away from Emma. "Does Daddy ever take you to work with him?"

"He takes me to work on *Take Your Daughter To Work Day*. And on *Earth Day*, because it's important to understand that our planet is dying and we need to respect it and not waste any more natural resources on producing bad movies."

"That's right! And do you know *where* your Daddy works?" he pressed.

Emma just nodded in response. Wacky Best Friend smiled at this.

"Think you could draw me a map?"

~

"...and he tells me that he wants to quit his job at this big company, where he makes a great living. He wants to go back to school, so he can feel more fulfilled in life. Whatever that means," Mrs. Carter told Girl Next Door, as she crimped the edges of the pie crust.

Girl Next Door was sitting on the counter, watching Mrs. Carter make the pie. She shook her head in response, saying, "Isn't that just typical? *They* want to feel fulfilled. Well, that's great. He goes and follows his heart or whatever, and you're still stuck here baking pies."

"I like baking pies. I have a degree in the culinary arts. I spent three years in France, learning how to cook from some of the top chefs," Mrs. Carter replied.

Girl Next Door shook her head with sympathy and said, "You poor woman."

"I marched in several anti-war protests back in the day too. I led my feminist study group in a *Take Back The Night* campaign. I once went to *Lilith Fair* and made out with a woman who had a mustache... Or, it might have been a monkey. I don't know. I was on a lot of shit that night."

Girl Next Door gasped and smiled as she said, "Oh my god, I went to college and pretended that I was a normal person for a while. I knew people just like you! We handed out flyers and yelled things at people and nodded our heads a lot like we understood things. Best. Week. Ever. I was researching a role. I was gonna play this lesbian college student in the 1970's who led a revolt and found love in the process. Only, I didn't get it. They said I wasn't gay enough."

Mrs. Carter didn't respond. Girl Next Door just smiled and nodded at her fond memories. She then turned her attention back to Mrs. Carter and said, "So, here you are, tied down to some crazed Christian extremist who likes to kill people. How does that happen?"

"Oh, no," Mrs. Carter smiled, as she brushed the pie with an egg wash and sprinkled it with sugar. "The only thing my husband hates more than celebrities are Christians."

"Really? Are you sure? 'Cause Political Advisor's character breakdown pretty clearly said—"

"Let's go!" came Starlette's voice from the other room.

~

Starlette and Heartthrob made their way down the stairs with haste. Their job was finished, and they had no desire to hang around that house.

Girl Next Door and Mrs. Carter hurried from the kitchen and met them in the foyer. Mrs. Carter seemed panicked when she saw Heartthrob's hands, which were covered in blood.

"Oh no. Please..." Mrs. Carter said, starting to cry. "My husband... Please tell me that he's still alive."

Starlette and Heartthrob exchanged a look. They both knew the answer to that question, and neither one of them wanted to be the one to deliver the news to the woman who would undoubtedly let out an ear-breaking scream.

Instead of answering the woman outright, Starlette simply said, "I guess it's possible."

She then turned her attention to Girl Next Door and asked, "Where is Wacky Best Friend? We need to get out of here. Now."

"He's watching the kid in the living room, so I could interrogate the wife in the kitchen," Girl Next Door told her.

Starlette turned to Heartthrob and said, "Get him."

With a nod, Heartthrob turned and headed for the living room. Once he was gone, Starlette looked to Mrs. Carter and said to her, "No matter what you see when you go upstairs, you will not tell anyone who was here. You will not describe us. You will not provide any details as to who did this. Do you understand me? We know where you live. We know where your daughter lives. We probably won't hurt her, but we know where she is. That's all I'm saying."

Mrs. Carter nodded as she held back sobs. She looked toward the stairs, wanting to run up them and see what had been done to her husband. Starlette couldn't help but think that if the woman knew what she would find, she would not be in so much of a hurry.

Within seconds, Hartthrob returned with Wacky Best Friend, who was shoving papers into his pocket. Starlette hoped that whatever he'd found in his search of the house, it was more than what she'd managed to get out of Michael Carter.

Once her team was assembled in the foyer, Starlette led the

way out of the house.

They rushed across the lawn, and down the street, where a van would be picking them up shortly. Moments after leaving the house, Mrs. Carter's scream could be heard across the entire neighborhood.

~

On the ride out of the suburbs, Starlette, Girl Next Door, Heartthrob and Wacky Best Friend all kept their eyes on the scenery around them. They watched as children ran and played in the sun. They observed the freedom of the fresh air from the safety of their heavily armored van. They looked across a world which seemed untouched and unchanged since the attacks, and none of them said a word.

~

The Director stood at the front of the conference room, as members of the various departments watched.

The actors sat in their normal chairs, with their minds drifting. They didn't listen to the discussion. They didn't watch the dailies, which played on the screens behind The Director. All that was displayed was the image of the suburban home from the outside, where the cameras could most safely observe without becoming a part of the action. They showed nothing of what occurred within.

"This shoot did not go according to plan," The Director said.

As those words were spoken, Wacky Best Friend glanced up and saw Head Writer looking his way and shaking his head.

"The interrogation of Michael Carter did not prove fruitful. What we walked away with... We have scraps. In her search of Carter's bedroom, Starlette managed to find this..." The Director said, holding up a plain white card, with a microchip built into it. "It appears to be a passkey. To what? We're not exactly sure. With luck, it will grant us access to one of Bookworm's buildings in the area. We just have to find out where this building is. To aid us in this search, Wacky Best Friend has retrieved some documents, which we have dubbed the Emma Carter Papers..."

Images began to flash across the monitors behind The Director. The images were of crudely drawn maps, with strange symbols and doodles which were meant to represent landmarks or street names. They could not be read. There were pictures of what appeared to be buildings, but which could have also been streets... or maybe trees. There were doodles of ponies and fish with smiley faces. There were scribbles and doodles.

As these images scrolled across the screen, they were accompanied by rather high-tech looking computer graphics which seemed to be scanning the documents and running some sort of advanced algorithms.

"The Emma Carter Papers currently provide us with our best hope of finding the location of the Bookworm stronghold. We have some of our best interns researching these papers, and it is our hope that with time, we might be able to discern their meaning. Until then, we will continue to do what we always do. We will fight. We will persevere. We will work toward a better tomorrow. Our work is far from over in this Studio, but we will win this war. One day, we will bathe in sunlight and breathe the more-or-less fresh ocean air. Each night brings with it the dawn of a new day," The Director told them. "Our day has not yet begun."

A round of applause rose across the room, and it spread throughout The Studio, where The Director's speech had been displayed on various monitors. The Studio was inspired to fight another day.

And the actors sat quietly.

~

"I feel like we should be in deep, reflective thought," Ember said as she towel-dried her hair and plopped down into the lawn chair next to Ethan. "I'm just not sure what my character should be reflecting on, so I'm just kinda doing this blank stare thing."

"You look very deep," Ethan replied.

Ember smiled and said, "Thanks. I've been practicing in front of a mirror."

Heartthrob walked out of his trailer, carrying a small cooler full of drinks and a radio, which was tuned to the only station that could be received within The Studio. It was an oldies station, which broadcast from within The Studio, thanks to a crew member's MP3 player and an FM transmitter which was meant for use in a car but had been craftily adapted to suit their needs.

He placed these things down in front of the lawn furniture and handed drinks to his two co-stars.

"Is it always like this?" Heartthrob asked. "Is it always bloody and violent?"

"Pretty much," Ethan replied.

Ember agreed, "Yup."

Heartthrob nodded and took a deep breath. He then said, "Good."

As they raised their drinks to another day of survival, Starlette emerged from her trailer, still in wardrobe. Her costars smiled as they saw her, and Heartthrob fished another drink from the cooler.

"Join us?" he asked her, holding out the drink.

Starlette accepted the drink and popped it open, but shook her head.

"Another time," she told them. "I have something I need to take care of."

She waved goodbye and headed off with her beverage in hand, leaving her co-stars behind.

They drank and laughed and listened to music, long into the night.

~

High above the city, Tessa Baker stood in her penthouse with all of the lights turned off. She had her curtains opened, and she watched the city below. It was dark and motionless. Far from the city that she had lived in and loved for so many years.

She held a drink in one hand and a cigarette in the other, daring someone to notice the glow of her cigarette as she took a puff. It was worth the risk.

Though she heard no noise and saw no reflection in the window before her, Tessa knew that someone was standing behind her. She smiled.

"You've returned once again," she said.

Starlette walked to her side and looked out the window. She said, "You were right. There are things that you can teach me. I'm not leaving The Studio and you don't have to come back there, but... I failed today. I dropped character, for just a second. He saw it. The man that I was questioning—he saw that I wasn't willing hurt his child; to be a monster."

"You sound ashamed of that," Tessa grinned, taking a sip of her drink.

Starlette hesitated for a moment before she replied. "More… surprised. I thought I was better than that. I thought that—"

"You thought that who you were going into all of this was dead. You thought that you were the beast that everyone expects you to be," Tessa nodded. "You play a bitch, so you're seen as a bitch. You play a victim, so you're seen as a victim. The truth is, no matter what they say in acting class, there is no *becoming* the character. The best we can hope for is the ability to empathize with the character. Your mistake wasn't feeling disgusted by the thought. Your mistake was allowing that disgust to show through your character. Your feelings should push you further, not hold you back."

"Further? You think that I should have used the kid?" Starlette asked.

"Dear God! We're actors! We *act*! *Act* as though you will use the child. Pretend that you will cut the man's finger off."

"I did cut his finger off."

"Well… Bully for you then," Tessa shrugged. "The problem with your generation is that you forget the craft of it all. Kids today play every part as though that character is just themselves on a bad day. *Seeming* natural doesn't mean that it must *be* natural. Our job is to project, not to be. You must know your movements. You must control them. You must not allow yourself to get carried away by the scene, because the moment someone throws an unexpected line at you, your eyes will betray you. Your eyes are the enemy, no matter who you may happen to be shooting at the time."

Starlette turned to look at Tessa, but Tessa did not meet her eyes. She continued to look out across the city, seeing it not as it was in that moment, but as it had once been.

Starlette said, "What happens if I don't know where the line is anymore? What if I don't know where Starlette ends? What if I can't go back when this is all over?"

Tessa laughed and finally turned to look at Starlette as she said, "This will never be over, dear. Your Studio simply will not allow it."

Tessa took another puff of her cigarette and a sip of her drink as Starlette watched her. She seemed so calm and collected for a woman in her situation. She seemed to somehow know things which Starlette did not—Things which Starlette wasn't sure she wanted to know at all.

Chapter Seven
THE CRIME SCENE

Starlette stood near one of the pillars on the stage and a smile formed on her face. She was just barely breaking a sweat. Ethan, on the other hand, was on the ground and looked as though he had just come in from the rain.

"I'm good," he told her, staying down. "I'll be back up again in no time. Really."

"We can just call it a day," she replied.

"No. No way. I'm not leaving here until I kick your ass."

He turned over and pushed himself off of the ground and to his feet. He took a moment to catch his breath, holding up a finger to let her know that he'd be with her again shortly.

"I was just letting you get a head start," he let her know.

She nodded, pretending to believe him. The smile on her face might have made it hard for him to believe her.

Life in The Studio could be taxing. There was no sunrise or sunset. There were only call times and lunch breaks. If you weren't on the schedule, you could find your life following the time zone of a country on the other side of the world. Too many night shoots took their toll on some, but Starlette preferred the darkness. The sun was a liar. It made things seem bright and hopeful, but the city that it shined down upon remained comatose.

At times, Starlette got the impression that some crew members disliked the actors. It could have been because the actors were living the life that many of those crew members once dreamed of. A number of them had hoped to be actors and to have their moment of glory. Most of those had settled into other positions because they loved the craft and wanted to remain a part of it. Others only took those jobs temporarily and were now locked into them due to the attacks. She couldn't blame them for holding a grudge against the actors who did get the opportunity to step out in front of the cameras and shoot the crap out of the bad guys.

Nobody voiced these grudges, but their eyes told the story. It wasn't all of the crew members. Just enough to make that line between cast and crew seem bold and impassable. It hadn't always been this way. In the years before the attacks, cast and crew were like family, joined by marriage and partnering in the creation of something important and beautiful.

In the months that followed the attacks, when The Studio was first coming together, this union held. Actors and crew members smiled and shared the dream of working together to bring down Bookworm and his minions, and to avenge the death of the Hollywood dream. But life can be a bitch at times, and the longer the cast and crew remained underground, the less time they spent laughing and dreaming with each other. With the passing of months and losses that only the actors could truly understand, the marriage had become strained. Now, each member of The Studio seemed to spend their off hours amongst their own kind. Within those circles, each cast seemed to form their own clique.

This was the saving grace of Studio life for Starlette. Without the friendships that she had formed with the actors with whom she worked, she didn't know what would have happened to her.

After so much loss and so much suffering, the possibility of falling into an emotional pit so dark and so cold that no humanity could survive was very real.

She was hardly the most social member of her cast. Rumors had circulated in the past, depicting Starlette as a snob who didn't want to spend her off hours with her co-stars. Stories were told in whispers, depicting Starlette as someone who demanded every little detail of every shoot to be exactly to her liking. The truth was, she didn't enjoy being around many people. Usually, she wanted to do her job and go home. She didn't want to talk about it. She didn't want to stand around, telling the story of where she was when the attacks happened. She didn't want to walk down memory lane with crew members who brought up those actors who hadn't made it this far.

The funny part was, she didn't hate people. She just hated when the only subjects that they brought up were the worst moments that she had ever been forced to experience; the moments that she relived on a regular basis, in her own mind.

With her co-stars, there was a deeper connection. She didn't have to say how deeply she hurt, because they knew. Each of them had experienced the same loss, and they saw the same bloody battles that she did, while shooting was taking place. They didn't press her to share. They didn't need to make awkward conversation about it. The subject was always there, but so was the unspoken understanding.

The result of this understanding was the ability to let her guard down and not worry about being punched in the gut by an unexpected reference to tragedies. She could just... be. The reason why those who didn't know her well thought of her as a bitch was because those who didn't know her well rarely knew her at all. They never saw her smile and joke around.

"If you want, I could spar with one hand tied behind my back," she offered Ethan.

He considered this offer for a moment. He looked off to the side and seemed to be deep in thought, and then he turned back to Starlette and said, "Would you be willing to go blindfolded?"

"I would, but Studio policy would probably require a stunt double for that sort of thing," she replied.

"Figures. Send us out to get shot at, but slap on a blindfold and they're suddenly worried about liability."

"Well, you know... they have to make sure we don't get injured during the shooting season."

Ethan cocked his head slightly and asked, "Is there an off-season?"

"Probably," Starlette answered. "I'm sure we'll get time off just as soon as this whole Bookworm arc is resolved."

"Unless it's a cliffhanger. Then we pick up right where we left off," Ethan noted.

"Which just means we have to kill the crap out of him, so there's no chance of a *to be continued*."

"Do you ever think we're taking this shtick too far?"

Starlette smiled at Ethan. She grabbed a bottle of water from a nearby cooler and brought it to him. As he drank, she said, "In the spirit of awkward segues... I recently discovered an aging actress in an abandoned building, and I've been going to her apartment so that she could impart her wisdom on me."

Ethan had a mouthful of water when he lowered the bottle and looked Starlette in the eyes. He didn't swallow right away, because he wasn't sure quite how he wanted to react. For a moment, Starlette thought that he might go for a spit-take, but he wasn't that kind of wacky.

When he did manage to swallow the water, Ethan turned away from her and gathered his thoughts. He then looked back to her and asked, "Why would you tell me this?"

"Because... Why wouldn't I?" she replied.

"Because!" was his very meaningful answer. "Does she have a name?"

"Tessa Baker."

His eyes widened and he put his hands on his head. This was big news for him. Very big.

"Stage name! I meant *stage* name! I don't need to know her real name!" he yelled.

"That is her stage name," Starlette told him. "Funny story, really. See, she was born—"

"No! Stop! Just... stop."

Ethan walked to one of the steps, near one of the giant fake-stone pillars. He sat down and tried to make sense of this situation in his head. Starlette sat next to him.

"She doesn't want to come into The Studio," she said, settling into the conversation.

Ethan nodded, understanding. After remaining silent for a few moments, he turned to Starlette and said, "Say nothing to anyone else. If The Director or Head Writer or any of the production staff ever find out that you told me this, they'll be pissed."

"I don't get it. Why?"

"Because... You're supposed to drag this secret out for an unnaturally long amount of time. Then it's supposed to come out in some big dramatic way that causes a stir throughout the entire Studio. If they find out that you're just willy-nilly telling people about this shady mentor figure... Starlette, this is a basic formula situation. You have to be careful with something like this. It has to be by the book. That means secrecy and suspicion, followed by a covert investigation and questions into your loyalty and trustworthiness."

"It's not that big a deal," she argued. "It's just some woman who doesn't want to come in."

Ethan seemed to grow more concerned by the moment, as the news of Starlette's interaction with Tessa sunk in. He leaned in a little bit closer and lowered his voice much more as he told her, "Tessa Baker isn't *some woman*. She's a person who could have influence within The Studio. She's a seasoned veteran. If she casts doubt on anything that's going on here, she could stir up a lot of dust. Be careful with this."

Starlette nodded her understanding of his warning. She didn't fully understand why it should be such a big deal, but if Ethan was warning her to tread lightly, that's what she would do. She trusted him and Ember more than anyone else in The Studio.

She said nothing else to Ethan before his eyes moved past her, to the entrance to the stage and he straightened up just a little bit. When she saw this, Starlette turned to see what he was looking at.

The Director walked onto the stage, carrying a folder along with him—He always seemed to be carrying a folder. Usually, it contained a new script or some sort of vital information. When she saw the folder, she knew that a shoot was being scheduled.

That made her happy.

Any hint of the smile that had been on her face while talking to Ethan was gone by the time The Director approached. She was all business now, as was Wacky Best Friend.

"Starlette," The Director said as he approached. "A moment of your time, please."

Starlette nodded and stepped toward him. Wacky Best Friend stayed back, pretending to study the craftsmanship of the stage.

"You're being sent out tonight," The Director told her.

"Where?" Starlette replied.

"Nothing fancy. It's strictly B-unit," The Director began to explain, but Starlette looked puzzled by this.

"Wait... if I'm on the team, doesn't that make it A-unit? Isn't this like Air Force One or something?" she asked him.

The Director smiled and said, "If that's how you want to look at it. Point is, it's just you and a small team. We want to test some new camera equipment in the field, so it's mostly pickup shots and b-roll. Some establishing shots of the streets. Stuff like that."

"Why are you sending me? Isn't this a job for the photo doubles?"

"Normally, maybe. But we want to really get in there and test this new equipment. Since we're limited in how we can use the doubles, and we don't want to pay stunt double salaries, we're using you. It might be boring, but it needs to get done. So, get Girl Next Door and Heartthrob and be ready to leave in two hours."

Wacky Best Friend stopped pretending to care about the scenery. He looked over at The Director, but The Director didn't meet his look.

Starlette wasn't sure what to make of the directions that she'd been given. She asked, "What about Wacky Best Friend?"

The Director hesitated for a moment and looked down to the folder before telling her, "We really didn't need the whole team for this one. It's just a small job. Nothing to worry about. He can sit this one out."

Starlette's mouth fell open, just slightly. Wacky Best Friend was as vital as Girl Next Door and more experienced than Heartthrob. She couldn't understand what reason there could be for leaving him off the call sheet.

The Director could obviously tell what she was thinking, but he offered no further information. He barely met her eyes, which told her that something was going on, and he didn't seem any more pleased by this turn of events than she did.

"Assemble your co-stars. Be in costume and ready to roll in two hours," The Director told her, and walked away.

Starlette was left standing there, in complete disbelief. She didn't know if this feeling was written all over her face, or if she had managed to maintain her steely character. She didn't care. Whatever was going on, she didn't like it.

Disbelief soon turned to anger. She turned to face Wacky Best Friend, whose mind was a million miles away. The look in his eyes told her that he was worried.

"I will get to the bottom of this," she promised him. "You are on *my* cast. I will get answers."

Ethan's eyes slowly drifted up to meet hers and she could see that his mind was racing. He wasn't scared exactly. He was thinking; calculating. Coming up with whatever course of action he would decide to take.

When he met her eyes, he shook his head and told her, "Don't do anything. Just leave this alone."

"The hell I will," she began to argue, but he stopped her.

"You will. You have to," he insisted. "Whatever this is, it's not your concern. I will not be responsible for dragging you into my problems."

"This isn't just your problem. I depend on you out there. I need you."

Ethan smiled as she said this. Whatever concern that had been in his eyes seemed to wash away.

"You don't need me," he told her, seemingly amused by her comment. "You're Starlette. The rest of us are just... filler."

"Ethan—"

"Don't worry about it. I'm fine. It's one shoot, and it's not even an important one. I'll be back out there with you for the next one," he smiled. "You should hit the showers. I really made you work during that sparring session. I'll let the others know that you're going out."

He walked past her and off the stage. Just like that.

Though Ethan had tried to play down the severity of the situation, Starlette knew better. She could see past his Wacky Best Friend act, and she knew that this turn of events was troubling him... and with good reason.

~

When Ethan got back to the trailers, he found Ember sitting on the front steps of her trailer with a notebook in hand and a pen tucked behind her ear. It was unusual to find her looking busy, but she seemed deep in thought as she stared at that notebook.

Though his mind was racing with all sorts of unpleasant thoughts, Ethan didn't blurt the situation out to her. He simply stood in front of her, waiting for her to look up, with a look of disbelief in his eyes.

When she looked up at him, she silently asked what he wanted with a faintly sibling-like annoyance in her eyes.

"I know you're probably swamped with incredibly deep thoughts," he told her, "but The Director wants you and Heartthrob suited up and ready to roll in two hours."

Ember lowered her notebook and seemed to grow more interested in Ethan when it became apparent that he was there on business. She asked "Where?"

"I think it's some equipment test or something. I don't know. Just make sure that the two of you are ready when you need to be."

After passing along the message, Ethan began to walk away from the trailers. As he walked, Ember called after him, "Shouldn't you take a shower? Wardrobe doesn't like when you start the day out all sweaty and gross."

"I'm not going with you, so it doesn't matter," he replied.

Ember chased after him and cut him off. She stood in front of him, now silently asking what was going on. He didn't immediately answer.

"Oh," Ember smiled, looking off into the distance. "I get it. You're too big and fancy for us now, with your super exciting writing career. You can't slum it on ho-hum shoots anymore."

He didn't respond, for fear that whatever he said would be dripping with a truth that he didn't wish to pass on to her just yet. He didn't want her to go on location with anything but a clear mind.

Ember continued to smile as she took on a rather excessive amount of sarcasm. She said, "That's cool. I get it. I'm actually thinking of branching out m'self. I have a log line all ready to go. Workin' up my pitch now. It's gonna be awesome. Way better than your stupid script."

"You don't wanna go there, Ember. Trust me."

"*Pshh!* I got this thing nailed, little man. I'm talking straight up musical episode, filled to the top with completely random pre-existing pop songs that I'll write the whole thing around. None of us will be in character. It won't make a lick of sense... I'm telling you, it's gonna be a ratings bo-nan-za."

Ethan couldn't help but smile at her. She did have a way of amusing him, even when he felt like worrying and brooding.

"Are you laughing at my musical idea?" she demanded.

"No," he replied, in a calm and steady tone. "I think it's brilliant. You should totally get on that."

"I will. And don't be surprised if you wind up in a blond wig and platform shoes, mister."

"Again?"

She didn't have a snappy comeback for that one. She just smiled, but narrowed her eyes just slightly, as though trying to read his mind. She then looked down at her notebook and said, "Well, I should go get ready. I have some cookies in the oven. I really think they might be edible this time."

"Awesome. I'll see you when you get back."

"See ya," she said, turning back toward her trailer and leaving him behind as she walked.

As Ethan watched her go, Heartthrob walked up beside him and patted him on the shoulder as he said, "Hey, man. I think I might have a lead on a possible *Pac-Man* coffee table arcade that's packed away in the storage section. Wanna help me dig it out later?"

Ethan looked Heartthrob squarely in the eyes and replied, "Yes. Yes I would."

~

Prop Master stood next to Starlette, looking over the camera equipment that Camera One was attaching to her outfit. It was small, lightweight and blended into her clothing well enough to remain inconspicuous. Still, he didn't seem convinced.

"We've seen the spy-cams before. The quality isn't high enough to blend with the standard cameras," he said to Camera One.

Camera One ran a cable around to Starlette's back, where he plugged her camera into a discrete battery pack. He shook his head and adjusted his baseball cap as he looked to Prop Master and told him, "This is new technology. We had some new chips smuggled in from Dallas. The quality should be there, in theory. New sensors. New lenses. I think they could work, but I'm concerned about battery life and the stabilizing software. I'm just not sure it's up to the challenge, given the type of action the actors normally see."

"And if they work, you'll have eyes on us for every shoot we're on? From now on, everything we say and see will be recorded? Like, close up?" Starlette asked, not masking her concern over the idea as well as she would have liked.

"That's the plan," Camera One told her.

"Neat," she came back.

She looked to Prop Master, who could tell that she wasn't thrilled with the idea of being filmed close up for every second of each shoot. Up until this point, they had relied on carefully positioned cameras to get shots from a distance. While inside a building, Starlette could go off-script when she saw fit, and the audio that was recorded for review at The Studio would rarely reflect just how far she strayed.

"The video will be compressed and saved to a drive that's built into the battery pack... I'm not sure how much we'll be able to store or whether the compression will hurt the quality. I'm hoping that this new algorithm will prevent degradation in the decompression process," Camera One went on.

Starlette and Prop Master looked at each other. They understood enough about what Camera One was saying, but neither had a response which seemed intelligent enough to say aloud.

"During the testing, I want you to go about a normal walk-through in the city. Head into buildings. We might have you spar a little bit, just to see how well the camera holds up during an action sequence," Camera One told her. "And let me know how comfortable it is. We don't want you too distracted by this thing."

While Camera One was fixing Starlette's camera, Camera Two was doing the same for Girl Next Door and Camera Three was working on Heartthrob. While Camera One and Camera Two seemed perfectly content to run wires and affix their cameras over the clothes of the actresses, Camera Three had insisted on Heartthrob removing his shirt, so they could test the cameras when they were run beneath clothing.

Starlette couldn't help but imagine Ethan rolling his eyes and making a snarky comment as Heartthrob once again found himself shirtless in the middle of The Studio.

She looked around the area and noticed a growing audience for Heartthrob's camera adjustments. It didn't exactly put a smile on her face, but she grinned on the inside.

As her mind drifted toward concerns for Ethan, Starlette looked to Prop Master, and she could see that he was reading her expression. When her eyes met his, he nodded just slightly. What he meant by this, she wasn't exactly sure.

~

While his cast was gearing up and preparing to hit the streets for a night of equipment testing and adventure, Ethan turned his attention to toward the craft service table. Since he wouldn't need to worry about high paced excitement on that night, he was willing to weigh himself down with empty carbs.

He browsed the table, choosing to ignore the deli meat platter and the baby carrots. He wondered what type of person actually enjoyed eating baby carrots as a snack, when not being forced at gunpoint. When he was a child, his mother regularly put them into his lunchbox, next to his sandwich, and snack-sized container of pudding. Somehow, little Ethan always seemed to grow full just before he got around to the carrots.

When his mother found out that he'd been selling his carrots to Gabby Wheeler for fifty cents each day, she let it be known in no uncertain terms that she was not pleased. From that point on, he found steamed carrots, mashed and spread across his sandwich like mayonnaise. He greatly preferred the baby carrots packed separately; especially on days when his mother made peanut butter and jelly.

He picked up a handful of chocolate chip cookies and put one in his mouth as he continued to browse the table. He put bite-sized candy bars in his pockets and a piece of licorice behind his ear.

"Wow," mused a female voice from behind him.

Ethan turned around and found the woman smiling at him, with her hands on her perfectly shaped hips. She had long red hair, which was flawlessly styled. She had polished nails and silver bracelets which looked as though they might actually be her own, and not the property of Wardrobe.

When she smiled at Ethan, she had a look in her eyes, as though she knew him. If they'd met before, he certainly didn't remember it.

"You're one of those emotional eaters, aren't you? Rough day, sweetheart?" she asked.

Ethan swallowed the cookie that was in his mouth and stepped toward her. He was trying to remember if they'd met and he had just forgotten her somehow... but it wasn't likely, considering how hot she was.

"Do we know each other?" he asked.

"Not really. I did background dancing in a commercial you did once. Remember, you were all *'Drink this cola, because it's really good'* or whatever, and there were about twenty desperate little things dancing behind you for some reason?"

"Yeah, I remember..."

"I was one of the desperate little things!" she smiled, walking toward him and extending a hand. "I'm Songstress, but my friends call me Sing."

"Were your parents psychic, or is that a stage name?" he replied, feeling very good about the smoothness of his delivery.

She walked past him, to the baby carrots and prepared to put one in her mouth. She said, "Funny, *Wacky Best Friend*. Mind if I call you Ethan? I never did like the name they stuck you with."

The sound of his own name surprised him. It was unusual for anyone to know his real name, considering the fact that he hadn't exactly been famous before the attacks. Given the day he'd been having up to that point, the sound of his own name was especially powerful when she said it.

"You know my name," he commented, removing the licorice from behind his ear and stuffing it into his pocket.

"You were the star of the commercial. I was absolutely captivated by you. The way you delivered that line was nothing short of inspired."

He picked up a hint of a southern accent now, and her entire personality was coming into focus. The perfect hair and makeup, despite the fact that she wasn't on a shoot. This was a southern woman.

"You seem to have the advantage here. I don't remember seeing you around The Studio," he said, still desperately searching his memory for any hint of her.

She nodded, grabbing a stick of celery, "Well you wouldn't have seen me. The way they hide my cast away, I'm pretty sure they've forgotten about us completely. Which is why I had to sneak out here... Y'all get the good snacks."

"Are you sure you know what snacks are? Because all I see you taking is rabbit food."

Sing shook her head and waved a finger at him, saying, "Uh-uh. Never do that. You never comment on the food that a girl's taking. It makes us self-conscious."

"Sorry. I didn't mean to—"

"Don't worry about it. I'm not as fragile as I *look*."

"You don't look fragile."

She smiled at him again and said, "We're all fragile these days. I'm just not as fragile as I look."

It was his turn to smile now. There was something about this girl that he couldn't quite put his finger on, but which made him want to keep talking to her for as long as he possibly could. Unfortunately, she turned away from the table and started to walk away.

"I better get back before the keeper knows I'm gone," she said as she walked.

He turned to watch her leave and called after her, asking, "What cast are you on? Where do they keep you, exactly."

She turned around and asked, "Are you planning to come looking?"

"I think I might, if I manage to live through the night."

"The amount of cookies you've been eating, I'm not so sure you will," she said. "But if you do, just walk the way I'm going until you find a dark and ominous hallway. Go down that, until you find a big and ominous door. Walk through that, into the incredibly flashy and not-so-ominous room, and ask for me."

She waved goodbye and walked away, chewing on a baby carrot as she went.

He watched her go... for a nice long while.

It was only after she was gone that he was able to think about the directions that she'd given him, and where those directions led. He knew that hallway, though he'd never walked down it. It was the hallway which led to a cast of the super elite. They were known as the *Triple Threats*, and called only under the most incredibly dire of circumstances.

No such circumstance had actually arisen yet... which just went to show how elite they were.

"Strange day," Ethan said to himself, as he grabbed another piece of licorice and stuck it behind his ear. "Very strange day."

He began to walk away from the snacks, toward his trailer. His mind was a million miles away, trying to recall that commercial that he'd been a part of, and the dancers behind him.

He was caught entirely off guard—and off balance—as Prop Master grabbed him and pulled him between two of the office trailers. Wacky Best Friend nearly fell over as Prop Master spoke.

"I noticed that you weren't on the call sheet," Prop Master said.

"Yeah, I—"

"I know what's going on. Starlette told me some and I guessed the rest. Take this..."

Prop Master shoved a small handgun into Wacky Best Friend's hand. Wacky Best Friend wasn't sure what to make of this gesture at first. He didn't know what he was supposed to do with the gun, seeing as how he didn't have a shoot to go on.

"Keep it on you. Hidden," Prop Master told him. "It's not logged in the system. Nobody will miss it. If you need to get out of here, you should have enough shots to get to the door. After that, just run and don't look back."

Wacky Best Friend said nothing in response. He didn't know

what he was supposed to say or think in that moment. Prop
Master didn't wait around for him to respond anyway. Before
Ethan could gather his thoughts, Prop Master was gone.

Ethan looked down at the gun and then stuffed it into the back
of his pants. He pulled his shirt over it and began to walk toward
his trailer once again, muttering along the way, "Strange day."

He made his way through The Studio and to the grouping of
trailers where he and his co-stars lived. He barely paid any
attention to where he was going, as his mind worked its way
down twisted paths of potential danger and exciting redheaded
actresses.

Because he was distracted, Ethan almost didn't see the two
rather muscular Studio security guards standing outside his
trailer, waiting for him to return. When he looked up and saw
them talking to each other, Ethan almost missed his chance to
duck behind Heartthrob's trailer, so that he wouldn't be seen.

There could have been any number of reasons why they would
be sent to Wacky Best Friend's trailer, but seeing them there sent
Ethan into full alert. Why two of them? Why get him when his co-
stars were away?

If he hadn't seen similar situations play out before, he probably
wouldn't have thought twice about it. But there were one or two
occasions when actors would be walked off to a meeting of some
sort, never to be heard from again. Their careers were over and
they were either dead or turned out onto the streets. It was hard
to say which fate would be worse.

When Ethan turned in his script, he knew that there were risks
involved. He knew that The Director might not like it. He knew
that Head Writer could resent him. He also knew that he was
blurring a line that no other actor in The Studio had dared to
approach since the attacks. He was upsetting the status quo, and
there was no telling what the repercussions would be for that.

The script had gone over well and the project had been given
the green light, but he received no credit for his work. Ripples had
been made on that day, and how far they would reach was
anybody's guess. Odds were, Studio Head would wish to nip the
situation in the bud, preventing Wacky Best Friend from telling
anyone that he was behind that script before ripples could turn

into waves.

He had good reason to worry. Token Black Guy had been disappeared for far less. From that day forward, Wacky Best Friend and most of the other actors in The Studio knew that this game had very strict rules and that Studio Head was sitting at the judge's table, taking notes and keeping tabs.

As he hid behind Heartthrob's trailer, Ethan didn't know what his plan would be. If he made a break for the exit, he might be able to get to the streets, but he had no supplies. He had nowhere to run. At the same time, he had no other choice. Time was of the essence.

He crept between trailers until he could be sure that those guards wouldn't see him leaving and when he reached the open floor of The Studio, he kept his eyes forward and walked quickly. Once he reached the doors, he hoped that nobody would notice or try to stop him. Starlette was more or less free to roam around because she was a lead actress and could afford to make demands of The Studio. Wacky Best Friend was—apparently—very expendable. For all he knew, they would open fire as soon as he was spotted.

His breathing was remarkably normal for such a high stress situation. His heart was not pounding in his chest, as he would have expected it to. He was too focused on the plot that was unfolding and his brain was doing all of the racing that his body needed.

It was going well. It was going *really* well, as far as he could tell. Nobody had stopped him. Nobody had yelled for guards to come and drag him away. Ethan was beginning to think that he just might make it out of there alive when he was grabbed by the arm and pulled behind some lighting equipment by The Director.

"What are you doing?" The Director asked.

Wacky Best Friend didn't know what he was supposed to say. What he heard come out of his mouth was, "Eating cookies."

"You're planning to run," The Director continued. "I can't let you do that."

"You'd rather see me die?"

"I have been trying to protect you from this. I will keep trying to protect you from this, but you have to realize that if you run, there's no coming back. Running now is career suicide. You might as well audition for a reality show after this."

"Well, staying here isn't really an option anymore, is it?"

"You don't have any other option. Out there, you will die."

"What else can I do?"

"Come with me. You're scheduled to meet with Studio Head."

"Like, in person? He never sees anyone in person."

"Over the phone. I'll be in there with you."

"And what happens in this meeting?"

"You make your case. Prove that you're role here is integral to the plot."

"And if he still decides that I should be killed off?"

The Director looked away and shook his head. He said, "I don't have all of the answers for you. All I have is your best option right now."

Wacky Best Friend said nothing right away. He looked at The Director, asking himself whether or not he could trust him. He thought about his options and his potential for survival. After seconds of deep and careful consideration, he decided.

"Well okay then," Wacky Best Friend declared, pulling a bite-sized candy bar from his pocket. "Let's do this thing."

~

Starlette hated equipment testing and wardrobe testing and any other type of testing that didn't push her any closer to taking down Bookworm once and for all. She found the process of being driven out to the middle of the city and dropped off so that she could roam through random buildings to be boring.

She had more pressing concerns on her mind. Just before she left The Studio, Wacky Best Friend had found himself in the middle of a more serious situation. She worried about him, but tried not to let it show as she went about her business.

Upon their arrival in the city, Starlette, Girl Next Door and Heartthrob began testing the cameras which were attached to their clothing. They were small and discrete, though there were little red lights which came to life whenever the camera was filming. For some reason, all of the high-tech equipment in The Studio had lights. Red lights, blue lights, blinking lights... Tracking devices which would otherwise go unnoticed were routinely discovered because of their large blinking lights and beeping sounds.

Sure, Prop Master had tried to take the lights out of his designs on many occasions, but the higher-ups wanted more style and flare. They wanted the audience to know that these devices were very high-tech, even if there was no audience tuning in at the time.

It had become a joke between Starlette and Prop Master, but both of them seemed to share in the belief that they would have tracked down Bookworm a lot sooner if their tracking devices had been more discrete.

After a few flips and punches into thin air, Starlette was already feeling bored with the camera testing. She told Girl Next Door and Heartthrob that they could collect situational samples if they split up and roamed through different buildings. So, that's what they did.

A half hour after splitting up, they were beginning to meet up in their agreed upon spot. As Starlette approached the area, she saw Girl Next Door with her back to a wall, peering around the corner.

Girl Next Door pulled her gun and turned the corner, yelling "Freeze!"

She fired a shot off into the night, and then reacted as though she had been punched in the stomach. Her gun dropped to the ground and slid out of reach.

Girl Next Door threw a punch into the air, and took another phantom punch to her face. She fell to the ground, hard. Leaping back to her feet, Girl Next Door went into an immediate roundhouse, followed by a backflip.

"I will stop you, bad guys! I shall also avenge the death of my half step-brother, Pancho, whom you unjustly killed in his sleep!" Girl Next Door shouted.

As Girl Next Door turned once again, she saw Starlette and started to walk toward her. She waved and smiled as she got closer to Starlette.

"Your half step-brother's name was Pancho?" Starlette asked, leaning up against a wall so that she could wait for Heartthrob to return and for this night to be over with.

"After the great Pancho Villa," Girl Next Door clarified.

"Because of your parents' obvious Mexican heritage?"

"We come from a long line of Chinese-Mexican-American warriors," Girl Next Door told Starlette. "It's all part of the scene that I have playing out in my mind. It helps pass the time and lets me get into all of this testing stuff. See, my half step-brother, Pancho, was killed by a horrible Irish-Italian-American mob boss, Shady Shamus Calzone..."

"I really don't need to know the whole story," Starlette cut in, holding up a hand. "I'm sure it's thrilling and all, but it's been a long and boring night, so I don't think I have the attention span for it right now."

"Whatever. Your loss," Girl Next Door sighed, as she leaned against the wall with Starlette. "By the way, your little red light is off."

Starlette looked down at her camera and to the little recording light, which was off. She tried pushing the *record* button, but it didn't come on. Running her hand behind her back, to where the camera's battery pack was, Starlette grabbed onto the power cable, which was unplugged.

"Shit," she said, plugging the cable back in. "It must have gotten snagged on something."

"You're totally gonna fail this test," Girl Next Door smiled.

Heartthrob rounded a nearby corner and began to walk toward Starlette and Girl Next Door. As he came toward, them, he grabbed Girl Next Door's gun off of the street. He held it up and asked, "Did one of you ladies happen to misplace your firearm?"

"Mine!" Girl Next Door replied, wincing at her own forgetfulness. "I would have failed right there with Starlette if I forgot that."

Heartthrob walked to Girl Next Door and handed her the gun, saying, "Your gun m'lady."

Girl Next Door took the gun, and Starlette noticed that her hand brushed against Heartthrob's just a little bit.

"Thank you," Girl Next Door said to him as she took the gun and smiled sweetly.

Heartthrob smiled back. It was perhaps the most unguarded Starlette had seen him since he arrived at The Studio, but it only lasted for a moment.

Starlette was just beginning to feel like a third wheel when a loud *BOOM* shook the street around them.

All three actors ducked at the sound, and drew their weapons, reacting to the explosion, but without any target to aim for.

"What was that?" Girl Next Door yelled, a little too loudly, while holding a hand to her ear.

"This way," Starlette ordered, leading her cast down the street.

As they ran, they kept low and ready for anything that might come their way. Starlette led them to the other side of the street, where they kept close to the building and rounded the corner.

They hurried down the next street, and dust that had been kicked into the air began to come down on them. Chunks of debris broke the silence of the street, and the glow of fire could be seen from within a building up ahead.

The front of the building had been blown off, but as the actors neared it, it became obvious to them what the building had once been. There was a broken marquee in the middle of the street, with lights and poster frames scattered around it. It was unmistakable.

"It's a movie theater," Girl Next Door said.

Starlette turned and looked at Girl Next Door, saying, "Yes, I see that."

Girl Next Door pointed to the camera on her clothing and said, "I'm saying it for the viewers at home."

"Bookworm?" Heartthrob asked.

"I don't know," Starlette replied, walking into the burning and crumbling building.

Following behind her, Heartthrob said, "Be careful."

As they searched through the rubble, Starlette kept an eye out for evidence. She needed to find something that would tell them who had done this and why.

"I don't see any bodies," Girl Next Door noted. "Doesn't Bookworm usually only take out places that have people inside? Theaters that are trying to show movies. Actor hideouts... stuff like that?"

"You'd have to be a pretty stupid actor to hide out in a theater... and most of them are already dead," Starlette replied, lifting debris and looking for something to take back to The Studio. "This has to be something else."

As the actors continued to sift through the debris, the fires continued to burn within the building. It was only a matter of time before the whole place came crashing down.

~

"Please state your name for the record," said the deep and menacing voice of Studio Head, over the speaker of the phone which was set in the middle of the conference room table where both Wacky Best Friend and The Director were sitting. Nobody else was in the room, and the lighting had been turned down to an intimidatingly dark level.

"Wacky Best Friend."

"Could you please state your *real* name and age range for me?" Studio Head asked.

Wacky Best Friend looked to The Director. He hated sharing his name with anyone, even if that person was already aware of this information. The Director gave Wacky Best Friend a slight nod, telling him to comply.

He shifted in his seat and leaned forward just slightly, as though this would make it easier for Studio Head to hear him when he said, "My name is Ethan Wehrli. I can play sixteen to twenty-three...ish."

"And how long have you been working at The Studio?"

Wacky Best Friend had to think about this. It seemed as though he'd been there forever. It was hard for him to remember a time when he awoke to anything but the artificial sunlight within The Studio. Time flowed differently there. It took him a moment to calculate how long he'd been working with Starlette, but he eventually came up with his answer, "Ten months."

"Thank you," Studio Head said, in an emotionless, almost robotic tone. "Do you know why you're contract is under review today?"

"I... think so," Wacky Best Friend answered, tentatively.

"You were hired to fill the role of sidekick to Starlette. Is this correct?"

"Yes."

"Did your contract stipulate any additional services that would be required on your part?"

"I didn't read the whole thing, but I think Casting Director mentioned something about back rubs."

"Mm-hmm... Did your contract mention anything that might pertain to writing?"

Again, Wacky Best Friend looked to The Director, who was taking notes as Studio Head spoke. When The Director looked up, he silently urged Wacky Best Friend to answer.

"No," Wacky Best Friend replied, "It didn't."

"So, you wrote that script on spec?"

"That's correct. Sir, if you don't mind my asking... My name wasn't on the final draft of that script. How did you find out about this?"

"I don't mind your asking," Studio Head replied. "Now, if you'll be so kind as to tell me... where did you get the idea for this script?"

"I thought of it myself."

"Based on your findings during the Heartthrob rescue mission?"

"That's right."

"So, would you describe the material in your scripts as being derived from a script that was written by Head Writer and his staff?"

The Director slid one of his notes across the table, to Wacky Best Friend. Wacky Best Friend read the note as quickly as possible and used it to form his answer to Studio Head.

"Sir," he said, "My script *was* based on material that originated on one of Head Writer's jobs. However, I believe that Head Writer is under contract with The Studio himself. Therefore, any work that he does is done with the understanding that his material is the property of The Studio. When I turned my script in, I submitted it to The Studio and it became Studio property as well. So... I don't think that you could accuse me of—"

"Thank you," Studio Head cut in. "You will find a small box in the corner of the room. Please place this box on the table and open it."

Wacky Best Friend hadn't seen a box when he entered the room. As he stood now, he kept replaying scenes from various movies in his mind. Boxes could hold within them some very dangerous plot twists, and it made him nervous to be given this order.

He walked to the back of the room and looked to the left corner. No box. In the right corner, he found a small metal box. It looked very heavy duty and serious, but when he picked it up he thought it was disappointingly light in weight.

He placed the box on the table and glanced to The Director once again. The Director didn't seem to know what was inside the box. He gave a slight shrug to Wacky Best Friend.

When Wacky Best Friend opened the box, he held his breath and stood back, just a little bit. He hardly expected it to explode in his face, but he wasn't entirely sure how these contract reviews were supposed to go. He'd never seen someone walk out of such a review, so they may very well have gotten the order to open an exploding box as well.

The box did not explode or spray a deadly gas into the air. There was some dry ice, which sent a thick cloud of vapor pouring out of the box and over the tabletop as Wacky Best Friend opened the box, but this was to be expected. Pretty much every box contained dry ice in this line of work.

When the vapor cleared, Wacky Best Friend could see into the box. What he saw caught him off guard. He didn't know what to say or how to react.

"When this review began, your trailer was searched. As it is also the property of The Studio, I'm sure that you'll agree that this was justified and proper call on our part. Your life seems to be incredibly boring, for the most part. That said, these two items did catch our eye... Do you care to explain them?"

Wacky Best Friend reached into the box and pulled out the ivory-handled knife and the gun that he had taken off of a Bookworm minion during the Heartthrob rescue shoot. He looked them over carefully, trying to appear as though he knew what was happening and that he wasn't pissed off over the invasion of his privacy.

After failing to come up with a reasonable response that he could be sure would not dig him even deeper into the hole that he was in, Wacky Best Friend looked to the phone and said, "I want to speak to my agent and union rep."

~

Searching the rubble was useless. Whatever hadn't been burned had been torn to shreds. Starlette was trying her best to find evidence to take back to The Studio, but it seemed useless.

Chunks of the building were beginning to fall into what had once been the main lobby, where Starlette and her cast now searched. They didn't have enough time to properly sift through what remained, but she knew that there was something to find. She just had to do it quickly.

Her determination was driven by the thought of Wacky Best Friend and whatever he was going through at that moment. She knew that it couldn't be pretty. There were few reasons to pull a primary cast member from a shoot, no matter how mundane that shoot might be, and none of those reasons sat well with her.

She needed evidence. Bringing something like this back to The Studio would attract attention, and any attention that was focused on this explosion would be attention not placed on Wacky Best Friend.

"Starlette, we need to get out of here," Girl Next Door told her, as she brushed dust out of her hair. "It's not safe. It's gonna come down any second now."

Starlette looked up to Girl Next Door and nodded. She said, "You're right. Go. Get outside and head for basecamp. Whoever did this might still be around."

"What about you?" Heartthrob asked her.

"I need to find something to bring back with us. We need evidence."

"Is it worth risking your life for?"

"Yes."

Heartthrob didn't know as much about Wacky Best Friend's situation as Starlette did. Even Girl Next Door was unaware of what was really going on. There was no way that either of them could have seen Starlette's logic or her motivation for staying in that building. Yet, when she told Heartthrob that it was worth risking her life, he and Girl Next Door looked at each other and came to a silent understanding. Without saying another word about leaving, both of them resumed the search for evidence.

"Do you have any guesses?" Heartthrob asked. "About who did this, I mean."

"I'm going with the crazed waiters," Girl Next Door replied.

Heartthrob seemed puzzled by this and asked, "Waiters?"

Girl Next Door shook her head and smiled, saying, "You haven't been back in town very long, have you? All those people who had big dreams of stardom and fame were just as lost as you and me after the attacks. Those who didn't have anything to go home to and no more dreams to comfort them at night—the ones who weren't already prostitutes—they just kinda lost it. Drugs and depression turned to violence and desperation. It's sad, when you think about it."

"Until they try to stab you to death with three different kinds of forks," Starlette chimed in.

"Yeah, until then," Girl Next Door agreed.

"So, you're pretty set on this not being Bookworm?" Heartthrob asked.

Girl Next Door shook her head and tossed aside a chunk of what had once been the theater's wall as she said, "The motive's not there. Empty theaters are like shrines to his greatest terrorist hits. Why would he blow one up?"

Heartthrob started to reply, saying, "What if he—" before stopping midsentence and crouching down.

He tossed aside some rubble and grabbed a small, very charred box. He pulled it free of the debris and held it in his hands as he stood up again.

"Check this out," he told the women, who turned to face him. Starlette smiled.

Girl Next Door raised her head and asked, "What is it?"

Heartthrob opened the box and looked inside as a healthy waft of dry ice vapor poured out. What he saw seemed to raise more questions than it provided answers. He did not immediately offer up a clear answer to Girl Next Door's question, because doing so would violate some of the most basic procedures within The Studio. Instead, he simply said, "It's our evidence."

He then looked at Starlette and Girl Next Door with a half grin on his face, and held that look for several seconds.

Starlette looked to Girl Next Door and said, "What's he doing?"

"Commercial break," Girl Next Door replied.

~

"Answer my questions," Studio Head demanded, still with his calm and even tone.

"I have rights," Wacky Best Friend told him.

"Where did you get these items, and why did you hide them?" Studio Head asked.

Wacky Best Friend crossed his arms in an act of defiance and refused to answer the questions.

The Director had his head in his hand, trying to figure out what he could say or do next, but answering these questions seemed unavoidable.

"Wacky Best Friend, please answer my questions," Studio Head insisted.

"You seem to have a story outlined already," Wacky Best Friend told him. "You know where this is going. You know what you want me to say and I'm guessing that you'll keep pressing me until I say it. So, just feed me my lines and we can get out of here while it's still early."

The Director kept his head in his hands, but shook his head now. Obviously, he did not think that this response would be helping Wacky Best Friend's case.

"During your mission to rescue Heartthrob, you mugged one of Bookworm's minions. Is this correct?" Studio Head asked.

"Yes," Wacky Best Friend replied. "Well, two really. But seeing as how his people killed thousands of us around the globe and forced the rest of us into hiding, I didn't see it as being that big a deal."

"Was this part of your shooting script?"

"No."

"What reason did you have for taking the wallet?"

"It's been forever since I had a good latte. I figured I might be able to afford one if the wallet had any cash in it."

"You're being sarcastic with me."

"I'm being *wacky*. It's part of my character description."

"Please answer my questions honestly."

"Ah, but if I don't answer your questions in character, I'll be in violation of my contract. Now, I'm not gonna suggest that you're trying to get me to do that on purpose... I'm just sayin'."

The Director looked up and at Wacky Best Friend now. The look in his eyes was not frustration or anger, as one might have expected. It was a look which asked if maybe Wacky Best Friend had a better handle on the situation than he had originally let on.

Wacky Best Friend had violated the terms of his contract when he submitted a spec script. Further breaches in that contract would leave him open for more brutal punishment. His options at this point were to either be cooperative with Studio Head and answer all of his questions, or to avoid being backed into a corner by using his contract as a shield.

It was a stupid plan, but it was a plan.

Wacky Best Friend was almost enjoying the back and forth with Studio Head. As soon as he'd been called into the conference room, he had assumed that this would be the end of his contract with The Studio and that his character would meet an untimely demise in the near future. As far as he could tell, he had nothing left to lose.

Under normal circumstances, this would have caused a person to become overwhelmed by fear. There was a time in his life when this type of situation would have turned Ethan into a quivering mess. But he'd seen a lot in the past year, and he was now the sort of person who could hold a live grenade in his hand, pull the pin and toss it at another human being with the hopes of killing that person. This had required a certain amount of disconnecting from who he had once been, in order to hold onto as much of that person as he could realistically hope for.

If he got stage fright while on a shoot, he would end up dead. He'd seen it before and he was sure that he would see it again. He refused to become one of those actors who were destroyed by their own fear of committing to the role that they'd been hired to play. Now, in his mind, the discussion with Studio Head had become just another shoot. It was up to him to dodge as many bullets as he could, and wait for an opportunity to get a shot or two off himself.

"Was this the first time that you had taken items from a shooting location without telling us?" Studio Head pressed on, as though he hadn't even heard Wacky Best Friend's other reply.

"I like to think that I take a little piece of every shoot home with me... in my heart."

"Clever."

"Thanks."

"What did you hope to accomplish by taking these items?"

"Umm... World peace. Education reform... Maybe gather support from others around the country and urge soda manufacturers to drop the high fructose corn syrup in favor of real sugar," Wacky Best Friend replied and then turned to The Director and said, "It really does make a world of difference."

The Director said nothing. He simply took down a note and turned his attention back to the discussion at hand.

Studio Head went on, "Are you aware of The Studio's policies on weaponry and gun ownership?"

"Umm... Aim for center mass?"

"The owning of such weaponry within The Studio is strictly prohibited. Weapons are to be utilized only under shooting conditions. Otherwise, they are to be logged and stored in the prop department in order to ensure the safety of everyone within The Studio. Do you understand these rules?"

"No. But I'm beginning to understand why so many of our people died in the attacks."

"What do you mean by that?"

"I mean..." Wacky Best Friend started, but The Director quickly shook his head, telling Wacky Best Friend to refrain from walking down that path. "I mean, obviously the attacks wouldn't have happened if rules like these had been in place for the population at large. You're so right."

"So, what were your intentions in regards to these weapons?"

"I intended to turn them over, but they somehow got misplaced. I thank you and your wonderfully burly guards for finding them and turning them in for me," Wacky Best Friend smiled.

"Are you still being... wacky?"

"I'm always wacky."

"It doesn't seem to me that this was your intention at all," Studio Head said.

"Oh? How do you figure?"

"When you found the wallet which led to the script that you wrote, you did not turn it in, just as you failed to turn in these weapons. I believe that you had no intention of turning these weapons in until you could find a way of using them in another script."

"So, you're saying—"

"I'm saying that, from where I'm sitting, it seems as though you've been plotting behind our backs for quite a while now. And this is a clear violation of the terms of your contract."

"Okay. I hear you and I value your thoughts," Wacky Best Friend replied. "Now, I'm going to open my emotion pouch and sprinkle you with some insight into *my* feelings, m'kay?"

The Director's face contorted into a *what the hell was that?* expression. Wacky Best Friend couldn't help but smile in response to the look.

"I have been working at The Studio for months, putting my ass on the line and trying to bring down Bookworm. Time and time again, I have been handed half-assed scripts and I have performed them as well as I possibly could, with the exception of the dialogue, which I normally just try to ignore completely. I do the work, and I do it with a smile on my face, because I believe in this project," Wacky Best Friend told Studio Head. "But the thing is, we can only draw this arc out for so long before we lose our target demographic for good. If we don't keep those bookish loonies in our sights, they'll be gone and we will be stuck living in this hole in the ground for the rest of our lives... And I'm not saying it's really ugly or anything, it's just *literally* a hole in the ground. Now, you might not agree with what I did. You might want me to stay quiet and play the role that you've hired me to play. But I saw an opportunity to really move this plot forward, and I took it. If I hadn't, we never would have gotten the wallet, which led us to the Carter house..."

"A shoot which provided none of the intended results," Studio Head noted.

"Yes, Michael Carter was a bust. Keep in mind, however, that we did get our hands on the Emma Carter documents, which could prove to be the single most substantial information that we've gotten to date... assuming that they can be translated."

"That's a rather big assumption."

"But it was worth it," Wacky Best Friend shot back. "And Girl Next Door did find out that Bookworm isn't a Christian extremist."

Studio Head grumbled, making it obvious that he still wasn't sold on that bit.

Wacky Best Friend took a deep breath and looked to the ceiling for a moment, gathering his thoughts before he turned back to the phone in the center of the room and said, "The Studio will crumble if we can't keep everyone motivated. We go on shoot after shoot, and come back with nothing that gets us any closer to taking down Bookworm and getting back to some semblance of our normal lives. Resentment is beginning to brew. Crew members are beginning to resent the actors for not getting the job done. The actors are beginning to resent the writers for not providing us with material that we can work with. The producers keep trying to dumb down the scripts, because they think that if we get too fancy out there on the streets, we'll lose popularity amongst the people that we're hoping to live with again someday..."

As Wacky Best Friend spoke, The Director's cell phone vibrated. The Director pulled it out of his pocket and looked at the message that had been sent to him. He then looked to Wacky Best Friend and said, "I'm sorry, but I have to go. I've just gotten some disturbing news from Starlette's latest shoot."

Wacky Best Friend could remain calm and quirky when his own life was on the line, but as soon as he heard that something had happened to Starlette and his other co-stars, Wacky Best Friend's heart dropped.

"What happened?" he asked The Director.

"I've received the same message and have other business to attend to," Studio Head replied. "My final decision on the matter of Wacky Best Friend will have to wait until we can resume our discussion."

"What happened?" Wacky Best Friend asked again, with more worry in his tone this time.

The phone line went dead. Studio Head was gone.

The Director turned to Wacky Best Friend and told him, "You'll have to stay in here until we can resolve this issue."

"I don't care. Just tell me if they're okay!"

"There was an explosion," The Director told him. "Starlette and your other co-stars were nearby."

"Are they hurt?"

"No. But there might be other... complications. I have to go now," The Director replied, exiting the room.

Wacky Best Friend was alone. He was left to wonder what had happened, and how he would be dealt with when Studio Head returned.

Looking down at the table, Wacky Best Friend said, "I didn't even get to finish my big monologue."

~

As the van pulled up to The Studio, Heartthrob held onto the box tightly. Until he was ready to make its contents known, he could not take the risk that the lid might blow off and someone would see what was inside. He wasn't sure exactly what it meant, but he could feel the weight of the box's contents (both literally and metaphorically) and the potential that it had to set The Studio abuzz.

He hopped out of the van and hurried down the stairs which led into The Studio. Once inside, he looked out across the group of people that was beginning to gather. Word had spread of the explosion, and many were waiting to see what it meant.

Had the attacks resumed? This was the question of the hour. For people who had been hiding for their own safety for nearly a year and who rarely got outside to see what had become of the world, the threat of explosions and death was the trigger to a deeper emotional scar.

Cabin fever was an old concept. When locked in a confined area, people can behave in unpredictable ways. Add a reasonable amount of paranoia to the mix, and there was a constant amount of pressure within The Studio. Each shoot provided an opportunity to vent this pressure, but each attack only added to it.

Bookworm had never really gone away. The attacks became more rare because there were fewer targets left for him to strike. On a good day, this calm could soothe people into a false sense of security and normalcy.

Heartthrob knew better than to feel any ounce of this security.

He had been on the run for months, and while The Studio provided shelter, he knew that the danger had never gone away. He had people to spend time with now. He had hot meals and a shower which was regularly accessible to him, but when he closed his eyes at night, everything that he had gone through came back to him. There was no question about whether or not he would have a nightmare when he went to sleep. The only question was in how bad that nightmare would be.

As each night passed in The Studio and he felt more at ease with his fellow actors, the nightmares grew more real and more intense. The pressure within him was building, just as it was building within The Studio as a whole. The difference was, he could process what was in the box. He understood it. He could live with it. He just wasn't so sure about everyone else.

He placed the box on a metal table, which was normally used to prepare props before a shoot. As he did this, The Director approached. He forced his way through the growing crowd, to Starlette and her cast, and he looked down at the box.

"What happened?" The Director asked.

"It was a theater. It exploded about a block away from us," Starlette replied.

The crowd began to whisper, as what had once been a rumor was now confirmed.

Camera One made his way through the crowd and stood next to The Director. He said, "We should be able to view the dailies from the cameras that they were testing. We'll be able to see everything from their point of view."

"Well, almost everything. Starlette's camera went all fizzle or something," Girl Next Door told him.

Starlette looked to Camera One and told him, "The power supply became unplugged. You might want to check that out."

"Son of a bitch," Camera One sighed, and his anger began to build. "Son of a bitch! Son of a fucking bitch! Why can't one thing work out like it's supposed to? Why do these stupid cameras always malfunction when there's no fucking reason for them to?! Why can't it just fucking work?!"

Everyone looked at Camera One, waiting for his rant to end. After punching the metal table once, his anger seemed to have passed.

Girl Next Door leaned in close to Heartthrob and whispered to him, "Just ignore him. He's really emotional about his projects."

The Director turned toward Starlette and asked her, "Were there any victims?"

"None that we could find," Starlette told him.

"What did you find?"

Starlette looked to Heartthrob and said, "Actually, it was Heartthrob who found it."

The Director looked at Heartthrob and gestured toward the box on the table. Heartthrob took his cue and went to the box. He opened it and placed the lid on the table.

The crowd seemed to be waiting for something which never came to be. Heartthrob turned to them and said, "Oh, I let the dry ice vapor out the first time I opened it."

The Director stepped closer to the box and looked inside. He seemed to be taken aback by what he saw. Starlette and Girl Next Door stepped closer as well.

When she saw what was in the box, Girl Next Door asked, "Are those scripts?"

"Yeah," Starlette replied.

Starlette reached into the box and pulled out a handful of script pages, which had been torn to shreds. She looked them over, and then looked to The Director and asked, "What does this mean?"

Girl Next Door reached into the box and pulled some script pieces out, so that she could have a look as well. As she read some of the dialogue on those fragments, she asked, "Is *Chance* a boy name or a girl name?"

The Director fished around in the box, looking for some other sign that might tell them where those script pages had come from. He placed pieces of the scripts on the table as he went, and each time that he placed a handful there, the crowd seemed to whisper just a little bit louder.

Heartthrob turned toward the crowd. He watched as they talked amongst themselves and shook their heads. They were confused and scared, and these feelings were growing more and more intense by the moment.

"I don't recognize any of these character names or the dialogue," Girl Next Door said, putting the script pieces down. "Maybe they were just left there a long time ago. I'm sure that there are a hundred scripts floating around Hollywood, right?"

"Yeah," The Director replied. "But how many of these are there?"

What he pulled out of the box next was a small laminated card, which had been badly burned. Though most of the writing on the card was unreadable, the logo on top was very recognizable. It was the image of a winged bull, with a faceless nude woman riding on its back, holding the world in her hand—the logo of The Studio.

"Is that a parking pass?" Starlette asked.

The Director nodded and put the pass down on the metal table. The crowd became much louder as panic began to set in.

"Oh my God," Girl Next Door said, picking the parking pass up and looking it over. "Why do we even have parking passes? There's no parking lot... We don't have cars."

Starlette looked into the box one more time and sifted through the pieces of script that remained inside of it. After a moment, she picked up the box and dumped its contents onto the table. She then looked to The Director and gestured for him to look inside.

As The Director leaned in and looked into the box, Heartthrob did the same. What he saw was a note, written in bold black marker, which said: YOU TURNED YOUR BACK ON ME.

The Director and Heartthrob looked at each other and then to Starlette.

"What does this mean?" Heartthrob asked.

The Director's words carried a great deal of weight with them as he replied, "I think it means that whoever blew up that building... was one of us."

As The Director said this, the panicking crowd turned into a screaming mob. Every person in The Studio had a question to ask and a concern to voice. Nobody knew how to respond to the news, or even what the news meant.

The Director put his hands up and yelled, "Quiet! Everybody quiet down!"

Around The Studio, production assistants began to yell,

"Quiet!"

After a few moments, the crowd's screaming calmed down and The Director could address them more properly.

"There is a note inside the box," he told them. "It says *'you turned your back on me.'* We don't know where this came from, or who left it. There is no need for alarm. None of us are in any danger."

"But that parking pass means that whoever did this was one of us, right?" a voice from the crowd asked.

"We don't know that," The Director replied.

"Yeah, for all we know, they could have just captured and killed one of us, so they could take a parking pass," Girl Next Door added.

Her words didn't seem to help matters.

"Please. Do not panic," The Director ordered. "We will figure out what's happening here."

"What if it is one of us?" came another voice. "What if it's one of the actors who have mysteriously disappeared?"

"There is no indication that this is a former employee of The Studio," The Director replied.

The voice in the crowd shot back, saying, "You mean, aside from the parking pass and the note that says that we turned our backs on him?"

The Director didn't respond to that. How could he? The truth was that this very probably was a former employee of The Studio. How could a situation like that possibly be made better with words? Nothing that The Director could say or do would ease the minds of the people of The Studio.

Over the next few hours, the crowd dissipated, but the buzzing continued. As Heartthrob went about his normal daily activities, he could hear whispers in every corner and catch knowing glances between different departments.

Rumors about who this former employee was were running rampant, but nobody knew for certain. Discussions turned toward the actors who had lived in The Studio at one time or another but who had parted ways with The Studio due to creative differences.

Other people spoke of those who had given their lives in service to The Studio, and whose names would be forever muddied if Studio members began to turn on each other.

But through all of this, the reaction that concerned Heartthrob the most were those who stopped talking whenever he came near. Members of each department would see him coming and they would turn the other way, quickly falling silent.

The one thing that was known about the person who had blown up the theater was that they were an actor. Suddenly, actors became very unpopular.

~

Starlette and Girl Next Door were walking with The Director, who had been trying to get Studio Head on the phone since the discovery of the box's contents. It wasn't unusual for Studio Head to be unreachable, but for some reason The Director seemed especially concerned over it this time.

"Where is Wacky Best Friend?" Starlette asked The Director.

"I can't tell you that," The Director replied.

"What can you tell me?" she pressed.

"I can tell you that this situation is getting heated very fast. We have to get it under control. Now."

"How? How can we track down an actor who we've already kicked out of The Studio?" Starlette asked.

"Especially since we don't know which one he or she is," Girl Next Door agreed.

"No actor has ever been kicked out of The Studio. Remember that. The option to renew their contracts was simply not exercised," The Director told them, in a very pointed tone.

"We all know that's just code," Starlette informed him. "Everyone here knows what happens when you don't play by the rules."

"Then why don't any of you ever play by the rules?" The Director asked.

"This problem isn't just going to be limited to actors in The Studio. It's opening up a whole big can of worms," Girl Next Door told both Starlette and The Director. "I've heard people talking. They're talking about how we turned our backs on other actors after the attacks. The waiters. The valets..."

"They're not even union," Starlette smirked. "How can anybody possibly count them as real actors?"

Girl Next Door shrugged and said, "I'm just saying what I've heard. People are blaming us for what happened to them. They're saying that we should do something."

"Like what?" The Director asked.

Girl Next Door shook her head and told him, "I don't know. But something big and earth-shattering. If they have to, some might even use the nuclear option... Y'know, hold a telethon."

The Director let this news sink in as he redialed his phone. He looked to Starlette and Girl Next Door and said, "I have to go. Keep listening and let me know what you hear people saying."

"What about Wacky Best Friend?" Starlette asked.

"I don't know," was all The Director could offer as he walked away.

~

Wacky Best Friend had been left alone in the conference room for hours. The last bit of information that he had been given was in regards to an explosion that somehow involved his castmates, and his mind had been spinning with all sorts of images ever since. Sure, he knew that they hadn't been hurt, but The Director and Studio Head had left the meeting in a hurry and Wacky Best Friend somehow doubted that they would do that if everything was fine.

For the first twenty minutes or so, he sat at the table, waiting for someone to come in and tell him what was going on, or release him. He expected *something*... But nobody came.

Soon, the waiting made him impatient and he began to create games in his own head, in order to keep himself busy. That didn't work for very long.

He counted floor tiles until he lost track of which tiles he'd already counted. He counted ceiling tiles until he realized that the ceiling didn't have tiles.

Then came the pacing. He paced back and forth for at least an hour, trying to imagine what turn of events could distract The Director and Studio Head for so long. He wondered if he'd simply been forgotten.

When pacing lost its ability to keep him adequately occupied, he began to run in place. He continued to do this for a half hour or so. Then he fell to the floor and did five sets of fifty pushups, which really impressed him even though he suspected himself of cheating.

After the pushups, he considered sit-ups. Since there was no way of anchoring his feet, he quickly scratched that plan.

And then he sat. He lost track of how much time had passed, but it felt like an eternity. His mind had gone through several possible outcomes and how he would react to each of them. He looked to the air ducts and wondered if he could squeeze through them, but he somehow doubted it.

The longer he waited, the less nervous he got. Eventually, he came to the conclusion that there was no way for him to prepare himself for what might come. He had no clue what might have happened with his co-stars, and he had no idea of what would happen when Studio Head reached his decision. All Wacky Best Friend could do was trust himself to think and react in the moment, and to go with whatever his gut told him to do.

He put his head on the table and closed his eyes. Soon, he began to drift off and his mind was flooded with irrational and disconnected thoughts which seemed to make sense in that moment, but would soon dissolve into a haze of gibberish when he awoke.

There was no way of knowing how long he spent drifting in and out of sleep, but he was awoken by the ringing of the phone in the center of the table.

Wacky Best Friend jolted up in his seat and hit the speakerphone button before he was fully awake.

"Hello?" he said, as though this were his own phone that he was answering.

"You've had enough time to consider your situation," Studio Head said to him. "Is there anything that you would like to change about your comments?"

Wacky Best Friend's first impulse was to tell Studio Head that he very much regretted not using the term *douchebag* more often in their interaction. Luckily, he was more awake and aware of himself, and he prevented himself from saying anything like that. Instead, he told Studio Head, "No, sir. I stand by every word."

"So, if given the option, you would commit the same actions again?"

Wacky Best Friend knew what Studio Head wanted to hear him say, but this was not the truth. Given the fact that he felt screwed either way, Wacky Best Friend said, "I might rethink the interrogation of Michael Carter. Other than that... Yes, I would do it all the same."

"Then I'm sorry to say that you leave me with very little choice. Your contract is terminated. Please turn in your par—"

As Studio Head spoke, the door to the conference room opened and The Director walked in. He closed the door behind him and walked to the table, so that he could be heard by Studio Head.

"Sir," The Director said, "I need to speak with you before you make your final decision."

"I'm afraid you're too late."

"Then I urge you to reconsider."

"I appreciate the fact that you are fond of Wacky Best Friend, however this decision cannot be based on your emotional connections."

Wacky Best Friend smiled to The Director, in an exaggeratedly adorable way. He was amused that Studio Head thought that The Director would be torn up over his dismissal.

The Director rolled his eyes and said, "This is not an emotional reaction, this is a logistical situation."

Studio Head took a moment before saying, "Go on."

"The recent explosion which involved Wacky Best Friend's cast has produced evidence that suggests that an actor may have been behind the bombing," The Director explained.

"I'm aware," Studio Head told him.

Wacky Best Friend was very much unaware of what had been discovered. He looked to The Director for more information, but The Director held up a hand and said, "The situation has caused a stir on the floor of The Studio. Tension is rising and people are wondering if we might be in some way responsible for this turn of events. Some are resenting the idea that we've turned our backs on some of our former employees. I'm worried that any further provocation could spark a backlash within The Studio."

"Then what action would you suggest we take?" Studio Head asked. "Are you suggesting that we simply release him without proper punishment?"

Wacky Best Friend nodded enthusiastically.

"No," The Director replied.

Wacky Best Friend frowned.

"He will pay his debt to The Studio," The Director told Studio Head. "We'll tell his co-stars that he has been admitted to the clinic for exhaustion—"

"Wait," Wacky Best Friend chimed in, no longer waiting for The Director to make his decisions. "My debt? I got us a big lead, remember? Shouldn't you be in debt to me?"

The Director ignored him and continued, saying, "In reality, Wacky Best Friend will be... Put on hiatus until further notice. Sir, if we terminate his contract, things will get ugly. If we kill him off, there will be chaos."

There was a long silence, which made Wacky Best Friend incredibly uncomfortable. He did not enjoy being spoken of as though he wasn't in the room. Even less when the conversation involved the possibility of killing him off.

What might have disturbed Wacky Best Friend the most was that there seemed to be some option on the table that he was not clear on. Something that the higher ranking members of The Studio were aware of, but which he and the rest of the actors and crew members were left in the dark about.

"I agree," Studio Head said, seeming to ignore Wacky Best Friend completely. "Wacky Best Friend is to be held in the vault until further notice."

The phone line went dead. Wacky Best Friend looked to The Director, still trying to process what just happened. He stood from his chair and backed away from the table, as though there was some way for him to avoid being taken.

He had never heard of the vault, but it was clear to him that while he was not being killed off, there was no promise of his return. His being kept alive was simply a means of leaving that door open and avoiding rebellion. He did not enjoy thinking about exactly what came next for him.

Wacky Best Friend pulled the gun that Prop Master had given him from behind his back. He looked down at the gun in his hand, wondering if he was really going to try to shoot The Director.

"There's an old saying about showing a gun in the first act,"

The Director said, in a quiet tone. "They say that you damn well better fire it in the third."

If Wacky Best Friend hadn't known better, he might have read into The Director's words, but after considering his options, he walked to the table and placed the gun down on it.

"Tell them that... Tell them that I'll see them soon."

~

It had been hours since she returned to The Studio. Girl Next Door and Heartthrob had gone to dinner, and Starlette was sitting alone in front of her trailer. She was waiting for Ethan to come home.

Starlette was fully aware of what could happen to him. She knew that others had been kicked out of The Studio, or worse. She was not naïve to the way things worked in The Studio. Yet, she did not believe that Wacky Best Friend would be one of these casualties of The Studio system. He had done good. How could they make him pay for that?

She sat on the front steps of her trailer for two hours, waiting for him. He never showed up.

She paced back and forth, and still, there was no sign of Ethan.

After a while, Ember and Heartthrob came home. They saw Starlette sitting outside of her trailer and they asked where Ethan was. When Starlette told them what was happening with him, Ember threw a fit. She yelled at Starlette for not telling her sooner, and cursed Ethan for pretending that everything was fine the last time she saw him.

Heartthrob remained quiet. The expression on his face betrayed no emotion. He simply sat with Starlette and Ember and he waited for news of Wacky Best Friend's situation. Starlette had to wonder if he felt as though he was not allowed to react to this news, being new to the group. For a moment or two, she wondered if he felt anything at all. Then she noticed that he was nervously bouncing his leg as he sat. Any reservation she had about him seemed to fade in that moment, and she realized that he was a part of their group. Come what may, he was one of them and that meant that he was her responsibility.

Her cast was suffering. Ethan was nowhere to be found. Ember was moments away from snapping completely. Heartthrob...

Starlette didn't even know what to expect from him.

Despite her best efforts to ensure a positive outcome for Ethan, she had failed. Now she was left to wonder how long it would take for someone else to figure out what she had done. She had gone into that theater knowing that her actions would kick up dust within The Studio, but she hoped that this would ensure Ethan's safety and that hope made it worth the risk. With Ethan gone, she was now left to wonder if causing the explosion had been worth it. The dust had yet to settle.

Chapter Eight
SPECIAL GUEST STAR

"They took him," Starlette said, balling her fists and pacing back and forth across the living room floor of Tessa Baker's penthouse.

Tessa watched from the comfort of her sofa, sipping what looked like simply cranberry juice, but Starlette had a hard time believing that it was *only* cranberry juice. Tessa wasn't known for her love of fruit juice, after all. She was known for her love of anything that might help her to forgive and forget. Maybe this was why the look on her face and the coolness of her disposition didn't match Starlette's level of anger.

Starlette felt like a wolf, just waiting for the wrong prey to cross her path. When it did, there would be no end to the amount of pain that she would inflict. Her only regret was that she couldn't go after the true source of her rage. To be honest, she didn't even know which specific person had done it... or even what had really been done.

"Took?" Tessa asked, looking down at her fingernails, as though she had forgotten to polish them and was just now making a mental note of it. "To whom are you referring?"

"Wacky Best Friend. He's my—"

"No. Let me guess..." Tessa cut in. "He's your *wacky* best friend?"

"He's my co-star."

"As in... *Domestic* co-star?"

Starlette looked at Tessa, wishing that the woman were just a smidge less drunk at the moment, so that she could hold a serious and meaningful conversation without all topics turning to domestic co-starships.

Her first instinct was to tell Tessa to shut up and listen to what she was saying, so that she might get some sage advice from the woman who had become like an actress hired to play a mother to her. She did not say what first came to mind. Instead, she took a deep breath and resumed her pacing.

"*Wacky Best Friend?*" Tessa commented. "My God, is that what they're naming people these days?"

"Aren't you listening to me? They took him," Starlette replied. "He's gone, and I don't know where."

"Where did they tell you he is?" Tessa asked.

"They told us that he admitted himself to the clinic, due to exhaustion."

Tessa looked up at Starlette with a slightly more serious tone than she had displayed up to that point. She took a sip of her drink, and then said, "We all know that *exhaustion* is never exhaustion. Do you know if he's been drinking? Is he a sex addict? A Republican, maybe?"

"You don't get it. You haven't lived in The Studio," Starlette told her. "Things aren't the same as they used to be."

"They sound the same to me. Some unseemly personality quirk pops up and they disappear your friend until they can make it go away. This is old school, sweetheart. Very old."

"So, where would they put him?"

"Did they tell you that he would be back?"

"They told us that they're hopeful that he might come back in the future."

Tessa shook her head and said, "How wonderfully vague they can be."

"Do you think he's dead?"

"I'm assuming that he didn't leave on good terms. What did he do that made them so angry?"

Starlette looked to the ground, thinking back on all of the events that led to this point, and she told Tessa, "He wrote a script on spec."

Tessa stared at her with a blank expression, as though she were waiting for something more. When Starlette didn't continue with some longer story, Tessa cocked her head just slightly and said, "I'm sorry, dear. I'm afraid I don't understand. Actors write scripts all the time. I have a stack of my own sitting in the closet. None finished, but all with absolutely amazing opening sequences. Would you like to see one?"

"No," Starlette told her. She hated when friends asked her to read scripts that they'd written, because they always wanted her to set them up with someone who might produce it.

Tessa smiled and said, "Good girl. Never read a friend's script unless you know they're good at writing. You wouldn't believe how many friends I've had to sleep with, just so they'd forget to ask what I thought of their script."

"I'm talking about a friend who's gone missing and you're spinning me yarns about screwing bad writers?"

"I simply don't understand the crisis at hand. I have told you a thousand times what the core of The Studio is. I've told you where they come from. I've told you how to survive, but I don't understand matters like this. I don't see how an actor would get thrown into rehab over writing a script."

Starlette sat down on a nearby chair and tried to bottle her energy even more securely, so that she could explain the situation to Tessa. She looked Tessa squarely in the eyes, but without any anger. She needed advice. She needed some idea of what to do, and Tessa was her best hope of that. So, she calmly explained, "This isn't old Hollywood. Not the Golden Age. Not the Digital Age. This is the *Dark* Age. It's war. People have jobs to do and roles to play and you really don't cross lines without a serious price to pay."

"Sounds terribly political."

"Basically, he's a drama club kid sitting at the jock table."

"And the only way for the principal to avoid chaos is to stick him in detention," Tessa caught on, taking another drink of her cranberry juice. "I love this metaphor. Now, who would be the saucy young teacher who likes to spank his students?"

"We don't have porn stars," Starlette told Tessa. "Their industry was largely ignored by Bookworm for some reason."

Tessa swallowed the last of her drink and held out her glass for Starlette to refill. Starlette took it and walked to the bar, where a bottle of cranberry juice was sitting. When she opened it, her theories regarding the drink were confirmed. As she poured, Tessa spoke.

"It seems to me that if you want to get your friend out of hock, you will have to play the system."

"I've tried that," Starlette replied. "Believe me... I tried that."

"And it didn't work?"

Starlette returned to Tessa with her drink and as she handed the glass over, she replied, "Umm... I'm gonna have to get back to you on that. It's still playing out."

"Then my advice to you is... let it. See how the story unfolds and be prepared to sway the outcome whenever the opportunity arises," Tessa suggested, taking a sip of her freshly refilled drink. "And always remember... You are the star. They need you. Don't be afraid to take advantage of that fact. Don't *ask* for anything. Demand *everything*."

As Tessa finished her sentence, she began to laugh. Starlette wasn't sure what was so funny about the line, but it was apparently very amusing after several glasses of cranberry juice.

~

With her mind still full of worry and her focus being placed on trying to get Wacky Best Friend back on her cast, Starlette walked out of Tessa's building and began to walk down the street without much thought given to her surroundings.

Because her mind was in another place, she failed to notice the man on a nearby corner, watching her exit Tessa's building. When she turned and walked away from him, she didn't notice that he was following her.

She didn't notice when a friend of this man walked out of a nearby shoe store and joined his partner's silent pursuit... At least, not right away.

As she walked, she was listening to the sounds around her, though paying them very little consideration. It took a few moments for her to hear a sound from behind. It wasn't the sound of footsteps that she heard, but the sound of shoes turning on the pavement; that grinding hiss which meant that someone was dragging their feet, just for a moment.

She stopped walking, and there was no more noise from behind. She stood silently, waiting for the next move to be made, but none immediately came.

Each window that wasn't broken along the street reflected the world around her, displaying a slightly different angle of the street. She scanned them carefully, forcing her eyes to focus *on* the windows, rather than *through* them. Finally, she caught a glimpse of the two men behind her. They wore dress pants which had been cut to the length of boardshorts, and white dress shirts which had the sleeves torn off.

They moved toward her stealthily, with the grace of someone who had been trained to carry a tray of fragile glasses through a crowded room. She couldn't see their faces, but she didn't have to. She knew the look in the eyes of each waiter and waitress that she had met over the previous months, and they were always the same. Lost. Sad. Driven to the edge of insanity, but never quite losing their ability to think situations through; to plot and maneuver.

Several months earlier, she had encountered a group of waiters from a five star restaurant in Beverly Hills. At first, they looted whatever they could carry. They waded through the rubble of the studios that once were, looking for guidance and safety, but finding none. They were not targets of Bookworm and did not have the protection of The Studio due to the fact that most of them were not yet union members, but their world had been destroyed just the same. Both sides of the battle had abandoned them, and the rest of the world had forgotten them. They went mad. Some took knives to their faces, destroying the beauty that they once hoped would guide them to stardom.

In the absence of celebrity, the streets of Hollywood were vulnerable, and the waiters had decided to take them. They were a cruel race. Those who stood in their way would not only have their silverware licked, they would also be torn to shreds. If they happened to find an actor on their streets, they were known to do to those actors what they had done to themselves: destroy the beauty that made them a star.

Starlette turned to face her pursuers, gently gripping a throwing knife with each hand. When she saw them, she saw that they were not disfigured. They were waiters whose beauty still existed, though hidden by grime and facial hair.

They slinked across the street like wild cats about to pounce, smiling when their eyes met hers. They wanted Starlette to fear them. They wanted her to turn and run so that they could chase her down and do whatever it was that they planned to do to her. Obviously, they did not know Starlette.

"Could you come back in five minutes?" Starlette asked. "I can't seem to make up my mind between disemboweling you and slitting your throats… they both just sound so darn good."

One of the waiters smiled at her and bit his bottom lip as he sized her up. He said, "You're her. The ghost of the Hollywood streets. The tormented actress who haunts our town and searches for her long lost career."

"You forgot the part about the disemboweling. I do that too. Not often, but enough."

"Tell me, ghost… What does your blood taste like?"

"Pennies. With a subtle spiciness that I can't quite put my finger on," Starlette replied.

The waiters slinked toward her and the one who remained silent pulled a steak knife from his belt. He gently waved it through the air and then licked it. Starlette watched this and wondered if he licked his knives often. Perhaps that was why he remained silent.

The first waiter pulled two knives of his own. These were bigger kitchen knives, and he held them as though he was about to give her an infomercial-style demonstration of their cutting abilities.

"I once caught an actress wandering my streets," the first waiter told her. "I sliced her up and served her for Thanksgiving dinner."

Starlette nodded and shot back, "I once under-tipped a waiter because he was a douche."

This seemed to anger the waiters, and they charged at Starlette with fury blinding their vision.

Knives cut through the air, and glistened with the reflection of the streetlights. Starlette used her own knives to block one of the first waiter's blades and the steak knife from the second waiter, and she bent backward to avoid the third blade that nearly sliced through her face.

As she deflected the two knives with her own, she kicked the silent waiter in the gut and sent him slamming into the brick wall of the building beside her.

She raised her arms and crossed her blades just in time to stop the first waiter from stabbing her. With a twist, she sent one of his knives flying through the air and onto the street, far enough away to ensure that it would not be a problem.

She spun and both of her knives sliced through the skin on the first waiter's face, leaving him with deep wounds that would scar him in just the same way as those waiters who had disfigured themselves.

Blood poured into his eye and he could not see her. He waved his remaining knife wildly through the air, but Starlette grabbed his arm, twisted it, and stabbed him repeatedly with his own knife. She was careful not to hit any vital organs. She didn't want him to die; not yet. She wanted him to go back to his friends and tell them what she had done to him. She wanted to send a message to the waiters of Hollywood, letting them know that this town was hers.

For good measure, she took the first waiter's knife from him and jammed it into his leg. He fell to the ground, making not so much as a slight whimper to show his pain.

The silent waiter had recovered and charged toward Starlette once again. With a backflip, she kicked him in the face and he stumbled backward. She spun and kicked him in the face again, and he stumbled some more.

At this point, she was just showing off.

When she was ready to end this fight, she grabbed the silent waiter by the hair and she slammed his face against the brick wall. She did this over and over again until she could feel his skull breaking.

She dropped him to the ground, where he lay twitching as she put her throwing knives away.

She resumed her walk down the street, never bothering to look back. She had nothing to fear. As she walked, she wiped away a bit of blood that had splattered onto the sleeve of her jacket and said, "The service in this place sucks."

~

It was late. Ordinarily, Ember would be sitting in bed, trying to figure out how to read a cookbook or which side of a knitting needle was up. Instead, she found herself sitting on one of the lawn chairs in front of her trailer, waiting.

She didn't even know what she was waiting for. She felt some sense of impatience toward something that she couldn't quite put her finger on. Under normal circumstances she would just go to one of her co-stars and hang out until she could remember what it was that she was supposed to be impatient about, but Ethan was gone and Starlette was walking around the outside world for some strange and unknown reason.

Heartthrob was in his trailer, but Ember didn't turn to him for comfort. Ever since coming into The Studio, he had made mention here and there about not getting enough sleep. She had seen him doze off once or twice during some especially boring production meetings, but she thought nothing of it because she usually only noticed him sleeping when she herself was just popping out of a near nap.

The more time that passed, the more tired he seemed. By the time Ethan was gone and Ember found herself sitting alone outside of the trailers, Heartthrob's sleeplessness had begun to manifest in more obvious ways.

She could hear him in his trailer from time to time, screaming. Usually, it would be one loud scream which apparently woke him up, but there were times when the screaming would last a minute or two and all she could do was listen. She didn't know what other options she had. She could offer to talk to him during the day, but over the previous months she had come to realize that very few people in The Studio wanted to open up and share their pain.

When she heard Heartthrob scream on that particular night, as she sat on the lawn chair with nobody else around, Ember found herself bursting into tears. She didn't know why. She didn't know how to make it stop. All she knew was that she felt incredibly broken.

She sobbed uncontrollably for several minutes, wondering how she must look with her puffy eyes and her runny nose, but still she couldn't stop. She tried to pull herself together several times and hold her breath so that she could break the cycle of tears, but it didn't work.

She didn't want to be seen like this. She couldn't afford being caught on film, looking like she had just been punched in the face by an angry gorilla who could make things ugly by punching them in the face.

That's a weird image, she thought to herself. She held onto the image of a wacky gorilla who went around punching people in the face, and it began to make her feel just a little bit better. She felt stupid for being so easily amused by herself, but this was the benefit of having an active imagination.

She closed her eyes and took a deep breath, telling herself, "The gorilla has a floppy white hat."

When she opened her eyes again, she found a production assistant standing in front of her, holding a walkie-talkie in one hand and a clipboard in the other. She was looking at Girl Next Door with a questioning look.

When Girl Next Door saw the production assistant, she wiped her tears away, smiled and said, "I was rehearsing for a shoot. They involve crying sometimes... and gorillas... with... Hey, what's up?"

The production assistant continued to look at Girl Next Door, but said nothing. After a moment, she spoke into the microphone that was attached to an earpiece, which all of the production assistants had for their walkie-talkies. She said, "Copy that. I'll get SGF down to wardrobe for a fitting."

Girl Next Door hated when they looked at her but spoke to someone else over the walkie-talkie. It made her feel like she should feel stupid for some reason.

At long last, the PA spoke to Girl Next Door and said, "Head Writer wanted to see you."

"Again?" Girl Next Door asked.

She didn't want to go see Head Writer. To the best of her knowledge, *nobody* wanted to go see Head Writer. He rarely asked actors to meet with him, because he didn't seem to care what any of them had to say about his writing or their character development. Yet, for some odd reason, he had been asking to see Girl Next Door more often in recent weeks.

With a sigh, Girl Next Door stood up and told the PA, "I'll be there in a minute."

The PA nodded and walked away, saying something into her walkie-talkie as she went. Girl Next Door took a moment to make sure that she didn't enter a meeting with Head Writer with cry-face. She didn't need him to know anything about her personal life or her inner most feelings, and she definitely didn't want him ripping off her gorilla idea.

When she made her way across The Studio, toward his office, she wondered why he would be asking to see her so late. She knew that the writers all worked well into the night most of the time, because they always had some strict deadline to meet, but why he chose to involve her in his late night work was beyond her.

It annoyed her that he kept calling her in for meetings, especially since they were mostly pointless chatter. He'd ask her what she thought of her character development and how she was getting along with her co-stars. He would pry into her emotional state. He would ask her if she'd ever considered a love interest.

He was a pain in her ass, and she would do everything in her power to avoid answering the more personal questions while appearing to be a professional, happy-go-lucky girl next door type.

On her way into Head Writer's office, Girl Next Door happened to glance toward the entrance to The Studio, where she saw The Director looking toward the door and then to his watch. He seemed to be waiting for someone—Probably Starlette, since she was the only one that Girl Next Door knew of who actually went out at night. He seemed very occupied with waiting for Starlette, as though he were keeping a close eye on her comings and goings; closer than usual.

As she walked into Head Writer's office, Girl Next Door saw The Director look her way. As their eyes met, he seemed as curious as to what she was doing as she was him. The moment was fleeting however, as she walked into the office and Head Writer greeted her.

He was sitting behind his desk, which was littered with crumpled up pieces of paper. Behind him, whiteboards were covered in notes which seemed to detail various aspects of shoots which the Starlette cast had been on, and some ideas for future scripts which Girl Next Door couldn't make heads or tails of. It all seemed like random words to her. *Surprise guest. Revolt. Ballroom. S-2.0? Floppy white hat.*

That one had to be a coincidence.

She tried not to dwell on things which couldn't possibly be known to her at that point. Instead, she sat down in one of the chairs in front of Head Writer's desk and looked at him, waiting for him to speak.

In her mind, she was imagining grabbing him and snapping his neck. She wanted to drive a knife through his gut and watch him bleed out all over his crumpled up notes. She wanted to grab one of the whiteboard markers and jam it in his eye.

Instead, she smiled politely and hoped that he didn't read any of those things in her expression.

"Thanks for coming," Head Writer said. "I didn't interrupt anything, did I? I mean, I know Starlette's out, but I wasn't sure if you and Heartthrob were busy... Training or rehearsing or something like that."

"It's fine. What did you need?"

"I was just hoping that maybe we could discuss your character a little bit. I'm really hoping to open you up and give you more to do. Especially..." he trailed off. He stopped himself short of saying, *especially now that Wacky Best Friend is gone.*

She wanted to grab the laptop off of his desk and beat him to death with it. Still, she smiled and said nothing. Thus far, she could think of nothing that he said which would require a response from her.

"Umm…" Head Writer began again, looking down at his notes. "Are you religious? Spiritual?"

"Is that an appropriate question?" she replied.

"I just mean… I'm working on developing different sides to your character and I was hoping to bring out more of… Well, *you*."

"I'm fine with whatever you want to make me," she replied.

"You don't have a preference?"

"I consider myself a Methodist actress, but I doubt that'll help you," she told him.

"A—umm. Okay."

"Well, I mean, I'm non-practicing. But that's how I would identify myself, I think. Though I tend to like to keep an open mind. I've explored some of those other belief systems out there. The thing with the crystals and the one with the space shippy thing… I saw something about this ritualistic atheism online once but my 3G went down before I could fully convert."

She was talking out of her ass, of course, but it always amazed her to see how seriously people would take what she said if she spoke with a serious tone. Her delivery was perfect and he was taking notes as she spoke. It amused her.

How any of this would end up in a script for some future shoot, she didn't know. She was curious to find out how long it would take Ritual Atheism to catch on in The Studio though, and she planned to convince everyone that she was a level twelve non-believer.

Head Writer finished writing his notes and he turned his attention from the pad in front of him, to her. He had his pen at the ready, just in case he felt a need to write something else, but he didn't write. He just said, "We should talk more about that sometime. Maybe over lunch. I'm fascinated by different religious beliefs."

"Methodist acting is not a religion," Girl Next Door corrected, holding up a finger. "It's a state of religious *being*."

She was beginning to wonder how long it would take her to convert him to one of her religions. He seemed to be very easily swayed by her.

"I'm sorry," he replied, still clinging to the pen as though it were a means of self-defense. "So, that covers that. Now, I'd love to get your input on some possible developments between you and your co-stars."

"Huh?"

"I mean... How do you think you relate to your co-stars? How well do you work together? Do you socialize at all with Heartthrob? I mean... Since he's new and all."

Head Writer swallowed hard, as though he was getting nervous. Girl Next Door was pretty sure that she knew why these questions would make him nervous. She kept a polite smile on her face, but her thoughts turned decidedly more violent once again.

"I have a great relationship with my co-stars," she replied, as sweetly as ever. "We socialize. We talk about our feelings. We plot deaths together. Namely, the death of whoever ratted out Wacky Best Friend."

She stared at Head Writer, waiting for him to confess his actions to her so that she could proceed to kick his ass. Instead, he stared blankly at her, as though waiting for her to continue speaking.

She shook her head and dropped the smile, saying, "I know it was you. There weren't a whole lot of people who knew that he really wrote that script, and only one that I know of who would hold a grudge about it."

Head Writer's mouth fell open. He sat back in his chair and tossed the pen onto the desk. He looked her in the eye with what almost looked like shock... She figured that he was surprised that someone could figure out what he had done.

"Wacky Best Friend is in rehab," he said, after taking his time to consider his words.

"The clinic," she corrected, with sarcasm dripping from every word. "For exhaustion... Or so they say."

"You don't believe it?"

"I haven't heard anything from him in days. None of us have. It's not like him to ditch us without saying a word about it. Which means that they're covering something up."

"I think you're jumping to conclusions."

"Am I?"

"You say it's not like him, but how well do you really know him?"

"I know my co-stars."

"Yeah?" Head Writer shot back, leaning forward in his chair once again. "Did you know that he was writing a script?"

Girl Next Door didn't answer. She hadn't known about the script before it was given the green light, but that didn't mean anything. There were probably plenty of things about her that nobody knew.

Head Writer nodded in a way that annoyed Girl Next Door. He said, "We all have secrets. Maybe Wacky Best Friend really is in the clinic for exhaustion. Maybe he's not. Maybe he's on a secret shoot without you... Maybe he's not."

"Wow. Thanks for clearing this up for me," she replied. It was all that she could think to say.

"If it makes you feel any better, just know that I didn't tell anyone about what he did. I wouldn't do that. Honestly, I'm surprised that you think I would."

"Why? You're always messing with us."

"I do what I have to do. Sometimes that makes life harder for you, but... I never enjoy putting you in those situations."

Girl Next Door had gone into that room with such a solid grasp on what she believed about Head Writer and what he had done to Ethan. Now, she didn't know what to believe. He could be a liar. Writers were always making stuff up, after all. But if he was telling the truth and he wasn't responsible for Ethan going missing, she didn't know who was.

"Are we done here?" she asked, getting up from her chair.

"You didn't answer my question," Head Writer told her. "How is your relationship with Heartthrob?"

Girl Next Door looked down at Head Writer and was about to reply when she realized that she didn't know what to say. So, rather than say anything at all, she just walked out of the office.

She had a plan. Her plan was to walk back to her trailer, lock the door, get into bed and pull the blankets over her head. Maybe she would wake up in the morning, or maybe she would stay in bed until things went back to normal. She missed the easy days of hunting down bad guys and shooting them in the face repeatedly.

Now everything was... messy.

Her plan hit a bump as soon as she walked out of Head Writer's office.

She could see Starlette walking through The Studio, on her way back to her own trailer. She wasn't covered in blood, so that was a good sign.

Girl Next Door was just about to call out for Starlette to wait for her so they could walk together, but The Director grabbed her arm and pulled her off to the side.

"I need to talk to you," he told her.

Girl Next Door sighed and asked, "Why does everyone want to talk to me in the middle of the night?"

"Does Starlette ever discuss her late night adventures with you?" The Director asked, ignoring Girl Next Door's question entirely.

"Not really. It's kinda her own business, right?"

"So she never tells you where she goes or what she does?"

"She told me about how she ran into a few recording artists from The Label a few weeks ago. They haven't tracked down Bookworm either, but promised to let us know if they do, so we won't be trapped down here twiddling our thumbs until we all die," Girl Next Door informed him. "I thought that was nice of them. Oh, and their guns are made of gold and have diamonds all over them... It's completely impractical, but how cool is that?"

"I want you to follow her. Take Heartthrob with you. The next time she goes on one of her walkabouts, you find out where she goes," The Director ordered.

"What?" Girl Next Door replied, caught entirely off guard by the directions that she had been given. "I won't spy on her. She's my lead actress. She's my friend. I can't do that to her."

"Would you rather I give the job to someone else?" The Director asked. "Someone who doesn't like Starlette and who would be just fine seeing her fall, so that there could be another opening for some rising star in The Studio?"

Girl Next Door thought about the question for a second or two before asking, "Couldn't we just let her do whatever it is that she does?"

"I've tried that. But I have a feeling about this, and it's telling me that we should know what she's up to."

"Then here's another crazy idea... Ask her."

"Do you think she'd tell me? Really?"

Girl Next Door didn't respond to that question. She just wanted to go back to her trailer and go to sleep. Unfortunately for her, The Director's instructions weren't something that she could turn down. Someone would be following Starlette, and the last thing that Girl Next Door needed was another co-star vanishing from her life.

After great hesitation, she looked down at her feet, already feeling guilty for what she was about to do, and said, "Okay. I'll do it."

~

When morning rolled around, Starlette found herself sitting outside of the trailers, waiting. She wasn't sure exactly what she was waiting for, but ever since Ethan disappeared there was a constant energy in the air. Change was coming.

Within The Studio, tensions were high. Ever since the explosion of the theater and the discovery of the evidence which suggested that it was one of their own who had done it, there was a certain level of distrust that was developing between the various departments.

Actors believed that The Studio was too willing to ignore the suffering of those who did not fall under The Studio's protection. After an actor disappeared or officially ended their contract with The Studio, it was common for life to go on as usual. The nature of the industry was that no job lasted forever and an actor had to know that they could be out of work at any moment. Each time they were sent out on location, they were fighting to prove their worthiness to continue at The Studio.

This philosophy seemed to be crumbling. Though no formal protests had begun, there was a feeling in the air. People were growing dissatisfied with the fluidity of their contracts and how easily they could be terminated.

More and more, Starlette had witnessed hushed conversations about those who were no longer under contract, or those who hadn't qualified in the first place.

On the other side of the aisle, a building had been blown up by an actor. Many within The Studio—those who were not actors—viewed this as nothing less than another act of terrorism. A theater had been taken out, which was akin to spitting in the face of each and every person who had ever played a part in the creation of film... according to some.

Though crew members would end their conversations whenever Starlette or any other actor walked by, she got the sense that there was a growing resentment toward her kind. For a long time, actors had been the ones who were allowed to go out and hunt down Bookworm and his minions. Actors were the ones who were allowed to fight the battles, in the hopes of someday taking back the entertainment industry's standing as the leaders of modern society. All the while, crew members would be relegated to behind the scenes operations. Intelligence gathering. Location scouting. Shooting the scenes from afar. Capturing audio while always remaining out of view. Their work was just as important, but lacked the glory and satisfaction of drawing blood.

To some, it seemed as though this power that the actors had been given was beginning to grow out of control. They worried that the actors were becoming rabid animals, with no sense of right or wrong. They were becoming entitled little whiners who always demanded to have everything their way, as though they were the end-all-be-all of The Studio.

Starlette sat back and watched all of the tension rise and all of the concerns come into light. She said nothing about what she had done or why she had done it. Instead, she allowed for those voices to be heard, because even if she hadn't blown up the theater, these tensions would eventually rise and the future of their cause depended on these issues being resolved.

Somewhere in the back of her mind, Starlette questioned her actions. She wondered if she had gone too far in her attempt to save Ethan from the same fate that had befallen the likes of Token Black Guy and the original Mother Figure.

Nobody had gotten hurt. The building had been abandoned for years, even before the attacks. The conclusion that she came to time and time again was that she would do exactly the same thing in the future, if she thought it would help.

This was what separated Starlette from the other actors in The

Studio. She didn't follow the ensemble mindset. She wasn't content to wait around for her chance in the spotlight. She was a *lead*.

She hadn't seen any sign of Girl Next Door or Heartthrob since she woke up that morning. She had been sitting outside, waiting for one of them to come out of their trailers, if only so that she wouldn't have to be alone with her thoughts. Each time they drifted toward Ethan, they always turned dark. She needed to focus on something else. She wanted a script to be delivered or a production meeting to attend, but there was nothing.

"You look tired," Heartthrob said to her, as he took one of the nearby lawn chairs. He was dripping wet, most likely with sweat.

Starlette was surprised when he sat down near her. She hadn't seen or heard him leave his trailer that morning.

Turning to him, she said, "You're one to talk."

"Early bird catches the worm. Have you ever seen the line at the gym after four in the morning?"

"I try to avoid it."

"I wish I could afford to."

"Hey, it's not about what you look like on the outside. It's about who you are on the inside—in your heart. That's what matters."

"Yeah, that really only works on fat people," Heartthrob replied, turning toward Ember's trailer. "Is she up yet?"

"I haven't seen her."

"I think she's taking it pretty hard. Ever since Wacky Best Friend—"

"Ethan."

Starlette knew that Ethan was notoriously hesitant about telling people his real name. Ever since the attacks, he feared for his family back home and what would happen to them if Bookworm ever found out that he was still alive. He hadn't given up on that life. He held onto it and the person he was with a fierce grip. But Heartthrob was one of them now. He deserved to know who he was acting with.

He seemed taken off guard when Starlette told him Ethan's real name; as though wondering whether or not he was entitled to know it. After a moment, he said, "She's been pretty upset since Ethan left."

Starlette didn't respond to that. She didn't know what there was to say. Girl Next Door had a right to be upset. She had a right to be pissed off. If anything, Starlette's only regret was not including her in her plan to help Ethan. Even if it didn't work, Ember deserved a chance to feel as though she had done something to help.

"Anyway, I'm going to take a shower," Heartthrob said, as he stood up and walked toward his trailer.

Once again, Starlette was back to sitting alone. It felt as though there should be something for her to do, but she spent most of her day sitting there, waiting.

Heartthrob came and went a few times throughout the day. He was still getting acquainted with The Studio and sometimes wandered aimlessly through the various departments and storage compartments, just to pass the time.

While Starlette smelled food cooking in Ember's trailer throughout the day, she didn't see her come out of the trailer at all. She could picture Ember, alone in her dark trailer, frantically trying to bake some bread or cookies or something of the like, too depressed to talk to anyone.

She felt bad for her co-star. She wanted to help her. She just didn't know how.

As night fell, Starlette once again began to grow impatient. The energy that had been building up in her all day long was dying to escape. She needed to get out of The Studio. She needed the open air and to escape the growing tension of her world within those walls.

As soon as she knew that the sun was set, Starlette grabbed a set of knives and a gun from the prop department, and she left The Studio. With luck, maybe she could find a bad guy to kill.

~

Girl Next Door had spent a good part of her day pacing back and forth in her trailer. When she looked through the blinds which covered her windows, she could see Starlette sitting outside, and she wanted to go and act as though it were any other day. Except, it wasn't any other day. Now, she was a traitor. She was a backstabber. She was a spy and a snitch. If she went outside to talk with Starlette, she would surely be discovered, and she had no desire to be on Starlette's bad side.

When it became apparent that Starlette would not be moving for the better part of the day, Ember turned her attention to cooking... or *trying* to cook.

First, she attempted to make a pie, using the methods that she'd seen used by Michael Carter's wife, when she was holding the woman at gunpoint. Unfortunately, she didn't have enough butter for the crust, and just the thought of using shortening made her feel disgusting. She also didn't have apples, so that plan was quickly scrapped.

She moved on to cookies, where she found the methods of Mrs. Carter to be completely useless. She regretted not shoving her gun in the woman's face and demanding a lesson in cookie-making.

It was a long, bad day. Her cookies were too thin and burned on the bottom, which she blamed on the crappy oven that she'd been given in her trailer.

Being trapped in the trailer was hell for her. She had energy to burn off, and she needed to discuss The Director's orders with Heartthrob, except she couldn't get past Starlette in order to talk to him. She couldn't talk. She couldn't bake. She couldn't kick anyone's ass.

Just when she had reached a point where she could take no more of that trailer, Ember looked through her blinds and saw what she had been waiting for all day. Starlette had moved.

She checked her watch and saw how late it was getting. Surely, Starlette was on her way out of The Studio. Ember needed to act fast if she wanted to get Heartthrob and her gear before losing Starlette's trail.

She hurried out of the trailer... and then hurried back inside to make sure that the oven was off. After she was sure, she ran back out of the trailer and over to Heartthrob's trailer, where she knocked on the door as urgently as she could manage.

There was no answer. He wasn't there.

She turned and looked around The Studio, as far as she could see from the cluster of trailers where she now stood. There was no sign of Heartthrob.

"Okay, just think..." she said to herself, trying to slow down and catch her breath. "Where would I be if I were a super hot guy in

The Studio?"

She looked over to Starlette's trailer and considered checking to see if Heartthrob was in there, but she quickly shook off the idea. Starlette hadn't shown any sign of being interested in anyone since Headliner, and the wounds from that loss were still far from mended.

Girl Next Door hurried away from Heartthrob's trailer and through The Studio with no destination in mind. As she walked, she scanned the crowd for Heartthrob, but he was nowhere to be seen.

With no time to spare, she walked to the nearest production assistant that she could find and caught his attention. She said, "I need you to get on your walkie-talkie and see if anyone knows where Heartthrob is."

"Why?" the PA asked in response.

"Because we have orders from The Director and I can't find him. Just do it!"

The PA nodded and took a few steps off to the side, to make the call without Girl Next Door being a part of the conversation. After a few nods and mumbled words into his walkie-talkie, the PA turned to Girl Next Door and said, "He's been spotted over by the viewing room."

"Good," Girl Next Door said. "Tell whoever sees him to get him over to Wardrobe's department, now."

With that she ran off, toward the wardrobe department. After two or three seconds, she turned around and ran back to the PA and said, "Please."

Once again, she ran toward Wardrobe's department.

It seemed to take forever, but within minutes, Girl Next Door was suited up in one of Wardrobe's stealthy black costumes. Just as she was putting on her shoes, Heartthrob rushed into the Wardrobe department, already unbuttoning his shirt and preparing to slip into a new outfit.

"What's going on?" he asked, as Wardrobe handed him a two hangers with his darker clothing on it.

He didn't bother to go into a changing room. Instead, he pulled off his shirt and tossed it onto a nearby chair, and did the same with his pants.

"You're going to wrinkle your clothes if you don't hang them up," Wardrobe warned him, as she collected some empty hangers and clothing bags, and walked into her back room mumbling, "They're your own clothes, so it's not my concern. I'm just warning you."

"Thanks," Heartthrob replied, still looking to Girl Next Door for an answer.

She hadn't answered right away, because her thoughts had suddenly been redirected upon his arrival. When she managed to pull her brain out of the gutter, she told Heartthrob what The Director had ordered them to do. He seemed confused by this.

"Follow her?" he asked. "Why would we follow her?"

"Because he wants to know where she goes."

"But... She might kill us."

"Maybe he thinks there's less chance of her killing us than someone else."

"But I'm new and she's probably not all that attached to me yet."

"Don't worry. I'll cover you."

As they left Wardrobe, Prop Master was already headed their way with a simple supply of guns. They strapped them on as quickly as they could, and Prop Master handed each of them a flashlight to go along with their supplies.

"Where are you two headed? The Director didn't tell me," Prop Master asked them, seeming to want to pry without wanting to seem like he was prying.

"Just... training. The Director wanted me to take Heartthrob out on the town, since it's been slow around here," Girl Next Door said, with a cute and innocent smile.

Heartthrob looked at her, wondering how she could lie with such ease. She felt bad about it, but hoped that this wasn't reflected on her face. If The Director hadn't told Prop Master, it was for good reason. Or... She thought it was *probably* for a good reason.

In what seemed like a blur of frantically rushing while trying to look cool and ho-hum about walking out of The Studio so as to not attract any attention, Girl Next Door and Heartthrob were on their way to tracking Starlette.

Upon their exiting The Studio, Starlette was nowhere to be seen. They hadn't taken a very long time to get ready and head out, but what time they did spend was time that Starlette had to slip out of their grasp.

Girl Next Door stood at the entrance to The Studio and looked out into the night, trying to figure out the next move.

"This way," Heartthrob told her, as he started to walk away from The Studio and down the street.

It didn't take long for Girl Next Door to remember that she might have been at The Studio for longer, but when it came to cast rankings, Heartthrob was the male lead. Whether or not he was ordering her to follow him, or simply choosing a direction and walking, she didn't know. Whichever it was, she was happy to oblige. She had no desire to lead. Too much responsibility made her break out in hives.

As they walked, Girl Next Door tried to keep up with Heartthrob, but he was walking fast and his legs were much longer than her own, which meant that she had to move at a near jog in order to keep pace.

"How do you know where you're going?" she asked him.

"There's only one road."

"Oh. Good call."

"I'm hoping that when we reach the main stretch, we'll be able to see her. If not, it'll be a best guess situation. I figure that she'll probably head toward the heart of the city, but there's no way of knowing for sure."

"Sounds about right," Girl Next Door agreed.

Silence fell between them. It seemed as though Heartthrob was focusing on the task at hand and wasn't very interested in small talk. From time to time though, she could have sworn that she saw him look over at her. By the time she looked to confirm her suspicion, he was looking straight ahead once again.

When they reached the main stretch of road, they had two options. By turning right, they would be taken around the edge of the city. Turning left would lead them toward the center. They stopped to consider their options.

Fortunately for them, when they looked to the left, they saw Starlette in the distance. She was standing under a street lamp, and while they couldn't see exactly what she was doing, her decision to stop gave them the opportunity to track her.

As they moved forward, Heartthrob led Girl Next Door off of the road and away from any street lights. He told her, "Stick to the shadows."

She nodded her reply and stayed close to him as he led the way. She didn't necessarily have to stay close to him, but she chose to anyway.

Girl Next Door wasn't sure what she expected to discover when following Starlette. She had never given much thought to it and had assumed that Starlette got something out of walking the dilapidated streets of a formerly great city. Maybe she enjoyed finding smalltime thugs and giving them the what for. She thought the idea of following Starlette sounded boring, especially if she couldn't join in the fight at some point.

For the longest time, it was boring. Starlette walked for what seemed like an eternity, turning down empty streets and finding nothing but crumpled up newspapers blowing in the wind.

She walked at a quick pace, which Heartthrob seemed just fine with, but which Girl Next Door became frustrated with after a short while. She wasn't built to go on power walks with supermodel types.

As time went on, Girl Next Door began to notice that Starlette wasn't slowing down at any turns. She wasn't stopping to think about where she wanted to go. She wasn't wandering; she was headed for a very specific destination.

"Where is she going?" Girl Next Door asked in a whisper, though she doubted that Starlette would have been able to hear her even if she spoke in her normal tone.

Heartthrob shook his head and said, "I don't know."

Turn after turn, they followed her. On the longer stretches of road, they stayed close to buildings and made their way from doorway to doorway, just in case Starlette turned around to see if she was being followed.

She never turned.

Finally, they watched as Starlette walked through the front door of a very tall building. It seemed as cold and as dead as any building in the city, so the appeal of it was lost on Girl Next Door.

As she and Heartthrob approached the building, they stayed away from the glass doors and windows. They looked inside while remaining as hidden as possible. There was no sign of Starlette.

"Let's go," Heartthrob said, in a hushed tone, while leading the way into the building through the same door that Starlette had used.

Girl Next Door was close behind him as they entered the rundown lobby of the building. They looked around, trying to find some sign of where Starlette might have headed off too, but she was gone.

They separated and looked over different sides of the room, quickly looking over what had presumably been a nice lobby at one point, but which had been torn apart by thieves, looters, and/or drunken rock stars. The Label was notorious for their talent's needlessly destructive habits. Just one of many reasons why Girl Next Door was glad that they rarely ever worked together. She hated when she was forced to work with musicians who had never acted a day in their lives, just for the sake of getting a boost in the ratings.

As she searched the lobby, she shined her flashlight across the room. For the most part, this just allowed her to get a better look at dead plants and overturned furniture, but her light also reflected off of something on the far side of the room and caught her eye.

Upon investigating, she found a framed photo which hung on a door. It was an old black and white glossy, featuring an older man with crazy hair, a tiny hat and glasses. He had a smile on his face which was welcoming while not very natural at all.

He was an actor. Girl Next Door recognized him from a hundred different movies and old television shows, but she had no idea what the man's name was.

"Over here," she yell-whispered to Heartthrob.

As he walked across the room to join her, Girl Next Door gestured toward the photo. He looked at it and squinted just a little bit before saying, "Ed Wynn."

"You recognize him?" she replied, impressed by his ability to name the actor whom even she could not easily put a name to.

"Yeah. He was all over the place, back in the day."

"I'm impressed."

Heartthrob looked from the photo, to Girl Next Door and half-smiled at her. He said, "Thanks."

For just a moment, they both seemed to forget why they were in the building. They stood and silently impressed each other for what could have either been seconds or hours. Girl Next Door wasn't really sure how much time had passed before they snapped out of their daze and turned toward the door.

"We should probably go through the door. It's a sign, right?" she asked.

"Probably, yeah."

Heartthrob pushed open the door and led the way inside.

They found themselves in a stairwell, which led upward. How many floors there were, Girl Next Door couldn't even imagine. It was dark and the building seemed to stretch upward, into infinity.

"Oh... Please be the second floor. Please be the second floor," she chanted to herself over and over again as they stepped onto the first stair.

On the wall next to the stairs, there was a strange object, which Girl Next Door couldn't immediately identify. It had blinking lights, which were going bonkers at the moment, and it was beeping. It wasn't until a display of numbers came to life that she realized what she was looking at and her eyes widened.

"Bomb," she said to Heartthrob, just as the numbers began to count down from ten seconds.

She looked to him, waiting for some signal to run and hide, or maybe for him to impress her even more by disarming the bomb. Instead, he just looked at it for a moment and then started to walk up the stairs.

"It's a fake," he told her. "Starlette just walked by here and it didn't blow up. The numbers reset."

Girl Next Door followed Heartthrob, but expected her back to be blown off at any moment as she said, "Are you sure?"

"Has it been more than ten seconds yet?"

Girl Next Door looked back to the bomb, just in time to see it go crazy once again.

"Who put that there?" she asked.

"I think we're about to find out."

"Please be the second floor. Please be the second floor."

By the time they reached the tenth floor, Girl Next Door was beginning to think that they might have to climb for a while. She was tired and her legs were killing her.

Heartthrob seemed to be doing better, though he was covered in sweat. She had seen him heading off to the gym many times since his arrival, and he never came back quickly, opting for ice cream rather than cardio, as she was known to do.

At the twentieth floor, just when Girl Next Door thought that she might have a heart attack, she came across two small bottles of water sitting on the stairs, next to one of Starlette's trademark throwing knives.

Upon seeing the water, Girl Next Door and Heartthrob looked at each other and she said, "I guess we weren't as stealthy as we thought."

"I'm usually pretty stealthy," Heartthrob said back.

"You're not usually talking to me on your way up an echo-y staircase."

"This is true."

Girl Next Door took one of the bottles and handed it to Heartthrob. She took the second for herself and sat on one of the steps so that she could catch her breath while taking a drink. She had a small bag full of cookies in her pocket, which she pulled out and began to eat.

She held out the bag and asked Heartthrob, "Want one? Freshly baked and everything."

He took a cookie and began to eat it. After the first bite, he sat next to her and said, "This is really good."

"I know, right?"

"I can't believe these are from the same woman who used cayenne pepper on her French toast, instead of cinnamon."

Girl Next Door frowned and told him, "They're not. I picked them up at the craft service table before we left."

She took a quick sip of her water and put the cookies back in her pocket as she stood up and continued to walk. The last thing she needed was to spend good quality time discussing how much her baking sucked.

When they reached the thirtieth floor, Girl Next Door and

Heartthrob found an open door, leading to a hallway. A light could be seen coming from one of the doorways. They walked toward it.

Through the door, there was a large and impressive apartment, full of ugly 1980's furniture and smelling faintly of dead roses.

They found Starlette sitting in the living room of the apartment. She hadn't even broken a sweat.

It took Girl Next Door a moment to realize that there was someone else in the room. Hidden in the shadows with just a few hints of dramatic lighting over her eyes, there was a woman. It wasn't immediately apparent who this woman was, but as she leaned forward, Girl Next Door found herself standing in the same room with a legend of the silver screen; an icon of American cinema; and perhaps the only woman over fifty in Hollywood who retained the ability to raise her eyebrows... Tessa Baker.

~

It had taken Starlette twice as long as usual to get up to Tessa's apartment. As soon as she realized that she was being followed, she had to wait around for Girl Next Door and Heartthrob to catch up with her, and then she had to make sure that they didn't lose her trail as they tried their best to remain stealthy in the streets.

They could have saved quite a bit of time and effort, if only they'd called out for her to wait up and asked her what she was up to. She had nothing to hide.

Tessa had grown rather reclusive since the attacks and seemed a little annoyed when Starlette told her that they would be having company. It quickly passed when she realized that her audience would be expanding to a level that she hadn't enjoyed in years—a crowd of three.

"Oh," was all that Girl Next Door could seem to get past her tongue at first. After some time and effort, she managed to squeeze out, "You're... Oh, wow."

Heartthrob walked across the room and extended his hand, saying "It's a pleasure to meet you, Ms. Baker. My name is Heartthrob."

"I'm sure it is. The pleasure is all mine, darling," Tessa replied, holding his hand just a little bit longer than he probably would have liked.

Tessa then turned toward Girl Next Door and asked, "And

whom might you be? No, let me guess... Catholic Schoolgirl? Slutty Librarian?"

Girl Next Door seemed frozen in place as she said, "Girl Next Door, ma'am."

Tessa smiled, "Right. Now, tell me... Don't you think that Sarah Palin is an absolute genius?"

"No ma'am! She's an abomination and a crime against humanity," Girl Next Door replied, standing straight and smiling widely, as though reciting the oath of a secret society.

Tessa's smile grew wider, "They've trained you well."

Girl Next Door stood proudly. She had passed the test and she was quite pleased with herself.

Heartthrob turned to Starlette and asked, "This is where you've been coming?"

"Only for a while," Starlette said with a nod. "She has a lot to teach us."

Girl Next Door began to walk around the room, looking at each piece of memorabilia. She reached out, as though to touch Tessa's Gimme award, but pulled back at the last moment.

Starlette watched Girl Next Door explore, and she couldn't help but miss Wacky Best Friend. She tried to think of some of the crazy things he would say when he met Tessa, but her mind didn't work like his and she couldn't hear his lines in her head. He was gone.

"The Director will want to know about this," Heartthrob told her. "He'll want to meet with you. I don't know what we're going to tell him."

Tessa looked to Starlette, who gave her a slight nod. Tessa didn't want to say what she was about to say, but she clenched her jaw and said it anyway.

"Starlette and I have been discussing what we would do when your Studio eventually discovered me here. I've known for a while that they wouldn't like the idea of my talking with her, and now with you. They wouldn't want me to sway you with my vast experience."

"So, what will you do?" Heartthrob asked.

"I will meet with your Director. Over lunch, of course. I don't *do* offices or conference rooms."

Girl Next Door moved away from the memorabilia and took a seat next to Starlette as she asked, "Does this mean that you'll be joining The Studio?"

"God, no," Tessa told her. "I have played their games in the past and I have no intention of joining their ranks once again."

Heartthrob seemed puzzled as he asked her, "So, why meet?"

"For the very simple reason that if I do not meet with your Studio, they will deny you all the opportunity to talk with me. They will send people here and they will pester me night and day... I am a rogue element now; suddenly of great interest because I pose a threat, even if they can't quite figure out what that threat might be. I will meet with your Director in order to put his mind at ease, so that none of you will be forced to play the middle man. And then, once I've turned down his offer to play some symbolic role in your Studio, I will return here and go about my life."

Tessa stood from her chair and grabbed a cigarette from a nearby table, which she proceeded to light. She breathed deeply of the smoke and allowed it to billow around her head as she exhaled.

"Now," she said, "if you'll excuse me, I need to fetch my coat and we can be on our way."

~

The walk down the stairs was much easier for Girl Next Door than the walk up had been. Even with Tessa along for the walk, they managed to get down at a relatively quick pace, and made their way to the lobby of the building without much fuss.

Upon seeing the lobby, Tessa seemed slightly surprised to find it in a state of such disrepair. As she stood and looked at the rotting plants and the overturned furniture, she put a hand on her chest and said, "My God... This must be what it's like to live in one of those states between California and New York."

"You haven't seen this before?" Girl Next Door asked. "I thought you put the picture and the fake bomb out here."

Tessa nodded, "I did. But that was months ago. I haven't had reason to come down to the lobby in ages."

"Where do you get food?"

"There must be hundreds of apartments in my building.

Apartments have kitchens with pantries full of canned goods. Freezers full of frozen food. Bathrooms filled with toiletries."

"And nobody packed this stuff up when they left?"

"My darling girl, I do not live in the slums of Pasadena. The people who live in a building like this do not pack when they leave home, they simply buy new things... and new homes, for that matter."

"Wow," Girl Next Door said with great wonder. "That is so cool."

Starlette and Heartthrob were already by the front doors by the time Girl Next Door and Tessa reached them. Heartthrob held the door open for the women as they made their way out onto the street.

Tessa took a look around and filled her lungs with somewhat fresh air. She closed her eyes and allowed a breeze to wash over her and then she turned to Starlette and asked, "So, where do we meet our chauffer?"

"There is no chauffer," Starlette told her.

"That's insane. Who will drive the limo?"

"There is no limo."

"Then, how shall we get back to your little Studio?"

"We walk."

"Oh," Tessa sighed. "Well... son of a bitch, then."

They began the walk back to The Studio, and toward what was sure to be a memorable homecoming.

After they had gone, a waiter stepped out of the shadows and watched them fade into the distance. Once they were gone, he turned and told his friends, "It's clear."

~

As The Studio door opened and Starlette stepped inside, life was going on as usual for everyone who worked and lived there. They barely noticed her at all. As she, Girl Next Door and Heartthrob walked into The Studio together, Starlette saw The Director look their way.

He seemed upset by the fact that they were all together, and that Girl Next Door and Heartthrob had blown their cover. He watched Starlette walk down the steps, and he walked toward her, undoubtedly intending to call her into a meeting.

The door behind Starlette and her co-stars did not get to close all the way before it was caught and opened once again. The Director was surprised by this. He looked up to the door just as Tessa walked through it and stood at the top of the steps, taking in the sight of The Studio below.

The Director's mouth fell open. He was speechless.

Upon seeing The Director's reaction, a crew member looked toward the door and saw Tessa. Then there was another crew member, and another. By the time the door slammed shut behind her, dozens of The Studio's residents were looking her way.

Starlette didn't look back right away, but she could imagine what the look on Tessa's face must have been like. She could picture Tessa taking in the drama of it all, and looking out across The Studio as a queen would look out over her kingdom.

When Starlette reached The Director, he asked, "You've been hiding her. How long?"

"Not long," Starlette replied. "She didn't want to bother with The Studio."

"You don't work for her," The Director reminded Starlette. "When you find something this big out there, you damn well better tell us about it."

"I brought her in, didn't I?"

"Only because you were found out."

"Is that why?" Starlette shot back and walked past The Director, toward a table where she could place her weapons and other assorted props.

Tessa had taught her well in the short time that they had known each other. By walking away from The Director, Starlette was focusing the power in their relationship on herself. She claimed the dramatic effect and it removed the sharpness of his authority over her.

She didn't look back to see his response, but Starlette could imagine that The Director would not be pleased with her.

As Tessa walked down the stairs, to The Studio floor, the crowd was buzzing. People were coming from all over The Studio to see the actress who had once been a legend of the old Hollywood.

Starlette turned and watched as Tessa walked to The Director and said, "Judging from the worn baseball cap and unkempt beard, I'm assuming that you are The Director of this show."

"I am," The Director replied. "It's a pleasure to meet you, Ms. Baker."

Tessa took another look at The Studio as she said "I'm sure it is."

"I have a feeling that we have a lot to talk about," The Director told her. "If you'll come with me, we can go to my office."

"I never meet a director in an office, my dear. It interferes with my creative process. We shall meet over lunch. I assume that you have a commissary of some sort."

"Of course," The Director replied, guiding Tessa toward the commissary. As he left, he turned and looked at Starlette. She couldn't be sure what he was thinking in that moment. She hoped it was along the lines of *good job*, but she doubted it.

As Starlette stood there, Girl Next Door and Heartthrob joined her.

"I think this is going really well," Girl Next Door commented.

~

As they sat down with plates of food in front of them, Tessa looked The Director in the eye, sizing him up. She had no intention of actually eating. After all, a proper actress always had to give the impression that they neither ate nor slept. They were machines, and always looked glamorous in spite of this fact.

The Director ate his French fries. After all, he had no need to worry about his on-screen appearance. Sitting *behind* a camera didn't add ten pounds.

"You've been out there all this time?" he asked her, "Alone?"

"I've been out there, alone, for much longer than you've been in here."

"What do you mean?"

"I mean, look at me. Until I walked through that door with three of your finest young things, you hadn't even thought that I might be out there, did you?"

"Most actors are dead. I assumed..."

"And before the attacks, did you ever consider me for a role?"

The Director hesitated, which was all the response that Tessa needed.

After he took a sip of his drink, he said to her, "I realize that mistakes were made in the past—"

"Leaving me out there as a target for an international terrorist who is bent on seeing us all dead? That mistake? Oh, think nothing of it. I'm sure we've all done it at one point or another," Tessa quipped, dripping with just the right amount of sarcasm to make The Director feel guilty. "Never mind it, my dear. As it turns out, I wasn't on *their* list of concerns either."

"Nobody came for you?"

"Would I be here if they had? I'm hardly doing backflips and spin-kicks at my age."

The Director looked down at his food, but didn't touch it. He pushed his plate away and looked at Tessa once again. He shook his head and said, "What an unbelievable oversight."

Tessa smiled, "Your sympathy toward my having not been murdered is appreciated."

"I wish to make it up to you."

"How?"

"By allowing you to come in from the cold."

"This is southern California. It doesn't get cold here. That's why I chose film over Broadway."

"I mean, come to The Studio. Join us. We'll audition you. Screen test. Interview you... Find you a role to play here."

"And then stick me with one of those stage names? What would I be?" she asked. "Withered Hag? Aging Crone?"

"We would think of something."

Tessa picked up her fork and began to poke at her food, to give the impression that she was eating it, while not placing any in her mouth. She said, "I don't audition for anyone, sweetheart. I've worked too long and too hard. I won't stoop to that level anymore. Furthermore, I don't appreciate the structure that you have in place here. I don't like being ordered around. I don't like being typecast and forced to do the bidding of whomever it is that gives you your orders. I've heard what goes on here, and I don't like it."

"You've heard...?" The Director asked, seeming unaware of what she was saying. "What is it that you think we do?"

"I think that you send innovative young actors to the *clinic*, to be treated for *exhaustion*."

The Director sat back in his seat, not pleased with having that thrown in his face. He told her, "You aren't aware of all the facts,

Ms. Baker. I assure you that I tried my best to handle that situation in a way that would turn out best for all of us."

"I'm sure you did," Tessa replied. "But you're not running this show, are you, love? You're just a puppet, being played with by the suits."

"Ma'am, if you don't mind my asking... Why did you come here if you aren't interested in accepting a role here?"

"I came here so that we could make things very clear between us. You and your type turned your back on me long ago, and I have no intention of coming back here now. Starlette is a good girl. She serves your interests well, but she humored my desire to remain in the background for as long as she could. She doesn't deserve to be punished for my actions."

"That's not your concern."

"Actually, it is. I've seen studios drive young actresses to drugs. To depression. To death. I've seen what your system is, and it reminds me of the way things once were. For all of those girls who gave their lives up to your kind in the past, I am making it my concern," Tessa demanded.

She pulled a cigarette from her pocket and lit it. As she blew smoke in The Director's direction, she said, "My concern is for the health and wellbeing of all industry professionals. Now, I understand that Starlette might be locked down and forbidden to see me again, but I want you to know... She is making a difference out there. People on the streets know her and fear her. If you lock her up, your icon will be gone. Your audience will leave. Your ratings will go down the tank. And when that happens, every person in this place will lose the will to fight... I assume. I mean, I haven't left my apartment in ages, so... You get my point, I'm sure."

"I do," The Director said.

He sat back in his chair and thought the situation over, eyeing Tessa as though she were some piece of the same memorabilia that she kept on her shelves at home. She expected him to argue with her. She thought he would be a pain in the ass, and demand that she comply with his demands. However, he didn't.

Instead, he asked, "Are you sure you won't reconsider? I really would feel better if I knew you were safe."

She knew that he had once been an actor, but for a moment

there she thought that he might have been genuinely concerned for her. She didn't trust this instinct, but she couldn't be sure. So, she simply smiled and said, "My dear, I wish someone in this city wanted me dead. Unfortunately... Nobody even remembers that I'm alive."

She put out her cigarette and looked down at her plate of food once again. This time, she allowed herself one French fry.

~

Tessa spent two hours in The Studio, getting a quick tour from Starlette and The Director. When it came time for her to leave, Starlette was told to escort her back to her apartment building. Girl Next Door and Heartthrob volunteered to join them—this time riding to her building in a van.

As they entered the apartment building and walked through the lobby, Starlette and Tessa led the way, while Girl Next Door and Heartthrob walked a few yards behind. She didn't know why Heartthrob had chosen to walk next to her, rather than taking the lead with Starlette, but Girl Next Door was grateful for the company.

The walk up the stairs was quiet. Heartthrob said nothing to her, and she was too caught up in her own thoughts to even think of speaking. She found herself overcome by a sadness that she couldn't quite put her finger on at first. It was like she'd lost something or forgotten something, but she couldn't remember what it was.

Mixed with the constant stream of baking-related thoughts, this sadness did not get much attention. It simply weighed on her and the silence of their walk seemed to make it worse.

It was only when she connected the silence with the sadness that she realized that she missed the noise in the background. The constant back and forth with Wacky Best Friend. He had been there for her since her first day at The Studio, when he told her that her name was stupid. Since that moment, they had bickered like siblings and now... she missed her brother.

"Million-dollar contract for your thoughts," Heartthrob said, as they reached the landing of the twentieth floor.

Girl Next Door snapped out of the daze that she didn't even realize she was in and put a smile on her face as she said,

"Biscuits. I haven't tried making those yet and I don't see how hard it can be to mix lard with flour."

Heartthrob shook his head, denying this response.

Girl Next Door dropped the smile and said, "I'm thinking that Ethan would be making some sarcastic comment about how we keep going up and down these thirty levels of stairs. I'm thinking that I suck at my job, because I can't even cook bacon and I'm the only pacifist I know who kills people on a near daily basis. I'm thinking that I'm... I'm just tired."

Heartthrob nodded and said, "I can work with that."

She smiled. This time, for real.

"You can?" she asked.

"Yeah. I mean... some of it. The baking thing, you should just give up. You don't like it, which is why you're not good at it."

"I'm supposed to be a girl next door."

"And which girl next door are you basing your performance on?"

"What do you mean?"

"I mean, if it's a *Mary-Ann* type, then yeah. She had about a billion types of pies on that little island. But there are the tomboy types. There are the sexy but sweet girls... There's not just one type. And honestly, you're kinda doing more of a mother hen act than a girl next door act."

"So my choices are to either get really offended that you just dissed my performance, or get super psyched that I don't have to bake anymore?"

"Please don't bake anymore," he quipped with a grin.

Heartthrob seemed like he was done talking and he was moving on, but then he paused for a moment and his entire body shifted in a way that Girl Next Door would never have been able to describe if someone had asked her. He just became... different.

"When I was younger..." Heartthrob started, and his voice was different too. His eyes were looking at the stairs ahead, but they were seeing something a million miles away. "I knew this girl. We grew up just down the street from each other. She was..." he smiled and tried to find the right words before saying, "She was a *nerd*. I mean, she had these 1950's glasses that she wore sometimes and she spent half her time reading books on databases or giga-whatsits, or whatever. She was awkward and brilliant and... There were some afternoons that I would sit outside my house and I couldn't stop watching her. She was just so off in her own world, doing her own thing and I was completely fascinated by her."

"Did you like her?"

Heartthrob looked at Girl Next Door and his smile faded, but only slightly, as he said, "I loved her. She didn't notice me until halfway through high school and we broke up after graduation. I didn't see her again for years, but she never lost that vibe. And it wasn't something that you can force or make people think you have when you don't. It's just there. And *you* don't even realize that you have it already."

She smiled at him but had no idea what to say next. She just watched as he kept that look in his eye for a moment, and it suddenly drained as the story played out in his head. She wanted to ask him what happened with this girl, or possibly forget all about that and do her best to comfort him by whatever means necessary. She had no time to do any of this however, because their attention was pulled to the loud *clang* that came from overhead as something slammed into the railing above them.

~

A blender hit the railing next to Starlette's hand as it fell past her and crashed to the floor at the base of the stairwell.

She looked upward into the darkness, and then to Tessa, who was looking over the railing, toward the ground floor.

"I believe that was my blender," Tessa commented.

"Stay here," Starlette told her, pulling a gun from her belt and keeping an eye on the stairs ahead of her.

They were on the twenty-eighth floor when the blender rushed by them. Girl Next Door and Heartthrob were trailing several floors below. Starlette didn't plan on waiting for them to catch up before she hurried up to the thirtieth floor and into Tessa's apartment.

With her gun at the ready, Starlette crept up the stairs as silently as possible.

As she got closer to the thirtieth floor, she began to smell the faint scent of liquor and heard the laughs of several people on

Tessa's floor. She heard glass breaking and wood being smashed.

When she reached the thirtieth floor, she kept her back to the wall by the door which led into the hallway, in order to avoid being seen before she was ready. She took a quick look through the doorway and down the hall. She saw nothing but the lights from Tessa's apartment and the shadows of those inside.

Keeping close to the wall, Starlette made her way down the hallway and to Tessa's door. She was just about to take a look inside when a bottle of whiskey flew past her and smashed into the wall across from where she stood.

Judging from the voices inside Tessa's apartment, Starlette guessed that there were three people that she would have to deal with. Perhaps more, depending on how quiet some were. She had no doubt that she could handle them. So, after taking a deep breath, Starlette turned and walked into Tessa's apartment.

She didn't stop to think or to consider who the people were before she shot two of them in the head. It was only as their friends dropped to the floor that the other four realized that they were under attack. For some reason, they seemed to find this funny.

~

Girl Next Door and Heartthrob ran up the stairs as soon as they saw the blender fall past them. Their weapons were drawn and they were ready for action by the time they encountered Tessa, who was sitting on the stairs, smoking a cigarette.

"What happened? Where's Starlette?" Heartthrob asked Tessa.

"She went upstairs to face the vandals who have invaded my home," Tessa replied. "I do hope she minds the carpet. It's nearly impossible to get a good cleaning service these days."

"Stay here," Heartthrob ordered Tessa, and she raised her cigarette as if to say *yes, sir.*

Heartthrob led the way as he and Girl Next Door hurried up the stairs. They only made it to the twenty-ninth floor however, when they came across a waiter and a waitress walking through the door which led to that floor's hallway. Each of them had an armful of knickknacks that they intended to steal.

The waiter was dressed in rags that looked as though they had been dragged through the sewer. His hair was a mess and he had the words *Tip Jar* carved into his forehead. Girl Next Door had to wonder if this was his name, or if he was just very crazy.

When Tip Jar saw the two actors coming, his eyes widened and he screamed like a little girl. He then proceeded to break the head off of a Hummel figurine and wave it through the air like a knife.

This answered Girl Next Door's question regarding his sanity.

The waitress had surprisingly clean clothes and her hair was pulled into a tidy ponytail. She had a green canvas messenger bag slung across her chest, filled with food, clothing and household cleaners that she had taken from one of the apartments. Girl Next Door was taken aback by the togetherness of this one, and worried that she might be an issue... until the waitress opened her mouth and blood poured onto the floor, along with a handful of thumbtacks which she had apparently been trying to eat.

The waitress smiled and muttered, "Cawn ow tack yow owder pwease?"

She then spit one more thumbtack onto the floor.

"Great Scott, these people are creepy," Girl Next Door said to Heartthrob, while keeping her gun aimed at the waitress' head.

"I know what you—" Heartthrob started to reply, before Tip Jar dropped most of his loot and charged toward them with his Hummel-shiv ready to do damage.

Heartthrob took a shot at center mass, but his bullet was met with a *clang* sound, which suggested that Tip Jar had something tucked under his shirt.

Heartthrob couldn't get off another shot before Tip Jar jumped on top of him and began to wave the Hummel-shiv in Heartthrob's face. Heartthrob blocked each of these attempted attacks.

Girl Next Door wanted to shoot the crap out of Tip Jar, but she couldn't get a clear shot. She couldn't risk shooting Heartthrob— Wacky Best Friend would never let her hear the end of it.

The waitress threw something at Girl Next Door. Without thinking, Girl Next Door took aim and pulled the trigger, and whatever the item had once been turned into a cloud of plaster dust. She smiled and said, "Like skeet!"

The waitress reached into her bag and pulled out a bottle of wood polish, which she threw at Girl Next Door. This time she charged toward Girl Next Door as the wood polish took Girl Next

Door's focus off of her. By the time Girl Next Door avoided the polish, the waitress was nearly on top of her.

Girl Next Door tried to shoot off another round, but the waitress knocked the gun away before proper aim could be achieved.

With the waitress so close, trying to use the gun was pointless. Girl Next Door had to resort to hand to hand combat, which grossed her out because the waitress was now covered in her own mouth blood.

The stairwell filled with blurs of motion and the grunts that came with fighting. Heartthrob and Tip Jar were scrambling on the ground, while Tip Jar continued to scream and slice through the air with his Hummel-shiv, and Heartthrob tried his best to avoid being cut; especially in the face and abs.

Girl Next Door was holding her own in the fight against the waitress. After a series of punches and kicks to the waitress' face, the waitress came back strong and punched Girl Next Door in the gut so hard that Girl Next Door fell backward, to the ground.

As the waitress charged at her once again, Girl Next Door began grabbing the random objects that the waitress and Tip Jar had dropped. She threw them at the waitress. Unfortunately, this did very little to slow the waitress down, and she charged at Girl Next Door while letting out what sounded like some sort of a battle cry.

The waitress jumped in the air and balled her fist, bringing it down as hard as she could toward Girl Next Door's face.

Girl Next Door rolled out of the way and let the waitress land beside her. She then spun around and grabbed the waitress with her legs. With a twist, the waitress was brought to the ground.

Girl Next Door felt around for something that could be used as a weapon, and found herself with a leather belt in her hand. She wrapped the belt around her fist and began beating the snot out of the waitress, as though the belt were a set of brass knuckles.

The waitress was beaten down enough to give Girl Next Door the time she needed to jump up to her feet, but it wasn't long before the waitress pulled herself off the ground and charged at Girl Next Door once again.

This time, Girl Next Door was prepared. As the waitress

charged, Girl Next Door moved forward and kneed her in the stomach. When the waitress doubled over, Girl Next Door grabbed the strap of the waitress' messenger bag, wrapped it around her neck and used the strap to gain leverage as she flung the waitress over the railing.

Rather than watch the waitress fall to her death, as intended, Girl Next Door watched as the messenger bag caught onto one of the finials of the art deco-style cast iron railing.

The waitress kicked and clawed at the strap around her neck, trying desperately to avoid being choked to death while apparently failing to realize that pulling herself free of the strap would not spare her life.

From below, Girl Next Door heard the sound of Tessa clapping.

When she got to Heartthrob, he was on top of Tip Jar, punching him repeatedly in the face.

"You good?" she asked him.

"Go help Starlette!" he replied.

Girl Next Door hurried past him and up the stairs, to the thirtieth floor. She ran down the hallway and into Tessa's apartment just in time to see a mangled waiter drop a lighter onto the floor, which burst into flames. The waiter was immediately engulfed as Starlette grabbed Girl Next Door's arm and pulled her back through the door, yelling, "Run!"

As Girl Next Door and Starlette ran down the hall, fire spread across the carpet with impressive speed. Soon, the entire floor was a mess of flames and smoke.

The fire seemed to be chasing the actresses down the hall, which Girl Next Door attributed to the vast amounts of alcohol that she only now felt soaking the carpet under her feet and saw splashed on the walls around her.

In order to escape the flames, Starlette shoved Girl Next Door down the stairs, while leaping over the railing herself.

Girl Next Door fell on top of Heartthrob, which drove the Hummel-shiv that Heartthrob was holding into Tip Jar's neck.

Starlette must not have had a plan for survival when she leapt over the railing, but she saw an opportunity and she took it. As she fell downward, she grabbed onto the legs of the waitress who had been struggling to survive up to that point. With Starlette's weight added, the waitress' neck snapped and she died at once.

For a moment, Starlette dangled there, swaying back and forth as chaos turned to silence in the stairwell, and the glow of fire from above flickered across the walls. Girl Next Door and Heartthrob raced down the stairs and helped to pull her up.

When all of them were safe once again, they found themselves standing next to Tessa, who was smoking a cigarette and slightly nodding to herself, taking in the scene around her.

"You know..." Tessa said in as cool a tone as ever, "I think I might just reconsider your Director's offer after all."

CHAPTER NINE
BAD PUBLICITY

The blinds were closed in Heartthrob's trailer, and only a few rays of light were able to creep past them. On the small table in the kitchen area of his trailer, there were paper plates that had been used for food, and notebooks filled with notes that he had been making about all of the scripts that he'd been given since joining The Studio.

He was not ordinarily one to spend his time keeping a journal full of his thoughts and feelings, but when his nights turned sleepless, he often found himself hunched over his table, working. Even if there was no work that needed to be done, he would scribble away at his pad and occupy his mind until it had calmed down enough to start the cycle all over again.

The cycle was simple. He would stay awake for as long as his body would allow, and then fall into bed where he would quickly fall asleep. As he drifted off, he would be jolted awake several times by flashes of horrible images or the feeling of falling from a high-up place. He would eventually find sleep and settle into a deep enough state to dream such vivid dreams that he could *smell* the dream world around him. He lived in that world every night, and with each night that passed, it took on more detail and became more real.

His dreams were abstract in some ways, but always focused on the life he had led in the time between the attacks and his being brought into The Studio. They always involved the same people, and they always ended with Heartthrob waking up in a bed that was so soaked in sweat that he had stopped to wonder once or twice if he had wet the bed.

In recent days when he awoke, he found himself in the middle of a fit of screams that he had somehow slept through until the images in his dreams scared him enough to wake him. He didn't know how long he had been screaming, or how loudly. He imagined that he had been heard by his fellow cast members, and probably others within The Studio, but nobody ever said a word to him. He wasn't sure if this made matters better or worse. On the one hand, he didn't have people prying into his life and trying to get him to share his pain with the world. On the other hand, he knew that they knew. He felt like people were watching and whispering behind his back.

When he woke, Heartthrob usually started his day by spending two or three hours in the gym. He barely had the energy to force his way through his workouts, but it helped him to refocus for the day. He ran, lifted and crunched until he no longer felt like sitting in a dark room for the rest of his life. Once the process was complete, he could compartmentalize and keep his eyes on the road in front of him, rather than behind.

So far, this method was working for him. He didn't expect it to last forever, but if he could manage to keep his life in order until he could look Bookworm in the eyes, put a gun to his forehead and pull the trigger, Heartthrob didn't care what came after.

In the days since Tessa Baker had been forced to join The Studio, life had been calm. There were no shoots to go on. No scenes to lock down. Heartthrob's life had become a game of *hurry up and wait*, without the benefit of knowing what he was waiting for.

As he walked toward his trailer, on his way back from the gym, Heartthrob kept his head down and tried to attract as little attention as possible. He didn't mean to come across as cold or rude, but he also didn't want to confirm his own suspicions that people were watching him and talking about him.

He told himself that it was all in his mind. After so many months of running and hiding and being the target of Bookworm's minions, he figured that paranoia was something that he was going to have to deal with. Still, he kept his eyes down for most of the walk back to his trailer.

It was only when he dropped his towel and bent over to pick it up that his eyes turned toward his surroundings. What he saw was confirmation of his crazy and irrational delusions. People *were* looking in his direction and they *were* whispering to each other.

Heartthrob froze. His eyes moved from person to person, and while he wasn't the focus of every eye in the house, there were enough people looking his way to make his heart beat just a little bit faster.

A hand grabbed his shoulder, and without a thought or a moment of hesitation, Heartthrob grabbed it and twisted, until the hand was being held behind the back of the person who had reached out for him.

"Ow!" Ember cried, though not in an angry or truly hurt way.

She broke free of his grip and twisted his own arm behind his back as she said, "Calm down, champ. It's just me."

Heartthrob's eyes widened as he realized who he had grabbed. He was scared that he had somehow hurt her without meaning to and began to say, "Oh, God. I'm sorry. I'm so sorry. I just didn't know—"

"It's fine. I probably shouldn't go around sneaking up on guys who normally carry guns and enjoy stabbing people," Ember replied.

"I don't *enjoy* it. It's just... therapeutic."

"Way less creepy."

"Is your arm okay? I didn't hurt you, did I?"

"*Pssh,*" Ember smirked. "Like you could hurt me, even if you wanted to? I take down thugs that are bigger than you all the time... And then I apologize and feel really bad about it, because I really do wish that we could just talk things out more often."

Heartthrob always seemed to find a grin on his face when Ember spoke. She had a way of saying things that didn't just distract him from all of his worries, but seemed to genuinely make them better somehow. She reminded him of a world that didn't revolve around gunplay and bloodshed.

Ember took a moment before continuing to speak, since she lacked a proper segue into what she actually came to say.

When she spoke, her eyes were filled with concern. She said, "I just wanted to come and make sure you're okay."

It seemed clear to him that she was talking about his screaming in the middle of the night. He had hoped that she was an incredibly sound sleeper and might have missed that quirk of his, but now it seemed that she hadn't.

He looked down and said, "I'm fine. I just have dreams sometimes, you know. I'm sorry if I—"

"Actually, I'm not talking about that," Ember cut in. "I mean, if you want to talk about that, we can. I'm here for anything you might... y'know... want. But I was talking about the other thing."

Now Heartthrob was lost. He had no idea what she was talking about, but he looked around and saw everyone staring at him and he began to feel like the kid in school who was always the last to hear about the cruel rumor or the slur that was painted on his locker.

He looked to Ember for some hint as to what she was talking about. For some reason, he couldn't figure out a way of asking what it was that he should be worried about.

Ember leaned closer and in a quiet tone she said, "I'm sorry. I figured you knew."

She reached into her back pocket and pulled out a piece of paper which had been folded. She opened it up and handed it to him, still trying to stay as close and quiet as possible. He could see her preparing for his reaction.

When he took the paper and looked at it, he saw that it was an article from a tabloid website called *The Celeb Spinner.* The headline on the article, written in big, bold letters read: *STUDIO HEARTTHROB RESPONSIBLE FOR FAMILY'S SLAUGHTER.*

He stopped breathing. His hands went numb. His brain would not form thoughts.

Everything that he had hoped to put behind him was now staring him in the face once again. Everything that he had hoped to keep private and never speak of again was now the talk of the town.

He didn't read the entire article. He could only see a word here and a word there, but from what those words suggested, it seemed as though his story was out—All of it.

"Talk to me," Ember said, but her voice sounded as though she were speaking from a distance.

She put a hand on his shoulder, and he felt his legs adjusting for the change in balance, but he could not feel her.

"Hey," she said, stepping toward him. "C'mon. We should get you back to your trailer."

Ember was looking around now. She could see everyone watching him and talking about him.

Heartthrob had spent years being photographed in his underwear. He had been ogled and touched in inappropriate ways by complete strangers. He had spent a good amount of time feeling awkward or slightly uncomfortable, yet this was the most naked he had ever felt in his life.

Ember tried to take him by the arm and lead him back to his trailer, but Heartthrob didn't move; he couldn't. Instead, he looked down at the article in his hands and stood perfectly still for what seemed like an hour.

In the back of his mind, he was yelling at himself to pull it together and act like a professional, but the sensible part of him had temporarily lost control of his body and the more he tried to fight this, the less control he had. Eventually, he found himself sitting on The Studio floor, staring at the article in his hand, while Ember stood over him and yelled at the people who tried to gawk.

~

Starlette was at the stage, alone. There was nobody for her to spar with, and she hated punching bags. When she threw a punch, she wanted to know that something was going to swing back. She wanted to feel the surge of adrenaline that came from being caught off guard.

The stage was as quiet a place as any in The Studio. A lot of the actors hated to rehearse, or preferred to do their training in the comfort of their own space. At certain times of the day, the stage would be crowded, but Starlette knew when she could go there and be alone, and that was why she found herself there at that particular moment.

Early that morning, she had been walking to breakfast when she heard the first rumblings of big news in the tabloids. She figured that they had discovered top secret information regarding an upcoming shoot, and the writers would have to rethink their plans in order to compensate.

It wasn't until she was sitting and eating that she saw the sound mixer's assistant, Boom Mike, reading an article on his cell phone. As he shook his head and let out a slight disapproving grunt, she caught a quick glimpse of the headline and saw Hearrthrob's name. Within a couple of seconds, that cell phone was in her hands and she was reading through the article while everyone around her waited to see how she would react.

She smirked as she read it. She tossed the cell phone down on Boom Mike's table and shook her head with a big smile on her face as she said, "People will believe anything they read on these websites."

And then she walked away.

She went to the stage, because she didn't want to go back to her trailer. She didn't want to be there when Heartthrob discovered what had happened to him, or see Ember crying the same way she cried when Ethan disappeared. She'd had her fill of pain in recent days, and if she was forced to endure one more tear from someone she cared about, she couldn't be held accountable for whatever actions she took as a result.

The stage was made to look like heavy marble pillars and to give the impression of grandeur. Some compared its appearance to Mount Olympus. The truth of its construction was that it was made of rather lightweight materials; wood and foam. Since the actors began using it as their sparring area, it had taken quite a beating.

Starlette stared at some of those dents and gashes, and seriously considered ripping the whole thing down. She was tired of the stage and the way it presented its users as mythical gods who couldn't be touched by the outside world. She wanted it gone, but she resisted the urge to destroy it.

"My word," came the voice of Tessa Baker, from the stage entrance. "Would you look at this?"

Tessa walked in with a cigarette in one hand and a glass of brown liquor in the other. She marveled at the sight of the stage as she made her way toward Starlette.

"I saw this on television back in the day, and it was impressive then. But now... I have half a mind to burst into some Greek tragedy. Perhaps a scene from that *Mamma Mia* movie."

Tessa made her way to Starlette and leaned against one of the nearby pillars, striking an adequately dramatic pose as she did.

This was the first time that Starlette had seen Tessa since the older actress joined The Studio. After her apartment was destroyed and Tessa returned with them to The Studio, she had been whisked away, in order to undergo proper assimilation procedures. Starlette imagined this as looking something like the scene from *The Wizard of Oz*, where Dorothy and her friends arrive in the Emerald City and get the full Oprah-style makeover.

"You seem to be doing well," Starlette told her. "I'm glad."

"This is what being an actress means. You don't always have to like where you work. Sometimes you take the job you don't want, just so that you'll eventually be able to take the job you do."

"What job do you want?"

"I want the job I used to have. Don't you?"

"Right now, I'd settle for a pony," Starlette sighed, before asking, "So, what job did they give you? Are you going to be out there with us, shooting up the bad guys?"

Tessa laughed a deep and hearty laugh which may or may not have been fake. She took a sip of her drink and said, "I am what they are affectionately calling a *Consulting Producer.*"

"What does that mean?"

"It means they have no job for me to do, but they want me to smile and pretend that I'm content to live by their rules. They don't want me to cause a stir, or tell people like you that the Star

System doesn't work quite as well for actors as it does for The Studio," Tessa said. "As long as I don't say anything like that, they'll be happy."

"Is that the name they gave you? Consulting Producer?"

"Oh good lord, no. I am still just the same old Tessa Baker that I've been for years, for the same reasons today as they gave me back then. It's calming and sounds friendly. Besides, nobody out there wanted me dead until a few days ago, so I don't think I'm a big priority for Bookcover."

"Bookworm."

"Whatever."

Tessa pushed off of her pillar and took a short stroll around the stage before taking a seat next to Starlette. She said, "The lighting in this place is absolutely disgusting. You can see everything."

Starlette didn't respond. She didn't have anything to say on the topic of lighting. It was not her department, and far from her main concern in that moment.

Tessa went on to say, "So, why are you sitting here, bathed in this wretched light?"

"I'm deep in thought. Waiting for the part of the story where I come to some obvious and cliché realization, and storm off to set things right."

"Set what right?"

"You haven't seen the headlines?" Starlette asked. "Heartthrob was torn to shreds in the rags and I have no clue what to say about it."

"Do people still read those things? I thought that the one good part of this... would you call it a genocide?"

Starlette shrugged.

"Well, whatever you'd call it... I would have thought that the one saving grace would be the total downfall of the tabloid press. They are nothing more than the bottom feeding motherfuckers who live for the moment when they can destroy one of us."

After saying this, Tessa took a moment to think and then added, "Though, when one phrases it in *that* way, I suppose it makes sense that they would still be around. They want us to suffer. They want us to fail. They want to see you and everyone you love inflicted with every sort of pain that can possibly be thrust upon you from afar."

Starlette listened to Tessa and her words set off a chain reaction of emotions. She came to connect the tabloids with the sort of print-loving terrorists that had destroyed her world. They were Bookworm's lowest minions, preying on the spirits of those who were already beaten down. They wanted to make her and her co-stars weak, so that they would be vulnerable to attack.

Starlette found herself growing angrier by the second. She was no longer content to ride out the wave of this tabloid invasion of her co-star's life. She would not sit by and wait for the next attack to take place. Instead, she would track down the source of this report and she would inflict a pain upon them that would send a message to Bookworm and his kind. It was time for the other side of this war to begin running.

When Tessa saw the resolve in Starlette's eyes, she took another drag of her cigarette and told Starlette, "The Director is waiting for you in the conference room."

Starlette turned to Tessa, slightly confused and said, "He was already planning a response?"

"The PR department has been working with the writers all morning," Tessa told her. "I was just coming here to make sure you were in the right frame of mind for the work you have to do. Call it... Consulting Producer-ing, or what have you."

~

"We're gonna kick some asses, right?" Girl Next Door asked, as she sat in her usual chair in the conference room, looking at The Director and then to the writers.

While these meetings could normally be attended by various crew members and department heads and the door would remain open, this meeting was different. Only The Director and two or three writers joined them in the room. The door was closed, which Girl Next Door was curious about, but didn't immediately question, because she figured that it would be explained at some point and she was more interested in her role there, rather than what everyone else *wasn't* going to be doing.

The chair next to her was empty, and had been ever since Wacky Best Friend went away. Heartthrob sat in the chair beside it, leaving a gap between Girl Next Door and himself which seemed really sweet and considerate until this particular day. Now, that space between them seemed like a million miles and he appeared isolated to her.

He had been different ever since seeing the article about his family. He eventually came out of his daze, but he wouldn't look Girl Next Door in the eye. He flinched whenever she tried to put a hand on his shoulder or comfort him. It seemed like a wall had been torn down inside of him, and the flood of his other life was now pouring into his life at The Studio.

"Tell me we're kicking asses," she pressed.

"We sincerely want to kick asses," The Director told her. "Our only problem now is that we don't know how to find the asses that we want to kick."

Girl Next Door furrowed her brow and asked, "Meaning what?"

"Meaning, websites can be updated from anywhere in the world. Our affiliate Studios are working with us to pinpoint exactly where this update might have come from but right now, we just don't know."

"Then why are we in here?" Starlette asked.

The Director adjusted his baseball cap just slightly and looked toward Head Writer for just a moment before looking back to Starlette and saying, "Because we wanted to discuss something with you. It's something that you're not going to like."

As though the day hadn't been plagued enough already. Girl Next Door had half a mind to cover her ears and start singing *la-la-la-la* so that she wouldn't hear what The Director had to say.

He paused before going on with whatever it was that he wanted to tell them. The longer he waited, the more dread Girl Next Door felt in her gut. She looked to Starlette who had her normal steely glare as she waited for The Director to continue. She then looked to Heartthrob, whose mind was wandering in an entirely different direction.

As Girl Next Door turned back to The Director, the door opened and a man walked into the room. He was good looking enough, with his hair and makeup already done. He was wearing dark clothes, which included skinny jeans and a black jean jacket over a dark purple t-shirt.

At first, she wondered which department he worked with. She

didn't recognize him, so she knew that he must be a recent transfer. Her mind didn't allow her to go to the most obvious conclusion until he closed the door, walked to the empty chair beside her and sat down.

As he settled in, this man smiled at her and gave her a little wave before turning back to The Director and saying, "Sorry I'm late. You wouldn't believe how long it took to get my hair right this morning. Hair was all like *'you're done'*, and then I was like, *'umm, no.'* So we had to start all over. It took for-ev-ver."

Girl Next Door's mouth dropped open and no words could properly express how she felt in that moment. She looked to Starlette, who was eyeing the man next to Girl Next Door with no expression on her face at all.

Starlette turned to The Director and asked the obvious question with only a look.

"I know what you're all thinking," The Director started.

"In that case, I'd like to apologize for my language," Girl Next Door said back.

The Director ignored her and continued, "This is Sassy Gay Friend. He'll be joining you until further notice."

"We already have a *Friend*. We don't need another *Friend*," Girl Next Door told The Director before turning to Sassy Gay Friend and saying, "No offense."

Sassy Gay Friend waved his hand in the air, letting her know that he thought nothing of it, and then proceeded to check out his nails. He winced when he saw the state they were in.

Starlette kept her expression as low-key as possible and betrayed no emotions at all when she said, "I thought you said that you were hoping for Wacky Best Friend to return."

"We are," The Director told her. "Sassy Gay Friend isn't a replacement for Wacky Best Friend. He's just crossing over from another cast to help fill out your cast for the time being. Right now, he's being considered a recurring guest star."

"Does his contract have the option for more?" Starlette pressed, in a tone that did not convey the type of anger that Girl Next Door was hoping to get from her.

It was hard for Girl Next Door to be angry. It did not fit the role that she had been given to play at The Studio, so she could never seem to find a good time to let loose and scream when she felt like it. Instead, she relied on Starlette to make the quips and to be the hard-ass in the room. She expected Starlette to stand up for what they all thought and felt, because she could get away with far more; because of both her character and her position as the lead in their cast.

In her mind, Girl Next Door was screaming for Starlette to act more upset. She wanted Starlette to throw something or hit someone. She wanted Starlette to wipe the smug look off of Head Writer's face.

Instead, Starlette remained fairly composed in the midst of all of the day's twists and turns.

"Sassy Gay Friend has a contract with The Studio. Whether he is on your cast or someone else's, he will be working here with us. So, yes, his contract does stipulate that he can be placed on any cast for as long as he's needed," The Director told them.

Girl Next Door placed her hands in her lap and balled her fists. She allowed her face to relax and she presented herself as a nice, sweet little co-star as she said, "How long until we can go after the tabloid?"

The Director looked to her and said, "I'll let you know as soon as any of us knows. Until then, we have another job to do here in The Studio."

Starlette straightened in her chair, just a little bit, and asked, "What kind of job?"

"The recent tabloid story is only one in a list of pieces that have been released in recent weeks. Certainly, it's the most damaging, but it's not the first."

On the monitors behind The Director, headlines from *The Celeb Spinner* appeared. They included article titles such as:

BOMBSHELL DEATH A SUICIDE?

SONGSTRESS LIP-SYNCS DURING VITAL SHOOT

And *GIRL NEXT DOOR CAUGHT IN FRIENDLY FIRE DRAMA*

Upon seeing her own name on the screen, Girl Next Door yelled, "It was *one* frickin' extra!"

"You shot an extra?" Sassy Gay Friend asked. "God, I've always wanted to shoot an extra."

"It was a mistake," Girl Next Door assured him.

Sassy Gay Friend winked and said, "If that's what you want to call it."

She didn't like him. She could tell already. He was acting as though she was a liar, and he was sitting in Wacky Best Friend's chair, and she did not like him even a little bit. She gave no indication of this fact, however. She was more professional than that.

"There was a notice posted this morning that more shocking and damaging revelations like Heartthrob's story will be posted over the next few days. We don't know who will be targeted or what will be said, but if this is true, it presents an obvious problem for us," The Director told them.

"So, we find the guy who runs the site and we stick our reboots up his harddrive," Girl Next Door declared, unable to resist the opening that Wacky Best Friend normally would have taken.

The Director nodded and said, "Yes, that is our primary goal. But a second unit will be working within The Studio. Since Starlette and Heartthrob will be needed for the primary shoot, I'd like for Girl Next Door to head up the second unit, and Sassy Gay Friend will back her up."

Girl Next Door didn't protest, but she hardly jumped for joy either.

"You think it's one of us? Someone in The Studio?" Starlette asked.

"We do. Someone has been leaking personal information from various actors, which would not be known to the outside world. As much as I hate to say it, that narrows the list considerably," The Director informed her.

"I never told anyone about..." Heartthrob started in a quiet voice, but he couldn't finish the sentence.

"I know," The Director nodded. "This leads us to believe that that information came from another source. Once we track down the person responsible for the website, we can question him about that source. Any questions?"

Yeah, how do I figure out who the leak is? popped into Girl Next Door's mind, but she didn't say it out loud. She figured that doing so might make her seem less than professional, so she remained quiet and tried to look like she knew what she was doing.

Nobody had anything else to add, so The Director took a look around and said, "Okay, then I guess we're done here. Remember, we're running on a small crew with this one for a reason. Keep it quiet out there."

With that, the meeting was over. The Director and Head Writer stayed where they were and continued talking with each other. Everyone else in the room, with the exception of Heartthrob stood and began to make their way out of the room. Girl Next Door was not happy. She planned to wait for Starlette and Heartthrob and then complain about Wacky Best Friend being replaced in a very hushed—but angry—tone.

As she walked out the door, she turned to see if Heartthrob was following yet. He was not.

Heartthrob was sitting in his chair, staring at one of the monitors at the back of the room, which was displaying nothing except The Studio logo. He was deep in thought.

Just when Girl Next Door was about to go back and get him, Heartthrob stood and walked to The Director and Head Writer and said, "I have an idea."

Girl Next Door was as curious as anyone to hear what he had to say, but he looked at her and silently told her that he was fine and that she should go.

She left him there, but continued to worry. The last thing they needed was for another actor to make an unsolicited pitch and go missing. But the ball was already rolling and there was nothing she could do to help him.

As she left the conference room, Girl Next Door looked around for Starlette. There was a lot to talk about and to plan. She wanted to ask for Starlette's thoughts on tracking down the in-house leak, but knew that she should probably refrain from talking about it in public areas. She also wanted to know how Starlette wanted to handle the tabloid blogger when they found him. There were options, after all. They could burn him, drown him, shoot him, stab him, blow him up, bury him alive... And those were only the options for the final kill. There might be hours of good clean fun before they even got to the killing part.

Starlette hadn't waited for Girl Next Door though. She was undoubtedly in some brooding hero zone, and for some reason, that always meant that she had to be off in her own mind. Girl Next Door would have loved—just for once—if the brooding hero zone somehow involved iced mochas and the two women talking about their feelings when it came to torture techniques. Not to mention the filler co-star that was suddenly thrust upon them.

She walked back to the trailers, hoping to find Starlette there, but Starlette was nowhere to be seen. Instead, Girl Next Door found Sassy Gay Friend standing outside of Ethan's trailer, holding about five suitcases and trying to open the door.

"Um... What are you doing?" Girl Next Door asked him as she walked up.

He turned and walked down the stairs of the trailer to greet her as he said, "I'm trying to move into the trailer they assigned to me, but I can't get the door open with all these bags in my hands. Could you help?"

She stood her ground and put her hands on her hips, saying "No."

"Umm... Okay. Rude, but okay."

"I mean, no you are not moving into that trailer. It's taken."

"I'm just doing what they told me to do."

"Then *they* are a bunch of incredibly stupid morons, because you are not using that trailer... The Director put me in charge of you, remember?"

"I think you misheard him."

"I think *you* misheard him."

~

Starlette had returned to her trailer and went inside to get something to drink before heading back to the lawn furniture. She was sure that Girl Next Door would want to talk with her and they had a lot to discuss.

After grabbing a bottle of water, she nearly opened the door and walked outside when she heard Ember yelling at someone. A quick glance through the blinds revealed that she was yelling at their new guest star, Sassy Gay Friend.

She considered her options. She could have gone out there and included herself in their discussion, but to do so would undoubtedly lead to her becoming a part of the bickering. Girl Next Door was so much better at that sort of thing than she was, so she decided to hold off on going back outside, and she went to the table in her kitchen area, where she sat and listened while drinking her water.

"Okay, there is no need for you to be getting all in my face about something I didn't do," Sassy Gay Friend yelled.

"Well, there's no need for you to keep acting like you are going to move into that trailer when I clearly just told you that you're not... And by the way, I will break every bone in your body if you put your hand on that door one more time."

"Is that a threat? Are you threatening me?"

"It's a promise."

"Oh. My. God. I can't even believe how homophobic you're being right now."

"I'm not being homophobic."

"Look, I get that yours is a very old and conservative people, but you don't have the right to cast judgment on me."

"Oh, that was so racist."

"Please, you're... I'm gonna go with Chinese or something. That barely even counts as another race. You might as well be white."

"Racist!"

"You wouldn't even be calling me that if I wasn't gay."

As Starlette listened to this back and forth, she could not help but be glad that she hadn't gone outside. It had to be one of the most idiotic arguments she had heard anyone have. Ever.

She listened to their back and forth for a while longer, taking small sips of her water so that she'd have something to occupy her time until the fighting ended.

Minutes passed, and Starlette could see a time-lapse video in her head. Flowers grew and died. The sun rose and set. But finally, the yelling stopped.

Starlette took a look through her blinds and saw Sassy Gay Friend's bags sitting on the floor outside of Ethan's trailer, but neither Ember nor Sassy Gay Friend were anywhere in sight.

She walked to her door and stepped outside. Nearly as soon as she was out of her trailer, she heard Sassy Gay Friend say, "Oh, I know you heard all that."

Starlette walked down her steps and turned to see Sassy Gay Friend sitting in one of the lawn chairs outside her trailer, where he could not be seen from her window.

She walked to him and said, "Yeah. And I'd appreciate it if you found another trailer to use while you're here."

Sassy Gay Friend looked her up and down, sizing her up and said, "I was going to anyway. The neighbors around here are a nightmare."

"She's been through a lot."

"Haven't we all?"

Now it was Starlette's turn to look him up and down, sizing him up. She had a knack for reading people and understanding them, but she was having a hard time getting a read on this one.

He stood up and walked to her, extending a hand and saying, "I'm Sassy Gay Friend, by the way. I don't think we were ever properly introduced."

Starlette shook his hand, and noted that he had a surprisingly firm grip. Somehow, she had expected a *dead-fish* handshake.

"And for the record," he told her, with a different tone than she'd heard him use before, "I'm not as sassy as they say I am. The Studio does like their stereotypes, but I want you to know that if we're out there and it's getting bad, you don't need to worry about me freaking out over a chipped nail."

Starlette narrowed her eyes and said, "So, that whole fight with Girl Next Door?"

Sassy Gay Friend smiled, "Was fun as hell. I like her."

"I'm pretty sure she hates you."

"She'll come around. She has to."

"You don't know Girl Next Door."

"No, I mean she *has* to. This is Hollywood, and I'm what I like to call The Studio's *my pet gay*. Whatever I do, no matter who I do it to, by the end of the episode we'll all be crying and talking about how great I am. I might even get Heartthrob to sing to me, because as far as the higher-ups are concerned, I'm like the retarded kid in school who everyone has to handle with kid gloves."

Starlette nodded and said, "I actually do find the term *retard* offensive."

"Sorry."

"And you're okay with this... *my pet gay* thing?"

"No, it's incredibly offensive, but have you ever tried to explain to someone that their bending over backwards trying not to offend you is more offensive than if they didn't care about offending you?"

"I'm pretty sure you lost me," Starlette said. "But I enjoyed our talk and I think that we understand each other a little bit better now. You are a *beautiful* human being, with an *amazing* soul and I just think you are *so* brave for being who you are."

"Fuck off."

Starlette smiled and turned to walk away. As she walked, she said, "I like you, kid... But don't get comfortable here. I do plan on getting Wacky Best Friend back."

"Bigot!"

"Whore."

~

The meeting in the conference room had just ended, and Heartthrob now stood alone with The Director and Head Writer. They were waiting for him to tell them his idea, but he didn't want to blurt it out. Being too forward would only serve to complicate his life even more than it already was.

"When I first came back to the city," he started, before trailing off for just a moment, trying to shake off the flash of images in his head; images of the events which led to his return. "When I first came back, I had only heard rumors of The Studio. Mostly from Bookworm's men who wanted to know where you were, so they could take you down forever."

The Director and Head Writer must have known that Bookworm would be looking for The Studio just as desperately as they were looking for him. They had to know that it was a race to see which side would track down and destroy the other. Yet, they looked at each other as though Heartthrob's confirmation of this was of some new interest.

"I didn't know where you were. I didn't know how to find you. All I knew was that I needed to be here, because I had nowhere else to go."

Heartthrob walked to the door and closed it, so that what he said would remain between him and the other two men in the room.

He continued, saying, "I roamed the streets for a couple of

weeks. I sifted through the rubble where the studios used to be. I hoped that at some point, I would just stumble upon one of your teams, or the woman that they call the *Ghost of Hollywood*... Starlette, I guess. But I never found you."

Heartthrob walked back to his seat at the table and sat down. He looked up at one of the monitors, which still had a tabloid headline displayed on it as he went on.

"Eventually, I saw this group of teenagers walking down the street, laughing and having a good time. Drunk. They looked like everything was perfectly normal and they were just headed out for a night of clubbing. Only there's not supposed to be clubbing anymore, right? So I followed them."

The Director sat on one of the tables, listening intently to Heartthrob's story. Head Writer jotted down notes as Heartthrob spoke, but seemed to be disinterested overall.

"There was this old building. It used to be an appliance store, I think. Cleared out now and just as dead as everything else, but in the basement, there was this hidden door."

The Director caught on, "A speakeasy."

Heartthrob nodded and said, "It's called the *Blind Tiger*. It's a place where people go to party and mingle. A lot of kids with nowhere else to go... And a lot of people claiming to be agents, offering to make those kids into stars in some made-up Hollywood revival."

"That's where you met the rogue agent?"

Heartthrob nodded and shifted in his seat, growing uncomfortable as he thought about the Blind Tiger, and all of the kids that were being preyed upon inside those walls.

"Not at first. At first, it was another guy. He sent his assistant over to me. She flirted and came on all hot and heavy. If I were new to this, I would have been completely taken by the scam. I'm sure he's sold more than his share of teenagers to people claiming to be producers. But I know the game. I knew what she was doing and what type of guy she worked for, so I had her introduce me," Heartthrob smirked a little bit. He said, "Neither of them recognized me at first. I guess I looked different or something. But I pressed for information about The Studio. He didn't have any, but after a few broken bones, he pointed me toward this other guy. The rogue agent that said he could put me in touch with you. And that's how I found The Studio."

Head Writer looked up from his notebook and said, "That's great, but it was all in your bio. What's your point?"

"My point is—" Heartthrob said, before being cut off.

"His point is that his *character* has ties to this underground," The Director chimed in, so that Heartthrob wouldn't have to say it himself and risk the same fate as Wacky Best Friend. "I was thinking the same thing myself, just a minute ago."

He was lying, of course, but Heartthrob knew what he was doing and didn't mind him taking credit for this one.

"If we can work those connections, we might be able to find an agent—maybe even the same one as before—who works as a go-between for the tabloid and its sources in The Studio."

"So, we get to write a club scene?" Head Writer asked, with a hopeful look in his eyes. "That's... Great. Do you know how tired I am of writing dingy old buildings? Almost as tired as trying to think up new and exciting fight sequences."

The Director nodded and said to Heartthrob, "Good. We'll prep the scene for you and Starlette."

"But the rogue agent has already seen Heartthrob and Starlette," Head Writer said to himself, trying to think up a solution to this problem. He shrugged it off and said, "Whatever. Nobody's ever going to put that together anyway, right?"

Heartthrob looked to The Director with a questioning look. The Director looked down and shook his head, unable to answer for the comment made by Head Writer.

"I'll tell Starlette to get ready," Heartthrob told The Director, and he headed out of the room.

Heartthrob hurried across The Studio, eager to fill Starlette in on the plan, though his eagerness only explained half of his haste. As he walked, he kept his head down and his eyes off of the other people in The Studio. He didn't want to see the expression in their eyes.

Logic dictated that if the story had been reported accurately, those around him would be watching him with sympathy. Many would undoubtedly be watching him with the same morbid curiosity that compelled them to stare at car accidents as they drove down the street, but for the most part, there would be sympathy. He would be the victim; the poor, damaged boy that everyone felt bad for.

He didn't want pity. For one thing, everyone in that place was a victim of Bookworm and he didn't feel a need to pretend that his pain was the worst of it. It was merely the current headline for them, and an event that he had already been working hard to put behind him for months.

With his eyes on the floor and avoiding the sympathy, his mind created images to fill in the blanks of the world around him. His mind was cruel and unforgiving, so the looks on the faces that he saw were not sympathetic. They were hateful. They were filled with anger. Some were the faces of those family members, still covered in the blood and dirt that he had last seen on them.

His mind created the image of Hell, with vengeful spirits reaching for him and demons just waiting for the right moment to pounce and rip him to shreds. He had been running from those demons for a long time, though he had managed to put a wall around them during the day, because he had been trained to keep his personal life separate from his work life. But the wall was wearing down and he feared that his nightmares would soon follow him into the artificial light of day that filled The Studio.

He picked up his pace. He needed to find Starlette and begin prepping their scene together, because it was the only way for him to become Heartthrob once again, and leave Ben behind for another day.

When he reached the trailers, he heard arguing. Ember was in the middle of a heated discussion with their new guest star, Sassy Gay Friend. If he approached, he would surely be dragged into that fight.

As much as he wanted to have Ember's back, he just could not bring himself to be drawn into behind the scenes drama at the moment, so he stayed out of sight and waited for the arguing to end.

After several minutes, he saw Ember walking off. She was most likely headed toward The Director's office, to voice a complaint about Sassy Gay Friend. He let her go without following her or trying to cool her down.

Before he could turn and head toward the trailers, he heard Starlette talking with Sassy Gay Friend, whose voice and inflections seemed to change between the time that Ember walked off and Starlette began talking with him.

The question of who he was or how much he could be trusted when he displayed two entirely different personalities amongst his co-stars would have to be saved for another time. Heartthrob didn't feel like dealing with him just then.

After a few moments, Heartthrob saw Starlette walking away. He hurried to catch up with her.

When he caught up to Starlette and began to walk beside her, she seemed to barely notice. She wasn't surprised or put off by him; she simply kept walking as though she had expected him to catch up to her.

"How did your talk with The Director go?" she asked.

"Good. You and I will be heading out tonight. There's a speakeasy where I think we might be able to gather some information about the tabloid," he told her.

He proceeded to fill her in on his experience with the speakeasy and the plan that he was hoping would bring them closer to taking down the tabloid.

As he spoke with her, Starlette showed no sign of pity for him or his situation. She acted as though nothing had happened and everything was exactly the same as it had been the day before. He appreciated this, because aside from the world knowing about the terrors that haunted him, everything *was* exactly as it had been the day before.

He needed for the buzz around his tabloid headline to go away and for everyone to start treating him the same as they always had. Starlette seemed to understand this. It would have seemed strange to anyone that he might have tried explaining it to, but in that moment, Starlette's complete lack of concern for him made her the best company that he could have asked for.

~

The last thing Starlette needed was drama. She had gone months without her cast being the topic of scandalous conversation in The Studio, and the idea that two of her co-stars were now being named on some tabloid rag website pissed her

off. It distracted from the work that they had to do, and made the
story more about the actors than the job.

As she walked beside Heartthrob and he filled her in on the
scene that was being written for them, she half expected him to
burst into tears and whine about his poor troubled past. While
she was concerned for him and cared about him, she needed him
to be focused. Especially if he was going to be the only actor
covering her back on this shoot.

She said nothing about the story that had broken earlier in the
day, because she figured that if he wanted to discuss it with her, he
would have brought it up at some point between the time he
arrived at The Studio and that day. Odds were, he would rather sit
down and have a heart to heart with Ember anyway. Starlette
noticed them growing closer, and it was only a matter of time
before they would introduce a baby to The Studio and auditions
would be held for child actors who could play the six year old that
would replace their baby a year later.

Upon thinking of this probable turn of events, Starlette
couldn't help but wonder how this classic ploy would hold up in
The Studio. Somehow, she doubted that real parents would
overlook their child rapidly aging and becoming a feisty,
precocious little co-star.

She shook off the thought. It was absurd.

By the time she got back to listening to Heartthrob, he was well
on his way to finishing the scene outline that she had only been
half-listening to. So far, he seemed to be holding it together, which
made her feel a little bit more confident in his ability to
compartmentalize, but she would be keeping her eye on him. If he
showed any sign of breaking character while they were on
location, she would call off the shoot and they would have to try
another take at some later point.

The idea of delaying this shoot was not one that sat well with
her. If given the choice, she would bench Heartthrob for a day or
two and let him deal with his personal issues while she and one of
her other co-stars took on the speakeasy scene. Unfortunately,
Girl Next Door would be held up dealing with the leak at The
Studio and Starlette hadn't worked with Sassy Gay Friend enough
to rely on him during such a vital shoot. Heartthrob was her only

choice.

As they walked and she tried to plan a strategy for handling the speakeasy scene in the event that he flubbed a line or missed his mark, she didn't notice Heartthrob looking at her.

He stopped her and looked her directly in the eyes, as though he could see that she was planning around him. He said, "Are you listening to me?"

"I was," she said. "For a while anyway."

"Look, I appreciate the fact that you didn't want to force a conversation about what happened, but if it's going to be an issue for you, I think we should talk about it."

"It's not an issue. I don't need to know anything you don't want to tell me."

"But you need to know that you can trust me. And I need to know that you're not going to relegate me to the background tonight because you're worried that I'm going to crack."

"Are you?"

He hesitated. Starlette made a mental note of this even as he went on to say, "What has the past year been like for you? How many people have you lost? How many people have to watched die? How many have you killed yourself?"

Starlette tried to think of an answer for him, but she couldn't easily come up with one. She'd lost count of the number of bodies she had seen and the screams that she had heard.

"None of us have had it easy," Heartthrob told her. "Any one of us could break, assuming we're not already broken."

She didn't say anything in response to this. She considered what he was saying, and couldn't help but agree. One only had to look around The Studio to see that he was right. People were on the verge of... something. Tensions were rising. Interdepartmental communications were falling apart. The commissary had gone from being an annoying loud mess at lunchtime, to nearly silent.

Since she had blown up the theater in an attempt to scare The Studio into keeping Wacky Best Friend around, the cracks that already existed in the foundation of The Studio had begun to grow wider and wider. Actors were beginning to wonder who had their backs and how easily they could be replaced.

He was right. Their whole system could crumble at any

moment, and all she could bring herself to think was, *oops.*

She took her time responding to Heartthrob, but finally told him, "I trust you."

She couldn't help but find that comment funny, considering the fact that she had protested even going to save his life in the first place, but it was true. She considered herself a good judge of character, and there was nothing about him that gave her legitimate reason to not trust him.

With that said, she added, "I just hope you can trust me."

As she said this, she heard a *chirp* coming from nearby. She turned to find the source of this sound and spotted one of the guys from the lighting department reach into his pocket and pull out his cell phone.

Heartthrob turned to see what she was looking at, and they both watched as the lighting guy read something on his phone. It did not seem like good news.

She heard more *beeps* and *chirps* in the distance, and knew that something was going on.

Starlette walked to the lighting guy, and asked "What's going on?"

The lighting guy looked at her, and for just a moment he seemed to question whether or not he should be talking to her. Finally, he said, "It's another update from the tabloid."

He handed Starlette his phone, as Heartthrob joined her. She read the report to him, "Studio closing in on Bookworm... Sources confirm that documents which were recently obtained by The Studio may bring them one step closer to bringing down the famed designer of the modern renaissance. The Celeb Spinner is in the process of trying to get copies of these documents, but our source tells us that they have been heavily guarded since their discovery."

"Son of a bitch," Heartthrob said under his breath.

Starlette handed the phone back to the lighting guy and grabbed Heartthrob by the arm. As they walked away, she spoke quietly to him, so that they could not be heard. She said, "I don't know how they caught wind of the Emma Carter papers, but we have to stop them from publishing. We have to find these people. Now."

~

Girl Next Door stood on The Studio floor, gazing out upon the crowd of potential leaks. Everyone was a suspect, and it was her job to narrow down that list and bring the guilty party to justice.

She just had to figure out how...

"If I were you, I would start with the tall ones. Tall people are notoriously guilty of things," Sassy Gay Friend spoke in her ear as he joined her and stood beside her with his arms crossed.

Girl Next Door wanted to cry. She *really* did not want to be stuck dealing with this replacement co-star for the rest of her life.

"Tell you what," she said to him, "why don't you start with the tall ones, and I'll start with my own suspects and then we'll never ever meet back here or discuss anything that we do ever again."

"That wasn't very *girl next door*-ish. Besides, I'm under strict orders to work with you. That means that we're partners, whether we like it or not."

Girl Next Door clenched her jaw, but said nothing in response.

Sassy Gay Friend smiled and stood straighter as he looked out over the crowd and said, "Now, since you technically outrank me, you lead the way. And since I outclass you, I'll do the talking."

"Just give me a minute. I'm preparing," she told him.

"Preparing what?"

"My angle. Look, there has to be a logical place to start this..."

Girl Next Door scanned the crowd and then pulled several pages of printed articles from her back pocket. She looked over the articles, studying them carefully.

In her mind, she kept trying to think of what Starlette would do first. She even asked herself what Wacky Best Friend would do, since he was into all of that plotting and planning stuff. But she had neither of them to rely on, so she had to figure it out on her own.

She looked from the articles, back to the crowd and said, "There aren't any visuals with the articles."

"Were you hoping for colorful pop-up pictures?"

"I mean... If the leak was someone from a visual department, they would have photos or film stills... In theory," she said, holding up the articles and flipping through them so that Sassy Gay Friend could see what she was talking about. "They have articles about stuff I did on shoots. Stuff that Bombshell did. Mother Figure. Exotic Beauty. Old Biker. They even have stuff that Starlette and Headliner did—"

"Ooh, I wish they had visuals for what Starlette and Headliner did," Sassy Gay Friend quipped. "Actually, I'm making up my own visuals now, so never mind... Oops, Starlette's gone. How weird."

Girl Next Door rolled her eyes and looked at Sassy Gay Friend with an angry expression. She said, "I get it. You're gay. Can we move on now? Look... They have all of this insider knowledge about what we did on shoots and no visuals. They even quote us once or twice. That means, it's probably one of the crew members that we're never supposed to acknowledge, but they're always there."

"So that limits our search down to six thousand? Good job."

"We can pare down the list more by checking internet access logs. There's no cell reception down here. Everyone is on wifi. That means that we can see who logs on and when. We can see which router they use. So, we can limit our search to the times between these specific shoots and the times when the articles were posted, and compare those records to specific crew accounts. Then we will have a smaller list of potential suspects that we can interview in person. We'll start with the lighting department. Then move on to audio and the production assistants. If we don't turn up anything with them, we'll move on to my next plan."

"Which would be?"

"I don't know. I'm still trying to think up this plan. Do you know how to do any of the stuff that I just said?"

"No."

"Frown."

~

If you were to look around the old, abandoned appliance store, you would not have known that anyone had recently stepped foot in there. That is, unless you looked down to where footprints cleared a path through the thick layer of dust that covered most of the floor. Even if Heartthrob hadn't told her which direction to head in, Starlette would have known.

Before leaving The Studio, she and Heartthrob had spent a

good amount of time in Wardrobe's department, as well as Hair and Makeup's trailer. Special attention was given to making them look different than they normally looked. The rogue agent that Heartthrob used to contact The Studio was a visitor to this speakeasy, and if he recognized either Starlette or Heartthrob, their scene would be blown.

Starlette was wearing a white tank top, beneath a black leather jacket. She had on a black skirt, which fit loosely and was cut below her knees. She had jeans on beneath the skirt, just in case she was forced into battle and didn't want to splash the tabloids with even more material than they already had. Paparazzi could be anywhere. They routinely stalked the rooftops of the city and hid in windows, waiting for a clear shot at a known actor, but they could be anywhere. Any person on the street could pull a camera at any moment, and many actors had been caught off guard by these sneak attacks.

Her hair was hidden beneath a bright red wig, and her makeup made her look like a disco slut, but she didn't look like Starlette, so their objective was accomplished.

Heartthrob had visited this place before, so hiding his appearance was vital. Wardrobe had given him some stylish sunglasses to hide his eyes, which were well known around the world, even before the attacks. He had a beanie to cover his hair and a loose fitting shirt to cover his abs. To the world, he was just another chiseled jaw.

As they made their way to the basement, there was a couple sitting outside of the entrance to the speakeasy. They were on the floor, falling all over each other and laughing about it. They couldn't have been more than sixteen years old, but they were drunk out of their minds. It disgusted Starlette. The world was a cruel enough place without kids helping it along by getting themselves killed.

Heartthrob showed her to a wall toward the back of the basement, where several shelves and coat hooks concealed any hidden latches. He pulled on one of the coat hooks and twisted it until the wall behind it popped open. It was only then that the music from within the speakeasy could be heard.

To call it music was perhaps too kind. There was no rhythm to this music. There was no soul. Like the film industry, the music industry had been hit in the attacks. It was as hard to find a good playlist these days as it was to find a movie to watch. So instead, the room was filled with this emotionless moaning techno sound. And still, the young'uns danced like they were on fire.

Starlette took in the room as she entered and the door closed behind her. There was no cover charge or security to keep out the undesirables. This place was designed for the weak and desperate. Waitresses in trashy clothes carried around trays of colorful and undoubtedly fruity drinks, along with bowls full of equally colorful pills.

Starlette looked to Heartthrob and shook her head. Even before the attacks, there were vultures in Hollywood who would prey on the fresh faced kids who had just stepped off the bus. Now, those kids had no more hope of fame or fortune and they wandered aimlessly through their lives. Some couldn't go home out of fear. Others simply couldn't afford to go home. All of them were lost, without so much as a dream to guide them.

"You don't even want to see the rooms in the back," Heartthrob told her.

"I really don't," she replied.

She tried to ignore what was going on around her. She had to keep her mind on the job that she was there to do, and that meant finding an agent who could lead them to the tabloid. Somehow, she got the feeling that none of the agents in this place would be like her late, beloved agent, Carla Saxman.

Her instinct, of course, was to roam the place until she spotted one of the slimy bastards, then beat the crap out of him until he gave up the information that they needed. This was not how the scene had been scripted, however.

"Go to the bathroom," she told Heartthrob. "It's time for us to do things the hard way, which will undoubtedly lead to us being attacked from behind when we least expect it."

He looked at her, confused, and said "Are you sure?"

"So it is written, so shall it be. Just walk off like you're going to the bathroom and leave me here alone for a few minutes."

Heartthrob reluctantly nodded and walked off toward the bathrooms, but Starlette knew that he would probably stop on the other side of the room and keep an eye on her from afar.

Once he was gone and she was alone, Starlette took off her leather jacket and acted like she wanted to place it on a nearby chair. She let it fall to the floor, and then bent down to pick it up. When she stood again, she straightened her clothes and looked around the place like she was as lost and intimidated as a girl could possibly be.

Within a minute, she heard a voice from behind her say, "It can be daunting, can't it?"

Starlette turned to face the person that was speaking to her. She found herself looking at a woman, much to her surprise. The woman was in her late 30's and dressed in a cute, gray pencil skirt, with a black belt and a white top. The shoes were four inch heels, but classy. She carried a glass of white wine with her.

Starlette smiled on the inside. She'd found her mark.

"I'm just new here," Starlette said, trying to sound like Girl Next Door. "It's all so... You know. Big and loud."

The agent smiled and said, "I know. It can be intimidating at first."

Starlette gave the agent a blank stare, as though she didn't understand what the agent just said. This prompted the agent to say, "Oh, it means *scary.*"

Starlette smiled and nodded.

"Was that your boyfriend?" the agent asked.

"Oh, yeah." Starlette replied. "I mean, we've been kinda dating for a while, but we're not exclusive or anything."

The agent nodded and took a sip of her drink. She said, "Have you guys ever considered being in the movies?"

Starlette smiled coyly. "I mean... It'd be cool, but the movies are gone, aren't they?"

"That's a myth," the agent told her. "There are some movies being made right in this very building, as we speak."

"Gosh, that's cool. And you think I could be in one?"

"You and your boyfriend."

Starlette allowed her smile to grow wider as she said, "It's like a dream come true."

"Now, I really think you'd be great for this, but I have to let you know that there is a small fee that you'll have to pay."

Starlette let her smile fade, but not completely. She wanted to give the impression that she was still holding out hope for that big break in the movies as she said to the agent, "Fee? What kind of fee?"

"Oh, it's not much. See, I'm just an agent. I can get you in with the producers of those movies and I'm sure you'll make money from them, but there are some overhead costs that we need to take into account."

"What kind of costs?"

The agent brushed the hair away from Starlette's eyes, so she could get a better look at Starlette's face. This gave Starlette the creeps.

The agent went on to say, "We'll have to take some pictures. That will cost money. And then we might put together a demo reel for you... You know, to show off your talents."

Starlette wanted to punch her hard. She imagined all of the naïve kids who would fall for this sort of crap and it infuriated her. Rather than beat down the agent right there, Starlette looked toward the bathroom, to see if she could find Heartthrob in the crowd.

When she spotted him, she smiled and waved him closer. She then turned back to the agent and said, "My boyfriend keeps all of my money for me."

"That's fine," the agent replied, taking another sip of her wine.

As Heartthrob approached, Starlette went to him and put her arms around him. She said, "Good news, baby. This woman's an agent. She wants to put us in movies."

Heartthrob caught on quickly and said, "That's great, baby."

He then extended his hand and for some reason used a southern accent as he said to the agent, "My name's Rock... You know, like the candy."

"She needs money, baby," Starlette said to him as he shook the agent's hand.

"Oh. I left all my money out in the car, baby," he said back, and then turned to the agent and said, "If you wanna come out and get it with me, we can."

The agent smiled and said, "That would be fine. And maybe we can run some lines while we're out there. See what kind of talent you kids have."

Heartthrob smiled and said, "I got all kinds of talent."

The agent took one last sip of her wine and placed her glass on a nearby table. She gestured toward the door and said, "Then let's go get that money."

Starlette grabbed her jacket and carried it with her as she and Heartthrob led the way out of the speakeasy, with the agent close behind.

They walked through the door and waited for it to close behind them before they did or said anything else to the agent.

Once they were in the dark and mostly empty basement of the appliance store, Starlette turned around to face the agent and asked, "Wanna see what I can do?"

"Sure," the agent replied, with a slimy grin.

Starlette smiled and grabbed the agent by the hair. She slammed the agent's face into a nearby wall twice before finally pinning the agent to the wall and saying, "You make me sick."

"Who are you? What's going on here?" the agent demanded.

Starlette leaned close. She wanted to try something that she'd never done before and while she wasn't sure that it would work, it would be cool if it did.

She whispered in the agent's ear, "I'm *Starlette.*"

The agent went crazy when she heard Starlette's name. She struggled and tried to get free, but Starlette wouldn't let her.

Starlette looked to Heartthrob, and he raised his eyebrows to let her know just how cool he thought that was.

"Let me go! I don't know anything! I swear!" the agent cried.

"You prey on those kids in there. You trick them into giving you their money and doing God-knows-what else. Tell me why the Hell I should let you go," Starlette shot back.

The agent had no reason to give. She had no earnest response that would lead to her being freed. All she could do was ask, "What do you want from me? Please, I will do anything. Just please, please don't hurt me."

The agent was crying by this point, which made Starlette feel pretty good about herself. Starlette slammed the agent against the wall one more time, for good measure and demanded, "Have you ever heard of a tabloid site called The Celeb Spinner?"

The agent, still crying, said, "Y—Yes."

"Do you know how to get in touch with them?"

"D—Does their site have an email address?"

Starlette looked to Heartthrob, who shrugged in reply. She figured that someone would have tried that before sending her out to get more information, so she slammed the agent against the wall once more and said, "Don't be cute. I need to get in touch with the owner of the site. Can you set that up?"

The agent started bawling now, "No. I can't. I don't know anyone. I don't have contacts."

"So, you just exploit teenagers and promise them fame and fortune so that you can take their money and get them trapped in a life of sleazy porn videos? Does that just about sum up what you do?" Starlette asked, pulling back on the agent's hair and causing her to scream in pain.

The drunk couple in the basement didn't seem to notice what was going on. Starlette could hear them laughing and playing around in the distance. If they had run off or even tried to attack her, she would have probably felt better about them. Their lack of response was disturbing.

"I'm sorry," the agent cried. "I'm so sorry. I won't do it again. I'll stop. I swear, I'll stop."

"Unfortunately, I'm not here on a mission of redemption and second chances. When I leave here, you'll slither back into your pit, lick your wounds and sharpen your fangs for your next night of exploitation. That is, unless I stop you."

The agent's fear gave her a surge of energy, which drove her to attempt an escape. She wiggled and pulled and tried to run off, but Starlette held onto her and drove her into the wall yet again.

Starlette turned to Heartthrob and asked, "Now, how should we go about this? Do you want to get the acid from the car while I wait here, or should we just douse her in alcohol and light her on fire?"

"The car's all the way down the street," Heartthrob replied, not sounding enthusiastic about making the trip out there.

"Fire it is then. You wanna run into the other room and get a couple of bottles?"

"Sure thing."

"Oh, and see if you can find some matches... And maybe some buffalo wings if they have any. I didn't eat before we came out here."

"Wait! Please wait!" the agent cried, with her face still against the wall and her eyes closed as though she could make this situation go away by simply not looking at it.

"Hmm?" Starlette asked.

"I can set you up with someone who has contacts. Another agent. He's not like me," the agent told them. "I promise. I swear, I can give him to you."

Starlette thought for a moment and then asked, "Is he here now?"

"Yes. I can get him. Please, let me get him. He can help you."

"Fine," Starlette agreed, letting go of the agent. "Just stop whining and clean yourself up. You look like shit."

~

Girl Next Door had a plan. In order to narrow her list of suspects, she was going to investigate the internet access logs from within The Studio. It was a plan that required far more technical savvy than she possessed, and Sassy Gay Friend didn't let her forget it.

She wished that she could just go to one of the tech departments and ask someone to help her, but the risk was too high. She was investigating a tabloid *blog* after all, and the tech departments were littered with people who knew how to use computers and who could have contacted that website.

Given the technical difficulties of that original plan, she knew that she had come up with a secondary course of action; and that's when it came to her.

"Duh!" she said to herself, as her eyes brightened and an excited smile formed on her face. "I'm not going to be able to *CSI* my way through this... This is different. This is old school. This is *Murder, She Wrote.*"

With that revelation in mind, she shifted the course of her entire investigation.

The last article to be posted—in regards to the Emma Carter documents—had been very telling. The article provided no solid description of these papers, which were clearly displayed on the monitors of the conference room after they were first discovered. This led Girl Next Door to the conclusion that whoever had leaked this information to the tabloid hadn't actually seen those documents. This meant that the culprit would not be a senior member of the crew.

She followed the string of information through The Studio, talking to different members of the cast and crew. She read through the tabloid website, looking at the information that had been leaked and she tried to figure out what the common point of view was for all of this information. The problem was, it was all so random. Some of it was based on information collected on shoots. Other bits were presented in the conference room at one point or another. But some of the articles contained information that was discussed privately, between cast members, within the walls of The Studio. She knew that she needed to find the key to this mystery, but once she found it and pieced together all of the information that she had gathered, she would know the identity of The Studio's leak.

She had been at it for hours and must have gone through half a dozen large cups of iced coffee drinks and a half a dozen bathroom breaks to go along with them. She was tired. Her eyes were aching. Her head was scrambled with tabloid reports about fellow actors within The Studio, and most of these reports were of the variety that she *really* didn't need to know about.

She nearly fell asleep as she poured over the information. Her body wanted to shut down and her mind was screaming for a break, but she fought her fatigue as hard as she possibly could. It was a valiant effort, though it ultimately failed.

The world around her faded to black.

"Sleeping on the job?" Sassy Gay Friend said from behind her, causing her to awaken with a jolt.

She looked around The Studio as Sassy Gay Friend took a seat in the lawn furniture beside her.

"How long have I been asleep?" she asked, more rhetorically than not.

"Depends on when you fell asleep. Either way, I'm guessing *too* long," he replied, skimming the papers around her.

"Well, I might not have dozed off if I'd had some help in this investigation."

"You made it perfectly clear that you didn't want any help from a gay man."

"I never said anything about you being gay."

"Umm... and I quote, *'I get it, you're gay. Can we move on now?'* If that wasn't hostile, I don't know what is," he told her.

"That wasn't hostility. But I could show you hostility if you really want me to."

He put his hand on his heart and said to her, "You are such a cruel and hateful person. Are you always like this, or is it just that time of the month?"

She said nothing in response. Their discussion was quickly becoming more annoying than she had the time to deal with at that moment. She needed to continue her work.

"Look, I don't know where you've been all this time, but if you want to go back there, that's fine with me. I have real work to do," she told him.

Sassy Gay Friend shrugged and said, "Actually, I was moving into my new trailer."

She looked at him with such a fiery glare that she could have melted steel, and asked "What trailer?"

He smiled in response, but said nothing.

"What trailer?" she asked again, this time more firmly. "I swear, if you moved into his trailer, I will beat you down."

Sassy Gay Friend gasped and leaned back, saying, "I am appalled! You know, you might want to keep it down, with that type of vitriol. The walls do have ears here, and the last thing you want is to wind up on this tabloid site with a big ol' *homophobe* label."

She was going to respond with something really scathing and brutal, but a light suddenly went off in her head. She stopped short of responding to him and looked down at all of the articles that she had printed. Each article that she skimmed seemed to push her closer and closer to the answer that had come to her.

She smiled, "I got it. Oh my God, I got it. I'm totally stupid and I actually figured this out!"

She paused for a moment, carefully thinking about the best course of action before adding, "Tomorrow morning, we have to get down to the prop department and move the Emma Carter documents. If my suspicion is correct, we don't have any time to lose. It *has* to be tomorrow morning!"

~

The prop department was dark. Given the late hour, one could be reasonably sure that Prop Master would be out for the night and that one could sneak their way past his security measures with relative privacy.

There was only a hint of light coming through the door that led into the prop department, and the person who crept through that door dared not make the room any brighter. To do so could draw attention.

The dark, shaded figure moved across the outer area of the prop department, toward the door that led to Prop Master's workshop and the storage area, where all of the important props were kept.

The door was locked, of course. Behind it, there were items which were vital to the safety and survival of The Studio. These items included the Emma Carter documents, which were stored there whenever they weren't be examined by Studio officials and interns who were trying to decipher them.

The dark and shaded person knelt next to the electronic lock on the door and pulled a tool kit from his pocket. He got to work, trying to break into the lock, but didn't get far before the lights in the room went on.

"Ladies and gentlemen, I give you our leak," Girl Next Door declared from behind the perp.

When he turned around, the whole room could see who he was. Standing next to Girl Next Door was The Director, Head Writer, several Producers, two Studio security guards, Sassy Gay Friend and Prop Master. Girl Next Door smiled widely as the guilty party turned and revealed his face.

His name was Michael Lefler, though in The Studio, he was more commonly known as Boom Mike. He was the assistant to The Studio's sound mixer, and regularly followed actors on shoots where he remained out of sight while holding the telescoping boom microphone and captured the audio of whatever scene was going down.

"I spent the better part of the night, trying to figure out who would be privy to all of this information. Who could be responsible for these leaks? I even considered the possibility that there was more than one leak in The Studio," Girl Next Door started.

"That's when I figured out that it was Boom Mike," Sassy Gay Friend stepped in. "He's the one man who always has his ear to the train tracks. He knows what's going on, even when we don't know he's there."

Girl Next Door looked to Sassy Gay Friend, shocked. She said, "I figured this out! You weren't even there most of the time!"

Sassy Gay Friend turned to face Girl Next Door and smiled politely as he said, "Look, I don't want to step on any toes. How 'bout we call it a team effort?"

"How 'bout we call it a *me* effort?" Girl Next Door shot back.

Sassy Gay Friend put a hand over his mouth and turned to The Director, choking up as he said, "This is how it's been all night. She just won't accept me as part of her group because I'm gay."

"What?!" Girl Next Door screeched.

The Director put his hand up, telling them both to shut up, and he said, "This is good work. Both of you."

Girl Next Door grumbled.

"We have our leak, and that's what's important," The Director continued. He then turned to the Producers and said, "Once we knew who it was, it was just a matter of laying the bait and waiting to confirm our suspicions. My actors figured that, if they were correct, Boom Mike would be listening to their investigation so he could stay ahead of them. They were sure to say that the documents would be moved in the morning, so Boom Mike would have to make his move tonight."

One of the Producers nodded and said, "Good work, all of you."

The Producer then gestured for the security guards to take Boom Mike away.

Boom Mike grumbled and glared as he was hauled away, saying, "You're not protecting us! You're keeping us trapped like animals! The Studio deserves to go down!"

The Producers, Head Writer and Prop Master followed Boom Mike and the guards out of the room, leaving Girl Next Door alone with The Director and Sassy Best Friend.

He looked at them with the stern expression of a father and said, "I think we all know what's going on here."

Sassy Gay Friend put his hand on his chest and continued to act as though he was going to cry at any moment. He said, "I just don't know why she can't accept me for what I am."

"A douchebag? Oh, I accept it," Girl Next Door fired back.

"Enough," The Director told her. "It took a lot of courage for Sassy Gay Friend to join your group and even more for him to stand up here tonight and speak with the strength and dignity that he did. Now, I know that you miss Wacky Best Friend, but you can't let that anger turn you into the type of person who would belittle someone just because they're different than you."

"I'm not! He's barely even gay! I've seen way gayer people and I'm fine with them. I was going to play gay in a movie once!" Girl Next Door argued.

The Director raised a hand and ordered her, "Apologize."

He then left the room. Once he was gone, Sassy Gay Friend smiled at her and said, "Have I ever told you about the *my pet gay* theorem?"

~

Starlette and Heartthrob stood by the entrance to the Blind Tiger speakeasy, keeping a careful eye on the agent as she reentered and moved through the crowd. Once or twice, she turned to see if they were keeping tabs on her and once she confirmed that they were, she picked up her pace.

The room was crowded with young people who were looking for a way to escape their lives. Each of them scared and desperate, but hiding those feelings beneath a thick layer of intoxication.

Agents roamed the room like sharks, eyeing Starlette and Heartthrob as they looked for their next victim. Starlette was no longer playing coy, and none of the agents dared approach her.

Both Starlette and Heartthrob remained quiet as they watched the female agent with whom they had been dealing. Starlette imagined that if Heartthrob were anything like her, he was probably thinking of fun ways to burn the building to the ground. But the sad truth was, it wouldn't make a difference. If they killed this nest, another would pop up someplace else. The best they could hope to do was plant the seeds of fear into the minds of the agents and let them know that their days were numbered.

The female agent made her way to the back of the room, to a booth in the corner. She bent down to speak with the person who was sitting at that booth, but Starlette couldn't see this person's face due to the crowd in front of her. All she could see was the female agent, speaking and pointing toward the door where Starlette and Heartthrob were waiting.

After a moment, the female agent stepped back and let the person in the booth get out. The crowd shifted and churned, and made it hard for Starlette to see the man. When she did catch a quick glimpse of his face, she recognized him immediately. It was the same rogue agent that had led her cast to Heartthrob—only after giving the same information to Bookworm's people.

Heartthrob noticed the rogue agent as well, and shifted just slightly. He seemed to be growing eager for their meeting with this rogue agent.

They didn't draw attention to themselves as the rogue agent grew near. They blended into the background as much as possible. Their plan was to let him walk out of the speakeasy first, and follow him.

As planned, the rogue agent passed by Starlette and Heartthrob, never noticing either of them. He walked through the exit and into the dark basement beyond.

Starlette and Heartthrob followed.

As they exited the speakeasy, they saw the rogue agent walking away from them. They made little noise as they pursued him, waiting for just the right moment to pounce.

Before they reached this perfect moment however, he stopped.

"Well... I guess it was only a matter of time before our paths crossed again," he said, before finally turning around.

Starlette and Heartthrob stood before him, unimpressed by his knowing that they were there.

The rogue agent looked to Heartthrob and said, "Congratulations on not being dead, by the way. I was rooting for you the whole time."

"Is that why you sold me out to Bookworm?" Heartthrob replied.

The rogue agent waved off the comment and said, "It's all business. You know how it is."

"I do," Heartthrob said. "In fact, I have some business of my own to tend to."

"Right. I read that story about you online, *Heartthrob*. Love the name, by the way. It projects an array of emotions," the rogue agent told him.

"You're going to tell us how to find the author of that site," Starlette stated, as though it weren't a question or a demand, but a simple fact.

"I would. Really. Except, that's not how I operate. See, I'm a middle man. You pass information to me, I pass it on to them, and so on and so forth. If I *cut out* the middle man, then they'll... y'know... cut out the middle man."

"I don't see how you're in a position to negotiate the terms of this agreement. You will do this or you will die," Starlette said.

The rogue agent held up a finger and responded by saying, "Ah, but there's a clause in the arrangement. Fine print, placed directly behind you."

As he said those words, Starlette noticed Heartthrob's eyes shift toward something behind her. She could read the warning in them before the words could make their way from his brain to his lips. When she turned to find out what both men were looking at, she was just in time to see a woman swing a baseball bat directly toward her head.

Given the way this scene had been playing out, Starlette was not at all surprised. Truth be told, this fit the formula perfectly.

Yup, Starlette thought to herself as the bat cut through the air, *that seems about right*.

~

At The Studio, cell phones began to chirp and computers began to notify their users of a new update to The Celeb Spinner. The latest headline read: TESSA BAKER AND THE MILLION DOLLAR BOOK DEAL.

CHAPTER TEN
MEDIA BLITZ

"Previously on..." Head Writer said, as he sat at the end of the table in the writers room. "We need to work on a *previously on*, because the cast was split up and we need everyone up to date once we get this ball rolling."

He looked around the room, as the rest of the writers were taking notes and trying to think of different ways to play their upcoming scenes. None of them responded. After several moments of waiting, Head Writer picked up his pen and began to scribble in his notebook.

He said, "Fine. I'll do it. I'll just put in references to Wacky Best Friend going off to the clinic to be treated for exhaustion, so I can remind people about Sassy Gay Friend coming into the cast. I can go into how he worked with Girl Next Door to track down the leak that we had in The Studio, which will hopefully put an end to the tabloid reports before any major spoilers get out…"

He wrote all of this down as he spoke, then paused to think about what else he might want to reference. As he turned back to the notebook, he said, "The latest tabloid report mentioned Tessa Baker signing a book deal, which can't be good for anyone… And I guess I'll cap it off by saying that Starlette and Heartthrob went off to some shady underground club, to try to find someone who might have contact information for the tabloid website that's been causing all this trouble."

He put the pen down and wondered aloud, "I wonder how that's working out for them."

~

The baseball bat was little more than a blur when Starlette saw it coming straight toward her face. Though she ducked in time to avoid getting hit by the bat, she could feel it brush by the top of her head, right before it slammed into the wall next to her.

Starlette pushed the rogue agent's personal assistant, Jennifer, away from her. This bought her enough time to get back to her feet and prepare a proper defense for the next attack.

Jennifer wasted no time in gathering herself, and charged toward Starlette once again. She swung the bat as hard as she could, but Starlette caught it before it could do any damage. Jennifer then leaped into the air and kicked off of Starlette, sending Starlette stumbling backwards while Jennifer rolled into a graceful backflip and landed on her feet. She still had the bat.

The rogue agent was not going to be joining the brawl. While Starlette was distracted with Jennifer, the rogue agent turned and ran toward the exit. Heartthrob wasted no time in chasing after him.

Given the slow pace of the rogue agent, due to a poor choice of footwear and an overall lack of regular exercise, Starlette had no doubt that Heartthrob would quickly catch him. The rogue agent's personal assistant apparently shared that confidence, because when Jennifer saw Heartthrob chasing after her boss, she panicked and threw the baseball bat toward Heartthrob's feet. This resulted in a fall that would have been somewhat comedic under normal circumstances, but which came off as cheesy at this particular moment.

Starlette charged toward Jennifer, confident that Heartthrob would be able to take care of the rogue agent on his own. She went for the full-on football tackle, lifting Jennifer off of her feet before she slammed her into the wall.

Jennifer had the wind knocked out of her, but didn't slow down. She took a swing at Starlette's face, which Starlette easily blocked. At the same time, Jennifer was kicking and squirming to get free. She was like a rabid animal, grunting with each attempt to inflict pain on Starlette.

Jennifer's skill was not refined. She had the ability to be a good fighter, but the execution of her attacks was sloppy. Though Starlette could easily block most of her attacks and the few hits that did make contact were not serious, the frantic speed with which they came made it hard for Starlette to put an end to the fight once and for all.

After a moment of holding Jennifer against the wall, Starlette backed up, hoping to regroup and go at Jennifer again. This time, she wanted to finish the job, so that she could track down Heartthrob and make sure that he had taken the rogue agent into custody.

As Jennifer moved away from the wall, she glared at Starlette. There was blood on her lower lip and sweat beginning to drip down her forehead. She reminded Starlette of one of those B-movie zombies that had no brain function except the drive to kill and eat.

"All this loyalty for a guy who tried to blow you up?" Starlette asked, hoping at the very least to slow Jennifer down.

"He's not the one who left me in there. You and your friends were," Jennifer shot back.

"To be fair, we didn't think he was gonna blow the place up. Did you know about that? Because I guess if you knew about that, it says something about you. How loyal you are; how devoted... How completely stupid."

Jennifer did not react well to being called stupid. She screamed and went for Starlette once again. She jumped into the air and kicked off of a nearby wall, propelling her into a spinning kick toward Starlette's face.

Starlette grabbed her mid-air, spun her around, and slammed

her into the wall once again. She dropped Jennifer to the ground, hoping that this blow to the head would at least knock the personal assistant unconscious.

This did not happen.

Jennifer leapt back to her feet, barely missing a beat. She stood before Starlette with fists at the ready, just waiting for the right moment to attack.

~

Heartthrob raced up the stairs, chasing after the rogue agent who should have only been a few paces ahead, but who seemed to vanish like a housefly in flight. As he reached the top of the stairs and entered the abandoned appliance store, he pulled his gun and slowed his pace.

As he moved, Heartthrob tried to make as little noise as possible. He listened to the store around him and kept his eyes on the thick layer of dust that covered the floor. If the rogue agent tried to find a hiding spot within the store, he would surely leave a trail.

There were no sounds, aside from Heartthrob's own breathing. The place was dark and it was hard to see anything at all. The rogue agent could have been in any number of places, and Heartthrob could easily overlook him entirely—but he wouldn't let that happen.

Heartthrob's investment in capturing the rogue agent was not limited to finding the tabloid reporter who had been spreading personal information and potential spoilers all over the internet. For Heartthrob, this was also about finding the man who had turned him over to Bookworm and his minions. The rogue agent was responsible for the days of torture that Heartthrob had endured, and there was no telling how many others he had done the same to in the past. Who knew how many more actors he would endanger in the future?

There was not a reason in the world why this rogue agent should be allowed to continue living, in Heartthrob's opinion. As soon as they got him back to The Studio and forced him to tell them everything he knew about the tabloid as well as Bookworm, Heartthrob planned on putting the rogue agent out of business for good.

The door to the appliance store opened and a group of young people walked in. They were not laughing and having a good time. In fact, they seemed rather broody and had a sickly look to them. As they walked through the store, they looked toward Heartthrob and saw his gun, but gave it very little thought.

Each person he saw that night stirred a strange sense of urgency in him. He had the irrational thought that if he worked harder and hurried to take care of Bookworm, maybe these people could be saved. He was tired of losing, and watching people around him wither and die. The world had a cancer of the most aggressive form, and until they cut that cancer out, the world would grow darker and weaker.

A rustling sound from behind caused Heartthrob to turn without even thinking. Before his eyes could focus on anything, his gun was trained on the area where that sound came from and he was ready to shoot.

His eyes found their focus and scanned through the darkness for the source of this rustling, but he could see nothing. There was no sign of the rogue agent, and no sign of Starlette coming to help track him down.

The door opened once again and this time, the sound of shoes on the sidewalk outside could be heard.

Heartthrob turned and saw the rogue agent running down the sidewalk outside. He aimed his gun and fired three times, shattering the store's glass windows, but the rogue agent did not go down. He covered his head with his arms and kept running as the glass from the window showered down over him like a spring rain.

Heartthrob ran across the store and through one of the shattered windows, wasting no time with doors that would only slow him down.

He hit the sidewalk with his gun once again at the ready and saw the rogue agent down the street, still running for his life and looking silly as he zigzagged in an attempt to avoid being shot. Heartthrob fired at the rogue agent twice more, but missed both times. Apparently, zigzagging worked.

After what Heartthrob had been through because of that rogue agent, he firmly believed that bottom-feeders like him were just as bad—and perhaps just as dangerous—as Bookworm. They were part of the disease. Heartthrob had no intention of letting him get away.

~

The kids who sat on the floor of the basement may or may not have been aware of Starlette's fight with Jennifer. They seemed to be looking in their general direction from time to time, but they never said a word and never reacted to anything they saw. They just... watched.

Jennifer had Starlette's arm twisted behind her back and had pulled hard enough to weaken Starlette, causing her knees to buckle, just slightly. Jennifer leaned forward and whispered into Starlette's ear, "You're a big fan of slamming people into walls, aren't you?"

After speaking those words, Jennifer threw Starlette against the wall, face first. Starlette's nose filled with the smell of copper as this happened. The smell was accompanied by a dull, almost numb pain. She hoped her nose wasn't broken. She did not want to have to walk around The Studio with a bandage on her nose, as crew members gossiped about whether or not she had gotten a nose job.

Jennifer pulled Starlette away from the wall and grabbed her hair, in an attempt to pull her head back. This plan backfired, as Starlette's wig came off, causing Jennifer to be thrown off for just a moment. This was long enough for Starlette to break free, twist around and punch Jennifer squarely in the jaw.

Jennifer was knocked against the wall and Starlette was about to move forward and continue her attack as a group of youngsters pushed their way past them. They looked like a gloomy bunch, and only one of them was polite enough to mumble what Starlette assumed was an *excuse me* under his breath.

Once they were past Starlette and Jennifer, they walked straight for the speakeasy, never thinking twice about the fight that was taking place.

Starlette shook her head and said to Jennifer, "Kids today."

To which Jennifer replied, "I know, right?"

Jennifer charged at Starlette once again, with the rage of a bull. As she charged, one of the two cell phones on Jennifer's belt vibrated, but Jennifer did not take the time to look at it as she continued her attack.

Starlette, meanwhile, jumped and grabbed onto an overhead pipe. She swung toward Jennifer, catching Jennifer's head between her legs. She then let go of the pipe and dropped with full force, bringing Jennifer quickly to the ground.

Starlette tumbled as she hit the ground and was quickly back on her feet.

As Jennifer scrambled to get back up, she instinctively pulled her cell phone off of her belt and looked at it. She rolled her eyes and sighed as she clipped it back to the belt and returned her attention to Starlette.

Starlette paused and put her hands on her hips, saying, "Seriously? Did you just check your messages in the middle of our fight? What, does your boss not remember where he parked the car?"

"Actually, I have his keys," Jennifer replied. "He's always losing them."

"And you put your life on the line for this guy?"

"He's the boss."

Jennifer raised her fists and prepared herself for the next round of fighting. Starlette shook her head and did the same. They stared each other down, just waiting for the moment when the fight would resume.

Starlette didn't know whether she would be the one to attack or if it would be Jennifer. She waited for the moment when instinct would tell her one way or the other. In her experience, Starlette had found fights like these to be something like a dance. There was a rhythm being followed, even if there was no music. She had to wait for the right beat before she could make her move, or her rhythm would be thrown off.

Instinct did not fail her this time. In the back of her brain, she felt the moment arrive when their fight would resume and just as she felt this, she saw Jennifer rush toward her. The way Jennifer was carrying herself told Starlette that she would be swinging from down low. Starlette prepared herself accordingly.

As Jennifer neared, she shifted her weight and threw herself into a flip which Starlette wasn't expecting. Jennifer's feet met

Starlette's chest and Jennifer put all of her weight into shoving Starlette backwards.

Starlette fell back, though only in part due to Jennifer's attack. She needed to adjust her strategy, so she allowed herself to go down, and she rolled as she hit the floor.

As she recovered, Starlette stayed low. In her hands, she now held two of the throwing knives that Prop Master included for all of her shoots.

Jennifer kicked off of the wall once again and spun in the air with her fist balled and meant to bring that fist down on Starlette as she landed.

Starlette moved out of the way and sliced through the air in an X pattern as Jennifer came in for the attack.

When Jennifer landed, she was cut across the chest and arm. She was bleeding badly and the shock of these wounds prevented her from landing on her feet. Instead, she flopped to the ground like a fish out of water, still squirming.

"You need to find a new job," Starlette told her as she looked around for some way of tying Jennifer's wrists.

~

Heartthrob followed the rogue agent down a dark alley. It seemed cliché, yet fitting. A rogue agent would probably spend a lot of his time in back alleys and shadowy corners. Heartthrob wouldn't be surprised if the rogue agent also lived in a cage and ate babies for breakfast—He was inhuman.

Once again, Heartthrob lost track of the rogue agent as he entered the alley. It seemed impossible, since there were few places to hide, but this rogue agent was slippery. He had a talent for vanishing into thin air.

Heartthrob walked softly down the alley, just as he had walked softly in the store. He knew that a person could only remain silent and still for so long, especially when pumped up on adrenaline. The rogue agent would reveal himself soon, and when he did, Heartthrob would be ready.

The alley filled with a faint *beeping*. It was not regular enough to be an alarm. The pattern of beeps sounded more like buttons being pushed on a cell phone.

The rogue agent was either calling someone or texting them,

but the echoes of the alley threw phantom beeps from every direction, making it difficult for Heartthrob to pinpoint their origin.

He kept moving forward, slowly and steadily. He knew that he must be close to the rogue agent. At any moment, the rogue agent would spring up from behind one of the few garbage cans in the area—or out from a doorway—and he would likely attempt to throw something at Heartthrob as a distraction, so he could run off and disappear once again.

"I know who you are," came a whisper, which echoed and repeated through the alley, just as the beeping had.

"Everyone knows who I am," Heartthrob replied, in a normal tone.

"But have they seen the *real* you?" came that whisper again. "The weak, scared, broken man who came to me for help? So desperate. So alone."

"I'm not alone anymore."

"Aren't you? How many of them call you by your real name? How many know the person you are deep down inside? How many of them did you tell about your family before that article came out?"

Heartthrob didn't respond. He was too busy trying to figure out where the whisper was coming from. He didn't owe this rogue agent any answers. He only owed him broken bones and bloodshed.

"You're a good actor," the rogue agent said. "But I can see right through you. I can see what's on the inside."

Still, Heartthrob remained silent. He moved steadily, with his eyes and ears open.

The rogue agent continued to press, "Do you sleep at night? Or do you see them every time you close your eyes? Do you cry for them? Do you feel their pain?"

Heartthrob got the location. He fired two shots at a dumpster several yards ahead, and the rogue agent jumped out from behind it like a scared cat. He grabbed a bag of garbage and hurled it at Heartthrob as he ran down the alley.

Heartthrob couldn't avoid the garbage entirely. He waited for it to come close and then swatted it out of his way as he ran after the rogue agent. He took aim as he ran and fired, just barely missing the rogue agent, who rounded the corner at the end of the alley.

When Heartthrob reached the end of the alley, he saw the rogue agent's car. It was a shiny red convertible, which Heartthrob could have guessed even without having seen it. The rogue agent was nowhere to be seen at first.

Heartthrob ducked low and looked under the car. He could see the rogue agent on the far end, crouching so as not to be seen. This time, he failed.

"Tell me," Heartthrob said in a cool and steady tone, "do you fear what you have coming to you? The pain? The endless hours of torture? Do you fear going through the same thing that you put me through?"

"I didn't do any of that to you."

"You sold me. *Twice*. And if my cast hadn't pulled me out of there, I would still be in that chair."

"I knew they'd save you."

"The question is... Who will save you?"

Heartthrob stepped around the car and aimed his gun at the rogue agent's head. The rogue agent threw his hands over his face and squirmed on the ground, as though he could move backwards despite being pressed against his car.

Heartthrob grabbed him and threw him against the hood of the car, holding him down by the neck as he holstered his gun.

The rogue agent was nervous and shaking, but he continued to push Heartthrob. He said, "Don't you worry about what they'd think, if they knew what you brought home to your own family? Do you believe they'd still have your back?"

Heartthrob lifted the rogue agent's head off of the hood and slammed it back down, saying, "Shut your mouth."

Heartthrob looked around the street, wondering how he was going to call the van to come and get him when he was so far from the pickup point. Though he had no means of handcuffing the rogue agent, he would have to move him through the alley and back toward the appliance store.

"Let's go," he said as he pulled the rogue agent off of the car and held his arm behind his back, immobilizing the prisoner.

He pushed the agent toward the alley, giving his arm enough of a tug to let the agent know that the arm could be broken—or at the very least, dislocated—at any moment.

As they walked down the alley, the rogue agent stumbled and breathed deeply. He was scared. This made Heartthrob feel warm inside.

"You can pretend you're fine," the rogue agent said to him. "You can put a smile on your face and push those memories to the back of your mind, but we both know the truth. Any moment now, you will break. Maybe you've come close to it already; maybe not. But it will happen, and when it does... Who will be the next person to die?"

"I said, shut your fucking mouth!" Heartthrob yelled in the rogue agent's ear, pulling the arm out of its socket.

The rogue agent screamed and crumbled onto the ground in pain. Heartthrob bent down and pulled him by the shirt, though the rogue agent would not use his legs and stand. He was in too much pain.

"You don't know me!" Heartthrob yelled in the rogue agent's face.

He threw a punch at the rogue agent and dropped him to the ground. He stomped his foot down on the rogue agent's stomach and then kicked him in the ribs, repeating, "You don't know me!"

He placed his foot on the rogue agent's neck and began to put pressure on it, telling the rogue agent, "You have no idea what I am."

"Heartthrob!" came Starlette's voice from the end of the alley.

He looked up and saw her running toward him, yelling, "Back off! Now!"

Heartthrob looked from Starlette, to the rogue agent. For the life of him, he couldn't remember how his foot had gotten on the rogue agent's neck.

Without saying a word, Heartthrob backed away from the rogue agent. When he reached a wall, he slid down it, keeping his eyes on the broken and bloody rogue agent on the ground, who was still crying in pain.

Once Starlette reached them, she stood over the rogue agent and looked at him for a moment. She then turned her attention to

Heartthrob and said, "I'm pretty sure you got him."

~

Tessa sat on the sofa in her dressing room, eating tiny sandwiches off of a disposable aluminum tray. The sandwiches were actually one sandwich, cut into quarters, but if she tried very hard she could make herself see them as four tiny, fancy sandwiches. If she squinted her eyes, she could see the disposable tray as a silver platter.

She missed her home. She missed her view, even if she did rarely get to open the curtains and look outside, especially at night. She missed her kitchen, which she had stocked with all of the caviar and pâté that the other tenants in her building had left behind. She missed her bar.

Oh, she could get passable martinis within The Studio, but it didn't seem the same. These martinis came at the cost of her freedom. Every move she made, every drink she took, she could feel the eyes and ears of The Studio on her. She could picture them counting each sip, and somehow being drunk suddenly felt as though it were something being done *to* her, rather than something that she was doing to herself.

She tried to count her blessings. At least she didn't have to live in one of those ridiculous little trailers. She had been given an office, which had been converted into a dressing room, in the Producers district. It was a loud place to live. During the day, producers screamed about budgetary issues and whatnot. They screamed at their assistants, for all sorts of reasons. They screamed at writers, directors, and all of the department heads, for whatever reasons struck their fancy; and at night, pretty young actors and actresses who were hoping to quickly rise through the ranks screamed as well, but in entirely different ways.

Tessa had looked at the menu upon arriving in her dressing room, and all of these actors looked like children to her. The thought of exploiting one turned her stomach.

She spent most of her time in her dressing room. Producers sometimes dropped off scripts for her to read. Usually, they were months old. This gave Tessa the impression that they wanted to keep her occupied. She supposed that they didn't want her wandering through The Studio, talking about the olden days and the system that had been in place back then.

She was fine, keeping to herself. She only sometimes enjoyed being hounded by young actresses who wanted to tell her how much their mothers loved her movies when they were kids. It was flattering on occasion, and highly insulting at other times.

The truth was, she had gotten used to being alone. For years, she was all but invisible. After the attacks, she was isolated entirely. Now, there were so many people around her; watching her; talking about her, and she was split on how she felt about that. On one hand, she was a star of the truest form and she loved being the center of attention. On the other hand, she could hear the faint whispers of all those baby-faced casting directors, telling her that she wasn't right for the part. She was too old, or too young. She was too pretty, or not pretty enough. She was too well known, or too distant a memory. Everywhere she turned, she felt judged. Being alone since the attacks was, in some ways, the most peace she had ever had.

To one side of the room, there was a table set up, with a lighted mirror. It was where she could apply makeup and fix her hair, but she sometimes sat in front of the brightly lit mirror and stared at herself, wondering how she had become the aging relic that she saw before her.

She boasted about being one of the few actresses in Hollywood over the age of fifty who could still raise her eyebrows, and she would never dare change that. She could see how those other actresses might be lured into the decision to have plastic surgery, however. She could see the appeal of the idea, despite knowing how awful it usually turned out.

Hollywood was a coldhearted bitch. It had been when Tessa was first coming up in the business, and it remained that way long after its collapse. In order to survive, you had to be a fighter.

She laughed as that thought entered her mind. It had always been true, but now it was also damn funny.

She took another bite of a tiny sandwich and imagined that she was sitting in the dressing room of some long ago film project. She imagined that any moment, a crew member would knock on her door and tell her that she was needed on the set.

"I'll be there when I'm damn ready," she muttered to herself.

"You cannot rush a star."

She picked up a glass of water, which had cucumber floating around in it for some unknown reason. She hadn't ordered her water with cucumber, but it had been delivered that way. She drank it and could only assume that it was a fancy modern Hollywood beverage, rather than a horrible mistake from the kitchen. She drank it, but she didn't like it. There was too much water and not enough vodka for her taste. Plus, the cucumber was stupid.

As she drank her cucumber-flavored water, she heard a *click*.

She put her glass down and looked around the room, wondering where on Earth that sound might have come from, but having not the faintest clue.

"Is someone at my door?" she called out.

There was no response.

Tessa stood and took another look around the room, figuring that there must have been some high-tech contraption that she wasn't aware of, which made clicking sounds. Though she knew her way around a smartphone, she hated technology with a passion. It robbed the world of its romance and mystery. In the days of text messaging and the internet, there was no need to get to know a person. Within an hour of meeting them, you could read a year's worth of their postings online and in most cases, find nude pictures to illustrate those trashy stories.

There was no elegance in technology. The mystique of celebrity was sacrificed to the vanity of seeing how many people you could have following your every sentence. Everything was gray and plastic. The entire civilization was mass produced and designed to be obsolete after a year. The idea of a Hollywood legend was dead before Hollywood was destroyed, and in the wake of its collapse, only one star had managed to remain shining above them all.

On top of all that philosophical crap, *technology* was now apparently clicking, which would surely drive her mad if she had to listen to it every day.

She looked at every electrical outlet in her room—because everything was tethered to the wall these days—yet she saw nothing unexpected. She looked under her bed and her sofa. She opened each drawer on her makeup table.

After failing to discover the source of this sound, she was beginning to think that it was all some sort of cucumber-induced hallucination. She stood in the middle of the room, wondering if she should just go back to her strict schedule of sitting and sometimes napping, but the sound echoed through her mind, growing louder with each encore.

There was something about the sound which didn't sit right with her. It wasn't a normal sound that you'd hear every day and move on with your life. This sound had weight to it, and it meant something that she was only aware of on a deep, instinctual level.

She decided to walk to the door and see if she could flag down some crew member to find out if they knew what she might have heard. Each step toward the door seemed more urgent to her somehow, and as she placed her hand on the knob, she came to a sudden realization: The door was locked.

Tessa didn't even have to turn the knob to know that it was locked; she just knew. She had been in two movies wherein she played a mental patient, confined to a small room. She played an alien abductee. She had played the victim of a masked serial killer. She knew what that clicking sound was in the back of her mind, because she had seen it all before, in her own movies.

Slowly, she tried to turn the doorknob, hoping that she was wrong. If the knob turned, she would simply consider herself a delusional old woman who had spent too much time by herself and who was in desperate need of a drink.

The knob turned.

Tessa smiled and the smile soon turned into a laugh as she considered how foolish she had been. Plotlines like that were created for the audience, not the talent. She had been suckered by her own knack for suspense.

As she shook her head and thanked God that nobody would ever know about her brief panic, she pulled on the door to open it.

The door did not open.

She pulled harder, figuring that it was simply stuck, but the door would not budge. She pulled on it again and again, suddenly feeling like a lab rat in a cage, or the character in some reality-bending episode of *The Twilight Zone*—which she had actually once been.

Tessa pounded on the door and yelled, "Let me out of here! Someone open this door at once!"

There was no response.

She backed away from the door, looking at it as though it could burst into flames at any moment. Her mind was racing, but Tessa struggled to get it under control. She was a professional. She stood in front of a camera on the day her first husband had died in a car accident, and she delivered one of the most upbeat performances of her life. She would not allow herself to react as they wanted her to react. If they wanted her to panic, she would sit on the sofa and eat her food. If they wanted her to kick and scream, she would remain passive.

Starlette was out with Heartthrob, and Girl Next Door did not tend to visit as much as Starlette, so Tessa would have to wait. Eventually, Starlette would return from her shoot and even if it took a while, she would begin to wonder where Tessa was. As long as she had that knowledge, Tessa would fear nothing.

She walked to her sofa and she spread herself out across it. She felt as though she were filming a scene, in the sense that she could feel someone watching her. If this was the case, they would see her looking as cool as one of the cucumbers in her water.

Tessa picked up one of the outdated scripts that had been given to her and she began to thumb through it as though it was a magazine. Though she wasn't really reading the script, she could tell that she would have passed on the project, had it been offered to her. The dialog was horrible and the number of spelling errors made her wonder how this person had ever gotten a job as a professional writer.

Still, she flipped through the script, all the while trying to think of some action that she might take, but she could think of none. The obvious reaction would be to run to the phone and try to make a call for help, but if the doors had been rigged with a remote lock, surely the phone had been killed as well... Or so she thought.

The phone began to ring.

Tessa's eyes moved to where the phone was sitting, on her makeup table, and she looked at it as though it was the enemy. She didn't know if she wanted to pick it up or not. Finally, she decided to let it ring. If she rushed to it and picked it up, she would seem desperate. By ignoring the phone, she forced the person on the other end of the line to wait for her. Undoubtedly, they would let it ring and ring, until she picked it up. She didn't have to worry about missing her one opportunity to get answers. So, she let them wait. After all, you cannot rush a star.

~

Girl Next Door stood by the entrance to The Studio, waiting for Starlette and Heartthrob to get back. Her night had been stressful and frustrating, and she had nobody to talk to. She didn't even *need* to talk. If they seemed annoyed or disinterested, she would be happy to just sit with people that she knew and trusted.

Sassy Gay Friend had been wandering around all night. She saw him walk past her, keeping an eye on her. She figured that he was probably looking for his next chance to swoop in and make her look like a fool. It pissed her off.

She was tired of feeling like this. Every day, since her arrival at The Studio, Ember had felt like she was struggling to stay afloat. She felt as though she constantly needed to prove herself worthy to The Studio, or else she would be kicked out. She feared going back to the streets. She didn't spend much time out there after the attacks, but what she did experience was horrible. She was constantly scared and lonely.

In The Studio, she felt safer. When she was around her co-stars, she felt like she had someone watching her back, and that they cared about what happened to her. As far as everyone else in The Studio was concerned, she was just filling out the cast. To the producers and the writers, and many others, she was expendable and easily replaced. Every time a producer said *hello* to her, she worried that it would be followed by *we need to talk*.

Maybe it was in her head. She considered that there was a chance that people did appreciate her for what she did in The Studio, but there was no way of knowing. They certainly didn't treat her with the same regard as Starlette, but then again, Starlette was the lead.

She started biting her nails as she waited for her co-stars to get back from their location shoot. Word had already come in that they found the same rogue agent that had turned Heartthrob over to Bookworm's minions. Ember wanted to meet that rogue agent. She wanted to sit down and ask him why he felt a need to behave in such a way. She wanted to know what childhood trauma had caused him to become such a vile human being.

She didn't like violence. If given the choice, Ember would vote for peaceful resolution every time. She believed in the power of conversation, but the attacks proved to her that you can't always fix your problems by talking them out. Sometimes, you needed to kill in order to protect yourself and those you cared for. The way she saw it, it was just Bookworm's karma biting him in the ass.

Ember must have looked nervous as she stood there, because when Sassy Gay Friend walked up and stood beside her, keeping his eyes on the entrance as well, he said "Opening night jitters?"

"Please go away," she replied.

He frowned and asked her, "Is that any way to talk to your partner in crime solving?"

"You mean, the guy who took all the credit for the work that *I* did?" Girl Next Door snapped back. "Because, yeah. That is *exactly* the way to talk to him."

"Let me guess… You're waiting here so that you can run up to Starlette and Heartthrob as soon as they walk through the door and whine to them about the big bad things that I've done?"

"I'm waiting here to make sure that they get home safely. Because I care about my co-stars, unlike some people," she replied. It was only partially a lie.

Sassy Gay Friend made a *tsk* sound and shook his head. He said, "And you wonder why nobody here takes you seriously."

The fact that he knew which buttons of hers to push pissed her off. She tried to remain calm in spite of his attempts to provoke her. So, while she may have wanted to beat the snot out of him, Girl Next Door simply looked at Sassy Gay Friend and said, "Look… I don't want to fight. I don't want anything from you. All I want is to be left alone. We can work together when we have to. I'll cover your back when people are shooting at you. We can get by just fine, but please, I am begging you… Just leave me alone."

"Jealousy is unbecoming."

She didn't want to respond, but she couldn't help herself. "Jealousy?"

"You're jealous because I solved the big mystery and saved the day."

"You did not solve the big mystery. I did," she told him, clenching her jaw as she said it. "How can you stand there and try to feed me the same lies you feed them, when we both know what really happened?"

"I guess I'm just a better actor than you."

Girl Next Door smiled and shook her head. She said, "You just feed off of the people around you, don't you? People like you make me sick."

Sassy Gay Friend put his hand on his chest and stepped back. He looked at her with tears in his eyes and said rather loudly, "People like me make you sick?"

"Oh, don't even..." she started, before changing directions, looking him in the eyes and rather sternly saying, "Yes. People like you make me sick. You're disgusting. You're immoral. You are everything that is wrong with the world we live in today. Just thinking about you makes me want to throw up."

She felt proud of herself. She was finally standing up for herself. She was finally stepping up and claiming some small amount of power. It was liberating—That is, until she stopped talking and looked around The Studio, where she saw countless actors and crew members staring at her.

In a split second, everything she had said with a raised voice replayed in her mind and she came to the realization that she had been played by Sassy Gay Friend once again.

Sassy Gay Friend didn't say anything. He simply stood there, with his mouth hanging open with feigned shock and tears in his eyes.

"No..." Girl Next Door said, looking to all of the people watching her. "I wasn't saying it like that. I was saying *he* makes me sick... Not because of the gay thing. He's just an ass, that's all."

All around her, people continued to glare and shake their heads. They didn't listen to her explanation, they just wrote her off. This once again confirmed how little people thought of her in The Studio.

Sassy Gay Friend walked closer to her once again and in a quiet voice said, "Remember, sweetie... It doesn't matter if you win or lose. It's all about how you play the game."

"Just get away from me," she replied, wanting nothing more to do with him. She couldn't even feel anger anymore; only fatigue.

Girl Next Door was going to turn and walk back to her trailer, so she could be alone in the dark and not have to face the people around her, but before she could leave, the door to The Studio opened.

The first person to walk through the door was the rogue agent, with his hands tied behind his back. His face was covered with a cloth shopping bag, but it was obvious that he was an agent by the way he was dressed. Starlette was behind him, forcing him down the stairs.

Following Starlette was another person with a bag over her head. For a moment, Girl Next Door wasn't sure who this person was, but when she saw the cell phones clipped to her belt, she knew that it was the rogue agent's assistant, Jennifer. Apparently, she had survived the explosion of the fast food restaurant where Girl Next Door had kicked her ass upon their first meeting.

"Son of a bitch," Girl Next Door said, under her breath. "A perfect end to a perfect day."

Heartthrob was behind Jennifer, guiding her down the stairs and into The Studio. There was a look in his eyes that Girl Next Door couldn't quite place. Though he didn't look injured, he seemed wounded somehow.

Girl Next Door walked toward her co-stars as they reached the bottom of the stairs. Behind her, The Director was approaching.

"Good work," The Director said to Starlette and Heartthrob. "We'll get them in for questioning. Normally, I'd ask you to do it, Heartthrob, considering your background in procedurals... But given the circumstances, I don't think you're the right man for this job."

Heartthrob nodded in agreement.

A couple of men from Studio security came to take the rogue agent and Jennifer away. Once they were gone, The Director said to Starlette, "Good work."

He then walked away, leaving the actors free to turn in their props, get changed and head back to their trailers for the night.

As Starlette and Heartthrob began to walk toward the prop

department, Girl Next Door kept pace with them. Unfortunately, so did Sassy Gay Friend.

"Are you okay?" Sassy Gay Friend asked, sounding as though he actually cared. "You look like it was a long night."

"We're fine," Starlette replied.

Starlette picked up her pace just a little bit, indicating that she didn't feel like talking. It was something that anyone who knew Starlette would pick up on, but Sassy Gay Friend didn't know Starlette. He kept up with her and walked beside her as she went.

Girl Next Door stayed back, with Heartthrob. He seemed distant, having not looked at her once since he arrived back at The Studio. From the look in his eyes, she could tell that his thoughts were a million miles away. She just didn't know what type of thoughts they were, but they seemed to weigh heavily on him.

As they walked, Girl Next Door slipped her hand into his. He squeezed it tightly.

~

The phone was still ringing. It had been for at least a half hour, and while the sound of its ringing annoyed Tessa to no end, she took pleasure in knowing that whomever it was that was trying to contact her was not only waiting, but probably incredibly frustrated by this point. Obviously, they had no choice but to wait for her.

After finishing one of those wretched scripts and downing the last of her cucumber water, Tessa calmly walked over to the phone, looked down at it for a moment, then picked up the receiver and put it to her ear.

"Yes?" she said into it coolly, as though she hadn't been letting it ring for a half hour.

There was silence on the other end of the line. Tessa wasn't sure whether the other person had fallen asleep or if they were taking a very long dramatic pause, but she didn't have patience for them either way. She waited only a couple of seconds before she pulled the phone from her ear, fully prepared to hang it up.

"Tessa Baker," came a voice on the other end of the line. It was cold; almost robotic.

She put the phone back to her ear and said, "Can I help you?"

"Do you know who I am?"

"It's not a video phone, darling."

"I am Studio Head. I am the one who makes all of the crucial decisions within The Studio. I decide what projects get the green light, and which don't. I decide who remains under contract and who does not."

"Well... Bully for you."

Tessa walked with the phone and sat on her sofa once again. She leaned back and looked at her nails as she chatted with Studio Head. She was not impressed by his rank.

"Do you know why I'm calling you?"

"I haven't the slightest clue, but I do wish you'd get on with it. I have a schedule to keep."

"Earlier tonight, a tabloid website was updated with an article which concerned you."

Tessa perked up. She hadn't been the topic of juicy tabloid gossip for ages, and the last time it happened, it was merely a piece on celebrity cellulite.

"What did it say?" she asked, never betraying her cool and collected demeanor.

"The article claimed that you have signed with a publisher. It says that you have a book deal."

Tessa deflated. This had to be the most boring revelation that they possibly could have discovered about her. She was half tempted to call the tabloid and tell them a secret or two, just to help them out.

"Darling, if that was the most shocking revelation they have about me, I should think your PR department can safely go home for the night."

"Then it's true?"

"No, it's not true. I do not currently have a book deal. I *did* have a book deal, several years ago, but it eventually fell through. Apparently, they were more interested in a book written by Paris Hilton's dog trainer or some such nonsense."

"Were you ever published?"

"I can't very well be published if I don't have a book deal, now can I?"

"Miss Baker, I do not believe you are taking this matter seriously."

Tessa switched ears and lit a cigarette as she said, "I might take it more seriously if you told me why this is such a big concern."

"Nearly one year ago, our industry was attacked by a literary known as Bookworm. Stop me if you've heard this story."

"*Bookworm.* Is this another one of your clever names? Tell me, why don't you call him by his real name?"

"The identity of Bookworm remains a mystery. Perhaps you could help us uncover it. Perhaps you could use your connections to his terrorist underworld."

"My *what* to his *whom*?"

"Your publishing ties."

Tessa broke into an all-out laugh when she heard Studio Head try to link her publishing connections to a terrorist organization. She took a drag from her cigarette and said to him, "Who is this really? Is this little Archie Hines? Burtie Larson? Dick Masterson? Which fresh faced little suit eventually climbed the ladder and made it all the way to the top?"

There was no response.

"I have been in this industry for a long time. I know you, even if I'm not sure which *you* I'm talking to. I was there when you were but an errand boy, fetching snacks for crew members in between takes. You may run this Studio, boy, but I am the foundation upon which it is built. Do not presume to group me with terrorists and criminals. When you wish to talk to me with the respect that I have earned, you have my number."

She hung up the phone and waited.

Moments passed, but the phone did not ring again. She imagined Studio Head, sitting at his oversized desk, in his oversized office, gritting his teeth and slamming his phone down. She imagined that he was collecting himself, and would call back soon, demanding that she answer his questions, lest she suffer the consequences.

In her mind, she prepared her approach for when the phone rang again. She decided that she would only let it ring a few times, and she would answer with grace and dignity. She would not sound angry or arrogant.

She imagined that she would kick the ball around a little bit more and finally tell Studio Head the truth of the situation: There was very little known about Bookworm, and to suspect her of treason against her own people merely because she had ties to the publishing world was not only silly, it was foolish. Countless movies had been based on the works of esteemed authors... She couldn't think of any off the top of her head, but surely there had been some.

She looked forward to walking around The Studio some more and seeing the culture that they had built there. She wondered how people like Studio Head had manipulated the fears of an already wounded people.

Tessa wasn't interested in being a role model for the actors and actresses in The Studio. She didn't need to lead a revolution, but she had been there before and she had seen this type of system at work in the past. She had seen desperate performers twisted beyond recognition, all because they were told that it was the only way for them to survive in the fierce atmosphere that was *Hollywood*.

When the phone rang, she planned on speaking gently to Studio Head and telling him exactly what was on her mind. She planned on telling him that what he was doing was disgusting and cruel; that his methods of picking who was and was not worthy of Studio protection was repulsive. She also planned on telling him that she would not be the one to remove him from his throne. The outside world was dangerous. Actors left to scatter would be picked off one by one, until their entire culture was extinct. They needed The Studio, in some form or another. Until Bookworm was gone and the actors would step out into the light of day without fear of being killed, they needed shelter. She only wished that it hadn't taken this form.

Tessa knew that history would repeat itself. She had faith in her people to free themselves of The Studio system and reclaim their power. Already, tensions were rising within The Studio. It was only a matter of time before a rebellion took shape, and Tessa wondered just how far that tension would rise if she were to suddenly disappear, like Starlette's other friend already had.

She waited for the phone to ring, but it never did.

Eventually, Tessa heard a *click*. The door had been unlocked.

~

After turning in their props and getting changed into their own clothes, Starlette and Heartthrob returned to their trailers, with Ember. The three of them were sitting outside of the trailers. They said nothing to each other; they simply did not want to go to sleep and did not want to be alone.

Heartthrob had been distant, ever since the news about his family had been made public. Starlette didn't want to press the subject, but what she saw in the alley gave her cause to worry. It wasn't the fact that he was beating the rogue agent which concerned her, it was the look in his eyes as he was doing it. It was an absent look; and the look in his eyes after she stopped him was the look of someone who didn't even realize what they were doing.

She wanted answers; she just didn't want to *ask* for answers. So, she sat there with Heartthrob and Ember, and she waited.

"Can I ask a question?" Heartthrob asked, still not looking at Starlette or Ember, but staring at his own hands.

Ember nodded and said, "Yeah, of course."

Heartthrob shifted in his seat. It seemed as though he didn't know quite how to approach the subject that he wanted to talk about. As he tried to figure it out, there was a look about him—as though he wished he hadn't said anything at all.

Finally, he asked, "Where were you during the attacks?"

Starlette and Ember looked at each other. It wasn't a popular subject in The Studio. People didn't typically spend their afternoons exchanging *where were you when* stories. To Starlette, it seemed like a completely different person who had gone through the attacks. She looked back on those memories as though they were a movie; as though she was watching it all from the outside. She had no desire to rewind and start it all over again.

"I was at a taco stand," Ember replied. She didn't seem eager to discuss it, and she did not deliver the story in her normal quirky tone. When she spoke of it, she sounded somehow older to Starlette. "I guess that's why nobody found me. I wasn't where I was supposed to be. I just took off that morning and I drove around. I didn't even know where I was going until I got there. It was this little place up the coast, and they were playing the awards on the radio, so I heard what was going on."

Ember paused, but her silence was heavy. It was as though she could see it all in front of her, happening again. After lingering for a moment, she shook it off and smiled, saying, "So I can safely say that cheapo fish tacos are not a good food to eat during the apocalypse."

Starlette didn't allow another silence to fall. She wanted to give Ember a chance to pack her baggage away once again. So, as soon as Ember was finished, Starlette said, "I was in England, filming a movie."

She tried to think of something more meaningful to say about it, but there didn't seem to be anything left. She shrugged and said, "Shots fired. Explosions. Knocked unconscious... pretty much the same as most people, I guess."

Images flashed through Starlette's mind. She saw her stunt double lying dead on the ground. She saw the dark figure who had stabbed her. She saw the bodies in the office trailer. Blood and violence, and a random act of fate which somehow saw her through it.

She didn't say anything about those images. She just let it go and hoped that she wouldn't have to revisit that night ever again.

"I was in New York," Heartthrob said. "It was snowing and I was attacked, but I got through it... It was that sort of powdery snow that swirls around whenever the wind blows. Everything else is a blur. I was running and hiding, and when it was all said and done... I was alone. I was in a city full of people, but I was completely alone. And I was scared."

He couldn't stay seated anymore. Talking about what happened made him uncomfortable, and he needed to move around, so he stood and he paced.

"I wasn't thinking," he told them. "I was in a daze, I guess. I didn't know what was going on... Maybe I just couldn't process it, I don't know. But I ran..."

He seemed to want to say more. Starlette could almost see the words lumped up in his throat, but he couldn't spit them out. The more he tried, the more his body resisted. The more he fought, the more pain she could see in his eyes. He didn't cry. To cry might have provided some release, but he didn't allow himself that release. He simply swallowed hard and tried to force his way through.

"I..." he said, still struggling. "I ran home."

He took a deep gulp of air, as though he'd been underwater and could hold his breath no longer. Starlette could see his hands shaking.

Ember moved to the edge of her seat. She wanted to go to him and help him, but she didn't. She gave him the space that he needed.

"I went home to my family, and I stayed there for a while. I let myself believe that it was over. I was just the kid who left there years ago, and I was back. I was going to have a simple life. I—" he looked at Ember and then quickly looked away once again. "I was going to marry my high school sweetheart."

Ember slid back in her chair.

Heartthrob put a hand over his mouth and shook his head, as though his body was telling him to stop talking. He fought the urge to fall silent and when he took his hand away from his mouth, he said, "When they came looking for me, I wanted to run again. I just wanted to get out of there, but my family wouldn't let me. They wanted to help me... I don't know why... I don't know what I was thinking was going to happen, but I let them."

He stopped pacing and turned to face Starlette and Ember as he said, "The rest was in the article. I wasn't even there for some of it. I didn't know exactly what happened. I just knew that they died because of me. They suffered for hours. They screamed. They bled, and they never gave me up. Not one of them. With a few words, they could have saved all their lives, but they didn't. And I hate them for that. I shouldn't hate them, but I do."

He looked off to the side for a moment, taking that time to collect himself and pull himself out of the details of those memories that he wasn't sharing. When he looked back to the actresses once again, he was the same Heartthrob that they had become accustomed to; troubled, but capable.

"I'm telling you this, because I need to you to know why I'm here. I need you to trust that I can do this. I am so messed up, I don't even know what sane is anymore, but I have nowhere to go but here. I have nobody to care about... except my cast. And I will not let that happen again. I swear to God, I will not let that happen again."

Starlette considered what he was saying, and she read the expression on his face as he said it. She tried to decide if he was completely insane or the normal brand of crazy that she was accustomed to.

Her conclusion was in his favor, but her reaction would have been the same either way. She stood from her seat and looked him in the eye as she said to him, "You're such a girl."

It was all that she needed to say. She wasn't going to get all sappy and give him a big hug. She wasn't going to tell him that it would be okay, because the odds were, it wasn't going to be okay. All she could offer him was the knowledge that even after everything that he had been through, he had family.

As she said it, there was a slight glimmer in his eye. He knew exactly what she meant.

With her message having been received, Starlette turned around and said, "I'm hitting the sack. G'night ladies."

She walked into her trailer and closed the door behind her.

Starlette didn't hear Ember say anything to Heartthrob after she left. Normally, she could hear entire conversations through the walls of her trailer.

When she let curiosity get the best of her, Starlette went to the window and took a quick look through her blinds. She couldn't help but smile as she saw Ember kissing Heartthrob.

~

"I spent the better part of the night in talks with the rogue agent," The Director told Starlette and her cast, who were gathered for an early morning meeting in the conference room. All of the department heads were there, listening intently to what he had to say. After all, nobody wanted to be the topic of the next news flash on The Celeb Spinner.

"By '*talks*', do you by any chance mean that you were beating him snotless?" Girl Next Door asked.

"The rogue agent has agreed to work with us in exchange for some... leniency," The Director told her. "Freedom wasn't on the table, but he will be confined for as long as he agrees to help us."

"You can't trust him," Starlette assured The Director. "He will play us all, and lead us to our deaths."

The Director nodded in agreement and said, "That may very well be the case. However, in this situation, we needed him."

The Director pressed a button on a remote control that was resting on the table in front of him. On the monitors behind him came appeared images of The Celeb Spinner website on either side, with a map of the city in the center.

"The rogue agent sent word through his network of connections, telling them that he had important spoilers to reveal about upcoming shoots that we are planning. He fed those contacts an e-mail address that we provided, and we waited to be contacted by the tabloid reporter. It didn't take long before we got an e-mail, asking for the information," The Director told everyone in the room.

Another press of a button brought up a map of the country, with several red dots which seemed to be radiating signals of some sort. A blue dot bounced between these red dots.

"The e-mail address that we provided was linked to a specific server, which was encoded with a tech-tech decoding tech, which would bounce a copy of the e-mail back to the sender, and work its way into the tech of the tech attempting to send the e-mail to us. The tech would then establish contact with us, letting us know where that computer is located."

Heartthrob leaned in closer to Girl Next Door and whispered, "Why does he keep saying 'tech' like that?"

Girl Next Door quietly replied, "It means that the writers haven't gotten in contact with the technical advisors yet, so they don't know what specific language to use in the script. It'll be added before we get the shooting script."

Heartthrob nodded his understanding and they turned their attention back to The Director.

"Everything went according to plan. We managed to trace the e-mail through a number of servers, scattered around the country. Apparently, the site owner is using a tech program to reroute his tech and make it hard to track, but our tech was better."

On the monitor which was displaying the map of the country, the animation displayed a visual representation of this signal bouncing all over the country. The dots made much more sense, when put in their proper context.

"So, where did it eventually track to?" Starlette asked. It seemed like an obvious question, but nobody else was asking it and The Director didn't appear to be continuing with the briefing until the question was out there, so she asked it.

"I'm glad you asked," The Director replied. "The signal bounced off of various servers in Iowa, North Dakota, New Mexico, Florida —"

"Oh! Florida! I've heard of that one!" Sassy Gay Friend declared. He then looked around the room and said, "I mean, I've *heard* of all those other ones too... I just always kind of thought they were made up for fantasy novels or something. I mean, *New Mexico*? Really? Who thought of that?"

The Director ignored Sassy Gay Friend's side comment and continued with what he was saying. "Where the signal eventually wound up should make everyone here pretty happy... The tabloid website is being run locally."

"Well, yeah..." Starlette said, in a ho-hum tone. "I just kinda figured that, since it made no reference at all to anyone outside of The Studio. I'd have been really surprised if it wound up being some random Network affiliate."

"Plus, we're the main characters, so... Don't they kinda have to be here?" Girl Next Door asked.

The room was silent for a moment after that question was asked. Nobody knew quite how to respond to it.

Eventually, The Director turned his attention back to the topic at hand. He said, "We tracked the location of the e-mail's origin to a local address. Starlette, you and your cast will head out in six hours. You will be responsible for not only shutting down the website, but gathering whatever information this guy has on us or any of the shoots that we have planned. If spoilers have been leaked, we need to know now, so that we can change the scripts without having to reshoot anything. Take whatever you can. Destroy the rest."

The meeting was over. Everyone knew their jobs and they knew how to prepare for them, so they began to file out of the conference room. As Starlette was preparing to leave, The Director waved her over to him.

As she approached him, Starlette asked The Director, "Do I ever get to just walk out of here without being called over for a secret follow-up meeting?"

"I thought you might like to know that we're making some progress with the Emma Carter papers," The Director told her. "Your cast gave up a lot to get those, and I want to assure you all, they're not being forgotten. In fact, we discovered something interesting on one of them."

The Director pressed a button on the remote control and one of the Emma Carter papers appeared on a monitor. It was a crude scribble, drawn in various colors of crayon. It seemed like complete nonsense to Starlette when she looked at it. She tried her best to seem intelligent enough to understand what this new revelation was, but it wasn't coming to her.

"It looks like nonsense, right?" The Director asked. "But when we scanned the paper into our computer and began fiddling with it in one of those tech-tech-tech programs, we were able to separate the layers of color. That's when we found this..."

Another press of a button pulled up another image. This image had the color of the paper changed from white to red and as a result, a lot of the scribblings were invisible. What remained had been accentuated with bold blacks, and Starlette could now see what the image was.

"It's a face," she said, still trying to make sense of what she was looking at.

The picture showed a crude drawing of a woman with short, light hair. When The Director looked to the image on the monitor, he told Starlette, "It's you. Somehow, your face wound up in these papers. We're still trying to figure out why you would be in this drawing, but it means something, Starlette. It means that you're important to our cause. More important than we ever thought possible."

Starlette nodded slightly, squinted her eyes and cocked her head. She then said, "Actually, I think it's Emma's mommy. She kinda looked like me in that *short-haired woman* kind of way."

Starlette then straightened up and added, "I could totally play her in a movie."

"We *are* working on it," The Director assured her, talking about the Emma Carter papers and not the movie wherein Starlette would play Mrs. Carter. He seemed a bit deflated, now knowing that this picture was not as important as he first suspected. "I won't let that shoot be for nothing."

She wanted to ask him where Wacky Best Friend really was. She wanted some way of tracking him down and getting him back, but she knew that if The Director could tell her anything, he would have. So, she played it cool. It was all she could do.

She patted him on the shoulder, but didn't say anything. She simply walked out of the room.

~

Starlette didn't know what she expected when she arrived at The Celeb Spinner's home office. Part of her expected to find it in the basement of some old lady's house, where her middle-aged son typed up the personal information of celebrities whenever he wasn't busy sitting in a parked car, outside of one of the local schools.

She just assumed that the person behind the tabloid must be some sort of deranged pervert with social disorders. What other type of person could possibly get their kicks from exposing the most horrible, painful, personal secrets of people they didn't even know?

When the van pulled up to a small office building in the middle of the city, Starlette was caught off guard. She double checked the address twice before getting out of the van, figuring that there must be some sort of mistake.

The building was old—looking to date back to the 1920's at the very least—but it wasn't the sort of old that looked rundown and ugly. Even though the city had been in a state of decay since the attacks and the street around this building showed signs of the same sort of thuggery and violence that she had been fighting on a nightly basis, the office building that she found herself in front of radiated a certain amount of old Hollywood charm. Not merely the old Hollywood from which Starlette came, but the *old* old Hollywood where every star was a vision of glamor and class, and the mysteries of their personal lives were more like urban legends than everyday gossip.

The images inside of her mind suddenly changed from the

basement of a pervert, to an art deco private detective office.

"Planning your strategy?" Girl Next Door asked her, as she approached Starlette's side, taking in the building.

Starlette didn't want to tell her that she was concocting a film noir scenario in her head, so she said, "Yeah. Something like that."

"Cool," Girl Next Door said. "To be honest, I was expecting more *Grams*, and less *gams*."

"So, what's the plan?" Sassy Gay Friend asked, holstering his pistol. "You ladies enter through the front and us gents will take up the rear?"

Starlette had heard about what Sassy Gay Friend had done to Girl Next Door by this point. Though Girl Next Door hadn't complained about it to Starlette, The Studio was all abuzz about Girl Next Door's homophobic tirade. She knew Girl Next Door, and trusted her. Neither of these things was true in regards to Sassy Gay Friend.

"Heartthrob is the male lead here," Starlette said. "He and Girl Next Door will take the other entrance and they'll meet us inside."

Sassy Gay Friend scrunched his nose and said, "Boy-girl, boy-girl? Hmm. Okay. I'll try anything once."

Without skipping a beat or waiting for further instructions, Heartthrob and Girl Next Door headed for the back of the building. They had their guns drawn and ready for whatever they might find.

Starlette intended to take this opportunity to get a read on Sassy Gay Friend. She needed to know if he was competent, or if he was simply playing his *my pet gay* system in order to get ahead in The Studio.

"I'm right behind you," she told him. There was no way in hell she was turning her back to him.

She thought he might have something to say about having to enter the building first. She wasn't sure that he had actually ever been on a shoot like this before, so she figured that he might want to hang back and let everyone else do the work. When he headed for the door without a second thought, Starlette was a little surprised.

Walking into the building was not the glamorous experience that she had imagined. There was no soulful saxophone music to accompany their search of the place. The lobby of the office building had been left to crumble, like most of the city. There were remnants of what the place had once been, and Starlette could almost see visions of people from long ago, going about the lives which must have seemed so ordinary to them, but which Starlette would now find thrilling. Even the calm of it would be alien to her.

In the lobby, there was a sign which listed all of the tenants of the building and which floors they could be found on. To Starlette's surprise, The Celeb Spinner was listed. In fact, it was the only listing that wasn't distorted or falling apart in any way. It was as though the tabloid website was any regular business which operated in the light of day, and not a sleazy underground gossip rag, bent on destroying the lives of relatively innocent people.

When Sassy Gay Friend saw the listing that Starlette was looking at, he smiled and said to her, "And here *we* are, living in a hole in the ground."

She didn't respond to him. Instead, she nodded toward the stairs which would lead them to the second floor.

Sassy Gay Friend once again followed her direction and began to climb.

They moved up the stairs slowly, waiting for a booby trap to go off or someone to open fire on them, but neither of these things happened. By the time they reached the second floor, Starlette was beginning to wonder if they would be met with any resistance at all. She might feel bad about shooting someone in the face if they weren't trying to do the same to her.

On the second floor, they found a hallway. It was dark and dusty, and in desperate need of a coat of paint or two, but Starlette could still feel the spirits of those who had walked that hallway before. Even if the place had been an accountant's office back in the 1930's, she couldn't help but think that there would have been some level of romance to that existence. She had grown up watching movies from that era and she once dreamed of becoming one of those actresses, with their fancy clothes and their fantasy lives. Part of her still dreamed of that.

Heartthrob and Girl Next Door made their way to the second floor shortly after Starlette and Sassy Gay Friend, using a different set of stairs. They had their guns drawn as well, but no shots were fired.

When Girl Next Door saw Starlette, she shrugged and looked as though she was asking what the heck was going on. Starlette returned the shrug.

They moved toward the door which had a sign which read *The Celeb Spinner* in bold letters, right on the window. All four of the actors met at that door, and Girl Next Door couldn't help but whisper, "What the hell? If you're going to be an evil mastermind, at least try to hide it. I'm really not feeling a lot of effort here."

"Maybe if you talk a little bit louder," Sassy Gay Friend replied, dripping with sarcasm.

Starlette ignored them both and put her hand on the doorknob. She checked with everyone to make sure that they were ready, and once they had confirmed to her that they were, she opened the door and moved through it.

The office was not in keeping with the deco vibe at all. It looked as though it had been redecorated at some point in the 1980's. The walls were covered in old, stained gray paint, with white trim. The floor was black and white checkerboard tile. The windows were covered with tightly closed blinds, so the only light in the office came from scribbles of pink and blue neon on the walls.

Starlette could practically feel her hair crimping at the sight of the place.

The office was difficult to navigate because there were boxes stacked from floor to ceiling, creating a maze that Starlette only assumed would lead them to the person responsible for the tabloid.

Heartthrob went to one of these boxes and opened the lid. He looked inside and pulled out a handful of files and photographs. As he looked them over, he shook his head and told her, "Information on actors, producers, news anchors... These are from fifteen years ago, at least."

"He's a gossip hoarder?" Girl Next Door winced.

"It would take us forever to go through all of these," Sassy Gay Friend added.

Starlette was about to respond when she heard a sound come from some distant, hard to reach corner of the office. It was the sound of fingers tapping away at a computer keyboard.

She quickly put a finger over her lips, telling her co-stars to be quiet. If they could hear this person typing, surely he could hear them talking. Why was there no response to their talking? Why did no alarm sound? Why did she not hear the pitter-patter of some sweaty overweight dude's feet, running for the hills?

Gripping her gun more tightly, Starlette began to move through the maze of boxes, trying her best not to make a sound. Behind her, her co-stars did the same.

When they reached a fork in the maze, Starlette quietly motioned for Heartthrob and Girl Next Door to take the path to the left, while she and Sassy Gay Friend continued to the right.

She moved quickly and with purpose, feeling each step bringing her closer to the oily-haired monster. Each step made the image in her head more vivid. She pictured him licking his lips as he sat down at the keyboard and breathing deeply as he stroked his keys.

She stopped there, because the image was getting a little more disturbing than she was comfortable with and she didn't even want to picture the moment when he clicked the button that uploaded the latest article.

Her concentration was blown when she heard a rustling behind her. When she turned, she found Sassy Gay Friend standing with his back pressed to one of the stacks of boxes. There was a look in his eyes which told Starlette that he had seen something disturbing, but she didn't know what.

He pointed toward the stack of boxes across from him. When she moved toward it, she could see that the wall of boxes was not quite as tall in one spot and that she could easily see over this area. This allowed her to see that these walls of boxes and been built to surround and enclose what had been there before. Desks, telephones and dusty old computers with clunky old monitors. Most disturbing though was the person sitting at this desk—long dead and rotting, as though this employee of the tabloid had either died while working, never to be moved, or they had been placed at their desk after death.

Either way, the sight of this corpse gave Starlette the chills. She looked around at all of the other stacks of boxes and began to wonder how many more desks this room could have held, and how many of them were still occupied when those walls were built.

One of the neon signs began to flicker, as though it could go out at any moment. In Starlette's head, it was a visual representation of a horror movie's musical score.

The light stopped flickering and the glow in the room was steady once again.

Starlette resumed her walk down the path, which seemed far creepier to her now. She found herself avoiding the walls of boxes, which she hadn't given a second thought to before.

There was a smell to the room, which she had interpreted as dusty with a hint of mildew before, and now she wondered how much of that smell could be attributed to the corpses that she assumed were littered around the entire office. How much of the dust that she was breathing in had once been the flesh of a person... or at least, the flesh of a tabloid reporter?

The tapping of the keyboard continued at a frenzied pace. There was a printer which came to life somewhere in the distance. It did not have the smooth, airy sound of a modern printer. It had the zippy, gravelly sound of a printer from decades earlier.

At last, Starlette could see the glow of computer monitors, which were blinking as images on the screen changed from dark to light and back again. She could tell that they were getting close to finding the person responsible for everything around her, and so much pain that could not be housed in this office of horrors.

The typing stopped, but the printing continued. The sound of a creaky old chair could be heard, followed by footsteps which sounded like the steps of someone struggling to move, with the step of one foot followed by the slide of the other across the tile.

Starlette didn't know what she expected to find anymore. The image of the sick, perverted, oily, sweaty monster did not seem to fit anymore. It had become so much worse than what she had first imagined that no picture which her brain could conjure seemed to do justice to the type of person that worked in *this* space and did *these* things.

As she turned a corner and made her way down the next segment of the path, she could see a clearing in front of her. It was where the light of computer monitors was coming from. It was where the printing was coming from. It was the end of the line.

She adjusted the aim of her gun to make sure that she was ready to kill whatever she found when she reached that clearing.

Sassy Gay Friend was by her side, and she could see his gun from the corner of her eye, reflecting the blue and pink neon. She could hear his breath, which seemed uneasy. The last thing she needed was for a panicked co-star to shoot her in the back by mistake.

Before she could reach the clearing, she saw a shadow on the floor. It was the shadow of a person moving toward her at a slow but steady pace. She stopped walking and held up a hand to tell Sassy Gay Friend to do the same.

She waited to see who would step out in front of her, and she prepared herself to shoot this person without a moment of hesitation.

When Heartthrob stepped out in front of her, Starlette nearly didn't take the time to recognize him. If she had been less in control of herself, she would have shot him dead.

Sassy Gay Friend fired his gun, blowing a hole in one of the boxes next to Heartthrob.

Heartthrob jumped out of the way and pointed his gun as Sassy Gay Friend out of instinct.

Starlette grabbed Sassy Gay Friend's arm and pushed it down. She turned to him and shoved him back against a wall of boxes.

Looking him in the eye with an angry glare, Starlette whisper-yelled, "What the fuck?"

"I didn't—I'm sorry," Sassy Gay Friend replied, clearly shaken by the fact that he almost killed a co-star.

While his incompetence was not reassuring, at least Starlette now knew that he would not *purposely* try to kill anyone on her cast.

She gave him one last shove as she pushed off of him and hurried toward Heartthrob at the clearing. He did not take time to linger on the fact that he was almost killed. Instead, Heartthrob greeted Starlette and guided her toward a desk, where computer monitors were displaying the tabloid website.

Girl Next Door was already fishing through stacks of papers

which covered the desk.

"Nobody was here when we found it," Heartthrob told Starlette.

"He was just here. I heard him," she replied.

She turned and looked around the area, trying to figure out which path the tabloid reporter could have taken to escape. She had to go after him. She needed to find him before he got away.

At the far end of the room, a door closed.

Starlette began moving before she had time to think about what she was doing. She told the others, "Stay here."

Leaving her co-stars behind, Starlette rushed through the path of boxes that she had just navigated, hoping with each turn that she had remembered the way from which she came and that she wouldn't find herself at a dead end.

When she reached the door, she hurried through it and into the hallway. There were two flights of stairs which the tabloid reporter could have taken to get out of the building. Given his lack of security measures, Starlette didn't take him as the type of person who would take the back stairs. He was bold and arrogant.

She ran for the main staircase which led to the lobby. She didn't see him anywhere along the way. He was slippery, but she was confident that she would catch him. She had no choice but to win this fight, because allowing him to roam free would mean endangering everything she had spent a year working toward.

When she rushed through the front door, she nearly ran into someone from the sound department, who was recording the audio of their shoot. It was a major mistake, but she didn't have time to slow down and lecture him on how to do his job, so she kept moving—they could always edit that part out in post.

She reached the sidewalk and looked to her right. There was nothing to see but an empty street.

When she looked to her left, she saw him. He was short and thin, with his back to her. He was wearing a dark suit and a fedora. She paused for a moment before going after him. She watched him walk, taking his sweet time. She thought that he would at least be in a hurry to get away from her, but the tabloid reporter was moving at a snail's pace.

She only half ran when she went after him. Though her shoes

were soft-soled and silent, the tabloid reporter stopped walking as she neared him. He knew she was there. He could sense her.

Starlette aimed her gun at him and said, "You're supposed to wait until I tell you to freeze."

The tabloid reporter raised one gloved hand. In it, he was holding a cell phone.

When he spoke, his voice was raspy and strained. He said, "You will let me go."

"Why would I do that?" she replied.

"Because if you do not, I will press a button and everything you know will end."

He turned around and looked at her. She was surprised to see that he was an old man. He was so frail and sickly that she almost wanted to look away. His eyes were sunken; the left eye, milky white. His cheek bones seemed as though they might cut through his skin, which looked like tissue paper. His lips were thin and cracked, barely covering his rotten teeth.

"What do you mean?" she asked. "What is that? A detonator? Is there a bomb planted in your office?"

He smiled and ugly smile, cracking a lip in the process. As blood dripped down his chin, he said, "You could call it that."

~

Girl Next Door was still sifting through the papers on the tabloid reporter's desk, looking through the various tips and stories that he might yet publish. She was hoping to find some information that would lead her to Bookworm or at least to an associate of Bookworm's, but she hadn't found anything useful thus far.

Heartthrob was sitting at the computer, looking through the files. He had an impressive USB flash drive, equipped with state of the art LED lights which blinked enough to look very high-tech, and he planned to use this flash drive to copy all of the tabloid files. This plan fell apart when Heartthrob failed to find a USB port on the tabloid's vintage PC.

Searching high and low for an alternative, he found a stack of blank CDs nearby and proceeded to search for the drive in which to use them. After attempting to slip a disc into a slot on the computer, which he eventually realized was a floppy disc drive, he discovered an external CD burner on the ground next to the computer and started the process of burning everything in the tabloid's system to disc. As the computer worked at a snail's pace, Heartthrob began reading through some of the files, not content to wait until they returned to The Studio before digging in.

As both Heartthrob and Girl Next Door looked for information, Sassy Gay Friend wandered through the room, opening boxes and skimming some of the files that they held inside. Girl Next Door wasn't comfortable taking her eyes off of him, but she had little choice in the matter. She needed to hurry and get her work done so that they could leave. She'd nearly been blown up in the past, when Starlette raced after another bad guy, and she had no intention of getting blown up this time because she decided to take her time.

A loud noise broke through the silence behind Girl Next Door, and a yellow light filled the room. As she turned to find the source of this light, she found Sassy Gay Friend standing by a window. He had opened the blinds.

"I could barely see in here," he told her.

She shook her head in annoyance and got back to work, flipping through papers quickly and stuffing those that she didn't have time to fully read into a reusable shopping bag that she found on the floor.

As she skimmed, she came across a paper which had a picture attached. It was a familiar face, and the story that was printed under that photo would very likely destroy the career of someone on her cast. She didn't know what to do with this information. It was the sort of thing that she wasn't sure The Studio *needed* to know, but they would definitely *want* to know.

Without time to think, Girl Next Door discretely folded the piece of paper and shoved it into her pocket. She would decide what to do with it later.

~

"There are no explosives connected to this device," the tabloid reporter told Starlette, as she pointed her gun at his head. "This bomb is of a different nature. You see, with the press of this button, my website will update and a flood of information will be released. When it does, all of you will drown."

"Why are you doing this?" she demanded.

"Because you're all so much fun. You live on high horses, pretending to be better than us, but you're not better. Without makeup, your faces are just as splotchy as anyone else. You live in mansions, but you suffer financial downfalls, just like anyone else. You portray fairy tale romance, but none of you ever truly know love. You can't possibly, because love is selfless and that is the opposite of your nature."

Starlette wasn't in the mood to try rationalizing with this man. He did, after all, have an office full of corpses. So, she changed directions.

"Do you know where Bookworm is?" she asked him.

He grinned that ugly grin again and told her, "I know it all. I know where he is. I know where you are. But I know that once either of you gets that information, my fun comes to an end; and you see, if you try to end my fun here tonight, I press this button and your fun ends as well."

"You'll tell him where we are," she concluded.

He raised an eyebrow in response, and she thought his forehead would crack just as his lip had.

She reaffirmed her aim and firmly demanded, "I think you'll find that I don't respond well to threats. Tell me where he is. Now. 'Cause honestly, I'm not having much fun anyway."

"No," the tabloid reporter said in response.

"I could kill you right here."

"And I you," he snapped. "But instead, I will tell you something that you will find interesting—something important to you—and in exchange, you will let me walk away. We both know how these scenes play out. We both know what your Studio wants. We've both read enough of these scripts to know that I am too important to kill. Oh, you might threaten me or smack me around a bit, but that's all you can do. You still need me for the big climax, after all. So, with that in mind, do we have a deal, Victoria?"

The sound of that name sent a chill up her spine. She nearly shot him right then.

"You will tell me where Bookworm is, and I'll *think* about it," she told him. She knew he was right; she was not supposed to kill him. The scene had not been written that way, but she hated that he knew this, and that this knowledge gave him power over her.

"That won't happen," he told her. "The information is not written down, nor stored on any computer, just as the location of your Studio did not exist outside of my head until I typed it into this cell phone."

The tabloid reporter licked his teeth and the roof of his mouth, and the movement of his tongue sounded like sandpaper to Starlette's ears. She wanted this encounter to be over, so she could begin to erase the image of him from her memory.

She didn't want to agree with anything he said. She wanted to finish this job and be done with it. She wanted to beat him to a pulp and drag his ass back to The Studio where they could properly interview him, but any movement could have caused him to hit that button and she couldn't afford that. So, the games continued.

"Fine," she finally agreed. "Tell me, and I'll walk away."

He wiped the blood from his chin, and said, "Good girl."

There was an awkward moment of hesitation, where Starlette began to wonder if maybe he had already forgotten their arrangement in his old age. She was getting ready to remind him of it, but before she could say anything, he spoke.

"Ethan is alive," he told her. "He is in The Studio, but I can't say how long that will last. If you want to see him again, I suggest you figure out a way of freeing him. And I would hurry if I were you."

"Where is he *exactly*?" she demanded.

Her heart was racing in her chest. Her hands were beginning to tingle, as though she had lost circulation in them.

"That, I don't know... But your Director does."

Just as he finished that sentence, and with that final *S* still rolling off of his tongue, Starlette shot him in the throat. The bullet severed his brain stem before he could press the button on his cell phone and he dropped to the ground, dead. The phone dropped beside him.

This was not how the scene had been written. She had gone off script.

Starlette hesitated for a moment, and then picked up the phone. She put it in her pocket and walked back to the building.

Only minutes later, the office was in flames. With it, the images that Starlette had of the building's glamorous past were destroyed. Though she had enjoyed those illusions, as she stood in the street and watched the building come down, she couldn't help but think that she preferred the fire.

CHAPTER ELEVEN
FIRST STRIKE

Starlette stood in Prop Master's department, with the tabloid reporter's cell phone sitting on Prop Master's desk. She hadn't officially turned the cell phone in. She was just bringing it to the prop department to get Prop Master's take on the situation.

"I've been looking through the bomb that he was going to drop on The Studio," she told him. "There are some pretty damning things. The truth about what happened to Token Black Guy... They didn't just kill him. They kept him locked away for weeks, trying to reprogram him. Trying to get him to comply with their way of thinking. When that didn't work, they dumped him on the streets. They left him to fend for himself."

"We all know who runs this show. Is any of this a surprise?" Prop Master asked her.

"Wacky Best Friend is here. They keep telling us that he's off getting some sort of medical help, hoping that the questions will eventually die down and nobody will notice when he doesn't come back. He's here right now, and we need to figure out a way of helping him."

Prop Master picked up the cell phone and looked over it. He thumbed through some of the titles from articles that hadn't yet been posted and he shook his head, saying, "You should have turned this in when you first came back. Now... We can't let anyone know this is here."

"I was hoping that we might find something on it that could give us leverage. Maybe if we have something on them, they'll have no choice but to let him go," Starlette suggested.

Prop Master looked at her like she was crazy, and asked, "Why? Because letting someone roam around here, knowing what he knows, would make them feel better? If they thought that you were hiding things from them, or planning to blackmail them like this, they would be telling people that you're off at some spa too."

"We can't do nothing."

"I agree," Prop Master told her. "Look around this place. Cabin fever is at an all-time high. Departments are turning into factions, and who knows where this will lead?"

"What are you saying?"

"I'm saying that we don't need to do anything at this point. You're an actor, so you probably don't hear everything that people are saying. I've heard people talking about that friend of yours, Tessa Baker."

"What do they have against her?"

"That book deal. As far as some people are concerned, she might as well be in bed with Bookworm."

"That's insane."

"This whole place is going insane. It might not make sense to you, but a lot of the people in here are tired of watching you draw blood. They're angry and they want someone that they can go after themselves. Ever since we heard about her book deal... I don't even know where it's coming from, but someone is whispering in the ears of the people out there. Things are about to get ugly," Prop Master told Starlette, glancing toward the door to make sure that nobody was listening to them. "When that happens, you need to be ready. You'll need to think on your feet, because *that* will be your chance to get Wacky Best Friend back. If you can't do it then, they'll probably just toss him and let that situation settle with the rest of the dust that gets kicked up."

Starlette nodded to let Prop Master know that she understood what he was telling her. She wondered how long the various crew members had been talking behind the backs of the actors, and what they were planning. She has been aware of the situation amongst the various casts in The Studio. She had been the one to plant the seeds of unease amongst the actors, hoping that one of the higher-ups would return Wacky Best Friend in an attempt to settle those tensions. Thus far, it hadn't happened. The tensions were on a constant simmer and she could feel that they would be coming to a full boil at any moment.

If Prop Master was correct, the situation was just as sensitive on the crew's side. Any spark could ignite them.

"Keep the phone," Starlette told Prop Master. "Look through it. See if you can piece together any of the contact information that could lead us to the tabloid's sources within Bookworm's camp. Just because The Studio doesn't know about it doesn't mean that we can't see if there's anything to know."

"What are you going to do?" Prop Master asked her, as he stuck the cell phone in his pocket.

"I'm going to go back to my normal routine and wait for my cue."

~

The Director walked into the green room and closed the door behind him. He was carrying a bottle of water and a small bag of chips.

He walked to the center of the room and looked to one of the two ugly gray couches in the room, where the rogue agent was sitting. The rogue agent didn't stand to greet The Director; he didn't have the option to stand. The rogue agent's wrists were cuffed together and those cuffs were chained to the feet of the couch, with just enough room to allow some slight movement, but not enough to stand or walk. The couch was bolted to the floor.

The rogue agent had been in the green room for two days, being unchained three times per day, just long enough to visit the bathroom under the watchful eye of a Studio security guard who did not love his job. Two meals were provided each day. They were small; just barely enough to keep the rogue agent alive but hungry.

As The Director looked down, the rogue agent smiled at him. It was a weak, tired smile. He said, "Are those for me?"

"No," The Director said, opening the bottle of water and taking a sip. "They're for me. I hope you don't mind. I haven't eaten in almost an hour and I'm getting kinda hungry."

"Torture is not an effective form of interrogation," the rogue agent told The Director. "Statistics show that you'll gain no useful information through torture. People will say anything to save themselves."

"Then we're both in luck. Because I'm here to listen to whatever you want to say in order to save yourself."

"It doesn't work that way. I have a business to run. I have a system."

"Where is Bookworm?"

"I would be more than willing to work with you, but my services are not free. I get a percentage... And then there is the matter of my up-front fee. Don't worry, it's small. Very affordable. We just need to get you in the system."

The Director opened the bag of chips and grabbed a few of them. He put them in his mouth and took his time to chew and swallow them. He then licked his fingers, took a sip of water, and said, "Where is Bookworm?"

"If I tell you that, I stand to lose a considerable amount of money. It would mean violating the trust of some vital contacts. I don't think that I'm prepared to do that for less than, say... eight million dollars."

"There will be no deal. I'm not one of those kids who's running around out there, naïve to the way this industry works. I've been doing this a long time, and I have seen hundreds of people like you come and go. Do you know *how* most of them go, mister— whatever the hell your name is?"

The rogue agent didn't respond. He simply tilted his head and blinked his eyes, which seemed slow to respond. He was tired. He needed sleep. His body was probably aching for a chance to lie down and rest, but he would not be allowed to sleep. The Director could keep him awake for as long as it took to make him beg for relief.

"Drug overdose. A rope around the neck. A bullet to the brain. People like you seem to have one thing in common," The Director told him. "By the end, they just want it all to be over."

"Is that true? Or did you just make that up to scare me?" the rogue agent asked, seeming to be unconcerned with what The Director was saying to him.

The Director put the cap back on his bottle of water and put the bottle on an end table next to the couch where he was sitting. He scooted forward on the couch and looked the rogue agent squarely in the eyes.

"I want you to imagine a table between us," The Director said to the rogue agent. "On that table, in front of you, I want you to image five little stacks of poker chips. They can be worth as much as you want, I guess. It doesn't really matter. What matters is that you have these five stacks and that's it. You can play the game all you want and you can try to bluff all you want, but when those chips are gone, you're going to have to leave the table."

"How many stacks of chips do you have?" the rogue agent replied, in a smug and sarcastic tone.

The Director smiled and stood. He walked to the rogue agent and punched him in the face with enough force to throw the rogue agent back, but only as far as his chains would allow. The Director then put his hand on the rogue agent's shoulder, which had just recently been popped back into its socket after Heartthrob dislocated it. He put pressure on the shoulder, threatening to dislocate it once again as he looked at the rogue agent with a cool and calm expression on his face.

With a tone just as calm, The Director said, "I don't gamble."

~

Starlette had been waiting for days. Each time she walked through The Studio, she could feel a change in the weather coming. It wasn't just that Prop Master had told her about what the crew members were saying behind the backs of the actors, it was the fact that the actors were beginning to wonder just how much their contracts with The Studio meant.

Ever since Starlette blew up the theater and gave credit to a banished actor, some of the supporting players had been calling upon their leads to do something or say something. Starlette's cast had been watching and waiting. They could feel something just as well as Starlette could, but aside from Sassy Gay Friend, none of them were pushing Starlette to say or do anything. They trusted her enough to know that she was fully aware of the situation and would handle it as best she could, when the opportunity presented itself.

She suspected that they knew about her blowing up the theater. Neither Heartthrob nor Girl Next Door actually said anything to her about it, but they were both there that night and had witnessed her camera malfunction. They were too smart to not even consider the possibility, and once they considered it, they would have to reflect on Wacky Best Friend's situation and the two would undoubtedly be related in their minds.

Girl Next Door had been particularly quiet at times, since they came back from taking down The Celeb Spinner. Sure, she seemed like her normal and friendly self when Starlette got her into a conversation, but she also seemed to be inside her own head much more than normal.

At first, Starlette wondered if the tension within The Studio was wearing on Ember, but there seemed to be something more to it. Every so often, Starlette would catch a glimpse of Ember looking at a piece of paper. When Ember saw Starlette coming her way, she would quickly fold the paper and shove it in her pocket.

Starlette never asked about it. If Ember wanted her to know, she would bring it up herself. Until then, Starlette had other things to focus her attention on.

Heartthrob continued to fight with the trauma that he had been through over the previous year. He tried his best to hide the fact that he was unrested and haunted by images of what had happened to his family. His sleeping hadn't improved since he opened up about those events. If anything, he seemed more withdrawn from those around him. Now that his secrets were out and everyone in The Studio was talking about them, Heartthrob couldn't even walk to the craft service table without feeling like he was being watched and whispered about. Even if he wasn't the true topic of discussion, he felt as though he was.

At times, Starlette would see Ember and Heartthrob sitting together outside their trailers, saying nothing. They weren't incredibly public with their displays of affection, but Starlette would notice them hold hands or lean against each other when one of them seemed to be having an especially bad day.

Starlette was happy to see that at least some people had managed to find time to lead their own lives. She didn't have that luxury. Until Wacky Best Friend was back and Bookworm was gone forever, she couldn't afford to let her guard down. She had to be ready whenever the time for action arrived.

The day she found her opening began slowly enough. She was sitting in one of the lawn chairs outside of her trailer, with Ember sitting nearby. Heartthrob was working out, as usual. Starlette admired his ability to maintain his strict routine, but she preferred to get her workout with weapons in hand, not by running on a treadmill or lifting dumbbells.

"Have you ever had information about someone that could hurt them?" Ember asked, staring off into space.

"Yeah," Starlette replied, though she didn't care to elaborate.

"What did you do?"

"Depends on the situation. Information is valuable. Are we talking about a friend or a foe?"

"Umm... I can't say."

"Are lives at risk if you don't share?"

"No."

"Then, why bother with it? If it weighs this heavily, I say you just forget you ever knew about it and move on with your life."

"I guess..."

Ember fell silent once again. Starlette didn't give her mysterious information another thought. Honestly, she didn't care to know anything that someone didn't want to tell her. She had enough to deal with as it was.

After a moment or two had passed, Sassy Gay Friend rushed up to the trailers. He had a dire look about him which caused Starlette to get to her feet before he opened his mouth.

"You need to get to the clinic," Sassy Gay Friend told her.

"Why? What happened?" Starlette asked in reply, with less

panic than dread in her tone.

Ember was on her feet by now as well. She asked, "Is it Hearthtthrob? Or Ethan?"

"No," Sassy Gay Friend replied. "It's Tessa. She was attacked last night. Someone found her on the ground in the Producers district this morning.

Though Starlette had already been prepared for bad news of some sort, when she heard that it was about Tessa, her heart began to pound in her chest. The sounds of The Studio around her seemed to dull.

She didn't react right away. She wasn't sure exactly what she was supposed to do. To the outside world, it must have seemed like she was overcome by concern for Tessa. While it was true that Starlette was concerned for her friend, the weight that came down on her in that moment was a far more serious and pressing weight.

This was it. This was the day when things would unravel within The Studio. She could feel it in the air. Tensions had spilled over and blood had been shed. She could all but see dark clouds gathering overhead, warning of an impending storm that would rattle the foundations of The Studio.

"Oh my God," Girl Next Door gasped, with panic in her eyes. She looked to Starlette and said, "Please tell me that you do have a plan. Because I've been banking on you having a plan."

Starlette looked to Girl Next Door, and was genuinely impressed by the fact that Girl Next Door had the same reaction.

Starlette nodded her head, to let Girl Next Door know that she had been preparing herself for this. She then said, "Right now, we get to the clinic."

They started to walk, but didn't run. Starlette was not going to allow herself to be seen in a panic at this moment, even if someone she cared about had just been attacked. Whoever had done this to Tessa was on The Studio floor and would be watching. She wanted them to see a resolute Starlette; one who would be coming for them.

As they walked, Girl Next Door couldn't help but ask, "But seriously, you do have a plan beyond going to the clinic, right?"

~

The clinic looked like any normal hospital that you would find in the real world. Set designers had taken a lot of time and effort over the previous years to piece together a clinic that was as close to the real thing as possible. Actors were injured on a regular basis. Many of them required medical care, and that could not be provided in a place that had no equipment and no staff.

After the attacks, when the people fled the city, hospitals were abandoned. Their patients were transferred to hospitals in other cities, and most of their equipment was taken as well. What was left behind eventually became free for the taking, which was exactly what the set designers and Prop Master did.

As Starlette, Girl Next Door and Sassy Gay Friend walked into the clinic, they weren't concerned with whether or not Tessa would be given adequate care, they were more concerned with the level of injuries sustained and whether she could recover from them.

Outside of the clinic, a crowd had gathered. As she walked through this crowd, Starlette noticed a divide. Actors seemed to be grouped together on one side, and crew on the other. Nobody was saying anything, but they all had the same look in their eyes: anger.

Studio security was standing outside the clinic doors, keeping the crowd from moving inside. As Starlette and her cast approached, they opened the doors and allowed them to enter. To Starlette's surprise, Heartthrob was already in the waiting room, with The Director. In the corner, Starlette saw several Producer types pacing and talking on phones, but they didn't strike her as being incredibly concerned with Tessa's medical condition. For them, it was all about managing the situation. They had to know that trouble was coming.

The Director and Heartthrob walked toward them, with somber expressions on their faces. Before Starlette could even ask a question, The Director was saying, "She was found by one of our other actresses this morning. She has at least two broken ribs that I know of, and her hand was broken. She was beaten pretty badly and there might be some internal bleeding. We have our top drama surgeons in with her now."

"That's good. Drama surgeons are good," Girl Next Door said, trying to sound upbeat. "It's those sitcom doctors that are iffy."

She looked off to the side and glared at Quirky Sitcom Doctor who was standing against a wall, staring off into space. When he snapped back to reality, he looked at her and said, "Why would you make tires out of marshmallows? They're obviously gonna melt when it gets hot out."

"I can't believe I used to date him," Girl Next Door muttered, shaking her head in disgust.

"We should know more about her condition soon," Heartthrob told them, moving on from whatever Girl Next Door was rambling about.

"Do we know who did this?" Starlette asked The Director.

He shook his head at her and said, "We're working on figuring that out. Tessa hasn't woken up yet, but as soon as she does, you can be in there and ask her whatever you need to ask. I want you to be in on this. I know you're close to the situation, but honestly... I trust you."

"I was going in there either way," Starlette told him. "But thanks."

There wasn't much more to be said. In her mind, Starlette was already plotting and planning, trying to figure out a way of making this situation work for her. She had to be careful. She couldn't afford to mess this up and destroy The Studio entirely. She couldn't dive into the pool of anger that she had walked through on her way into the clinic. She needed to remain outside of the group of actors; she couldn't be one of them.

In the waiting room, silence fell. Girl Next Door and Heartthrob found chairs and they sat, quietly talking amongst themselves. Sassy Gay Friend stood near Starlette, but didn't say anything to her for most of the time that they spent waiting.

The Director did not stand with the Producers. He did not stand amongst the actors either. Instead, he positioned himself somewhere in the middle, by himself. He spoke with nobody. He looked at nobody.

The Director had once been an actor. Starlette always felt that his experience helped him to work with actors in ways that other directors couldn't quite understand. She was fortunate to have him working with her cast, as she had seen other casts fall apart due to poor direction.

She had to wonder which side he would choose, if he were ever forced into that situation. She thought he was an honorable man, but he played both sides of the business and she could not put all of her faith in his loyalty to the actors.

As she ran through strategies and considered the loyalties of those around her, Starlette didn't keep track of how much time had passed. When Sympathetic Nurse came into the waiting room, she walked toward Starlette, and The Director came closer as well.

"She's awake," Sympathetic Nurse told them. "She's going to need some surgery but our guys are confident that she'll be fine. They're prepping now, getting some last minute lessons from the medical consultants, but she wanted to speak with you before she goes in."

Sympathetic Nurse led Starlette back to the room where Tessa was being treated. At first, Starlette wondered if The Director would be standing over her shoulder as she spoke with Tessa, but he didn't follow her to Tessa's room. A more pushy, power hungry director might have forced his way in, but he remained in the waiting room.

She wanted to believe that he was on her side, but she couldn't afford to have faith in his loyalty. After all, she knew without a doubt that he was withholding information about Wacky Best Friend.

The room where Tessa was being treated was small. It looked like any hospital room that one might have found in the real world. The set designers had managed to capture the smell of a real hospital as well, which Starlette wasn't overly fond of.

Tessa was lying in bed, covered with a thin blanket. She was wearing a hospital gown, and her hand was already in a cast.

As Starlette walked into the room, Tessa turned to see her. This was when Starlette saw the bruises on Tessa's face and the split lip which had been stitched. Starlette wanted to gasp, but she didn't.

Sympathetic Nurse left the room and closed the door behind her, leaving Starlette alone with Tessa.

Tessa's eyes never seemed to lock onto Starlette. She appeared to be heavily drugged and groggy, but she was smiling.

"They hate me," she grinned. "They really hate me."

"Who did this to you?" Starlette replied, standing over Tessa.

"Oh, who cares? Really, it's an honor just to be incapacitated."

Starlette wished that Tessa was more clear-minded. She wished that she could get easy answers and find the person who attacked her.

She asked the question once again, "Who did this? Did you see them?"

"I barely had time to realize what was happening, my dear. One moment, I was walking toward my dressing room. The next, I was being dragged into the shadows. I never saw her face."

"*Her?* So, it was a woman who did this?"

"It's so hard to tell in this place, but I think so. I distinctly remember a female voice."

"Did she speak? What did she say?"

"Only in a whisper. She said that I was a bitch, and I kindly responded that I wasn't the one pummeling an old woman. I think that she probably would have beaten me to death if she'd been given the chance."

"What stopped her?"

"Her cell phone vibrated," Tessa replied, looking as though she was about to fall asleep. "But I don't remember which one."

As Tessa spoke that sentence, a realization washed over Starlette. It felt like she'd been zapped with a low voltage stun gun. Every muscle tensed. Her fists clenched. She knew exactly who had attacked Tessa. The only question was how it was possible.

Tessa's eyes were closed and she was no longer talking. Starlette was ready to leave the room so that she could go and beat the crap out of someone, so she didn't try to stir Tessa or get more information.

Quietly, Starlette turned and headed for the door. She was just about to pull it open when Tessa spoke to her once again.

"It doesn't matter who did this to me," Tessa told her, barely able to get the words out in her grogginess. "The question is... It's... Who told them do to this on me?"

Tessa drifted to sleep once more and while Starlette knew very well what Tessa had meant to say, she took a moment to ponder Tessa's meaning.

Whatever Tessa was trying to say, Starlette's reaction would be the same. She hurried out of the room and down the hall, toward the waiting room. When she walked into the waiting room, she scanned the area for The Director. She needed to talk to him.

Girl Next Door and Heartthrob stood when they saw her. They could see that something was wrong and Girl Next Door was beginning to panic.

"What's wrong?" Girl Next Door asked. "Is she okay?"

"Where's The Director?" Starlette asked, ignoring Girl Next Door's questions.

Heartthrob replied, "He said he had to check on a project, but he'd be back as soon as he can."

"So, his office?" Starlette asked.

Heartthrob nodded, with a slight shrug thrown in because he couldn't be entirely sure of where The Director was.

Starlette hurried out of the clinic. Her co-stars followed her, unaware of what was going on, but knowing that whatever it was couldn't be good.

As they left the clinic and began to walk through The Studio, people from the crowd were yelling.

"She's a traitor!" came one voice from the crew side of the crowd. "She should be shot!"

"Burn the book-whore!"

Obviously, they were no fans of Tessa Baker. Starlette couldn't imagine why such a fury had arisen, but she knew that none of these people were to blame. She couldn't stop herself from scanning the crowd for the face of the woman responsible for this, but she highly doubted that Jennifer would be roaming around, waiting to be seen by Starlette or her cast.

Someone grabbed Starlette's arm and began to tug at her, screaming, "How can you side with her? How can you trust someone who follows Bookworm?"

"She doesn't follow Bookworm," Starlette replied, turning toward the crew member and shoving him away from her. "Tessa Baker is more Hollywood than all of you combined, so I'd watch my tone if I were you. And the next time your hand touches me, I'm keeping it."

From the actor side of the crowd, Starlette could hear more cries.

"What are we going to do?!" came one female voice?

"Who did this to her?" came another.

"We're not even safe in The Studio!" came a third.

There were more cries from both sides, but they tended to blend together. People were looking to Starlette for answers, but she had none to give—Not yet, anyway. She needed to speak with The Director.

Turning to her co-stars, Starlette said, "I need you to watch this situation. Make sure nothing gets started before I get back."

Heartthrob nodded, but Girl Next Door asked, "How do we do that?"

Starlette didn't have time to answer. She kept walking toward The Director's office. If she didn't find him there, she would track him down, wherever he was. There was no time to wait. The time for action was now.

~

The Director walked into the green room once again, this time with a folder in hand. He sat on the couch opposite the rogue agent and placed the folder on the cushion next to him.

"Have you reconsidered?" The Director asked the rogue agent.

"Have you?"

"I don't pay agents up front. If you connect us with Bookworm and we get the job done, you will be compensated," The Director said, reaffirming what he had already told the rogue agent.

"How long are you willing to wait?" the rogue agent asked him. "How many more of your actors have to die? How much tension will have to build within your Studio?"

"You'll be dead before another actor is injured," The Director replied. "You're starving as it is. You're dehydrated. Weak. Fragile. How long are you willing to wait before you give in and tell us what we want to know?"

"What happens to me if I do?"

"You live. For a while, at least."

"Well, that sounds lovely. But *where* do I live?"

"That all depends on the information you give us and how useful it turns out to be," The Director told the rogue agent. "If we take down Bookworm, I could see a scenario where you breathe fresh air someday. If the information you give us turns out to be bogus... Fresh or not, you're breathing days will be over."

The rogue agent couldn't help but chuckle at that comment. He shifted in his seat, but only as much as his chains would allow. He did not respond to what The Director was saying to him.

"I have a theory," The Director said after a moment. "My theory is that you're bluffing. You think that as long as I believe you know how to contact Bookworm, I'll keep you alive, and I think you're willing to bet everything on this bluff."

"If I didn't know how to contact Bookworm, how could I have sold your actor to him?"

The Director shrugged and said, "Things change. Cell phones get tossed. Contacts go cold. Buildings are abandoned. For all I know, you bumped into a minion of his at a party and wound up sealing the deal. None of this tells me that you really know anything of any use to me right now."

The rogue agent shrugged and said, "You could be absolutely right. Or, you could be throwing away your only chance to get information that could end this war of yours. You let me go and pay me an insane amount of money, and once I'm clear, I will contact you with information on how to find Bookworm. Keep me here and yes, I might very well die. But you will be in this prison for the rest of your life."

"I'm not dealing with you," The Director assured the rogue agent. "I am telling you that you will either tell me what you know, or you will be locked away in a place where things only go to die. Forgotten. Lost to the ages. By the time they find your rotting corpse, you will be considered the archaeological find of the decade."

"Hmm," the rogue agent muttered thoughtfully. "Y'know, that sounds kinda neat. I could *be* someone. For all we know, they'll think I'm royalty."

The Director had no response. The rogue agent looked into his eyes, as though trying to read The Director's thoughts, but he said nothing. The Director was giving him nothing to work with. The rogue agent's bluff was failing.

"I don't believe you have anything to offer," The Director told him. "In fact, I will have no trouble at all walking out of this room, knowing that by this time tomorrow, you will be a fading memory. But, I'm a fair guy."

The Director stood and grabbed his folder. From it, he pulled several pieces of paper. They were copies of the Emma Carter papers. He proceeded to pin them to the wall across from the rogue agent.

"You have one more chance. If you cannot tell me something useful within the next six hours, you're done," The Director told the rogue agent.

The rogue agent looked at the papers on the wall, not comprehending their meaning at all. He asked, "What are those?"

"Clues. Beyond that, it's up to you to tell me what you see."

"Well, I can safely tell you that your artistry leaves something to be desired," the rogue agent replied, still looking over the pictures.

The fact that the rogue agent hadn't simply glanced at the images and moved on told The Director that the rogue agent was panicking. If he could make something of those images, he would, because he knew that this was the only way that he could survive.

"Six hours," The Director said once again, before walking out of the room and leaving the rogue agent alone to ponder his future.

As The Director left the green room and proceeded down the hall which would lead him back to his office, Starlette turned the corner in front of him. As she walked toward him, he could see fury in her eyes.

~

The crowd's anger seemed to be growing, rather than fading, and it was making Girl Next Door uncomfortable. She didn't know what was going to come of this anger, but she knew that it couldn't possibly be good.

She was standing in the middle of the line between cast and crew, and she was being pushed and shoved from both sides. Nobody seemed concerned with her or for her, they were more interested in screaming back and forth.

"I am sick and tired of being second-class citizens in this

place!" yelled an actress called Mother Figure, from within the acting section.

"Second class? You get everything you want, and your own trailers on top of that! Try living with a bunch of sweaty cameramen!" came a voice from the other side, which Girl Next Door didn't recognize.

She had to stop for a moment to wonder if it was insensitive of her to not know who that crew member was. On the one hand, she didn't like to be elitist and pretend that the actors were the end-all-be-all of The Studio, but then again, there were about a billion crew members and not all of them worked with her cast.

She decided that she wasn't a snob after all.

Mother Figure had more to say. As she spoke, the group of actors cleared around her, giving her something of a stage from which to deliver her thoughts. She was a well-respected member of the acting community. Though she was not well known by name, anyone who watched television would recognize her from a slew of commercials and guest roles on family dramas.

"We put our lives on the line every day. Some more than others, but we're all out there," Mother Figure declared. "Yet, what support do we have from The Studio?"

"This isn't good," Heartthrob whispered in Girl Next Door's ear.

She turned to exchange troubled looks with him and scanned the crowd for Starlette. She wished that Starlette was there, so they wouldn't have to worry about holding back the mob on their own.

"Where is Token Black Guy?" Mother Figure asked. "He was a valued member of my cast and he was simply kicked out for no apparent reason."

"He was a Republican!" yelled someone from the crew side.

"Oh..." Mother Figure replied. She didn't seem to know that before she made her comment. "Nevertheless, there are serious questions to be asked about how this place works. How safe is it for us here when our valued elders are attacked right in our own home? This is meant to be a sanctuary for all of us in the industry, and we now have one of our own laying in the bed of a hospital set."

"What about the unnamed actor who blew up that theater?"

asked a man with a long beard, dressed in jeans and leather. His name was Biker #1. "If that wasn't a cry for help, I don't know what is. And what did we do about it? Nothing!"

"We totally should have tracked down the mad bomber and invited him back here!" shouted a sarcastic member of the crew that looked very familiar, but whose name Girl Next Door still didn't know.

"What he did was meant to highlight a problem that we have here!" Biker #1 declared. "We might work for The Studio, but none of our contracts are iron-clad. None of us are truly secure in the work that we have here! Not the actors, and certainly not the crew! When they want us gone, we just disappear!"

"Has anyone actually *seen* Wacky Best Friend lately?" asked another woman with reddish hair. She looked like an actress, but Girl Next Door hadn't seen her around.

Having someone outside of her own cast mention Wacky Best Friend gave Girl Next Door the chills. Until this point, it had been *their* concern and *their* worry. Having someone else bring him up made him seem like some sort of missing person.

She leaned over to Heartthrob and asked, "Who is that?"

Heartthrob shrugged. Sassy Gay Friend then leaned in closer to them and said, "They call her Songstress. She's a Triple Threat."

"Gosh," Girl Next Door nodded, genuinely impressed and a little intimidated.

Sassy Gay Friend put a hand on Girl Next Door's shoulder and said to her, "Don't worry, sweetie. You're getting by just fine without any talent."

Girl Next Door was going to say something to him. She wanted to snap back with some sarcastic comment about how stupid he was or how ugly his hair looked, but she stopped herself. Instead, she turned her attention back to the crowd, which seemed to be on a steady path toward chaos.

~

Starlette walked into The Director's office, with The Director close behind. She had somehow managed to avoid screaming at him in the middle of a public area, which would have surely gotten her a reputation for being a difficult actress to work with. It took all of the restraint that she had within her.

Once he closed the door, The Director looked to Starlette and calmly said, "What's going on?"

Starlette clenched her jaw and took a moment to properly channel her anger. She didn't want to scream and yell like a child. She wanted to make herself perfectly clear without an hint of tantrum throwing.

"I am going to ask you about two things," she said to him. "How you answer my questions will determine how this day goes for you and the people who give you your orders."

The Director's eyes narrowed as she said this. He didn't like the tone of her voice, but he obviously had no idea why she was so upset. Her opening the discussion with a threat could not have sat well with him.

"First, where is the rogue agent's personal assistant? Where's Jennifer?"

His eyes narrowed a little bit more and he sat on the corner of his desk. As if he hadn't been clueless enough before, The Director seemed even more lost now.

He shook his head and replied, "She was taken into custody. She was transferred to a more permanent holding area as soon as we were done questioning her."

"Are you lying to me?" Starlette asked. "Or do you really not know?"

"Know what? Starlette, I saw them walk her away in chains. I saw the paperwork."

"And nobody mentioned her escaping?"

"Would you mind telling me what the hell you're talking about?"

Starlette looked at The Director's face, and the way he was holding himself. He wasn't carrying himself like a man who was trying to cover something up. He seemed genuinely at a loss.

"Get on the phone," she told him. "Call down to wherever the hell you said she was and have someone check on her. I want to have actual eyes on her, not paperwork."

The Director nodded and picked up the phone. He seemed just as curious as Starlette was.

As he dialed and waited for an answer, he asked her, "Is this about Tessa? Is Jennifer the one who attacked her?"

"If she did," Starlette told him in as cool a tone as she'd ever spoken with, "someone here is going to have a lot of explaining to do, and I don't think they're going to have an easy time of it with my fist down their throat."

When someone on the other end of the line picked up, The Director said, "This is The Director. I need eyes on the prisoner that we sent down there a couple days ago. Jennifer."

He waited a moment, listening to the voice on the other end of the phone. He then said, "The Director of *Starlette*... No, not that guy. He directs another cast and crew. Look up my ID number, alpha-five-seven-seven-six-two."

The Director went silent once again as his identity was confirmed. He pushed the button which activated the speakerphone and put down the handset. Peppy soft rock music played in the background as they waited for more information regarding Jennifer.

It seemed to take forever for them to get back on the phone. Starlette expected that as soon as someone came back, he would pick up the handset and she would have to get her information secondhand.

Instead, when the music stopped, The Director left the speakerphone on.

"Sir?" came a male voice from the other end of the line.

"Yes. Tell me you have her down there," The Director said.

"We do, sir. She's right where she is supposed to be."

Starlette was confused by this. She was sure that Jennifer would be missing and that Tessa's attack was more than just another crazy crew member. She could feel it in her gut.

"Thank you," The Director said into the phone, before pressing the button to hang it up. "I don't know who attacked Tessa or what's going on here, but we will figure it out. I'm on your side, Starlette. Trust me."

"You want me to trust you?" Starlette asked, "Then tell me where Wacky Best Friend is."

As soon as the question was asked, The Director's eyes went to the ground. It was only for a moment, and then he looked back to Starlette. By this point she knew what he was going to say.

"I've told you, Wacky Best Friend is in the clinic, being treated for exhaustion."

"I know what you've told me. Now tell me the truth."

The Director didn't say anything. It seemed to Starlette that he didn't know what to say. She obviously wasn't buying into the lies, and he couldn't just come out and tell her the truth.

"You keep telling me to trust you. You tell me that you're on my side. Then why are you a part of this?"

"We all answer to someone," he told her, not seeming proud of this fact.

Starlette nodded calmly, accepting the answer. She took a moment to think about her next move, and then said, "Well, as of today... you all answer to *me*."

She turned and walked out of the office, leaving The Director to find out exactly what she meant by this.

~

The crowd was still building to their eventual eruption. Girl Next Door could do nothing but stand back and watch, having given up on trying to figure out a way of stopping a full-on riot.

In the clear area where actors were speaking their minds, Up-and-Comer was yelling, "I worked a fifteen hour day last week! That violates my rights!"

The crowd was upset by this. Girl Next Door shook her head in disgust. As much as she may have wanted to stop the riot, she couldn't disagree with their reasoning. She couldn't deny the fact that actors had been horribly mistreated.

"If The Studio won't stand up for us, why should we stand up for them?!" Mother Figure yelled to the crowd, like a minister trying to get an *amen* from her parishioners.

"The names they give us are offensive!" screamed Fat Chick Who We'll Pretend Is Sexy.

Next to her, Exotic Model Type rolled her eyes.

"Enough!" came the booming voice of a man in the crowd.

The crowd was silenced as this man made his way to the speaking area. When Girl Next Door saw him, she recognized the animal skins and fringe at once. He was one of their most respected character actors, Wise Native-American Elder. Girl Next Door met him several years before the attacks. His name was Tony. She wasn't entirely sure that he really was Native-American at all.

"Our people have suffered greatly," Wise Native-American Elder told the crowd, in a voice that reached the corners of The Studio, but didn't seemed raised at all. "For too long, we have been content to let the suited man tell us how we should live our lives. Our spirits grow heavy with the weight of this oppression. We have been called to action by the spirits of those actors who came before us. They have touched one who walks amongst us. They have chosen our leader; the one who walks apart from us, but who *is* us."

"I have no idea what he's saying, but he is *so* wise," Girl Next Door said to Heartthrob.

"Let her guide us to a better way," Wise Native-American Elder told them.

"Who?" Mother Figure asked. "Who is this leader that you're talking about?"

Wise Native-American Elder pointed his finger toward the crowd. One by one, the actors began to part as they realized that they were not essential enough to be considered the leader of The Studio's actors.

Finally, the parting crowd left one person standing before them. Whispers and gasps rippled through the crowd.

"She's perfect," said one voice.

Girl Next Door couldn't see over the head of the person in front of her. She tried to stand on her toes, but this didn't help. She looked to Heartthrob, and he looked down at her with a smile on his face. He took Ember's hand and she knew that whoever they were talking about, it was the right person.

As their new leader made her way to the front of the crowd, Girl Next Door finally saw who it was. When Starlette's face was revealed to her, she heard herself yelling, "Holy shit-balls!"

She then slapped her hand over her mouth and looked down, so as to avoid seeing everyone look in her direction.

In spite of her embarrassment, Girl Next Door was happy.

~

When she walked out of The Director's office, Starlette was pissed. She didn't know exactly what she was going to do or how she was going to do it, but she knew that she had to show The

Studio that she was a force to be reckoned with.

As she left the hallway which led from The Director's office to the main Studio floor, she wondered how she would convince people to join her in whatever plan she was about to devise.

The fact that she had no clue what she was doing didn't scare her somehow. She knew that as each moment came, she would be able to make a decision that would lead her in the right direction. She had faith in her abilities and her instincts.

Stepping onto the main floor of The Studio, Starlette looked at the crowd in front of her. She was just in time to see them step aside and look at her with an expression in their eyes that she had always seen reserved for the truly important people in the world, like royalty and whichever old person was about to receive the Golden Me Awards' trophy for lifetime achievement.

As they looked upon her with respect and trust, she felt as though things were falling into place.

She walked through the parted crowd, keeping her eyes on the man at the front, Wise Native-American Elder, who was pointing at her.

Midway through the crowd, she heard Ember shout "Holy shit-balls!"

She tried not to grin or look toward Ember. She kept a somber look on her face and her head held high. She was becoming more than the lead of one cast; she was becoming the lead of every actor in The Studio.

When she reached Wise Native-American Elder, he placed his hand on her shoulder and in a low voice that only she could hear, he said to her, "What up, player?"

She nodded at him, as though he were saying something wise and important to her. He then stepped aside, allowing her to address the crowd.

"It's true," she began. "We have lived in this place and fought this war for almost exactly one year now. We have watched beloved friends and co-stars sacrifice their lives for our cause. We have seen treasured members of the acting community hurt time and time again, and we chalked those things up to part of the job; what we signed up for. What we did *not* sign up for was a war within The Studio. We did not agree to live in a place where we could not feel safe, just walking home at night. We should not have to live in fear of those people who surround us."

People in the crowd began to cheer and display their agreement with her on the actors' side of the crowd. From the crew side, there were jeers and the shaking of fists in the air.

"I do not believe that the crew is our enemy," Starlette told her crowd. "I believe that they are hardworking members of this Studio, who work side by side with us on a daily basis. They can't be blamed for wanting to be a more active part of the fight. They have a right to be mad. We should *all* be mad!"

Cheers arose from both sides of the crowd. Starlette could feel a new energy beginning to wash over them and into her. There was a growing unity amongst the citizens of The Studio.

"They blame Tessa because she had a book deal, but they're not mad at her. They're mad at the fact that we have been spinning our wheels for a year now, and we still don't even know what Bookworm's real name is!"

More cheers from all around her. Because she had appeared on three different sitcom pilots in her youth, Starlette knew how to wait for those cheers to die down before she continued.

"Wacky Best Friend," Starlette said, in a more somber tone than she had been using thus far. "Token Black Guy. The third and sixth Up-and-Comers. How many others have there been? How many actors or crew members have just... disappeared? How long will we allow this to continue before we speak out and say: *Enough!*"

Cheers came from both sides of the crowd. A few people tried to begin a chant of Starlette's name, but it didn't catch on.

"What do we do about it?" came a voice from an actor, who Starlette didn't see.

"We fight!" Biker #2 yelled back. "We show them who's in charge around here!"

"Fight!" yelled several more actors and crew members as the anger in the crowd rose to a new high.

Starlette raised her hands, calming the crowd so that she could speak once again. Once she was sure that she could be heard, she said, "We do take action. We do show them how valuable each member of this Studio really is. But we do not do this by acting like drunken soccer fans when their team loses. We don't riot and tear apart our own home. We get our message across in a different way."

Starlette took a moment to gather her thoughts and to let the drama of the moment build. She looked to various members of her community, and she connected with them in a way that assured them that they did have someone representing them now.

And then she said, in a soft tone, "Tessa Baker has told me stories of the Hollywood that was. Of the people who fought back against a corrupt system and who fought for the right to live their own lives. Their legacy is an inspiration to us all. As we eventually take down Bookworm and rebuild this industry, we must do so with those honored heroes in our hearts. Today, I tell you that we will fight back and will drive our message home, but we do this not with bloodshed. We do it the same way those actors, actresses, writers, directors, and various members of the crews that came before us did... We strike."

~

The Director was watching Starlette speak on a monitor in his office, which displayed all of the goings-on on the floor of The Studio. He would have liked to have been out there, watching her speak in person. She impressed him, and he would have loved to support her. The truth was, there were things that were going on within The Studio that he was no fan of either, but he could not be as bold as Starlette. He had to play the game and wait for his opportunity to make a move of his own.

Fortunately, Starlette had a way of providing him with many opportunities when dealing with Studio Head, and other higher-ups. He was hoping that he would be able to use this current situation to raise some concerns and make a few changes, but he needed to be smart. He needed to wait for just the right moment.

As he sat at his desk, The Director waited for the phone call that he knew was coming. If he could see what was happening on the Studio floor, then so could all of the other high-ranking members of The Studio. Producers were probably watching, and trying to put together a logical plan of action, complete with schedules and budgets. The Executives were probably reviewing contracts and seeing if anything that Starlette or the other actors were doing could be in violation of those contracts.

The Director was willing to bet that there was some clause that would give The Studio grounds to terminate contracts if they saw fit. However, if they chose to clean house, there were not many actors who could replace Starlette or her cast. If they got rid of the Bikers, Mother Figure or Wise Native-American Elder, the outrage would only grow. They might be able to get rid of some of the bit players, if they wanted to make an example out of them, but even then they would be risking more fury.

The best strategy for The Studio at this point was to work with the actors and the crew. They had to show their employees that they really were on their side and that they supported them during this war against Bookworm.

Studio Head was not known for his great support of his acting troops. He would make promises of major actions to be taken, or speak of ending the war once and for all, but in the end he was more likely to be found putting golf balls in his office than looking for ways of resolving the more major issues.

The Director suspected that Studio Head enjoyed the level of control that he had now. He would never come out and say this to anyone, but Studio Head never seemed to be troubled by making actors disappear, or terminating the contracts of high level crew members. He never showed his face to the members of The Studio who did the ground work. He took sick days whenever he might be called upon to attend a Studio memorial service.

The Director was no fan of Studio Head. He spent a large amount of his time trying to figure out ways of working around Studio Head or manipulating Studio Head's decisions. At first, it was easy. When The Director first started working with his cast, he barely registered as a blip on Studio Head's radar. But Starlette and her co-stars were an extraordinary bunch, and this brought attention from the upper ranks.

At long last, Starlette's rise within The Studio was reaching a peak, and this would undoubtedly draw more attention and require more maneuvering on The Director's part.

He waited for it. He watched the clock on his desk. Each second that passed without his phone ringing actually surprised him a little bit.

When the phone rang at long last, The Director did not jump to pick it up. He looked at it, and the little red button that blinked on and off with each ring, and he waited for the right moment to grab the handset. He needed to make it seem as though he was hard at work on the Starlette situation, and not simply sitting there, waiting to con Studio Head into doing exactly what he had been waiting for ever since the night of the theater explosion.

He picked up the phone and tried to sound busy as he said, "Yeah?"

"This is how you answer your phone?" Studio Head asked, in his level, emotionless voice.

"Sorry, sir. I'm having a bit of a situation down here right now," The Director said, rustling some papers for Studio Head's benefit.

"I can see that you have a situation. It would seem that we all have a situation."

"I'm doing my best to resolve it, sir."

"And how might you do that?"

"I'm still working on that. I don't suppose we could just go on a firing spree," The Director quipped, knowing full well that Studio Head couldn't afford such a bold swipe at The Studio's workers.

There was a pause, as though Studio Head was actually considering it. For just a moment, The Director was beginning to worry.

Finally, Studio Head said, "I suppose not."

The Director could have sworn he heard a golf ball falling into the cup of Studio Head's putting green.

The Director took a deep breath and tried to sound as though he was as troubled by the situation as any good Studio Head lackey would be. After a moment, he said in a serious tone, "Sir, I believe that I'm close to getting a lead on Bookworm. If I can track him down, we might really have a chance at ending this war once and for all. Frankly, we can't afford to let this strike last for very long. We have scenes to shoot and schedules to keep."

Logical. Reasonable. Nothing that Studio Head could disagree with, without sounding like a complete fool. The Director seemed to have covered all of his bases, with just the right amount of urgency. If Starlette had seen him at work here, she never would have doubted his acting talent.

"Do you have any suggestions?" Studio Head asked him.

"We need to manage the situation carefully," The Director replied. "They're upset because they don't feel safe. They don't feel respected. They don't feel like they are being heard, or that they are making a difference. We need to make them believe that we are on their side and that we respect what they do here. Simply put... We need to play them."

He wondered if that last part went too far. Coming out and boldly saying that he wanted to con the actors into thinking that The Studio cared about them might have been overstepping just a little bit. He was hoping that Studio Head was too busy playing office games to be fully listening to what he was saying.

After another pause, Studio Head said, "What do you want to do?"

"Make them an offering. Give them something that they thought they lost."

"Such as?"

The Director took a deep breath before making his proposal. This was the moment that would make or break his conversation with Studio Head.

~

The Studio's vault was a cold and dark place. Hidden deep in the shadows of the cavernous hangar where The Studio had made its home, there was a thickly armored door, with a locking mechanism that could not be broken into by even the most talented of bank robber types.

Behind that door, there was very little light and very little heat. The place was designed to store original film prints, props and set pieces that nobody ever thought they would need again, but wanted to keep around just in case. Nothing that went into the vault was ever expected to come out; it was where little pieces of Hollywood went to fade into distant memories.

Moving past the vast expanse of shelves which held film cans that spanned the decades, there was another section of the vault. This section was relatively new; built after the attacks on Hollywood.

In this stretch of the vault, heavy cages had been built. They were equipped with only the basic plumbing requirements and old cots that were discovered in the hangar before it became The Studio.

A Studio security guard walked across this expanse. He could barely see where he was going, but he had been given orders and he was determined to follow them, even if it meant bumping into more than one obstacle.

When he reached the prisoner's cage, only a dim light was shining from high above. The prisoner was little more than a shadow which moved through this light, but when this prisoner heard the security guard coming, he stood and turned toward the cage door.

"Damnit... I specifically said that I wouldn't be taking visitors today," the prisoner quipped in a raspy whisper, shaking his head as he watched the guard unlock the door. "Receptionists just aren't what they used to be. I think I might need to find a new girl."

~

It was dark and hot beneath the cloth sack had been placed over his head as he was dragged out of his cage and transported to wherever it was that he was going. He remained quiet the entire way, because there was no use in wasting his sarcasm on low level security guards.

His wrists and ankles had been chained together, to ensure that he could not attack or escape, and though his face was covered, he could smell the smoke that had been pumped into the hallways before him. He could see yellow lights flashing through the burlap which covered his head, telling him that his transport had been deemed a security threat.

He was ordered to walk slowly and to make no sudden movements, and while he remained silent, he heard a generic power ballad blasting from speakers around him, most likely because The Studio could not clear the rights to an appropriate Trisha Yearwood number.

He was unsure whether the loud music was to prevent him from yelling to whoever might be nearby, or simply for effect.

What he could hear even more than the sound of that music was the sound of his own breathing, heavy and uneven. His heart was pounding in his chest. His palms were sweaty. He was ready

for whatever awaited him at the end of this walk. To fight would
be preferable, but he fully expected to die. Either way, he was not
scared. He had been preparing for this moment, and now that it
had arrived, adrenaline was surging through him like a raging fire.

A drop of sweat dripped down his face. He swallowed hard,
though his mouth was dry. He closed his eyes for just a second or
two and allowed the moment to wash over him. He couldn't help
but smile.

When he was brought into a room and led to a chair where he
sat down, the cloth sack was pulled off of his head. As it was
removed, the sack tugged on his long beard and shaggy hair,
which had only recently been acquired.

"Sorry about the theatrics," The Director said, from the other
side of the table, where Wacky Best Friend found himself sitting.
"We couldn't afford for you to be recognized on your way in here."

"Because I usually have the bag over my head…" Wacky Best
Friend said, pulling off the fake beard and wig. He put his hands
on the table in a polite manner, looked around the room and
asked, "Where am I?"

"An unused office, in a part of The Studio where nobody ever
goes," The Director replied, watching the security guard leave the
room.

"And still no window."

"Before the phone rings, I want to tell you… It's good to see you
again. A lot's happened since you were away, so let me lead the
conversation and we should get out of here just fine."

"Out of here being… Like, *out* of here?"

"Back to your trailer and your co-stars."

"Oh. That's good too, I guess."

The phone in the center of the table rang. Wacky Best Friend
and The Director exchanged a look. The Director silently asked if
Wacky Best Friend was ready to do this, and Wacky Best Friend
nodded—because really, what choice did he have?

During his time in the cage, Wacky Best Friend had a lot of
time to think. He had little ability to do anything else.

He had been dreaming of a moment such as this for a while by
the time he found himself in that room with The Director and a
phone on the table in front of him. He had a list of things that he

wanted to say to Studio Head. Now that he was in the moment, he wondered how many of those things he would have the nerve to say.

The Director turned on the speakerphone and said, "We're here."

"Good," came that robotic voice over the phone. "I trust that you're in good health, Mr. Wehrli?"

Wacky Best Friend couldn't help but shoot The Director a look in response to this question. The look asked a question somewhere along the lines of: *Did he really just ask me that?* Though it could have just as easily been a: *What the hell?* Considering the fact that Studio Head had sent Wacky Best Friend to the vault to begin with, the question was almost humorous.

"Your status has been brought up for review," Studio Head said. "Tell me... Do you feel that your time in the vault has been well spent? Have you considered the actions which led you to this point?"

The Director nodded at Wacky Best Friend, telling him to answer in the affirmative.

"I did, sir," Wacky Best Friend replied. "I spent every day thinking about it."

"And what conclusions did you come to?"

"Obviously, it's wise to know your place in The Studio," Wacky Best Friend explained. He kept his eyes on The Director, to make sure that he was following the right path with his responses as he continued. "My contract with The Studio was an acting contract, not a writing contract. I shouldn't have tried to step outside the boundaries of that arrangement."

"Why?" Studio Head asked.

Wacky Best Friend looked to The Director for guidance. Honestly, he had no clue why they were so opposed to the idea of actors expanding their resumes, but he knew that this would not make for a great answer.

"Sir, if I may," The Director chimed in. "Wacky Best Friend and I had a moment to talk before you called, and during that time I think I managed to get a pretty good feel for his current mindset. When he tried to convey to me the respect that he has for the structure of The Studio and how easily that structure could collapse if people started overstepping, I could hear the emotion in his voice. I could see the tear in his eye."

Wacky Best Friend raised his brow, as if to say, *I didn't cry.*

The Director held up a hand, to make sure that Wacky Best Friend didn't say anything.

Wacky Best Friend remained silent. For the moment, he was content to listen.

~

In the hours since Starlette declared the strike, The Studio had fallen into a strange lull. For a people who were accustomed to hardcore violence, their chosen form of protest was remarkably peaceful. All of the members of the cast and crew stayed together. Some sat on the floor. Others stood.

The speaking area had become a stage, where people could voice concerns, share the story of how they survived the attacks, or perform a prepared monologue.

Girl Next Door was sitting on the floor next to Heartthrob, with her head on his shoulder. They were taking in the view of the place and the calm of the moment.

"It's strange, isn't it?" Heartthrob commented.

Without taking her head off of his shoulder, Ember replied, "What's that?"

"The day started out with violence. It grew to the breaking point... and then she took over. The strongest warrior. The fiercest leader..."

"Every soldier needs a day off," Ember told him. "But when she tells us it's time to fight, these people darn well better fight."

Starlette approached them and sat beside Girl Next Door. She looked out at the peaceful protest and said, "If any of these people start bouncing beach balls around, I'm nuking the place. I swear, if I knew that a work stoppage would be this flowery, I'd have staged a revolt instead."

"You did good," Ember told her. "You gave them a voice."

"Yay for me. So, I went to check on Tessa. She's still sleeping, but they managed to stop all the bleeding they caused when they opened her up."

"What's your plan?" Heartthrob asked.

"Y'know, I do plan to come up with one of those. I really do,"

Starlette smiled. "Until then, I'm winging it. All I know is that something smells rotten in here. Tessa's attack—She told me her attacker had two cell phones on her belt."

"Jennifer?" Girl Next Door asked. "I knew she would pop up again. I didn't say it out loud because I didn't want to sound stupid if it didn't happen, but I *knew* it."

"Thing is, The Director checked and Jennifer's in lockup," Starlette told them, raising one eyebrow to increase the mysterious tone of the comment.

Girl Next Door was intrigued by this. She tried her best to figure out what it could all mean, but she couldn't understand who else would have attacked Tessa, aside from about a thousand crew members who were screaming for Tessa's blood earlier that morning. But Girl Next Door knew that Starlette was intrigued by this mystery, so she nodded and narrowed her eyes so that she would look like she was deep in thought.

She then began to wonder if the commissary workers were on strike too.

~

The Director was still sitting across from Wacky Best Friend, listening to Studio Head question him as though the decision to free Wacky Best Friend hadn't already been made.

So far, it seemed to be going well. The Director was nervous that some slip of Wacky Best Friend's tongue would cause Studio Head to lash out irrationally, throwing Wacky Best Friend back in the cage despite the fact that it would keep the strike going for even longer than it had already.

Any minor thing could throw Studio Head into as large a rage as The Director could imagine him having without expressing any emotion whatsoever.

The back and forth of questions did not seem to intimidate Wacky Best Friend. He was keeping his sarcasm down to a respectable level, but he didn't seem worried in the least. In fact, he didn't seem very invested in this conversation at all.

The Director figured that Wacky Best Friend had already seen what could happen to him. There was nothing left to threaten him with, except death, and Wacky Best Friend had been in enough life or death situations over the previous year to keep a cool head under those conditions.

This attitude lent itself well to dealing with Studio Head. If Wacky Best Friend had put up more of a fight, there was no telling what could have happened. An excess of sarcasm did not go over well when Wacky Best Friend was first questioned by Studio Head, and only The Director's quick thinking after a fortunately timed theater bombing had saved Wacky Best Friend from being written off for good.

Though the situation was stressful for The Director and he wanted to be there to lead Wacky Best Friend through the conversation, this would not be possible.

The Director had brought a walkie-talkie with him into the meeting, telling Studio security that he was only to be interrupted if it was truly an emergency. There were a number of situations which he could need to tend to in a hurry. Tessa Baker was in the clinic, recovering from a severe beating at the hand of an unknown attacker who could still be walking freely around The Studio. The casts and crew of The Studio had declared a strike, which could turn violent at any moment, though The Director trusted Starlette to keep that situation in check.

The situation that pulled The Director from his meeting with Studio Head and Wacky Best Friend was neither of these. Instead, it was his questioning of the rogue agent; a situation that he would have happily ignored for a while longer, if only Studio Head hadn't heard the call come in over the walkie-talkie and ordered The Director to handle it at once... After all, sitting on one's hands after being told that the rogue agent had important information regarding Bookworm's whereabouts would not sit well with anyone in The Studio.

Wacky Best Friend looked The Director squarely in the eye upon hearing the conversation on the walkie-talkie and he silently told The Director to go. He knew as well as anyone that any opportunity to get this information must be seized at once.

Though The Director didn't like leaving that meeting, he did. He made the long walk back to his office, using hallways that would keep him away from the main Studio floor where the sit-down strike was currently being held.

He had to appreciate the fact that it was a *sit-down* strike.

Though he and Starlette often went back and forth yelling at each other due to the positions they held, he often felt as though there was an unspoken partnership between them. Too often it seemed as though convenient situations just happened to present themselves when he needed leverage. He didn't ask questions, but there was something more to those situations than lucky twists of fate.

He arrived at the green room and stood outside the door for a moment, trying to switch gears between the subtle manipulation he had been using in his meeting with Studio Head, and the type of force with which the rogue agent must be dealt. After he was confident that he had lost all subtlety, The Director walked into the room and took his seat on the couch across from the rogue agent.

He said nothing. He simply sat there, looking at the rogue agent, waiting for the rogue agent to begin speaking.

The rogue agent seemed to have trouble spitting out whatever it was that he was going to say. Obviously, he was planning to violate some sacred code of pathetic con artists everywhere.

"I walk," the rogue agent finally said.

The Director wasn't sure if this was a statement or a question. Either way, he replied, "You walk when Bookworm is dead."

It was a fair enough offer to make. Once the war was over and Bookworm was gone, life would go on. Movies would be made and actors would go back to really making a difference in the world. At that point, it would just be strange for them to keep people as prisoners.

The rogue agent took a moment to consider the deal. He looked at The Director and said, "Nobody knows it was me?"

"Not unless you piss me off."

"And the place you put me until he's gone... It's nice?"

"Like a hotel," The Director lied. "In fact, we just had the VIP suite open up."

He would have felt horrible about lying like this, if the man he was lying to hadn't been a heartless, manipulative predator who placed one of The Director's actors in the hands of Bookworm. Given the circumstances, he really didn't feel too bad about it.

The rogue agent nodded as he considered the offer once again.

"You called me down here," The Director said. "If you don't have anything you want to tell me, I have more important things to do. For starters, I have to figure out what kind of fabric that couch your sitting on is covered with, and then I have to figure out how to get blood and brain matter out of whatever fabric that couch is covered with."

After the rogue agent failed to speak up, The Director got to his feet. Shaking his head, he said, "You know... We have people for that sort of stuff. I'm not even gonna bother with the couch thing."

"It's a college," the rogue agent blurted, as though it would hurt less if he said it quickly.

The Director turned to him and said, "What?"

"That one picture on the wall. Three in, from the left."

The Director looked at the copies of the Emma Carter papers that were pinned to the wall. Three in from the left, there was a scribbling that looked like a distorted zebra holding a house.

He turned back to the rogue agent and said, "I don't see it."

"The drawing is of a falcon carrying a book in its talons," the rogue agent said.

Looking back to the picture, The Director cocked his head and tried to see what the rogue agent was describing, but the picture still looked like a zebra and a house to him.

"He's named Diomedes, after an ancient something-or-other that makes college kids feel smart when they reference him. Name aside, it's a simple mascot for a think tank at Princedale University."

"I've never heard of it," The Director replied, in regards to the university.

"You wouldn't have," the rogue agent explained. "It's a smaller college. Very elite. Only the best and the brightest of the kids who can't get into a real school are able to attend Princedale."

The Director pulled the drawing from the wall and looked at it carefully. He then looked at the rogue agent and said, "You're sure about this?"

"I'm sure. My sister went to Princedale... So by telling you this, I'm not violating the trust of any of my contacts. Let's be clear on that."

"Sure. You're a good and honorable man," The Director replied with as much sarcasm as he could muster.

There was a strange feeling in each of The Director's limbs. His body was suddenly overflowing with energy, screaming at him to run and tell someone that they had a lead on Bookworm at long last.

He remained cool, however. Keeping his eyes on the paper, he said, "So if Emma Carter was drawing a picture of her father's office..."

"...I'd say you just found yourself a Bookworm stronghold."

~

"We have to think about those actors who don't get to work on location very often! We have to consider the fact that they don't have as much as we do! We must help them increase the residual payments they get for the work they do!" cried Strong Professional Woman.

Around The Studio, there were claps here and there. Nobody seemed to be incredibly supportive of her comments.

"Are we supposed to be getting paid?" Girl Next Door asked.

Starlette shrugged. She had been listening to the concerns of The Studio's employees for hours by this point and while they were all very interesting, she just wanted to get back to work. She wanted to track someone down and kick their ass. She wanted to shoot someone.

Starlette had a million questions that needed answering. She would not return to her job until someone could explain to her where Ethan was, or who attacked Tessa. Until she could track down Bookworm and take him down, she needed to focus on the problems that she could *solve*. At that particular moment, this meant dealing with the problems at home. She figured that there would probably be no slitting of throats on this front, but she didn't rule it out entirely.

The Director stepped onto The Studio floor, and the entire crowd turned to look at him. Those who were seated got to their feet, including Starlette.

People began to scream and yell at him, demanding answers. Some threw empty cups or scraps of food at him, but The Director didn't seem to care.

Calmly, he walked to the speaking area. Starlette was trying to get a read on his body language, so she could figure out what he might have to say, but he betrayed no emotion. He remained perfectly at ease as he prepared to address the people of The Studio.

Starlette and her cast moved forward through the crowd, until they were at the front. The Director looked at her.

"Your concerns have been recognized. We have taken into account all of what you've had to say. But the strike must end now," he told her.

"Or what? The Studio makes us disappear?" Starlette replied.

"No," he replied. "Look, we could drag this out for weeks or months. You make demands, they make counter demands. You want better hours, they want harder work. You want respect, they want respect. It goes back and forth and in the end, none of you get what you really want. But if you end this now, and if you trust *me*, I can give you what you want."

"What does that mean?"

"It means... I've been conducting extensive interrogations with the rogue agent that you brought in. I've been questioning him and breaking him down since he got here, and as a result... I have the location of a Bookworm stronghold which will lead us directly to Bookworm himself. If we act *fast* and we act *together*, Bookworm will be dead in a matter of days."

Truth be told, Starlette was sold on the idea then and there. There was no way that she was going to let Bookworm slip through their fingers; no way that she was going to miss the chance to make him suffer, the same way that everyone in The Studio had suffered. She had spent the day hearing their stories, and she would see to it that it ended now.

Yet, she did not respond to The Director. She did not flinch, even as those around her began to stir and get worked up over the idea.

He met her look, and did not react to her lack of response for several seconds. Then, something in his eyes changed. Right then and there, she knew that all of her maneuvering and all of this *power to the people* crap had paid off.

"We know that none of you are simply going to fall in line and obey the orders that you're given," The Director continued. "We have told you time and time again that The Studio is not in the habit of '*disappearing*' people. Some leave. Some die. But the men in charge want you to know that they grieve with you when that happens. To prove this... I have asked Wacky Best Friend to end his treatment early, so that he might be a part of this historic occasion."

The Director held up a hand, directing everyone's attention to the back of the crowd. As they turned and stepped aside, so that Starlette and her cast could see, Wacky Best Friend stepped into view. He looked as though he just came from a spa, with a fresh haircut and clothes that did not fit his normal character wardrobe at all. They were... cool.

Part of Starlette wanted to scream and jump up and down, and run to Ethan. Despite this, she did not betray her steely character. She began to walk toward Ethan, with a smile in her eyes, but not on her lips. She walked calmly and slowly.

Meanwhile, Girl Next Door threw her arms in the air and screamed. She jumped up and down and ran to Wacky Best Friend, tackling him and taking him to the ground.

Around the room, the crowd broke into applause, welcoming home their long lost comrade.

Heartthrob reached Wacky Best Friend before Starlette, and helped him off of the ground. As they shook hands, Starlette couldn't hear what they were saying over all of the cheers around them, but they were smiling as they talked and she liked seeing her family smile for once. She could have stopped right there and watched them for a while, but she chose not to.

As she got closer, Wacky Best Friend walked to meet her. Though she extended a hand for him to shake, he put his arms around her and hugged her tightly.

The noise from the crowd died down, and Starlette said to Wacky Best Friend, "I think they want you to say something."

"Why?"

With a grin, she told him, "You're the boy at the bottom of the well."

"I have no clue what that means."

"Just talk."

Wacky Best Friend turned toward the crowd, and with his co-stars behind him, he said, "Umm... Thanks? If I had known that taking some time off would be this big a deal, I might have reconsidered. But I was really... *exhausted*. If you only knew how often I... yawned... It was a lot. But I'm back now and I'm ready to join my cast in taking down the son of a bitch who put us in this hole in the first place. Let's kill that guy."

The crowd began to cheer once again.

The strike was over. They had a lot of work ahead of them. There were shoots to plan, scenes to rehearse, and locations to scout. But for that one night, Starlette's cast would be happy to hang out on their lawn furniture.

Starlette, Wacky Best Friend, Girl Next Door, Heartthrob and Sassy Gay Friend began their walk back to the trailers to rest up for what was to come. As they walked, Wacky Best Friend leaned close to Starlette and asked her, "Who is this peppy guy that's walking with us?"

Sassy Gay Friend threw a snap in the air.

Wacky Best Friend leaned close to Starlette again and said, "Sorry... I mean the *sassy* guy."

~

Hours earlier...

The Director had left the room, leaving Wacky Best Friend alone with the speakerphone and the voice of Studio Head which was asking him question after question.

Wacky Best Friend wanted to get back to his co-stars and to his life. He knew what he had to do to make this happen, and he was prepared to do it. He just wished that it could be hurried along just a little.

"What is your favorite movie?" Studio Head asked. "That story that you can see when you close your eyes. The one which you can almost recite line for line."

Wacky Best Friend thought about it for a moment, but he found it hard to think of a favorite movie in that particular situation. He finally picked from his go-to list of favorites and said, "*Signs*... I guess."

"Why?"

Wacky Best Friend had no interest in talking about movies with Studio Head, but he played along. He said, "I don't know. I like the fact that two people can look at it and see two entirely different movies. I like that it isn't what it's supposed to be."

"And you enjoy favoring a film that most of the world hates, because you like to buck the system," Studio Head added.

"That too."

"I've always loved *The Time Machine*... The original, of course. The elegance of the story. The direct honesty of what it was," Studio Head told Wacky Best Friend. "The opposite of your choice, I suppose. Have you seen it?"

"Yeah," Wacky Best Friend replied, leaving off the fact that the movie was on his list of favorites and making a mental note to reevaluate the film, seeing as how Studio Head enjoyed it so much.

"In the story, a man travels to the distant future. He sees a world which has been torn apart; destroyed. And he finds a barbaric race of people who live beneath the earth. They've become inhuman; monsters. This happened because their civilization was thrown into chaos. Anarchy prevailed. Eventually, they could not even tolerate the light," Studio Head explained.

At first Wacky Best Friend wasn't sure why this topic had come up, but as Studio Head went on, he began to see some relevance to the topic and began to wonder if he could have chosen a more fitting movie for his own selection, to counter Studio Head's.

Studio Head went on to say, "Our society belongs in the light, Mr. Wehrli. We need to return to that light, and in order to do that, we must prevent ourselves from becoming like the Morlocks. We need structure. We need guidance. Do you understand?"

Wacky Best Friend thought about his answer for a moment, and then said, "Yes."

"When you disappeared, your friends were told that you were being treated for exhaustion, at the clinic," Studio Head told him.

Wacky Best Friend had to wonder if they had actually bought that story. In what world did people actually check into a clinic to be treated for exhaustion?

Studio Head continued, "If you return to your cast, what will you tell them of your time away."

Wacky Best Friend didn't need to take a moment to consider his answer. He knew what Studio Head wanted to hear, and what his own motivation was. Every word out of his mouth had to count toward his ultimate goal.

"I would tell them that I was being treated for exhaustion. At the clinic," he responded.

Studio Head was silent for a moment. Wacky Best Friend decided that this would be a good time to take advantage of Studio Head's knack for dramatic pauses.

"That is to say, I *might* tell them that," Wacky Best Friend said, in an even tone. "Sir."

"Excuse me?"

Wacky Best Friend leaned closer to the phone for reasons that he did not quite understand. He stared down the speaker as though Studio Head could see him through it.

"When I was locked up in that cage, I had a lot of time to think. I thought about what I would say or do if this situation ever came up," Wacky Best Friend explained. "And then, when I got pulled in here... I threw all of that out the window. You know why?"

There was silence on the other end of the phone.

"Don't worry, I'll tell you anyway. See, I realized that something was going on out there. I know that you would love nothing more than to toss me out the nearest break-away window, but for some reason, here I am. And I have to ask myself what that's all about."

"I do not appreciate your banter, Mr. Wehrli."

"I don't mind. I have a large following amongst teenagers, and I tend to play toward my audience," Wacky Best Friend shot back. "So here we are, renegotiating my contract."

"Excuse me?"

"If I recall, you specifically said that my contract with The Studio had been terminated. This means that what we have here is a renegotiation. And since something must have happened that would force you to drag me down here, I will graciously listen to whatever your proposal might be."

"Mr. Wehrli—"

"Call me Wacky. Please."

"You have a chance to return to your cast; to sleep in a bed with sheets. You have an opportunity to reclaim the life you had here. I would not be so quick to toss it aside."

"Oh, I'm not tossing," Wacky Best Friend told him. "I intend to get those things back. But as they sang in that classic episode of *Gilligan's Island*... *'You need me'*. So here's the deal, Mr. Phoneface... I will return to my cast and my trailer and my awesome hoodies, but I want more."

"Money?"

"I wasn't gonna ask for that, but now that you mention it... Sure," Wacky Best Friend replied, feeling a rush as he dealt with Studio Head. He had missed putting up fights.

Continuing with his demands, Wacky Best Friend said, "In addition to your generous donation, I want a *Producer* credit, so that I can be sure that I'll never end up back here for doing what I do. And I want script approval."

"Absolutely not."

"If having me out there to help you quell the Morlocks isn't valuable enough to you, then you can send me back to the cage and hope for the best."

There was silence on the other end of the line, as Studio Head considered his options.

Wacky Best Friend began to wonder if his gamble would pay off. He did not want to go back to the cage, but he had to grab this opportunity while he could.

Finally, Studio Head said, "I agree to your terms. The paperwork will be sent at once."

Wacky Best Friend was relieved. He couldn't help but smile and say, "Awesome."

"Do not forget the terms of our arrangement, Mr. Wehrli. If you tell them where you were, you will be in violation of this contract."

"Right-o," Wacky Best Friend nodded. Before the line could go dead, he lost the smile and said, "And sir... You might not have been my target demographic before... But I'm aiming for you now."

Chapter Twelve
THE RED PAGES

As they sat on the lawn furniture near their trailers, sipping cold drinks and pretending to tan in the sun, Starlette couldn't help but take in the feeling of being with her full cast once again. Since Ethan came home, things felt normal to her once again—and the fact that any of this felt normal scared her just a little bit.

They didn't need to talk. There was an unspoken connection between her cast members and herself; something which helped ease the mind, even when things were getting difficult.

There is a storm coming. It was a line that she had seen a hundred times, in scripts for the television series that she starred in, back in another life. Usually, it would appear in the episode right before the finale, when the tension was near a breaking point and all of that season's plotlines were about to be resolved. But this was not a story. This was Starlette's real life, and for the first time she was beginning to understand how her character had felt for all those years.

Of course, looking back, she had played those scenes far too dramatically. The feeling of impending change wasn't something that brought tears to the eyes of a hero or scared them. There was a reason why people often referred to the calm before a storm. Though she knew that her home could be blown down within the next few days, Starlette was strangely at ease.

This was more than she could say for Heartthrob. At night, he could still be heard screaming until he eventually woke up from his nightmares, which undoubtedly involved watching his entire family tortured and killed for the sake of protecting him.

He acted fine during the day, but she could see him drifting from time to time, and she wondered if he might eventually crumble irreparably. She had doubted him before ever meeting him and she had not been very excited about his joining her cast. Now, though her concerns were more real than ever before, she could not turn her back on him. To do so could cost lives—his included.

For that moment however, he was safely under Ember's watchful eye. She was good for Heartthrob, and he was good for her. Since meeting him, she had stopped trying to force herself to bake. This was something which Starlette would be eternally grateful for.

Since Wacky Best Friend returned to their cast, Starlette had been waiting for him to show some hint of damage. She highly doubted that he would check himself into a clinic and leave his co-stars to fight the evil Bookworm forces on their own, while he brushed up on his yoga, or whatever one was supposed to do while being treated for exhaustion. Yet, aside from pulling all of the breakdowns and synopses for all of the shoots that he had missed, Ethan was as cool and relaxed as ever. He hadn't been back for very long, so she thought that maybe his trauma would present itself at some later point, but in the hours since his return he had spent most of his time reviewing the shoots, all while sipping drinks and cracking jokes with his friends.

And then there was Sassy Gay Friend, who had pulled up a metal folding chair and was sitting with the main cast members, despite still being classified only as a guest star. Starlette wasn't sure what she thought of him yet.

The silence had lasted longer than Starlette expected it to. Since becoming the leader of The Studio's employee rebellion, people had started coming to her with their concerns and their problems. Luckily, Mother Figure and Wise Native-American Elder offered to help manage these responsibilities for Starlette so that she could prepare for her impending takedown of Bookworm's army. Trying to balance killing people with paperwork would be difficult for anybody.

She enjoyed the silence, but knew that it had to end soon, and she could have predicted that Ember would be the one to break it.

"So, where were you?" Ember asked, turning to Ethan.

"Rehab," he replied, looking over some of the recaps of the shoots that he missed.

"I thought you were being treated for exhaustion," Ember pressed.

Ethan looked up from his papers and said, "Oh. Right. Then... That's where I was."

"Seriously, where were you?" Ember continued. "Because I know you and you would not check in to the clinic because you're exhausted. You're far too lazy to be exhausted."

"Seriously..." Wacky Best Friend said, in a tone that sounded strangely stern as he looked at Girl Next Door. He then changed his tone to a much lighter one and said to Ember, "Oh, I heard about your new hobby, by the way."

A curious look came over Ember and she took the bait. She asked, "What hobby?"

"Y'know, the whole *homophobia* thing..."

Sassy Gay Friend raised a hand as if to say *stop*, and said, "Oh, don't even get me started on that one."

"I am not!" Ember yelled. "I love gay people. *All* gay people, regardless of their individual personalities."

"So, you didn't go on a homophobic tirade?" Wacky Best Friend asked, and Starlette could not help but note the effectiveness of his redirecting the conversation.

Ember emphatically replied, "I did not."

Sassy Gay Friend made a slight *hmph* sound as he crossed his arms and looked at Girl Next Door like she was the biggest liar in the world.

Ethan held up his cell phone. On it, a video played, showing Girl Next Door and Sassy Gay Friend talking on the main Studio floor. As the video began, Sassy Gay Friend said, "People like me make you sick?"

As the video went on, Girl Next Door mumbled something that the camera didn't pick up as she turned away from Sassy Gay Friend. When she turned back to him, she yelled, "Yes. People like you make me sick. You're disgusting. You're immoral. You are everything that is wrong with the world we live in today. Just thinking about it makes me want to throw up."

As the video came to an end, Girl Next Door was looking around The Studio, realizing that people were watching her. The video froze on her embarrassed face as the word *homophobe* appeared on the screen.

Wacky Best Friend put his cell phone down.

"Oh. Snap," Sassy Gay Friend snarked, sitting back in his folding metal chair.

"Shut up," Ethan told him, rather bluntly dismissing the guest star.

"I hadn't seen that video before," Heartthrob winced.

Starlette couldn't help but cringe as she said, "It does look pretty bad."

Ember was mortified. She looked like she was about to either burst into tears or break someone's face in. She looked around the area, as though she was expecting a mob of villagers to come looking for her with pitchforks and torches in hand.

She then turned to Ethan and said, "So, where were you again? Because I'm not really easily distracted."

Ethan grinned, and looked back to his papers. He seemed amused by Ember's persistence. He told her, "I was hired by the CIA to track down top secret documents pertaining to third world dictators, in the hopes of aiding the efforts to oust said dictators."

Ember's eyes widened and she said, "Seriously?"

Laughing, Ethan replied, "No! Not seriously. Dude, I'm just an actor. I don't know how to do CIA stuff."

Before Ember could press the subject, a production assistant approached and said, "Excuse me. Girl Next Door is needed in Head Writer's office."

Girl Next Door looked up at the production assistant and asked, "For real? Again? Why am I the only one who gets called to his office?"

The production assistant did not seem amused with Girl Next Door. She ignored the question and walked away.

"Did it just get cold in here?" Ethan asked as Girl Next Door started to get up.

Before Girl Next Door could get to her feet, Heartthrob grabbed her arm and said, "Hey."

She turned and looked at him, but he said nothing. He simply gave her a sympathetic, supportive nod and a quick kiss.

"Thanks," she said to him, and then got up.

As Girl Next Door walked away from the group, she made sure to kick Ethan's chair.

Once she was gone, Sassy Gay Friend smiled and said, "I guess she doesn't like seeing what she looks like to the rest of us."

Wacky Best Friend didn't look up from his papers as he said, "Leave."

Sassy Gay Friend seemed shocked. He said, "Excuse me?"

Ethan didn't say another word. He simply looked up from his papers, to Sassy Gay Friend and his expression conveyed all that he wanted to say.

Sassy Gay Friend quickly stood and walked away from the group. He seemed somewhat less Sassy as he did this.

"Well... I guess *I'm* gonna be on the internet now," Ethan muttered as he looked back to his papers.

"I'm going to hit the gym before we're called into a meeting," Heartthrob told them, standing up and preparing to take off.

"Didn't you work out this morning?" Starlette asked, in a more concerned tone than she intended.

"Can't hurt to loosen up before we kill some bad guys, right?" Heartthrob responded, and he walked away from them.

Starlette was worried. He was obviously using his exercise as a distraction from everything else that was going on, and that was fine with her. But more working out meant that he needed more distraction, and that was a troubling thought; especially as they prepared for their most important shoot yet.

She couldn't blame him for being tired. They could have all used a vacation at that point, and she certainly wouldn't hold it against him. Still, she needed to be careful. She could not allow anyone or anything to prevent them from taking down Bookworm once and for all.

"That's a heavy look," Ethan commented in regards to Starlette's expression, once Heartthrob was gone. "Related to his tabloid story?"

Starlette sat back in her chair and brushed the hair out of her face, "I don't know. I just need to keep an eye on a lot of people right now."

"I hear ya," Ethan replied.

Starlette looked around the area to make sure that they were alone. Once she was sure that they were, she leaned forward and quietly spoke to Ethan. She said, "Listen. I talked to The Director and I asked him to hold you back on this shoot. I told him that *officially*, you need to get acclimated before you dive into work."

"And unofficially?" Ethan asked, seeming to be unfazed by his being benched.

"I need you to check in with Tessa as soon as she wakes up," Starlette told him.

Ethan held up a hand and asked, "Tessa?"

Realizing that Ethan wasn't entirely up to date, she told him, "Remember how I told you that I found Tessa Baker? Well, we brought her into The Studio, but there was some controversy with her having a book deal a while back, so some people were all upset."

"That's stupid," Ethan replied, fishing through his papers to find anything that might mention Tessa. He pulled several sheets and began skimming them.

Starlette continued, "She was attacked and sent to the clinic. She was operated on, and hasn't woken up yet. At least, not that I know of. But before she was put under, she told me that her attacker was a woman with two cell phones on her belt."

"So, we're thinking that this was a personal assistant?" Ethan asked. After a moment of thinking, he deduced, "We brought in the rogue agent. That means that his assistant was probably taken down too."

"Jennifer. Only, she's supposed to be in lockup somewhere."

Ethan looked off to the side, as though trying to recall something. Starlette didn't know what he was thinking, but she didn't press him on the subject. She was okay with the fact that he couldn't tell her everything.

"So you want me to check things out while you're gone? See who could have attacked Tessa if Jennifer's in the clink?"

"Or, who could have let Jennifer out long enough to attack Tessa," Starlette added.

Wacky Best Friend seemed to understand what was going on better than Starlette expected him to. He nodded slightly, as his brain went to work. He asked only one more question: "Do you want Heartthrob to hang back with me?"

Starlette considered it for a moment. She hadn't decided what to do with Heartthrob yet. She thought that he could be of use to Wacky Best Friend's investigation, but she finally decided against it. She told Wacky Best Friend, "I'm not going to be the one to keep him away from this."

"Cool," Wacky Best Friend said, turning back to his papers. "I'll do some digging on my own then."

~

As Girl Next Door walked through The Studio, on her way to Head Writer's office, she kept her head down. She felt like people were watching her and judging her. She felt like a fool. She felt like a criminal.

Of course, there was the hope that she was simply imagining things. She hoped that she was being paranoid and that nobody in The Studio was even thinking about the video that Ethan had found online, but the video was put up by someone out there, and if Ethan found it, that meant that others probably had as well.

She didn't want to look up and see whether she was being paranoid or not. She wanted to cling to that hope, but walking through a crowded building generally required some amount of attention to be paid to others. She had no choice but to look up from time to time, and though she did not intend to look directly at anyone when she did this, she couldn't help it. She looked... and so did they.

Not everyone was staring at her. She wasn't that important a figure, even in The Studio. Those who did look were not pleased however, and this made Girl Next Door feel like she was about an inch tall.

She could have tried to explain herself. She could stop someone and tell them that she wasn't a homophobe, and that she very specifically hated Sassy Gay Friend. If they refused to give her any slack, she could even tell them his deep dark secret, which she had discovered in the office of The Celeb Spinner, shortly before it was destroyed.

But she wouldn't do that. No matter how much she might want to destroy Sassy Gay Friend, this particular secret was something which was not hers to spill. She could not be that type of person, no matter what the cost.

She looked down once again and kept walking. It wouldn't take her that long to reach Head Writer's office, and once she was in there, she would at least be sheltered from the judgmental eyes of Studio workers.

When she reached his door, it was closed. She knocked, but didn't bother to wait for an answer before she opened the door and walked inside. She quickly closed the door behind her, still keeping her eyes on the ground.

The room was darker than normal. There was only one small light turned on, which sat on a shelf on the far side of the office.

Though dim, the light allowed her to see the room clearly. When she looked up, she could see Head Writer sitting at his desk, with his head resting in his hands.

On the markerboard behind him, the word *homophobe* was written in red ink, with several lines under it.

Her jaw dropped when she saw the word.

"You wouldn't believe the type of headache I have," Head Writer told her. "Between the Bookworm stronghold shoot and this..."

Without looking back, he raised one hand, gesturing toward the markerboard.

He looked up at her, looking more tired than she had ever seen him before and he said, "Don't worry though. I know you. I know your character. I will try to find some way of resolving this thread without damage to you."

"You will?" Girl Next Door replied, somewhat shocked. "I mean... Thanks."

"The question I have is: where do you see yourself going?"

"What do you mean? I'm supposed to go find Bookworm any minute now."

"I mean, long-term," Head Writer said. "You have to have some thoughts about where you'd like to take your whole arc."

"I tend to just kinda go with whatever happens," Girl Next Door told him.

"Has that worked well for you? Starlette took over the entire Studio. Wacky Best Friend has his own thing going on. Heartthrob is buried in drama. And you... the best you've had is this whole *homophobe* thing," Head Writer told her, causing Girl Next Door to reflect on her role within her cast. "I'm not judging you. I think you're doing a great job. I was just wondering if maybe you'd be interested in fleshing out your character. Maybe—I don't know—add a love interest?"

Girl Next Door suddenly became very uncomfortable. She looked Head Writer in the eyes, but didn't say anything in response to him. He stood from his chair and walked around his desk, where he sat down closer to her.

Looking down at the ground rather than at her, Head Writer asked, "I was thinking maybe you and I could get coffee sometime."

"What?" she replied, partly relieved that he wasn't going to be prying into her relationship with Heartthrob. "I can't. I mean... You're *Head Writer.*"

"I like you," he explained. "That's why I've been bringing you in here so much. I just wanted to get to know you more. I wanted you to get to know me."

"I don't think I should be here right now," she said, looking toward the exit. "Look, I'm flattered. Really. And I hope that I don't come off as snotty or anything like that, but I don't like you..."

While this statement was true as-is, she thought that it came out sounding a little harsh, so she added, "...in that way."

Also technically true. She didn't like him in *that* way, or any other way.

"I think you could like me if you got to know me," he said.

She stood and put a hand on his shoulder as she said, "I don't think that's going to happen."

With that, she turned and started to walk toward the door. Before she could reach it, he said, "I really wish you would change your mind."

The tone with which he said that did not sit well with her, but she ignored it. She opened the door and walked out of the office, leaving Head Writer alone.

As she walked away, she felt the strong need for a bath. Unfortunately for her, she did not even make it back to her trailer before she was told to meet The Director in the conference room.

~

Heartthrob was on his way to the gym, preparing to push his muscles to their limits in the hopes of making himself so tired that his mind could not possibly force his body to wake up in the middle of the night.

Working out cleared his mind. Whether he was on the treadmill or lifting weights, the repetitive motions allowed him to fall into a calm unlike anything else he could find in any other corner of his world. His mind would wander and drift in any direction that it wanted to go, and he allowed it to. Whether that direction was a pleasant thought of Ember, or the darkest memory of his past, he allowed his mind to go there.

The harder it was to cope with a memory, the harder he pressed his body. The more pain his mind was in, the more pain he put his body through. It wasn't a conscious decision to torture himself, but it seemed to do the job. For hours after a good workout, he could function like a normal person, without getting flashes of memories or lashing out at people around him.

He knew how to hide his mood. He could walk off when he felt anger or confusion setting in, and he could stay away from people until that mood had passed. It had only slipped out in front of people on a few occasions; the worst of which was when Starlette witnessed him nearly kill the rogue agent that he was supposed to be capturing. Now, he had to try even harder to be normal, because he knew that she was watching him. Any sane person would watch him after they heard his screams at night and witnessed him losing control in a dark alley. He couldn't blame Starlette for being concerned, and any energy she wasted on him was energy that she was not focusing on her primary job. More guilt. More pain. More working out.

He needed to find a way to control himself. It would be so much easier if he could just sleep. Ember made him feel better, but he worried that if she ever saw what was going on in his head, she would be too scared to stay with him. He had lost too much as it was, and couldn't stand the thought of losing her as well.

"You look tired," came the voice of a man behind him.

Heartthrob stopped walking and turned around. He found himself looking at a man in a suit—obviously not an actor. Judging by the haircut and the shoes, Heartthrob guessed that he was an Executive.

"You don't know me," the man said. "That's fine. I haven't introduced myself. You can call me Co-Executive Producer. I take care of a lot of the business that goes on behind the scenes here."

The man extended a hand, and Heartthrob shook it. He couldn't quite put his finger on it, but something about this man made him uncomfortable.

"I'm on my way somewhere," Heartthrob told the man. "I don't mean to be rude, but…"

"You're wondering what I want," the man replied, with a smile. "Truth is, some of us who share an interest in how you perform have been a little worried about you lately."

"I'm fine."

"Oh, I know. I'm not accusing you of anything. You just seem… tired," Co-Executive Producer said, in a tone that seemed to blend concern with accusation. "It's nothing we haven't seen before. The long hours you work; the stress you're under. Who wouldn't feel a little rundown?"

Heartthrob still wasn't getting the point of this conversation, and the look on his face must have said as much. Co-Executive Producer read this expression and held up a hand, telling Heartthrob to hold on a second.

Co-Executive Producer reached into his pocket and pulled out a small plastic bag. The bag was clear, and Heartthrob could see pills inside of it.

"I know what you're thinking, but let me explain," Co-Executive Producer said. "The red pills will give you a little added boost. Like caffeine, but better. The blue pills will make it easier for you to sleep at night, so you won't need the red pills. The green pills... Well, the green pills just make it a little easier to get through the day, if you need them."

"I'm not taking pills," Heartthrob said, without so much as a second thought.

He was a guy who didn't eat dark meat. He stayed away from flavored coffee drinks, and only allowed himself one cup of black coffee per day. He worked out more than some athletes. He was not in the habit of throwing toxins into his body.

"I'm not saying that you have to," Co-Executive Producer insisted. "Your union prevents me from doing that anymore. I'm just saying that you're wearing down. If you stay on this path, we couldn't send you out on shoots in good conscience. You'd be a danger to yourself and to your co-stars. So, if you ever feel like you might need a little help nipping that problem in the bud, I wanted to give you the option."

Co-Executive Producer tossed the bag to Heartthrob, who caught it out of reflex and not desire.

"You're needed in the conference room," Co-Executive Producer told him with a pleasant smile. "I promised a cute little PA that I'd let you know that."

Co-Executive Producer turned and started to walk away without saying another word.

Heartthrob was left holding the bag, though he had no intention of opening it.

~

The conference room was nearly empty. Starlette found herself sitting at the table next to her co-stars, and there was nobody else in the room at all. The door was closed. The blue lights which had been placed around the room to add atmosphere had been replaced by red lights.

The monitors on the wall displayed no images of importance, only The Studio's logo, which featured a nude, faceless woman riding on the back of a winged bull while holding the world in the palm of her hand. Starlette couldn't take her eyes off of that image as she waited.

Girl Next Door was talking to her, telling her that Head Writer had asked her on a date. Starlette didn't look at Girl Next Door, but she must have made a face in reaction to this news, because Girl Next Door said, "I know, right?!"

"Did you say yes?" Sassy Gay Friend asked her.

"No. He's gross."

Shaking his head, Sassy Gay Friend said, "He may be gross, but he could do wonders for your career... I'm just saying. And you could use all the help you can get."

"Yeah, because of you."

"I don't make haters. I just expose them for what they are."

"I'm not a hater."

"Should we go to the instant replay one more time?"

"Enough," Starlette cut in. "Just stop bickering, would you?"

Starlette turned to look at her co-stars and saw Heartthrob talking with Wacky Best Friend. She couldn't hear what they were saying, but she could see a bag full of pills in Heartthrob's hand.

"What is that?" she asked him.

Everyone turned their attention to Heartthrob, who showed them the bag.

"Wow, that's a lot of vitamins," Girl Next Door gasped.

"They're not vitamins," Heartthrob told her.

Looking past everyone, to Starlette, Wacky Best Friend asked, "What do we know about Co-Executive Producer?"

"Which one?" Starlette replied.

Wacky Best Friend looked to Heartthrob for the answer, but Heartthrob couldn't provide one. He just shrugged and said, "He had nice shoes."

"And apparently a drug store," Wacky Best Friend added.

"Can I have some?" Sassy Gay Friend asked, without a second thought or any hint of hesitation.

When everyone looked at Sassy Gay Friend as though he was made of 100% pure homegrown crazy, he shrank in his chair and quietly said, "Kidding."

The door opened and The Director walked into the room. He closed the door behind him.

Heartthrob put the plastic bag into one of the pockets of his cargo pants, and Wacky Best Friend quietly warned him, "Do not take those."

"If I was going to take them, would I have told you about them?" Heartthrob whispered back.

"Sorry for making you wait," The Director said.

"Heartthrob has drugs!" Sassy Gay Friend called out, like a kid tattling to the teacher.

"That's nice," The Director said and quickly moved on, saying, "As you can probably tell, this is a low profile shoot. We're going in guerrilla-style. No scouts. No background. Wacky Best Friend will be sitting this one out, while he gets reacclimated, so it will just be the four of you going in."

"What?" Girl Next Door asked. "No fair. Why can't you make Sassy Gay Friend get reacclimated?"

"It's cool," Wacky Best Friend told her. "I have some stuff to catch up on anyway."

"Can I just say that I am getting tired of her constant stream of hurtful, hateful, vitriolic diatribes?" Sassy Gay Friend complained, in a tone that suggested that he might cry.

"I'll show you hurtful," Girl Next Door fired back.

"Enough," The Director told them. "We don't have time for this right now. If you two don't think that you can work together on this shoot, we will find actors who can."

Girl Next Door straightened up and said, "No. We're good."

The Director looked to Sassy Gay Friend, who nodded slightly in agreement, though still moping. The Director then went on to say, "Good. Because this shoot will make or break our entire season. This is the first time in the year since the attacks that we have a lead on Bookworm. While he may not be at this location himself, we believe that this is one of the key hubs for his operations in this area and this site should house vital information. We're looking for anything on Bookworm himself, including his real name and any pictures. Most importantly, we need a location. Where is he now? Where are his bases around the world?"

"So basically, you want us to get everything there is to know," Starlette summed up.

"Yes," The Director nodded. "And there is no way to verbalize how important it is that you get this information back to us, by whatever means necessary."

The Director paused for a moment, to think about what he *wanted* to say and what he *needed* to say. When he spoke again, he told them, "We've never been inside a Bookworm stronghold before. You've never had this many minions on your ass at one time. Do not take this scene lightly. I cannot stress that point enough."

The Director went on to outline the shoot for them, working off of a script that he would not allow out of the conference room when they were done there. Because they wanted to prevent news of this shoot from leaking, only those who absolutely needed to know about it were filled in.

The Director brought up images on the monitors. These images were taken from Princedale University's website, prior to the attacks on the entertainment industry. The images featured a layout of the campus, as well as several images of supposed students who smiled as they went about their studies. Several of these supposed students were believed to be models and were probably now dead.

He ran down the areas of interest, which included the computer lab and the library. Since the attacks, the university's student population was believed to have dropped significantly as people fled the region. Regardless, the actors would be entering the university under the cover of night, when only a handful of classes were being held for those minions who had day jobs.

The meeting in the conference room lasted longer than normal, because this was not the time for improv. Since their scripts would not be leaving the conference room, each actor was required to know their part before leaving.

Once The Director was finished laying everything out, he reached into his pocket and pulled out a white plastic card, which had a microchip built into it. He placed it in front of Starlette.

"This is the card which you recovered from Michael Carter's residence. With luck, it will grant you access to the information that we're looking for... If not, this is what you need to take off of someone else in order to gain access to the information that we're looking for," The Director told her.

He ended the meeting by taking each script and shredding them. As the actors stood and prepared to leave the conference room, The Director said, "Girl Next Door, can you hang back for a moment?"

Girl Next Door seemed surprised at first and shot Starlette a look of concern. She stayed behind in the conference room as the rest of the actors began to walk toward their trailers. Their clothes for this shoot would not be provided by Wardrobe. They would be dressing themselves, with the goal of blending in with university students.

As they walked, Starlette grabbed Wacky Best Friend's arm and held him back so that she could speak with him and not be heard by anyone else. She spoke in a quiet tone and said, "Do you have things covered here?"

"I'm on my way to see if Tessa's awake now," he replied. "If I don't see you before you leave... Good luck."

"You too," she told him.

As they parted ways, Starlette got a nagging feeling in her gut. The last time she went on a shoot without him, he vanished. Though she would have liked to believe that the nagging was a result of what happened before, she couldn't help but feel as though this night would be more than a normal shoot and a happy return to The Studio.

On this night, their future would be dictated. If they succeeded, they stood the chance of reclaiming their former lives. If they failed, none of it would have meant anything.

~

Wacky Best Friend walked away from Starlette and started to walk toward the clinic. He wasn't sure exactly what he was expecting to discover when he asked Tessa about her attack, but whatever it was, he was sure that it would lead him on an interesting adventure.

As he walked, he spotted two crew members looking in the direction of the conference room. He heard one of them say "What a crazy bitch."

Naturally, this caused Wacky Best Friend to turn around. When he did, he saw Ember standing just outside the conference room. She wasn't walking; only looking around The Studio with an uncertain air about her. After a moment, she began to walk toward her trailer.

"I heard that she's pretty easy though," the second crew member said to his friend.

"Easy until you wake up in a pool of your own blood," the first one laughed.

"No wonder Heartthrob's always screaming," the second one quipped.

Wacky Best Friend laughed, which caused the two crew members to look in his direction. He wandered over to where they were standing and said, "*I heard a smacking sound and then a thud.*"

As the crew members looked at him with confusion in their eyes, Wacky Best Friend grabbed the first guy and smashed his face into the second guy's face. They both fell to the ground with a *thud*.

Wacky Best Friend continued on his way to the clinic.

Once he entered the clinic, he was greeted by Sympathetic Nurse. She asked him how he was doing and told him that she was sorry that she missed seeing him during his stay at the clinic. He had to wonder if she really believed the story about his being there the whole time, or if she was merely playing her part.

After the pleasantries, Sympathetic Nurse led Wacky Best Friend down the hallway, toward Tessa's room. She didn't go in with him.

As he entered the room, Wacky Best Friend expected to see the typical, brightly lit hospital set. Maybe there would be a heart monitor or a breathing machine involved. The reality was nothing like this, however. The room was dark, with only hints of light shining through the mostly-closed blinds which covered the windows.

If one were to open the windows they would find no view of the outside, of course. While some of the windows in The Studio had matte paintings outside of them, the clinic windows had panels of lights, made to resemble sunlight. These were hidden by frosted glass and blinds. Now those blinds were only barely open, and the light that shone through cut into the darkness like a knife.

Tessa sat in a wheelchair near one of these windows, looking through the blinds as though there were something to see.

Wacky Best Friend couldn't help but be impressed. Tessa oozed drama from every pore. She had taken that hospital room and transformed it into an extension of that drama. As he walked into that room, Wacky Best Friend half expected tension-filled background music to begin playing.

"Close the door," Tessa said, in a deep, quiet voice.

He closed the door behind him and stepped deeper into the room.

"Those are the footsteps of a man," Tessa said. "Not one of the clinic actors. You walk with purpose and control."

"You sit with drama and your ass," Wacky Best Friend replied.

Tessa chuckled slightly, still staring out the viewless window. She said, "You're back. Starlette was worried about you."

"I haven't introduced myself—"

"Wacky Best Friend," Tessa nodded. "Ethan."

"Yeah. I guess you've met the others."

"I have. None of them made me laugh."

"You should see me do my George Burns impersonation."

"Another time, perhaps. You've come for a reason."

"I have."

Tessa looked away from the window and turned her wheelchair so that she could face him. Now, the light was behind her and her hair seemed to glow while her face remained in shadows.

She said to him, "I'd ask if you brought any liquor, but I don't think the doctor types would approve of my drinking right now."

"I'll owe you."

"And I'll love you for it. What can I do for you?"

"Tell me about the person who attacked you."

"What's there to tell? I couldn't see her face, but she grunted like a whore during business hours each time she hit me."

"I wasn't expecting *that* mental image, but I'll take it," Wacky Best Friend quipped. "Do you remember what she was wearing?"

"Blue jeans, I think. But pockets on the legs, like those... What do you call them?"

"Cargo pants?"

"Sure. She wore a sweatshirt, but it didn't look too trashy on her, as they tend to do."

"And her belt?"

"A normal belt, I suppose. With two of those cell phone holsters that make you wonder if people know what pockets are for."

Wacky Best Friend had no idea what Jennifer was wearing when she was captured by Starlette. He would have to track down whatever records he could find of her interviews. But the more information he could get from Tessa, the better.

He pressed on, asking, "Did you see what her hair looked like?"

"She was wearing one of those ski masks that are all the rage with the villainous sort."

"Did she say anything when she attacked you?"

Tessa thought for a moment, trying to recall the details of the attack. As she did this, she put her hand on her ribs, as though they were made to hurt worse by the memories.

"She told me that she was a big fan," Tessa told him.

"She said that?"

"I'm not making it up, darling."

"Doesn't it strike you as odd that a woman who was beating the crap out of you was a fan?"

"It wasn't the thing that struck me the most," Tessa quipped in a dry sort of way. "But I do suppose that it was strange."

"Do you remember anything else about the attack?"

"Aside from the excruciating pain?"

"Yeah, aside from that."

"I'm sorry, but it just… happened. There was no matchbook left at the scene of the crime. No rambling monologue wherein my attacker detailed her every thought and motivation. It was what it was."

Wacky Best Friend tried to think of another question to ask her, but he was out of them. She had told him everything that she knew about the attacker, and she had done it with style. In fact, she didn't seem very traumatized at all. This realization intrigued him.

"You seem to be handling this all very well," he told her.

"Would you have me flinch every time someone came near?" she asked. "Perhaps I could cry a little bit. I could do that if you'd like, but I'd rather not slam my fists against any tables. I'm still sore, you know."

"You aren't curious?"

"Curious about what?"

"Curious about why she attacked you. Don't you want to know her motivation?"

Tessa smiled. She took a deep breath through her nose and closed her eyes as she released it. She then said, "I was ignored before the attacks. In spite of my long and honored career, I was left jobless and forgotten by studios and producers. Nobody wanted anything to do with me. I was ignored *during* the attacks. Forgotten, I suppose. Overlooked. I simply didn't matter."

"That's not right," Wacky Best Friend said, before quickly adding, "Not that I think you should have been killed. I just mean that most people didn't forget you."

"They didn't forget who I was. But nobody wanted to see me as an aging relic of Hollywood history," Tessa told him. "When Starlette first discovered me, I was thrilled to have someone to talk to. Someone to whom I could relate. Someone to mentor, perhaps. And you see, that was the problem."

"I don't see."

"I came into The Studio reluctantly. I didn't want anything to do with this place."

"Why?"

"Because I've seen it all before. In another form perhaps, but the same animal. They questioned me about my book deal, but that's not really what concerned them. They wanted to know whether or not I was going to play their game. They wanted to know if I was going to tell people what Hollywood was like, behind the scenes, during the so-called *Golden Age*. How they changed our names and our entire personalities. How they created illusions for the public to consume and forced us to hide who we really were.

"Even though I was a child, it was all about being what the audience wanted me to be. And when an actor couldn't handle that made-up life—when their minds simply wouldn't allow it— they did their best to alter those minds. They pumped actors full of drugs. They forced young actresses to have... 'procedures', all in order to preserve that golden image on the screen.

"They talk about the days when the government was looking for communists in Hollywood, and they act as though it's the most absurd idea in the world. The wonderful, brilliant part of that whole affair was that there *was* communism in Hollywood. Nothing in cahoots with the Russians or whatnot. But a regime of all their very own, and it was happening right before the eyes of everyone who paid the price of a ticket."

Wacky Best Friend allowed her thoughts to play out, with a reasonable amount of silence following them. He absorbed what she was saying, and took a deep breath before saying, "Wow. Just wow. That monologue was brilliantly delivered. You're a genius."

Tessa smiled and waved her hand through the air in order to thank him and play off the compliment.

"But we have a system in place to prevent this sort of exploitation. We have a union. We have people keeping an eye on our rights..." Wacky Best Friend said, more to hear her response than to voice a belief of his own.

"How long did that union exist before the Star System burned out the first time around?" Tessa asked. "For that matter, how often does your union—the people who are supposed to be looking out for *your* interests—make a decision that you disagree with but have no say in? You are a Republican, aren't you?"

Wacky Best Friend straightened up and his eyes widened. He said, "No. I'm—No."

His heart was pounding in his chest. His palms were sweating. Little in this world could cause him to panic by that point, but the threat of being found out and having his entire life's work thrown out the window made him feel like a deer in headlights.

As he reacted to Tessa, he realized that her point had been made. He lived in fear of being found out. He lived in denial of who he really was, and it was all because the system in place would not allow for his kind to survive.

Tessa smiled. She said, "Don't worry, dear. If I had a penny for every secret I've kept for Hollywood's elite, I would be far richer than I am today—Which is pretty fucking rich, I must say."

"Why would people stand for that kind of oppression?" Wacky Best Friend asked. "Why wouldn't they just walk away?"

Tessa's smile grew into a momentary laugh. She threw her

head back dramatically and then her smile faded and she looked at Wacky Best Friend with serious eyes.

"Could you just walk away?" she asked him. "Even after everything that's happened and everything you've been through, could you just turn your back on this industry?"

He looked down, and that was all the response he needed to give. Because both of the people in that room were true actors to the core of their being, they both knew that they would endure the pains of their industry, simply for the sake of being a part of it.

Tessa sat back in her chair and seemed to grow a little sad as she said, "I couldn't walk away either. They abuse us. They lie to us. They make us feel worthless, and we always come back to them.

He wanted to deny what she was saying, but he couldn't. It was true. As much as they may wish to hide from the fact, at the end of the day, they were all slaves to their craft.

~

Starlette, Girl Next Door, Heartthrob and Sassy Gay Friend had walked out of The Studio without drawing attention to themselves. As far as anyone in The Studio would know, Starlette would simply be going for one of her nighttime walks and her friends had just decided to tag along.

They had weapons tucked beneath their jackets, hidden from view of anyone who might have looked their way. They did not have dire, serious expressions on their faces as they left The Studio. They did not walk in slow motion to add an element of importance to what they were doing. They walked casually, and at full speed.

Once they left The Studio, the actors walked up the stairs which led to the outside world. The fresh air seemed cold on Starlette's face when she first stepped into it, but the air surrounding Hollywood could never really be considered cold.

Outside The Studio, a black SUV was parked. It was not normal for actors to drive themselves from The Studio to a location, but there could be no sign of strange activity, so even the drivers were left out of the loop. The Director had parked this SUV there himself.

In the back of the SUV, there were backpacks, which were

loaded with books that had been recovered from various locations in the past and kept by The Studio, just in case they needed props on a shoot.

Starlette wondered if The Director had informed Prop Master about what they were planning for that night. If so, she could probably find a few explosives or extra guns beneath the books. If not, she imagined that Prop Master would spend his night going crazy after realizing that some of his props were missing. He kept close tabs on what was stored in the prop department. She had no doubt that he would notice.

Starlette climbed into the passenger seat of the SUV. She had never been a big fan of driving, and would not be taking up the habit now.

Girl Next Door sat in back. She also refused to drive, though her objection was more about the fact that the SUV was needlessly guzzling gas and emitting dangerous greenhouse gasses into the atmosphere.

Behind the wheel, Heartthrob took his seat. He managed to grab that spot before Sassy Gay Friend could get the chance, so Sassy Gay Friend was forced to sit in back with Girl Next Door. Neither of them seemed pleased.

"Are we there yet?" Girl Next Door asked, before Heartthrob could even pull away from The Studio.

The car's navigation system was programmed with the address of the university. Once in the car, Starlette pressed the button which plotted their course, taking into account which route had the least traffic. Given the fact that they lived in a city where the streets were mostly empty, Starlette did not worry about being late to class.

~

Heartthrob parked the car down the street from the main entrance to the university. They did not want to drive down any streets which might have Bookworm minions roaming around, so they would make the last leg of the journey on foot.

The campus was surrounded by a large wall, with several gates that allowed access while sufficiently isolating the university population from the rest of the world.

Within the walls of the campus, large trees provided shade

during the day, and added cover for actors who were sneaking in during the night. Vines crept up the wall that surrounded the campus, as well as the walls of every building that housed classrooms and dormitories. While the fancy university campuses of the north might only have lush greenery during the spring and summer months, the campus of Princedale University was green year-round. The grass had been recently mowed, giving the area a deceptively welcoming scent.

It was quiet as they approached, which made Girl Next Door more uncomfortable than if there were air raid sirens blaring and spotlights swinging back and forth across the lawn.

Though she had not been on many college campuses in the past, Girl Next Door had always imagined that they would be more lively. She imagined music blasting and young people dressed in bed sheets that they were calling togas, running up and down the lawn, screaming and consuming vast amounts of alcohol. She imagined that college would be fun.

This was anything but fun. Most of the buildings that they walked past were completely dark. In the distance, one of the dorms seemed to be well populated, but there was no pop music bleeding through its walls. Instead, as they got closer to this dorm, Girl Next Door heard classical music playing loudly within.

Of course, she told herself, *Bookworm killed all the pop stars, but he appreciated orchestras and classical music. He hadn't killed any opera singers or violin players.*

She was nervous. More nervous than she had been about a shoot in a long while. This was bigger and more important than anything she had done since joining The Studio, which included the rescue of Heartthrob. Important as that may have been, it did not bring about the destruction of the Bookworm empire.

There were thoughts racing though Girl Next Door's mind as she followed Starlette and Heartthrob across the lawn. She thought about all of the things that she had neglected to do or say to people. She was about to enter a metaphorical hornets nest which was packed with angry, hostile villains. There was so much that she wanted to say to people, just in case, but there wasn't time. Starlette and Heartthrob were deeply in character and she dared not pull them aside for a chat.

Sassy Gay Friend, on the other hand, seemed to be strolling across the lawn like it was a sunny Sunday afternoon and he had not a care in the world.

She grabbed his arm and slowed him down so that she could talk with him, without Starlette or Heartthrob overhearing.

"Hold on a sec," she said. "I want to talk to you."

"Is this going to be one of those moments where you realize that you're a small-minded, hateful person and vow to change your ways? Because I love those scenes. Let me get my hanky," Sassy Gay Friend replied.

"No," Girl Next Door told him. "This is the moment where I'm going to try to overlook the fact that you're irritating as hell, and I'm going to try to relate to you as though you're an actual human being. Because I finally understand why you are the way you are —Which is not nearly as sassy as you could be, by the way."

"Oh, God. Please don't let this be a comment about the 'environment versus genetics' debate."

"I'm not talking about the gay thing. Well, I am, but I'm not. I'm talking about the reason why you're such an unbearable tool."

"Why is that?"

"I know your secret, Sassy Gay Friend," she said, in a voice that was even more quiet than before. "I know what you're hiding from everyone here. I know what you're living with every day of your life. The thing that you don't want anyone to know."

He tried to force a smile, but it didn't work. He tried to look as though he had no idea what she was talking about, but she could see vulnerability in his eyes. He was worried about what she was going to say.

"Don't worry. I'm not going to tell anyone," she assured him. "I've known ever since I read about it in that tabloid office, and I kept the paper out of the files we turned in to The Studio. It's none of their business. It's nobody's business, and if you don't want to share it with anyone, that's your prerogative. But I hope that you will, someday. I hope that you won't feel a need to hide who you really are, because I think that the person that's hiding in there might actually be pretty beautiful. Once you stop snapping at people and trying to impress The Studio so they won't ask questions—Once you can accept it yourself."

"Just shut up," he told her, looking as though he was about to cry. "I have no idea what you're talking about. You're high or something."

"You're straight, Sassy Gay Friend," she replied, as bluntly as she could. "And until you stop living this lie, you're going to be missing out on a real life. You're going to be missing out on the chance to love and be happy."

"I am not straight," he snapped. "Just shut up."

"I saw a picture of you. Kissing a woman," Girl Next Door told him.

"We've all experimented. Maybe it was before I came out," he fired back, defensively.

She could have pressed the issue even more. She could have pushed him into admitting the truth about who he was, but he wasn't ready for that truth. She could see in his eyes that he hadn't come to terms with it himself, so there was no way that he could be ready to share it with anyone. Pushing him would only make it harder. It would only drive him deeper into the closet. So, she pulled back.

"You're not ready," she acknowledged. "I get that. But I want you to know that when you are ready, I will be there to support you and to love you, no matter what happens. Because I know the *real* you. I can see it hiding behind this bully act."

He was on the verge of breaking down. He was vulnerable at a moment when they were going to be entering a highly dangerous environment. He could have fallen apart right then and there, but he chose not to. As soon as she was done talking, Sassy Gay Friend pulled himself together and became the person she had known all along.

"That would make it easy for you, wouldn't it?" he smirked. "If I were straight, you wouldn't have to deal with a disgusting homo anymore. I know how much you hate people like me. But I'm not like you. I'm *nothing* like you. I have talent. And flare. And I— unlike you—am absolutely fabulous. So, you can take your little homophobic self and you can sashay your ass right across that lawn and away from my sight. Because you, girlfriend, disgust me."

He threw a snap in her face, and shoved her hard enough to

nearly make her fall backwards as he walked away from her and caught up to Starlette and Heartthrob.

As she watched him go, Girl Next Door could no longer feel the blinding hatred that she had held for him before. Now, she felt sorry for him. Even more after talking to him than she had when she was holding his secret on her own.

No matter how he might try to hurt her, or annoy her, or bully her, or make The Studio hate her, she would only be able to see the scared person hiding behind that hostility; afraid to show the world who he really was.

She hurried to catch up to her co-stars—and her very special guest star—as they trekked across the campus lawn. As they made their way toward the heart of the university campus, they came closer and closer to that dorm room which was alive with the sound of classical music. Through the windows of the bottom floor, Girl Next Door could see much activity. There were shadows moving across the light. People were bouncing and spinning inside.

Either they were enduring a rather amusing form of combat training, or they were dancing the night away, while she and her fellow actors plotted to destroy the culture that they were attempting to build atop the rubble of the society that they had destroyed one year earlier.

It figured that they would be partying. Aside from being university students, they had a lot to celebrate, from their point of view. It had been a year since the attacks—almost to the day. Over the course of that year, the entertainment industry had been silenced. Aside from the battles which they fought from time to time, Hollywood was a fading memory in the minds of a world that was beginning to move on.

Bookworm was out to change the world. He was pushing books on innocent American citizens, whether they wanted them or not. He was replacing synthetic beats and auto-tuned pop divas with intricate melodies and soothing, raw talent. Girl Next Door appreciated black and white movies as much as the next girl, but Bookworm was bastardizing modern culture and it made her sick.

The closer she got to the dorm where that celebration was being held, the more she felt like crashing that party and burning everyone within that building to death, just as they had done to countless innocent industry professionals, who simply wanted to entertain the world and influence the way people thought and how they dressed.

She caught herself in this thought, and she was amazed by what she had become. A year and a half earlier, she would have thrown a bucket of red paint in her own face, and screamed at herself for being a baby killer, perpetuating the war machine that was destroying the world. Now, she was fantasizing about burning people alive after driving across town in an SUV that wasn't even a hybrid, much less an electric car which relied on no fossil fuel at all in order to power itself.

She had been urging Sassy Gay Friend to be honest with himself about who he really was, and the funny part to all of this was that she had no idea who *she* was anymore. None of what she did fit with what she once believed. She felt as though she was drowning and she had no idea which way was up.

~

Wacky Best Friend left Tessa in the clinic and tried to figure out where to go next. As he looked across the floor of The Studio, he watched the various actors and crew members going about their daily business and Tessa's words played in his mind, over and over again. He thought about how each of those people was given a specific role to play or a specific job to do in The Studio, and if they deviated from their assignment, they would be punished.

Tessa had spoken of the old Star System and how it had gotten out of hand. She spoke of the communist trials in Hollywood and the things which were overlooked. She filled his head with deep and meaningful thoughts about subjects that he didn't need to be thinking about in that particular moment.

He pushed those thoughts out of his mind. He tried to focus on the attack and what Tessa had told him about her assailant. He knew that it was a female, who Starlette suspected to be Jennifer. The woman wore a mask and said nothing, except that she was a big fan of Tessa's. Aside from the cell phones, there was little to go by.

There were papers back in his trailer which covered just about all of the developments that took place while he was away. He remembered seeing the breakdown of Jennifer's capture, but there were no pictures in that file. Police may have taken mug shots, but The Studio was not a police station, and unless you were an actor, there was no need for a headshot.

He thought about trying to review the footage from The Studio's cameras, but there were certain people that he did not want knowing about what he was doing. Even with his new status as a Producer, he could not access that footage without drawing attention to himself.

Closing his eyes, he tried to force his mind to work harder and to think of another piece to this puzzle. He ran through the conversation with Tessa again and again, but nothing about what she said jumped out at him.

When he opened his eyes, he was beginning to get annoyed with himself. He thought that he should have been able to figure out what was going on, just like all of those super smart TV Detectives, and he wished that he could have just gone over and asked them to help him out, but that would require bringing more people into this investigation. More people would mean more attention. He couldn't risk it.

"Think," he whispered to himself, but his brain refused to listen.

After failing to make any progress with the old *close your eyes and wish for it* method of investigation, Wacky Best Friend decided that he needed to change his approach. He was not a detective type. He would never be chosen to play a detective. What he was good at—aside from kicking ass, taking names, and remembering many pages of dialog at a time—was breaking down scripts. He could look at a script and his mind would project that story before his eyes. He could spot plot holes from a mile away. He could smooth out dialog that didn't seem to fit a character. Being able to connect with the script was what made him a good actor, and potentially a good writer. So, he took a different approach to his investigation. He looked at the story that had played out.

This time, when he played Tessa's comments back in his mind, Wacky Best Friend looked for mistakes. He looked for anything that didn't make sense to the story, and that was when he thought of the mask.

Thinking of the mask made him think of Wardrobe, and he remembered that everyone who came into The Studio after a shoot was photographed by Wardrobe, to make sure that she could match their outfit from that shoot at a later date, if needed.

He hurried to Wardrobe's department and went inside. He found Wardrobe sitting at a table, pinning a piece of fabric. Her back was to him as he entered, and she did not hear him.

"Wardrobe?" he said to her as he walked closer.

"Yes?"

"I need your help with something."

Wardrobe turned around and looked at Wacky Best Friend. She was looking over her glasses, which were sitting at the tip of her nose. There was a pencil tucked behind her ear, and a pin held between her lips, which she removed when she turned away from her project.

"I don't recall any shoots planned for you today," Wardrobe told him.

"There aren't any. I need your help finding information on a shoot that happened while I was away," Wacky Best Friend explained. "I was hoping to get a look at your binder. I'm trying to find out what the rogue agent's personal assistant was wearing when she was brought into The Studio."

Wardrobe stared at Wacky Best Friend for a moment and he wasn't sure that she was going to help him at first. There was no reason why she wouldn't help him, but Wardrobe always seemed annoyed with the actors that came into her department and it usually seemed like she was just a moment away from smacking them in the face.

After considering his request, Wardrobe stood from her chair and walked to a nearby desk, where several binders were sitting. She picked up one of those binders and began to flip through the plastic pages which held her photographs. After finding the picture that she was looking for, she turned the album around and held it out for Wacky Best Friend.

When he took the album from her, he saw the picture that he was looking for. He saw Jennifer being held by two Studio security guards. She did not look happy at all, but this was of little concern to Wacky Best Friend.

In the photo, Jennifer was wearing a pair of form fitting slacks and a white button-up blouse, which was tucked in. She had her belt with the cell phone holsters, but aside from this one detail, nothing that Jennifer was wearing in that picture resembled what Tessa had described of her attacker.

The look on his face must have told Wardrobe that he wasn't seeing what he was looking for, because she said, "Is something wrong?"

"I was just expecting to see something different," he told her.

"I'm sorry," she replied, taking the binder back and placing it on her desk. "If there's nothing else you need..."

"No, that's it," he said, as he started to turn and walk toward the door. After a second, he stopped himself and turned around. He asked, "Are you missing any ski masks?"

Wardrobe perked up when he mentioned this. She told him, "Yes, and I'm getting tired of people coming in here, thinking that they can browse the racks and take whatever they want. This isn't a store, after all."

"Is something else missing?"

"A pair of pants and a sweatshirt."

"Cargo jeans?"

"Yes."

"Tell me... Would those missing pants be around the right size to fit the personal assistant?"

Wardrobe thought about it for a moment and then confirmed, "Yes, they'd be about right."

Wacky Best Friend smiled and said to her, "I promise, whoever took those clothes will die tonight."

He then hurried for the door, as Wardrobe called out, "That's a bit much, isn't it?!"

~

They reached the point of their walk across the university lawn where they would be parting ways. Heartthrob and Sassy Gay Friend were tasked with investigating the computer lab, where they would be looking for any data that could be useful in their hunt for Bookworm.

Meanwhile Starlette and Girl Next Door were to go to the library that was located near the center of the campus. Since Bookworm's teachings were heavy on the literature and classical methods of learning, it was suspected that the library would be a key location for his minions.

As they prepared to part ways, Starlette allowed Girl Next Door to take a moment to say goodbye to Heartthrob. In their line of work, there was no knowing when tragedy would strike and she couldn't blame Girl Next Door for being worried about her man.

Truth was, Starlette didn't like the idea of letting Heartthrob lead the second unit at that particular moment. She was uncertain of his mental condition; a situation made worse by the fact that someone within The Studio had become concerned enough to take matters into their own hands and supply Heartthrob with drugs in order to keep him manageable.

Unfortunately, she didn't have much choice. Heartthrob was the male lead of their cast, and since Wacky Best Friend had other business to tend to, Heartthrob was the only option. Though Girl Next Door had more experience with Starlette, she was still classified as a supporting actress. The Studio did not have faith in her ability to take the lead on any location shoots.

Once they were on their way toward the library, Starlette and Girl Next Door decided on a much more stealthy approach than they had been using up to that point. The closer they got to that building, the more security they expected to encounter. There were only two of them by this point, and this was no time to slip up and risk the entire shoot because they were spotted just a little bit too early.

The library building was not the cozy little shack that Starlette always pictured when the word *library* was thrown into a conversation. There didn't seem to be any fireplaces that one could bundle up next to with a glass of brandy and a good book. This was a relatively modern looking building, with five levels. It was the only building that she had seen which was brightly lit and seemed to have a reasonable amount of activity surrounding it, though she imagined that it would be far more lively during the day.

She and Girl Next Door crouched behind a bush, looking at the library and craftng their plan for attack.

"Maps from their website show four public entrances. Figure at least a couple of fire exits on top of that," Girl Next Door said, in a low voice. "How do you want to do this?"

Starlette evaluated the situation and watched a man dressed in all black as he walked in front of the library. He reminded her of the first Bookworm minion that she had ever seen, but there was no way that it could be the same man. Most Bookworm minions looked the same to her, as though he could only afford to use the same dozen or so extras to fill out the scene. But he was not The Studio and they were not extras. The only conclusion that she could come to was that she was somewhat bigoted against Bookworm minions, and she was kinda okay with that.

"If we try to sneak around to a side entrance, we're more likely to draw attention to ourselves," Starlette told Girl Next Door.

"So, you're saying that we're..."

"Going in through the front door? Yeah. That's what I'm saying."

Starlette stood up and straightened her clothes. Girl Next Door did the same, though she seemed far less comfortable with this idea than Starlette.

"Try to look like you think you're smarter than everyone," Starlette told her, and they started to walk. "College kids always think they're smarter than everyone."

As they got closer to the library, Starlette adjusted the shoulder strap on her backpack, which suddenly felt heavier and more obvious than it had before. In the back of her mind, as she tried to prepare whatever character it was that she was planning to play, she began to wonder if the backpack was too much. It seemed like a reasonable prop to have on a university campus shoot, but if she were a Bookworm minion, would she be carrying a backpack?

There was no way of answering that question. She had never been in enemy territory like this before. She had encountered minions in other places, sure, but they were never going about their normal lives in those situations.

She began to wonder if they should be wearing all black, because all of the Bookworm minions that she'd encountered had a tendency to wear black. But once again, they were never in their natural environment when she came across them.

Despite the questions that were circling around her head, Starlette maintained a steady and confident pace. Girl Next Door actually had a pleasant smile on her face, which impressed Starlette, because she knew that Girl Next Door must be asking a dozen times the number of questions that Starlette was asking.

As they reached the sidewalk that led to the front door, Starlette spotted a minion standing guard at the door. The door itself had a fancy looking lock mechanism, which would require a special passkey. With luck, the card that Starlette had in her pocket would grant them access. If not, they would have to try to take out this minion and any others who might be in the area before they could alert the entire campus to the presence of the actors in their midst.

The minion at the door stood a little straighter when he saw the women walking toward him. He was a heavy guy, who seemed like he could inflict some damage if he knew how to use that weight to his advantage. He had neatly combed hair and no facial hair.

"What can I do for you ladies?" he asked them as they neared the door.

Starlette smiled at him and said, "If you want, you could do our work for us. That'd be great."

"Ah. Missing out on the big party tonight? I know how that feels," he replied. "So, what type of work are you doing?"

Starlette had no idea how to answer that question. She didn't seem to know what it was that Bookworm minions did when they weren't killing the people she loved. She assumed that there must have been some big plan, but she had no clue what the day-to-day business of that goal would look like.

"Oh, you know... Gathering some information that the boss might be able to use for that... y'know... *Tech*," she said, stumbling over her words. She then smiled and said, "Okay, maybe I went to the party for a couple of minutes. My brain isn't firing on all cylinders tonight."

"We're doing an in-depth study of the various ways in which the motion picture industry has savaged our nation and reduced our population to a pile of mindless goo that sits on couches and eats too much junk food. We're running a comparative analysis of some South American tribes which lack modern day luxuries and examining how their communities are better off for it," Girl Next Door chimed in.

Starlette wanted to hug her. With the bulk of her recent career being devoted to a more action-based genre, Starlette hadn't spent much time working on the smaller, quieter roles that would have helped her out in a situation like this. She felt like a fool, but Girl Next Door had her back.

"Wow," the guard replied to Girl Next Door. "That sounds like it could take a while. I'm actually kinda jealous. I haven't had a chance to hit the books in weeks."

"Well, we'll do enough hitting for everyone," Girl Next Door joked.

"Thanks," the guard replied and Starlette could have sworn that he had a smitten look in his eyes as he looked at Girl Next Door.

He stepped aside, to let them enter the building. Their first obstacle was out of the way, but Starlette still had to use the card to get into the building and if it didn't work, they were screwed.

She stepped up to the door and pulled the key from her pocket. She didn't hesitate to try scanning it, because if it didn't work, she wanted to get it over with as quickly as possible.

A light on the lock turned from red to green, and there was a *beep-beep-beep* sound to let them know that the card had scanned correctly. Starlette released the breath that she hadn't realized she'd been holding and she pushed the library door open.

They entered the library and the door closed behind them. The air inside was cool and heavily filtered. The smell of all-purpose cleaner was heavy in the air, bringing Starlette to the conclusion that the janitor had just left.

There were two people that she could see on the ground floor. Both appeared to be in their late twenties, well groomed, with their faces buried in books of some kind. They were taking notes and too focused on their own tasks to even notice that anyone else had entered the building.

The library had windows on all sides and was very well lit. Anyone who just happened to be passing by the building outside could glance over and see Starlette and Girl Next Door at any moment, which meant that they probably didn't want to do their work on the ground floor if given any other option.

As they walked deeper into the library, Girl Next Door grabbed a pamphlet from the librarian's desk and began to skim through it.

They made their way to the stairs in the center of the library, which led to the upper floors. It was a large, very exposed staircase, but they had no other options.

As they reached the landing for the second floor, Girl Next Door gestured for Starlette to keep walking up the stairs, to the third floor. Starlette didn't ask any questions. She simply walked as quickly and quietly as she possibly could without drawing attention to herself.

When they reached the third floor, Girl Next Door led the way to the maze of bookcases, which stood taller than either woman. Once they were standing between two of these bookcases, they were hidden from anyone who happened to walk by or look through the windows.

Girl Next Door showed Starlette the pamphlet, which had a map of the library's many levels and a detailed guide to which books could be found in which section. Starlette looked it over as Girl Next Door whispered to her.

"I think there's an administrative office on this floor, toward the back," Girl Next Door said, pausing for a moment, as though testing to see if her voice was echoing through the entire library before she continued. "If we can get in there, we can look through their files and systems without being seen."

"I agree," Starlette said.

Girl Next Door was about to fold up the pamphlet and put it away, but Starlette stopped her. She grabbed the pamphlet from Girl Next Door and examined it a little more closely.

"What are you looking for?" Girl Next Door asked.

Starlette pointed to the map of the library, noting the various entrances and exits. She said, "Aside from the main doors on the ground level, there are fire escapes through a few windows. Roof access..."

Starlette flipped the pamphlet over, and looked through it a little bit more, before adding, "There's a tunnel under the main level, which leads to one of the other buildings..."

Girl Next Door nodded as she followed along and said, "Plus, it has vending machines."

"Do you remember the exits, just in case?" Starlette asked her.

"I got it."

"Then let's go."

They quickly made their way through the maze of books, toward the back of the third floor. They saw no other people as they went along, and Starlette looked to the ceiling to see if there were security cameras, but she didn't spot any.

There was a door at the back of the third floor. When they reached that door, Starlette tested the knob. She was not surprised to find that it was locked. It was a simple lock, which would only take moments to pick, but those moments could lead to disaster if they were spotted.

Girl Next Door kept watch as Starlette pulled a lock pick set from her bag and got to work. Within seconds, the door was open. They entered and closed the door behind them as quickly as possible.

They hurried down a short hallway, which led to a much heavier door, secured by two deadbolts and one of the electronic security locks that they had encountered on the outside of the building. While this proved to them that this office contained something worth protecting, it also prevented them from just gliding into the office and taking whatever they wanted.

"I don't suppose that key card would work again?" Girl Next Door asked, though not very seriously.

"Michael Carter was a low level minion, keeping guard over Heartthrob. No way he'd have access to this. If we try to use it, the alarms could go off," Starlette responded, looking over the deadbolts.

Starlette took a moment to think and she studied the wall around the highly guarded door. As she ran her hand along the wall, stopping once or twice to softly knock on it, Girl Next Door stood by and watched the entrance to the hallway, just in case someone decided to do some late night paperwork.

"What are you thinking?" Girl Next Door asked.

"I'm thinking, I hope this doesn't make too much noise,"

Starlette replied as she knelt on the ground and pulled her backpack off of her shoulder. She put the pack on the ground and began to fish through it.

When she finally found the knife that she was looking for, Starlette remained kneeling on the floor and said, "Keep watch. This could take a while."

As Girl Next Door continued to watch, Starlette got to work. She did not stab the drywall, which would have made far too much noise. Instead, she used the tip of the knife to drill a hole in the wall. She would then try her best to gently saw a hole big enough for herself and Girl Next Door to climb through.

~

Wacky Best Friend walked into the prop department, making sure that nobody was behind him. Prop Master was not in the front area when Wacky Best Friend entered, so he wandered a little bit deeper and said, "Hello?"

"Hold on a sec," Prop Master replied, from the back room where all of the props were stored.

Wacky Best Friend waited for a few seconds, until Prop Master came out of that back room, wiping his hands down with a shop rag. He looked as though he had been hard at work with some sort of machinery, because his hands were covered in grease.

"What can I do for you?" Prop Master asked, wiping the sweat from his brow.

Wacky Best Friend wasn't sure how to approach the topic that he needed to discuss, so he tried to ease his way into it, saying, "Umm... Do you remember a while back, you kinda gave me a gun in case I needed to shoot my way out of The Studio and make a break for it?"

"Vaguely, yeah," Prop Master replied.

"Cool," Wacky Best Friend said. "So, do you think that I could maybe have another one?"

"Does this look like a fast food restaurant to you? Do you think you can just walk up to the counter, say *'give me the number three'* and I'll whip it right up for you?"

"I was kinda hoping it'd be like that."

Prop Master looked at Wacky Best Friend with hard, intimidating eyes for several seconds. He then said, "Yeah. I got a gun for you."

As Prop Master walked to his desk and opened a drawer to find the gun that he wanted to give to Wacky Best Friend, he said, "The last time I gave you one of these, you didn't use it."

"I was in the middle of a Studio full of people who could have taken me down with the wave of Studio Head's hand."

"So, I'm assumin' that's what *exhausted* you for all that time?"

"It was really stressful."

Prop Master handed Wacky Best Friend the gun, which Wacky Best Friend quickly tucked into his pants and covered with his shirt.

"Anything going on here that you want to tell me about?" Prop Master asked.

"It's probably better if I don't," Wacky Best Friend replied. "At least, not until I have more information."

"Is that what the gun's for?"

"Nine out of ten doctors recommend it."

"The gun's not logged. If you ditch it, there's no way it's tracing back to me. If you wipe it clean, it's not tracing back to you."

"Thanks."

"Be careful."

"If I were careful, I'd be dead by now."

Wacky Best Friend left Prop Master's department with a gun and the nagging feeling that he would be firing that gun by the end of the day.

Next, he went to the commissary. He wasn't interested in eating, but he knew the schedule of shift changes and lunch breaks for certain Studio employees, so he knew where to find them when he wanted them.

He sat in the commissary, at an empty table, and waited. It wouldn't be long.

Minutes later, a Studio security guard entered the commissary. His official name was Security Guard #17, but his co-workers just called him Danny. This was not the name that his mother had given him, as Studio policy dictated that stage names were required, but a name like Security Guard #17 wasn't exactly personal either. His fellow security guards had taken to calling him Danny Boy, due to the fact that he was Irish.

Danny didn't see Wacky Best Friend when he first entered the commissary. He walked to the counter and picked out his food, all while Wacky Best Friend kept an eye on him.

Once Danny was ready to sit down and turned to find a table to sit at, Wacky Best Friend raised his hand, urging Danny to come and sit with him.

Danny didn't seem pleased to see Wacky Best Friend, and did not want to sit down with him. He chose to sit at an empty table instead.

Wacky Best Friend rolled his eyes and walked over to Danny's table, where he sat down.

"See how that works? I can use these legs of mine to walk over here. It's pretty easy. Y'know, when I don't run into a cage wall or something," Wacky Best Friend said.

Wacky Best Friend had met Danny while serving his time in the vault. Danny was one of the few security guards with access to the vault; one of the few people in The Studio who even know that the vault existed.

During his time in the cage, Wacky Best Friend would shoot witty comments to the security guards as they made their rounds. In return, the security guards would slam their nightsticks against his cage and demand that he shut his mouth.

He rarely shut his mouth.

"Go on," Wacky Best Friend said to Danny. "Eat your food. Try to be quick though, we have plans."

"What the hell are you talking about?" Danny asked, looking around as though he didn't want to be seen talking to Wacky Best Friend.

"There's a chick in the vault. A personal assistant. You're going to bring me to see her."

Danny chuckled, "The hell I am."

"You are. Trust me."

"I don't take orders from someone at your level. My orders come from Studio Head himself. Anything else I do for anyone in this place, I do as a favor. And I ain't doing you any favors."

"Do you want to know who *my* orders come from?" Wacky Best Friend asked. He didn't wait for a response before saying, "My orders come from Starlette. As in, the person who could have you drawn and quartered by any person in this room right now, with nothing more than a nod and the sparkle in her eye."

Danny seemed unimpressed by the mention of Starlette. This didn't surprise Wacky Best Friend, since Danny spent most of his time locked in the vault, away from Studio headlines.

Wacky Best Friend saw an actor by the name of Androgynous Teen walking by with a bowl full of French fries. Androgynous Teen was about as innocent and harmless as anyone in The Studio. He had overly styled hair and wore skinny-jeans which Wacky Best Friend thought should be a federal crime for anyone who checked the *male* box on job applications, but he was a solid actor as far as Wacky Best Friend could tell. He waved the boy over.

"What's up?" Androgynous Teen asked with a smile.

Wacky Best Friend smiled back and said, "Not much... Say, let me ask you a question."

"Shoot," Androgynous Teen replied.

"Okay. Say I told you that Starlette needed someone in The Studio killed. She had her reasons, but they were confidential. What would you say to that?"

Androgynous Teen smiled, raised his hand and jokingly said, "Ooh, ooh, pick me! I'll do it!"

"Good boy," Wacky Best Friend said. "Now leave."

Androgynous Teen waved and left Wacky Best Friend to talk to Danny.

"That doesn't impress me," Danny said.

"It should. Because any one of these people would reply the same way. They trust Starlette to do what's right for this place," Wacky Best Friend told Danny. "And if I shot you dead right here, none of them would blink an eye. Because they know that I'm her co-star. I'm one of two—maybe three—people who she trusts without a doubt in this place."

Danny didn't respond. He started eating his meal, seemingly unmoved by Wacky Best Friend's argument. So, Wacky Best Friend took another approach.

"What if I told all of your buddies that you let the personal assistant out of her forced hiatus? What if I told them that she slipped through your fingers and wound up brutally attacking a beloved member of The Studio's acting community?"

Danny didn't seem to like the idea that someone had slipped out of the vault. Wacky Best Friend saw a question form in Danny's head, which he didn't want to speak aloud; at least, not to Wacky Best Friend.

Wacky Best Friend answered this question anyway, saying, "Tessa Baker. *The* Tessa Baker was attacked by a woman the other day. I've pieced together evidence from Tessa's description of the woman, along with Wardrobe's details about missing clothes, and I've determined that the attacker was a personal assistant, Jennifer, who we recently captured. She was supposed to be in the vault the entire time. That means that someone let her out. She attacked Tessa. And I'm assuming, someone snuck her back in. If it wasn't you, you have a crooked guard on your hands."

Danny put his food down. Despite his being a rather large asshole, in Wacky Best Friend's opinion, Danny was a guard with morals and standards. He would not stand for a traitor amongst his own co-workers.

Within minutes, they were on their way to the vault.

Shortly after reaching the vault, they found Jennifer's cage. Empty.

~

Heartthrob and Sassy Gay Friend crept across the university lawn, into an area that was perhaps even more dark and shadowy than what they had seen before.

The music from the dormitory building was just barely audible at this distance and they saw no Bookworm minions walking through the area, but they remained hidden and stealthy as they made their way toward the computer lab, just in case there were other methods of security that they were not aware of.

The two men did not say much to each other as they went along. Though Heartthrob had no serious issues with Sassy Gay Friend, aside from the fact that Sassy Gay Friend had destroyed the reputation of the woman that Heartthrob was falling in love with, he did not make pleasant conversation. While he was in charge, Heartthrob wanted to focus.

Sassy Gay Friend did not even try to change this. He stayed behind Heartthrob, practically mimicking Heartthrob's every move. He made no suggestions and offered no comments.

Heartthrob might as well have been doing his work alone, because he felt no backup coming from Sassy Gay Friend. He did not feel as though he could leave it up to Sassy Gay Friend to keep an eye out for Bookworm minions, so he kept his own eyes on the entire area.

Some people may have disliked a scene partner who did not pull their weight, but Heartthrob was fine with Sassy Gay Friend, just so long as he kept up and stayed out of the way.

As he neared the computer lab building, Heartthrob took cover behind a tree and scoped things out.

The building was dark. It looked as though nobody was inside, but he could not trust appearances. It looked as though there was no security, but he could not bet his life on that observation. He had to assume that such a valuable building would be monitored and that there were people inside.

They wouldn't be going through the front door. Assuming they could bypass and locks on the building, the front door would be the most heavily guarded entrance. Windows would be wired to any alarms, so they were out of the question as well.

Fortunately, there was a fire escape which Heartthrob could see near one of the second story windows. It led all the way to the roof, and on the roof there would most likely be a way of getting into the building.

He hurried across the lawn, with Sassy Gay Friend close behind him. *Very* close behind him. When Heartthrob stopped next to the building, Sassy Gay Friend nearly ran into him.

Heartthrob put up a hand, telling Sassy Gay Friend to step back as he reached for the retractable ladder of the fire escape.

As the ladder came down, it made far more noise than Heartthrob would have liked, but there seemed to be no reaction from inside the building. For the moment it looked as though nobody had heard the ladder.

Heartthrob made his way up the ladder, to the roof. Sassy Gay Friend joined him quickly, as Heartthrob was looking for a way to gain access to the building.

There was a door on the roof, which led into the building. Heartthrob considered using this door, but surely it would be locked and guarded.

There was an air vent not far from the door, which would provide a much less obvious entrance. It was possible that this entrance would not be guarded and they could make their way into the building without alerting anyone, assuming the sound of the ladder hadn't already done so.

Heartthrob opened the air vent with little difficulty and looked inside. It was wide enough for him to fit, but there was a fan between him and the inner duct. He quickly reached into his bag and pulled out a tool kit, which he used to remove the fan from the vent, and he tossed the fan onto the roof.

He climbed into the duct and pressed his legs and back against the sides, keeping himself from dropping into the building as he made his way downward.

Once inside, he found his way to a vent which was wide enough for him to drop out of. He opened it and dropped to the floor of a hallway within the computer lab building.

Sassy Gay Friend dropped soon after, landing with the stealth of a cat.

The hallway was dark and smelled of mildew. There was no sign of life, aside from something which sounded like a rat, scurrying in the distance.

They made their way through the computer lab building, quickly navigating the hallways and looking into the various rooms as they went along, expecting to find a massive computer system behind one of those doors, but they found nothing except silence. The few computers that remained behind were non-operational. Some had been ripped open and their components had been stripped.

In the last room that they searched, which was at the end of a long hallway on the ground floor, Heartthrob stopped to think. Obviously, there was nothing to find here, but it made no sense to him.

Sassy Gay Friend walked to one of the bookcases and looked through some of the empty boxes that littered its shelves. He pulled one box and looked it over. It was an empty video game box.

"I had a friend who did a voice for this game," Sassy Gay Friend said, not even trying to be quiet. He put the box back on the shelf and said, "He's dead now."

Heartthrob was beginning to understand. He looked to Sassy Gay Friend and said, "That's it… Computer geeks like the entertainment industry. They *like* streaming videos and pirating music. They *like* video games and comic book movies. They wouldn't be on Bookworm's team."

Sassy Gay Friend nodded in agreement and said, "Which means, anything that there is to find on this campus is probably in the library. Old school."

Heartthrob wanted to run out of the building and race to the library so that he could provide backup to Girl Next Door and Starlette, but he knew that he couldn't burst in there now. It was up to them to get the information on their own.

Sassy Gay Friend put his hands on his hips and said, "Well, at least this means that there was probably nobody around to reprogram the locks after y'all stole that key card from that guy."

~

It took Starlette a while, but she finally managed to create a hole in the drywall that was big enough for herself and Girl Next Door to slip through.

Once they were in the office, they turned on the lights. There were no windows. There was nothing to fear from turning on the lights.

The office was large and full of file cabinets, bookcases and a heavy wood desk, which had a computer sitting on it.

Starlette wasn't sure where to begin at first, but she had to keep her pace up and get through this quickly. She told Girl Next Door to look through the file cabinets, while she went to the desk and began looking through it.

Neither the desk nor the file cabinets were locked. Apparently, whoever worked in this office did not believe that there was a big outside threat that could find its way into the place. It was a fortunate mistake, as far as Starlette was concerned.

The desk was littered with mail, memos and protest literature —it was still a college campus after all. Sitting beneath a mess of papers, Starlette found a manuscript, bound together.

On the cover sheet of this manuscript, a note was scribbled. It read: *Howard, I would appreciate your thoughts and feedback. All the best, L.C.*

The title of this manuscript was *The Formation of the New American Society, Through Means of Media Transformation and Literary Education.*

It was a Bookworm manifesto. Starlette couldn't believe what she was holding in her hands. It was his formula for rebuilding what he had torn down; American society. And to make the situation even more surreal, the manuscript had the name of the author—the true identity of Bookworm himself—Professor Luscious Cartwright.

Starlette stared at that manuscript for a moment before saying to Girl Next Door, "His name is Luscious Cartwright."

Girl Next Door turned from her work and said, "Who? The guy who works here?"

"Bookworm," Starlette said. "We know who he is. We can take him down. This is it."

Girl Next Door's jaw dropped as her eyes shifted down to the manuscript in Starlette's hand. She didn't know what to say.

A moment passed and neither of the actresses moved. Finally, Girl Next Door looked to Starlette and with a puzzled expression asked, "Are you sure that's him? 'Cause I was expecting it to be someone we know. Doesn't the formula dictate that it be like some big, shocking reveal? I was sort of expecting it to be Tessa."

"You thought Tessa was Bookworm?"

"Kinda," Girl Next Door shrugged, seeming a just a tad disappointed. "Are we sure this Professor guy is really him?"

Starlette looked down at the manuscript as just a little bit of doubt sank in. She quickly shook off this doubt, reminding herself that this was real life, and not a television show. She shoved the manuscript in her backpack and said, "Keep working. We have to keep working."

Both of the actresses went back to work. Starlette skimmed through all of the papers on the desk, but found nothing. She then turned on the computer, but a password was required before she could search its files.

She wasn't sure what to do at first, but she remembered an episode of her television series in which her character was in a similar situation. She remembered her character looking for the password hidden somewhere nearby, so she began to look. She looked in the drawers and on the corkboard on the wall. She looked under the desk calendar, but found nothing.

She then looked where her character had found the password in that episode of her series; she looked under the stapler. There, she found the word *trebuchet* written on a piece of tape. She entered this password and was granted access to the computer.

She immediately went to the email program, because she wanted to see what business was going on at that moment. It was more urgent than looking through old files, she figured, and she was right.

There were many emails from Luscious Cartwright, ranging from casual conversation about the tides of their political revolution, to making dinner plans for the next time Cartwright was in town.

Most interestingly, there was an invitation. When Starlette opened this invitation, she immediately knew where this entire journey had been leading. She knew where the story would end. She knew where she would win back the life that had been taken from her.

A party was to be held in three days. This party would mark the one year anniversary of Bookworm's destruction of the entertainment industry. At this party, Bookworm would be honoring his financial backers, his most outstanding pupils, and those administrators who helped him manage his grand undertaking.

Starlette planned to be at that party, with bells on.

~

Upon finding Jennifer's cage empty, Danny pulled her file and looked it over. According to their records, she should still be in that cage. According to the checklist from the last patrol of the vault, Jennifer was present and accounted for.

This patrol had been conducted by Security Guard #7; also known as Mac, due to his fondness for macaroni and cheese.

Mac was still on duty when Danny led Wacky Best Friend to him. He was surprised to see Wacky Best Friend in the vault once again, and could tell at once that his being there was not a good thing.

Wacky Best Friend and Danny wasted no time in disabling Mac and locking him in one of the cages. Wacky Best Friend kept his gun aimed at Mac's head as they pressed him for answers.

Despite being threatened, Mac was not easily swayed. He resisted answering, and only chuckled when Danny called him a traitor.

After a bit of time, and after threats had turned to violence, Mac turned cocky. As he spit blood and told Wacky Best Friend that his days were numbered, Wacky Best Friend's suspicions were growing stronger.

He asked Mac, "How do you think our bosses are going to react when they hear what you did? Do you think they're going to let you walk away?"

He asked these questions in the standard interrogational tone, but he had another motive. He wanted to see the look in Mac's eyes when he was asked these questions. He wanted to hear the tone of his voice as he replied, regardless of what he said.

If eyes could smile, Mac's would have been as he looked up to Wacky Best Friend and said, "I'll just have to take my chances."

There was something about Mac during this questioning. He wasn't scared. He wasn't exactly defiant either. He was playing along. Wacky Best Friend was an actor. He was trained to add nuance and subtlety to his characters, but Mac was untrained. He could put on an act, but a real actor could easily see through it. He had the look and tone of someone who was trying to hide a surprise party from their friend; like he was in on a joke that Wacky Best Friend and Danny weren't supposed to get.

At this point, Wacky Best Friend was trying to confirm suspicions more than anything else. He knew who was behind all of this and what he had to do in response, but he was hoping for some solid, undeniable evidence before he did what he was planning to do. He wanted to know that he wasn't simply basing his reaction on grudges and hunches. He wanted confirmation, but confirmation wasn't coming. He would have to make the decision to press on in spite of this. He would have to trust his gut.

Turning to Danny, Wacky Best Friend said, "Put him in a cage and watch him."

"Where are you going?" Danny asked.

"You probably don't want details, just in case I lose this one," Wacky Best Friend replied. "But, um... Would you happen to know where Studio Head's office is?"

Danny told Wacky Best Friend where Studio Head's office was. After that, he read the confused expression on Wacky Best Friend's face and proceeded to draw him a map.

Wacky Best Friend left the vault and began the long walk through parts of The Studio that few crew members and no actors had ever walked. He walked through passages and down hallways that he never knew existed. Every step of the way, he felt as though he was being watched and would be attacked from behind at any moment, but when he turned around to take a look, nobody was there.

Outside of Studio Head's office, there was a rather nice reception area. There was a desk where a secretary sat during the day, but it was late now and she was gone for the night. Her computer had a plastic cover over it, similar to those once used to cover typewriters at the end of the workday.

To one side of the reception area, there was a water cooler, with paper cups stacked on top. Standing at the water cooler, with her back to Wacky Best Friend, was Jennifer. She was sipping water from one of the paper cups. He quietly leveled his gun at her.

As she crushed her cup and threw it in the garbage, she said, "Do you have an appointment?"

"Yeah," Wacky Best Friend replied. "It should be on the calendar; under *I have a gun to your head.*"

Jennifer grabbed the stack of paper cups and threw them back at Wacky Best Friend. He easily swatted them out of the way, but Jennifer took this opportunity to rush across the room, preparing for attack.

He took a shot at her, but his aim was off and he blew a hole in the water cooler instead. It began to soak the ground *glugging* away as it did so.

Jennifer grabbed his arm and tried to twist the gun out of it, but Wacky Best Friend kneed her in the gut and smacked her in the face with his elbow.

She recovered and punched him across the face. She tried to flip him to the ground next, but he surprised himself by kicking off of the secretary's desk and reversing the flip. He landed on his feet and threw Jennifer to the ground. While she was down, he tried to stomp her face with his boot, but she moved out of the way and grabbed his foot. With a twist, he was on the ground next to her.

He kicked toward her head, but missed and hit the desk instead. She flipped up to her feet and grabbed a letter opener from the secretary's desk. She went at Wacky Best Friend, screaming as she attempted to drive the letter opener through his chest.

Wacky Best Friend caught her before she could kill him, and held her there for a moment as he said, "So, I take it you found a new boss."

"Looks like," she replied.

"How's that working out for you?"

"The hours suck," she told him. "But there are benefits."

Wacky Best Friend kicked her off of him and got to his feet as she stumbled back. He prepared for her next attack, waiting for her to charge at him. He waited for several seconds before remembering that he had a gun in his hand.

As she started to rush toward him with the letter opener in hand, Wacky Best Friend could not properly aim, but he managed to avoid her letter opener attack and whacked her over the head with the butt of the gun.

She flopped over to the side and grabbed her head, but threw a kick which caught him off guard and sent his gun flying across the room. As the gun hit the floor, Jennifer was still holding onto her head, hunched over. Blood was pouring down her face and into her eye, making it impossible for her to see.

Wacky Best Friend did not give her a chance to recover. He grabbed her by the shirt and the belt with two cell phone holsters and he swung her around, sending her head-first into the water cooler. The half-empty jug of water fell on top of her, and she was out.

Wacky Best Friend walked over to her and kicked her foot, but Jennifer didn't move.

"You wait here," he told her, as he turned and walked toward Studio Head's office. He picked up his gun along the way.

He opened the door and walked through it without the least bit of hesitation.

Studio Head's office was a grand set indeed. It looked like a throwback to classic designs of the 1940's or 50's, with a full wet bar, club chairs and a fake view that would take a person's breath away if it were real.

To Wacky Best Friend's surprise, one wall of Studio Head's office was lined with shelves that were packed full of leather-bound books.

On the far side of the room, there was a large, heavy looking desk. Behind the desk, there was an older gentleman who wore an expensive suit. He was slightly heavier than Wacky Best Friend would have imagined. He had a beard, which seemed to be more for the purpose of hiding a double chin than anything else. It didn't work.

 Despite not meeting Wacky Best Friend's expectations on a physical level, it was obvious that this was Studio Head. He did not react to Wacky Best Friend entering the office and when he spoke, it was with that very level, somewhat robotic voice that Wacky Best Friend had grown to know very well.

"You seem to have found my office," Studio Head said. "I suppose it was only a matter of time."

"You had Tessa Baker attacked," Wacky Best Friend blurted, jumping right in.

"Did I?"

"Your new personal assistant wasn't exactly subtle."

"Nor efficient. If she'd done the job right, there would have been nobody alive that could have described her."

"I'd say you should fire her, but it seems kinda moot at this point in the game."

"Why? Do you plan to kill me?"

"I've been considering it, yeah."

Wacky Best Friend walked closer to Studio Head's desk. As he walked, he kept an eye on Studio Head's hands, which were on the desk. There was a stack of papers in front of him, and many gaudy, decorative objects. Wacky Best Friend's attention was immediately drawn to a gun that was sitting near Studio Head's hands. It was the same gun that Wacky Best Friend had taken off of one of Bookworm's minions on the night that they rescued Heartthrob.

"You recognize it?" Studio Head asked.

"Yes."

As Wacky Best Friend looked at the gun, he began to wonder why it was there. Why would Studio Head keep such an unimportant piece of evidence?

He then recalled the meeting in the conference room, shortly before he was sent to the vault. He remembered an image of this gun and the knife that he found appearing on a monitor, but the items themselves were not in the room. They were taken from Wacky Best Friend's trailer and apparently brought directly to Studio Head. But why?

Placing this much attention on the gun brought Wacky Best Friend to a realization. He had been under the impression that he was locked away because he had broken character by submitting a spec script. Now, he wasn't so sure.

"This is why you did it," Wacky Best Friend said, as that realization came over him. "This is why you locked me up."

"I regret letting you go now," Studio Head said in a matter-of-fact tone. "At the time, it was a choice between the entire Studio being up in arms, or one lowly supporting actor. Apparently, I made the wrong decision."

Wacky Best Friend wasn't listening to what Studio Head was saying. He was still focused on the gun. He said, "The inscription..."

Though he knew it was of some importance, he didn't know what that importance was. Not right away.

As he tried to piece everything together, his eyes wandered to the wall behind Studio Head. There, he saw a degree from Princedale University.

Still confused, he said, "You went to Princedale?"

"I did," Studio Head said, getting out of his chair and walking to the wet bar.

Wacky Best Friend kept his gun aimed at Studio Head, but he was more interested in getting answers than killing him at that particular moment.

"You're a Bookworm minion?" Wacky Best Friend asked.

Studio Head laughed. It was unnatural and wrong for a man with his lack of personality, but he laughed. He said to Wacky Best Friend, "No. No, I'm not a minion. I simply knew the man years ago. We were roommates in college; friends in our youth."

"The gun?"

"A gag gift that I gave him when we were in school. The quote inscribed on it—"

Wacky Best Friend cut in, reciting the quote from memory, "'What strange developments of humanity, what wonderful advances upon our rudimentary civilization, I thought, might not appear when I came to look nearly into the dim elusive world that raced and fluctuated before my eyes...'"

"From *The Time Machine*. The book. It was supposed to be a joke at the time, putting it on a gun like that," Studio Head said. "I never thought he'd take it so seriously."

"He was there? He was in the same building as Heartthrob?" Wacky Best Friend asked, "I fought Bookworm?"

The more pieces that fit together in Wacky Best Friend's head, and the clearer the larger picture became, the more he realized that this situation had become so much bigger than he had ever imagined. He thought that Tessa was attacked because Studio Head was power hungry, but now his suspicion was growing into something entirely different. His perspective had shifted so quickly that he was still having a hard time keeping up with it.

As he tried to make sense of all of this information in his own mind, Wacky Best Friend asked, "Did you know about the attacks? Before they happened?"

Studio Head took a sip of his rum, which he had splashed with cranberry juice, and he replied, "It's not like I was *in* on them. I haven't spoken to the man in years. I didn't plan them. I didn't carry them out. I didn't even necessarily *want* them to happen, but there was nothing I could do to stop them. So... I did this. I prepared."

As Wacky Best Friend absorbed Studio Head's response, he could feel his trigger finger growing itchy.

~

Based on the information that Starlette found on the computer of the person who had, in her mind, come to be known as The Librarian, Girl Next Door's search of the file cabinets had become more specific. She was now looking for any information that she could find on investors that would be invited to Bookworm's party.

Given the number of filing cabinets, Starlette expected Girl Next Door's search to take longer. She was looking through computer files, trying to find anything of use, as Girl Next Door worked. But her search of the computer didn't last long.

"Got it," Girl Next Door said, pulling a stack of files from the cabinet and bringing them to the desk.

Starlette stood and began to look over the files with Girl Next Door. The papers were tax forms. Apparently, Bookworm's cause had found support from several politicians who pushed through the paperwork necessary to have a division of Bookworm's empire considered a religious institution, thereby making donations to his cause tax deductible.

"Seriously?" Girl Next Door muttered as she looked over these forms. "They're seriously siding with the guy who killed thousands of people all over the world?"

"It's not about siding with him. It's about fear. They don't fear us because they know that we're not the ones who are going to hunt them down and kill them. We just want our lives back. Bookworm has a way of slaughtering those who don't comply with him," Starlette replied. "He took out Hollywood. Who's to say he couldn't take down Washington?"

"Who's to say that some of his students aren't already there?" Girl Next Door pondered.

"We have to get this information back to The Studio."

Starlette began to shove papers into her bag, which was becoming quite full. Once she had everything that they needed, she and Girl Next Door closed out all of the e-mails that they had opened and the file cabinets that they had searched through. They didn't want to make it very obvious that they had discovered what they had discovered. With luck, The Librarian would have to scramble and search his entire office, trying to figure out what was taken. This would give The Studio time to plan their attack.

Girl Next Door was the first one to leave the office, through the hole in the wall. Once she was out, Starlette shoved the backpack through the hole and proceeded to climb out herself.

In the hallway, there was a large potted plant. For the sake of slightly slowing down any investigation into what they had done there, Starlette pulled that potted plant in front of the hole in the wall. With luck, nobody would notice that hole until The Librarian got to work in the morning.

Girl Next Door led the way down the hallway and through the door which would take them back to the main library. If things had gone smoothly, the actresses would have been able to walk down the stairs and slip out of the library without drawing any attention to themselves. However, things did not go smoothly.

As soon as Girl Next Door left the hallway and reentered the public area of the library, she stopped short and her eyes widened. Starlette stopped short as well, though she couldn't see what Girl Next Door was reacting to.

"Actor!" came a male voice from the library. "We have an actor up here!"

Girl Next Door pulled a gun from her bag and fired one shot, killing the man who was screaming. The gunshot echoes throughout the entire library.

An alarm began to sound. Within seconds, Bookworm minions would be pouring into the library and up the stairs. The actresses had to think fast.

"Let's go!" Starlette said to Girl Next Door as she hurried toward one of the fire escapes.

When they reached the window which led to the fire escape, Starlette turned its lock and forced it open. She stepped aside, to allow Girl Next Door to leave before her.

Girl Next Door didn't move.

When Starlette realized this, she turned around and said, "Let's go! Move!"

Girl Next Door's eyes locked onto Starlette, filling with tears. In that moment, she was not quirky or fun. Her voice was oddly commanding as she said, "I'm not going. You go."

"Girl Next Door, I told you to move. Now!" Starlette insisted, grabbing Girl Next Door's arm, but Girl Next Door pulled free.

"Listen to me," Girl Next Door said, trying her best to hold back her emotions. "They know there's one of us in here. They're not going to stop looking until they get someone. This is where they live. There are too many of them. We can't both get out. You *know* that. One of us needs to distract them... *I* need to distract them."

Starlette was trying to think of an argument, but adrenaline was pumping and her mind wasn't clear. Obviously, there had to be another way to end this scene. There needed to be some clever improv that she could whip up, or a line of dialogue that she was forgetting from the script, but nothing came to her. She felt powerless.

They could hear minions rushing up the stairs below. They would be on top of the actresses at any moment.

"I'll stay," Starlette insisted, tensing every muscle in her body. "You go. Get this information back to The Studio."

Girl Next Door shook her head and told Starlette with pride, "They need you. They need you to lead them out of this fight and back into the world. They don't need me..." Tears began to roll down Girl Next Door's cheek as she finished, forcing out the words, "They don't even *like* me."

For the first time in a year, Starlette could feel herself fighting back tears of her own. She shook her head and said, "No. No, I'm not leaving you. We'll die her together if we have to, but I will *not* leave you."

"I know," Ember told her, smiling warmly.

Girl Next Door punched Starlette in the face as hard as she could, throwing Starlette off balance. She then shoved Starlette through the window and locked her out.

As Starlette scrambled to get back to her feet, she saw Ember press her hand against the glass for just a moment before turning and rushing toward the library's staircase.

Starlette threw herself against the glass, trying to scream and kick and find some way to fight back against this, but there was no fight to be had.

Girl Next Door was gone.

~

"It started with letters," Studio Head said. "We got threatening letters all the time. I didn't believe any of them. Not at first. But they kept coming. And then, they became more specific. Finally, I realized who was sending them. I knew then what was going to happen."

"And you didn't tell anybody?" Wacky Best Friend asked.

"I didn't have time. What he was doing took *years*. It was global. There was no way to stop it, so I prepared The Studio. I decided that if *he* was going to take out the industry, *I* would put it back together. I would restore it to its former glory."

"Like this? By controlling people? By keeping them locked up and suffering?"

"Look at what we've created here. Look at the people you work with. Aside from Girl Next Door, there have been no major scandals. No sex tapes. No reality shows. We are on our way to becoming the Hollywood that existed years ago. The true icon."

"You're insane. You could have stopped this. You could have saved lives with one phone call, but you didn't. You chose to let those attacks take place and when I was starting to get to close, you had me locked up. When Tessa was threatening to remind people about what we were becoming, you tried to have her killed..." Wacky Best Friend started.

As he said these things, Wacky Best Friend came to a realization. He stopped dead in his tracks and his heart tightened in his chest.

After taking a moment, he asked, "Why did you mention Girl Next Door?"

Studio Head did not reply.

"Answer me!" Wacky Best Friend demanded, reaffirming his aim at Studio Head's head.

Studio Head remained silent, but his eyes drifted toward his desk. When Wacky Best Friend turned and looked at the desk, he saw that there were a couple sheets of paper which stood out amongst the stacks of papers. These sheets of paper were red.

"Red pages..." Wacky Best Friend said to himself as he walked to the desk and picked them up. As he realized what they were, he said, "An alternate ending."

"We can rebuild what we once had," Studio Head told him. "But not all of us will survive. Some will need to be sacrificed for the greater good."

Wacky Best Friend read the pages, and he remembered seeing Girl Next Door walk out of The Director's office after their meeting. He remembered the look that she had in her eyes, and in that moment, he knew that she had been ordered to make sure that the information was recovered, even if it meant sacrificing herself.

The blood drained from his limbs. Everything around him seemed to grow darker.

"You son of a bitch," Wacky Best Friend said under his breath, finding that his normal voice was failing him.

He then looked back to Studio Head and pulled the trigger of his gun, over and over again. With each pull of the trigger, the reality of the situation sank in just a little bit more. With each pull, his rage grew. With each pull, he choked back the urge to vomit.

Studio Head fell backwards and slumped to the ground, dead. Blood stained the wall behind him, and then the ground beneath him. The smell of urine filled the room.

For all the power that he wielded and all of the calm that he had tried to convey, Studio Head's biopic would end on the floor, soaked in bodily fluids.

"Fuck your greater good," Wacky Best Friend said, and he ran out of the office.

~

Starlette climbed down the fire escape as quickly as she could. Through the windows of the library, she could see Girl Next Door rush down a section of the stairs before leaping over the banister and landing on the ground floor.

Bookworm minions were pouring through the front door. There were dozens of them. Far more than Girl Next Door could handle on her own. Even more than the two of them could have handled together.

As Starlette reached the ground, minions were beginning to hurry around the sides of the building, to secure the perimeter, but Starlette was hidden behind bushes and trees. She could put distance between herself and the library without being seen.

She kept to the shadows and made her escape, only stopping to turn around once as she went.

When she turned, she could see through the windows of the library. She saw Girl Next Door putting up a fight, spinning and kicking and flipping. She saw her fire her gun and take down more than one minion. She made Starlette proud, and then she made Starlette cry.

Starlette then saw Girl Next Door disabled. Several of the minions fired their weapons at her, and Girl Next Door fell to the ground, out of view. Minions swarmed over her like ants over a discarded lollipop.

Through all of this, Starlette heard no gunshots as the minions fired on Girl Next Door. She saw no blood. She saw no body. She was in shock and unable to process any of what was happening around her. All she knew was that she needed to get that information back to The Studio.

~

Wacky Best Friend's heart was pounding in his chest. He could hear it pounding in his ears. Though he was running as fast as his legs would carry him, *running* was not the reason for his pounding heart.

He was in the far reaches of The Studio, away from where the actors and crew members lived and worked. He wanted to be back there and to do something that could help Girl Next Door, but he was helpless. He couldn't move fast enough.

The world seemed to slow down around him. Each step that he took seemed to take minutes.

As he ran, he tried to talk himself out of believing what was happening. He told himself that Heartthrob had already been held hostage once. He himself had gone missing. Tessa had been attacked. To have Girl Next Door killed would be *stupid*. It would be *redundant*. It would be horrible, horrible writing.

He then remembered who Head Writer was and he tried to run faster, but his legs simply could not do it.

~

Starlette ran across the campus lawn with her backpack on her shoulder. She found Heartthrob and Sassy Gay Friend waiting for her as she neared the spot where they last saw each other.

"Go!" Starlette demanded as she neared them.

She did not want to stop. She didn't want Bookworm's minions to have time to catch them, but more than that, she feared that if they slowed down, none of them would be able to start moving again.

Heartthrob did not start running. He looked around and asked, "Where is she?"

Starlette wanted to keep moving more than anything in the world at that point. She would have given anything to not have to face Heartthrob, but she couldn't stop that moment from coming.

She stopped running, but couldn't look at him as she said, "She's not coming."

"What? Why? Where is she?" Heartthrob asked, as though he didn't understand. But Starlette knew that he understood all too well.

She told him, "We have to go. We have to leave now."

"We have to go back. We have to get her," Heartthrob insisted, as he began moving toward the library.

Starlette grabbed his arm, and though he tried to pull away, she would not let go. She caught a glimpse of his eyes as he spun around. She saw the desperation in them; the rage. She could tell that he wanted to hit her, but he held back. Instead, he grabbed her hand and pulled it from his arm.

"I'm going. You can leave me if you want to, but I will not abandon her. I won't let her—"

He couldn't even bring himself to finish that sentence. Instead, he began to walk away from Starlette.

Starlette rushed to get ahead of Heartthrob. She stood in his path and asked him, "Do you think I would? Do you think I just decided to walk out of there?"

Heartthrob didn't answer. He also didn't throw her to the ground and keep walking. Instead, he stopped and listened, though he hated every word that came out of her mouth.

"She gave herself up because she believed that we had to get this information back to The Studio. She did it to save us... It's too late for her right now. If we go back there, we lose and she did this for nothing," Starlette told him, lying to herself as much as she was to him. What happened to Girl Next Door was senseless, but it was over. There was no going back.

In that moment, as Heartthrob realized what was happening, Starlette saw him slip away. Whatever he had been hanging onto —whatever had prevented him from going insane up to this point —was gone.

~

Wacky Best Friend was getting closer. He was once again amongst the casts and crew of The Studio and he would soon reach The Director's office. He wasn't sure exactly what he would say once he got there. He knew that The Director must have been aware of the red pages.

He imagined that he would yell and scream at The Director. He wanted to beat the crap out of Head Writer. He wanted to get into a van and rush to the university, so he could prevent that scene from going down.

He was a *Producer* now. There had to be something he could do to change things. Studio Head was gone. The way things had been done was no longer the way they had to be done. Nobody needed to be sacrificed for the sake of The Studio.

He would fight. He would hit anyone that he had to hit. He would shoot anyone that he had to shoot. He would kill as many people as he needed to kill, but he would not allow Girl Next Door to go down like this. She was too good... She was the best of them.

As he neared The Director's office, Wacky Best Friend was stopped in his tracks.

Starlette, Heartthrob and Sassy Gay Friend were standing with The Director. They had returned from their shoot, and Girl Next Door was not with them.

Wacky Best Friend felt the air leave his lungs. He fell to his knees.

He had lost.

Around The Studio, word of Starlette's shoot was spreading. People came from all around and looked at the stack of information that was recovered.

Cheers erupted.

A celebration began.

Chapter Thirteen
THE FINAL CHAPTER

8:23 AM...

The morning sun shone most brightly through the back window of the Hume house. As its rays reflected off of the swimming pool water, it caused the light that bathed the living room to dance across the walls in wavy, shimmering patterns.

Nancy Hume was at a full jog on her treadmill that morning, as she was on most mornings. She believed in taking care of one's self; mind, body and... well, she didn't believe in anything like a soul, but she believed in the human spirit. She believed in persistence, and unrelenting determination. She believed that the world would only ever be as good or beautiful as each person tried to make it.

She was firm in her political beliefs, as well as her philosophical. She did not believe in holding back and trying to be polite when someone disagreed with her. She did not believe in pretending that certain beliefs were not childish, foolish and absolutely insane.

Was she a bigot? Well, if being of strong will and conviction made someone a bigot, then she would be most happy to accept that title, but she did not see herself in that light. She saw herself as being in a unique position. She had been raised with enough money to attend the best schools. She had studied under the best professors. She had seen what a difference those great minds could make in the world, and she was caring enough to want to spread the wealth of her education to everyone in the world. The uninformed masses who had been polluted for decades by mindless forms of entertainment had no idea what they were missing. They could not see the world as it was, only as it was presented to them.

She hoped to change that. She was a humanitarian, on a mission of relief from the unnatural disaster that was the Hollywood machine.

Everyone knew that tobacco was poison. Everyone important knew that mankind was destroying the environment and that something must be done to prevent its complete annihilation. Everyone knew that the hungry should be fed and the poor should be sheltered. Everyone knew that the sick deserved to be cured. These causes held no interest for Nancy. She would cut a check here and there in support of a worthy cause that could handle the heavy lifting on those fronts, but most of her money and most of her support went to her primary cause.

Different people had different names for it. There were several branches of the cause—it was a full cultural revolution after all—but the term which best encompassed the movement in Nancy's eyes was: *Awakening*.

It was an awakening from the slumber that the world had been in for far too long. It was an awakening of the mind. It was an opening of the eyes. It was the dawn of a new day.

Nancy was hardly the most influential member of this cause.

She wasn't even high ranking. She was simply an observer of the great things that were unfolding, and by giving of herself—that is to say, her money—Nancy could claim some small piece of that awakening as her own.

The sun was shining. The birds were chirping. It had been a year since the beginning of the revolution and thus far, everything was going swimmingly.

To commemorate the anniversary of the cultural revolution, the founder of her cause, Professor Luscious Cartwright was going to be holding a party. There would be wine and the honoring of key members of their movement. There would be celebration of all that they had accomplished.

Nancy had known Professor Cartwright for years. He was a teacher of hers when she went to college, and she would spend every day of his class in awe of his vision. He had taken the clay of her mind and sculpted it into a work of art, capable of thinking freely and forming educated opinions about matters which she never could have considered before.

To that very day—even as she entered her late 20's—Nancy would read Professor Cartwight's thoughts and opinions on a subject and she would be amazed with how true and pure they rang inside of her, though she hadn't even been able to convey those feelings before.

He was a genius, and it put a smile on her face to see the world changing around them.

When Nancy's parents died, she inherited a fortune. Her father had been a high ranking employee of an oil company and now that Nancy could get her hands on his money, she could finally use some of it to undo the damage caused by his kind of people.

After setting aside enough money for herself to live comfortably on for a few decades—a mere hundred and fifty million or so—Nancy used the remaining five million to further Professor Cartwright's cause.

She was looking forward to attending his gala. Though he probably wouldn't even recognize her, given her shyness and knack for sitting in the back of his classroom back in her college days, she wanted to be there to commemorate that truly momentous event.

She had a million things to do. She had to get her dress from the dry cleaner. She had to get her date's tux from the tailor. She had to get her date from the escort service. She had some time to kill, but she could not wait for that night to come. She imagined herself as *Cinderella*, going to the ball.

She was picturing the *Cinderella* of the book, not from a movie, of course.

As she jogged on the treadmill, she imagined how the evening might play out and she could almost see it before her eyes.

What she didn't see was the dark figure walking through the room behind her.

~

12:52 PM...

Robert Forester was a business man, plain and simple. He prided himself on his talent for numbers and his bold grasp of logic and reason. There was no room for imagination. There was no justification for spending countless hours glued to a television. There was only time for the things that mattered; the things that you could hold in your hands and use to put food on the table.

His boyfriend felt the same way... or, he did before he left Robert for a younger model. But Robert didn't mind being alone. He was pushing thirty and had his whole life ahead of him. Sure, almost nobody had seen him outside of the office in nearly a decade, but what did that matter? It wasn't as though he hadn't made a difference. He was important.

When Robert was in college, he attended the lectures of Professor Luscious Cartwright and he listened to the man go on about the corruption of the human mind. It was so true. So much time had been wasted by so many people; time that could have been spent doing something truly important, like solving world hunger or finally proving the theory of evolution once and for all, so that those stupid religious types would shut the fuck up.

It infuriated him to no end. It drove him mad to think that people would put their faith in God and Hollywood. This was why Robert volunteered to be a part of Professor Cartwright's anti-religious sect, dubbed *Ritual Atheism* for the purpose of attaining a tax exempt status. Ritual Atheism was not a religion, though they were claiming to be. They were the lack of religion. They held meetings to discuss their joint belief in the non-existence of a higher being. They lit candles to represent what was true and provable in the world; that fire is the result of matter changing from a solid to a gas, and not some magic as those religious types would have people believe. They recited pre-written chants in unison, to focus their minds on the fact that religious people were strange and did stupid things.

If Robert had gotten his way, the cultural revolution would have taken out religions right along with Hollywood, but this would have threatened their tax exempt status and their government connections assured them that attacking religious institutions would surely see them labeled as terrorists, even if their cause was just and noble.

It didn't matter. Their intellectual views on religion were merely one facet of the overall doctrine of Professor Luscious Cartwright. It was one aspect of society that would have to be reformed once their movement took root. Once the world returned its attention to true worldly concerns and stopped distracting themselves with mindless Hollywood entertainment, progress of the mind would leave no option but to accept the truth. There was only what we could see and touch and prove, and nothing else.

In the months following the attacks, libraries across the country had seen a boom in their business. People were reading once again. They were opening their minds to ideas that they might not have before. They were learning to live in the world that Hollywood had taken away from them, and this warmed Robert's heart. It made him feel hope, where hope hadn't existed in a very long time.

He accepted that people would be reading fiction, as well as non-fiction. He didn't like the fact that Professor Cartwright was allowing an industry which had been in cahoots with the Hollywood machine for so long to continue, but he accepted that reading was the gathering of information and the planting ground of thought. He accepted that even works of fiction—save for insipid serials—opened the minds of the reader to new ideas and made them think. It was far different than movies or television or pop music, which asked their audience to tune the world out and stop thinking for the duration.

In Professor Cartwright's world, people were brought off of their couches and into the world.

Hallelujah! Robert thought to himself, in a purely rational and logical, non-religious way, of course.

He sat in his office, atop a twenty-five story building and he looked out across the world. He drank it in. From this office, he had filed the paperwork necessary to secure transportation and housing for Professor Cartwright's soldiers on the ground. From that very office, Robert had played his part in the revolution which was one year in progress and looking fine.

He couldn't wait to attend the event which would honor the work of Professor Cartwright and all of those who joined together in their common goal, to take down Hollywood. It would be his first time attending such an event. His work was normally done in solitude, but he could feel the brotherhood of all those others. He dreamed of embracing those brothers and never letting go.

As he dreamed of the night that would soon come to be, his mind wandered toward all of the possibilities. The future was bright and he was a part of something truly great. His parents would have been so proud, if he hadn't killed them and hidden their bodies years earlier because of their ridiculously outdated belief in gods and mystics. Luckily, their film careers had dwindled long before he killed them, so nobody ever even noticed that they were gone.

All that went unnoticed now was the shadowy figure that slipped through his office door as he took in the view outside.

~

5:16 PM...

Howie Pavel lived a secluded life. He didn't want to see anyone or talk to anyone on most days. He preferred to spend his time with books and numbers. He enjoyed the security of knowing that books were always the same and numbers were always reliable. People were not. People were unpredictable. They died. They cheated. They became obsessed with pretty-boy vampires who had absolutely no logical reason for not being the demonic killers that vampires were meant to be.

It made no sense!

When Howie was younger, he was what most people would consider normal. Though, if you were to ask him now, he would have told you that *normal* wasn't normal. Normal was flawed.

There was a time in his life when Howie enjoyed parties and dating girls and having a good time. There was a time before his eyes were opened to the realities of the world, when he could spend hours enthralled by the projections of life, as seen through the eyes of Hollywood professionals. They were liars. They were manipulators. They played the emotions of their audience, but there was no logic to it; no reason.

Sex sells. Violence sells. The people weren't real, and the more Howie watched those stories on television, the more he began to see the flaws in their construction... And then there were the deleted scenes. How could you delete scenes from a person's life? How could someone be expected to believe in the reality of those characters when entire portions of their lives could simply be plucked out, as though they never happened?

People died, but they weren't dead in the deleted scenes. How could they be both alive and dead? How could the endings be both happy and sad? Which one was real and which one was fake?

The characters within books breathed and felt. They were real. They didn't have deleted chapters which could be added or subtracted on a whim with no thought or concern. They didn't have different endings that could easily be interchanged and swapped out, depending on which button a person pressed on a remote control.

Stories were meant to be life. Life was a series of facts, leading to one inescapable conclusion. The numbers added up, but not in movies.

When Howie heard Professor Luscious Cartwright speak for the first time, it was as though the world suddenly made sense, and the stories within all of those movies were adding up to one inescapable conclusion. They needed to end. There were no deleted scenes that could spare them.

Howie followed Professor Cartwright's movement online and he began to detail the events that were leading them to the conclusion of the Hollywood story. He did the math and he fed those numbers to Professor Cartwright, telling him how it would need to play out.

He did this all through e-mails and chat rooms, of course. Howie lived in the woods, far away from the rest of the world. He didn't want to see the rest of the world anymore; not until it was cleansed and the stories made sense again.

The walls of Howie's cabin were lined with papers, detailing which movies were in production in which places around the world at the time of the attacks. Professor Cartwright had hundreds or thousands of pupils, who could be placed around the world. Some posed as crew members in order to gain access to these sets. Others simply tracked their targets.

With each report that came in, and each target confirmed dead, Howie marked those papers with a red *X*. By the end of the night, most of those papers were marked. In the days that followed, there were even more.

A year later, the world was in the process of transforming into something new and beautiful.

Yet, the numbers suggested that no matter how many targets were confirmed dead, there would be some overlooked. There would be errors. He spent most of his time trying to figure out how many there were and where they might be. He could not leave his home until he knew how to finish what had been started. Even if it meant missing the party, which he had been invited to through e-mails.

He wanted to meet Professor Cartwright. He wanted to shake the hand of the author of the new world. But his work was not finished. There were more.

The thing that disturbed Howie the most was that logic dictated that any survivors would be working toward revenge. The more time that passed, the closer they would come. The closer they came, the more exposed Professor Cartwright would be.

The natural symmetry of the story suggested that this party would be the perfect endpoint. But how would it end? Who would end it?

Howie's numbers failed to make sense to him. The reason for this was the fact that he had overlooked the possibility that some of those people who were thought dead were in fact alive.

Without knowing exactly who was in play, every survivor was an unknown variable, and any one of those variables could pop up at any time and wreak havoc on the natural flow of the story.

There was a noise in the room behind Howie. This startled him, because he knew every sound that was supposed to be in his home, and this noise was not normal.

Someone was in his house... This was an unexpected twist.

~

9:17 PM...

Anita Kwon was barely in her twenties. If anyone were to look at her and take a guess of her age, they might think that she was more like fifteen or sixteen. She didn't mind this most of the time, but looking like a kid sometimes made her *feel* like a kid. Especially when it came to dealing with her parents.

As a teenager, Anita was into movies and television, as most teenagers were. She enjoyed watching movies about vampires and swooning over them. Vampires were sexy, and she didn't care what any of those werewolf fans had to say about it.

Her parents did not think that these movies were very intelligent. They urged Anita to read the books instead, though even reading the books would not make her parents happy. They wanted her to stop acting like such a normal girl and put her brain to good use. They wanted her to be more like them, whether she wanted to or not.

There were times when she hated her parents growing up, but she respected them enough to not tell them that she hated them. She tried to make them as happy as she could, while living her own life.

This didn't work out very well.

When Anita graduated from high school, her parents insisted on her going to college. They wanted her to become a doctor or a lawyer, or something equally valuable to society. They chose her courses for her, which included classes taught by Professor Luscious Cartwright.

She thought the Professor was a self-righteous blowhard, but she went to his classes and wrote the papers that he wanted to see, all so that her parents would not disown her.

Anita enjoyed having money, and as long as she had that

money, she would try to make her parents happy. If she wound up marrying into money, she could please her parents while possibly going on to live a life that she could tolerate. Until then, she would just get by.

Professor Cartwright had some pretty radical ideas. He often spoke of the corruption of the human mind by the entertainment industry. When Anita wasn't secretly listening to music on her MP3 player during his classes, she was more than a little skeptical of the ideas that he was pushing. All of the other kids seemed to appreciate what he was saying though, so she played along and figured that she must have missed some crucial piece of the puzzle which would make his teachings more understandable.

Her parents read the teachings of Professor Cartwright and they bought into what he was saying. They even attended one or two of his special lectures and seemed enthusiastic about his lessons. They loved that their daughter was being taught by someone of his caliber.

When Professor Cartwright began taking his lessons to the next level, looking for students to aid him in his mission to educate the world, Anita was asked to join his legion. She was offered a position as one of the pupils who would infiltrate the entertainment industry and feed information back to Professor Cartwright. She might have even been one of the pupils who eventually killed members of the entertainment industry, but her parents didn't like the idea of their daughter traveling away from home and spending time amongst the enemy.

Instead, they supported Professor Cartwright by making a rather large donation to his cause, in Anita's name.

Just like that, Anita Kwon was a key financial backer for the cause which would result in countless deaths around the world. Yet still, she felt uneasy about that cause.

On the night of Professor Cartwright's revolutionary campaign against the entertainment industry, Anita watched the news unfold on the internet. While her parents took delight in seeing their ideals spread across the world, Anita wanted to throw up.

Overnight, she lost access to movies and television. Internet fan groups died down. Her parents even managed to replace all of her favorite music with classical and opera.

Anita kept quiet. She buried her nose in books about vampires and werewolves fighting for sexy dominance. When she finished with those, she resorted to books about prepubescent wizards. And after those, she was lost.

She eventually came to pick up a copy of *Dracula*. Then *Frankenstein*. Then, because these books weren't quite as appealing to her romantic side, she turned to books by Jane Austen. From there, she found herself swimming in a sea of authors that her parents actually approved of... and she liked them.

She could hold her own in Professor Cartwright's classes, now led mainly by his assistants. She could debate the merits of different authors. She could discuss the nuance of certain classical composers. She could blather on about the evils of the Hollywood machine and the bright future that awaited them at the end of this revolution.

She had even taken an interest in cookbooks and the techniques used to create some of her favorite foods. But with the sweet, there also came sour.

Taking down Hollywood was just the beginning. From there, the movement would spread. Once Professor Cartwright opened the eyes of the dumbed-down masses, his ideals would become the next logical evolution of human thinking; at least, according to Cartwright's followers and several of Anita's papers.

Her parents continued to make donations in her name and she came to appreciate some of what she had avoided in the past, but Anita was never convinced, and she had a hard time deciding whether or not she should even attend the celebration of Professor Cartwright's revolution. Being a major investor, she was invited to attend as an honored guest. Her parents would be attending, but Anita couldn't decide whether or not she should go.

She sat alone in her bedroom, in an over-sized house that her parents had purchased for her, and she stared at that invitation. Somehow, it seemed wrong.

As Anita tried to make her final decision, she kept her back turned to her bedroom door. She never would have noticed if someone had walked into the room behind her.

~

8:47 AM...

Nancy finished with her workout and walked up the stairs of her home, wiping the sweat from her forehead with a towel, which she promptly threw in the garbage. She hated doing laundry, so it was easier to simply purchase new towels whenever she needed to.

The master bedroom of Nancy's home was decorated very simply. There was no clutter or mess. There was only a bed and a dresser, and a nightstand on which she kept a very basic alarm clock and a lamp which she used when reading in bed.

Of course, she had three other bedrooms in the house, which were decorated in different styles. She would sleep in one of those rooms if she was ever in the mood for change. In recent months, she had begun to consider burning down the house entirely, and starting from scratch.

The master bathroom in Nancy's house was large, with white tile floors which she paid a lovely old woman to clean twice a week. The bathtub had an old fashioned design with ball-and-claw feet. The shower was tiled in marble. All of the hardware in the bathroom was stainless steel.

Her towels were red on this particular day. Though she worried about the possibility of the dye from those towels rubbing off on her wet skin, she was in the mood for red. It was such a lovely reminder of the passion with which Professor Luscious Cartwright had enacted his plan and destroyed the Hollywood machine.

Red was a celebration of their victory over the entertainment industry.

For the following day, she was thinking of something regal, in anticipation of the big celebration. Perhaps purple.

As Nancy closed the bathroom door and walked toward the bathtub, she did not notice the darkly dressed woman behind her. The woman remained perfectly quiet as Nancy walked to the tub and turned on the water.

While the tub filled with water, Nancy stepped back and kicked off her running shoes. In her mind, she was thinking about all of the shopping that she needed to do that day. There was dinner to buy, and an escort to pick out of a catalog. She needed to find shoes to match her dress for the party.

The darkly dressed woman began to approach from behind and Nancy caught a glimpse of this woman in the bathroom mirror. She was only a blur as Nancy turned to look, and by the time the blur turned into a real human form, there was something wrapped around Nancy's neck, being pulled tight... it felt like the belt of a bath robe.

Nancy tried to struggle, but it seemed like the more she fought, the tighter the belt became and the less she could breath.

"Happy anniversary," the woman whispered in Nancy's ear.

In that moment, Nancy came to realize that she was not being attacked by some random street hood. She was being attacked by something far worse; she was being attacked by an actress.

She began to fight harder, but couldn't break free. She couldn't breathe and she could feel herself losing this battle. This meant death, and Nancy simply had too many things to do that day. Death was not an option.

She kicked her feet out, hitting the bathroom cabinet in front of her.

The actress who was attacking her shoved her forward and smashed her head into the mirror, shattering it. Blood began to pour down Nancy's face.

"How does it feel?" the actress asked. "How does it feel to know that you will be dying today? To know that the people you love and work with will be dead by the end of the week? To know that Professor Luscious Cartwright will be dead?"

Nancy's eyes widened in shock when she heard the actress use the Professor's name. They weren't supposed to know. How could they know?

"We know who you are. You hide like vermin, but we've discovered your nest. Soon, everything that you worked for will be gone and we will win this war," the actress told her.

The actress pulled Nancy away from the cabinet and the mirror and threw her into the tub. She held Nancy's bleeding head underwater for several seconds. Nancy was sure that this would be the end.

The actress then grabbed Nancy's hair and pulled her face out of the water with great force.

"When you die, I want you to know who it was that killed you. I want my name to be the last thing you ever hear," the actress said, in a voice that was filled with a pure, animalistic rage. "Maybe you've heard of me. I'm the ghost of Hollywood. The one who hunts your kind and takes pleasure in their killing. I am the one who will stop at nothing to make sure that each and every one of you pays for what you've done to my people. I'm the one who will bring Hollywood back into the light. I am Starlette."

Once that name was spoken, Nancy's head was once again shoved beneath the water. She could feel her nose break as it slammed against the bottom of the tub.

As her energy left her and life began to slip away, Nancy could see nothing but the red of her own blood as it mixed with the water that filled her lungs. In that moment, Nancy considered that perhaps *red* had not been the best choice of towel color for that day.

~

12:58 PM...

Robert enjoyed the view from his office, but there was much to be done. The Professor's movement would soon be taking their campaign to the next level. They would step out of the shadows and become the guiding force of the intellectual revolution. First, they would spread their cause across America, and then they would spread it across the world.

Creating an international icon, beloved by everyone who was smart enough to recognize his greatness, was no easy task.

As Robert turned to resume working, he found himself sitting before a darkly dressed woman. Had he been straight, Robert surely would have lost his breath at the sight of such an unusually attractive woman. Yet, he suffered no breathlessness. Instead, his mind went to the place which was most logical and reasonable.

"You're an actress," he said in a matter-of-fact tone.

She didn't respond. She simply stared at him with cold eyes, which were hidden behind a thick layer of dark makeup.

"How did you find me?" he asked.

She started to move around his desk. He responded by quickly standing up and moving around the other side.

She pulled a small knife from her belt and began to play with it between her fingers. Robert kept his eyes on the knife, wondering just what she intended to do with it. Obviously, she had come to his office with the intention of killing him, but he was a man of business. Business meant negotiation.

"We can discuss this," he told her. "I can make sure you're not killed."

As he looked back on that comment in the seconds that followed, Robert began to believe that perhaps he could have found some better way of opening those negotiations.

The actress threw the knife, which struck Robert before he knew what was happening. It stuck into his arm and he could feel the pain of that wound radiating throughout his entire right side.

He could not help but let out a scream of pain.

"We're not alone! There are people in the offices around me!" he warned her.

"Not anymore," she replied.

A chill ran up Robert's spine. He turned and ran for the door, but the woman was fast. She caught up with him and grabbed the back of his jacket, jerking him backwards and causing him to fall to the ground. He tried to crawl away as tears filled his eyes, but she kicked him in the face and he could no longer move due to the pain.

"What makes a man decide that it's acceptable to slaughter thousands of people?" the actress asked him. "And what makes a person pathetic enough to follow that lunatic?"

Robert didn't answer those questions. He took offense to them, naturally, but he thought this was hardly the time for political discussions.

The actress stood over Robert and looked down at him with those eyes. In her hand, she was now holding a gun. He knew that there was no way for him to escape his fate.

"How do you sleep at night, minion?" the actress asked him.

"Wh—what?" he replied.

"How do you sleep? Do you sleep well, with the blood of my people on your hands?"

He didn't answer her. In response to his silence, the actress blew a hole through his leg. He screamed.

She pressed, "Do you sleep well?"

"I... I don't know," he said, still suffering the pain of his fresh wound and unable to think of an intelligent answer.

She shot his other leg. Again, he screamed.

"Why are you doing this to me?!" he asked, as soon as he could form words again. He suddenly found courage and told her, "I will not tell you where he is. I will not tell you anything."

"You're reading too much into this," the actress told him. "I don't care what you have to tell me. I don't want information from you. You're not important."

"Then... why?"

The actress smiled. It was a beautiful smile; he couldn't deny that.

She said, "If I tell you why I'm here, you will realize just how worthless you are. To me. To him. You will see that your life has been wasted and that when you die, nobody will even miss you... Do you still want to know why I'm here?"

Robert thought about what she said, and he feared the truth of it. So, he shook his head and closed his eyes. He could feel a tingling in his nose as tears began to form. In that moment, he saw his life flash before his eyes. Then, the flash of something else.

As he died, Robert could have sworn that he smelled something burning.

~

5:22 PM...

Howie didn't turn when he heard the noise behind him. He didn't rush to find a weapon and defend himself. He remained seated, with his back to the door, and he smiled.

"If I don't see you, you don't exist," he said.

"I exist," came the voice of a woman. She sounded hot.

"If I don't see you, you have no power," he told her.

"I have power," the woman replied.

Howie shook his head. He didn't accept that answer. He took a sip of the whiskey that he had sitting on the desk in front of him. He had laced it with some sort of drug, but he couldn't remember exactly what. It didn't matter.

"Characters have faces, they can't just be voices," he told her. "If I don't see you, there's no description. There's no character. You have no substance."

There was a silence, but Howie felt the woman get closer. Then, she whispered in his ear, "This story isn't from your point of view. It's from mine."

Howie's heart skipped a beat. He had never considered this idea. He always just assumed that he was the focus of the story, because his life had the most detail to it. He had never even considered the possibility that he could be a small part of a much larger story.

The variable was right. The more he thought about it, the more it made sense. He was alone. He did nothing of importance. There was so much happening in the world that he was not a part of. If he was the main character, the story was boring.

The woman walked around the room, taking a look at all of his papers and information. Not studying them, as she would have to in order to fully grasp the complexity of his work, but looking them over and getting the gist of what it all meant.

"You planned it?" she asked him.

"I didn't plan it. I helped coordinate..." he told her, not wanting to take any credit from the man who actually brought it all together.

"How do you justify killing all of those people?"

"It had to be done."

"Why?"

"Why did we need to drop the bomb in Japan?"

"That was to end a war. You did this to *start* a war."

"But it had to be done. For the future."

"You believe that?"

"The numbers back it up."

"Your numbers are shit."

"You're wrong."

"Did you predict my coming here?"

Howie paused for a moment, and then said, "No."

"Then you're not the genius you think you are. You're just crazy."

Howie stopped and considered what she was saying. He tried to do the math in his head, but it wasn't working anymore. He couldn't see the patterns. If he couldn't see the patterns, he couldn't be sure that he was right. If he couldn't be sure that he was right, what did he know anymore?

Finally, he had to concede, "That makes sense."

"Repent."

Howie shook his head, "I can't. I wouldn't mean it."

"Then I have no choice..."

"I understand."

A hand reached around Howie from behind. In the hand was a knife. Its blade moved across his neck without the least bit of resistance.

As he died, Howie finally remembered why he thought Hollywood was evil: There was too much violence in movies.

~

10:33 PM...

Anita crawled into bed and stared at the ceiling. It was a crazy world and she seemed to be right at the center of the lunacy.

She was tired, but not sleepy. She wished that she could close her eyes and drift off, but her mind was racing at a million miles per hour as she tried to make sense of what her life had become.

Was she really a part of some war against Hollywood? Was she really going to a party with a charismatic leader who had somehow talked his students into killing thousands of people around the world?

It all seemed like a dream. Part of her wanted to wake up and turn on the television, but she didn't know what she would want to watch, even if it were an option. Her new instinct was to reach for a book and sink into a fantasy world, lulling her mind into its nightly slumber with thoughts of faraway places in long ago times. But she didn't feel like reading on that night.

She stared at the ceiling for what seemed like forever, trying to figure out whether or not she wanted to go to that party which Professor Cartwright was holding in honor of his brightest pupils and his biggest investors. She seemed to be counted amongst one or both of those groups, thanks to her parents.

There was a shadow which moved across the outside window and caught Anita's eye. She sat up in her bed and looked to see if anyone was standing on the balcony outside, but nobody was there.

She shook off the feeling that she was being watched and closed her eyes. In that moment, as she considered what it would be like to have someone come into her home and kill her, Anita's mind was made up.

She would not be attending the party. If her parents had a problem with that decision, they could kick her to the curb and she could make her own way in the world. Part of her wanted it that way.

Anita would never know how lucky she was. She would never know that if another Bookworm minion needed to be killed on that night, she would have been it. As far as anyone knew, she was just as guilty as the next minion, and by remaining silent for so long, perhaps she deserved that reputation.

But Starlette had killed all that she needed to kill that day. Anita would be spared.

~

Starlette walked into The Studio and she could feel all eyes on her. They looked on with pride as she returned home, knowing that what she carried with her was the key to their victory.

She ignored them. She had no time for—nor interest in—playing the role of hero to them. Not anymore. Frankly, she couldn't care less if most of the people in The Studio dropped dead at that point, because that was as much respect as they'd shown Ember.

Just thinking about it made Starlette want to kill somebody... Though she'd been doing that all day and it didn't seem to help her very much. She couldn't believe how quickly and easily everyone had turned on Ember and how they spoke of her after her death—

Ember wasn't dead. Starlette had to stop herself from considering that possibility. There was no body, and everyone knows that if you don't see the body, there is no death. It's just a ratings stunt waiting to happen.

Until Ember returned, Starlette had work to do. Bookworm's party was being held in one day. They'd already wasted enough time devising their course of action for the hours leading up to that event. Even as she walked into The Studio, Wacky Best Friend was in the conference room with The Director, Head Writer and all of the other writers, working on their outline for the primary attack. They'd been in there ever since Starlette and Girl Next Door pulled that information from Bookworm's library at Princedale and Starlette brought it back to The Studio.

As she walked across the floor of The Studio, Sassy Gay Friend caught up to her and walked beside her.

"You're back," he said, stating the obvious. "I assume you got the job done?"

"I did," she replied.

"You know, I could have gone with you. I could have helped."

"You've helped plenty."

Starlette tried to walk faster, hoping that Sassy Gay Friend would take her hint and leave her alone, but he did not.

He said to her, "I've been offered a regular role on your cast... I haven't accepted it yet."

Starlette's response to this was a smirk. She told him, "There is no regular role on my cast anymore. This is it. Series finale. After we take down Bookworm, we all go our own separate ways."

"Do you think it's that simple?"

"I'm making it that simple," she said, and stopped walking so that she could look Sassy Gay Friend directly in the eyes. "I will not spend the rest of my life in this place. I will not have them tell me that I have to work with you, after what you did."

"What I did?"

"You made them hate her. Everyone in this place is laughing and joking about her death because of you."

"I—I didn't mean... This is what they wanted me to do. This is my role."

Starlette turned and started to walk away, but she stopped herself. She turned back to Sassy Gay Friend and said, "When we were in that library and Ember was trying to convince me that she should be the one to stay behind, do you know what she told me? Do you know why she sacrificed herself?"

She gave Sassy Gay Friend a moment to think about the question. She wanted him to hang on it and to really hear her when she gave him the answer.

After taking that moment, she continued, "She told me... She said that the people here didn't even like her anymore. She gave herself up and saved me because she knew that nobody here had her back. Nobody cared whether she lived or died. And *that* is on you."

She didn't know how good an actor Sassy Gay Friend was. She hadn't ever really seen him try to stand out in a scene. So, she couldn't tell whether or not his reaction was sincere. But as she told him about Ember's last moments, Sassy Gay Friend's mouth fell open and he stepped back. She could have sworn that she saw his eyes begin to tear up, but he didn't allow himself to cry.

For the longest time, he said nothing. It looked like he wanted to say something, but he didn't. After taking his time, Sassy Gay Friend looked to the ground and then turned away. He walked off, leaving her alone.

She didn't have time to care about him. She had business to tend to, and that meant heading to the conference room.

When she got there, she found the tables covered in food wrappers, empty water bottles and crumpled up pieces of paper. There was an odd smell in the room as well.

In the corner, The Director was pacing back and forth while talking on his cell phone. Ever since Studio Head was taken out of the game and an Executive had been chosen to fill his job until a more permanent replacement was found, communications with the upper levels had become strained. Some were calling for Wacky Best Friend to be interviewed about the killing of Studio Head, but The Director was taking the brunt of their communications and defending Wacky Best Friend while Wacky Best Friend worked with the writers on developing their script for Bookworm's demise.

The Director hung up the phone and saw Starlette standing in the doorway. He said to her, "Who would have thought that killing the guy in charge of The Studio would lead to so many headaches?"

"My bad," Wacky Best Friend quipped, standing from his chair and moving toward Starlette as she walked to her regular spot at the table. The Director joined her as well.

Starlette reached into her coat pocket and pulled out the plastic ID cards that she had taken from each of her marks on that day. She also had paper invitations, addressed to each of those marks.

"Nancy Hume," Starlette said, picking Nancy's ID from the stack and looking at the picture on it. She showed it to Wacky Best Friend and said, "I could play her, right?"

Wacky Best Friend nodded. He fished through the cards and said, "Which one is me? Robert Forester? Howard Pavel?"

"Neither. Playing the part of Howie Pavel will be Heartthrob. Sassy Douchebag will be taking Robert," Starlette told Wacky Best Friend.

Wacky Best Friend seemed puzzled and asked, "What about me?"

"Nancy's got a thang for the man-whores," Starlette told him, with a grin. "You're my whore-date."

"I'm man candy?" Wacky Best Friend replied, at first looking appalled, but then excited. He said, "Awesome!"

"Well, you know... Nancy's cheap," Starlette quipped.

"I have no problem being the whore at the bottom of the bargain bin," Wacky Best Friend replied, "But isn't Heartthrob our usual shirtless wonder?"

"First of all, it's not like you're going to the party in a banana-hammock."

Wacky Best Friend put his best pouty face on.

"Second," Starlette continued, ignoring his pouty face, "I think Heartthrob's better suited to Howie Pavel these days."

Wacky Best Friend picked up Howie's ID and looked at the picture. Howie was long-bearded, scruffy, worn and not exactly a looker. Wacky Best Friend turned to Starlette and held up the picture with a questioning look.

"He's reclusive. Nobody's probably ever seen him in person—at least, not much. So, we stick a beard on Heartthrob and put him in a suit that doesn't immediately spell *underwear model*, and he should be fine. Plus, he can be... Quirky."

"Quirky is an interesting way of putting it," The Director told her.

"How's he doing?" Starlette asked. "Any progress?"

As she asked that question, Wacky Best Friend and The Director looked at each other. Judging by their expressions, she was guessing that there hadn't been much progress.

~

Stand-In #1 flew across the stage and slammed into one of the faux marble pillars. As he hit the ground, the entire set was rocking and looked as though it could easily tip over at any moment.

Stand-In #2 rushed toward Heartthrob with rage in his eyes. As he approached, he threw a punch in Heartthrob's direction, but Heartthrob grabbed his fist before it could ever make contact. With a twist, Heartthrob sent Stand-In #2 to the ground.

By the time Stand-In #2 was on the ground, Stand-In #3 and Stand-In #4 were approaching from behind. Together, they hoped to take Heartthrob down and put an end to this marathon training session, which had already ruined the day of eight Stunt Doubles, the Bikers, two Gangstas, a Hood and Up-N-Comer's tutor, who just happened to be walking by at an unfortunate moment.

Heartthrob hadn't slowed down all day. He hadn't slowed down ever since he returned from Princedale University without Ember. He didn't plan on slowing down anytime soon. His body was worn down. He ached like he had never ached before, but he could not stop. If he tried to take a break, he would fall into a pit that he would never be able to crawl out of.

He could feel the shadowy hands of the demons that he carried with him, wrapping themselves around his legs, waiting for their opportunity to pull him into that pit. At some point, he became unable to tell whether these hands were metaphorical or if they were real. All he knew was that if he stopped, they won.

As soon as he returned to The Studio from his shoot at Princedale, he wanted to gear up and turn around, to find Girl Next Door. He tried to convince The Director to let him go. He tried to talk Head Writer into making it work for them, but nobody would relent. Even Wacky Best Friend had told him that going back to look for Ember would be a mistake.

In his rage, Heartthrob grabbed a chair and threw it halfway across The Studio. It nearly hit three actresses who were running lines and minding their own business, but he didn't care.

He tried to pull himself together, but the more time that passed, the more he felt himself slipping away. He could no longer pretend to be normal. He could no longer act like the person they wanted him to be. He *was* rage.

~

Once the plans were sketched out and work had begun on fully outlining and scripting the shoot that would take place at Bookworm's party, Wacky Best Friend stepped out of the conference room. As a Producer, he could pitch in and help with the writing elements, but he had other responsibilities to consider.

As he stood outside of the conference room, stretching his legs and trying to regain feeling in his ass, Head Writer moved past him, mumbling "Excuse me," as he went.

At first, Wacky Best Friend ignored him. He had no interest in Head Writer on most days, so ignoring him had become second nature. After a moment, however, as the haze of work in his mind cleared and the realities of life set back in, Wacky Best Friend turned and watched Head Writer walk into his office.

Ember was gone.

It was a thought that he hadn't even managed to fully process before diving into his work. The initial shock of what happened to her struck him hard, but he wasn't given time to react to it. Almost as soon as he had been given the news, The Director was asking him what happened to Studio Head.

Once The Director knew the details of what had happened in Studio Head's office—including the discovery that Studio Head had been given advance warning of the attacks and still let them happen—he was thrown into a frenzy of business. Executives wanted to know what happened and who was there. They scurried to find a temporary replacement while The Director did his best to keep Wacky Best Friend free of that insanity, so that he could focus on the more pressing insanity.

Starlette had a wealth of information in her bag when she returned from Princedale University. Diving into that information had distracted him. Staying buried beneath it kept his mind from settling to the point where he could remember that Ember was gone. *Really* gone.

He watched Head Writer walking into his office and he found himself walking in behind him. When he closed the door, Head Writer turned and seemed a little surprised.

"Did you need something else?" Head Writer asked, picking a ream of paper up from his desk.

"I want to know what it felt like," Wacky Best Friend said. "When you wrote those red pages, what did it feel like?"

When he asked the question, Wacky Best Friend wasn't angry. His voice wasn't accusatory or full of hate. It was a genuine question, and he was looking for a genuine answer. But Head Writer didn't respond right away. He just looked down, as though he didn't know what to say.

"You had a thing for her, right?" Wacky Best Friend asked. "You asked her out?"

Head Writer looked up again. He seemed surprised that Wacky Best Friend knew this at first, but his shock quickly melted away. It only made sense that she would have told people, so there was no reason for him to be surprised.

"When did you write those pages?"

And there was the accusatory question. It surprised Wacky Best Friend almost as much as it did Head Writer. Somehow, it just slipped out.

"Are you suggesting that I wrote her out because she turned me down for a date?" Head Writer replied, genuinely insulted. "I would never..."

As he trailed off, Head Writer looked away from Wacky Best Friend, toward a corner of the office. He was trying to pull his thoughts together. Neither man was nearly as awake as they should have been for this conversation. They had been working long and hard, and needed rest, but this was when the conversation came about. So, they went all in.

"You all think I'm just doing what I do because I'm a giant asshole. Like I take pleasure in putting people in danger or... killing them off. You think it's easy for me to watch you all come back, broken or bleeding, and to know that I put you in that position and maybe if I was better at what I do, it wouldn't have come to this," Head Writer said. "But I do what I'm told. I have notes coming down from countless suits and if they don't get their way, they'll cancel all of us and start over. Do you know that I'm officially an Executive Producer around here? But what good does that do me? With all of the notes coming from The Studio, and more notes coming from The Network, how am I supposed to balance that? Do you think The Network takes responsibility for what happened to Headliner? It was the other Head Writer who paid for that decision."

Head Writer sat at his desk and looked as though he might fall asleep right then and there. Wacky Best Friend thought that if he looked half as worn as Head Writer did, there was no way he'd be able to convincingly play a man-whore.

"I'm tired," Head Writer continued. "And Girl Next Door was... She was the one person who could put a smile on my face. When I wrote for her, it was like I knew what this whole thing was about. I knew what we were fighting for. And when they told me to write that alternate ending, just in case... I knew that no matter what we do here, we lose."

Head Writer looked down at his hands, as though there was blood on them. He rubbed his fingers together and then turned his attention back to Wacky Best Friend as he said, "I asked her out after I wrote those pages. Her answer had nothing to do with what I wrote. I just needed to know."

Wacky Best Friend could feel himself on the verge of breaking down. It had nothing to do with what Head Writer was saying; just the fact that their conversation involved Girl Next Door being dead. As he heard the business end of that decision, her death became real to him.

She was gone. Right then, Wacky Best Friend knew that after all of this was over, he would never write again.

~

No matter how many people crawled away from the stage looking as though they were about to bleed out, Heartthrob did not feel ready to stop fighting. When there were no people left for him to hit, he stirred like a lion in a cage. He needed to vent. He needed an outlet. He needed *something*.

He punched one of the faux marble pillars, but felt none of the pain that he expected to feel. He thought he might break his hand when he hit it, but that didn't happen. The pillar rocked back and forth, but did not fall.

He punched it again. This time, he left a spot of blood on the pillar, but still he felt nothing. He punched it again and again, until a chunk of the pillar fell to the ground, and then he stopped for a moment to look at that chunk of the pillar.

There were two of these pillars on either side of the stage. These pillars originally supported other pieces of the set, but those upper pieces had been removed at some point and now they supported nothing.

Heartthrob had found his next sparring partner.

He attacked that pillar without holding back, as he had with all of the people with whom he had been training. He punched at it until it fell to the ground and broke into pieces. Then, he attacked the next pillar.

When that pillar fell, Heartthrob picked up one of the broken pieces and he threw it through one of the windows on the stage. He ripped through the stage like a violent storm, tearing it apart and ripping it down. He attacked it until there was nothing left to attack.

Still, his need to fight was not satisfied. He looked around the area, but there were no people to spar with. There was no other set to rip apart. He had done all that he could do there, so he made his way back to his trailer.

As he walked, the world around him was a blur. He could see nothing clearly, nor hear it. He could barely feel the ground beneath his feet.

When he entered his trailer, he didn't know what to do with himself. He grabbed a glass off of the table and threw it against the wall. He punched the mirror. He tried to go crazy and rip the place apart, but it wasn't much of a target.

When he reached the kitchen area and swiped a stack of paper plates off of the counter, his eye caught something that had been behind them. It was a clear plastic bag, filled with three smaller bags. Within those smaller bags were pills, given to him by a man who had introduced himself as Co-Executive Producer.

He considered giving in. He considered taking one or two of those pills, just for the sake of getting some sleep. He even told himself that his taking those pills might be better for his cast, since he was falling apart more and more each moment.

Then, he considered taking more than one or two of those pills. It would have been so easy to grab a handful or two and finally be done with the mess that his life had become. But no matter how hard he might wish for it to be over, he knew that it wasn't. As long as there was a battle to fight and Bookworm was still breathing, even death couldn't soothe his troubled soul.

As easy as it would have been to take those pills, the temptation wasn't strong enough to twist his mind into wanting them. He had spent too many years taking care of his body and avoiding drugs. He didn't even drink alcohol.

He wanted for there to be temptation. He wanted some illusion of relief, but there was none. His pain would not relent. His suffering would not end.

He just wanted to fight.

~

Morning. The promise of a new day and a new life was just beyond her grasp. Starlette could almost feel it at her fingertips.

She had forced herself to sleep the night before, because she knew that rest was essential to the work of an actress. To deny rest would make her sloppy and there could be no chance of messing this up. They had come too far and sacrificed too much to let it go now.

As Starlette stepped out of her trailer, the first thing she saw were the lawn chairs that had been set up in front of them for nearly as long as she had been in The Studio. Usually, she could find someone sitting out there, sipping a drink or making some sarcastic comment. Now, they were empty. They looked different to her now; like relics of some long ago time.

As she walked down the stairs from her trailer, she heard Ember's trailer door open. At first, she didn't think anything of it. It was a sound that she was used to and expected. After that fleeting moment however, she was struck by the realization that this sound should not be.

She looked to the trailer, just as a couple of crew members began to walk down the steps. Each of them was carrying a cardboard box, full of Ember's belongings.

Starlette walked toward them at a normal pace and without great emotion. When she met up with them, she tried to remain as calm and cool as she could manage to be as she kindly asked them, "What the fuck are you doing?"

So, the wording was perhaps a bit too harsh. At least her tone was polite.

One of the crew members looked at her as though she was speaking a different language and said, "Clearing out the trailer. Nobody lives here anymore, right?"

Starlette swallowed her initial reaction, which would have come out sounding harsh no matter how she delivered those lines. Instead, she said, "I would appreciate it if you would hold off on emptying her trailer."

"Hold off 'til when?"

"I don't know," Starlette said. "Maybe you could let the body get cold before you pawn her shit for beer money."

The body. Those words echoed through Starlette's mind after she said them. She couldn't allow herself to believe that Girl Next Door was dead, but here she was, talking about her as though she was nothing but a corpse.

"We have our orders," the crew member told her.

"Well, I'm giving you new orders," Starlette replied. "And you really have to ask yourself... Between me and the other guy who gave you orders, who's more likely to kill you right now?"

"It's not worth it," the second crew member told his friend. "Let's just put the boxes back and wait. Odds are, we're gonna be emptying the whole place out soon enough anyway."

The first crew member looked to his buddy and then back to Starlette. He didn't seem thrilled, but he was probably more annoyed that he had wasted his time. As he shrugged and said, "Whatever," he and the second crew member put their boxes back in the trailer and walked off.

As they left, The Director approached and said "I was going to handle that. Glad to see I don't have to."

"Who gave the order?" Starlette asked.

"I could tell you, but then you'd have to kill them. I'd rather not have anyone else killed in The Studio for the next couple days."

"Fair enough," Starlette nodded. "Are we still on schedule?"

"For the most part."

Wacky Best Friend chose that moment to walk out of his trailer. He looked as though he had been run down by a cartoon train as he joined Starlette and The Director, yawning.

"We have some last minute preparations to make, of course. Obviously, this is a bigger shoot than we're used to, and we're going to need more than just your cast," The Director told them.

"Crossover?" Wacky Best Friend asked.

"To say the least," The Director confirmed. "We're going to need a lot of background as well, which is where you come in."

Wacky Best Friend didn't quite catch the meaning of that sentence, so he said, "I come in where?"

"I was hoping you'd be interested in working with me. Kinda like a Second Assistant Director," The Director told him. "Work with background and get them prepped while I work with some of the normal actors."

"Do you have a First Assistant Director? I don't think I've ever seen a First AD roaming around here," Wacky Best Friend mused, getting off topic. He then turned to Starlette and said, "Did you know that Head Writer is actually an Executive Producer?"

"I knew that," Starlette replied. "I just didn't care."

The Director cut in and said, "Will you do it?"

"Sure. I guess," Wacky Best Friend said with a nod and a shrug.

"Good. Then let's get to work. Tonight's the night," The Director told them.

Before The Director could walk away, Starlette stopped him by saying, "Hey..."

He turned around and waited for her to speak. She didn't know what to say at first. Her eyes went back to Girl Next Door's trailer and then to the ground. She knew that she wanted to say something about Girl Next Door. She wanted to make sure that she was somehow considered in all of this, but she didn't know what it was that she wanted from The Director.

Seeing Starlette struggle to find words, The Director looked to the trailer and then to the actors. He said, "I'm trying to put together a memorial. I want to dedicate this shoot to her... It's just that..."

He trailed off. Now he was the one who didn't know what to say. It took him a few seconds, but he finally managed to spit it out, saying, "Nobody's willing to come to a memorial."

"That's bullshit," Wacky Best Friend blurted. "She was a hero. *Their* hero."

"I know that. You know that," The Director replied. "They only know what they *think* they know and they don't care about anything else."

Wacky Best Friend was pissed off. He demanded, "Then tell me why any of us should fight for them. Why should I risk losing more of my people for *them*?"

"Because," Starlette told him. "That's what Ember sacrificed herself for."

Wacky Best Friend didn't say anything in response to that. At least, not while The Director was there.

After a moment, The Director said, "I'm sorry," and he walked off to do his work.

Wacky Best Friend stood with Starlette and all he could seem to do was shake his head. She waited for him to speak. She knew that it was coming, but it took him a while to get to the point where he could say anything.

"This place..." was all he said. He then walked away.

He didn't need to say anything more. The stress of The Studio was getting to everyone. People needed to get their lives back. The tensions had been cooled for a little while after Starlette called for her strike and they got their victory in the form of Wacky Best Friend's return. This was not a permanent fix, however. Eventually, those tensions would rise once more. Today, that hostility was directed toward Girl Next Door.

Starlette hoped that by the following day, it would no longer matter. By taking down Bookworm, she would put an end to life within The Studio's walls. She would free all who had been held prisoner there.

~

As Wacky Best Friend walked toward the extras' holding area, his mind was racing in a hundred different directions at once. He was trying to map out his own performance for the party, while trying to figure out how to prepare the extras, while trying to think of a way to put his cast back together.

Heartthrob was dying. Girl Next Door was dead. Starlette didn't believe that Ember was dead, which was either a form of denial or a form of self-motivation; Wacky Best Friend couldn't quite figure out which.

He would have loved to believe that she was alive. He wanted to believe it more than anything, but he couldn't afford to believe it. He had to accept what he had been told and move forward, or else he risked their entire climax. If he thought for one second that Ember was still alive, he would have no choice but to find her; Bookworm be damned.

But she had given herself up for a reason. She did what she had to do and that meant that he had to do what he *had* to do.

"You look like your brain's about to come pourin' out your ears," came a friendly voice, with a southern drawl.

Wacky Best Friend didn't stop walking right away. Sing caught up with him and kept pace, with a smile on her face.

"And by that, I mean that you look all kinds of perturbed," she said. "Did I use that word right? I don't think I've ever used it before in my life."

Wacky Best Friend stopped walking. He wanted to tell her that he didn't have time to make pleasant chit-chat, but as soon as he looked at her and the smile on her face, he could tell that she wasn't just making chit-chat. She was trying to perk him up.

"I heard about what happened to Girl Next Door," she said, finally losing the smile. She tilted her head slightly to the side and shook it as she said, "I'm so sorry."

As she said it, he saw a tear in her eye. It seemed strange to him, that she could feel genuine emotion for a woman she didn't know. Yet, Sing didn't seem to be acting.

"Thanks," was all he could think to say in response.

"If there's anything I can do to help you or your friends, you let me know. I mean that. I'm from the south, so I'm not just being nice here. I have casseroles standing by."

"They actually do that in the north too, I think," he told her.

"Really? I always kinda assumed they just gave people the finger and told them to get over it up there."

Wacky Best Friend couldn't help but smile. He said, "Maybe in Connecticut."

"They do seem shifty in the eyes," Sing replied. She quickly followed that with, "Well, I just wanted to make sure that y'all were doing okay and to let you know that I'm here if you need me."

"I appreciate it."

Flashing that smile of hers once more, Sing turned and started to walk away, humming some song that Wacky Best Friend didn't recognize as she went.

"Hey," he called after her. When she turned, he asked, "Are you on board for this shoot tonight?"

"I haven't been approached."

"Consider yourself approached. Get your team together and tell The Director I sent you."

Her smile grew wider and she said, "This might be fun."

With a wave, she turned and started to walk again. Wacky Best Friend watched her for a moment, listening to her hum.

~

Starlette knocked on Heartthrob's trailer door. There was no answer.

She knew that he was inside. She'd heard enough noise coming from his trailer to know that he hadn't gone off to beat up some other set in The Studio.

The fact that he didn't respond to her knock didn't surprise Starlette, but it did concern her. She needed him to pull himself together, at least enough to get through the night. She was down one cast member and didn't trust another, so she only had Heartthrob and Wacky Best Friend to fall back on.

She knocked again and said, "Heartthrob, open up. It's me."

She didn't know whether or not the fact that it was her knocking would have helped or hurt her cause. She didn't know how much he cared for her at that particular moment, considering the fact that she had left Girl Next Door behind at the library.

It wasn't her choice. She didn't want to do it. She didn't like doing it... She had to keep repeating those facts to herself each time the memory of that library scene came to mind.

Heartthrob wasn't answering. She hoped that this meant that he was finally asleep and would be well rested for the party, but she doubted that he was sleeping. He had a hard enough time sleeping on *good* days.

She debated whether or not she should push the matter. She could have gotten into the trailer if she really wanted to, but she didn't know how Heartthrob would respond to that. So, she let him have his alone time, but she told him, "Listen... We're going after Bookworm tonight. Be ready."

As she walked away from his trailer, things felt wrong. She had long imagined what it would be like when they could finally take down Bookworm and go back to their normal lives, but somehow this was not it.

She walked across The Studio and she could see some crew members and actors rushing around, making preparations. Others were sitting by, watching.

One of the crew members that she passed along the way said "Kick some ass for me tonight."

She nodded and kept walking.

Another crew member said, "I guess I never should have given up acting classes. Give 'em hell."

She just kept walking.

A third crew member handed her a rabbit foot keychain and said, "Shove this down that bastard's throat for me, huh?"

It had been a year since the attacks on Hollywood. For a year, the people in The Studio had been hiding in the shadows, waiting for their day in the sun. Now that it was here, only the A-listers were going to be getting the revenge that they all deserved.

Too many of her friends and loved ones were gone. They would never know the victory that Starlette planned to attain that night. All of the others were there and alive. They deserved more than watching the dailies after it was all over.

Starlette saw The Director walking up ahead. He stopped and looked out across the floor of The Studio, taking it all in. When his eyes met Starlette's from that distance, she knew that he could tell what she was thinking. He had been an actor in another life. He knew what it was like to be the person standing front and center, getting praised for the work of hundreds.

"Listen up!" The Director called, as loudly as he could.

Everyone in The Studio stopped and turned to face him. They listened with great interest as he said, "Tonight is it. Tonight, we will march into Bookworm's world and we will rip out its heart!"

Cheers erupted all around. The Director allowed this to go on for a moment, and then held up his hand to quiet them down.

"For a year, we have lived here together, working toward our common goal. We have fought side by side. Eaten together. Cried together. Tonight is the night that it all ends. By morning... By morning, we can go home."

More cheers. Several people threw hats and clipboards into the air. The hats that came down were met with a far nicer response than the clipboards.

"Each person here has a right to be angry," The Director continued. "Each person here has a right to claim a piece of that victory as their own. Each person here has a right to vengeance. So, that is what I am offering to you now. To anyone who wishes to join our cast as we march into battle, the line starts here! Let's turn this attack into a siege!"

The crowd had cheered before, but now it screamed. Casts and crew alike, the people of The Studio rushed to answer the open casting call to war.

In the hours that followed, preparations took on a new face. Their effort was no longer limited to attacking the party and taking down Bookworm. Those heading into battle were no longer counted by the dozens, but by the hundreds. They would use the information gathered by Starlette and Girl Next Door to attack members of Bookworm's organization who were not in attendance at the party.

Strongholds, like Princedale University and office buildings all around the city would be overtaken. The call went out all across The Network, to every Affiliate around the world. On this night, the people of the entertainment industry would rise from the ashes and send the souls of their enemies into the underworld, screaming and writhing in pain.

~

Wacky Best Friend walked into the extras holding area, which was an isolated room, off to the side of The Studio.

Though this room was connected to The Studio that he had lived in for nearly a year, he had never stepped foot in there. He was shocked at what he saw when he did.

Make-shift tents had been constructed throughout the room, crafted from the tattered rags of the extras' wardrobe options. They did not normally get to visit Wardrobe. They did not have the luxury of Hair or Makeup. These people had been living on their own, with limited access to food and water, while the rest of The Studio had gone on with their daily lives just beyond the door. While Wacky Best Friend and his cast had been shooting regularly, the extras had been left waiting.

As he walked through the holding area, extras looked up at him from where they were sitting on the ground and in folding chairs. Some had been reading books. Others had been conversing with their fellow extras, but as he walked through that room, they all looked at him with eyes that screamed to him to pick them and take them from that room, if only for a little while.

He didn't know if they were up to it. He didn't know if they had the skills required, or the energy to push through the shoot that they had scheduled for that night, but he needed them. So, in the short time that he had left, he would choose them; all of them. He would set them up and give them their cues. By the time they left for the party location, he would see to it that they were ready to charge into battle while not blocking the cameras or speaking any line of dialogue.

~

High atop a hill, far away from the broken down city that had once been home to movie stars and skanky heiresses, there was a mansion. It was large and imposing, and could have quite easily been mistaken for a museum or a school of some sort. There were many windows and many rooms, which made it the perfect location for Bookworm's celebration.

Spotlights shot into the air and crisscrossed in the sky above the mansion. In front, cars were pulling up. Their doors were opened by valets who helped the well dressed women get to their feet.

It was a night to remember, and so there were photographers hired to take photos of the event. Bookworm wanted the world to see the glory of intelligence and the superiority of the well learned. The party would be written of in books and journals all across the world.

A banner was hanging over the entrance to the mansion, honoring the one year anniversary of the cultural revolution. Guests at the party stopped to have their photos taken in front of that banner, as they smiled wide and proud.

As her limo pulled up to the party, she pulled a small mirror from her bag and looked at her reflection. Her hair was longer than normal, thanks to the wig that Hair had provided for her. Her makeup was far more subdued, as Makeup wanted to give her more chance to blend into the crowd.

She wore a dress which sparkled and showed off her curves, while allowing her the freedom to move and hide weapons. For one split second as she looked at her reflection in the mirror, she didn't feel like Starlette. She felt like that young, naïve actress who had died in the English countryside.

The feeling quickly faded. She put the mirror away and looked to Wacky Best Friend, who was dressed in a tuxedo, sitting next to her. His hair was neatly combed, which was unusual for him. Starlette thought that he looked as though he might actually be a high-priced man-whore.

He looked to her and gave her a slight nod. They had come a long way together, and it was all boiling down to the moment when their efforts and sacrifices would pay off at long last.

The car came to a stop and Starlette's door was opened by a valet. As he helped her out of the car and she nodded her *thank you*, the valet stared. At first, she thought that he must have recognized her. Many valets had dreamed of becoming famous actors in Hollywood, and like the waiters out there, many of them had taken to the streets and lost their sanity after the attacks.

She assumed that the valets at the party were of the other sort; college kids, trying to earn their way through school. Possibly brought in from some other city for the party, to ensure that no Hollywood sympathizers would be employed by Bookworm. Yet, as that valet looked at her, she had to wonder.

Wacky Best Friend walked around the car and took her arm, leading her up the walkway, toward the entrance. As they walked, he smiled and leaned close to say, "Relax. You look hot. That's why he was staring."

Starlette hadn't even considered that possibility before. Somehow, she had forgotten that she was a young, attractive woman and not just an action star.

As they neared the entrance, Wacky Best Friend pulled Starlette to the side. Their photo was snapped in front of the banner and while Starlette had little expression on her face at all in that moment, Wacky Best Friend had a big smile and gave a thumbs-up as the picture was taken.

"I'm gonna want that one for my mantle," he said to her. "Y'know, when I don't live in a home that has wheels."

They walked to the main entrance and Starlette handed Nancy's invitation to one of the many minions guarding the place. He graciously granted Starlette and Wacky Best Friend entrance to the mansion and said, "Have a pleasant evening."

"I plan to," Starlette replied.

The main foyer in the house was grand indeed. One could have possibly fit a smaller house in that foyer, and visitors to the mansion would have commented on what a bold choice of artwork that smaller house was.

The foyer was full of guests, mingling and sipping champagne before the main event. At the far end of the foyer, Starlette spotted Sassy Gay Friend. He was sipping his drink and talking to a few of the younger guests in attendance. They seemed to be hanging on his every word, which was a good sign.

"He spent the day researching his role," Wacky Best Friend commented, in an incredibly low voice. "I think it's the first time I've ever seen him work."

She didn't reply. She tried not to stare at Sassy Gay Friend, but she kept an eye on him as often as possible. If anything went wrong, their entire script would have to be thrown out the window.

Head Writer and his team were sitting in a van, about a half a mile down the road; hidden behind trees and bushes. They had their laptops at the ready, just in case there was a need for a last minute rewrite.

Each actor on Starlette's cast was wearing one of the hidden cameras that Camera One had been working on and fine tuning for weeks. The cameras, as well as microphones were well hidden. This time, Starlette would not be disconnecting her power pack. She wanted every detail of this shoot caught on video.

Cameramen were positioned at a distance around the mansion. Their cameras were mounted on top of the line stabilizers, which would give each camera operator more freedom to move and adjust their angles as the night's festivities progressed.

So far, everything was going according to plan. Starlette could only hope that things remained on course as she saw Heartthrob enter the building.

Heartthrob's costume and makeup altered his appearance more than any of the other actors. He wore a fake beard and a wig, which Starlette had her doubts about when she first heard of these details, but Hair and Makeup had worked magic on Heartthrob. Wardrobe threw in a pair of glasses, which made his nose look bigger than it actually was. She also put him in an ill-fitting tuxedo.

He looked awkward and uncomfortable. He was the sort of person nobody would want to talk to at the party, but nobody would think twice about his being there. It was a look that worked for him in his current situation.

Heartthrob did not even attempt to mingle or blend in. He stood by the doors which led to the ballroom, waiting for those doors to be opened so that he could take his assigned seat.

When Starlette first entered the party, there was a small part of her who didn't see the enemy. The people in that mansion were not the typical minions that she had been killing for the past year. They were well dressed, respectable-looking people, who were drinking and talking and having a good time. They seemed so normal upon first glance that Starlette could have forgotten about who they were if she chose to.

She longed for the days of fancy parties with pretty gowns and cameras flashing in every direction, but this was not the world she longed for. It wasn't even close.

As she and Wacky Best Friend wandered through the foyer, they did not stop to talk to anyone. Instead, they listened to the conversations that people were having as they walked by.

Once she could put sound to the picture and all of those high-class partiers were revealed as the minions that they truly were, there wasn't any hint of that voice in her head. There was no mistaking those people for normal.

As she listened, she could hear those men and women joking about the attacks on Hollywood. More than once, she heard someone reference a bomb at the box office and the people they were speaking to would laugh in an annoying, snotty, elitist sort of way.

Some of the snotty men would go on about how they wished they could have been out in the field, fighting those damned actors with their bare hands, rather than working in the offices or simply supporting Professor Cartwright financially. Looking at those men, Starlette wished that they had been out there, attacking actors… That way more actors would have lived and more Bookworm minions would have died.

The women tried to sound more civilized most of the time, criticizing Hollywood and the damage that films and television did to the minds of today's youth. They spoke of the horrible amounts of violence that children were exposed to at the hands of Hollywood. According to them, it was fortunate that the entertainment industry was taken down… Somehow, they glossed over the violence that went into those attacks and the many child actors who were exposed to that violence.

Other topics of discussion ranged from saving the environment to figuring out a way to bring about world peace. Somehow, all of those people seemed to think that by killing off the entertainment industry, they were making real progress in the world.

To Starlette, they sounded stupid. They overlooked the facts. They glossed over the realities of the world. Hollywood was a pioneer of social change. Actors and well known directors had routinely traveled around the world in their private jets, speaking on issues like global warming and feeding the poor.

Activism in the hands of these madmen was a dangerous thing for Hollywood's unfortunate people, and for the world.

The more she listened, the more disgusted she was. These people—most of them anyway—were doing nothing to better the world, aside from talking big and occasionally throwing money at a cause that they thought would do the job for them. They were fools, and their inability to think for themselves was what resulted in the deaths of thousands. They threw all of their support and all of their faith into some hollow leader, whom they viewed as charismatic for some unknown reason.

They needed to be done away with. Any sway they had over the world's cultures had to be taken away as soon as possible, and

The Studio was the force to do this ridding. After that… Well, Starlette wasn't thinking beyond the scope of this evening at this point. She only wanted to accomplish the goal at hand. Everything she was, she invested in that goal.

The lights in the foyer dimmed and brightened three times, and the party guests began to move toward the ballroom, where low-ranking minions were opening the doors and welcoming people inside.

Starlette thought it strange that Bookworm would signal his guests by using a method common to theatres and opera houses at intermission. It wasn't entirely breaking with his normal style. He hadn't completely destroyed the world's musicians, only those who performed modern forms of music. Orchestras and opera singers were allowed to live in Bookworm's world, though Starlette did not imagine that they lived in comfort. One wrong move and Bookworm would have them killed. One stylized beat added to a song and the guilty party would be put up against a wall and shot.

At least, according to the rumors that trickled back to The Studio from their allies within the music industry, who had gathered under The Label.

As thoughts of those allies crossed her mind, Starlette couldn't help but wonder if she should have sent word of their final shoot to them.

She shrugged this thought off. The Company would have clashed with the Triple Threats, whom they viewed as traitors, and this would have put the whole shoot in jeopardy. The Studio was better off going in alone.

Heartthrob was the first actor to enter the ballroom. Starlette and Wacky Best Friend paced their entrance to ensure that there would not be a clump of actors walking in at once.

Once inside the ballroom, they saw that it was filled with dining tables. Each table had assigned seats for its guests. Starlette had taken this into account when she selected the characters that she and her co-stars would be portraying. Each of them was well known enough to get an invitation, but unimportant enough that the actors could replace the real people without being noticed.

This meant that their seats were not up front, as Starlette would have liked. Heartthrob was located toward the middle of the room; the closest to the stage of all the actors.

Starlette and Wacky Best Friend were not quite at the back of the room, but they would have to fight their way to the front once *action* was called, because Bookworm would undoubtedly be toward the front, if not on stage.

Sassy Gay Friend was about even with Starlette and Wacky Best Friend, though on the opposite side of the room.

The stage must have been constructed for this event, but one never would have known it. There were impressive red curtains covering most of the stage, hiding whatever was on the stage from all of the guests until the presentation started.

Off to the side of the stage, there was a small orchestra. They played classical music with ease and coolness, though their eyes betrayed their fear. They looked skinny and worn. Surely, their year of playing for Bookworm had not been easy, and Starlette would not hold any grudges against these prisoners of war.

She noticed one of the orchestra members scanning the audience. They locked eyes for a moment and he seemed to know who she was. She looked away as quickly as possible, so that there would be no suspicion of her character having been recast at the last moment.

There were other people sitting at the table with Starlette and Wacky Best Friend, dressed to the nines and having a great time. Each of them was the enemy. Each would be dead within a matter of minutes.

Once all of the guests had taken their seats, the doors which led into the ballroom were closed. Starlette waited to hear the *click* of those doors being locked, but she couldn't hear any such sound over the low rumble of party guests talking amongst themselves.

Minutes passed and there was no sign of Bookworm. She wasn't sure what he looked like, but she knew that when he entered, there would be cheers. He was the leader of their literary cult, after all.

Just as Starlette was beginning to settle in for a prolonged wait, the lights in the ballroom dimmed. The curtains on the stage pulled back, and the orchestra stopped playing their music.

Behind the curtains, there was a large display screen. At first, this scene was black. Then the familiar voice of Bookworm poured from the speakers like a disgusting goo; thick and oozing.

It was the message that he had delivered to Hollywood on the night of the attacks, which said, "Good evening... Right now, you are all thinking to yourselves, 'Oh, my God. I wonder if my hair looks okay.'"

The people inside the ballroom laughed heartily at this joke. It was a far better reception than he had gotten the first time this speech played.

" However," the voice went on, "at any moment, you will look up at this screen and you will realize that something is not going according to plan. You will see that there is a rather ominous looking man speaking to you from an undisclosed location, and this is rarely a good thing."

The audience in the ballroom listened intently. Some put their hands on their hearts. Others closed their eyes and absorbed the sound of this speech as though they were listening to the sermon of a beloved pastor.

On the screen appeared the words: *ONE YEAR AGO...*

Bookworm's infamous speech continued, "You will wonder who I am, but it does not matter. You will wonder why I am doing what I am about to do, but in truth, that will matter even less, so I won't bore you with my reasoning. I will simply tell you that ours is a world corrupted."

In the crowd, someone yelled "Yes!"

"Corrupted by greed."

"Amen!" came another voice, "But in a non-religious way!"

"Corrupted by envy."

"I concur!"

"Corrupted by celebrity."

And now the crowd erupted in cheers.

"Our children grow fat and waste away, while watching endless hours of television. Our lives have become meaningless and hollow..."

On the screen, images began to flash. They were images of the attacks, taken from the point of view of the minions who carried out those attacks. The bloody corpses of beloved movie stars were displayed on the screen, while Bookworm minions posed for pictures as though they were tourists.

On the screen, a word flashed: *CORRUPTION.*

More images flashed across the screen, followed by the word: *GREED.*

More images flashed, and then: *CHANGE.*

Wacky Best Friend leaned close to Starlette and whispered, "This actually has some pretty good production value."

Starlette ignored him and watched the display.

The recording of Bookworm went on, "This answer is simple. I am going to kill all of you and bring an end to the reign of Hollywood buffoonery."

And the screen went black once again. The audience waited with baited breath for whatever would come next.

Bookworm knew how to wield the power of the dramatic pause. At the height of the tension from that pause, the blackness vanished and on the screen there appeared video, captured on a cell phone and copied from a popular video hosting website for the purpose of Bookworm's presentation.

In the video, an actress was running through an electronics store, trying to escape death at the hands of one of Bookworm's minions. Starlette knew this actress. They had attended network parties together in the past. Her name was Casey Dale, and she did not deserve to die.

Starlette and Wacky Best Friend watched in horror as the minion grabbed Casey by the hair and threw her to the ground. In the background of this video, people watched and did nothing to help her.

Casey screamed and struggled, and the crowd pulled out their cameras to film what was happening. The minion grabbed a video camera and used it to beat Casey to death, and Starlette looked at the table in front of her, rather than watch the video on the screen.

As the video ended, the audience cheered.

Bookworm's voice came over the speakers. This time, it was not a recording. He said, "That was then. Over the past year, we have changed the face of the world!"

Taking that cue, the words *THREE DAYS AGO* appeared on the

screen. Starlette looked back to the screen just in time to see a new video begin.

In the video, Girl Next Door stood, surrounded by Bookworm minions. They cheered as she was tased and fell to the ground, twitching as electricity shot through her body. They rushed toward her and kicked her in the stomach. They threw books at her face, screaming "Knowledge is power!"

Starlette's stomach turned. She looked to Wacky Best Friend whose eyes were locked on the screen, though he managed to keep a blank expression on his face.

She turned her attention to Heartthrob, expecting him to stab someone right then and there, but he did not move. From what she could see, it looked as though his eyes were on the ceiling, rather than on the screen.

There was a noise to Starlette's side. It was the sound of a glass tipping over and the scurry to clean up the resulting mess. Starlette's eyes moved toward this sound and found Sassy Gay Friend struggling to regain his composure. She tried not to draw attention to herself by staring.

Back on the screen, Girl Next Door was bleeding. Her body was being dragged across a floor, leaving a trail of blood behind it. She was propped up in a chair, and Bookworm minions gathered to have their picture taken with her. Each held her head up as they smiled for the camera. Each dropped it again once they were through.

The screen went black.

As the audience roared, a man walked onto the stage. As he made his way to center stage, the applause grew in intensity. This had to be him. This had to be Bookworm.

Starlette was underwhelmed. She had spent a year imagining him as a Kelsey Grammar or John Noble type. She pictured a sophisticated-looking man with a red smoking jacket. He had none of these features. Instead, he was a man who never could have been an actor of any kind. He was ordinary. Neither fat nor thin. Not bald, but without a lush head of hair. It was not black, but not gray, settling somewhere in the middle.

He had a beard, but it did not make him seem more impressive to her; nor did his choice of plaid sweater-vest, paired with his tuxedo.

"We have made a difference!" Bookworm yelled. "And we will continue to sweep this world and bring forth a new age for humanity!"

The crowd cheered and rose to their feet in order to support their leader. Starlette and her co-stars did not want to rise, but they had no choice. The role demanded it.

The applause lasted quite a while and seemed to pick up energy once or twice before finally settling down. Once all of the well-dressed minions had taken their seats, Bookworm continued.

"As honored as I am to be your leader, I could not have accomplished this great... accomplishment... on my own. So, tonight I will take pride in honoring all of you and your..." he winced as he said, "...accomplishments."

The crowd seemed to overlook Bookworm's lack of verbal skills, but Starlette knew Wacky Best Friend and could see a laugh in his eyes, even if there was not one on his lips. She had to look away from him in order to avoid laughing herself.

"Ladies and gentlemen, presenting the plaque for most creative slaying of a supporting actress in a comedy or musical is —"

Before Bookworm could finish that sentence, the lights in the ballroom went out. The room was thrown into complete darkness.

At first, the audience seemed to think that this was a part of the ceremony, but Bookworm chuckled and said "Please pardon the technical difficu—"

His microphone went dead.

Starlette's heart began to pound in her chest. Adrenaline began pumping through her, and her muscles were screaming for violence. But, being the professional actress that she was, she waited.

Soon, a spotlight lit up the room. It came from the ceiling and shined straight down in the center of the room, casting light upon one person and one person only: Sing.

As she looked into an audience that she could not see, Sing began to sing a familiar song, whose name and lyrics would not be recorded in the days to follow, due to legal matters concerning copyrights and licensing—they really should have contacted The

Label.

Regardless of these legal facts, Starlette knew the song well. It was a classic rock tune from the 1980's, and while it started slow, Starlette anticipated the increase in its pace.

She was impressed by Sing's choice to sing the song in its original language. The use of German threw off Bookworm and his minions, causing them to look at each other for a few moments, with no idea what was happening.

Behind Sing, the orchestra joined in, playing along as the speed of the song picked up and Starlette's cast rose to their feet.

The lights in the ballroom came back on. Sing did not miss a beat in her song. She continued to sing as Bookworm backed up and minions screamed for security to come and help them.

But security would not come.

"Action!" Wacky Best Friend yelled.

Across the room, Heartthrob wasted no time in pulling his weapons and opening fire. After he had killed all of the Bookworm followers at his table, he moved toward the center of the room, continuing to shoot everyone that he could.

Starlette, Wacky Best Friend and Sassy Gay Friend pulled their guns and took aim just as the ballroom doors burst open and a flood of Studio employees rushed into the room.

Starlette shot two of her table-mates in the head before turning her attention to the stage, where she saw Bookworm backing away and looking as though he was about to take off.

Sing continued with her song as she flipped and kicked, all in very impressive and rhythmic ways.

From the sides of the stage, more of the Triple Threats emerged, singing backup. They were moving in perfect sync as they blocked Bookworm's path and began laying down cover fire for the rest of the cast and crew.

Starlette pushed past Wacky Best Friend, determined to reach Bookworm. She watched the stage as Bookworm dropped and rolled off of it. Minions surrounded him as he landed on the ground, and returned fire against the cast and crew. She couldn't tell at first whether he was injured or not, but as she struggled to get closer, she saw him stand.

He looked right at her as two of the well-dressed minions

grabbed her and tried to throw her to the ground. She flipped backwards and broke free of their grip. She then shot one in the chest and pulled a throwing knife that was hidden on her belt. She used it to slit the throat of the second minion.

She looked back to Bookworm and he smiled at her as his minions grabbed him and shoved him through a trap door which led beneath the stage.

She would not let him escape.

As they pressed on, fires erupted around the room. One of the Triple Threats was hit by a make-shift Molotov cocktail. She fell to the ground, screaming and rolling around. Her fellow Triple Threats rushed to her aid.

As she got close to the stage, Starlette could see the trap door, hidden behind three large minions. She was determined to make sure that they would not be slowing her down.

She shot one of the minions as she got closer to the stage. Her bullet hit him in the upper chest and while he did not die right away, he did fall to his knees and begin clawing at his friends for help.

The other two minions did not pay their companion any attention. They pulled guns of their own and fired at Starlette. As her mind processed the fact that she was being shot at, everything around her slowed down. Sounds became muffled. The people became a blur.

She had no illusion of being a superhero who could dodge or catch bullets, but as soon as she saw those minions reaching for their guns, Starlette twisted to the side and leapt into the air. Her sudden and unpredictable movement threw off the aim of the Bookworm minions, but not enough for her to avoid being hit entirely.

One bullet caught Starlette in the arm. It ripped through her flesh and she was not lucky enough to escape with a slight scrape this time. The bullet dug in and pain shot through Starlette's entire left side.

She did not land on her feet. Thrown by the shock of the bullet striking her, Starlette landed on her side and quickly rolled behind a table, kicking it over so that she could avoid being struck by more bullets.

The guests who had been sitting at the table were not fighters. They did not have weapons. They were simple-minded followers who just happened to have a lot of money that they could throw into a cause that made them feel special.

As Starlette hid behind their table, these guests were standing nearby, afraid to run for the doors or try to make it to the walls, where many of Bookworm's other followers were standing. The working theory for this particular group seemed to be that if they didn't move at all, nobody would notice them.

One of the men became bold when he saw an injured actress on the ground, taking cover behind an overturned table. He picked up a chair and moved toward Starlette, preparing to slam it down on top of her.

He was older and slower than she was. He was also much slower than the bullet which shot from her gun and struck him in the stomach.

His wife screamed and yelled, "Winthrop!"

Starlette now had to keep her eye on the group of followers from that group. Though they were distracted by Winthrop falling to the ground and groaning, Starlette could not afford to assume that those people no longer posed a threat. At the same time, she could not ignore the armed minions who had shot at her while protecting the trap door under the stage.

Starlette tried to count the number of bullets which remained in her gun as she took cover behind the table. There were two armed minions and countless unarmed.

Winthrop was bleeding everywhere. Starlette had to pull her dress away from the line of blood that was making its way across the floor, toward her. She would hate to bring the dress back to Wardrobe with blood all over it.

"Medic! We need a medic!" Winthrop's wife screamed across the room.

Starlette turned to her and wanted to ask the woman if she honestly believed that someone was going to rush across the room to her aid.

"You're a monster!" the woman screamed at Starlette. "You wonder why we wanted you all dead? Well, this is why!"

Starlette shot the woman in the face. One less bullet to put toward the armed minions.

As Winthrop's wife slumped down across her husband's bleeding chest, Winthrop continued to scream.

One of the other party guests nearby put a hand over her heart and said, "My word!"

Starlette didn't shoot her. She figured that she'd let one of the supporting actors handle it.

A chunk of the table blew off near Starlette's head. The armed minions were aiming for her, hoping to draw her out. She did not plan to disappoint them.

~

As soon as the action began, Heartthrob grabbed the table where he was sitting and tossed it on top of the Bookworm followers who were sitting opposite him. He pulled his gun and shot the person next to him in the head, never stopping to think or consider his actions.

As he got to his feet, Heartthrob shot the people under the table. They died without a fight.

The room was filling with more actors and various crew members who had decided to take The Director up on his offer to let them make a cameo appearance in the background of this shoot. Heartthrob did not slow down to consider where each of these Studio employees were or what they were doing.

He charged into the middle of the room and began taking out Bookworm followers left and right. At first, he didn't even remember that he was wearing the wig or fake beard. He was too focused on the job at hand and his thirst for vengeance. He wanted these people to pay. He wanted them to suffer.

Heartthrob didn't shoot all of the Bookworm followers in the head or chest. Many of them, he shot in the stomach. They would die slow, painful deaths. They would be forced to endure the type of torture that his family had suffered. They would be forced to watch their world crumble, as all of those other actors had. And they would die bloody for what they had done to Ember. He didn't know exactly what happened to her, but he knew that whatever it was, these people deserved to pay for it.

As he took out follower after follower, he began to sweat. The sweat dripped down his face and he became aware of the beard that was glued to his face and the wig on his head. He ripped the wig off, but the beard was not as easy. He pulled at it and pulled at it, but he could only pull chunks of it off of his face. Spots of beard remained and when combined with the mess of his real, sweat-soaked hair, Heartthrob looked like a crazy shell of the man he once was.

He resumed shooting. He pulled the trigger time and time again, and never stopped to see if his aim had been true. He didn't care. He only cared about taking as many of those people down as he possibly could.

When his gun ran out of bullets, he pulled his backup gun and fired that one into the crowd as well.

Behind him, there rose a shriek. It was a horrible, ear-shattering shriek which caused him to turn with his gun prepared to fire. As he turned, he felt something smash against him. A bottle broke against his shoulder and he was drenched in what smelled like whiskey.

The woman who had slammed the bottle against him was standing in her party dress, with rage in her eyes that was normally reserved for armed minions, not investors. As she threw a lighter at him, Heartthrob assumed that she was one of the honored party guests who had taken part in the original slayings.

As he burst into flames, Heartthrob grabbed the woman and they both fell to the ground. He was on top of her and his flames became her flames. She was wearing far fewer layers than him, so as the fire burned his clothes, it burned her flesh. She screamed in pain, and he watched.

~

After Starlette left him behind to charge after Bookworm, Wacky Best Friend tried to provide as much cover for her as he could while remaining behind to help direct the swarm of actors, crew members and extras who were pouring through the door of the ballroom.

More than one follower of Bookworm tried to go after Starlette with a knife or a vase, and Wacky Best Friend took them out. He doubted that Starlette ever even knew that they were there.

He glanced toward the door and saw that extras were beginning to gather in one corner of the room, not moving into the battle. He pointed at one and screamed, "You, go!"

That extra rushed across the room, though still appearing to be uncertain of his action.

Wacky Best Friend hurried to the corner of the room where the extras were gathered and he yelled "What the hell are you doing? I said to go on *action!*"

"We couldn't hear anyone say *action!*" one of the extras replied. "It's too loud in here!"

"And I'm not even sure what's going on!" another extra yelled. "Are we supposed to react to the fight?"

"Should we really fight? Or should we pantomime it?" asked another.

"Just *move!*" Wacky Best Friend yelled at them. "Kill people! And for the love of God, *stop talking!* You're extras!"

Wacky Best Friend shoved a couple of the extras toward the fight before turning his attention back to the action that was taking place. First, he saw Sing, spinning and flipping in unison with the other Triple Threats who had leaped off of the stage and had joined the fight on the ballroom floor. They moved with precision, ease and remarkable flexibility.

Next, Wacky Best Friend saw Starlette taking cover behind a table. He had enough sense to know that she wasn't hiding, but regrouping. There were two armed minions moving toward her, with guns at the ready.

If the room had been more clear, Wacky Best Friend could have easily taken aim and shot the two armed minions for Starlette. As it was, he needed to move closer before he could help her.

He hurried to make his way across the ballroom floor toward Starlette, but as he moved a burst of light caught his eye. When he looked to see where this light was coming from, he saw Heartthrob in flames, resting on top of a female Bookworm minion. It didn't seem like Heartthrob was planning on putting out the fire himself, so Wacky Best Friend changed his plans and rushed toward Heartthrob.

Along the way, Wacky Best Friend grabbed a tablecloth. When he reached Heartthrob, he pulled him off of the female minion and used the tablecloth in an attempt to put out the fire. Instead of accomplishing this task, the tablecloth burst into flames.

Wacky Best Friend tossed the tablecloth on top of the female minion, who continued to scream. He then grabbed Heartthrob's jacket and pulled it off; a task that was easily accomplished, as the jacket was badly burned and nearly fell apart in his hands. As he pulled off the jacket, Heartthrob pulled on the shirt beneath it, and soon he was free of the flames. Fortunately, the clothing had been so loose-fitting that Heartthrob's skin was not badly burned.

Upon once again finding Heartthrob shirtless for no good reason, Wacky Best Friend could not help but yell, "Oh, come on!"

~

Tessa was due to be released from the clinic that day, but she could not find anyone to give her the official permission to return home.

Finding the clinic empty, she wandered out to the floor of The Studio. The place which was normally filled with people, sounds and a certain amount of chaos was now like a ghost town. There was no sign of life for as far as the eye could see.

She wandered around The Studio for a bit. Once again forgotten, Tessa placed her hands on her hips and with all of the glamour that one would expect, she said, "Well... Fuck."

~

Another chunk of the table blew off. This time, Starlette heard the shot being fired. She could tell that the armed minions were getting closer to her and were still gunning for her.

She could have risen from behind that table with bullets flying and people dying all around her. It would have been a perfectly valid option for most action sequences, but it was predictable. They would have seen it coming.

Instead, Starlette turned herself around and put her feet against the table. She kicked it forward and as the table slid across the floor, Starlette remained low on the ground, firing her gun up at the armed minions who had been expecting her to jump up before shooting.

She caught them off guard just long enough to shoot one of the minions. As he fell to the ground, he knocked into his partner, throwing that partner off balance. Starlette jumped to her feet and shot the second minion before he could regain his footing.

The trap door which led beneath the stage was clear now, but

Starlette did not immediately rush toward it. Instead, she turned and looked across the ballroom at the action that was unfolding. She saw Sassy Gay Friend pinned to a table by two followers of Bookworm, but before she could move to help him, he managed to kick one in the head and break himself free. He then shot both of the followers.

Heartthrob ran across Starlette's field of vision, screaming and shirtless. She wondered for a split second how he had managed to find himself shirtless once again, but she did not linger on this fact as she watched him dive on top of an armed minion that Starlette hadn't seen rushing her way.

Next, she saw Wacky Best Friend. He was shooting his gun and hitting several of Bookworm's men while waving Starlette on and yelling, "Go! Go! Go!"

As she turned and began to rush toward the trap door, Starlette could see armed minions pouring into the ballroom from backstage. She had to make a decision. She had to decide between leaving her friends and co-workers to deal with all of the armed minions, as well as the unarmed followers of Bookworm, or staying there to help them fight.

While the decision was not difficult to make, it was difficult to follow through on. As she hurried through the trap door, she wondered if her co-stars would be able to handle the fight without her. She wondered how many of them would be left standing when she returned.

She didn't have time to linger on this thought as she closed the trap door behind her and took in the view of where she was.

Under the stage, all of the sounds of the fight were muffled. There was little light, but she could see at once that Bookworm was nowhere nearby. He had escaped somehow, but she could not tell where another door might be.

She had to crouch as she made her way across the open space beneath the stage, and she kept her gun at the ready, just in case Bookworm popped up unexpectedly.

As she made her way toward the back of this space, she saw a light. It was small and easy to miss, but after she saw it she could see that it was creeping in around the edges of a door. She moved toward it.

Since the stage had been built specially for that party, the door was only half-accessible. She had to reach up, behind the structure of the stage in order to grab and turn the knob. When she did, the door opened into a hallway.

She moved into the hallway and closed the door behind her. Now, the fight seemed like a distant memory. The hallway was brightly lit, with cream colored walls and a red carpet resting atop hardwood floors.

The décor looked as though it had been ripped from the library at the White House. It was classic and elegant, but cold at the same time.

Starlette scanned the area for Bookworm, but he had enough of a head start to avoid being seen.

Keeping her gun at the ready, Starlette began to move down the hallway. She moved slowly. The high heeled shoes that she wore had felt attached to the bottoms—compliments of Wardrobe —making her steps extra stealthy.

As she passed each doorway, she looked into each room. All were dark and empty. Though she did not have the time to conduct a full search of each room, she knew that Bookworm was not in any of them. She could *feel* him at a distance, though she was growing closer.

Down the hall, around a corner, she heard a noise. It was the sound of a door closing.

She picked up her pace and hurried to find the source of that noise.

~

Wacky Best Friend hit the ground hard. He hadn't been expecting an attack from behind, and when he was struck by a chair to the back, he had no chance to adjust his balance or to block the attack.

As soon as he hit the ground he knew that he was in trouble. All around him, people were shooting and fighting and dropping like flies. Few of them ever got back up.

He flipped over and saw a middle-aged man in a tuxedo, holding the chair over his head. The man looked like he was at the end of his rope. He was not a heavy man. In fact, he looked like he took pretty good care of himself. But there was something about the guy which looked sickly; like he could have a heart attack and drop at any moment.

The Bookworm follower seemed determined to take as many Hollywood types out with him as possible, if he was going to die on that night.

He prepared to bring the chair down on Wacky Best Friend, and probably planned on beating him with the chair until he was dead.

Upon hitting the floor, Wacky Best Friend's gun fell from his hands. He didn't know where it was at the moment, so he had to fight back with nothing but his hands and feet to work with. Luckily, it was enough.

As the follower prepared to strike, Wacky Best Friend kicked him in the groin. The follower doubled over, dropping the chair. Wacky Best Friend then kicked him in the face, but the man did not fall over. Instead, he stumbled backward, trying to get away from Wacky Best Friend.

Out of nowhere, a bullet blew a hole in the man's head. The wound send a mist of blood into the air around the follower's head, which lingered even after the Bookworm follower dropped to the ground, dead.

A hand was extended and Wacky Best Friend took it. Sassy Gay Friend helped him to his feet and handed Wacky Best Friend the gun that he'd dropped after being hit.

As Wacky Best Friend looked around the room, he saw that there were plenty of Bookworm followers going down, but they were not alone. Many of the crew members and lesser-used actors from The Studio had fallen in this battle. Though victory was within reach, it would not be without its losses.

An armed minion raised his weapon to Wacky Best Friend's head, just as Wacky Best Friend turned and saw him. There was nothing that Wacky Best Friend could do in time to prevent being shot. Luckily, Heartthrob tacked the minions and took him to the ground.

While on top of the minion, Heartthrob beat his face until it was broken and bloody. He then grabbed something off of the ground and began stabbing the minion in the chest over and over and over again. Blood flew each time Heartthrob pulled his weapon out of the minion's chest, and Wacky Best Friend watched in shock of the savage nature of Heartthrob's attack.

"Wow," Sassy Gay Friend said. "All that with a butter knife?"

Wacky Best Friend shook his head and looked a little closer before saying, "I think it's a spoon."

Sassy Gay Friend winced.

Heartthrob was finished with the armed minion and he stood once again. He was covered in blood and soot from the fires that burned around the room. He scanned the area, and then asked Wacky Best Friend, "Where's Starlette?"

Wacky Best Friend gestured toward the trap door and said, "She went after Bookworm."

Without skipping a beat, Heartthrob ran for the trap door, leaving Wacky Best Friend and Sassy Gay Friend behind.

"Don't worry," Wacky Best Friend said with great sarcasm, though Heartthrob couldn't hear him. "We've got this covered. You go."

~

Starlette turned the corner and half expected to come face to face with Bookworm right there. Instead, she found herself standing outside the door that she had heard closing. It was a large, heavy door with an antique knob and lock.

She kicked it open.

Beyond the door there was a library. It was a grand, two level library with thousands of books on dozens of shelves. There was a spiral staircase which led from the first level to the second, and a fireplace which burned to one side of the room.

It was stunning, sure, but there was nobody inside the library.

Starlette moved forward with her gun in front of her, ready to aim and shoot with little warning. She expected to be attacked by a swarm of minions, or by Bookworm himself, but all she heard was the crackling of the fire.

As she looked around the library, she began to wonder which of the books she would need to pull on in order to open the secret passage through which Bookworm had undoubtedly escaped. It would take her forever to test them all, and she did not have time.

She looked to the floor, hoping to spot footprints which could lead her right to Bookworm, or the marks of a bookcase which had been opened, but she didn't see any. The floors were spotless.

She moved deeper into the room, preparing to go nuts and rip the books from the shelves as quickly as possible. If that didn't work, she would move to the fireplace and push, pull or twist anything she could find on it. Surely, there had to be a lever.

A gentle breeze brushed across Starlette's face as she prepared to launch into her search. As she turned to find the source of this breeze, she saw a large window in the back of the room, swinging in the wind. Beneath the window, there was a book which appeared to have been dropped and now rested open on the floor; its pages flapping in the wind.

It seemed too unimaginative. Who escaped from a large and imposing mansion through the window? Yet, when Starlette rushed toward that window and looked out into the hills that stretched into the distance, she could see the faint outline of a man running for those hills.

She jumped through the window and landed on the grass outside. Though she could hear a battle being waged on the front lawn, this was beyond her view. She did not let it distract her. Instead, she kicked off her heels, pulled off her wig and ran.

Bookworm was not fast as he ran across the lawn. He was older and out of shape. It was not hard for Starlette to catch up to him, despite his head start.

As she got closer, Starlette pulled a knife from her belt. She stopped running and threw the knife, which planted itself in Bookworm's leg. He stumbled, but did not drop. Instead, he turned.

The moonlight shined across Bookworm's face as he stood in the middle of that dark lawn, struggling to catch his breath.

Starlette stopped running and finished her pursuit at a walking pace. She was having no trouble breathing.

An explosion in the front lawn rocked the area. A fireball that Starlette did not turn to see lit up Bookworm's face, for just a moment.

She expected him to be more scared. She expected him to be more guarded, but here he was, alone and looking her in the eye with a slight smile on his face.

"It's you," he said. "I knew it would be you."

"So did I," Starlette replied, raising her gun to take aim at his head.

"Look at the world we've created. Isn't it beautiful?"

"We?"

"You and I. The balance. We did this together."

Starlette shook her head just slightly and said, "I didn't do anything except survive."

"Exactly," Bookworm replied. "We all just want to survive, and now we will."

"Not you."

"Won't I? Oh, you might kill me tonight, my dear, but my cause will continue. My people will thrive. After tonight, I will not simply be a leader of the cause, I will be a martyr to it. In some ways, I will be more present in the world after I'm dead."

"Your people are falling," Starlette told him. "I fell some of them myself."

"Those who survive will fight back. Just like you did."

"Then we will hunt them down and kill them. Just like we did you."

Bookworm laughed. He said, "And the cycle continues."

He took a step toward Starlette, but she reaffirmed her aim and this caused Bookworm to stop. He put his hands up and said, "You kill me. They kill you. Your friends kill them... My people are prepared to die."

"My people are prepared to live."

He ignored her and continued, saying, "And the longer we fight these battles, the longer your kind will be out of the minds of the masses. That's all that really matters. We sacrifice ourselves so that the future can know a world without movie stars."

Bookworm stopped talking, waiting for Starlette to say something. He expected her to make some sort of joke or to argue against his point. She did not give him the satisfaction.

He continued, saying, "I am a figure to your people as well as my own. I have given you something to fight toward; to aim for. I created the person you are today... And you will create the next hero to come from all of this. He or she will see what you do here tonight and they will become just like you. They will struggle and fight. In the end, you will find yourself in my position and your people will once again be the target of an impressive raid such as that which I perpetrated one year ago, and which you are undertaking tonight. Because of you, I am no longer a man. I am a legend. Behold Ares, the god of war."

Starlette looked to the ground and nodded slightly as she took in his long and rambling monologue. She then looked him in the eyes once again and said, "Well, Ares... The difference between you and me is that you failed to finish the job one year ago. Because you suck at what you do, I was created. And because I fucking rock at what I do, your kind will spend the rest of their short lives running. And my kind will have a hundred scripts optioned by morning."

"Perhaps," Bookworm replied. "You may very well be right. But you could also be very wrong. I am the lid to Pandora's box. If you kill me, you unleash an evil unto the world, the likes of which you cannot possibly see coming. You think that you will simply go home? You can never go home. You are Death. You will never stop fighting; never stop killing. You live for it. You need it."

"Oh, I'm not going to kill you..." Starlette said. "I don't need to."

BAM!

The shot rang through the night and echoed into the distance. Bookworm's head exploded in front of Starlette and his body dropped to the ground.

"I'm going to let him do it," Starlette finished.

Heartthrob stood at a distance, to Starlette's side. Bookworm had never seen him coming. He had planned for Starlette to kill him. Heartthrob had never even been considered. To Starlette, that one simple fact proved that Bookworm's insane rant had been wrong. She was nothing like him. She did not live for death. She hated it.

She walked closer to Bookworm's body and looked down at it. She said, "There was one thing left in Pandora's box once the evil was released..."

~

Fires burned across the lawn of Princedale University. Bookworm minions were being dragged from their dorm rooms and thrown onto the grass. Some cursed actors and spit at the feet of those who were attacking them—but these were not all actors.

Amongst those who took part in the raid on Princedale were lighting technicians, grips, gaffers, van drivers and many other crew members who had spent a year underground, filling their reserves with rage, hate, and creative ways of killing people. Now, they vented.

Prop Master led this raid on Princedale University. He oversaw the deaths of those who would have been more than happy to kill him first, if only they had been given the chance. He ordered the burning of the dorms and lecture halls. As for the library... He wanted to take care of that one himself.

Prop Master walked through the building with a backpack full of explosives. He started at the uppermost level and placed those explosives next to the load-bearing walls. He made his way through the entire building like this, until he reached the ground floor and happened across a trail of blood. Someone had been dragged.

In his ear, Prop Master could hear what was happening at the mansion in the hills. As he walked, slowly following the trail of blood, Prop Master listened to the audio feed from Starlette's camera. He had listened to the speech that Bookworm had given. He heard Songstress' musical call to violence. He had heard Starlette fight the fight that they had long been waiting for. Now on this feed, Prop Master heard the voice of Bookworm, speaking not on a stage, but to Starlette herself. He listened with bated breath, though never taking his eyes off of that trail of blood on the floor.

"—I am the lid to Pandora's box," Bookworm said. "If you kill me, you unleash an evil unto the world, the likes of which you cannot possibly see coming. You think that you will simply go home? You can never go home. You are Death. You will never stop fighting; never stop killing. You live for it. You need it."

"Oh, I'm not going to kill you..." Starlette said. "I don't need to."

Prop Master found himself walking down a flight of stairs which, according to signs on the wall, led to an underground tunnel. Midway down those stairs, his eardrum was nearly burst by the sound of a single gunshot on Starlette's feed. He couldn't help but flinch, but he kept moving. Though she may have finished her job, he had not yet finished his.

The smell within the tunnel was familiar, but unpleasant. It was the smell of rotting flesh, and it grew stronger. As he followed the trail of blood downward, he felt as though he were descending into the bowls of Hell itself.

The audio from Starlette's feed cut out as Prop Master reached the tunnel. Static took its place. It stayed with him as he continued to walk.

The overhead lights in the tunnel were flickering. Flyers for various on-campus protests were scattered across the floor. There were snack machines against one wall in the tunnel, and an old payphone, which had been broken and unused for years.

The stench grew stronger the farther he walked. The overhead lights soon gave out entirely, leaving only the red glow of his gun-mounted flashlight to light his way. The static in his ear began to break in and out as bits and pieces of the transmission made their way through the tunnel walls.

Prop Master saw a pile of debris in the distance. At first, he believed that this debris came from the tunnel collapsing in on itself, but there did not seem to be any damage to the tunnel.

Growing closer, he came to realize that this debris was not from the building. He was looking at a stack of bodies; Hollywood professionals who had been assumed dead after the attacks, but who had apparently managed to live for months afterward. Regardless of when it happened, their fate was the same.

On top of this pile of bodies, Prop Master found the end to the trail of blood that he had been following. He walked to her and choked back a tear as he placed an explosive on her chest and wrapped her arms around it. He put a hand on her head and said his silent goodbye.

"There was one thing left in Pandora's box once the evil was released..." came Starlette's voice over the audio feed, just as Prop Master noticed the explosives on Girl Next Door's chest moving ever so slightly up and down.

"Hope."

~

Heartthrob stood with his arm extended, holding his gun for the longest time. He didn't move. He didn't say a word.

After a few moments, his gun dropped to the ground. He fell to his knees and stared at Bookworm's body. His breathing became heavy and tears formed in his eyes. He began to sob.

He cried in honor of all those industry professionals who had died in the attacks. He cried for those who had been running ever since. He cried for his family and all the others who had been tortured and killed by Bookworm's men. He cried for Ember.

Starlette stood there with him, shedding not one tear.

~

Around the world, battles were fought that night. Bookworm's minions were killed, or left to scramble into hiding.

By morning, the world was changed. Though it would never be quite as it was before the attacks which had destroyed the entertainment industry, it was a world that could once again dare to dream. It was a world of movie stars and summer blockbusters, coming soon to a theater near you.

Of all the discoveries made in the Bookworm strongholds around the world, perhaps none was more surprising than that of Girl Next Door, found—and nearly blown up—by Prop Master, in the tunnel beneath the library at Princedale.

Though badly beaten and left in a coma from which she may never awaken, Girl Next Door was alive. While most of Hollywood cursed her name, to Starlette and her cast, she was a symbol of everything that they had fought for. They had no doubt that someday the fallen actress would open her eyes and emerge into the world that she had long been dreaming of.

The spirit of Hollywood was strong within Ember, and Hollywood cannot be destroyed.

~

FADE TO BLACK

ROLL CREDITS

Find Starlette Online:

www.StarletteNovel.com

facebook.com/StarletteNovel

@StarletteNovel

Find Kyle Andrews Online:

authorkyleandrews.wordpress.com

kyle@starlettenovel.com